SELECTED NON-DRAMATIC WRITINGS

OF BERNARD SHAW

✳   ✳   ✳

RIVERSIDE EDITIONS

RIVERSIDE EDITIONS

UNDER THE GENERAL EDITORSHIP OF

Gordon N. Ray

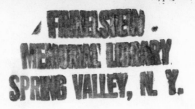
Selected Non-Dramatic Writings

of

Bernard Shaw

An Unsocial Socialist
The Quintessence of Ibsenism
Essays and Reviews

EDITED BY

Dan H. Laurence
NEW YORK UNIVERSITY

HOUGHTON MIFFLIN COMPANY · BOSTON
The Riverside Press Cambridge

Contents

III

Introductory Note

To those who know Shaw chiefly through his plays and prefaces, this volume should come as something of a revelation. Mr. Dan Laurence, Shaw's bibliographer and the editor of his correspondence, has here brought together a representative selection from his non-dramatic writings during the period in which he was rising to fame. The fiction that occupied him during his early years in London is exampled by *An Unsocial Socialist*, the last and most idiosyncratic of the five "Novels of his Nonage." The critical journalism by which he supported himself after he ceased to be a novelist is represented by two major essays, *The Quintessence of Ibsenism* and *The Sanity of Art* (as "A Degenerate's View of Nordau" is more familiarly known). The shorter pieces which make up the remainder of the book have been shrewdly chosen from among Shaw's polemical and autobiographical essays to provide a view of his personality and opinions during his formative years. Throughout Mr. Laurence has used early texts, thus avoiding the sometimes extensive retouching which Shaw permitted himself when he republished his work.

George Bernard Shaw was born in Dublin in 1856. His father was a civil servant turned ne'er-do-well grain wholesaler, his mother an accomplished musician who was "utterly unfit" for "ordinary domestic mothering and wifing." He had little formal schooling, but his parents' habit of treating him as a small adult rather than as a child gave him a precocious insight into the realities of life, and he had free access to books, pictures, and music. When he left Ireland to join his mother, who had become a concert singer in London, he was quite unlike the ordinary young man of twenty. Without experience of social life, he was untrained in accepted behavior. He held none of the received opinions or prejudices about questions of the day; indeed he regarded everything as an open question. He now moved to London, the great stronghold of English respectability and conformity. As he himself later remarked, his "attitude to conventional British life ever since has been that of a missionary striving to understand the superstitions of the natives in order to make himself intelligible to them."

From the first, Shaw's aim was to make himself a great writer, and to this aim he consistently subordinated all other considerations. "I was an able-bodied and able-minded young man in the strength of my youth; and my family, then heavily embarrassed, needed my help urgently," he afterwards recalled. "I did not throw myself into the struggle for life; I threw my mother into it." For several years his routine hardly varied. He spent his days at the British Museum and his evenings wandering about London. His sole apparent employment was to write each day five pages of a novel which no one showed any interest in publishing.

Shaw dated his intellectual awakening from his reading of Henry George's *Progress and Poverty* in 1881 and the French translation of the first volume of *Das Kapital* in 1883. George persuaded him that all other issues were insignificant in comparison with the economic issue. Marx's book was a revelation to him because of its "appeal to an unnamed, unrecognized passion — a new passion — the passion of hatred in the more generous souls among the respectable and educated sections for the accursed middle-class institutions that had starved, thwarted, misled and corrupted them from their cradles." Henceforth Shaw had a potent anti-bourgeois gospel to preach, in the formulation of which his economic studies had "played as important a part as a knowledge of anatomy does in the work of Michael Angelo."

Shaw's new conviction of "the importance of the economic basis" soon made him a socialist. For many years he spoke in favor of socialism nearly every Sunday, often two or three times, and on weekdays as well before any audience that would listen to him. He became a member of the nascent Fabian Society. Two of his novels were published serially in socialist periodicals. These activities brought him into notice, and in 1885 he began a thirteen-year stint as a critic of art, music, and latterly drama which made his name familiar in the London literary world. In 1892 his career as a playwright was launched with a performance of *Widowers' Houses* by the Independent Theatre, but it was not until 1904 that he achieved a West End production by a commercially responsible company. Yet persons of discernment soon saw that a new power in literature had emerged. At the first night of *Arms and the Man* in 1894 an audience which had assembled to condemn the play gave it an ovation after the final curtain. When Shaw came to the front of the house, he was greeted by a single "boo" from the gallery. Shaw said: "I assure the gentleman in the gallery that he and I are of exactly the same opinion, but what can we do against a whole house who are of the contrary opinion?" Yeats, who tells this story, remarks that "from that moment Bernard Shaw became the most formidable man in modern letters."

Such briefly is the background against which Mr. Laurence's selections from Shaw's early writings should be read. They are the work of a confirmed outsider, whose aim is "to stick pins into pigs." But this "conscientious intellectual revolutionary" is at war with his readers only for their own good, and his objective is always to make a beneficial difference in their lives. This accounts for the spirit of genial magnanimity which is so attractive a feature of all the pieces in this volume. The two most considerable call for individual comment.

As a novel *An Unsocial Socialist* has consistently met with the lack of success which it certainly deserves. Regarding the fiction of his time as the last refuge of unreality, Shaw could not bring himself to take novel-writing seriously. He has his fun in this book with Chichester Erskine, who writes drama "without regard to the exigencies of the stage," but it never seems to have occurred to Shaw that fiction has its exigencies as well. The result is a novel which falls somewhere between Harriet Martineau's *Illustrations of Political Economy* and W. H. Mallock's *New Republic*. Ideas are exampled and discussed endlessly, but the true stuff of fiction is largely missing. Shaw was proud of his conception of Sidney Trefusis, the "poor devil of a millionaire" who forgoes the advantages of wealth and position provided by his Manchester "Cottontot" father to masquerade as Jefferson Smilash, a member of "the undeserving poor." No doubt this impersonation had its shock value for Shaw's contemporaries, but today the joke quickly palls, and Smilash after a time becomes as tedious as a comic representative of the lower orders in a play by Boucicault.

Nonetheless, *An Unsocial Socialist* is a capital document in Shaw's intellectual history. Trefusis is his creator's *alter ego,* and in telling his story Shaw is vicariously playing out that grand public rejection of the Victorian social order which his narrow circumstances gave him no opportunity of making in his own person. Shaw intended the novel to be "a gigantic grapple with the whole social problem" from the perspective imposed by his recent study of Marx. In the event he finished only two chapters, "chapters of colossal length but containing the merest preliminary matter." Yet fragmentary though his novel may be, it offers a comprehensive indictment of the thought and morality of late Victorian England. Shaw's punning title hardly conveys the import of his book; a more suitable name would be that suggested by a sentence in chapter nine: *Nothing Sacred.*

The Quintessence of Ibsenism is a better book than *An Unsocial Socialist,* but it too is chiefly interesting for what it reveals about Shaw and his work. In 1891 it was a valiant *livre de combat* which helped immeasurably in gaining a hearing for the Norwegian master. Ibsen's theatre now ranks with Shakespeare's and Molière's, however, and Shaw's method of "telling the stories of the plays" a little in the manner of Charles and Mary Lamb no longer seems very enlightening, no matter how excellent its execution. But when Shaw describes a society in which there are 700 Philistines and 299 idealists to every realist, when he asserts that "the real slavery of today is slavery to ideals of virtue," when he insists that "there is no golden rule — that conduct must justify itself by its effect upon happiness and not by its conformity to any rule or ideal," he is setting forth the quintessence of Shavianism, the assumptions that underlie his own dramatic masterpieces. He writes in his first chapter:

> First there was man's duty to God, with the priest as assessor. That was repudiated; and then came Man's duty to his neighbour, with Society as the assessor. Will this too be repudiated, and be succeeded by Man's duty to himself, assessed by himself?

It is precisely to the ramifications of this question, which brilliantly sums up the moral history of the last 200 years, that Shaw addresses himself in his plays.

Despite his enormous success, Shaw was not altogether lucky in the pattern of his career. As the prophet of a radical gospel, he had some reason to expect that his views would retain much of their novelty throughout his lifetime. But as early as 1913 Max Beerbohm exhibited a cartoon in which he showed himself gazing at Shaw standing on his head. The caption reads: "Mild surprise of one who, revisiting England after long absence, finds that the dear fellow has not moved." The guns which sounded in August of the following year set in motion a process of accelerating change in all areas of human life which by the nineteen-twenties had made Shaw's essentially fixed ideas seem old-fashioned, at least in advanced circles. To persuade his audience and perhaps himself that he remained in the vanguard of opinion, Shaw became ever more strident and assertive in the last decades of his long life, until for many people the character of GBS, "the jester at the court of King Demos," grew simply tiresome.

The writings collected in this volume are free from the grandiose delusions of his later years. No doubt Shaw is intent upon dramatizing himself, but the joyousness and zest with which he goes about his campaign "to get selected" as a man of genius deprive it of offense. So he begins an address to the respectable Shelley Society, whose members preferred to see in their hero Arnold's "beautiful and ineffectual angel," by announcing, "I, like Shelley, am a socialist, an atheist, and a vegetarian." Shaw's vegetarianism, indeed, was the source of some of his most successful effects. When he fell ill in 1898, his physician urged meat upon him. He promptly wrote an article for the *Academy* concerning the dilemma in which he was placed.

> My situation is a solemn one. Life is offered to me on condition of eating beefsteaks. My weeping family crowd about me with Bovril and Brand's Essence. But death is better than cannibalism. My will contains directions for my funeral, which will be followed not by mourning coaches, but by herds of oxen, sheep, swine, flocks of poultry, and a small travelling aquarium of live fish, all wearing white scarves in honor of the man who perished rather than eat his fellow-creatures. It will be, with the exception of the procession into Noah's Ark, the most remarkable thing of the kind ever seen.

His most determined opponents found such fun irresistible at the time, and it remains irresistible today.

Finally, not only *The Quintessence of Ibsenism* but all of these early works lead directly to Shaw's plays. They are full of anticipations of the characters, situations, dialogue, and key monologues of his theatre. And as the reader engages in the fascinating game of comparing such passages with what they became in *Pygmalion* and *Man and Superman,* in *Arms and the Man* and *The Doctor's Dilemma,* he will also discover how it happened that by submitting to the exigencies of a demanding art form, Shaw achieved the control, the concentration, and particularly the liberation from self which made him a great master of the drama.

GORDON N. RAY

A Note on the Texts

From the start of his literary career Bernard Shaw insisted upon an idiosyncratic styling of his published works. His spelling sometimes was archaic: *Shakspere* (later *Shakespear*), *shew* for *show,* etc.; more often it was phonetic. "I always use the American termination *or* for *our* [*labor* rather than *labour*]," he noted in *The Author* in April 1902. "Theater, somber, center, etc., I reject only because they are wantonly anti-phonetic: theatre, sombre, etc., being nearer the sound. Such abominable Frenchifications as programme, cigarette, etc., are quite revolting to me. Telegram, quartet, etc., deprive them of all excuse. I should like also to spell epilogue epilog, because people generally mispronounce it, just as they would mispronounce catalogue if the right sound were not so familiar. That is the worst of unphonetic spelling: in the long run people pronounce words as they are spelt; and so the language gets senselessly altered."

He reserved his greatest scorn for non-essential apostrophes. "The apostrophes in ain't, don't, haven't, etc., look so ugly that the most careful printing cannot make a page of colloquial dialogue as handsome as a page of classical dialogue. Besides, shan't should be sha"n't, if the wretched pedantry of indicating the elision is to be carried out. I have written aint, dont, havnt, shant, shouldnt and wont [also *wernt*] for twenty years with perfect impunity, using the apostrophe only where its omission would suggest another word: for example, hell for he'll. There is not the faintest reason for persisting in the ugly and silly trick of peppering pages with these uncouth bacilli. I also write thats, whats, lets, for the colloquial forms of that is, what is, let us; and I have not yet been prosecuted."

Inevitably he clashed with publishers and printers who were not as concerned as he for the aesthetics of typography, and who insisted on "peppering" the page with conventional punctuation. One outraged editor, D. Gordon of the Walter Scott Publishing Company (which had contracted to reissue *Cashel Byron's Profession*), informed

Shaw on 21 February 1889: "I object entirely to such typographical aberrations and monstrosities . . . signs which no doubt have enormous significance for the individual who conceived them, but which are simply an aggravation and a puzzle to the ordinary person who tries to decipher them. I beg to inform you, then, that I shall instruct my printer to print the usual contractions in the usual way." [Shaw archive, British Museum.] But when Shaw threatened to cancel the contract, the editor capitulated: "All right; have it your own evil way. To be strictly logical I think you should 'agglutinate' the whole page; a series of continuously unbroken lines would probably look much better typographically than the present series of lines conventionally divided into words. I hope however that the 'youves' and the 'youds' don't abound too piteously in *Cashel Byron*." [Shaw archive, British Museum.]

Swan Sonnenschein and Company, which published *An Unsocial Socialist* in 1887, also remonstrated with Shaw, but they too were intimidated finally into accepting at least some of the author's peculiar dicta on style. Editors of London newspapers and journals, however, adamantly refused for the most part to indulge Shaw in his eccentricities, setting his work according to prescribed house rules.

In later years, whenever Shaw re-published any of his early writings (particularly in the Collected Edition, 1930–32), he freely re-styled (and extensively revised) the texts, sometimes quite inconsistently from page to page. The editor of the present volume, lacking the same license, has chosen to follow the safe method of reproducing the texts exactly as they originally appeared, except for the occasional correction of obvious typographical errors and the arbitrary deletion of a series of superfluous commas anarchistically set before dashes by the editor in the text of "A Degenerate's View of Nordau."

The text of *An Unsocial Socialist* is set from the first edition (1887) and the Appendix from the "cheap" edition (1888). The *Quintessence* is set from the first edition (1891) and the added chapter "The Last Four Plays" from the edition of 1913. "In the Days of My Youth" is reproduced from a reprint in *T. P.'s and Cassell's Weekly* (19 July 1934), and "The Illusions of Socialism" from its first book appearance (1897). "Socialism for Millionaires" is set from Fabian Tract No. 107 (1901), the editor preferring this revision, with its useful sub-headings, to the earlier serial text. The remaining pieces are set from first serial appearance, as indicated in the headnotes.

D. H. L.

An Unsocial Socialist

An Unsocial Socialist, written in 1883, appeared serially in the Socialist journal *To-day* from March to December 1884. It was revised for book publication in 1887. When the publisher, prompted by poor sales, issued the remaining sheets of the edition in a cheap binding in April 1888, Shaw added an Appendix, purporting to be a letter to the author from Sidney Trefusis, the novel's principal character. An unauthorized edition of the novel, including the Appendix, was published in New York in 1900. When the novel was reprinted in 1930 in the Collected Edition of Shaw's works (called the Ayot St. Lawrence Edition in America), Shaw provided a brief Foreword; except for minor stylistic changes, however, the text was unaltered.

An Unsocial Socialist

BOOK I

*

CHAPTER I.

In the dusk of an October evening, a sensible looking woman of forty came out through an oaken door to a broad landing on the first floor of an old English country-house. A braid of her hair had fallen forward as if she had been stooping over book or pen; and she stood for a moment to smooth it, and to gaze contemplatively — not in the least sentimentally — through the tall, narrow window. The sun was setting, but its glories were at the other side of the house; for this window looked eastward, where the landscape of sheepwalks and pasture land was sobering at the approach of darkness.

The lady, like one to whom silence and quiet were luxuries, lingered on the landing for some time. Then she turned towards another door, on which was inscribed, in white letters, CLASS ROOM NO. 6. Arrested by a whispering above, she paused in the doorway, and looked up the stairs along a broad smooth handrail that swept round in an unbroken curve at each landing, forming an inclined plane from the top to the bottom of the house.

A young voice, apparently mimicking someone, now came from above, saying,

"We will take the *Études de la Vélocité* next, if you please, ladies."

Immediately a girl in a holland dress shot down through space; whirled round the curve with a fearless centrifugal toss of her ankle; and vanished into the darkness beneath. She was followed by a stately girl in green, intently holding her breath as she flew; and also by a large young woman in black, with her lower lip grasped between her

3

teeth, and her fine brown eyes protruding with excitement. Her passage created a miniature tempest which disarranged anew the hair of the lady on the landing, who waited in breathless alarm until two light shocks and a thump announced that the aerial voyagers had landed safely in the hall.

"Oh law!" exclaimed the voice that had spoken before. "Here's Susan."

"It's a mercy your neck aint broken," replied some palpitating female. "I'll tell of you this time, Miss Wylie; indeed I will. And you, too, Miss Carpenter: I wonder at you not to have more sense at your age and with your size! Miss Wilson cant help hearing when you come down with a thump like that. You shake the whole house."

"Oh bother!" said Miss Wylie. "The Lady Abbess takes good care to shut out all the noise we make. Let us ——"

"Girls," said the lady above, calling down quietly, but with ominous distinctness.

Silence and utter confusion ensued. Then came a reply, in a tone of honeyed sweetness, from Miss Wylie.

"Did you call us, *dear* Miss Wilson?"

"Yes. Come up here, if you please, all three."

There was some hesitation among them, each offering the other precedence. At last they went up slowly, in the order, though not at all in the manner, of their flying descent; followed Miss Wilson into the class-room; and stood in a row before her, illumined through three western windows with a glow of ruddy orange light. Miss Carpenter, the largest of the three, was red and confused. Her arms hung by her sides, her fingers twisting the folds of her dress. Miss Gertrude Lindsay, in pale sea-green, had a small head, delicate complexion, and pearly teeth. She stood erect, with an expression of cold distaste for reproof of any sort. The holland dress of the third offender had changed from yellow to white as she passed from the grey eastern twilight on the staircase into the warm western glow in the room. Her face had a bright olive tone, and seemed to have a golden mica in its composition. Her eyes and hair were hazel-nut colour; and her teeth, the upper row of which she displayed freely, were like fine Portland stone, and sloped outward enough to have spoilt her mouth, had they not been supported by a rich under lip, and a finely curved, impudent chin. Her half cajoling, half mocking air, and her ready smile, were difficult to confront with severity; and Miss Wilson knew it; for she would not look at her even when attracted by a convulsive start and an angry side glance from Miss Lindsay, who had just been indented between the ribs by a finger tip.

"You are aware that you have broken the rules," said Miss Wilson quietly.

"We didnt intend to. We really did not," said the girl in holland, coaxingly.

"Pray what was your intention then, Miss Wylie?"

Miss Wylie unexpectedly treated this as a smart repartee instead of a rebuke. She sent up a strange little scream, which exploded in a cascade of laughter.

"Pray be silent, Agatha," said Miss Wilson severely. Agatha looked contrite. Miss Wilson turned hastily to the eldest of the three, and continued,

"I am especially surprised at you, Miss Carpenter. Since you have no desire to keep faith with me by upholding the rules, of which you are quite old enough to understand the necessity, I shall not trouble you with reproaches, or appeals to which I am now convinced that you would not respond" (here Miss Carpenter, with an inarticulate protest, burst into tears); "but you should at least think of the danger into which your juniors are led by your childishness. How should you feel if Agatha had broken her neck?"

"Oh!" exclaimed Agatha, putting her hand quickly to her neck.

"I didnt think there was any danger," said Miss Carpenter, struggling with her tears. "Agatha has done it so oft — oh dear! you have torn me." Miss Wylie had pulled at her schoolfellow's skirt, and pulled too hard.

"Miss Wylie," said Miss Wilson, flushing slightly: "I must ask you to leave the room."

"Oh no," exclaimed Agatha, clasping her hands in distress. "Please dont, dear Miss Wilson. I am so sorry. I beg your pardon."

"Since you will not do what I ask, I must go myself," said Miss Wilson sternly. "Come with me to my study," she added to the two other girls. "If you attempt to follow, Miss Wylie, I shall regard it as an intrusion."

"But I will go away if you wish it. I didnt mean to diso ——"

"I shall not trouble you now. Come, girls."

The three went out; and Miss Wylie, left behind in disgrace, made a surpassing grimace at Miss Lindsay, who glanced back at her. When she was alone, her vivacity subsided. She went slowly to the window, and gazed disparagingly at the landscape. Once, when a sound of voices above reached her, her eyes brightened, and her ready lip moved; but the next silent moment she relapsed into moody indifference, which was not relieved until her two companions, looking very serious, re-entered.

"Well," she said gaily: "has moral force been applied? Are you going to the Recording Angel?"

"Hush, Agatha," said Miss Carpenter. "You ought to be ashamed of yourself."

"No, but you ought, you goose. A nice row you have got me into!"

"It was your own fault. You tore my dress."

"Yes, when you were blurting out that I sometimes slide down the bannisters."

"Oh!" said Miss Carpenter slowly, as if this reason had not occurred to her before. "Was that why you pulled me?"

"Dear me! It has actually dawned upon you. You are a most awfully silly girl, Jane. What did the Lady Abbess say?"

Miss Carpenter again gave her tears way, and could not reply.

"She is disgusted with us, and no wonder," said Miss Lindsay.

"She said it was all your fault," sobbed Miss Carpenter.

"Well, never mind, dear," said Agatha soothingly. "Put it in the Recording Angel."

"I wont write a word in the Recording Angel unless you do so first," said Miss Lindsay angrily. "You are more in fault than we are."

"Certainly, my dear," replied Agatha. "A whole page, if you wish."

"I b-believe you *like* writing in the Recording Angel," said Miss Carpenter spitefully.

"Yes, Jane. It is the best fun the place affords."

"It may be fun to you," said Miss Lindsay sharply; "but it is not very creditable to me, as Miss Wilson said just now, to take a prize in moral science and then have to write down that I dont know how to behave myself. Besides, I do not like to be told that I am ill-bred."

Agatha laughed. "What a deep old thing she is! She knows all our weaknesses, and stabs at us through them. Catch her telling me, or Jane there, that we are ill-bred!"

"I dont understand you," said Miss Lindsay, haughtily.

"Of course not. That's because you dont know as much moral science as I, though I never took a prize in it."

"You never took a prize in anything," said Miss Carpenter.

"And I hope I never shall," said Agatha. "I would as soon scramble for hot pennies in the snow, like the street boys, as scramble to see who can answer most questions. Dr. Watts is enough moral science for me. Now for the Recording Angel."

She went to a shelf and took down a heavy quarto, bound in black leather, and inscribed, in red letters, My Faults. This she threw irreverently on a desk, and tossed its pages over until she came to one only partly covered with manuscript confessions.

"For a wonder," she said, "here are two entries that are not mine. Sarah Gerram! What has she been confessing?"

"Dont read it," said Miss Lindsay quickly. "You know that it is the most dishonourable thing any of us can do."

"Pooh! Our little sins are not worth making such a fuss about. I always like to have my entries read: it makes me feel like an author; and so in Christian duty I always read other people's. Listen to poor Sarah's tale of guilt. '1st October. I am very sorry that I slapped Miss Chambers in the lavatory this morning, and knocked out one of her teeth. This was very wicked; but it was coming out by itself; and she has forgiven me because a new one will come in its place; and she was only pretending when she said she swallowed it. Sarah Gerram.' "

"Little fool!" said Miss Lindsay. "The idea of our having to record in the same book with brats like that!"

"Here is a touching revelation. '4th October. Helen Plantagenet is deeply grieved to have to confess that I took the first place in algebra yesterday unfairly. Miss Lindsay prompted me; and ——"

"Oh!" exclaimed Miss Lindsay, reddening. "That is how she thanks me for prompting her, is it? How dare she confess *my* faults in the Recording Angel?"

"Serve you right for prompting her," said Miss Carpenter. "She was always a double-faced cat; and you ought to have known better."

"Oh, I assure you it was not for her sake that I did it," replied Miss Lindsay. "It was to prevent that Jackson girl from getting first place. I dont like Helen Plantagenet; but at least she is a lady."

"Stuff, Gertrude," said Agatha, with a touch of earnestness. "One would think, to hear you talk, that your grandmother was a cook. Dont be such a snob."

"Miss Wylie," said Gertrude, becoming scarlet: "you are very — Oh! oh! Stop Ag — oh! I will tell Miss W — oh!" Agatha had inserted a steely finger between her ribs, and was tickling her unendurably.

"Sh-sh-sh," whispered Miss Carpenter anxiously. "The door is open."

"Am I Miss Wylie?" demanded Agatha, relentlessly continuing the torture. "Am I very — whatever you were going to say? Am I ——? am I ——? am I?"

"No, no," gasped Gertrude, shrinking into a chair, almost in hysterics. "You are very unkind, Agatha. You have hurt me."

"You deserve it. If you ever get sulky with me again, or call me Miss Wylie, I will *kill* you. I will tickle the soles of your feet with a feather" (Miss Lindsay shuddered, and hid her feet beneath the chair) "until your hair turns white. And now, if you are truly repentant, come and record."

"You must record first. It was all your fault."

"But I am the youngest," said Agatha.

"Well, then," said Gertrude, afraid to press the point, but determined not to record first, "let Jane Carpenter begin. She is the eldest."

"Oh, of course," said Jane, with whimpering irony. "Let Jane do all the nasty things first. I think it's very hard. You fancy that Jane is a fool; but she isnt."

"You are certainly not such a fool as you look, Jane," said Agatha gravely. "But I will record first, if you like."

"No, you shant," cried Jane, snatching the pen from her. "I am the eldest; and I wont be put out of my place."

She dipped the pen in the ink resolutely, and prepared to write. Then she paused; considered; looked bewildered; and at last appealed piteously to Agatha.

"*What* shall I write?" she said. "You know how to write things down; and I dont."

"First put the date," said Agatha.

"To be sure," said Jane, writing it quickly. "I forgot that. Well?"

"Now write, 'I am very sorry that Miss Wilson saw me when I slid down the bannisters this evening. Jane Carpenter.' "

"Is that all?"

"That's all: unless you wish to add something of your own composition."

"I hope it's all right," said Jane, looking suspiciously at Agatha. "However, there cant be any harm in it; for it's the simple truth. Anyhow, if you are playing one of your jokes on me, you are a nasty mean thing, and I don't care. Now, Gertrude, it's your turn. Please look at mine, and see whether the spelling is right."

"It is not my business to teach you to spell," said Gertrude, taking the pen. And, whilst Jane was murmuring at her churlishness, she wrote in a bold hand,

I have broken the rules by sliding down the bannisters to-day with Miss Carpenter and Miss Wylie. Miss Wylie went first.

"You wretch!" exclaimed Agatha, reading over her shoulder. "And *your* father is an admiral!"

"I think it is only fair," said Miss Lindsay, quailing, but assuming the tone of a moralist. "It is perfectly true."

"All my money was made in trade," said Agatha; "but I should be ashamed to save myself by shifting blame to your aristocratic shoulders. You pitiful thing! Here: give me the pen."

"I will strike it out if you wish; but I think ——"

"No: it shall stay there to witness against you. Now see how I confess my faults." And she wrote, in a fine, rapid hand,

This evening Gertrude Lindsay and Jane Carpenter met me at the top of the stairs, and said they wanted to slide down the bannisters and would do so if I went first. I told them that it was against the rules, but they said that did not matter; and as they are older than I am, I allowed myself to be persuaded, and slid.

"What do you think of that?" said Agatha, displaying the page.

They read it, and protested clamorously.

"It is perfectly true," said Agatha, solemnly.

"It's beastly mean," said Jane energetically. "The idea of your finding fault with Gertrude, and then going and being twice as bad yourself! I never heard of such a thing in my life."

" 'Thus bad begins; but worse remains behind,' as the Standard Elocutionist says," said Agatha, adding another sentence to her confession.

> But it was all my fault. Also I was rude to Miss Wilson, and refused to leave the room when she bade me. I was not wilfully wrong except in sliding down the bannisters. I am so fond of a slide that I could not resist the temptation.

"Be warned by me, Agatha," said Jane impressively. "If you write cheeky things in that book, you will be expelled."

"Indeed!" replied Agatha significantly. "Wait until Miss Wilson sees what *you* have written."

"Gertrude," cried Jane, with sudden misgiving: "has she made me write anything improper? Agatha: *do* tell me if ——"

Here a gong sounded; and the three girls simultaneously exclaimed "Grub!" and rushed from the room.

CHAPTER II.

One sunny afternoon, a hansom drove at great speed along Belsize Avenue, St. John's Wood, and stopped before a large mansion. A young lady sprang out; ran up the steps; and rang the bell impatiently. She was of the olive complexion, with a sharp profile: dark eyes with long lashes: narrow mouth with delicately sensuous lips: small head, feet, and hands, with long taper fingers: lithe and very slender figure moving with serpent-like grace. Oriental taste was displayed in the colours of her costume, which consisted of a white dress, close-fitting, and printed with an elaborate china blue pattern; a yellow straw hat covered with artificial hawthorn and scarlet berries; and tan-coloured gloves reaching beyond the elbow, and decorated with a profusion of gold bangles.

The door not being opened immediately, she rang again, violently, and was presently admitted by a maid, who seemed surprised to see her. Without making any inquiry, she darted upstairs into a drawing-room, where a matron of good presence, with features of the finest Jewish type, sat reading. With her was a handsome boy in black velvet, who said,

"Mamma: here's Henrietta!"

"Arthur," said the young lady excitedly: "leave the room this instant; and dont dare to come back until you get leave."

The boy's countenance fell; and he sulkily went out without a word.

"Is anything wrong?" said the matron, putting away her book with the unconcerned resignation of an experienced person who foresees a storm in a teacup. "Where is Sidney?"

"Gone! Gone! Deserted me! I ——" The young lady's utterance failed; and she threw herself upon an ottoman, sobbing with passionate spite.

"Nonsense! I thought Sidney had more sense. There, Henrietta: dont be silly. I suppose you have quarrelled."

"No! No!! No!!!" cried Henrietta, stamping on the carpet. "We had not a word. I have not lost my temper since we were married, mamma: I solemnly swear I have not. I will kill myself: there is no other way. There's a curse on me. I am marked out to be miserable. He —— "

"Tut tut! What has happened, Henrietta? As you have been married now nearly six weeks, you can hardly be surprised at a little tiff arising. You are so excitable! You cannot expect the sky to be always cloudless. Most likely you are to blame; for Sidney is far more reasonable than you. Stop crying, and behave like a woman of sense; and I will go to Sidney and make everything right."

"But he's gone; and I cant find out where. Oh, what shall I do?"

Henrietta writhed with impatience. Then, forcing herself to tell her story, she answered,

"We arranged on Monday that I should spend two days with aunt Judith instead of going with him to Birmingham to that horrid Trade Congress. We parted on the best of terms. He c — *couldnt* have been more affectionate. I will kill myself: I dont care about anything or anybody. And when I came back on Wednesday he was gone; and there was this lett ——" She produced a letter, and wept more bitterly than before.

"Let me see it."

Henrietta hesitated; but her mother took the letter from her; sat down near the window; and composed herself to read without the least regard to her daughter's vehement distress. The letter ran thus: —

Monday night.

MY DEAREST: *I am off — surfeited with endearment — to live my own life, and do my own work. I could only have prepared you for this by coldness or neglect, which are wholly impossible to me when the spell of your presence is upon me. I find that I must fly if I am to save myself.*

I am afraid that I cannot give you satisfactory and intelligible reasons for this step. You are a beautiful and luxurious creature: life is to you full and complete only when it is a carnival of love. My case is just the reverse. Before three soft speeches have escaped me, I rebuke myself for folly and insincerity. Before a caress has had time to cool, a strenuous revulsion seizes me: I long to return to my old lonely ascetic hermit life; to my dry books; my Socialist propagandism; my voyage of discovery through the wilderness of thought. I married in an insane fit of belief that I had a share of the natural affection which carries other men through lifetimes of matrimony. Already I am undeceived. You are to me the loveliest woman in the world. Well, for five weeks I have walked and talked and dallied with the loveliest woman in the world; and the upshot is that I am flying from her, and am for a hermit's cave until I die. Love cannot keep possession of me: all my strongest powers rise up against it and will not endure it. Forgive me for writing nonsense that you wont understand; and do not think too hardly of me. I have been as good to you as my selfish nature allowed. Do not seek to disturb me in the obscurity which I desire and deserve. My solicitor will call on your father to arrange business matters; and you shall be as happy as wealth and liberty can make you. We shall meet again — some day.

Adieu, my last love.
SIDNEY TREFUSIS.

"Well?" cried Mrs. Trefusis, observing through her tears that her mother had read the letter, and was contemplating it in a daze.

"Well, certainly!" said Mrs. Jansenius, with emphasis. "Do you think he is quite sane, Henrietta? Or have you been plaguing him for too much attention. Men are not willing to give up their whole existence to their wives, even during the honeymoon."

"He pretended that he was never happy out of my presence," sobbed Henrietta. "There never was anything so cruel. I often wanted to be by myself for a change; but I was afraid to hurt his feelings by saying so. And now he has no feelings. But he *must* come back to me. Mustnt he, mamma?"

"He ought to. I suppose he has not gone away with anyone?"

Henrietta sprang up, her cheeks vivid scarlet. "If I thought that, I would pursue him to the end of the earth, and murder her. But no: he is not like anybody else. He hates me. Everybody hates me. You dont care whether I am deserted or not, nor papa, nor anyone in this house."

Mrs. Jansenius, still indifferent to her daughter's agitation, considered a moment, and then said placidly,

"You can do nothing until we hear from the solicitor. In the meantime you may stay with us, if you wish. I did not expect a visit from you so soon; but your room has not been used since you went away."

Mrs. Trefusis ceased crying, chilled by this first intimation that her father's house was no longer her home. A more real sense of desolation came upon her. Under its cold influence she began to collect herself, and to feel her pride rising like a barrier between her and her mother.

"I wont stay long," she said. "If his solicitor will not tell me where he is, I will hunt through England for him. I am sorry to trouble you."

"Oh, you will be no greater trouble than you have always been," said Mrs. Jansenius calmly, not displeased to see that her daughter had taken the hint. "You had better go and wash your face. People may call; and I presume you dont wish to receive them in that plight. If you meet Arthur on the stairs, please tell him he may come in."

Henrietta screwed her lips into a curious pout, and withdrew. Arthur then came in, and stood at the window in sullen silence, brooding over his recent expulsion. Suddenly he exclaimed, "Here's papa; and it's not five o'clock yet!" whereupon his mother sent him away again.

Mr. Jansenius was a man of imposing presence, not yet in his fiftieth year, but not far from it. He moved with dignity, bearing himself as if the contents of his massive brow were precious. His handsome aquiline nose and keen dark eyes proclaimed his Jewish origin, of which he was ashamed. Those who did not know this, naturally believed that he was proud of it, and were at a loss to account for his permitting his children to be educated as Christians. Well instructed in business, and subject to no emotion outside the love of family, respectability, comfort, and money, he had maintained the capital inherited from his father, and made it breed new capital in the usual way. He was a banker; and his object as such was to intercept and appropriate the immense saving which the banking system effects, and so, as far as possible, to leave the rest of the world working just as hard as before banking was introduced. But as the world would not on these terms have banked at all, he had to give them some of the saving as an inducement. So they profited by the saving as well as he; and he had the satisfaction of being at once a wealthy citizen and a public benefactor, rich in comforts and easy in conscience.

He entered the room quickly; and his wife saw that something had vexed him.

"Do you know what has happened, Ruth?" he said.

"Yes. She is upstairs."

Mr. Jansenius stared. "Do you mean to say that she has left already?" he said. "What business has she to come here?"

"It is natural enough. Where else should she have gone?"

Mr. Jansenius, who mistrusted his own judgment when it differed from that of his wife, replied slowly, "Why did she not go to her mother?"

Mrs. Jansenius, puzzled in her turn, looked at him with cool wonder, and remarked, "I am her mother, am I not?"

"I was not aware of it. I am surprised to hear it, Ruth. Have you had a letter too?"

"I have seen the letter. But what do you mean by telling me that you do not know I am Henrietta's mother? Are you trying to be funny?"

"Henrietta! Is *she* here? Is this some fresh trouble?"

"I dont know. What are you talking about?"

"I am talking about Agatha Wylie."

"Oh! I was talking about Henrietta."

"Well, what about Henrietta?"

"What about Agatha Wylie?"

At this Mr. Jansenius became exasperated; and she deemed it best to relate what Henrietta had told her. When she gave him Trefusis's letter, he said, more calmly, "Misfortunes never come singly. Read that," and handed her another letter, so that they both began reading at the same time.

Mrs. Jansenius read as follows.

> To Mrs. Wylie,
> *Acacia Lodge, Chiswick.*
>
> Alton College, Lyvern.
>
> Dear Madam: *I write with great regret to request that you will at once withdraw Miss Wylie from Alton College. In an establishment like this, where restraint upon the liberty of the students is reduced to a minimum, it is necessary that the small degree of subordination which is absolutely indispensable be acquiesced in by all without complaint or delay. Miss Wylie has failed to comply with this condition. She has declared her wish to leave; and*

has assumed an attitude towards myself and my colleagues which we cannot, consistently with our duty to ourselves and her fellow students, pass over. If Miss Wylie has any cause to compain of her treatment here, or of the step which she has compelled us to take, she will doubtless make it known to you.

Perhaps you will be so good as to communicate with Miss Wylie's guardian, Mr. Jansenius, with whom I shall be happy to make an equitable arrangement respecting the fees which have been paid in advance for the current term.

> *I am, Dear Madam,*
> *Yours faithfully,*
> MARIA WILSON.

"A nice young lady, that!" said Mrs. Jansenius.

"I do not understand this," said Mr. Jansenius, reddening as he took in the purport of his son-in-law's letter. "I will not submit to it. What does it mean, Ruth?"

"I dont know. Sidney is mad, I think; and his honeymoon has brought his madness out. But you must not let him throw Henrietta on my hands again."

"Mad! Does he think he can shirk his responsibility to his wife because she is my daughter? Does he think, because his mother's father was a baronet, that he can put Henrietta aside the moment her society palls on him?"

"Oh, it's nothing of that sort. He never thought of us."

"But I will make him think of us," said Mr. Jansenius, raising his voice in great agitation. "He shall answer for it."

Just then Henrietta returned, and saw her father moving excitedly to and fro, repeating, "He shall answer to me for this. He shall answer for it."

Mrs. Jansenius frowned at her daughter to remain silent, and said soothingly, "Dont lose your temper, John."

"But I will lose my temper. Insolent hound! Damned scoundrel!"

"He is *not*," whimpered Henrietta, sitting down and taking out her handkerchief.

"Oh, come, come!" said Mrs. Jansenius peremptorily: "we have had enough crying. Let us have no more of it."

Henrietta sprang up in a passion. "I will say and do as I please," she exclaimed. "I am a married woman; and I will receive no orders. And I will have my husband back again, no matter what he does to hide himself. Papa: wont you make him come back to me? I am dying. Promise that you will make him come back."

And, throwing herself upon her father's bosom, she postponed further discussion by going into hysterics, and startling the household by her screams.

CHAPTER III.

One of the professors at Alton College was a Mrs. Miller, an old-fashioned schoolmistress who did not believe in Miss Wilson's system of government by moral force, and carried it out under protest. Though not ill-natured, she was narrow-minded enough to be in some degree contemptible, and was consequently prone to suspect others of despising her. She suspected Agatha in particular, and treated her with disdainful curtness in such intercourse as they had — it was fortunately little. Agatha was not hurt by this; for Mrs. Miller was an unsympathetic woman, who made no friends among the girls, and satisfied her affectionate impulses by petting a large cat named Gracchus, but generally called Bacchus by an endearing modification of the harsh initial consonant.

One evening Mrs. Miller, seated with Miss Wilson in the study, correcting examination papers, heard in the distance a cry like that of a cat in distress. She ran to the door and listened. Presently there arose a prolonged wail, slurring up through two octaves, and subsiding again. It was a true feline screech, impossible to localize; but it was interrupted by a sob, a snarl, a fierce spitting, and a scuffling, coming unmistakably from a room on the floor beneath, in which, at that hour, the older girls assembled for study.

"My poor Gracchy!" exclaimed Mrs. Miller, running downstairs as fast as she could. She found the room unusually quiet. Every girl was deep in study except Miss Carpenter, who, pretending to pick up a fallen book, was purple with suppressed laughter and the congestion caused by stooping.

"Where is Miss Ward?" demanded Mrs. Miller.

"Miss Ward has gone for some astronomical diagrams in which we are interested," said Agatha, looking up gravely. Just then, Miss Ward, diagrams in hand, entered.

"Has that cat been in here?" she said, not seeing Mrs. Miller, and speaking in a tone expressive of antipathy to Gracchus.

Agatha started, and drew up her ankles as if fearful of having them bitten. Then, looking apprehensively under the desk, she replied, "There is no cat here, Miss Ward."

"There is one somewhere: I heard it," said Miss Ward carelessly, unrolling her diagrams, which she began to explain without further parley. Mrs. Miller, anxious for her pet, hastened to seek it elsewhere. In the hall she met one of the housemaids.

"Susan," she said: "have you seen Gracchus?"

"He's asleep on the hearthrug in your room, maam."

"But I heard him crying down here a moment ago. I feel sure that another cat has got in, and that they are fighting."

Susan smiled compassionately. "Lor' bless you, maam," she said, "that was Miss Wylie. It's a sort of play-acting that she goes through. There is the bee on the window-pane, and the soldier up the chimley, and the cat under the dresser. She does them all like life."

"The soldier in the chimney!" repeated Mrs. Miller, shocked.

"Yes, maam. Like as it were a follower that had hid there when he heard the mistress coming."

Mrs. Miller's face set determinedly. She returned to the study and related what had just occurred, adding some sarcastic comments on the efficacy of moral force in maintaining collegiate discipline. Miss Wilson looked grave; considered for some time; and at last said, "I must think over this. Would you mind leaving it in my hands for the present?"

Mrs. Miller said that she did not care in whose hands it remained provided her own were washed of it, and resumed her work at the papers. Miss Wilson then, wishing to be alone, went into the empty class-room at the other side of the landing. She took the Fault Book from its shelf, and sat down before it. Its record closed with the announcement, in Agatha's handwriting.

> Miss Wilson has called me impertinent, and has written to my uncle that I have refused to obey the rules. I was not impertinent; and I never refused to obey the rules. So much for Moral Force!

Miss Wilson rose vigorously, exclaiming, "I will soon let her know whether — ." She checked herself, and looked round hastily, superstitiously fancying that Agatha might have stolen into the room unobserved. Reassured that she was alone, she examined her conscience as to whether she had done wrong in calling Agatha impertinent, justifying herself by the reflection that Agatha had, in fact, been impertinent. Yet she recollected that she had refused to admit this plea on a recent occasion when Jane Carpenter had advanced it in extenuation of having called a fellow-student a liar. Had she then been unjust to Jane, or inconsiderate to Agatha?

Her casuistry was interrupted by some one softly whistling a theme from the overture to Masaniello, popular at the college in the form of an arrangement for six pianofortes and twelve hands. There was only one student unladylike and musical enough to whistle; and Miss Wilson was ashamed to find herself growing nervous at the prospect of an encounter with Agatha, who entered whistling sweetly, but with a lugubrious countenance. When she saw in whose presence she stood, she begged pardon politely, and was about to withdraw, when Miss Wilson, summoning all her judgment and tact, and hoping that they would — contrary to their custom in emergencies — respond to the summons, said,

"Agatha: come here. I want to speak to you."

Agatha closed her lips; drew in a long breath through her nostrils; and marched to within a few feet of Miss Wilson, where she halted with her hands clasped before her.

"Sit down."

Agatha sat down with a single movement, like a doll.

"I dont understand that, Agatha," said Miss Wilson, pointing to the entry in the Recording Angel. "What does it mean?"

"I am unfairly treated," said Agatha, with signs of agitation.

"In what way?"

"In *every* way. I am expected to be something more than mortal. Everyone else is encouraged to complain, and to be weak and silly. But I must have no feeling. I must be always in the right. Everyone else may be home-sick, or huffed, or in low spirits. I must have no nerves, and must keep others laughing all day long. Everyone else may sulk when a word of reproach is addressed to them, and may make the professors afraid to find fault with them. I have to bear with the insults of teachers who have less self-control than I, a girl of seventeen! and must coax them out of the difficulties they make for themselves by their own ill temper."

"But, Agatha, —— "

"Oh, I know I am talking nonsense, Miss Wilson; but can you expect me to be always sensible? — to be infallible?"

"Yes, Agatha: I do not think it is too much to expect you to be always sensible; and —— "

"Then you have neither sense nor sympathy yourself," said Agatha.

There was an awful pause. Neither could have told how long it lasted. Then Agatha, feeling that she must do or say something desperate, or else fly, made a distracted gesture, and ran out of the room.

She rejoined her companions in the great hall of the mansion, where they were assembled after study for "recreation," a noisy process which always set in spontaneously when the professors withdrew. She usually sat with her two favourite associates on a high window seat near the hearth. That place was now occupied by a little girl with flaxen hair, whom Agatha, regardless of moral force, lifted by the shoulders and deposited on the floor. Then she sat down and said,

"Oh, *such* a piece of news!"

Miss Carpenter opened her eyes eagerly. Gertrude Lindsay affected indifference.

"Someone is going to be expelled," said Agatha.

"Expelled! Who?"

"You will know soon enough, Jane," replied Agatha, suddenly grave. "It is someone who made an impudent entry in the Recording Angel."

Fear stole upon Jane; and she became very red. "Agatha," she said: "it was you who told me what to write. You know you did; and you cant deny it."

"I cant deny it, cant I? I am ready to *swear* that I never dictated a word to you in my life."

"Gertrude knows you did," exclaimed Jane, appalled, and almost in tears.

"There," said Agatha, petting her as if she were a vast baby. "It shall not be expelled, so it shant. Have you seen the Recording Angel lately, either of you?"

"Not since our last entry," said Gertrude.

"Chips," said Agatha, calling to the flaxen haired child: "go upstairs to No. 6; and, if Miss Wilson isnt there, fetch me the Recording Angel."

The little girl grumbled inarticulately, and did not stir.

"Chips," resumed Agatha: "did you ever wish that you had never been born?"

"Why dont you go yourself?" said the child pettishly, but evidently alarmed.

"Because," continued Agatha, ignoring the question, "you shall wish yourself dead and buried under the blackest flag in the coal cellar if you dont bring me the book before I can count sixteen. One — two —— "

"Go at once and do as you are told, you disagreeable little thing," said Gertrude sharply. "How dare you be so disobliging?"

" — nine — ten — eleven — " pursued Agatha.

The child quailed; went out; and presently returned, hugging the Recording Angel in her arms.

"You are a good little darling — when your better qualities are brought out by a judicious application of moral force," said Agatha, good-humouredly. "Remind me to save the raisins out of my pudding for you tomorrow. Now, Jane, you shall see the entry for which the best hearted girl in the college is to be expelled. *Voilà!*"

The two girls read, and were awestruck: Jane opening her mouth and gasping: Gertrude closing hers and looking very serious.

"Do you mean to say that you had the dreadful cheek to let the Lady Abbess see that?" said Jane.

"Pooh! she would have forgiven that. You should have heard what I said to her! She fainted three times."

"That's a story," said Gertrude, gravely.

"I beg your pardon?" said Agatha, swiftly grasping Gertrude's knee.

"Nothing," cried Gertrude, flinching hysterically. "Dont, Agatha."

"How many times did Miss Wilson faint?"

"Three times. I will scream, Agatha: I will indeed."

"Three times, as you say. And I wonder that a girl brought up as you have been, by moral force, should be capable of repeating such a falsehood. But we had an awful row, really and truly. She lost her temper. Fortunately, I never lose mine."

"Well, I'm blowed!" exclaimed Jane incredulously. "I like that."

"(For a girl of county family, you are inexcusably vulgar, Jane). I dont know what I said; but she will never forgive me for profaning her pet book. I shall be expelled as certainly as I am sitting here."

"And do you mean to say that you are going away?" said Jane, faltering as she began to realize the consequences.

"I do. And what is to become of you when I am not here to get you out of your scrapes, or of Gertrude without me to check her inveterate nobbishness, is more than I can foresee."

"I am not nobbish," said Gertrude, "although I do not choose to make friends with everyone. But I never objected to you, Agatha."

"No: I should like to catch you at it. Hallo, Jane!" (who had suddenly burst into tears): "what's the matter? I trust you are not permitting yourself to take the liberty of crying for me."

"Indeed," sobbed Jane indignantly, "I know that I am a f — fool for my pains. You have no heart."

"You certainly are a f — fool, as you aptly express it," said Agatha, passing her arm round Jane, and disregarding an angry attempt to shake it off; "but if I had any heart, it would be touched by this proof of your attachment."

"I never said you had no heart," protested Jane; "but I hate when you speak like a book."

"You hate when I speak like a book, do you? My dear silly old Jane! I shall miss you greatly."

"Yes, I dare say," said Jane, with tearful sarcasm. "At least my snoring will never keep you awake again."

"You dont snore, Jane. We have been in a conspiracy to make you believe that you do: that's all. Isnt it good of me to tell you?"

Jane was overcome by this revelation. After a long pause, she said with deep conviction, "I always *knew* that I didnt. Oh, the way you kept it up! I solemnly declare that from this time forth I will believe nobody."

"Well, and what do you think of it all?" said Agatha, transferring her attention to Gertrude, who was very grave.

"I think — I am now speaking seriously, Agatha — I think you are in the wrong."

"Why do you think that, pray?" demanded Agatha, a little roused.

"You must be, or Miss Wilson would not be angry with you. Of course, according to your own account, you are always in the right, and everyone else is always wrong; but you shouldnt have written that in the book. You know I speak as your friend."

"And pray what does your wretched little soul know of my motives and feelings?"

"It is easy enough to understand you," retorted Gertrude, nettled. "Self-conceit is not so uncommon that one need be at a loss to recognize it. And mind, Agatha Wylie," she continued, as if goaded by some unbearable reminiscence: "if you are really going, I dont care whether we part friends or not. I have not forgotten the day when you called me a spiteful cat."

"I have repented," said Agatha, unmoved. "One day I sat down and watched Bacchus seated on the hearthrug, with his moony eyes looking into space so thoughtfully and patiently that I apologized for comparing you to him. If I were to call him a spiteful cat he would only not believe me."

"Because he *is* a cat," said Jane, with the giggle which was seldom far behind her tears.

"No; but because he is not spiteful. Gertrude keeps a recording angel inside her little head; and it is so full of other people's faults, written in large hand and read through a magnifying glass, that there is no room to enter her own."

"You are very poetic," said Gertrude; "but I understand what you mean, and shall not forget it."

"You ungrateful wretch," exclaimed Agatha, turning upon her so suddenly and imperiously that she involuntarily shrank aside: "how often, when you have tried to be insolent and false with me, have I not driven away your bad angel — by tickling you? Had you a friend in the college, except half-a-dozen toadies, until I came? And now, because I have sometimes, for your own good, shewn you your faults, you bear malice against me, and say that you dont care whether we part friends or not!"

"I didnt say so."

"Oh, Gertrude: you know you did," said Jane.

"You seem to think that I have no conscience," said Gertrude querulously.

"I wish you hadnt," said Agatha. "Look at me! I have no conscience; and see how much pleasanter I am!"

"You care for no one but yourself," said Gertrude. "You never think that other people have feelings too. No one ever considers me."

"Oh: I like to hear you talk," cried Jane ironically. "You are considered a great deal more than is good for you; and the more you are considered the more you want to be considered."

"As if," declaimed Agatha theatrically, "increase of appetite did grow by what it fed on. Shakspere!"

"Bother Shakspere," said Jane, impetuously: " — old fool that expects credit for saying things that everybody knows! But if *you* complain of not being considered, Gertrude, how would you like to be *me*, whom everybody sets down as a fool? But I am not such a fool as —— "

"As you look," interposed Agatha. "I have told you so scores of times, Jane; and I am glad that you have adopted my opinion at last. Which would you rather *be*, a greater fool than y—— "

"Oh, shut up," said Jane, impatiently: "you have asked me that twice this week already."

The three were silent for some seconds after this: Agatha meditating: Gertrude moody: Jane vacant and restless. At last Agatha said,

"And are you two also smarting under a sense of the inconsiderateness and selfishness of the rest of the world? — both misunderstood? — everything expected from you, and no allowances made for you?"

"I dont know what you mean by *both* of us," said Gertrude, coldly.

"Neither do I," said Jane, angrily. "That is just the way people treat me. You may laugh, Agatha; and she may turn up her nose as much as she likes: you know it's true. But the idea of Gertrude wanting to make out that she isnt considered, is nothing but sentimentality, and vanity, and nonsense."

"You are exceedingly rude, Miss Carpenter," said Gertrude.

"My manners are as good as yours, and perhaps better," retorted Jane. "My family is as good, anyhow."

"Children, children," said Agatha, admonitorily: "do not forget that you are sworn friends."

"We didnt swear," said Jane. "We were to have been three sworn friends; and Gertrude and I were willing; but you wouldnt swear, and so the bargain was cried off."

"Just so," said Agatha; "and the result is that I spend all my time in keeping peace between you. And now, to go back to our subject, may I ask whether it has ever occurred to you that no one ever considers *me?*"

"I suppose you think that very funny. You take good care to make yourself considered," sneered Jane.

"You cannot say that *I* do not consider you," said Gertrude reproachfully.

"Not when I tickle you, dear."

"I consider you; and I am not ticklesome," said Jane, tenderly.

"Indeed! Let me try," said Agatha, slipping her arm about Jane's ample waist, and eliciting a piercing combination of laugh and scream from her.

"Sh — sh," whispered Gertrude, quickly. "Dont you see the Lady Abbess?"

Miss Wilson had just entered the room. Agatha, without appearing to be aware of her presence, stealthily withdrew her arm, and said aloud,

"How *can* you make such a noise, Jane? You will disturb the whole house."

Jane reddened with indignation, but had to remain silent; for the eyes of the principal were upon her. Miss Wilson had her bonnet on. She announced that she was going to walk to Lyvern, the nearest village. Did any of the sixth form young ladies wish to accompany her?

Agatha jumped from her seat at once; and Jane smothered a laugh.

"Miss Wilson said the *sixth* form, Miss Wylie," said Miss Ward, who had entered also. "You are not in the sixth form."

"No," said Agatha, sweetly; "but I want to go, if I may."

Miss Wilson looked round. The sixth form consisted of four studious young ladies, whose goal in life for the present was an examination by one of the Universities, or, as the college phrase was, "the Cambridge Local." None of them responded.

"Fifth form, then," said Miss Wilson.

Jane, Gertrude, and four others, rose and stood with Agatha.

"Very well," said Miss Wilson. "Do not be long dressing."

They left the room quietly, and dashed at the staircase the moment they were out of sight. Agatha, though void of emulation for the Cambridge Local, always competed with ardour for the honour of being first up or down stairs.

They soon returned, clad for walking, and left the college in procession, two by two: Jane and Agatha leading: Gertrude and Miss Wilson coming last. The road to Lyvern lay through acres of pasture land, formerly arable, now abandoned to cattle, which made more money for the landlord than the men whom they had displaced. Miss Wilson's young ladies, being instructed in economics, knew that this proved that the land was being used to produce what was most wanted from it; and if all the advantage went to the landlord, that was but natural, as he was the chief gentleman in the neighbourhood. Still, the arrangement had its disagreeable side; for it involved a great many cows, which made them afraid to cross the fields; a great many tramps, who made them afraid to walk the roads; and a scarcity of gentlemen subjects for the maiden art of fascination.

The sky was cloudy. Agatha, reckless of dusty stockings, waded through the heaps of fallen leaves with the delight of a child paddling in the sea; Gertrude picked her steps carefully; and the rest tramped along chatting subduedly, occasionally making some scientific or philo-sophical remark in a louder tone in order that Miss Wilson might over-hear and give them due credit. Save a herdsman, who seemed to have caught something of the nature and expression of the beasts he tended, they met no one until they approached the village, where, on the brow of an acclivity, masculine humanity appeared in the shape of two curates: one tall, thin, close shaven, with a book under his arm, and his neck craned forward: the other middle-sized, robust, upright, and aggressive, with short black whiskers, and an air of protest against such notions as that a clergyman may not marry, hunt, play cricket, or share the sports of honest laymen. The shaven one was Mr. Josephs: his companion, Mr. Fairholme. Obvious scriptural perversions of this brace of names had been introduced by Agatha.

"Here come Pharaoh and Joseph," she said to Jane. "Joseph will blush when you look at him. Pharaoh wont blush until he passes Gertrude; so we shall lose that."

"Josephs, indeed!" said Jane, scornfully.

"He loves you, Jane. Thin persons like a fine armful of a woman. Pharaoh, who is a cad, likes blue blood on the same principle of the attraction of opposites. That is why he is captivated by Gertrude's aristocratic air."

"If he only knew how she despises him!"

"He is too vain to suspect it. Besides, Gertrude despises everyone, even us. Or rather she doesnt despise anyone in particular, but is contemptuous by nature, just as you are stout."

"Mf! I had rather be stout than stuck-up. Ought we to bow?"

"I will, certainly. I want to make Pharaoh blush, if I can."

The two parsons had been simulating an interest in the cloudy firma-ment as an excuse for not looking at the girls until close at hand. Jane sent an eyeflash at Josephs with a skill which proved her favourite assertion that she was not so stupid as people thought. He blushed, and took off his soft, low-crowned felt hat. Fairholme saluted very solemnly; for Agatha bowed to him with marked seriousness. But when his gravity and his stiff silk hat were at their highest point, she darted a mocking smile at him; and he too blushed, all the deeper because he was enraged with himself for doing so.

"Did you ever see such a pair of fools?" whispered Jane, giggling.

"They cannot help their sex. They say women are fools; and so they are; but thank Heaven they are not quite so bad as men! I should like to look back and see Pharaoh passing Gertrude; but if he saw me he would think I was admiring him; and he is conceited enough already without that."

The two curates became redder and redder as they passed the column of young ladies. Miss Lindsay would not look to their side of the road; and Miss Wilson's nod and smile were not quite sincere. She never spoke to curates, and kept up no more intercourse with the vicar than she could not avoid. He suspected her of being an infidel, though neither he nor any other mortal in Lyvern had ever heard a word from her on the subject of her religious opinions. But he knew that "moral science" was taught secularly at the college; and he felt that where morals were made a department of science, the demand for religion must fall off proportionately.

"What a life to lead! and what a place to live in!" exclaimed Agatha. "We meet two creatures, more like suits of black than men; and that is an incident — a startling incident, in our existence!"

"I think they're awful fun," said Jane; "except that Josephs has such large ears."

The girls now came to a place where the road dipped through a plantation of sombre sycamore and horse chestnut trees. As they passed down into it, a little wind sprang up; the fallen leaves stirred; and the branches heaved a long rustling sigh.

"I hate this bit of road," said Jane, hurrying on. "It's just the sort of place that people get robbed and murdered in."

"It is not such a bad place to shelter in if we get caught in the rain, as I expect we shall before we get back," said Agatha, feeling the fitful breeze strike ominously on her cheek. "A nice pickle I shall be in with these light shoes on! I wish I had put on my strong boots. If it rains much I will go into the old chalet."

"Miss Wilson wont let you. It's trespassing."

"What matter! Nobody lives in it; and the gate is off its hinges. I only want to stand under the veranda — not to break into the wretched place. Besides, the landlord knows Miss Wilson: he wont mind. There's a drop."

Miss Carpenter looked up, and immediately received a heavy rain-drop in her eye.

"Oh!" she cried. "It's pouring! We shall be drenched."

Agatha stopped; and the column broke into a group about her.

"Miss Wilson," she said: "it is going to rain in torrents; and Jane and I have only our shoes on."

Miss Wilson paused to consider the situation. Someone suggested that if they hurried on they might reach Lyvern before the rain came down.

"More than a mile," said Agatha scornfully; "and the rain coming down already!"

Someone else suggested returning to the college.

"More than two miles," said Agatha. "We should be drowned."

"There is nothing for it but to wait here under the trees," said Miss Wilson.

"The branches are very bare," said Gertrude anxiously. "If it should come down heavily, they will drip worse than the rain itself."

"Much worse," said Agatha. "I think we had better get under the veranda of the old chalet. It is not half a minute's walk from here."

"But we have no right —— " Here the sky darkened threateningly. Miss Wilson checked herself, and said, "I suppose it is still empty."

"Of course," replied Agatha, impatient to be moving. "It is almost a ruin."

"Then let us go there, by all means," said Miss Wilson, not disposed to stand on trifles at the risk of a bad cold.

They hurried on, and came presently to a green hill by the wayside. On the slope was a dilapidated Swiss cottage, surrounded by a veranda on slender wooden pillars, about which clung a few tendrils of withered creeper, their stray ends still swinging from the recent wind, now momentarily hushed as if listening for the coming of the rain. Access from the roadway was by a rough wooden gate in the hedge. To the surprise of Agatha, who had last seen this gate off its hinges and only attached to the post by a rusty chain and padlock, it was now rehung and fastened by a new hasp. The weather admitting of no delay to consider these repairs, she opened the gate and hastened up the slope, followed by the troop of girls. Their ascent ended with a rush; for the rain suddenly came down in torrents.

When they were safe under the veranda, panting, laughing, grumbling, or congratulating themselves on having been so close to a place of shelter, Miss Wilson observed, with some uneasiness, a spade — new, like the hasp of the gate — sticking upright in a patch of ground that someone had evidently been digging lately. She was about to comment on this sign of habitation, when the door of the chalet was flung open; and Jane screamed as a man darted out to the spade, which he was about to carry in out of the wet, when he perceived the company under the veranda, and stood still in amazement. He was a young labourer with a reddish brown beard of a week's growth. He wore corduroy trousers, and a linen-sleeved corduroy vest: both, like the hasp and spade, new. A coarse blue shirt, with a vulgar red-and-orange neckerchief, also new, completed his dress; and, to shield himself from the rain, he held up a silk umbrella with a silver-mounted ebony handle, which he seemed unlikely to have come by honestly. Miss Wilson felt like a boy caught robbing an orchard; but she put a bold face on the matter, and said,

"Will you allow us to take shelter here until the rain is over?"

"For certain, your ladyship," he replied, respectfully applying the spade handle to his hair, which was combed down to his eyebrows. "Your ladyship does me proud to take refuge from the onclemency of the yallowments beneath my 'umble rooftree." His accent was barbarous; and he, like a low comedian, seemed to relish its vulgarity. As he spoke, he came in among them for shelter, and propped his spade against the wall of the chalet, kicking the soil from his hobnailed blucher boots, which were new.

"I come out, honoured lady," he resumed, much at his ease, "to house my spade, whereby I earn my living. What the pen is to the poet, such is the spade to the working man." He took the kerchief from his neck; wiped his temples as if the sweat of honest toil were there; and calmly tied it on again.

"If you'll 'scuse a remark from a common man," he observed; "your ladyship has a fine family of daughters."

"They are not my daughters," said Miss Wilson, rather shortly.

"Sisters, mebbe?"

"No."

"I thought they mout be, acause I have a sister myself. Not that I would make bold for to dror comparisons, even in my own mind; for she's only a common woman — as common a one as ever you see. But few women rise above the common. Last Sunday, in yon village church, I heard the minister read out that one man in a thousand had he found; 'but one woman in all these,' he says, 'have I not found'; and I thinks to myself, 'Right you are!' But I warrant he never met your ladyship."

A laugh, thinly disguised as a cough, escaped from Miss Carpenter.

"Young lady a ketchin' cold, I'm afeerd," he said, with respectful solicitude.

"Do you think the rain will last long?" said Agatha, politely.

The man examined the sky with a weather-wise air for some moments. Then he turned to Agatha, and replied humbly, "The Lord only knows, Miss. It is not for a common man like me to say."

Silence ensued, during which Agatha, furtively scrutinizing the tenant of the chalet, noticed that his face and neck were cleaner and less sunburnt than those of the ordinary toilers of Lyvern. His hands were hidden by large gardening gloves, stained with coal dust. Lyvern labourers, as a rule, had little objection to soil their hands: they never wore gloves. Still, she thought, there was no reason why an eccentric workman, insufferably talkative, and capable of an allusion to the pen of the poet, should not indulge himself with cheap gloves. But then the silk, silver-mounted umbrella ———

"The young lady's hi," he said suddenly, holding out the umbrella, "is fixed on this here. I am well aware that it is not for the lowest of the low to carry a gentleman's brolly; and I ask your ladyship's pardon for the liberty. I come by it accidental-like, and should be glad of a reasonable offer from any gentleman in want of a honest article."

As he spoke, two gentlemen, much in want of the article, as their clinging wet coats shewed, ran through the gateway, and made for the chalet. Fairholme arrived first, exclaiming, "Fearful shower!" and briskly turned his back to the ladies in order to stand at the edge of the veranda, and shake the water out of his hat. Josephs came next, shrinking from the damp contact of his own garments. He cringed to Miss Wilson, and hoped that she had escaped a wetting.

"So far I have," she replied. "The question is, how are we to get home?"

"Oh, it's only a shower," said Josephs, looking up cheerfully at the unbroken curtain of cloud. "It will clear up presently."

"It aint for a common man to set up his opinion again' a gentleman wot have profesh'nal knowledge of the heavens, as one may say," said the man; "but I would 'umbly offer to bet my umbrellar to his wide-awake that it dont cease raining this side of seven o'clock."

"That man lives here," whispered Miss Wilson; "and I suppose he wants to get rid of us."

"Hm!" said Fairholme. Then, turning to the strange labourer with the air of a person not to be trifled with, he raised his voice, and said, "You live here, do you, my man?"

"I do, sir, by your good leave, if I may make so bold."

"What's your name?"

"Jeff Smilash, sir, at your service."

"Where do you come from?"

"Brixtonbury, sir."

"Brixtonbury! Where's that?"

"Well, sir, I dont rightly know. If a gentleman like you, knowing jography and such, cant tell, how can I?"

"You ought to know where you were born, man. Havent you got common sense?"

"Where would such a one as me get common sense, sir? Besides, I was only a foundling. Mebbe I warnt born at all."

"Did I see you at church last Sunday?"

"No, sir. I only come o' Wensday."

"Well, let me see you there next Sunday," said Fairholme shortly, turning away from him.

Miss Wilson looked at the weather; at Josephs, who was conversing with Jane; and finally at Smilash, who knuckled his forehead without waiting to be addressed.

"Have you a boy whom you can send to Lyvern to get us a conveyance — a carriage? I will give him a shilling for his trouble."

"A shilling!" said Smilash, joyfully. "Your ladyship is a noble lady. Two four-wheeled cabs. There's eight on you."

"There is only one cab in Lyvern," said Miss Wilson. "Take this card to Mr. Marsh, the jobmaster; and tell him the predicament we are in. He will send vehicles."

Smilash took the card, and read it at a glance. He then went into the chalet. Reappearing presently in a sou'wester and oilskins, he ran off through the rain and vaulted over the gate with ridiculous elegance. No sooner had he vanished than, as often happens to remarkable men, he became the subject of conversation.

"A decent workman," said Josephs. "A well mannered man, considering his class."

"A born fool, though," said Fairholme.

"Or a rogue," said Agatha, emphasizing the suggestion by a glitter of her eyes and teeth, whilst her schoolfellows, rather disapproving of her freedom, stood stiffly dumb. "He told Miss Wilson that he had a sister, and that he had been to church last Sunday; and he has just told you that he is a foundling, and that he only came last Wednesday. His accent is put on; and he can read; and I dont believe he is a workman at all. Perhaps he is a burglar, come down to steal the college plate."

"Agatha," said Miss Wilson gravely: "you must be very careful how you say things of that kind."

"But it is so obvious. His explanation about the umbrella was made up to disarm suspicion. He handled it and leaned on it in a way that showed how much more familiar it was to him than that new spade he was so anxious about. And all his clothes are new."

"True," said Fairholme; "but there is not much in all that. Workmen nowadays ape gentlemen in everything. However, I will keep an eye on him."

"Oh, thank you so much," said Agatha.

Fairholme, suspecting mockery, frowned; and Miss Wilson looked severely at the mocker. Little more was said, except as to the chances — manifestly small — of the rain ceasing, until the tops of a cab, a decayed mourning coach, and three dripping hats, were seen over the hedge. Smilash sat on the box of the coach, beside the driver. When it stopped, he alighted; re-entered the chalet without speaking; came out with the umbrella; spread it above Miss Wilson's head; and said,

"Now, if your ladyship will come with me, I will see you dry into the shay; and then I'll bring your honoured nieces one by one."

"I shall come last," said Miss Wilson, irritated by his assumption that the party was a family one. "Gertrude: you had better go first."

"Allow me," said Fairholme, stepping forward, and attempting to take the umbrella.

"Thank you: I shall not trouble you," she said frostily, and tripped away over the oozing field with Smilash, who held the umbrella over her with ostentatious solicitude. In the same manner he led the rest to the vehicles, in which they packed themselves with some difficulty. Agatha, who came last but one, gave him threepence.

"You have a noble 'art, and an expressive hi, Miss," he said, apparently much moved. "Blessings on both! Blessings on both!"

He went back for Jane, who slipped on the wet grass and fell. He had to put forth his strength as he helped her to rise.

"Hope you aint sopped up much of the rainfall, Miss," he said. "You are a fine young lady for your age. Nigh on twelve stone, I should think."

She reddened and hurried to the cab, where Agatha was. But it was full; and Jane, much against her will, had to get into the coach, considerably diminishing the space left for Miss Wilson, to whom Smilash had returned.

"Now, dear lady," he said, "take care you dont slip. Come along."

Miss Wilson, ignoring the invitation, took a shilling from her purse.

"No, lady," said Smilash, with a virtuous air. "I am an honest man, and have never seen the inside of a jail except four times, and only twice for stealing. Your youngest daughter — her with the expressive hi — have paid me far beyond what is proper."

"I have told you that these young ladies are not my daughters," said Miss Wilson, sharply. "Why do you not listen to what is said to you?"

"Dont be too hard on a common man, lady," said Smilash, submissively. "The young lady have just given me three 'arf-crowns."

"Three half-crowns!" exclaimed Miss Wilson, angered at such extravagance.

"Bless her innocence, she dont know what is proper to give to a low sort like me! But I will not rob the young lady. 'Arf-a-crown is no more nor is fair for the job; and 'arf-a-crown will I keep, if agreeable to your noble ladyship. But I give you back the five bob in trust for her. Have you ever noticed her expressive hi?"

"Nonsense, sir. You had better keep the money now that you have got it."

"Wot! Sell for five bob the high opinion your ladyship has of me! No, dear lady: not likely. My father's very last words to me was —— "

"You said just now that you were a foundling," said Fairholme. "What are we to believe? Eh?"

"So I were, sir; but by my mother's side alone. Her ladyship will please to take back the money; for keep it I will not. I am of the lower orders, and therefore not a man of my word; but when I do stick to it, I stick like wax."

"Take it," said Fairholme to Miss Wilson. "Take it, of course. Seven and sixpence is a ridiculous sum to give him for what he has done. It would only set him drinking."

"His reverence says true, lady. The one 'arf-crown will keep me comfortably tight until Sunday morning; and more I do not desire."

"Just a little less of your tongue, my man," said Fairholme, taking the two coins from him, and handing them to Miss Wilson, who bade the clergymen good afternoon, and went to the coach under the umbrella.

"If your ladyship should want a handy man to do an odd job up at the college, I hope you will remember me," Smilash said, as they went down the slope.

"Oh: you know who I am, do you?" said Miss Wilson drily.

"All the country knows you, Miss, and worships you. I have few equals as a coiner; and if you should require a medal struck to give away for good behaviour or the like, I think I could strike one to your satisfaction. And if your ladyship should want a trifle of smuggled lace —— "

"You had better be careful, or you will get into trouble, I think," said Miss Wilson sternly. "Tell him to drive on."

The vehicles started; and Smilash took the liberty of waving his hat after them. Then he returned to the chalet; left the umbrella within; came out again; locked the door; put the key in his pocket; and walked off through the rain across the hill without taking the least notice of the astonished parsons.

In the meantime, Miss Wilson, unable to contain her annoyance at Agatha's extravagance, spoke of it to the girls who shared the coach with her. But Jane declared that Agatha only possessed threepence in the world, and therefore could not possibly have given the man thirty times that sum. When they reached the college, Agatha, confronted with Miss Wilson, opened her eyes in wonder, and exclaimed, laughing, "I only gave him threepence. He has sent me a present of four and ninepence!"

CHAPTER IV.

Saturday at Alton College, nominally a half holiday, was really a whole one. Classes in gymnastics, dancing, elocution, and drawing, were held in the morning. The afternoon was spent at lawn tennis, to which lady guests resident in the neighbourhood were allowed to bring their husbands, brothers and fathers: Miss Wilson being anxious to send her pupils forth into the world free from the uncouth stiffness of schoolgirls unaccustomed to society.

Late in October came a Saturday which proved anything but a holiday for Miss Wilson. At half-past one, luncheon being over, she went out of doors to a lawn that lay between the southern side of the college and a shrubbery. Here she found a group of girls watching Agatha and Jane, who were dragging a roller over the grass. One of them, tossing a ball about with her racket, happened to drive it into the shrubbery, whence, to the surprise of the company, Smilash presently emerged carrying the ball; blinking; and proclaiming that, though a common man, he had his feelings like another, and that his eye was neither a stick nor a stone. He was dressed as before; but his garments, soiled with clay and lime, no longer looked new.

"What brings you here, pray?" demanded Miss Wilson.

"I was led into the belief that you sent for me, lady," he replied. "The baker's lad told me so as he passed my 'umble cot this morning. I thought he were incapable of deceit."

"That is quite right: I did send for you. But why did you not go round to the servants' hall?"

"I am at present in search of it, lady. I were looking for it when this ball cotch me here" (touching his eye). "A cruel blow on the hi nat'rally spiles its vision and expression, and makes a honest man look like a thief."

"Agatha," said Miss Wilson: "come here."

"My dooty to you, Miss," said Smilash, pulling his forelock.

"This is the man from whom I had the five shillings, which he said you had just given him. Did you do so?"

"Certainly not. I only gave him threepence."

"But I showed the money to your ladyship," said Smilash, twist-ing his hat agitatedly. "I gev it you. Where would the like of me get five shillings except by the bounty of the rich and noble? If the young lady thinks I hadnt ort to have kep the tother 'arf-crown, I would not object to its bein' stopped from my wages if I were given a job of work here. But —— "

"But it's nonsense," said Agatha. "I never gave you three half-crowns."

"Perhaps you mout 'a made a mistake. Pence is summat similar to 'arf-crowns; and the day were very dark."

"I couldnt have," said Agatha. "Jane had my purse all the earlier part of the week, Miss Wilson; and she can tell you that there was only threepence in it. You know that I get my money on the first of every month. It never lasts longer than a week. The idea of my having seven and sixpence on the sixteenth is ridiculous."

"But I put it to you, Miss, aint it twice as ridiculous for me, a poor labourer, to give up money wot I never got?"

Vague alarm crept upon Agatha as the testimony of her senses was contradicted. "All I know is," she protested, "that I did not give it to you; so my pennies must have turned into half-crowns in your pocket."

"Mebbe so," said Smilash gravely. "I've heard, and I know it for a fact, that money grows in the pockets of the rich. Why not in the pockets of the poor as well? Why should you be su'prised at wot 'appens every day?"

"Had you any money of your own about you at the time?"

"Where could the like of me get money? — asking pardon for mak-ing so bold as to catechise your ladyship."

"I dont know where you could get it," said Miss Wilson testily: "I ask you, had you any?"

"Well, lady, I disremember. I will not impose upon you. I dis-remember."

"Then you have made a mistake," said Miss Wilson, handing him back his money. "Here. If it is not yours, it is not ours; so you had better keep it."

"Keep it! Oh, lady, but this is the heighth of nobility! And what shall I do to earn your bounty, lady?"

"It is not my bounty: I give it to you because it does not belong to me, and, I suppose, must belong to you. You seem to be a very simple man."

"I thank your ladyship: I hope I am. Respecting the day's work, now, lady: was you thinking of employing a poor man at all?"

"No, thank you: I have no occasion for your services. I have also to give you the shilling I promised you for getting the cabs. Here it is."

"Another shillin'!" cried Smilash, stupefied.

"Yes," said Miss Wilson, beginning to feel very angry. "Let me hear no more about it, please. Dont you understand that you have earned it?"

"I am a common man, and understand next to nothing," he replied reverently. "But if your ladyship would give me a day's work to keep me goin', I could put up all this money in a little wooden savings bank I have at home, and keep it to spend when sickness or old age shall, in a manner of speaking, lay their 'ands upon me. I could smooth that grass beautiful: them young ladies'll strain themselves with that heavy roller. If tennis is the word, I can put up nets fit to catch birds of paradise in. If the courts is to be chalked out in white, I can draw a line so straight that you could hardly keep yourself from erectin' an equilateral triangle on it. I am honest when well watched; and I can wait at table equal to the Lord Mayor o' London's butler."

"I cannot employ you without a character," said Miss Wilson, amused by his scrap of Euclid, and wondering where he had picked it up.

"I bear the best of characters, lady. The reverend rector has known me from a boy."

"I was speaking to him about you yesterday," said Miss Wilson, looking hard at him; "and he says you are a perfect stranger to him."

"Gentlemen is so forgetful," said Smilash sadly. "But I alluded to my native rector — meaning the rector of my native village, Auburn. 'Sweet Auburn, loveliest village of the plain,' as the gentleman called it."

"That was not the name you mentioned to Mr. Fairholme. I do not recollect what name you gave; but it was not Auburn, nor have I ever heard of any such place."

"Never read of sweet Auburn!"

"Not in any geography or gazetteer. Do you recollect telling me that you have been in prison?"

"Only six times," pleaded Smilash, his features working convulsively. "Dont bear too hard on a common man. Only six times, and all through drink. But I have took the pledge, and kep' it faithful for eighteen months past."

Miss Wilson now set down the man as one of those keen half-witted country fellows, contemptuously styled originals, who unintentionally make themselves popular by flattering the sense of sanity in those whose faculties are better adapted to circumstances.

"You have a bad memory, Mr. Smilash," she said good-humouredly. "You never give the same account of yourself twice."

"I am well aware that I do not express myself with exactability. Ladies and gentlemen have that power over words that they can always say what they mean; but a common man like me cant. Words dont come natural to him. He has more thoughts than words; and what words he has dont fit his thoughts. Might I take a turn with the roller, and make myself useful about the place until nightfall, for ninepence?"

Miss Wilson, who was expecting more than her usual Saturday visitors, considered the proposition, and assented. "And remember," she said, "that as you are a stranger here, your character in Lyvern depends upon the use you make of this opportunity."

"I am grateful to your noble ladyship. May your ladyship's goodness sew up the hole which is in the pocket where I carry my character, and which has caused me to lose it so frequent. It's a bad place for men to keep their characters in; but such is the fashion. And so hurray for the glorious nineteenth century!"

He took off his coat; seized the roller; and began to pull it with an energy foreign to the measured mill-horse manner of the accustomed labourer. Miss Wilson looked doubtfully at him, but, being in haste, went indoors without further comment. The girls, mistrusting his eccentricity, kept aloof. Agatha determined to have another and better look at him. Racket in hand, she walked slowly across the grass, and came close to him just as he, unaware of her approach, uttered a groan of exhaustion, and sat down to rest.

"Tired already, Mr. Smilash?" she said mockingly.

He looked up deliberately; took off one of his wash-leather gloves; fanned himself with it, displaying a white and fine hand; and at last replied, in the tone and with the accent of a gentleman,

"Very."

Agatha recoiled. He fanned himself without the least concern.

"You — you are not a labourer," she said at last.

"Obviously not."

"I thought not."

He nodded.

"Suppose I tell on you," she said, growing bolder as she recollected that she was not alone with him.

"If you do, I shall get out of it just as I got out of the half-crowns; and Miss Wilson will begin to think that you are mad."

"Then I really did not give you the seven and sixpence," she said, relieved.

"What is your own opinion?" he answered, taking three pennies from his pocket, jingling them in his palm. "What is your name?"

"I shall not tell you," said Agatha with dignity.

He shrugged his shoulders. "Perhaps you are right," he said. "I would not tell you mine if you asked me."

"I have not the slightest intention of asking you."

"No? Then Smilash shall do for you; and Agatha will do for me."

"You had better take care."

"Of what?"

"Of what you say, and — Are you not afraid of being found out?"

"I am found out already — by you; and I am none the worse."

"Suppose the police find you out!"

"Not they. Besides, I am not hiding from the police. I have a right to wear corduroy if I prefer it to broadcloth. Consider the advantages of it! It has procured me admission to Alton College, and the pleasure of your acquaintance. Will you excuse me if I go on with my rolling, just to keep up appearances. I can talk as I roll."

"You may, if you are fond of soliloquizing," she said, turning away as he rose.

"Seriously, Agatha, you must not tell the others about me."

"Do not call me Agatha," she said impetuously.

"What shall I call you, then?"

"You need not address me at all."

"I need, and will. Dont be ill natured."

"But I dont know you. I wonder at your —— " She hesitated at the word which occurred to her, but, being unable to think of a better one, used it. " —— at your cheek."

He laughed; and she watched him take a couple of turns with the roller. Presently, refreshing himself by a look at her, he caught her looking at him, and smiled. His smile was commonplace in comparison with the one she gave him in return, in which her eyes, her teeth, and the golden grain in her complexion seemed to flash simultaneously. He stopped rolling immediately, and rested his chin on the handle of the roller.

"If you neglect your work," said she maliciously, "you wont have the grass ready when the people come."

"What people?" he said, taken aback.

"Oh, lots of people. Most likely some who know you. There are visitors coming from London: my guardian, my guardianess, their daughter, my mother, and about a hundred more."

"Four in all. What are they coming for? To see you?"

"To take me away," she replied, watching for signs of disappointment on his part.

They were at once forthcoming. "What the deuce are they going to take you away for?" he said. "Is your education finished?"

"No. I have behaved badly; and I am going to be expelled."

He laughed again. "Come!" he said: "you are beginning to invent in the Smilash manner. What have you done?"

"I dont see why I should tell you. What have *you* done?"

"I! Oh: I have done nothing. I am only an unromantic gentleman, hiding from a romantic lady who is in love with me."

"Poor thing!" said Agatha sarcastically. "Of course, she has proposed to you; and you have refused."

"On the contrary: I proposed; and she accepted. That is why I have to hide."

"You tell stories charmingly," said Agatha. "Good-bye. Here is Miss Carpenter coming to hear what we are talking about."

"Good-bye. That story of your being expelled beats —— Might a common man make so bold as to inquire where the whitening machine is, Miss?"

This was addressed to Jane, who had come up with some of the others. Agatha expected to see Smilash presently discovered; for his disguise now seemed transparent: she wondered how the rest could be imposed on by it. Two o'clock, striking just then, reminded her of the impending interview with her guardian. A tremor shook her; and she felt a craving for some solitary hiding-place in which to await the summons. But it was a point of honour with her to appear perfectly indifferent to her trouble; so she stayed with the girls, laughing and chatting as they watched Smilash intently marking out the courts and setting up the nets. She made the others laugh too; for her hidden excitement, sharpened by irrepressible shootings of dread, stimulated her; and the romance of Smilash's disguise gave her a sensation of dreaming. Her imagination was already busy upon a drama, of which she was the heroine and Smilash the hero; though, with the real man before her, she could not indulge herself by attributing to him quite as much gloomy grandeur of character as to a wholly ideal personage. The plot was simple, and an old favourite with her. One of them was to love the other, and to die broken-hearted because the loved one would not requite the passion. For Agatha, prompt to ridicule sentimentality in her companions, and gifted with an infectious spirit of farce, secretly turned for imaginative luxury to visions of despair and death; and often endured the mortification of the successful clown who believes, whilst the public roar with laughter at him, that he was born a tragedian. There was much in her nature, she felt, that did not find expression in her popular representation of the soldier in the chimney.

By three o'clock, the local visitors had arrived; and tennis was proceeding in four courts, rolled and prepared by Smilash. The two curates were there, with a few lay gentlemen. Mrs. Miller, the vicar, and some mothers and other chaperons looked on and consumed light refreshments, which were brought out upon trays by Smilash, who had borrowed and put on a large white apron, and was making himself officiously busy.

At a quarter past the hour, a message came from Miss Wilson, requesting Miss Wylie's attendance. The visitors were at a loss to account for the sudden distraction of the young ladies' attention which ensued. Jane almost burst into tears, and answered Josephs rudely when he innocently asked what the matter was. Agatha went away apparently unconcerned, though her hand shook as she put aside her racket.

In a spacious drawing-room at the north side of the college, she found her mother, a slight woman in widow's weeds, with faded brown hair, and tearful eyes. With her were Mrs. Jansenius and her daughter. The two elder ladies kept severely silent whilst Agatha kissed them; and Mrs. Wylie sniffed. Henrietta embraced Agatha effusively.

"Where's Uncle John?" said Agatha. "Hasnt he come?"

"He is in the next room with Miss Wilson," said Mrs. Jansenius coldly. "They want you in there."

"I thought somebody was dead," said Agatha: "you all look so funereal. Now, mamma, put your handkerchief back again. If you cry, I will give Miss Wilson a piece of my mind for worrying you."

"No, no," said Mrs. Wylie, alarmed. "She has been so nice!"

"So good!" said Henrietta.

"She has been perfectly reasonable and kind," said Mrs. Jansenius.

"She always is," said Agatha complacently. "You didnt expect to find her in hysterics, did you?"

"Agatha," pleaded Mrs. Wylie: "dont be headstrong and foolish."

"Oh, she wont: I know she wont," said Henrietta coaxingly. "Will you, dear Agatha?"

"You may do as you like, as far as I am concerned," said Mrs. Jansenius. "But I hope you have more sense than to throw away your education for nothing."

"Your aunt is quite right," said Mrs. Wylie. "And your Uncle John is very angry with you. He will never speak to you again if you quarrel with Miss Wilson."

"He is not angry," said Henrietta; "but he is so anxious that you should get on well."

"He will naturally be disappointed if you persist in making a fool of yourself," said Mrs. Jansenius.

"All Miss Wilson wants is an apology for the dreadful things you wrote in her book," said Mrs. Wylie. "You'll apologize, dear, wont you?"

"Of course she will," said Henrietta.

"I think you had better," said Mrs. Jansenius.

"Perhaps I will," said Agatha.

"That's my own darling," said Mrs. Wylie, catching her hand.

"And perhaps, again, I wont."

"You will, dear," urged Mrs. Wylie, trying to draw Agatha, who passively resisted, closer to her. "For my sake. To oblige your mother, Agatha. You wont refuse me, dearest?"

Agatha laughed indulgently at her parent, who had long ago worn out this form of appeal. Then she turned to Henrietta, and said, "How is your *caro sposo?* I think it was hard that I was not a bridesmaid."

The red in Henrietta's cheeks brightened. Mrs. Jansenius hastened to interpose a dry reminder that Miss Wilson was waiting.

"Oh, she does not mind waiting," said Agatha, "because she thinks you are all at work getting me into a proper frame of mind. That was the arrangement she made with you before she left the room. Mamma knows that I have a little bird that tells me these things. I must say that you have not made me feel any goody-goodier so far. However, as poor Uncle John must be dreadfully frightened and uncomfortable, it is only kind to put an end to his suspense. Good-bye." And she went out leisurely. But she looked in again to say in a low voice, "Prepare for something thrilling. I feel just in the humour to say the most awful things." She vanished; and immediately they heard her tapping at the door of the next room.

Mr. Jansenius was indeed awaiting her with misgiving. Having discovered early in his career that his dignified person and fine voice caused people to stand in some awe of him, and to move him into the chair at public meetings, he had grown so accustomed to deference that any approach to familiarity or irreverence disconcerted him exceedingly. Agatha, on the other hand, having from her childhood heard Uncle John quoted as wisdom and authority incarnate, had begun in her tender years to scoff at him as a pompous and purseproud city merchant, whose sordid mind was unable to cope with her transcendental affairs. She had habitually terrified her mother by ridiculing him with an absolute contempt of which only childhood and extreme ignorance are capable. She had felt humiliated by his kindness to her (he was a generous giver of presents); and, with the instinct of an anarchist, had taken disparagement of his advice and defiance of his authority as the signs wherefrom she might infer surely that her face was turned to the light. The result was that he was a little afraid of her without being quite conscious of it; and she not at all afraid of him, and a little too conscious of it.

When she entered with her brightest smile in full play, Miss Wilson and Mr. Jansenius, seated at the table, looked somewhat like two culprits about to be indicted. Miss Wilson waited for him to speak, deferring to his imposing presence. But he was not ready; so she invited Agatha to sit down.

"Thank you," said Agatha sweetly. "Well, Uncle John: dont you know me?"

"I have heard with regret from Miss Wilson that you have been very troublesome here," he said, ignoring her remark, though secretly put out by it.

"Yes," said Agatha contritely. "I am so very sorry."

Mr. Jansenius, who had been led by Miss Wilson to expect the utmost contumacy, looked to her in surprise.

"You seem to think," said Miss Wilson, conscious of Mr. Jansenius's movement, and annoyed by it, "that you may transgress over and over again, and then set yourself right with us" (Miss Wilson never spoke of offences as against her individual authority, but as against the school community) "by saying that you are sorry. You spoke in a very different tone at our last meeting."

"I was angry then, Miss Wilson. And I thought I had a grievance — everybody thinks they have the same one. Besides, we were quarrelling — at least I was; and I always behave badly when I quarrel. I am so *very* sorry."

"The book was a serious matter," said Miss Wilson gravely. "You do not seem to think so."

"I understand Agatha to say that she is now sensible of the folly of her conduct with regard to the book; and that she is sorry for it," said Mr. Jansenius, instinctively inclining to Agatha's party as the stronger one, and the least dependent on him in a pecuniary sense.

"Have you seen the book?" said Agatha eagerly.

"No. Miss Wilson has described what has occurred."

"Oh, *do* let me get it," she cried, rising. "It will make Uncle John scream with laughing. May I, Miss Wilson?"

"There!" said Miss Wilson, indignantly. "It is this incorrigible flippancy of which I have to complain. Miss Wylie only varies it by downright insubordination."

Mr. Jansenius too was scandalized. His fine colour mounted at the idea of his screaming. "Tut, tut!" he said: "you must be serious, and more respectful to Miss Wilson. You are old enough to know better now, Agatha — quite old enough."

Agatha's mirth vanished. "What have I said? What have I done?" she asked, a faint purple spot appearing in her cheeks.

"You have spoken triflingly of — of the volume by which Miss Wilson sets great store, and properly so."

"If properly so, then why do you find fault with me?"

"Come, come," roared Mr. Jansenius, deliberately losing his temper as a last expedient to subdue her: "dont be impertinent, Miss."

Agatha's eyes dilated: evanescent flushes played upon her cheeks and neck: she stamped with her heel. "Uncle John," she cried: "if you *dare* to address me like that, I will never look at you, never speak to you, nor ever enter your house again. What do you know about good manners, that you should call me impertinent? I will not submit to intentional rudeness: that was the beginning of my quarrel with Miss Wilson. She told me I was impertinent; and I went away and told her that she was wrong by writing it in the fault book. She has been wrong all through; and I would have said so before, but that I wanted to be reconciled to her, and to let bygones be bygones. But if she insists on quarrelling, I cannot help it."

"I have already explained to you, Mr. Jansenius," said Miss Wilson, concentrating her resentment by an effort to suppress it, "that Miss Wylie has ignored all the opportunities that have been made for her to reinstate herself here. Mrs. Miller and I have waived merely personal considerations; and I have only required a simple acknowledgment of this offence against the college and its rules."

"I do not care *that* for Mrs. Miller," said Agatha, snapping her fingers. "And you are not half so good as I thought."

"Agatha," said Mr. Jansenius: "I desire you to hold your tongue."

Agatha drew a deep breath; sat down resignedly; and said, "There! I have done. I have lost my temper; so now we have all lost our tempers."

"You have no right to lose your temper, Miss," said Mr. Jansenius, following up a fancied advantage.

"I am the youngest, and the least to blame," she replied.

"There is nothing further to be said, Mr. Jansenius," said Miss Wilson, determinedly. "I am sorry that Miss Wylie has chosen to break with us."

"But I have not chosen to break with you; and I think it very hard that I am to be sent away. Nobody here has the least quarrel with me except you and Mrs. Miller. Mrs. Miller is annoyed because she mistook me for her cat, as if that was my fault! And really, Miss Wilson, I dont know why you are so angry. All the girls will think I have done something infamous if I am expelled. I ought to be let stay until the end of the term; and as to the Rec — the fault book, you told me most particularly when I first came that I might write in it or not just as I pleased, and that you never dictated or interfered with what was written. And yet the very first time I write a word you disapprove of, you expel me. Nobody will ever believe now that the entries are voluntary."

Miss Wilson's conscience, already smitten by the coarseness and absence of moral force in the echo of her own "You are impertinent," from the mouth of Mr. Jansenius, took fresh alarm. "The fault book," she said, "is for the purpose of recording self-reproach alone, and is not a vehicle for accusations against others."

"I am quite sure that neither Jane nor Gertrude nor I reproached ourselves in the least for going downstairs as we did; and yet you did not blame us for entering that. Besides, the book represented moral force — at least you always said so; and when you gave up moral force, I thought an entry should be made of that. Of course I was in a rage at the time; but when I came to myself I thought I had done right; and I think so still, though it would perhaps have been better to have passed it over."

"Why do you say that I gave up moral force?"

"Telling people to leave the room is not moral force. Calling them impertinent is not moral force."

"You think then that I am bound to listen patiently to whatever you choose to say to me, however unbecoming it may be from one in your position to one in mine?"

"But I said nothing unbecoming," said Agatha. Then, breaking off restlessly, and smiling again, she said, "Oh, dont let us argue. I am very sorry, and very troublesome, and very fond of you and of the college; and I wont come back next term unless you like."

"Agatha," said Miss Wilson, shaken: "these expressions of regard cost you so little, and when they have effected their purpose, are so soon forgotten *by you,* that they have ceased to satisfy me. I am very reluctant to insist on your leaving us at once. But as your uncle has told you, you are old and sensible enough to know the difference between order and disorder. Hitherto you have been on the side of disorder, an element which was hardly known here until you came, as Mrs. Trefusis can tell you. Nevertheless, if you will promise to be more careful in future, I will waive all past cause of complaint; and at the end of the term I shall be able to judge as to your continuing among us."

Agatha rose, beaming. "Dear Miss Wilson," she said, "you are *so* good! I promise, of course. I will go and tell mamma."

Before they could add a word, she had turned with a pirouette to the door, and fled, presenting herself a moment later in the drawing-

room to the three ladies, whom she surveyed with a whimsical smile
in silence.

"Well?" said Mrs. Jansenius peremptorily.

"Well, dear?" said Mrs. Trefusis, caressingly.

Mrs. Wylie stifled a sob and looked imploringly at her daughter.

"I had no end of trouble in bringing them to reason," said Agatha,
after a provoking pause. "They behaved like children; and I was like
an angel. I am to stay, of course."

"Blessings on you, my darling," faltered Mrs. Wylie, attempting a
kiss, which Agatha dexterously evaded.

"I have promised to be very good, and studious, and quiet, and
decorous, in future. Do you remember my castanet song, Hetty?

Tra! lalala, la! la! la!
Tra! lalala, la! la! la!
Tra! lalalalalalalalalalala!"

And she danced about the room, snapping her fingers instead of
castanets.

"Dont be so reckless and wicked, my love," said Mrs. Wylie. "You
will break your poor mother's heart."

Miss Wilson and Mr. Jansenius entered just then; and Agatha became motionless and gazed abstractedly at a vase of flowers. Miss
Wilson invited her visitors to join the tennis players. Mr. Jansenius
looked sternly and disappointedly at Agatha, who elevated her left
eyebrow and depressed her right simultaneously; but he, shaking his
head to signify that he was not be conciliated by facial feats, however
difficult or contrary to nature, went out with Miss Wilson, followed by
Mrs. Jansenius and Mrs. Wylie.

"How is your Hubby?" said Agatha then, brusquely to Henrietta.

Mrs. Trefusis's eyes filled with tears so quickly that, as she bent her
head to hide them, they fell, sprinkling Agatha's hand.

"This is such a dear old place," she began. "The associations of my
girlhood ——"

"What is the matter between you and Hubby?" demanded Agatha,
interrupting her. "You had better tell me, or I will ask him when I
meet him."

"I was about to tell you, only you did not give me time."

"That is a most awful cram," said Agatha. "But no matter. Go on."

Henrietta hesitated. Her dignity as a married woman, and the reality of her grief, revolted against the shallow acuteness of the schoolgirl. But she found herself no better able to resist Agatha's domineer-
ing than she had been in her childhood, and much more desirous of

obtaining her sympathy. Besides, she had already learnt to tell the story herself rather than leave its narration to others, whose accounts did not, she felt, put her case in the proper light. So she told Agatha of her marriage; her wild love for her husband; his wild love for her; and his mysterious disappearance without leaving word or sign behind him. She did not mention the letter.

"Have you had him searched for?" said Agatha, repressing an inclination to laugh.

"But where? Had I the remotest clue, I would follow him barefoot to the end of the world."

"I think you ought to search all the rivers: you would have to do that barefoot. He must have fallen in somewhere, or fallen down some place."

"No, no. Do you think I should be here if I thought his life in danger? I have reasons — I know that he is only gone away."

"Oh, indeed! He took his portmanteau with him, did he? Perhaps he has gone to Paris to buy you something nice, and give you a pleasant surprise."

"No," said Henrietta dejectedly. "He knew that I wanted nothing."

"Then I suppose he got tired of you and ran away."

Henrietta's peculiar scarlet blush flowed rapidly over her cheeks as she flung Agatha's arm away, exclaiming, "How dare you say so? You have no heart. He adored me."

"Bosh!" said Agatha. "People always grow tired of one another. I grow tired of myself whenever I am left alone for ten minutes; and I am certain that I am fonder of myself than anyone can be of another person."

"I know you are," said Henrietta, pained and spiteful. "You have always been particularly fond of yourself."

"Very likely he resembles me in that respect. In that case he will grow tired of himself and come back; and you will both coo like turtle doves until he runs away again. Ugh! Serve you right for getting married. I wonder how people can be so mad as to do it, with the example of their married acquaintances all warning them against it."

"You dont know what it is to love," said Henrietta, plaintively, and yet patronizingly. "Besides, we were not like other couples."

"So it seems. But never mind: take my word for it, he will return to you as soon as he has had enough of his own company. Dont worry thinking about him; but come and have a game at lawn tennis."

During this conversation they had left the drawing-room, and made a detour through the grounds. They were now approaching the tennis courts by a path which wound between two laurel hedges through the shrubbery.

Meanwhile, Smilash, waiting on the guests in his white apron and gloves (which he had positively refused to take off, alleging that he was a common man, with common hands such as born ladies and gentlemen could not be expected to take meat and drink from) had behaved himself irreproachably until the arrival of Miss Wilson and her visitors, which occurred as he was returning to the table with an empty tray, moving so swiftly that he nearly came into collision with Mrs. Jansenius. Instead of apologizing, he changed countenance, hastily held up the tray like a shield before his face, and began to walk backward from her, stumbling presently against Miss Lindsay, who was running to return a ball. Without heeding her angry look and curt rebuke, he half turned and sidled away into the shrubbery, whence the tray presently rose into the air; flew across the laurel hedge; and descended with a peal of stage thunder on the stooped shoulders of Josephs. Miss Wilson, after asking the housekeeper, with some asperity, why she had allowed that man to interfere in the attendance, explained to the guests that he was the idiot of the countryside. Mr. Jansenius laughed, and said that he had not seen the man's face, but that his figure reminded him forcibly of some one: he could not just then recollect exactly whom.

Smilash, making off through the shrubbery, found the end of his path blocked by Agatha and a young lady whose appearance alarmed him more than had that of Mrs. Jansenius. He attempted to force his way through the hedge, but in vain: the laurel was impenetrable; and the noise he made attracted the attention of the approaching couple. He made no further effort to escape, but threw his borrowed apron over his head, and stood bolt upright with his back against the bushes.

"What is that man doing there?" said Henrietta, stopping mistrustfully.

Agatha laughed, and said loudly, so that he might hear, "It is only a harmless madman that Miss Wilson employs. He is fond of disguising himself in some silly way, and trying to frighten us. Dont be afraid. Come on."

Henrietta hung back; but her arm was linked in Agatha's and she was drawn along in spite of herself. Smilash did not move. Agatha strolled on coolly, and as she passed him, adroitly caught the apron between her finger and thumb, and twitched it from his face. Instantly Henrietta uttered a piercing scream, and Smilash caught her in his arms.

"Quick," he said to Agatha: "she is fainting. Run for some water. Run!" And he bent over Henrietta, who clung to him frantically. Agatha, bewildered by the effect of her practical joke, hesitated a moment, and then ran to the lawn.

"What is the matter?" said Fairholme.

"Nothing. I want some water — quick, please. Henrietta has fainted in the shrubbery: that is all."

"Please do not stir," said Miss Wilson authoritatively: "you will crowd the path, and delay useful assistance. Miss Ward: kindly get some water and bring it to us. Agatha: come with me and point out where Mrs. Trefusis is. You may come, too, Miss Carpenter: you are so strong. The rest will please remain where they are."

Followed by the two girls, she hurried into the shrubbery, where Mr. Jansenius was already looking anxiously for his daughter. He was the only person they found there. Smilash and Henrietta were gone.

At first the seekers, merely puzzled, did nothing but question Agatha incredulously as to the exact spot on which Henrietta had fallen. But Mr. Jansenius soon made them understand that the position of a lady in the hands of a half-witted labourer was one of danger. His agitation infected them; and when Agatha endeavoured to reassure him by declaring that Smilash was a disguised gentleman, Miss Wilson, supposing this to be a mere repetition of her former idle conjecture, told her sharply to hold her tongue, as the time was not one for talking nonsense. The news now spread through the whole company; and the excitement became intense. Fairholme shouted for volunteers to make up a searching party. All the men present responded; and they were about to rush to the college gates in a body when it occurred to the cooler among them that they had better divide into several parties, in order that search might be made at once in different quarters. Ten minutes of confusion followed. Mr. Jansenius started several times in quest of Henrietta, and, when he had gone a few steps, returned and begged that no more time should be wasted. Josephs, whose faith was simple, retired to pray, and did good, as far as it went, by withdrawing one voice from the din of plans, objections and suggestions which the rest were making: each person trying to be heard above the others.

At last Miss Wilson quelled the prevailing anarchy. Servants were sent to alarm the neighbours and call in the village police. Detachments were sent in various directions under the command of Fairholme and other energetic spirits. The girls formed parties among themselves, which were reinforced by male deserters from the previous levies. Miss Wilson then went indoors, and conducted a search through the interior of the college. Only two persons were left on the tennis ground: Agatha and Mrs. Jansenius, who had been surprisingly calm throughout.

"You need not be anxious," said Agatha, who had been standing aloof since her rebuff by Miss Wilson. "I am sure there is no danger. It is most extraordinary that they have gone away; but the man is no

more mad than I am; and I know he is a gentleman. He told me so."
"Let us hope for the best," said Mrs. Jansenius, smoothly. "I think
I will sit down — I feel so tired. Thanks." (Agatha had handed her
a chair.) "What did you say he told you? — this man."

Agatha related the circumstances of her acquaintance with Smilash,
adding at Mrs. Jansenius's request, a minute description of his personal appearance. Mrs. Jansenius remarked that it was very singular,
and that she was sure Henrietta was quite safe. She then partook of
claret-cup and sandwiches. Agatha, though glad to find someone disposed to listen to her, was puzzled by her aunt's coolness, and was
even goaded into pointing out that though Smilash was not a labourer,
it did not follow that he was an honest man. But Mrs. Jansenius only
said, "Oh: she is safe — quite safe. At least, of course I can only hope
so. We shall have news presently," and took another sandwich.

The searchers soon began to return, baffled. A few shepherds, the
only persons in the vicinity, had been asked whether they had seen
a young lady and a labourer. Some of them had seen a young woman
with a basket of clothes, if that mout be her. Some thought that Phil
Martin the carrier would see her if anybody would. None of them had
any positive information to give.

As the afternoon wore on, and party after party returned tired and
unsuccessful, depression replaced excitement; conversation, no longer
tumultuous, was carried on in whispers; and some of the local visitors
slipped away to their homes with a growing conviction that something
unpleasant had happened, and that it would be as well not to be mixed
up in it. Mr. Jansenius, though a few words from his wife had surprised and somewhat calmed him, was still pitiably restless and uneasy.

At last the police arrived. At sight of their uniforms, excitement
revived: there was a general conviction that something effectual would
be done now. But the constables were only mortal; and in a few moments a whisper spread that they were fools. They doubted everything
told them, and expressed their contempt for amateur searching by entering on a fresh investigation, prying with the greatest care into the
least probable places. Two of them went off to the chalet to look for
Smilash. Then Fairholme, sunburnt, perspiring, and dusty, but still
energetic, brought back the exhausted remnant of his party, with a
sullen boy, who scowled defiantly at the police, evidently believing
that he was about to be delivered into their custody.

Fairholme had been everywhere, and, having seen nothing of the
missing pair, had come to the conclusion that they were nowhere. He
had asked everybody for information, and had let them know that he
meant to have it too, if it was to be had. But it was not to be had.

The sole result of his labour was the evidence of the boy whom he didnt believe.

"Hm!" said the inspector, not quite pleased by Fairholme's zeal, and yet overborne by it. "You're Wickens's boy, aint you?"

"Yes I am Wickens's boy," said the witness, partly fierce, partly lachrymose; "and I say I seen him; and if anyone sez I didnt see him, he's a lie."

"Come," said the inspector sharply: "give us none of your cheek; but tell us what you saw, or you'll have to deal with me afterwards."

"I dont care who I deal with," said the boy, at bay. "I cant be took for seein' him, because there's no lor agin it. I was in the gravel pit in the canal meadow ——"

"What business had you there?" said the inspector, interrupting.

"I got leave to be there," said the boy insolently, but reddening.

"Who gave you leave?" said the inspector, collaring him. "Ah," he added, as the captive burst into tears: "I told you you'd have to deal with me. Now hold your noise, and remember where you are and who you're speakin' to; and perhaps I maynt lock you up this time. Tell me what you saw when you were trespassin' in the meadow."

"I sor a young 'oman, and a man. And I see her kissin' him; and the gentleman wont believe me."

"You mean you saw him kissing her, more likely."

"No I dont. I know wot it is to have a girl kiss you when you dont want. And I gev a screech to friken 'em. And he called me and gev me tuppence, and sez, 'You go to the devil,' he sez; 'and dont tell no one you seen me here, or else,' he sez, 'I might be tempted to drownd you,' he sez, 'and wot a shock that would be to your parents!' 'Oh yes, very likely,' I sez, jes' like that. Then I went away, because he knows Mr. Wickens; and I was afeerd of his telling on me."

The boy being now subdued, questions were put to him from all sides. But his powers of observation and description went no further. As he was anxious to propitiate his captors, he answered as often as possible in the affirmative. Mr. Jansenius asked him whether the young woman he had seen was a lady; and he said yes. Was the man a labourer? Yes — after a moment's hesitation. How was she dressed? He hadnt taken notice. Had she red flowers in her hat? Yes. Had she a green dress? Yes. Were the flowers in her hat yellow? (Agatha's question.) Yes. Was her dress pink? Yes. Sure it wasnt black? No answer.

"I told you he was a liar," said Fairholme contemptuously.

"Well: I expect he's seen something," said the inspector; "but what it was, or who it was, is more than I can get out of him."

There was a pause; and they looked askance upon Wickens's boy.

His account of the kissing made it almost an insult to the Janseniuses to identify with Henrietta the person he had seen. Jane suggested dragging the canal, but was silenced by an indignant "sh-sh-sh," accompanied by apprehensive and sympathetic glances at the bereaved parents. She was displaced from the focus of attention by the appearance of the two policemen who had been sent to the chalet. Smilash was between them, apparently a prisoner. At a distance, he seemed to have suffered some frightful injury to his head; but when he was brought into the midst of the company, it appeared that he had twisted a red handkerchief about his face as if to soothe a toothache. He had a particularly hangdog expression as he stood before the inspector with his head bowed and his countenance averted from Mr. Jansenius, who, attempting to scrutinize his features, could see nothing but a patch of red handkerchief.

One of the policemen described how they had found Smilash in the act of entering his dwelling; how he had refused to give any information or to go to the college, and had defied them to take him there against his will; and how, on their at last proposing to send for the inspector and Mr. Jansenius, he had called them asses, and consented to accompany them. The policeman concluded by declaring that the man was either drunk or designing, as he could not or would not speak sensibly.

"Look here, governor," began Smilash to the inspector: "I am a common man — no commoner goin,' as you may see for ——"

"That's 'im," cried Wickens's boy, suddenly struck with a sense of his own importance as a witness. "That's 'im that the lady kissed, and that gev me tuppence and threatened to drownd me."

"And with a 'umble and contrite 'art do I regret that I did not drownd you, you young rascal," said Smilash. "It aint manners to interrupt a man who, though common, might be your father for years and wisdom."

"Hold your tongue," said the inspector to the boy. "Now, Smilash: do you wish to make any statement? Be careful; for whatever you say may be used against you hereafter."

"If you was to lead me straight away to the scaffold, colonel, I could tell you no more than the truth. If any man can say that he has heard Jeff Smilash tell a lie, let him stand forth."

"We dont want to hear about that," said the inspector. "As you are a stranger in these parts, nobody here knows any bad of you. No more do they know any good of you neither."

"Colonel," said Smilash, deeply impressed: "you have a penetrating mind; and you know a bad character at sight. Not to deceive you, I am that given to lying, and laziness, and self-indulgence of all sorts, that the only excuse I can find for myself is that it is the nature of the race so to be; for most men is just as bad as me, and some of 'em worser. I do not speak pers'nal to you, governor, nor to the honourable gentlemen here assembled. But then you, colonel, are a hinspector of police, which I take to be more than merely human; and as to the gentlemen here, a gentleman aint a man — leastways not a common man: the common man bein' the slave wot feeds and clothes the gentleman beyond the common."

"Come," said the inspector, unable to follow these observations: "you are a clever dodger; but you cant dodge me. Have you any statement to make with reference to the lady that was last seen in your company?"

"Make a statement about a lady!" said Smilash indignantly. "Far be the thought from my mind!"

"What have you done with her?" said Agatha, impetuously. "Dont be silly."

"You're not bound to answer that you know," said the inspector, a little put out by Agatha's taking advantage of her irresponsible unofficial position to come so directly to the point. "You may if you like, though. If you've done any harm, you'd better hold your tongue. If not, you'd better say so."

"I will set the young lady's mind at rest respecting her honourable sister," said Smilash. "When the young lady caught sight of me, she fainted. Bein' but a young man, and not used to ladies, I will not deny but that I were a bit scared, and that my mind were not open to the sensiblest considerations. When she unveils her orbs, so to speak, she ketches me round the neck, not knowin' me from Adam the father of us all, and sez, 'Bring me some water; and dont let the girls see me.' Through not 'avin' the intelligence to think for myself, I done just what she told me. I ups with her in my arms — she bein' a light weight and a slender figure — and makes for the canal as fast as I could. When I got there, I lays her on the bank, and goes for the water. But what with factories, and pollutions, and high civilizations of one sort and another, English canal water aint fit to sprinkle on a lady, much less for her to drink. Just then, as luck would have it, a barge came along, and took her aboard; and ——"

"No such a thing," said Wickens's boy stubbornly, emboldened by witnessing the effrontery of one apparently of his own class. "I sor you two standin' together, and her a kissin' of you. There wornt no barge."

"Is the maiden modesty of a born lady to be disbelieved on the word of a common boy that only walks the earth by the sufferance of the landlords and moneylords he helps to feed?" cried Smilash indignantly.

"Why, you young infidel, a lady aint made of common brick like you. She dont know what a kiss means; and if she did is it likely that she'd kiss me when a fine man like the inspector here would be only too happy to oblige her. Fie, for shame! The barge were red and yellow, with a green dragon for a figurehead, and a white horse towin' of it. Perhaps you're colour-blind, and cant distinguish red and yellow. The bargee was moved to compassion by the sight of the poor faintin' lady and the offer of 'arf-a-crown; and he had a mother that acted as a mother should. There was a cabin in that barge about as big as the locker where your ladyship keeps your jam and pickles; and in that locker the bargee lives, quite domestic, with his wife and mother and five children. Them canal boats is what you may call the wooden walls of England."

"Come: get on with your story," said the inspector. "We know what barges is as well as you."

"I wish more knew of 'em," retorted Smilash: "perhaps it 'ud lighten your work a bit. However, as I was sayin', we went right down the canal to Lyvern, where we got off; and the lady she took the railway omnibus, and went away in it. With the noble openhandedness of her class, she gave me sixpence: here it is, in proof that my words is true. And I wish her safe home; and if I was on the rack I could tell no more, except that when I got back I were laid hands on by these here bobbies, contrary to the British constitooshun; and if your ladyship will kindly go to where that constitooshun is wrote down, and find out wot it sez about my rights and liberties — for I have been told that the working-man has his liberties, and have myself seen plenty took with him — you will oblige a common chap more than his education will enable him to express."

"Sir," cried Mr. Jansenius suddenly: "will you hold up your head, and look me in the face?"

Smilash did so, and immediately started theatrically, exclaiming, "Whom do I see?"

"You would hardly believe it," he continued, addressing the company at large; "but I am well beknown to this honourable gentleman. I see it upon your lips, governor, to ask after my missus; and I thank you for your condescending interest. She is well, sir; and my residence here is fully agreed upon between us. What little cloud may have rose upon our domestic horizon has past away; and, governor," — here Smilash's voice fell with graver emphasis — "them as interferes betwixt man and wife now will incur a nevvy responsibility. Here I am, such as you see me; and here I mean to stay, likewise such as you see me. That is, if what you may call destiny permits. For destiny is a rum thing, governor. I came here thinking it was the last place in the world I should ever set eyes on you in; and blow me if you aint a'most the first person I pops on."

"I do not choose to be a party to this mummery of ——"

"Asking your leave to take the word out of your mouth, governor: I make you a party to nothink. Respecting my past conduct, you may out with it or you may keep it to yourself. All I say is that if you out with some of it I will out with the rest. All or none. You are free to tell the inspector here that I am a bad un. His penetrating mind have discovered that already. But if you go into names and particulars, you will not only be acting against the wishes of my missus, but you will lead to my tellin' the whole story right out afore everyone here, and then goin' away where no one wont never find me."

"I think the less said the better," said Mrs. Jansenius, uneasily observant of the curiosity and surprise this dialogue was causing. "But understand this, Mr. ——"

"Smilash, dear lady: Jeff Smilash."

"—— Mr. Smilash. Whatever arrangement you may have made with your wife, it has nothing to do with me. You have behaved infamously; and I desire to have as little as possible to say to you in future."

"I desire to have *nothing* to say to you —— *nothing!*" said Mr. Jansenius. "I look on your conduct as an insult to me, personally. You may live in any fashion you please, and where you please. All England is open to you except one place —— my house. Come, Ruth." He offered his arm to his wife; she took it; and they turned away, looking about for Agatha, who, disgusted at the gaping curiosity of the rest, had pointedly withdrawn beyond earshot of the conversation.

Miss Wilson looked from Smilash —— who had watched Mr. Jansenius's explosion of wrath with friendly interest, as if it concerned him as a curious spectator only —— to her two visitors as they retreated. "Pray do you consider this man's statement satisfactory?" she said to them. "*I* do not."

"I am far too common a man to be able to make any statement that could satisfy a mind cultivated as yours has been," said Smilash; "but I would 'umbly pint out to you that there is a boy yonder with a telegram trying to shove hisself through the 'iborn throng."

"Miss Wilson!" cried the boy shrilly.

She took the telegram; read it; and frowned. "We have had all our trouble for nothing, ladies and gentlemen," she said, with suppressed vexation. "Mrs. Trefusis says here that she has gone back to London. She has not considered it necessary to add any explanation."

There was a general murmur of disappointment.

"Dont lose heart, ladies," said Smilash. "She may be drowned or murdered for all we know. Anyone may send a telegram in a false name. Perhaps it's a plant. Let's hope for your sakes that some little accident — on the railway, for instance — may happen yet."

Miss Wilson turned upon him, glad to find someone with whom she might justly be angry. "*You* had better go about your business," she said. "And dont let me see you here again."

"This is 'ard," said Smilash plaintively. "My intentions was nothing but good. But I know wot it is. It's that young varmint a-saying that the young lady kissed me."

"Inspector," said Miss Wilson: "will you oblige me by seeing that he leaves the college as soon as possible."

"Where's my wages?" he retorted reproachfully. "Where's my lawful wages? I am su'prised at a lady like you, chock full o' moral science and political economy, wanting to put a poor man off. Where's your wages fund? Where's your remuneratory capital?"

"Dont you give him anything, maam," said the Inspector. "The money he's had from the lady will pay him very well. Move on here, or we'll precious soon hurry you."

"Very well," grumbled Smilash. "I bargained for ninepence; and what with the roller, and opening the soda water, and shoving them heavy tables about, there was a decomposition of tissue in me to the tune of two shillings. But all I ask is the ninepence, and let the lady keep the one and threppence as the reward of abstinence. Exploitation of labour at the rate of a hundred and twenty-five per cent., that is. Come: give us ninepence; and I'll go straight off."

"Here is a shilling," said Miss Wilson. "Now go."

"Threppence change!" cried Smilash. "Honesty has ever been ———"

"You may keep the change."

"You have a noble 'art, lady; but you're flying in the face of the law of supply and demand. If you keep payin' at this rate, there'll be a rush of labourers to the college; and competition 'll soon bring you down from a shilling to sixpence, let alone ninepence. That's the way wages goes down and deathrates goes up, worse luck for the likes of hus, as has to sell ourselves like pigs in the market."

He was about to continue, when the policeman took him by the arm; turned him towards the gate; and pointed expressively in that direction. Smilash looked vacantly at him for a moment. Then with a wink at Fairholme, he walked gravely away, amid general staring and silence.

CHAPTER V.

What had passed between Smilash and Henrietta remained unknown except to themselves. Agatha had seen Henrietta clasping his neck in her arms, but had not waited to hear the exclamation of "Sidney, Sidney," which followed, nor to see him press her face to his breast in his anxiety to stifle her voice as he said, "My darling love, dont screech, I implore you. Confound it, we shall have the whole pack here in a moment. Hush!"

"Dont leave me again, Sidney," she entreated, clinging faster to him as his perplexed gaze, wandering towards the entrance to the shrubbery, seemed to forsake her. A din of voices in that direction precipitated his irresolution.

"We must run away, Hetty," he said. "Hold fast about my neck; and dont strangle me. Now then." He lifted her upon his shoulder, and ran swiftly through the grounds. When they were stopped by the wall, he placed her atop of it; scrambled over; and made her jump into his arms. Then he staggered away with her across the fields, gasping out, in reply to the inarticulate remonstrances which burst from her as he stumbled and reeled at every hillock, "Your weight is increasing at the rate of a stone a second, my love. If you stoop you will break my back. Oh Lord, here's a ditch!"

"Let me down," screamed Henrietta in an ecstasy of delight and apprehension. "You will hurt yourself; and — Oh *do* take ——"

He struggled through a dry ditch as she spoke, and came out upon a grassy place that bordered the tow-path of the canal. Here, on the bank of a hollow where the moss was dry and soft, he seated her; threw himself prone on his elbows before her; and said, panting,

"Nessus carrying off Dejanira was nothing to this! Whew! Well, my darling: are you glad to see me?"

"But ——"

"But me no buts, unless you wish me to vanish again and for ever. Wretch that I am, I have longed for you unspeakably more than once since I ran away from you. You didnt care, of course."

"I did. I did indeed. Why did you leave me, Sidney?"

"Lest a worse thing might befall. Come, dont let us waste in explanations the few minutes we have left. Give me a kiss."

"Then you are going to leave me again. Oh, Sidney ——"

"Never mind to-morrow, Hetty. Be like the sun and the meadow, which are not in the least concerned about the coming winter. Why do you stare at the cursed canal, blindly dragging its load of filth from place to place until it pitches it into the sea — just as a crowded street pitches its load into the cemetery? Stare at *me*; and give me a kiss."

She gave him several, and said coaxingly, with her arm still upon his shoulder, "You only talk that way to frighten me, Sidney: I know you do."

"You are the bright sun of my senses," he said, embracing her. "I feel my heart and brain wither in your smile; and I fling them to you for your prey with exultation. How happy I am to have a wife who does not despise me for doing so — who rather loves me the more!"

"Dont be silly," said Henrietta, smiling vacantly. Then, stung by a half intuition of his meaning, she repulsed him and said angrily, "*You* despise *me*."

"Not more than I despise myself. Indeed, not so much; for many emotions that seem base from within, seem lovable from without."

"You intend to leave me again. I feel it. I know it."

"You think you know it because you feel it. Not a bad reason, either!"

"Then you *are* going to leave me?"

"Do you not feel it and know it? Yes, my cherished Hetty: I assuredly am."

She broke into wild exclamations of grief; and he drew her head down, and kissed her with a tender action which she could not resist, and a wry face which she did not see.

"My poor Hetty, you dont understand me."

"I only understand that you hate me, and want to go away from me."

"That would be easy to understand. But the strangeness is that I *love* you and want to go away from you. Not for ever. Only for a time."

"But I dont want you to go away. I wont let you go away," she said, a trace of fierceness mingling with her entreaty. "Why do you want to leave me if you love me?"

"How do I know? I can no more tell you the whys and wherefores of myself than I can lift myself up by the waistband and carry myself into the next county, as some one challenged a speculator in perpetual motion to do. I am too much a pessimist to respect my own affections. Do you know what a pessimist is?"

"A man who thinks everybody as nasty as himself, and hates them for it."

"So, or thereabout. Modern English polite society, my native sphere, seems to me as corrupt as consciousness of culture and absence of honesty can make it. A canting, lie-loving, fact-hating, scribbling, chattering, wealth-hunting, pleasure-hunting, celebrity-hunting mob, that, having lost the fear of hell, and not replaced it by the love of justice, cares for nothing but the lion's share of the wealth wrung by threat of starvation from the hands of the classes that create it. — If you interrupt me with a silly speech, Hetty, I will pitch you into the canal, and die of sorrow for my lost love afterwards. — You know what I am, according to the conventional description: a gentleman with lots of money. Do you know the wicked origin of that money and gentility?"

"Oh, Sidney: have you been doing anything?"

"No, my best beloved: I am a gentleman, and have been doing nothing. That a man can do so and not starve is now-a-days not even a paradox. Every halfpenny I possess is stolen money; but it has been stolen legally; and, what is of some practical importance to you, I have no means of restoring it to the rightful owners even if I felt inclined to. Do you know what my father was?"

"What difference can that make now? Dont be disagreeable and full of ridiculous fads, Sidney dear. I didnt marry your father."

"No; but you married — only incidentally, of course — my father's fortune. That necklace of yours was purchased with his money; and I can almost fancy stains of blood ——"

"Stop, Sidney. I dont like this sort of romancing. It's all nonsense. *Do* be nice to me."

"There are stains of sweat on it, I know."

"You nasty wretch!"

"I am thinking, not of you, my dainty one, but of the unfortunate people who slave that we may live idly. Let me explain to you why we are so rich. My father was a shrewd, energetic and ambitious Manchester man, who understood an exchange of any sort as a transaction by which one man should lose and the other gain. He made it his object to make as many exchanges as possible, and to be always the gaining party in them. I do not know exactly what he was; for he was ashamed both of his antecedents and of his relatives; from which I can only infer that they were honest and therefore unsuccessful people. However, he acquired some knowledge of the cotton trade; saved some money; borrowed some more on the security of his reputation for getting the better of other people in business; and, as he accurately told me afterwards, started *for himself*. He bought a factory and some raw cotton. Now you must know that a man, by labouring some time on a piece of raw cotton, can turn it into a piece of manufactured cotton fit for making into sheets and shifts and the like. The manufactured cotton is more valuable than the raw cotton, because the manufacture costs wear and tear of machinery, wear and tear of the factory, rent of the ground upon which the factory is built, and human labour, or wear and tear of live men, which has to be made good by food, shelter, and rest. Do you understand that?"

"We used to learn all about it at college. I dont see what it has to do with us, since you are not in the cotton trade."

"You learned as much as it was thought safe to teach you, no doubt; but not quite all, I should think. When my father started for himself, there were many men in Manchester who were willing to labour in this way; but they had no factory to work in, no machinery to work with, and no raw cotton to work on, simply because all this indispensable plant, and the materials for producing a fresh supply of it, had been appropriated by earlier comers. So they found themselves with gaping stomachs, shivering limbs, and hungry wives and children, in a place called their own country, in which nevertheless every scrap of ground and possible source of subsistence was tightly locked up in the hands of others and guarded by armed soldiers and policemen. In this helpless condition, the poor devils were ready to beg for access to a factory and to raw cotton on any conditions compatible with life. My father offered them the use of his factory, his machines, and his raw cotton, on the following conditions. They were to work long and hard, early and late, to add fresh value to his raw cotton by manufacturing it. Out of the value thus created by them, they were to recoup him for what he supplied them with: rent, shelter, gas, water, machinery, raw cotton — everything; and to pay him for his own services as superintendent, manager, and salesman. So far he asked nothing but just remuneration. But after this had been paid, a balance due solely to their own labour remained. 'Out of this,' said my father, 'you shall keep just enough to save you from starving; and of the rest you shall make me a present to reward me for my virtue in saving money. Such is the bargain I propose. It is, in my opinion, fair and calculated to encourage thrifty habits. If it does not strike you in that light, you can get a factory and raw cotton for yourselves: you shall not use mine.' In other words, they might go to the devil and starve — Hobson's choice! — for all the other factories were owned by men who offered no better terms. The Manchesterians could not bear to starve or to see their children starve; and so they accepted his terms and went into the factory. The terms, you see, did not admit of their beginning to save for themselves as he had done. Well, they created great wealth by their labour, and lived on very little; so that the balance they gave for nothing to my father was large. He bought more cotton, and more machinery, and more factories with it; employed more men to make wealth for him; and saw his fortune increase like a rolling snowball. He prospered enormously; but the workmen were no better off than at first; and they dared not rebel and demand more of the money they had made; for there were always plenty of starving wretches outside willing to take their places on the old terms. Sometimes he met with a check: as, for instance, when, in his eagerness to increase his store, he made the men manufacture more cotton than the public needed; or when he could not get enough of raw cotton, as happened during the civil war in America. Then he adapted himself to circumstances by turning away as many workmen as he could not find customers or cotton for; and they, of course, starved or subsisted on charity. During the war-time a big subscription was got up for these poor wretches; and my father subscribed one hundred pounds, in spite, he said, of his own great losses. Then he bought new machines; and, as women and children could work these as well as men, and were cheaper and more docile, he turned away about seventy out of every hundred of his *hands* (so he called the men), and replaced them by their wives and children, who made money for him faster than ever. By this time he had long ago given up managing the factories, and paid clever fellows who had no money of their own a few hundreds a year to do it for him. He also purchased shares in other concerns conducted on the same principle; pocketed dividends made in countries which he had never visited by men whom he had never seen; bought a seat in Parliament from a poor and corrupt constituency; and helped to preserve the laws by which he had thriven. Afterwards, when his wealth grew famous, he had less need to bribe; for modern men worship the rich as gods, and will elect a man as one of their rulers for no other reason than that he is a millionaire. He aped gentility; lived in a palace at Kensington; and bought a part of Scotland to make a deer forest of. It is easy enough to make a deer forest, as trees are not necessary there. You simply drive off the peasants; destroy their houses; and make a desert of the land. However, my father did not shoot much himself: he generally let the forest out by the season to those who did. He purchased a wife of gentle blood too, with the unsatisfactory result now before you. That is how Jesse Trefusis, a poor Manchester bagman, contrived to become a plutocrat and gentleman of landed estate. And also how I, who never did a stroke of work in my life, am overburdened with wealth; whilst the children of the men who made that wealth are slaving as their fathers slaved, or starving, or in the workhouse, or on the streets, or the deuce knows where. What do you think of that, my love?"

"What is the use of worrying about it, Sidney? It cannot be helped now. Besides, if your father saved money, and the others were improvident, he deserved to make a fortune."

"Granted; but he didnt make a fortune: he took a fortune that others had made. At Cambridge they taught me that his profits were the reward of abstinence — the abstinence which enabled him to save. That quieted my conscience until I began to wonder why one man should make another pay him for exercising one of the virtues. Then came the question: what did my father abstain from? The workmen abstained from meat, drink, fresh air, good clothes, decent lodgings, holidays, money, the society of their families, and pretty nearly everything that makes life worth living, which was perhaps the reason why they usually died twenty years or so sooner than people in our circumstances. Yet no one rewarded them for their abstinence. The reward came to my father, who abstained from none of these things, but indulged in them all to his heart's content. Besides, if the money was the reward of abstinence, it seemed logical to infer that he must abstain ten times as much when he had fifty thousand a-year as when he had only five thousand. Here was a problem for my young mind. Required, something from which my father abstained and in which his workmen exceeded, and which he abstained from more and more as he grew richer and richer. The only thing that answered this description was hard work; and as I never met a sane man willing to pay another for idling, I began to see that these prodigious payments to my father were extorted by force. To do him justice, he never boasted of abstinence. He considered himself a hard-worked man; and claimed his fortune as the reward of his risks, his calculations, his anxieties, and the journeys he had to make at all seasons and at all hours. This comforted me somewhat until it occurred to me that if he had lived a century earlier; invested his money in a horse and a pair of pistols; and taken to the road: his object — that of wresting from others the fruits of their labour without rendering them an equivalent — would have been exactly the same, and his risk far greater; for it would have included risk of the gallows. Constant travelling with the constable at his heels, and calculations of the chances of robbing the Dover mail, would have given him his fill of activity and anxiety. On the whole, if Jesse Trefusis, M.P., who died a millionaire in his palace at Kensington, had been a highwayman, I could not more heartily loathe the social arrangements that rendered such a career as his not only possible, but eminently creditable to himself in the eyes of his fellows. Most men make it their business to imitate him, hoping to become rich and idle on the same terms. Therefore I turn my back on them. I cannot sit at their feasts knowing how much they cost in human misery, and seeing how little they produce of human happiness. What is your opinion, my treasure?"

Henrietta seemed a little troubled. She smiled faintly, and said caressingly, "It was not your fault, Sidney. *I* dont blame you."

"Immortal powers!" he exclaimed, sitting bolt upright, and appealing to the skies: "here is a woman who believes that the only concern all this causes me is whether she thinks any the worse of me personally on account of it!"

"No, no, Sidney. It is not I alone. Nobody thinks the worse of you for it."

"Quite so," he returned, in a polite frenzy. "Nobody sees any harm in it. That is precisely the mischief of it."

"Besides," she urged, "your mother belonged to one of the oldest families in England."

"And what more can man desire than wealth with descent from a county family! Could a man be happier than I ought to be, sprung as I am from monopolists of all the sources and instruments of production — of land on the one side, and of machinery on the other? This very ground on which we are resting was the property of my mother's father. At least the law allowed him to use it as such. When he was a boy, there was a fairly prosperous race of peasants settled here, tilling the soil; paying him rent for permission to do so; and making enough out of it to satisfy his large wants and their own narrow needs without working themselves to death. But my grandfather was a shrewd man. He perceived that cows and sheep produced more money by their meat and wool than peasants by their husbandry. So he cleared the estate. That is, he drove the peasants from their homes, as my father did afterwards in his Scotch deer forest. Or, as his tombstone has it, he developed the resources of his country. I dont know what became of the peasants: *he* didnt know, and, I presume, didnt care. I suppose the old ones went into the workhouse, and the young ones crowded the towns, and worked for men like my father in factories. Their places were taken by cattle, which paid for their food so well, that my grandfather, getting my father to take shares in the enterprise, hired labourers on the Manchester terms to cut that canal for him. When it was made, he took toll upon it; and his heirs still take toll; and the sons of the navvies who dug it and of the engineer who designed it pay the toll when they have occasion to travel by it, or to purchase goods which have been conveyed along it. I remember my grandfather well. He was a well-bred man, and a perfect gentleman in his manners; but, on the whole, I think he was wickeder than my father, who, after all, was caught in the wheels of a vicious system, and had either to spoil others or be spoiled by them. But my grandfather — the old rascal! — was in no such dilemma. Master as he was of his bit of merry England, no man could have enslaved him; and he might at least have lived and let live. My father followed his example in the matter of the deer forest; but that was the climax of his wickedness, whereas it was only the beginning of my grandfather's. Howbeit, whichever bears the palm, there they were, the types after which we all strive."

"Not all, Sidney. Not we two. I hate tradespeople and country squires. We belong to the artistic and cultured classes; and we can keep aloof from shopkeepers."

"Living, meanwhile, at the rate of several thousand a year on rent and interest. No, my dear: this is the way of those people who insist that when they are in heaven they shall be spared the recollection of such a place as hell, but are quite content that it shall exist outside their consciousness. I respect my father more — I mean I despise him less — for doing his own sweating and filching than I do the sensitive sluggards and cowards who lent him their money to sweat and filch with, and asked no questions provided the interest was paid punctually. And as to your friends the artists, they are the worst of all."

"Oh, Sidney: you are determined not to be pleased. Artists dont keep factories."

"No; but the factory is only a part of the machinery of the system. Its basis is the tyranny of brain force, which, among civilized men, is allowed to do what muscular force does among schoolboys and savages. The schoolboy proposition is, 'I am stronger than you: therefore you shall fag for me.' Its grown-up form is, 'I am cleverer than you: therefore you shall fag for me.' The state of things we produce by submitting to this, bad enough even at first, becomes intolerable when the mediocre or foolish descendants of the clever fellows claim to have inherited their privileges. Now, no men are greater sticklers for the arbitrary dominion of genius and talent than your artists. The great painter is not satisfied with being sought after and admired because his hands can do more than ordinary hands, which they truly can; but he wants to be fed as if his stomach needed more food than ordinary stomachs, which it does not. A day's work is a day's work, neither more nor less; and the man who does it needs a day's sustenance, a night's repose, and due leisure, whether he be painter or ploughman. But the rascal of a painter, poet, novelist, or other voluptuary in labour, is not content with his advantage in popular esteem over the ploughman: he also wants an advantage in money, as if there were more hours in a day spent in the studio or library than in the field; or as if he needed more food to enable him to do his work than the ploughman to enable him to do his. He talks of the higher quality of his work, as if the higher quality of it were of his own making! — as if it gave him a right to work less for his neighbour than his neighbour works for him! — as if the ploughman could not do better without him than he without the ploughman! — as if the value of the most celebrated pictures has not been questioned more than that of any straight furrow in the arable world! — as if it did not take an apprenticeship of as many years to train the hand and eye of a mason or blacksmith as of an artist! — as if, in short, the fellow were a god, as canting brain worshippers have for years past been assuring him he is. Artists are the high priests of the modern Moloch. Nine out of ten of them are diseased creatures, just sane enough to trade on their own neuroses. The only quality of theirs which extorts my respect is a certain sublime selfishness which makes them willing to starve and to let their families starve sooner than do any work they dont like."

"*Indeed* you are quite wrong, Sidney. There was a girl at the Slade school who supported her mother and two sisters by her drawing. Besides, what can you do? People were made so."

"Yes: I was made a landlord and capitalist by the folly of the people; but they can unmake me if they will. Meanwhile I have absolutely no means of escape from my position except by giving away my slaves to fellows who will use them no better than I, and becoming a slave myself; which, if you please, you shall not catch me doing in a hurry. No, my beloved: I must keep my foot on their necks for your sake as well as for my own. — But you do not care about all this prosy stuff. I am consumed with remorse for having bored my darling. You want to know why I am living here like a hermit in a vulgar two-roomed hovel instead of tasting the delights of London society with my beautiful and devoted young wife."

"But you dont intend to stay here, Sidney."

"Yes, I do; and I will tell you why. I am helping to liberate those Manchester labourers who were my father's slaves. To bring that about, their fellow slaves all over the world must unite in a vast international association of men pledged to share the world's work justly; to share the produce of the work justly; to yield not a farthing — charity apart — to any full-grown and ablebodied idler or malingerer; and to treat as vermin in the commonwealth persons attempting to get more than their share of wealth or give less than their share of work. This is a very difficult thing to accomplish; because working men, like the people called their betters, do not always understand their own interests, and will often actually help their oppressors to exterminate their saviours to the tune of 'Rule Britannia,' or some such lying doggrel. We must educate them out of that, and, meanwhile, push forward the international association of labourers diligently. I am at present occupied in propagating its principles. Capitalism, organized for repressive purposes under pretext of governing the nation, would very soon stop the association if it understood our aim; but it thinks that we are engaged in gunpowder plots and conspiracies to assassinate crowned heads; and so, whilst the police are blundering in search of evidence of these, our real work goes on unmolested. Whether I am really advancing the cause is more than I can say. I use heaps of postage stamps; pay the expenses of many indifferent lecturers; defray the cost of printing reams of pamphlets and hand-bills which hail the labourer flatteringly as the salt of the earth; write and edit a little socialist journal; and do what lies in my power generally. I had rather spend my ill-gotten wealth in this way than upon an expensive house and a retinue of servants. And I prefer my corduroys and my two-roomed chalet here to our pretty little house, and your pretty little ways, and my pretty little neglect of the work that my heart is set upon. Some day, perhaps, I will take a holiday; and then we shall have a new honeymoon."

For a moment Henrietta seemed about to cry. Suddenly she exclaimed with enthusiasm, "I will stay with you, Sidney. I will share your work, whatever it may be. I will dress as a dairymaid, and have a little pail to carry milk in. The world is nothing to me except when you are with me; and I should love to live here and sketch from nature."

He blenched, and partially rose, unable to conceal his dismay. She, resolved not to be cast off, seized him and clung to him. This was the movement that excited the derision of Wickens's boy in the adjacent gravel pit. Trefusis was glad of the interruption; and, when he gave the boy twopence and bade him begone, half hoped that he would insist on remaining. But though an obdurate boy on most occasions, he proved complaisant on this, and withdrew to the highroad, where he made over one of his pennies to a phantom gambler, and tossed with him until recalled from his dual state by the appearance of Fairholme's party.

In the meantime, Henrietta urgently returned to her proposition. "We should be so happy," she said. "I would housekeep for you; and you could work as much as you pleased. Our life would be a long idyll."

"My love," he said, shaking his head as she looked beseechingly at him: "I have too much Manchester cotton in my constitution for long idylls. And the truth is, that the first condition of work with me is your absence. When you are with me, I can do nothing but make love to you. You bewitch me. When I escape from you for a moment, it is only to groan remorsefully over the hours you have tempted me to waste, and the energy you have futilized."

"If you wont live with me, you had no right to marry me."

"True. But that is neither your fault nor mine. We have found that we love each other too much — that our intercourse hinders our usefulness; and so we must part. Not for ever, my dear: only until you have cares and business of your own to fill up your life and prevent you from wasting mine."

"I believe you are mad," she said petulantly.

"The world is mad now-a-days, and is galloping to the deuce as fast as greed can goad it. I merely stand out of the rush, not liking its destination. Here comes a barge, the commander of which is devoted to me because he believes that I am organizing a revolution for the abolition of lock dues and tolls. We will go aboard and float down to Lyvern, whence you can return to London. You had better telegraph from the junction to the college: there must be a hue and cry out after us by this time. You shall have my address; and we can write to one another or see one another whenever we please. Or you can divorce me for deserting you."

"You would like me to, I know," said Henrietta, sobbing.

"I should die of despair, my darling," he said complacently. "Ship aho-o-o-y! Stop crying, Hetty, for God's sake. You lacerate my very soul."

"Ah-o-o-o-o-o-oy, master!" roared the bargee.

"Good-arternoon, sir," said a man who, with a short whip in his hand, trudged beside the white horse that towed the barge. "Come up!" he added malevolently to the horse.

"I want to get on board, and go up to Lyvern with you," said Trefusis. "He seems a well fed brute, that."

"Better fed nor me," said the man. "You cant get the work out of a hunderfed 'orse that you can out of a hunderfed man or woman. I've bin in parts of England where women pulled the barges. They come cheaper nor 'orses because it didnt cost nothing to get new ones when the old ones was wore out."

"Then why not employ them?" said Trefusis, with ironical gravity. "The principle of buying labour-force in the cheapest market and selling its product in the dearest has done much to make Englishmen — what they are."

"The railway comp'nies keeps 'orspittles for the like of '*im*," said the man, with a cunning laugh, indicating the horse by smacking him on the belly with the butt of the whip. "If ever you try bein' a labourer in earnest, governor, try it on four legs. You'll find it far preferable to trying on two."

"This man is one of my converts," said Trefusis apart to Henrietta. "He told me the other day that since I set him thinking he never sees a gentleman without feeling inclined to heave a brick at him. I find that Socialism is often misunderstood by its least intelligent supporters and opponents to mean simply unrestrained indulgence of our natural propensity to heave bricks at respectable persons. Now I am going to carry you along this plank. If you keep quiet, we may reach the barge. If not, we shall reach the bottom of the canal."

He carried her safely over, and exchanged some friendly words with the bargee. Then he took Henrietta forward, and stood watching the water as they were borne along noiselessly between the hilly pastures of the country.

"This would be a fairy journey," he said, "if one could forget the woman down below, cooking her husband's dinner in a stifling hole about as big as your wardrobe, and —— "

"Oh, dont talk any more of these things," she said crossly: "I cannot help them. I have my own troubles to think of. *Her* husband lives with her."

"She will change places with you, my dear, if you make her the offer."

She had no answer ready. After a pause he began to speak poetically of the scenery, and to offer her loverlike speeches and compliments. But she felt that he intended to get rid of her; and he knew that it was useless to try to hide that design from her. She turned away and sat down on a pile of bricks, only writhing angrily when he pressed her for a word. As they neared the end of her voyage, and her intense protest against desertion remained, as she thought, only half expressed, her sense of injury grew almost unbearable.

They landed on a wharf, and went through an unswept, deeply rutted lane up to the main street of Lyvern. Here he became Smilash again, walking deferentially a little before her, as if she had hired him to point out the way. She then saw that her last opportunity of appealing to him had gone by; and she nearly burst into tears at the thought. It occurred to her that she might prevail upon him by making a scene in public. But the street was a busy one; and she was a little afraid of him. Neither consideration would have checked her in one of her ungovernable moods; but now she was in an abject one. Her moods seemed to come only when they were harmful to her. She suffered herself to be put into the railway omnibus, which was on the point of starting from the innyard when they arrived there; and though he touched his hat; asked whether she had any message to give him; and in a tender whisper wished her a safe journey, she would not look at nor speak to him. So they parted; and he returned alone to the chalet, where he was received by the two policemen who subsequently brought him to the college.

CHAPTER VI.

The year wore on; and the long winter evenings set in. The studious young ladies at Alton College, elbows on desk and hands over ears, shuddered chillily in fur tippets whilst they loaded their memories with the statements of writers on moral science, or, like men who swim upon corks, reasoned out mathematical problems upon postulates. Whence it sometimes happened that the more reasonable a student was in mathematics, the more unreasonable she was in the affairs of real life, concerning which few trustworthy postulates have yet been ascertained.

Agatha, not studious, and apt to shiver in winter, began to break Rule No. 17 with increasing frequency. Rule No. 17 forbade the students to enter the kitchen, or in any way to disturb the servants in the discharge of their duties. Agatha broke it because she was fond of making toffee, of eating it, of a good fire, of doing any forbidden thing, and of the admiration with which the servants listened to her ventriloquial and musical feats. Gertrude accompanied her because she too liked toffee, and because she plumed herself on her condescension to her inferiors. Jane went because her two friends went; and the spirit of adventure, the force of example, and the love of toffee, often brought more volunteers to these expeditions than Agatha thought it safe to enlist. One evening, Miss Wilson, going downstairs alone to her private wine cellar, was arrested near the kitchen by sounds of revelry, and, stopping to listen, overheard the castanet dance (which reminded her of the emphasis with which Agatha had snapped her fingers at Mrs. Miller); the bee on the window pane; "Robin Adair" (encored by the servants); and an imitation of herself in the act of appealing to Jane Carpenter's better nature to induce her to study for the Cambridge Local. She waited until the cold and her fear of being discovered spying forced her to creep upstairs, ashamed of having enjoyed a silly entertainment, and of conniving at a breach of the rules rather than face a fresh quarrel with Agatha.

There was one particular in which matters between Agatha and the college discipline did not go on exactly as before. Although she had formerly supplied a disproportionately large number of the confessions in the fault book, the entry which had nearly led to her expulsion was the last she ever made in it. Not that her conduct was better: it was rather the reverse. Miss Wilson never mentioned the matter, the fault book being sacred from all allusion on her part. But she saw that though Agatha would not confess her own sins, she still assisted others to unburden their consciences. The witticisms with which Jane un-suspectingly enlivened the pages of the Recording Angel were con-clusive on this point.

Smilash had now adopted a profession. In the last days of autumn he had whitewashed the chalet; painted the doors, windows, and veranda; repaired the roof and interior; and improved the place so much that the landlord had warned him that the rent would be raised at the expiration of his twelvemonth's tenancy, remarking that a tenant could not reasonably expect to have a pretty, raintight dwelling-house for the same money as a hardly habitable ruin. Smilash had imme-diately promised to dilapidate it to its former state at the end of the year. He had put up a board at the gate with an inscription copied from some printed cards which he presented to persons who hap-pened to converse with him.

JEFFERSON SMILASH

PAINTER, DECORATOR, GLAZIER, PLUMBER & GARDENER.

*Pianofortes tuned.   Domestic Engineering in all its
Branches.   Families waited upon
at table or otherwise.*

CHAMOUNIX VILLA,

(N.B.—ADVICE GRATIS.   LYVERN.
No reasonable offer refused.)

The business thus announced, comprehensive as it was, did not flour-ish. When asked by the curious for testimony to his competence and respectability, he recklessly referred them to Fairholme, to Josephs, and in particular to Miss Wilson, who, he said, had known him from his earliest childhood. Fairholme, glad of an opportunity to show that he was no mealy-mouthed parson, declared, when applied to, that Smilash was the greatest rogue in the country. Josephs, partly from benevolence, and partly from a vague fear that Smilash might at any moment take an action against him for defamation of character, said he had no doubt that he was a very cheap workman, and that it would be a charity to give him some little job to encourage him. Miss Wilson confirmed Fairholme's account; and the church organist, who had tuned all the pianofortes in the neighbourhood once a year for nearly a quarter of a century, denounced the new-comer as Jack of all trades and master of none. Hereupon the radicals of Lyvern, a small and disreputable party, began to assert that there was no harm in the man, and that the parsons and Miss Wilson, who lived in a fine house and did nothing but take in the daughters of rich swells as boarders, might employ their leisure better than in taking the bread out of a poor workman's mouth. But as none of this faction needed the services of a domestic engineer, he was none the richer for their support; and the only patron he obtained was a housemaid who was leaving her situation at a country house in the vicinity, and wanted her box repaired, the lid having fallen off. Smilash demanded half-a-crown for the job; but on her demurring, immediately apologized and came down to a shilling. For this sum he repainted the box; traced her initials on it; and affixed new hinges, a Bramah lock, and brass handles, at a cost to himself of ten shillings and several hours' labour. The housemaid found fault with the colour of the paint; made him take off the handles, which, she said, reminded her of a coffin; complained that a lock with such a small key couldnt be strong enough for a large box; but admitted that it was all her own fault for not employing a proper man. It got about that he had made a poor job of the box; and as he, when taxed with this, emphatically confirmed it, he got no other commission; and his signboard served thenceforth only for the amusement of pedestrian tourists, and of shepherd boys with a taste for stone throwing.

One night a great storm blew over Lyvern; and those young ladies at Alton College who were afraid of lightning, said their prayers with some earnestness. At half-past twelve, the rain, wind, and thunder made such a din, that Agatha and Gertrude wrapped themselves in shawls; stole downstairs to the window on the landing outside Miss Wilson's study; and stood watching the flashes give vivid glimpses of the landscape, and discussing in whispers whether it was dangerous to stand near a window, and whether brass stair-rods could attract lightning. Agatha, as serious and friendly with a single companion as she was mischievous and satirical before a larger audience, enjoyed the scene quietly. The lightning did not terrify her; for she knew little of the value of life, and fancied much concerning the heroism of being indifferent to it. The tremors which the more startling flashes caused her, only made her more conscious of her own courage and its contrast with the uneasiness of Gertrude, who at last, shrinking from a forked zigzag of blue flame, said,

"Let us go back to bed, Agatha. I feel sure that we are not safe here."

"Quite as safe as in bed, where we cannot see anything. How the house shakes! I believe the rain will batter in the windows be- fore —— "

"Hush," whispered Gertrude, catching her arm in terror. "What was that?"

"What?"

"I am sure I heard the bell — the gate bell. Oh, do let us go back to bed."

"Nonsense! Who would be out on such a night as this? Perhaps the wind rang it."

They waited for a few moments: Gertrude trembling; and Agatha feeling, as she listened in the darkness, a sensation familiar to persons who are afraid of ghosts. Presently a veiled clangour mingled with the wind. A few sharp and urgent snatches of it came unmistakably from the bell at the gate of the college grounds. It was a loud bell, used to summon a servant from the college to open the gates; for though there was a porter's lodge, it was uninhabited.

"Who on earth can it be?" said Agatha. "Cant they find the wicket, the idiots!"

"Oh, I hope not! Do come upstairs, Agatha."

"No, I wont. Go you, if you like." But Gertrude was afraid to go alone. "I think I had better waken Miss Wilson, and tell her," con- tinued Agatha. "It seems awful to shut anybody out on such a night as this."

"But we dont know who it is."

"Well, I suppose you are not afraid of them, in any case," said Agatha, knowing the contrary, but recognizing the convenience of shaming Gertrude into silence.

They listened again. The storm was now very boisterous; and they could not hear the bell. Suddenly there was a loud knocking at the house door. Gertrude screamed; and her cry was echoed from the rooms above, where several girls had heard the knocking also, and had been driven by it into the state of mind which accompanies the climax of a nightmare. Then a candle flickered on the stairs; and Miss Wil- son's voice, reassuringly firm, was heard.

"Who is that?"

"It is I, Miss Wilson, and Gertrude. We have been watching the storm; and there is some one knocking at the —— " A tremendous battery with the knocker, followed by a sound, confused by the gale, as of a man shouting, interrupted her.

"They had better not open the door," said Miss Wilson, in some alarm. "You are very imprudent, Agatha, to stand here. You will catch your death of —— Dear me! What can be the matter?"

She hurried down, followed by Agatha, Gertrude, and some of the braver students, to the hall, where they found a few shivering servants watching the housekeeper, who was at the keyhole of the house door, querulously asking who was there. She was evidently not heard by those without; for the knocking recommenced whilst she was speaking; and she recoiled as if she had received a blow on the mouth. Miss Wilson then rattled the chain to attract attention; and demanded again who was there.

"Let us in," was returned in a hollow shout through the keyhole. "There is a dying woman and three children here. Open the door."

Miss Wilson lost her presence of mind. To gain time, she replied, "I — I cant hear you. What do you say?"

"Damnation!" said the voice, speaking this time to someone outside. "They cant hear." And the knocking recommenced with increased urgency. Agatha, excited, caught Miss Wilson's dressing gown, and repeated to her what the voice had said. Miss Wilson had heard distinctly enough; and she felt, without knowing clearly why, that the door must be opened; but she was almost overmastered by a vague dread of what was to follow. She began to undo the chain; and Agatha helped with the bolts. Two of the servants exclaimed that they were all about to be murdered in their beds, and ran away. A few of the students seemed inclined to follow their example. At last the door, loosed, was blown wide open, flinging Miss Wilson and Agatha back, and admitting a whirlwind that tore round the hall; snatched at the women's draperies; and blew out the lights. Agatha, by a flash of lightning, saw for an instant two men straining at the door like sailors at a capstan. Then she knew by the cessation of the whirlwind that they had shut it. Matches were struck, the candles relighted, and the new comers clearly perceived.

Smilash, bareheaded, without a coat, his corduroy vest and trousers heavy with rain. A rough looking middle-aged man, poorly dressed like a shepherd, wet as Smilash, with the expression, piteous, patient, and desperate, of one hard driven by ill-fortune, and at the end of his resources. Two little children, a boy and a girl, almost naked, cowering under an old sack that had served them as an umbrella. And, lying on the settee where the two men had laid it, a heap of wretched wearing apparel, sacking, and rotten matting, with Smilash's coat and sou'-wester: the whole covering a bundle which presently proved to be an exhausted woman with a tiny infant at her breast. Smilash's expression, as he looked at her, was ferocious.

"Sorry fur to trouble you, lady," said the man, after glancing anxiously at Smilash as if he had expected him to act as spokesman; "but my roof and the side of my house has gone in the storm; and my missus has been having another little one; and I am sorry to ill-convenience you, Miss; but — but —— "

"Inconvenience!" exclaimed Smilash. "It is the lady's privilege to relieve you — her highest privilege!"

The little boy here began to cry from mere misery; and the woman roused herself to say, "For shame, Tom! before the lady," and then collapsed, too weak to care for what might happen next in the world. Smilash looked impatiently at Miss Wilson, who hesitated, and said to him,

"What do you expect me to do?"

"To help us," he replied. Then, with an explosion of nervous energy, he added, "Do what your heart tells you to do. Give your bed and your clothes to the woman; and let your girls pitch their books to the devil for a few days, and make something for these poor little creatures to wear. The poor have worked hard enough to clothe *them*. Let them take their turn now and clothe the poor."

"No, no. Steady, master," said the man, stepping forward to propitiate Miss Wilson, and evidently much oppressed by a sense of unwelcomeness. "It aint any fault of the lady's. Might I make so bold as to ask you to put this woman of mine anywhere that may be convenient until morning. Any sort of a place will do: she's accustomed to rough it. Just to have a roof over her until I find a room in the village where we can shake down." Here, led by his own words to contemplate the future, he looked desolately round the cornice of the hall, as if it were a shelf on which somebody might have left a suitable lodging for him.

Miss Wilson turned her back decisively and contemptuously on Smilash. She had recovered herself. "I will keep your wife here," she said to the man. "Every care shall be taken of her. The children can stay too."

"Three cheers for moral science!" cried Smilash, ecstatically breaking into the outrageous dialect he had forgotten in his wrath. "Wot was my words to you, neighbour, when I said we should bring your missus to the college; and you said, ironical-like, 'Aye, and bloomin' glad they'll be to see us there.' Did I not say to you that the lady had a noble 'art, and would shew it when put to the test by sech a calamity as this?"

"Why should you bring my hasty words up again' me now, master, when the lady has been so kind?" said the man with emotion. "I am humbly grateful to you, Miss; and so is Bess. We are sensible of the ill-convenience we —— "

Miss Wilson, who had been conferring with the housekeeper, cut his speech short by ordering him to carry his wife to bed, which he did with the assistance of Smilash, now jubilant. Whilst they were away, one of the servants, bidden to bring some blankets to the woman's room, refused, saying that she was not going to wait on that sort of people. Miss Wilson gave her warning almost fiercely to quit the college next day. This excepted, no ill will was shown to the refugees. The young ladies were then requested to return to bed.

Meanwhile, the man, having laid his wife in a chamber palatial in comparison with that which the storm had blown about her ears, was congratulating her on her luck, and threatening the children with the most violent chastisement if they failed to behave themselves with strict propriety whilst they remained in that house. Before leaving them, he kissed his wife; and she, reviving, asked him to look at the baby. He did so, and pensively apostrophized it with a shocking epithet in anticipation of the time when its appetite must be satisfied from the provision shop instead of from its mother's breast. She laughed and cried shame on him; and so they parted cheerfully. When he returned to the hall with Smilash, they found two mugs of beer waiting for them. The girls had retired; and only Miss Wilson and the housekeeper remained.

"Here's your health, mum," said the man, before drinking; "and may you find such another as yourself to help you when you're in trouble, which Lord send may never come!"

"Is your house quite destroyed?" said Miss Wilson. "Where will you spend the night?"

"Dont you think of me, mum. Master Smilash here will kindly put me up 'til morning."

"His health!" said Smilash, touching the mug with his lips.

"The roof and south wall is blowed right away," continued the man, after pausing for a moment to puzzle over Smilash's meaning. "I doubt if there's a stone of it standing by this."

"But Sir John will build it for you again. You are one of his herds: are you not?"

"I am, Miss. But not he: he'll be glad it's down. He dont like people livin' on the land. I have told him time and again that the place was ready to fall; but he said I couldnt expect him to lay out money on a house that he got no rent for. You see, Miss, I didnt pay any rent: I took low wages; and the bit of a hut was a sort of set-off again' what I was paid short of the other men. I couldnt afford to have it repaired, though I did what I could to patch and prop it. And now most like I shall be blamed for letting it be blew down, and shall have to live in half a room in the town and pay two or three shillin's a week, besides walkin' three miles to and from my work every day. A gentleman like Sir John dont hardly know what the value of a penny is to us labourin' folk, nor how cruel hard his estate rules and the like comes on us."

"Sir John's health!" said Smilash, touching the mug as before. The man drank a mouthful humbly; and Smilash continued, "Here's to the glorious landed gentry of old England: bless 'em!"

"Master Smilash is only jokin'," said the man apologetically. "It's his way."

"You should not bring a family into the world if you are so poor," said Miss Wilson severely. "Can you not see that you impoverish yourself by doing so — to put the matter on no higher grounds."

"Reverend Mr. Malthus's health!" remarked Smilash, repeating his pantomime.

"Some say it's the children; and some say it's the drink, Miss," said the man submissively. "But from what I see, family or no family, drunk or sober, the poor gets poorer and the rich richer every day."

"Aint it disgustin' to hear a man so ignorant of the improvement in the condition of his class?" said Smilash, appealing to Miss Wilson.

"If you intend to take this man home with you," she said, turning sharply on him, "you had better do it at once."

"I take it kind on your part that you ask me to do anythink, after your up and telling Mr. Wickens that I am the last person in Lyvern you would trust with a job."

"So you are — the very last. Why dont you drink your beer?"

"Not in scorn of your brewing, lady; but because, bein' a common man, water is good enough for me."

"I wish you good-night, Miss," said the man; "and thank you kindly for Bess and the children."

"Good-night," she replied, stepping aside to avoid any salutation from Smilash. But he went up to her and said in a low voice, and with the Trefusis manner and accent,

"Good-night, Miss Wilson. If you should ever be in want of the services of a dog, a man, or a domestic engineeer, remind Smilash of Bess and the children, and he will act for you in any of those capacities."

They opened the door cautiously, and found that the wind, conquered by the rain, had abated. Miss Wilson's candle, though it flickered in the draught, was not extinguished this time; and she was presently left with the housekeeper, bolting and chaining the door, and listening to the crunching of feet on the gravel outside dying away through the steady pattering of the rain.

CHAPTER VII.

Agatha was at this time in her seventeenth year. She had a lively perception of the foibles of others, and no reverence for her seniors, whom she thought dull, cautious, and ridiculously amenable by commonplaces. But she was subject to the illusion which disables youth in spite of its superiority to age. She thought herself an exception. Crediting Mr. Jansenius and the general mob of mankind with nothing but a grovelling consciousness of some few material facts, she felt in herself an exquisite sense and all-embracing conception of nature, shared only by her favourite poets and heroes of romance and history. Hence she was in the common youthful case of being a much better judge of other people's affairs than of her own. At the fellowstudent who adored some Henry or Augustus, not from the drivelling sentimentality which the world calls love, but because this particular Henry or Augustus was a phœnix to whom the laws that govern the relations of ordinary lads and lasses did not apply, Agatha laughed in her sleeve. The more she saw of this weakness in her fellows, the more satisfied she was that, being forewarned, she was also forearmed against an attack of it on herself. Much as if a doctor were to conclude that he could not catch small pox because he had seen many cases of it; or as if a master mariner, knowing that many ships are wrecked in the British channel, should venture there without a pilot, thinking that he knew its perils too well to run any risk by them. Yet, as the doctor might hold such an opinion if he believed himself to be constituted differently from ordinary men; or the shipmaster adopt such a course under the impression that his vessel was a star, Agatha found false security in the subjective difference between her fellows seen from without and herself known from within. When, for instance, she fell in love with Mr. Jefferson Smilash (a step upon which she resolved the day after the storm), her imagination invested the pleasing emotion with a sacredness which, to her, set it far apart and distinct from the frivolous fancies of which Henry and Augustus had been the subject, and she the confidant.

"I can look at him quite coolly and dispassionately," she said to herself. "Though his face has a strange influence that must, I know, correspond to some unexplained power within me, yet it is not a perfect face. I have seen many men who are, strictly speaking, far handsomer. If the light that never was on sea or land is in his eyes, yet they are not pretty eyes — not half so clear as mine. Though he wears his common clothes with a nameless grace that betrays his true breeding at every step, yet he is not tall, dark, and melancholy, as my ideal hero would be if I were as great a fool as girls of my age usually are. If I am in love, I have sense enough not to let my love blind my judgment."

She did not tell anyone of her new interest in life. Strongest in that student community, she had used her power with goodnature enough to win the popularity of a school leader, and occasionally with unscrupulousness enough to secure the privileges of a school bully. Popularity and privilege, however, only satisfied her when she was in the mood for them. Girls, like men, want to be petted, pitied, and made much of, when they are diffident, in low spirits, or in unrequited love. These are services which the weak cannot render to the strong, and which the strong will not render to the weak, except when there is also a difference of sex. Agatha knew by experience that though a weak woman cannot understand why her stronger sister should wish to lean upon her, she may triumph in the fact without understanding it, and give chaff instead of consolation. Agatha wanted to be understood and not to be chaffed. Finding herself unable to satisfy both these conditions, she resolved to do without sympathy and to hold her tongue. She had often had to do so before; and she was helped on this occasion by a sense of the ridiculous appearance her passion might wear in the vulgar eye.

Her secret kept itself, as she was supposed in the college to be insensible to the softer emotions. Love wrought no external change upon her. It made her believe that she had left her girlhood behind her, and was now a woman with a newly developed heart capacity at which she would childishly have scoffed a little while before. She felt ashamed of the bee on the window-pane, although it somehow buzzed as frequently as before in spite of her. Her calendar, formerly a monotonous cycle of class times, meal times, play times, and bed time, was now irregularly divided by walks past the chalet and accidental glimpses of its tenant.

Early in December came a black frost; and navigation on the canal was suspended. Wickens's boy was sent to the college with news that Wickens's pond would bear, and that the young ladies should be welcome at any time. The pond was only four feet deep; and as Miss Wilson set much store by the physical education of her pupils, leave was given for skating. Agatha, who was expert on the ice, immediately proposed that a select party should go out before breakfast next morning. Actions not in themselves virtuous often appear so when performed at hours that compel early rising; and some of the candidates for the Cambridge Local, who would not have sacrificed the afternoon to amusement, at once fell in with her suggestion. But for them, it might never have been carried out; for when they summoned Agatha, at half-past six next morning, to leave her warm bed and brave the biting air, she would have refused without hesitation had she not been shamed into compliance by these laborious ones who stood by her bedside, bluenosed and hungry, but ready for the ice. When she had dressed herself with much shuddering and chattering, they allayed their internal discomfort by a slender meal of biscuits; got their skates; and went out across the rimy meadows, past patient cows breathing clouds of steam, to Wickens's pond. Here, to their surprise, was Smilash, on electro-plated acme skates, practising complicated figures with intense diligence. It soon appeared that his skill came short of his ambition; for, after several narrow escapes, and some frantic staggering, his calves, elbows, and occiput smote the ice almost simultaneously. On rising ruefully to a sitting posture, he became aware that eight young ladies were watching his proceedings with interest.

"This comes of a common man putting himself above his station by getting into gentlemen's skates," he said. "Had I been content with a humble slide, as my fathers was, I should ha' been a happier man at the present moment." He sighed; rose; touched his hat to Miss Ward; and took off his skates, adding, "Good-morning, Miss. Miss Wilson sent me word to be here sharp at six to put on the young ladies' skates; and I took the liberty of trying a figure or two to keep out the cold."

"Miss Wilson did not tell me that she ordered you to come," said Miss Ward.

"Just like her to be thoughtful and yet not let on to be! She is a kind lady, and a learned — like yourself, Miss. Sit yourself down on the camp-stool; and give me your heel: if I may be so bold as to stick a gimlet into it."

His assistance was welcome; and Miss Ward allowed him to put on her skates. She was a Canadian, and could skate well. Jane, the first to follow her, was anxious as to the strength of the ice; but when reassured, she acquitted herself admirably; for she was proficient in out-door exercises, and had the satisfaction of laughing in the field at those who laughed at her in the study. Agatha, contrary to her custom, gave way to her companions; and her boots were the last upon which Smilash operated.

"How d'you do, Miss Wylie?" he said, dropping the Smilash manner now that the rest were out of earshot.

"I am very well, thank you," said Agatha, shy and constrained. This phase of her being new to him, he paused with her heel in his hand, and looked up at her curiously. She collected herself; returned his gaze steadily; and said, "How did Miss Wilson send you word to come? She only knew of our party at half-past nine last night."

"Miss Wilson did not send for me."

"But you have just told Miss Ward that she did."

"Yes. I find it necessary to tell almost as many lies now that I am a simple labourer as I did when I was a gentleman. More, in fact."

"I shall know how much to believe of what you say in future."

"The truth is this. I am perhaps the worst skater in the world; and therefore, according to a natural law, I covet the faintest distinction on the ice more than immortal fame for the things in which nature has given me aptitude to excel. I envy that large friend of yours — Jane is her name, I think — more than I envy Plato. I came down here this morning, thinking that the skating world was all a-bed, to practise in secret."

"I am glad we caught you at it," said Agatha, maliciously; for he was disappointing her. She wanted him to be heroic in his conversation; and he would not.

"I suppose so," he replied. "I have observed that Woman's dearest delight is to wound Man's self-conceit, though Man's dearest delight is to gratify hers. There is at least one creature lower than Man. Now, off with you. Shall I hold you until your ankles get firm?"

"Thank you," she said, disgusted: "*I* can skate pretty well; and I dont think you could give me any useful assistance." And she went off cautiously, feeling that a mishap would be very disgraceful after such a speech.

He stood on the shore, listening to the grinding, swaying sound of the skates, and watching the growing complexity of the curves they were engraving on the ice. As the girls grew warm and accustomed to the exercise, they laughed; jested; screamed recklessly when they came into collision; and sailed before the wind down the whole length of the pond at perilous speed. The more animated they became, the gloomier looked Smilash.

"Not two-penn'orth of choice between them and a parcel of puppies," he said; "except that some of them are conscious that there is a man looking at them, although he is only a blackguard labourer. They remind me of Henrietta in a hundred ways. Would I laugh, now, if the whole sheet of ice were to burst into little bits under them?"

Just then the ice cracked with a startling report; and the skaters, except Jane, skimmed away in all directions.

"You are breaking the ice to pieces, Jane," said Agatha, calling from a safe distance. "How can you expect it to bear your weight?"

"Pack of fools!" retorted Jane indignantly. "The noise only shows how strong it is."

The shock which the report had given Smilash answered him his question. "Make a note that wishes for the destruction of the human race, however rational and sincere, are contrary to nature," he said, recovering his spirits. "Besides, what a precious fool I should be if I were working at an international association of creatures only fit for destruction! Hi, lady! One word, Miss." This was to Miss Ward, who had skated into his neighbourhood. "It bein' a cold morning, and me havin' a poor and common circulation; would it be looked on as a liberty if I was to cut a slide here, or take a turn in the corner all to myself?"

"You may skate over there if you wish," she said, after a pause for consideration, pointing to a deserted spot at the leeward end of the pond, where the ice was too rough for comfortable skating.

"Nobly spoke!" he cried, with a grin, hurrying to the place indicated, where, skating being out of the question, he made a pair of slides, and gravely exercised himself upon them until his face glowed and his fingers tingled in the frosty air. The time passed quickly: when Miss Ward sent for him to take off her skates, there was a general groan and declaration that it could not possibly be half-past eight o'clock yet. Smilash knelt before the camp-stool, and was presently busy unbuckling and unscrewing. When Jane's turn came, the camp-stool creaked beneath her weight. Agatha again remonstrated with her, but immediately reproached herself with flippancy before Smilash, to whom she wished to convey an impression of deep seriousness of character.

"Smallest foot of the lot," he said critically, holding Jane's boot between his finger and thumb as if it were an art treasure which he had been invited to examine. "And belonging to the finest built lady."

Jane snatched away her foot; blushed; and said, "Indeed! What next, I wonder?"

"T'other un next," he said, setting to work on the remaining skate. When it was off, he looked up at her; and she darted a glance at him as she rose which showed that his compliment (her feet were in fact small and pretty) was appreciated.

"Allow me, Miss," he said to Gertrude, who was standing on one leg, leaning on Agatha, and taking off her own skates.

"No, thank you," she said coldly. "I dont need your assistance."

"I am well aware that the offer was overbold," he replied, with a self-complacency that made his profession of humility exasperating. "If all the skates is off, I will, by Miss Wilson's order, carry them and the campstool back to the college."

Miss Ward handed him her skates and turned away. Gertrude placed hers on the stool and went with Miss Ward. The rest followed, leaving him to stare at the heap of skates, and consider how he should carry them. He could think of no better plan than to interlace the straps, and hang them in a chain over his shoulder. By the time he had done this, the young ladies were out of sight; and his intention of enjoying their society during the return to the college was defeated. They had entered the building long before he came in sight of it.

Somewhat out of conceit with his folly, he went to the servants' entrance, and rang the bell there. When the door was opened, he saw Miss Ward standing behind the maid who admitted him.

"Oh," she said, looking at the string of skates as if she had hardly expected to see them again. "So you have brought our things back."

"Such were my instructions," he said, taken aback by her manner.

"You had no instructions. What do you mean by getting our skates into your charge under false pretences? I was about to send the police to take them from you. How dare you tell me that you were sent to wait on me, when you know very well that you were nothing of the sort?"

"I couldnt help it, Miss," he replied submissively. "I am a natural born liar — always was. I know that it must appear dreadful to you that never told a lie, and dont hardly know what a lie is, belonging as you do to a class where none is ever told. But common people like me tells lies just as a duck swims. I ask your pardon, Miss, most humble; and I hope the young ladies 'll be able to tell one set of skates from t'other; for I'm blest if I can."

"Put them down. Miss Wilson wishes to speak to you before you go. Susan: show him the way."

"Hope you aint been and got a poor cove into trouble, Miss."

"Miss Wilson knows how you have behaved."

He smiled at her benevolently, and followed Susan upstairs. On their way they met Jane, who stole a glance at him, and was about to pass by, when he said,

"Wont you say a word to Miss Wilson for a poor common fellow, honoured young lady? I have got into dreadful trouble for having made bold to assist you this morning."

"You neednt give yourself the pains to talk like that," replied Jane, in an impetuous whisper. "We all know that you are only pretending."

"Well: you can guess my motive," he whispered, looking tenderly at her.

"Such stuff and nonsense! I never heard of such a thing in my life," said Jane, and ran away, plainly understanding that he had disguised himself in order to obtain admission to the college, and enjoy the happiness of looking at her.

"Cursed fool that I am!" he said to himself: "I cannot act like a rational creature for five consecutive minutes."

The servant led him to the study, and announced, "The man, if you please, maam."

"Jeff Smilash," he added, in explanation.

"Come in," said Miss Wilson sternly.

He went in, and met the determined frown which she cast on him from her seat behind the writing table, by saying courteously,

"Good-morning, Miss Wilson."

She bent forward involuntarily, as if to receive a gentleman. Then she checked herself and looked implacable.

"I have to apologize," he said, "for making use of your name unwarrantably this morning — telling a lie, in fact. I happened to be skating when the young ladies came down; and as they needed some assistance which they would hardly have accepted from a common man — excuse my borrowing that tiresome expression from our acquaintance Smilash — I set their minds at ease by saying that you had sent for me. Otherwise, as you have given me a bad character — though not worse than I deserve — they would probably have refused to employ me; or at least I should have been compelled to accept payment, which I of course do not need."

Miss Wilson affected surprise. "I do not understand you," she said.

"Not altogether," he said, smiling. "But you understand that I am what is called a gentleman."

"No. The gentlemen with whom I am conversant do not dress as you dress, nor speak as you speak, nor act as you act."

He looked at her; and her countenance confirmed the hostility of her tone. He instantly relapsed into an aggravated phase of Smilash.

"I will no longer attempt to set myself up as a gentleman," he said. "I am a common man; and your ladyship's hi recognizes me as such and is not to be deceived. But dont go for to say that I am not candid when I am as candid as ever you will let me be. What fault, if any, do you find with my putting the skates on the young ladies, and carryin' the camp-stool for them?"

"If you are a gentleman," said Miss Wilson, reddening, "your conduct in persisting in these antics in my presence is insulting to me. Extremely so!"

"Miss Wilson," he replied, unruffled: "if you insist on Smilash, you shall have Smilash: I take an insane pleasure in personating him. If you want Sidney — my real Christian name — you can command him. But allow me to say that you must have either one or the other. If you become frank with me, I will understand that you are addressing Sidney. If distant and severe, Smilash."

"No matter what your name may be," said Miss Wilson, much

annoyed, "I forbid you to come here or to hold any communication whatever with the young ladies in my charge."

"Why?"

"Because I choose."

"There is much force in that reason, Miss Wilson; but it is not moral force in the sense conveyed by your college prospectus, which I have read with great interest."

Miss Wilson, since her quarrel with Agatha, had been sore on the subject of moral force. "No one is admitted here," she said, "without a trustworthy introduction or recommendation. A disguise is not a satisfactory substitute for either."

"Disguises are generally assumed for the purpose of concealing crime," he remarked sententiously.

"Precisely so," she said, emphatically.

"Therefore, I bear, to say the least, a doubtful character. Nevertheless, I have formed with some of the students here a slight acquaintance, of which, it seems, you disapprove. You have given me no good reason why I should discontinue that acquaintance; and you cannot control me except by your wish: a sort of influence not usually effective with doubtful characters. Suppose I disregard your wish; and that one or two of your pupils come to you and say, 'Miss Wilson: in our opinion Smilash is an excellent fellow: we find his conversation most improving. As it is your principle to allow us to exercise our own judgment, we intend to cultivate the acquaintance of Smilash.' How will you act in that case?"

"Send them home to their parents at once."

"I see that your principles are those of the Church of England. You allow the students the right of private judgment on condition that they arrive at the same conclusions as you. Excuse my saying that the principles of the Church of England, however excellent, are not those your prospectus led me to hope for. Your plan is coercion, stark and simple."

"I do not admit it," said Miss Wilson, ready to argue, even with Smilash, in defence of her system. "The girls are quite at liberty to act as they please; but I reserve my equal liberty to exclude them from my college if I do not approve of their behaviour."

"Just so. In most schools children are perfectly at liberty to learn their lessons or not, just as they please; but the principal reserves an equal liberty to whip them if they cannot repeat their tasks."

"I do not whip my pupils," said Miss Wilson indignantly. "The comparison is an outrage."

"But you expel them; and, as they are devoted to you and to the place, expulsion is a dreaded punishment. Yours is the old system of making laws and enforcing them by penalties; and the superiority of Alton College to other colleges is due, not to any difference of system, but to the comparative reasonableness of its laws, and the mildness and judgment with which they are enforced."

"My system is radically different from the old one. However, I will not discuss the matter with you. A mind occupied with the prejudices of the old coercive despotism can naturally only see in the new a modification of the old, instead of, as my system is, an entire reversal or abandonment of it."

He shook his head sadly, and said, "You seek to impose your ideas on others, ostracising those who reject them. Believe me, mankind has been doing nothing else ever since it began to pay some attention to ideas. It has been said that a benevolent despotism is the best possible form of Government. I do not believe that saying, because I believe another one to the effect that hell is paved with benevolence, which most people, the proverb being too deep for them, misinterpret as unfulfilled intentions. As if a benevolent despot might not by an error of judgment destroy his kingdom, and then say, like Romeo when he got his friend killed, 'I thought all for the best!' Excuse my rambling: I meant to say, in short, that though you are benevolent and judicious, you are none the less a despot."

Miss Wilson, at a loss for a reply, regretted that she had not, before letting him gain so far on her, dismissed him summarily instead of tolerating a discussion which she did not now know how to end with dignity. He relieved her by adding unexpectedly,

"Your system was the cause of my absurd marriage. My wife acquired a degree of culture and reasonableness from her training here which made her seem a superior being among the chatterers who form the female seasoning in ordinary society. I admired her dark eyes, and was only too glad to seize the excuse her education offered me for believing her a match for me in mind as well as in body."

Miss Wilson, astonished, determined to tell him coldly that her time was valuable. But curiosity took possession of her in the act of utterance; and the words that came were, "Who was she?"

"Henrietta Jansenius. She is Henrietta Trefusis; and I am Sidney Trefusis, at your mercy. I see I have roused your compassion at last."

"Nonsense!" said Miss Wilson hastily; for her surprise was indeed tinged by a feeling that he was thrown away on Henrietta.

"I ran away from her and adopted this retreat and this disguise in order to avoid her. The usual rebuke to human forethought followed. I ran straight into her arms — or rather she ran into mine. You remember the scene, and were probably puzzled by it."

"You seem to think your marriage contract a very light matter,

Mr. Trefusis. May I ask whose fault was the separation? Hers, of course."

"I have nothing to reproach her with. I expected to find her temper hasty; but it was not so: her behaviour was unexceptionable. So was mine. Our bliss was perfect; but unfortunately I was not made for domestic bliss: at all events, I could not endure it; so I fled; and when she caught me again I could give no excuse for my flight, though I made it clear to her that I would not resume our connubial relations just yet. We parted on bad terms. I fully intended to write her a sweet letter to make her forgive me in spite of herself; but somehow the weeks have slipt away and I am still fully intending. She has never written; and I have never written. This is a pretty state of things, isnt it, Miss Wilson, after all her advantages under the influence of moral force and the movement for the higher education of women?"

"By your own admission, the fault seems to lie upon your moral training, and not upon hers."

"The fault was in the conditions of our association. Why they should have attracted me so strongly at first, and repelled me so horribly afterwards, is one of those devil's riddles which will not be answered until we shall have traced all the yet unsuspected reactions of our inveterate dishonesty. But I am wasting your time, I fear. You sent for Smilash; and I have responded by practically annihilating him. In public, however, you must still bear with his antics. One moment more. I had forgotten to ask you whether you are interested in the shepherd whose wife you sheltered on the night of the storm?"

"He assured me, before he took his wife away, that he was comfortably settled in a lodging in Lyvern."

"Yes. Very comfortably settled indeed. For half-a-crown a week he obtained permission to share a spacious drawing-room with two other families in a ten-roomed house in not much better repair than his blown-down hovel. This house yields to its landlord over two hundred a year, or rather more than the rent of a commodious mansion in South Kensington. It is a troublesome rent to collect; but on the other hand there is no expenditure for repairs or sanitation, which are not considered necessary in tenement houses. Our friend has to walk three miles to his work, and three miles back. Exercise is a capital thing for a student or a city clerk; but to a shepherd who has been in the fields all day, a long walk at the end of his work is somewhat too much of a good thing. He begged for an increase of wages to compensate him for the loss of the hut; but Sir John pointed out to him that if he was not satisfied, his place could be easily filled by less exorbitant shepherds. Sir John even condescended to explain that the laws of political economy bind employers to buy labour in the cheapest market; and our poor friend, just as ignorant of economics as Sir John, of course did not know that this was untrue. However, as labour is actually so purchased everywhere except in Downing Street and a few other privileged spots, I suggested that our friend should go to some place where his market price would be higher than in merry England. He was willing enough to do so, but unable from want of means. So I lent him a trifle; and now he is on his way to Australia. Workmen are the geese that lay the golden eggs; but they fly away sometimes. I hear a gong sounding, to remind me of the flight of time and the value of your share of it. Good-morning."

Miss Wilson was suddenly moved not to let him go without an appeal to his better nature. "Mr. Trefusis," she said: "excuse me; but are you not, in your generosity to others, a little forgetful of your duty to yourself; and ——"

"The first and hardest of all duties!" he exclaimed. "—— I beg your pardon for interrupting you. It was only to plead guilty."

"I cannot admit that it is the first of all duties; but it is sometimes perhaps the hardest, as you say. Still, you could surely do yourself more justice without any great effort. If you wish to live humbly, you can do so without pretending to be an uneducated man, and without taking an irritating and absurd name. Why on earth do you call yourself Smilash?"

"I confess that the name has been a failure. I took great pains, in constructing it, to secure a pleasant impression. It is not a mere invention, but a compound of the words smile and eyelash. A smile suggests good humour: eyelashes soften the expression and are the only features that never blemish a face. Hence Smilash is a sound that should cheer and propitiate. Yet it exasperates. It is really very odd that it should have that effect, unless it is that it raises expectations which I am unable to satisfy."

Miss Wilson looked at him doubtfully. He remained perfectly grave. There was a pause. Then, as if she had made up her mind to be offended, she said, "Good-morning," shortly.

"Good-morning, Miss Wilson. The son of a millionaire, like the son of a king, is seldom free from mental disease. I am just mad enough to be a mountebank. If I were a little madder, I should perhaps really believe myself Smilash instead of merely acting him. Whether you ask me to forget myself for a moment, or to remember myself for a moment, I reply that I am the son of my father, and cannot. With my egotism, my charlatanry, my tongue, and my habit of having my own way, I am fit for no calling but that of saviour of mankind — just of the sort they like." After an impressive pause, he turned slowly and left the room.

"I wonder," he said, as he crossed the landing, "whether, by judiciously losing my way, I can catch a glimpse of that girl who is like a golden idol."

Downstairs, on his way to the door, he saw Agatha coming towards him, occupied with a book which she was tossing up to the ceiling and catching. Her melancholy expression, habitual in her lonely moments, shewed that she was not amusing herself, but giving vent to her restlessness. As her gaze travelled upward, following the flight of the volume, it was arrested by Smilash. The book fell to the floor. He picked it up and handed it to her, saying,

"And, in good time, here *is* the golden idol!"

"What?" said Agatha, confused.

"I call you the golden idol," he said. "When we are apart, I always imagine your face as a face of gold, with eyes and teeth of bdellium, or chalcedony, or agate, or any wonderful unknown stones of appropriate colours."

Agatha, witless and dumb, could only look down deprecatingly.

"You think you ought to be angry with me; and you do not know exactly how to make me feel that you are so. Is that it?"

"No. Quite the contrary. At least — I mean that you are wrong. I am the most commonplace person you can imagine — if you only knew. No matter what I may look, I mean."

"How do you know that you are commonplace?"

"Of course I know," said Agatha, her eyes wandering uneasily.

"Of course you do not know: you cannot see yourself as others see you. For instance, you have never thought of yourself as a golden idol."

"But that is absurd. You are quite mistaken about me."

"Perhaps so. I know, however, that your face is not really made of gold, and that it has not the same charm for you that it has for others — for me."

"I must go," said Agatha, suddenly in haste.

"When shall we meet again?"

"I dont know," she said, with a growing sense of alarm. "I really must go."

"Believe me, your hurry is only imaginary. Do you fancy that you are behaving in a manner quite unworthy of yourself, and that a net is closing round you?"

"No. Nothing of the sort!"

"Then why are you so anxious to get away?"

"I dont know," said Agatha, affecting to laugh as he looked sceptically at her from beneath his lowered eyelids. "Perhaps I do feel a little like that; but not so much as you say."

"I will explain the emotion to you," he said, with a subdued ardour that affected Agatha strangely. "But first tell me whether it is new to you or not."

"It is not an emotion at all. I did not say that it was."

"Do not be afraid of it. It is only being alone with a man whom you have bewitched. You would be mistress of the situation if you only knew how to manage a lover. It is far easier than managing a horse, or skating, or playing the piano, or half a dozen other feats of which you think nothing."

Agatha coloured, and raised her head.

"Forgive me," and said, interrupting the action. "I am trying to offend you in order to save myself from falling in love with you; and I have not the heart to let myself succeed. On your life, do not listen to me or believe me: I have no right to say these things to you. Some fiend enters into me when I am at your side. You should wear a veil, Agatha."

She blushed, and stood burning and tingling, her presence of mind gone, and her chief sensation one of relief to hear — for she did not dare to see — that he was departing. Her consciousness was in a delicious confusion, with the one definite thought in it that she had won her lover at last. The tone of Trefusis's voice, rich with truth and earnestness; his quick insight; and his passionate warning to her not to heed him, convinced her that she had entered into a relation destined to influence her whole life.

"And yet," she said remorsefully, "I cannot love him as he loves me. I am selfish, cold, calculating, worldly, and have doubted until now whether such a thing as love really existed. If I could only love him recklessly and wholly, as he loves me!"

Smilash was also soliloquizing as he went on his way.

"Now I have made the poor child — who was so anxious that I should not mistake her for a supernaturally gifted and lovely woman — as happy as an angel; and so is that fine girl whom they call Jane Carpenter. I hope they wont exchange confidences on the subject."

CHAPTER VIII.

Mrs. Trefusis found her parents so unsympathetic on the subject of her marriage, that she left their house shortly after her visit to Lyvern, and went to reside with a hospitable friend. Unable to remain silent upon the matter constantly in her thoughts, she discussed her husband's flight with this friend, and elicited an opinion that the behaviour of

Trefusis was scandalous and wicked. Henrietta could not bear this, and sought shelter with a relative. The same discussion arising, the relative said,

"Well, Hetty, if I am to speak candidly, I must say that I have known Sidney Trefusis for a long time; and he is the easiest person to get on with I ever met. And you know, dear, that you are very trying sometimes."

"And so," cried Henrietta, bursting into tears, "after the infamous way he has treated me, I am to be told that it is all my own fault."

She left the house next day, having obtained another invitation from a discreet lady who would not discuss the subject at all. This proved quite intolerable; and Henrietta went to stay with her uncle Daniel Jansenius, a jolly and indulgent man. He opined that things would come right as soon as both parties grew more sensible; and, as to which of them was in fault, his verdict was, six of one and half a dozen of the other. Whenever he saw his niece pensive or tearful, he laughed at her, and called her a grass widow. Henrietta found that she could endure anything rather than this. Declaring that the world was hateful to her, she hired a furnished villa in St. John's Wood, whither she moved in December. But, suffering much there from loneliness, she soon wrote a pathetic letter to Agatha, entreating her to spend the approaching Christmas vacation with her, and promising her every luxury and amusement that boundless affection could suggest and boundless means procure. Agatha's reply contained some unlooked-for information.

ALTON COLLEGE. LYVERN.
14th December.

DEAREST HETTY: *I dont think I can do exactly what you want, as I must spend Xmas with mamma at Chiswick; but I need not get there until Xmas Eve, and we break up here on yesterday week, the 20th. So I will go straight to you and bring you with me to mamma's, where you will spend Xmas much better than moping in a strange house. It is not quite settled yet about my leaving the college after this term. You must promise not to tell anyone; but I have a new friend here — a lover. Not that I am in love with him, though I think very highly of him — you know I am not a romantic fool —; but he is very much in love with me; and I wish I could return it as he deserves. The French say that one person turns the cheek and the other kisses it. It has not got quite so far as that with us: indeed, since he declared what he felt, he has only been able to snatch a few words with me when I have been skating or walking. But there has always been at least one word or look that meant a great deal.*

And now, who do you think he is? He says he knows you. Can you guess ? He says you know all his secrets. He says he knows your husband well; that he treated you very badly; and that you are greatly to be pitied. Can you guess now? He says he has kissed you — for shame, Hetty! Have you guessed yet? He was going to tell me something more when we were interrupted; and I have not seen him since except at a distance. He is the man with whom you eloped that day when you gave us all such a fright, — Mr. Sidney. I was the first to penetrate his disguise; and that very morning I had taxed him with it, and he had confessed it. He said then that he was hiding from a woman who was in love with him; and I should not be surprised if it turned out to be true; for he is wonderfully original — in fact what makes me like him is that he is by far the cleverest man I have ever met; and yet he thinks nothing of himself. I cannot imagine what he sees in me to care for, though he is evidently ensnared by my charms. I hope he wont find out how silly I am. He calls me his golden idol ——

Henrietta, with a scream of rage, tore the letter across, and stamped upon it. When the paroxysm subsided, she picked up the pieces; held them together as accurately as her trembling hands could; and read on.

— but he is not all honey, and will say the most severe things sometimes if he thinks he ought to. He has made me so ashamed of my ignorance that I am resolved to stay here for another term at least, and study as hard as I can. I have not begun yet, as it is not worth while at the eleventh hour of this term; but when I return in January I will set to work in earnest. So you may see that his influence over me is an entirely good one. I will tell you all about him when we meet; for I have no time to say anything now, as the girls are bothering me to go skating with them. He pretends to be a workman, and puts on our skates for us; and Jane Carpenter believes that he is in love with her. Jane is exceedingly kindhearted; but she has a talent for making herself ridiculous that nothing can suppress. The ice is lovely, and the weather jolly: we do not mind the cold in the least. They are threatening to go without me — good-bye!

Ever your affectionate
AGATHA.

Henrietta looked round for something sharp. She grasped a pair of scissors greedily, and stabbed the air with them. Then she became conscious of her murderous impulse, and shuddered at it; but in a moment more her jealousy swept back upon her. She cried, as if suffocating, "I dont care: I should like to kill her!" But she did not take up the scissors again.

At last she rang the bell violently, and asked for a railway guide. On being told that there was not one in the house, she scolded her maid so unreasonably that the girl said pertly that if she were to be spoken to like that, she should wish to leave when her month was up. This check brought Henrietta to her senses. She went upstairs, and put on the first cloak at hand, which was fortunately a heavy fur one. Then she took her bonnet and purse; left the house; hailed a passing hansom; and bade the cabman drive her to St. Pancras.

When the night came, the air at Lyvern was like iron in the intense cold. The trees and the wind seemed ice-bound, as the water was; and silence, stillness, and starlight, frozen hard, brooded over the country. At the chalet, Smilash, indifferent to the price of coals, kept up a roaring fire that glowed through the uncurtained windows, and tantalized the chilled wayfarer who did not happen to know, as the herdsmen of the neighbourhood did, that he was welcome to enter and warm himself without risk of rebuff from the tenant. Smilash was in high spirits. He had become a proficient skater, and frosty weather was now a luxury to him. It braced him, and drove away his gloomy fits; whilst his sympathies were kept awake, and his indignation maintained at an exhilarating pitch, by the sufferings of the poor, who, unable to afford fires or skating, warmed themselves in such sweltering heat as overcrowding produces in all seasons.

It was Smilash's custom to make a hot drink of oatmeal and water for himself at half-past nine o'clock each evening, and to go to bed at ten. He opened the door to throw out some water that remained in the saucepan from its last cleansing. It froze as it fell upon the soil. He looked at the night, and shook himself to throw off an oppressive sensation of being clasped in the icy ribs of the air; for the mercury had descended below the familiar region of crisp and crackly cold, and marked a temperature at which the numb atmosphere seemed on the point of congealing into black solidity. Nothing was stirring.

"By George!" he said: "this is one of those nights on which a rich man darent think!"

He shut the door; hastened back to his fire; and set to work at his caudle, which he watched and stirred with a solicitude that would have amused a professed cook. When it was done, he poured it into a large mug, where it steamed invitingly. He took up some in a spoon, and blew upon it to cool it. Tap, tap, tap, tap! hurriedly at the door.

"Nice night for a walk," he said, putting down the spoon. Then, shouting, "Come in."

The latch rose unsteadily; and Henrietta, with frozen tears on her cheeks, and an unintelligible expression of wretchedness and rage, appeared. After an instant of amazement, he sprang to her and clasped her in his arms; and she, against her will, and protesting voicelessly, stumbled into his embrace.

"You are frozen to death," he exclaimed, carrying her to the fire. "This seal jacket is like a sheet of ice. So is your face" (kissing it). "What is the matter? Why do you struggle so?"

"Let me go," she gasped, in a vehement whisper. "I h — hate you."

"My poor love, you are too cold to hate anyone — even your husband. You must let me take off these atrocious French boots. Your feet must be perfectly dead."

By this time her voice and tears were thawing in the warmth of the chalet and of his caresses. "You shall not take them off," she said, crying with cold and sorrow. "Let me alone. Dont touch me. I am going away — straight back. I will not speak to you, nor take off my things here, nor touch anything in the house."

"No, my darling," he said, putting her into a capacious wooden armchair, and busily unbuttoning her boots: "you shall do nothing that you dont wish to do. Your feet are like stones. Yes, yes, my dear: I am a wretch unworthy to live. I know it."

"Let me alone," she said piteously. "I dont want your attentions. I have done with you for ever."

"Come: you must drink some of this nasty stuff. You will need strength to tell your husband all the unpleasant things your soul is charged with. Take just a little."

She turned her face away, and would not answer. He brought another chair, and sat down beside her. "My lost, forlorn, betrayed one —— "

"I am," she sobbed. "You dont mean it; but I am."

"You are also my dearest and best of wives. If you ever loved me, Hetty, do, for my once dear sake, drink this before it gets cold."

She pouted; sobbed; and yielded to some gentle force which he used, as a child allows itself to be half persuaded, half compelled, to take physic.

"Do you feel better and more comfortable now?" he said.

"No," she replied, angry with herself for feeling both.

"Then," he said cheerfully, as if she had uttered a hearty affirmative, "I will put some more coals on the fire; and we shall be as snug as possible. It makes me wildly happy to see you at my fireside, and to know that you are my own wife."

"I wonder how you can look me in the face and say so," she cried.

"I should wonder at myself if I could look at your face and say anything else. Oatmeal is a capital restorative: all your energy is coming back. There: that will make a magnificent blaze presently."

"I never thought you deceitful, Sidney, whatever other faults you might have had."

"Precisely, my love. I understand your feelings. Murder, burglary, intemperance, or the minor vices you could have borne; but deceit you cannot abide."

"I will go away," she said despairingly, with a fresh burst of tears. "I will not be laughed at and betrayed. I will go barefooted." She rose, and attempted to reach the door; but he intercepted her, and said,

"My love: there is something serious the matter. What is it? Dont be angry with me."

He brought her back to the chair. She took Agatha's letter from the pocket of her fur cloak, and handed it to him with a faint attempt to be tragic.

"Read that," she said. "And never speak to me again. All is over between us."

He took it curiously, and turned it to look at the signature. "Aha!" he said: "my golden idol has been making mischief, has she?"

"There!" exclaimed Henrietta. "You have said it to my face! You have convicted yourself out of your own mouth!"

"Wait a moment, my dear. I have not read the letter yet."

He rose and walked to and fro through the room, reading. She watched him, angrily confident that she should presently see him change countenance. Suddenly he drooped as if his spine had partly given way; and in this ungraceful attitude he read the remainder of the letter. When he had finished, he threw it on the table; thrust his hands deep into his pockets; and roared with laughter, huddling himself together as if he could concentrate the joke by collecting himself into the smallest possible compass. Henrietta, speechless with indignation, could only look her feelings. At last he came and sat down beside her.

"And so," he said, "on receiving this, you rushed out in the cold, and came all the way to Lyvern. Now, it seems to me that you must either love me very much ——"

"I dont. I hate you."

" —— or else love yourself very much."

"Oh!" And she wept afresh. "You are a selfish brute; and you do just as you like without considering anyone else. No one ever thinks of me. And now you wont even take the trouble to deny that shameful letter."

"Why should I deny it? It is true. Do you not see the irony of all this? I amuse myself by paying a few compliments to a schoolgirl for whom I do not care two straws more than for any agreeable and passably clever woman I meet. Nevertheless, I occasionally feel a pang of remorse because I think that she may love me seriously, although I am only playing with her. I pity the poor heart I have wantonly ensnared. And, all the time, she is pitying me for exactly the same reason! She is conscience-stricken because she is only indulging in the luxury of being adored by 'by far the cleverest man she has ever met,' and is as heart-whole as I am! Ha, ha! That is the basis of the religion of love of which poets are the high-priests. Each worshipper knows that his own love is either a transient passion or a sham copied from his favourite poem; but he believes honestly in the love of others for him. Ho, ho! Is it not a silly world, my dear?"

"You had no right to make love to Agatha. You have no right to make love to anyone but me; and I wont bear it."

"You are angry because Agatha has infringed your monopoly. Always monopoly! Why, you silly girl, do you suppose that I belong to you, body and soul? — that I may not be moved except by your affection, or think except of your beauty?"

"You may call me as many names as you please; but you have no right to make love to Agatha."

"My dearest: I do not recollect calling you any names. I think you said something about a selfish brute."

"I did not. You called me a silly girl."

"But, my love, so you are."

"And so *you* are. You are thoroughly selfish."

"I dont deny it. But let us return to our subject. What did we begin to quarrel about?"

"I am not quarrelling, Sidney. It is you."

"Well, what did I begin to quarrel about?"

"About Agatha Wylie."

"Oh pardon me, Hetty: I certainly did not begin to quarrel about her. I am very fond of her — more so, it appears, than she is of me. — One moment, Hetty, before you recommence your reproaches. Why do you dislike my saying pretty things to Agatha?"

Henrietta hesitated, and said, "Because you have no right to. It shows how little you care for me."

"It has nothing to do with you. It only shows how much I care for her."

"I will not stay here to be insulted," said Hetty, her distress returning. "I will go home."

"Not to-night: there is no train."

"I will walk."

"It is too far."

"I dont care. I will not stay here, though I die of cold by the roadside."

"My cherished one: I have been annoying you purposely because you show by your anger that you have not ceased to care for me. I am in the wrong, as I usually am; and it is all my fault. Agatha knows nothing about our marriage."

"I do not blame you so much," said Henrietta, suffering him to place her head on his shoulder; "but I will never speak to Agatha again. She has behaved shamefully to me; and I will tell her so."

"No doubt she will opine that it is all your fault, dearest; and that I have behaved admirably. Between you I shall stand exonerated. And now, since it is too cold for walking; since it is late; since it is far to Lyvern and farther to London, I must improvise some accommodation for you here."

"But —— "

"But there is no help for it. You must stay."

CHAPTER IX.

Next day, Smilash obtained from his wife a promise that she would behave towards Agatha as if the letter had given no offence. Henrietta pleaded as movingly as she could for an immediate return to their domestic state; but he put her off with endearing speeches; promised nothing but eternal affection; and sent her back to London by the twelve o'clock express. Then his countenance changed: he walked back to Lyvern, and thence to the chalet, like a man pursued by disgust and remorse. Later in the afternoon, to raise his spirits, he took his skates and went to Wickens's pond, where, it being Saturday, he found the ice crowded with the Alton students and their half-holiday visitors. Fairholme, describing circles with his habitual air of compressed hardihood, stopped and stared with indignant surprise as Smilash lurched past him.

"Is that man here by your permission?" he said to Farmer Wickens, who was walking about as if superintending a harvest.

"He is here because he likes, I take it," said Wickens stubbornly. "He is a neighbour of mine, and a friend of mine. Is there any objections to my having a friend on my own pond, seein' that there is nigh on two or three ton of other people's friends on it without as much as a with-your-leave or a by-your-leave?"

"Oh no," said Fairholme, somewhat dashed. "If you are satisfied, there can be no objection."

"I'm glad on it. I thought there mout be."

"Let me tell you," said Fairholme, nettled, "that your landlord would not be pleased to see him here. He sent one of Sir John's best shepherds out of the country, after filling his head with ideas above his station. I heard Sir John speak very warmly about it last Sunday."

"Mayhap you did, Muster Fairholme. I have a lease of this land — and gravelly, poor stuff it is —; and I am no ways beholden to Sir John's likings and dislikings. A very good thing too for Sir John that I have a lease; for there aint a man in the country 'ud tak' a present o' the farm if it was free to-morrow. And what's a' more, though that young man do talk foolish about the rights of farm labourers and such-like nonsense; if Sir John was to hear him layin' it down concernin' rent and improvements, and the way we tenant farmers is put upon, p'raps he'd speak warmer than ever next Sunday."

And Wickens, with a smile expressive of his sense of having retorted effectively upon the parson, nodded and walked away.

Just then Agatha, skating hand in hand with Jane Carpenter, heard these words in her ear. "I have something very funny to tell you. Dont look round."

She recognized the voice of Smilash, and obeyed.

"I am not quite sure that you will enjoy it as it deserves," he added, and darted off again, after casting an eloquent glance at Miss Carpenter.

Agatha disengaged herself from her companion; made a circuit; and passed near Smilash, saying, "What is it?"

Smilash flitted away like a swallow; traced several circles around Fairholme; and then returned to Agatha and proceeded side by side with her.

"I have read the letter you wrote to Hetty," he said.

Agatha's face began to glow. She forgot to maintain her balance, and almost fell.

"Take care. And so you are not fond of me — in the romantic sense?"

No answer. Agatha dumb, and afraid to lift her eyelids.

"That is fortunate," he continued; "because — good evening, Miss Ward: I have done nothing but admire your skating for the last hour — because men were deceivers ever; and I am no exception, as you will presently admit."

Agatha murmured something; but it was unintelligible amid the din of skating.

"You think not? Well, perhaps you are right: I have said nothing to you that is not in a measure true: you have always had a peculiar charm for me. But I did not mean you to tell Hetty. Can you guess why?"

Agatha shook her head.

"Because she is my wife."

Agatha's ankles became limp. With an effort she kept upright until she reached Jane, to whom she clung for support.

"Dont," screamed Jane. "You'll upset me."

"I must sit down," said Agatha. "I am tired. Let me lean on you until we get to the chairs."

"Bosh! I can skate for an hour without sitting down," said Jane. However, she helped Agatha to a chair, and left her. Then Smilash, as if desiring a rest also, sat down close by on the margin of the pond.

"Well," he said, without troubling himself as to whether their conversation attracted attention or not: "what do you think of me now?"

"Why did you not tell me before, Mr. Trefusis?"

"That is the cream of the joke," he replied, poising his heels on the ice so that his skates stood vertically at legs' length from him, and looking at them with a cynical air. "I thought you were in love with me, and that the truth would be too severe a blow to you. Ha! ha! And, for the same reason, you generously forbore to tell me that you were no more in love with me than with the man in the moon. Each played a farce, and palmed it off on the other as a tragedy."

"There are some things so unmanly, so unkind, and so cruel," said Agatha, "that I cannot understand any gentleman saying them to a girl. Please do not speak to me again. Miss Ward! Come to me for a moment. I — I am not well."

Miss Ward hurried to her side. Smilash, after staring at her for a moment in astonishment, and in some concern, skimmed away into the crowd. When he reached the opposite bank, he took off his skates, and asked Jane, who strayed intentionally in his direction, to tell Miss Wylie that he was gone, and would skate no more there. Without adding a word of explanation, he left her, and made for his dwelling. As he went down into the hollow where the road passed through the plantation on the college side of the chalet, he descried a boy, in the uniform of the post office, sliding along the frozen ditch. A presentiment of evil tidings came upon him like a darkening of the sky. He quickened his pace.

"Anything for me?" he said.

The boy, who knew him, fumbled in a letter case, and produced a buff envelope. It contained a telegram.

From JANSENIUS, *London.*

To J. SMILASH, *Chamounix Villa, Lyvern.*

Henrietta	*dangerously*	*ill*	*after*	*journey*
wants	*to*	*see*	*you*	*doctors*
say	*must*	*come*	*at*	*once*

There was a pause. Then he folded the paper methodically, and put it in his pocket, as if quite done with it.

"And so," he said, "perhaps the tragedy is to follow the farce, after all."

He looked at the boy, who retreated, not liking his expression.

"Did you slide all the way from Lyvern?"

"Only to come quicker," said the messenger, faltering. "I came as quick as I could."

"You carried news heavy enough to break the thickest ice ever frozen. I have a mind to throw you over the top of that tree instead of giving you this half-crown."

"You let me alone," whimpered the boy, retreating another pace.

"Get back to Lyvern as fast as you can run or slide, and tell Mr. Marsh to send me the fastest trap he has, to drive me to the railway station. Here is your half-crown. Off with you; and if I do not find the trap ready when I want it, woe betide you."

The boy came for the money mistrustfully, and ran off with it as fast as he could. Smilash went into the chalet, and never reappeared. Instead, Trefusis, a gentleman in an ulster, carrying a rug, came out; locked the door; and hurried along the road to Lyvern, where he was picked up by the trap, and carried swiftly to the railway station, just in time to catch the London train.

"Evening paper, sir?" said a voice at the window, as he settled himself in the corner of a first-class carriage.

"No, thank you."

"Footwarmer, sir?" said a porter, appearing in the newsvendor's place.

"Ah: that's a good idea. Yes: let me have a footwarmer."

The footwarmer was brought; and Trefusis composed himself comfortably for his journey. It seemed very short to him: he could hardly believe, when the train arrived in London, that he had been nearly three hours on the way.

There was a sense of Christmas about the travellers and the people who were at the terminus to meet them. The porter who came to the carriage door reminded Trefusis by his manner and voice that the season was one at which it becomes a gentleman to be festive and liberal.

"Wot luggage, sir? Ensom or fourweoll, sir?"

For a moment Trefusis felt a vagabond impulse to resume the language of Smilash, and fable to the man of hampers of turkey and plum-pudding in the van. But he repressed it; got into a hansom; and was driven to his father-in-law's house in Belsize Avenue, studying in a gloomily critical mood the anxiety that surged upon him and made his heart beat like a boy's as he drew near his destination. There were two carriages at the door when he alighted. The reticent expression of the coachmen sent a tremor through him.

The door opened before he rang. "If you please, sir," said the maid in a low voice, "will you step into the library; and the doctor will see you immediately."

On the first landing of the staircase, two gentlemen were speaking to Mr. Jansenius, who hastily moved out of sight, not before a glimpse of his air of grief and discomfiture had given Trefusis a strange twinge, succeeded by a sensation of having been twenty years a widower. He smiled unconcernedly as he followed the girl into the library, and asked her how she did. She murmured some reply, and hurried away, thinking that the poor young man would alter his tone presently.

He was joined at once by a grey whiskered gentleman, scrupulously dressed and mannered. Trefusis introduced himself; and the physician looked at him with some interest. Then he said,

"You have arrived too late, Mr. Trefusis. All is over, I am sorry to say."

"Was the long railway journey she took in this cold weather the cause of her death?"

Some bitter words that the physician had heard upstairs made him aware that this was a delicate question. But he said quietly, "The proximate cause, doubtless. The proximate cause."

"She received some unwelcome and quite unlooked-for intelligence before she started. Had that anything to do with her death, do you think?"

"It may have produced an unfavourable effect," said the physician, growing restive, and taking up his gloves. "The habit of referring such events to such causes is carried too far, as a rule."

"No doubt. I am curious because the event is novel in my experience. I suppose it is a commonplace in yours."

"Pardon me. The loss of a lady so young and so favourably circumstanced, is not a commonplace either in my experience or in my opinion." The physician held up his head as he spoke, in protest against any assumption that his sympathies had been blunted by his profession.

"Did she suffer?"

"For some hours, yes. We were able to do a little to alleviate her pain — poor thing!" He almost forgot Trefusis as he added the apostrophe.

"Hours of pain! Can you conceive any good purpose that those hours may have served?"

The physician shook his head, leaving it doubtful whether he meant to reply in the negative, or to deplore considerations of that nature. He also made a movement to depart, being uneasy in conversation with Trefusis, who would, he felt sure, presently ask questions or make remarks with which he could hardly deal without committing himself in some direction. His conscience was not quite at rest. Henrietta's pain had not, he thought, served any good purpose; but he did not want to say so, lest he should acquire a reputation for impiety and lose his practice. He believed that the general practitioner who attended the family, and had called him in when the case grew serious, had treated Henrietta unskilfully; but professional etiquette bound him so strongly that, sooner than betray his colleague's inefficiency, he would have allowed him to decimate London.

"One word more," said Trefusis. "Did she know that she was dying?"

"No. I considered it best that she should not be informed of her danger. She passed away without any apprehension."

"Then one can think of it with equanimity. She dreaded death, poor child! The wonder is that there was not enough folly in the household to prevail against your good sense."

The physician bowed, and took his leave, esteeming himself somewhat fortunate in escaping without being reproached for his humanity in having allowed Henrietta to die unawares.

A moment later the general practitioner entered. Trefusis, having accompanied the consulting physician to the door, detected the family doctor in the act of pulling a long face just outside it. Restraining a desire to seize him by the throat, he seated himself on the edge of the table, and said cheerfully,

"Well, doctor: how has the world used you since we last met?"

The doctor was taken aback; but the solemn disposition of his features did not relax as he almost intoned, "Has Sir Francis told you the sad news, Mr. Trefusis?"

"Yes. Frightful, isnt it? Lord bless me, we're here to-day and gone to-morrow."

"True, very true!"

"Sir Francis has a high opinion of you."

The doctor looked a little foolish. "Everything was done that could be done, Mr. Trefusis; but Mrs. Jansenius was very anxious that no stone should be left unturned. She was good enough to say that her sole reason for wishing me to call in Sir Francis was that you should have no cause to complain."

"Indeed!"

"An excellent mother! A sad event for her! Ah yes, yes! Dear me! A very sad event!"

"Most disagreeable. Such a cold day too. Pleasanter to be in heaven than here in such weather, possibly."

"Ah!" said the doctor, as if much sound comfort lay in that. "I hope so: I hope so: I do not doubt it. Sir Francis did not permit us to tell her; and I, of course, deferred to him. Perhaps it was for the best."

"You would have told her, then, if Sir Francis had not objected?"

"Well, there are, you see, considerations which we must not ignore in our profession. Death is a serious thing, as I am sure I need not remind you, Mr. Trefusis. We have sometimes higher duties than indulgence to the natural feelings of our patients."

"Quite so. The possibility of eternal bliss and the probability of eternal torment are consolations not to be lightly withheld from a dying girl, eh? However, what's past cannot be mended. I have much to be thankful for, after all. I am a young man, and shall not cut a bad figure as a widower. And now tell me, doctor: am I not in very bad repute upstairs?"

"Mr. Trefusis! Sir! I cannot meddle in family matters. I understand my duties, and never overstep them." The doctor, shocked at last, spoke as loftily as he could.

"Then I will go and see Mr. Jansenius," said Trefusis, getting off the table.

"Stay, sir! One moment. I have not finished. Mrs. Jansenius has asked me to ask — I was about to say that I am not speaking now as the medical adviser of this family; but although an old friend — and — ahem! Mrs. Jansenius has asked me to ask — to request you to excuse Mr. Jansenius, as he is prostrated by grief, and is, as I can — as a medical man — assure you, unable to see anyone. She will speak to you herself as soon as she feels able to do so — at some time this evening. Meanwhile, of course, any orders you may give — you must be fatigued by your journey, and I always recommend people not to fast too long: it produces an acute form of indigestion — any orders you may wish to give will, of course, be attended to at once."

"I think," said Trefusis, after a moment's reflection, "I will order a hansom."

"There is no ill-feeling," said the doctor, who, as a slow man, was usually alarmed by prompt decisions, even when they seemed wise to him, as this one did. "I hope you have not gathered from anything I have said —— "

"Not at all: you have displayed the utmost tact. But I think I had better go. Jansenius can bear death and misery with perfect fortitude when it is on a large scale, and hidden in a back slum. But when it breaks into his own house, and attacks his property — his daughter was his property until very recently — he is just the man to lose his head and quarrel with me for keeping mine."

The doctor was unable to cope with this speech, which conveyed vaguely monstrous ideas to him. Seeing Trefusis about to leave, he said in a low voice, "Will you go upstairs?"

"Upstairs! Why?"

"I — I thought you might wish to see —— " He did not finish the sentence; but Trefusis flinched: the blank had expressed what was meant.

"To see something that was Henrietta, and that is a thing we must cast out and hide, with a little superstitious mumming to save appearances. Why did you remind me of it?"

"But, sir, whatever your views may be, will you not as a matter of form, in deference to the feelings of the family —— ?"

"Let them spare their feelings for the living, on whose behalf I have often appealed to them in vain," cried Trefusis, losing patience. "Damn their feelings!" And, turning to the door, he found it open, and Mrs. Jansenius there listening.

Trefusis was confounded. He knew what the effect of his speech must be, and felt that it would be folly to attempt excuse or explanation. He put his hands into his pockets; leaned against the table; and looked at her, mutely wondering what would follow on her part.

The doctor broke the silence by saying, tremulously, "I have communicated the melancholy intelligence to Mr. Trefusis."

"I hope you told him also," she said sternly, "that, however deficient we may be in feeling, we did everything that lay in our power for our child."

"I am quite satisfied," said Trefusis.

"No doubt you are — with the result," said Mrs. Jansenius, hardly. "I wish to know whether you have anything to complain of."

"Nothing."

"Please do not imply that anything has happened through our neglect."

"What have I to complain of? She had a warm room and a luxurious bed to die in, with the best medical advice in the world. Plenty of people are starving and freezing to-day that we may have the means to die fashionably: ask *them* if they have any cause for complaint. Do you think I will wrangle over her body about the amount of money spent on her illness? What measure is that of the cause she had for complaint? I never grudged money to her — how could I? seeing that more than I can waste is given to me for nothing. Or how could you? Yet she had great reason to complain of me. You will allow that to be so."

"It is perfectly true."

"Well, when I am in the humour for it, I will reproach myself and not you." He paused, and then turned forcibly on her, saying, "Why do you select this time, of all others, to speak so bitterly to me?"

"I am not aware that I have said anything to call for such a remark. Did *you*" (appealing to the doctor) "hear me say anything?"

"Mr. Trefusis does not mean to say that you did, I am sure. Oh no. Mr. Trefusis's feelings are naturally — are harrowed. That is all."

"My feelings!" cried Trefusis impatiently. "Do you suppose my feelings are a trumpery set of social observances, to be harrowed to order and exhibited at funerals? She has gone as we three shall go soon enough. If we were immortal, we might reasonably pity the dead. As we are not, we had better save our energies to minimize the harm we are likely to do before we follow her."

The doctor was deeply offended by this speech; for the statement that he should one day die seemed to him a reflection upon his professional mastery over death. Mrs. Jansenius was glad to see Trefusis confirming her bad opinion and report of him by his conduct and language in the doctor's presence. There was a brief pause; and then Trefusis, too far out of sympathy with them to be able to lead the conversation into a kinder vein, left the room. In the act of putting on his overcoat in the hall, he hesitated, and hung it up again irresolutely. Suddenly he ran upstairs. At the sound of his steps, a woman came from one of the rooms, and looked inquiringly at him.

"Is it here?" he said.

"Yes, sir," she whispered.

A painful sense of constriction came in his chest; and he turned pale and stopped with his hand on the lock.

"Dont be afraid, sir," said the woman, with an encouraging smile. "She looks beautiful."

He looked at her with a strange grin, as if she had uttered a ghastly but irresistible joke. Then he went in, and, when he reached the bed, wished he had stayed without. He was not one of those who, seeing little in the faces of the living, miss little in the faces of the dead. The arrangement of the black hair on the pillow, the soft drapery, and the flowers placed there by the nurse to complete the artistic effect to which she had so confidently referred, were lost on him: he saw only a lifeless mask that had been his wife's face; and at sight of it his knees failed, and he had to lean for support on the rail at the foot of the bed.

When he looked again, the face seemed to have changed. It was no longer a waxlike mask, but Henrietta, girlish and pathetically at rest. Death seemed to have cancelled her marriage and womanhood: he had never seen her look so young. A minute passed; and then a tear dropped on the coverlet. He started; shook another tear on his hand; and stared at it incredulously.

"This is a fraud of which I have never even dreamed," he said. "Tears and no sorrow! Here am I crying! growing maudlin! whilst I am glad that she is gone and I free. I have the mechanism of grief in me somewhere: it begins to turn at sight of her though I have no sorrow; just as she used to start the mechanism of passion when I had no love. And that made no difference to her: whilst the wheels went round she was satisfied. I hope the mechanism of grief will flag and stop in its spinning as soon as the other used to. It is stopping already, I think. What a mockery! Whilst it lasts I suppose I am really sorry. And yet, would I restore her to life if I could? Perhaps so: I am therefore thankful that I cannot." He folded his arms on the rail, and gravely addressed the dead figure, which still affected him so strongly that he had to exert his will to face it with composure. "If you really loved me, it is well for you that you are dead — idiot that I was to believe that the passion you could inspire, you poor child, would last. We are both lucky: I have escaped from you; and you have escaped from yourself."

Presently he breathed more freely, and looked round the room to help himself into a matter-of-fact vein by a little unembarrassed action, and the commonplace aspect of the bedroom furniture. He went to the pillow, and bent over it, examining the face closely.

"Poor child!" he said again, tenderly. Then, with sudden reaction, apostrophizing himself instead of his wife, "Poor ass! Poor idiot!

Poor jackanapes! Here is the body of a woman who was nearly as old as myself, and perhaps wiser; and here am I moralizing over it as if I were God Almighty and she a baby! The more you remind a man of what he is, the more conceited he becomes. Monstrous! I shall feel immortal presently."

He touched the cheek with a faint attempt at roughness, to feel how cold it was. Then he touched his own, and remarked,

"This is what I am hastening toward at the express speed of sixty minutes an hour!" He stood looking down at the face and tasting this sombre reflection for a long time. When it palled on him, he roused himself, and exclaimed more cheerfully,

"After all, she is not dead. Every word she uttered — every idea she formed and expressed, was an inexhaustible and indestructible impulse." He paused; considered a little further; and relapsed into gloom, adding, "And the dozen others whose names will be with hers in the *Times* to-morrow? Their words too are still in the air, to endure there to all eternity. Hm! How the air must be crammed with nonsense! Two sounds sometimes produce a silence: perhaps ideas neutralize one another in some analogous way. No, my dear: you are dead and gone and done with; and I shall be dead and gone and done with too soon to leave me leisure to fool myself with hopes of immortality. Poor Hetty! Well: good-bye, my darling. Let us pretend for a moment that you can hear that: I know it will please you."

All this was in a half articulate whisper. When he ceased, he still bent over the body, gazing intently at it. Even when he had exhausted the subject, and turned to go, he changed his mind, and looked again for a while. Then he stood erect, apparently nerved and refreshed, and left the room with a firm step. The woman was waiting outside. Seeing that he was less distressed than when he entered, she said,

"I hope you are satisfied, sir!"

"Delighted! Charmed! The arrangements are extremely pretty and tasteful. Most consolatory." And he gave her half-a-sovereign.

"I thank you, sir," she said, dropping a curtsey. "The poor young lady! She was anxious to see you, sir. To hear her say that you were the only one that cared for her! And so fretful with her mother, too. 'Let him be told that I am dangerously ill,' says she, 'and he'll come.' She didnt know how true her word was, poor thing; and she went off without being aware of it."

"Flattering herself, and flattering me. Happy girl!"

"Bless you, I know what her feelings were, sir: I have had experience." Here she approached him confidentially, and whispered, "The family were again' you, sir; and she knew it. But she wouldnt listen to them. She thought of nothing, when she was easy enough to think at all, but of your coming. And — hush! Here's the old gentleman."

Trefusis looked round, and saw Mr. Jansenius, whose handsome face was white and seamed with grief and annoyance. He drew back from the proffered hand of his son-in-law, like an overworried child from an ill-timed attempt to pet it. Trefusis pitied him. The nurse coughed, and retired.

"Have you been speaking to Mrs. Jansenius?" said Trefusis.

"Yes," said Jansenius offensively.

"So have I, unfortunately. Pray make my apologies to her. I was rude. The circumstances upset me."

"You are not upset, sir," said Jansenius, loudly. "You do not care a damn."

Trefusis recoiled.

"You damned my feelings; and I will damn yours," continued Jansenius, in the same tone. Trefusis involuntarily looked at the door through which he had lately passed. Then, recovering himself, he said quietly,

"It does not matter. She cant hear us."

Before Jansenius could reply, his wife hurried upstairs; caught him by the arm; and said, "Dont speak to him, John. And you," she added, to Trefusis: *"will* you begone."

"What!" he said, looking cynically at her. "Without my dead! Without my property! Well: be it so."

"What do you know of the feelings of a respectable man?" persisted Jansenius, breaking out again in spite of his wife. "Nothing is sacred to you. This shows what Socialists are!"

"And what fathers are, and what mothers are," retorted Trefusis, giving way to his temper. "I thought you loved Hetty; but I see that you only love your feelings and your respectability. The devil take both! She was right: my love for her, incomplete as it was, was greater than yours." And he left the house in dudgeon.

But he stood awhile in the avenue to laugh at himself and his father-in-law. Then he took a hansom, and was driven to the house of his solicitor, whom he wished to consult on the settlement of his late wife's affairs.

CHAPTER X.

The remains of Henrietta Trefusis were interred in Highgate Cemetery the day before Christmas Eve. Three noblemen sent their carriages to the funeral; and the friends and clients of Mr. Jansenius, to a large number, attended in person. The bier was covered with a profusion of costly flowers. The undertaker, instructed to spare no expense, provided long-tailed black horses, with black palls on their backs, and black plumes upon their foreheads; coachmen decorated with scarves and jack-boots; black hammercloths, cloaks, and gloves; with many hired mourners, who, however, would have been instantly discharged had they presumed to betray emotion, or in any way over-step their function of walking beside the hearse with brass-tipped batons in their hands.

Among the genuine mourners were Mr. Jansenius, who burst into tears at the ceremony of casting earth on the coffin; the boy Arthur, who, pre-occupied by the novelty of appearing in a long cloak at the head of a public procession, felt that he was not so sorry as he ought to be when he saw his papa cry; and a cousin who had once asked Henrietta to marry him, and who now, full of tragic reflections, was enjoying his despair intensely.

The rest whispered, whenever they could decently do so, about a strange omission in the arrangements. The husband of the deceased was absent. Members of the family and intimate friends were told by Daniel Jansenius that the widower had acted in a blackguard way, and that the Janseniuses did not care two-pence whether he came or stayed at home; that, but for the indecency of the thing, they were just as glad that he was keeping away. Others, who had no claim to be privately informed, made inquiries of the undertaker's foreman, who said he understood the gentleman objected to large funerals. Asked why, he said he supposed it was on the ground of expense. This being met by a remark that Mr. Trefusis was very wealthy, he added that he had been told so, but believed the money had not come from the lady; that people seldom cared to go to a great expense for a funeral unless they came into something good by the death; and that some parties, the more they had, the more they grudged. Before the funeral guests dispersed, the report spread by Mr. Jansenius's brother had got mixed with the views of the foreman, and had given rise to a story of Trefusis expressing joy at his wife's death with frightful oaths in her father's house whilst she lay dead there, and refusing to pay a farthing of her debts or funeral expenses.

Some days later, when gossip on the subject was subsiding, a fresh scandal revived it. A literary friend of Mr. Jansenius's helped him to compose an epitaph, and added to it a couple of pretty and touching stanzas, setting forth that Henrietta's character had been one of rare sweetness and virtue, and that her friends would never cease to sorrow for her loss. A tradesman who described himself as a "monumental mason" furnished a book of tomb designs; and Mr. Jansenius selected a highly ornamental one, and proposed to defray half the cost of its erection. Trefusis objected that the epitaph was untrue; and said that he did not see why tombstones should be privileged to publish false statements. It was reported that he had followed up his former misconduct by calling his father-in-law a liar, and that he had ordered a common tombstone from some cheap-jack at the East-end. He had, in fact, spoken contemptuously of the monumental tradesman as an "exploiter" of labour, and had asked a young working mason, a member of the International Association, to design a monument for the gratification of Jansenius.

The mason, with much pains and misgiving, produced an original design. Trefusis approved of it, and resolved to have it executed by the hands of the designer. He hired a sculptor's studio; purchased blocks of marble of the dimensions and quality described to him by the mason; and invited him to set to work forthwith.

Trefusis now encountered a difficulty. He wished to pay the mason the just value of his work, no more and no less. But this he could not ascertain. The only available standard was the market price, and this he rejected as being fixed by competition among capitalists who could only secure profit by obtaining from their workmen more products than they paid them for, and could only tempt customers by offering a share of the unpaid-for part of the products as a reduction in price. Thus he found that the system of withholding the indispensable materials for production and subsistence from the labourers, except on condition of their supporting an idle class whilst accepting a lower standard of comfort for themselves than for that idle class, rendered the determination of just ratios of exchange, and consequently the practice of honest dealing, impossible. He had at last to ask the mason what he would consider fair payment for the execution of the design, though he knew that the man could no more solve the problem than he, and that, though he would certainly ask as much as he thought he could get, his demand must be limited by his poverty and by the competition of the monumental tradesman. Trefusis settled the matter by giving double what was asked, only imposing such conditions as were necessary to compel the mason to execute the work himself, and not make a profit by hiring other men at the market rate of wages to do it.

But the design was, to its author's astonishment, to be paid for separately. The mason, after hesitating a long time between two-pounds-ten and five pounds, was emboldened by a fellow-workman, who treated him to some hot whiskey and water, to name the larger sum. Trefusis paid the money at once, and then set himself to find out how much a similar design would have cost from the hands of an eminent Royal Academician. Happening to know a gentleman in this position, he consulted him, and was informed that the probable cost would be from five hundred to one thousand pounds. Trefusis expressed his opinion that the mason's charge was the more reasonable, somewhat to the indignation of his artist friend, who reminded him of the years which a Royal Academician has to spend in acquiring his skill. Trefusis mentioned that the apprenticeship of a mason was quite as long, twice as laborious, and not half so pleasant. The artist now began to find Trefusis's Socialistic views, with which he had previously fancied himself in sympathy, both odious and dangerous. He demanded whether nothing was to be allowed for genius. Trefusis warmly replied that genius cost its possessor nothing; that it was the inheritance of the whole race incidentally vested in a single individual; and that if that individual employed his monopoly of it to extort money from others, he deserved nothing better than hanging. The artist lost his temper, and suggested that if Trefusis could not feel that the prerogative of art was divine, perhaps he could understand that a painter was not such a fool as to design a tomb for five pounds when he might be painting a portrait for a thousand. Trefusis retorted that the fact of a man paying a thousand pounds for a portrait proved that he had not earned the money, and was therefore either a thief or a beggar. The common workman who sacrificed sixpence from his week's wages for a cheap photograph to present to his sweetheart, or a shilling for a pair of chromolithographic pictures or delft figures to place on his mantelboard, suffered greater privation for the sake of possessing a work of art than the great landlord or shareholder who paid a thousand pounds, which he was too rich to miss, for a portrait that, like Hogarth's Jack Sheppard, was only interesting to students of criminal physiognomy. A lively quarrel ensued: Trefusis denouncing the folly of artists in fancying themselves a priestly caste when they were obviously only the parasites and favoured slaves of the moneyed classes; and his friend (temporarily his enemy) sneering bitterly at levellers who were for levelling down instead of levelling up. Finally, tired of disputing, and remorseful for their acrimony, they dined amicably together.

The monument was placed in Highgate Cemetery by a small band of workmen, whom Trefusis found out of employment. It bore the following inscription:

THIS IS THE MONUMENT OF

HENRIETTA JANSENIUS

WHO WAS BORN ON THE 26TH JULY, 1856,

MARRIED TO SIDNEY TREFUSIS ON THE 23RD AUGUST, 1875,

AND WHO DIED ON THE 21ST DECEMBER IN THE SAME YEAR.

Mr. Jansenius took this as an insult to his daughter's memory, and, as the tomb was much smaller than many which had been erected in the cemetery by families to whom the Janseniuses claimed superiority, cited it as an example of the widower's meanness. But by other persons it was so much admired that Trefusis hoped it would ensure the prosperity of its designer. The contrary happened. When the mason attempted to return to his ordinary work, he was informed that he had contravened trade usage, and that his former employers would have nothing more to say to him. On applying for advice and assistance to the trades-union of which he was a member, he received the same reply, and was further reproached for treachery to his fellow-workmen. He returned to Trefusis to say that the tombstone job had ruined him. Trefusis, enraged, wrote an argumentative letter to the *Times,* which was not inserted; a sarcastic one to the trades-union, which did no good; and a fierce one to the employers, who threatened to take an action for libel. He had to content himself with setting the man to work again on mantelpieces and other decorative stone-work for use in house property on the Trefusis estate. In a year or two his liberal payments enabled the mason to save sufficient to start as an employer, in which capacity he soon began to grow rich, as he knew by experience exactly how much his workmen could be forced to do, and how little they could be forced to take. Shortly after this change in his circumstances, he became an advocate of thrift, temperance, and steady industry; and quitted the International Association, of which he had been an enthusiastic supporter when dependent on his own skill and taste as a working mason.

During these occurrences, Agatha's school-life ended. Her resolution to study hard during another term at the college had been formed, not for the sake of becoming learned, but that she might become more worthy of Smilash; and when she learned the truth about him from his own lips, the idea of returning to the scene of that humiliation became intolerable to her. She left under the impression that her heart was broken; for her smarting vanity, by the law of its own existence, would not perceive that it was the seat of the injury. So she bade Miss Wilson adieu; and the bee on the window-pane was heard no more at Alton College.

The intelligence of Henrietta's death shocked her the more because she could not help being glad that the only other person who knew of her folly with regard to Smilash (himself excepted) was now silenced for ever. This seemed to her a terrible discovery of her own depravity. Under its influence she became almost religious, and caused some anxiety about her health to her mother, who was puzzled by her unwonted seriousness, and, in particular, by her determination not to speak of the misconduct of Trefusis, which was now the prevailing topic of conversation in the family. She listened in silence to gossiping discussions of his desertion of his wife; his heartless indifference to her decease; his violence and bad language by her deathbed; his parsimony; his malicious opposition to the wishes of the Janseniuses; his cheap tombstone with the insulting epitaph; his association with common workmen and low demagogues; his suspected connection with a secret society for the assassination of the royal family and blowing up of the army; his atheistic denial, in a pamphlet addressed to the clergy, of a statement by the Archbishop of Canterbury that spiritual aid alone could improve the condition of the poor in the East-end of London; and the crowning disgrace of his trial for seditious libel at the Old Bailey, where he was condemned to six months' imprisonment: a penalty from which he was rescued by the ingenuity of his counsel, who discovered a flaw in the indictment, and succeeded, at great cost to Trefusis, in getting the sentence quashed. Agatha at last got tired of hearing of his misdeeds. She believed him to be heartless, selfish, and misguided; but she knew that he was not the loud, coarse, sensual and ignorant brawler most of her mother's gossips supposed him to be. She even felt, in spite of herself, an emotion of gratitude to the few who ventured to defend him.

Preparation for her first season helped her to forget her misadventure. She "came out" in due time; and an extremely dull season she found it. So much so, that she sometimes asked herself whether she should ever be happy again. At the college there had been goodfellowship, fun, rules and duties which were a source of strength when observed and a source of delicious excitement when violated, freedom from ceremony, toffee making, flights on the bannisters, and appreciative audiences for the soldier in the chimney. In society there were silly conversations lasting half-a-minute, cool acquaintanceships founded on such half-minutes, general reciprocity of suspicion, overcrowding, insufficient ventilation, bad music badly executed, late hours, unwholesome food, intoxicating liquors, jealous competition in useless expenditure, husband-hunting, flirting, dancing, theatres, and concerts. The last three, which Agatha liked, helped to make the contrast between Alton and London tolerable to her; but they had their drawbacks; for good partners at the dances, and good performances at the spiritless opera and concerts, were disappointingly scarce. Flirting she could not endure: she drove men away when they became tender, seeing in them the falsehood of Smilash without his wit. She was considered rude by the younger gentlemen of her circle. They discussed her bad manners among themselves, and agreed to punish her by not asking her to dance. She thus got rid, without knowing why, of the attentions she cared for least (she retained a schoolgirl's cruel contempt for "boys"), and enjoyed herself as best she could with such of the older or more sensible men as were not intolerant of girls.

At best, the year was the least happy she had ever spent. She repeatedly alarmed her mother by broaching projects of becoming a hospital nurse, a public singer, or an actress. These projects led to some desultory studies. In order to qualify herself as a nurse, she read a handbook of physiology, which Mrs. Wylie thought so improper a subject for a young lady, that she went in tears to beg Mrs. Jansenius to remonstrate with her unruly girl. Mrs. Jansenius, better advised, was of opinion that the more a woman knew, the more wisely she was likely to act; and that Agatha would soon drop the physiology of her own accord. This proved true. Agatha, having finished her book by dint of extensive skipping, proceeded to study pathology from a volume of clinical lectures. Finding her own sensations exactly like those described in the book as symptoms of the direst diseases, she put it by in alarm, and took up a novel, which was free from the fault she had found in the lectures, inasmuch as none of the emotions it described in the least resembled any she had ever experienced.

After a brief interval, she consulted a fashionable teacher of singing as to whether her voice was strong enough for the operatic stage. He recommended her to study with him for six years, assuring her that at the end of that period — if she followed his directions — she should be the greatest singer in the world. To this there was, in her mind, the conclusive objection that in six years she should be an old woman. So she resolved to try privately whether she could not get on more quickly by herself. Meanwhile, with a view to the drama in case her operatic scheme should fail, she took lessons in elocution and gymnastics. Practice in these improved her health and spirits so much that her previous aspirations seemed too limited. She tried her hand at all the arts in succession, but was too discouraged by the weakness of her first attempts to persevere. She knew that as a general rule there are feeble and ridiculous beginnings to all excellence; but she never applied general rules to her own case, still thinking of herself as an exception to them, just as she had done when she romanced about Smilash. The illusions of adolescence were thick upon her.

Meanwhile her progress was creating anxieties in which she had no share. Her paroxysms of exhilaration, followed by a gnawing sense of failure and uselessness, were known to her mother only as "wildness" and "low spirits"; to be combated by needlework as a sedative, or beef tea as a stimulant. Mrs. Wylie had learnt by rote that the whole duty of a lady is to be graceful, charitable, helpful, modest and disinterested whilst awaiting passively whatever lot these virtues may induce. But she had learnt by experience that a lady's business in society is to get married; and that virtues and accomplishments alike are important only as attractions to eligible bachelors. As this truth is shameful, young ladies are left for a year to two to find it out for themselves: it is seldom explicitly conveyed to them at their entry into society. Hence they often throw away capital bargains in their first season, and are compelled to offer themselves at greatly reduced prices subsequently, when their attractions begin to stale. This was the fate which Mrs. Wylie, warned by Mrs. Jansenius, feared for Agatha, who, time after time when a callow gentleman of wealth and position was introduced to her, drove him brusquely away as soon as he ventured to hint that his affections were concerned in their acquaintanceship. The anxious mother had to console herself with the fact that her daughter drove away the ineligible as ruthlessly as the eligible; formed no unworldly attachments; was still very young; and would grow less coy as she advanced in years and in what Mrs. Jansenius called sense.

But as the seasons went by, it remained questionable whether Agatha was the more to be congratulated on having begun life after leaving school, or Henrietta on having finished it.

BOOK II

✳

CHAPTER XI.

Brandon Beeches, in the Thames valley, was the seat of Sir Charles Brandon, seventh baronet of that name. He had lost his father before attaining his majority, and had married shortly afterwards; so that in his twenty-fifth year he was father to three children. He was a little worn, in spite of his youth; but he was tall and agreeable, had a winning way of taking a kind and soothing view of the misfortunes of others, could tell a story well, liked music and could play and sing a little, loved the arts of design and could sketch a little in water colours, read every magazine from London or Paris that criticized pictures, had travelled a little, fished a little, shot a little, botanized a little, wandered restlessly in the footsteps of women, and dissipated his energies through all the small channels that his wealth opened and his talents made easy to him. He had no large knowledge of any subject, though he had looked into many just far enough to replace absolute unconsciousness of them with measurable ignorance. Never having enjoyed the sense of achievement, he was troubled with unsatisfied aspirations that filled him with melancholy and convinced him that he was a born artist. His wife found him selfish, peevish, hankering after change, and prone to believe that he was attacked by dangerous diseases when he was only catching cold.

Lady Brandon, who believed that he understood all the subjects he talked about because she did not understand them herself, was one of his disappointments. In person she resembled none of the types of beauty striven after by the painters of her time; but she had charms to which few men are insensible. She was tall, soft and stout; with ample and shapely arms, shoulders and hips. With her small head, little ears, pretty lips and roguish eye, she, being a very large creature, presented an immensity of half womanly, half infantine loveliness which smote even grave men with a desire to clasp her in their arms and kiss her. This desire had scattered the desultory intellectual culture of Sir Charles at first sight. His imagination invested her with the taste for the fine arts which he required from a wife; and he married her in her first season, only to discover that the amativeness in her temperament was so little and languid that she made all his attempts

111

at fondness ridiculous, and robbed the caresses for which he had longed of all their anticipated ecstasy. Intellectually she fell still further short of his hopes. She looked upon his favourite art of painting as a pastime for amateur, and a branch of the house furnishing trade for professional artists. When he was discussing it among his friends, she would offer her opinion with a presumption which was the more trying as she frequently blundered upon a sound conclusion whilst he was reasoning his way to a hollow one with his utmost subtlety and seriousness. On such occasions his disgust did not trouble her in the least: she triumphed in it. She had concluded that marriage was a greater folly, and men greater fools, than she had supposed; but such beliefs rather lightened her sense of responsibility than disappointed her; and, as she had plenty of money, plenty of servants, plenty of visitors, and plenty of exercise on horseback, of which she was immoderately fond, her time passed pleasantly enough. Comfort seemed to her the natural order of life: trouble always surprised her. Her husband's friends, who mistrusted every future hour, and found matter for bitter reflection in many past ones, were to her only examples of the power of sedentary habits and excessive reading to make men hipped and dull.

One fine May morning, as she cantered along the avenue at Brandon Beeches on a powerful bay horse, the gates at the end opened, and a young man sped through them on a bicycle. He was of slight frame, with fine dark eyes and delicate nostrils. When he recognized Lady Brandon he waved his cap; and when they met he sprang from his inanimate steed, at which the bay horse shied.

"Dont, you silly beast!" she cried, whacking the animal with the butt of her whip. "Though it's natural enough, goodness knows! How d'ye do? The idea of any one rich enough to afford a horse, riding on a wheel like that!"

"But I am not rich enough to afford a horse," he said, approaching her to pat the bay, having placed the bicycle against a tree. "Besides, I am afraid of horses, not being accustomed to them; and I know nothing about feeding them. My steed needs no food. He doesnt bite, nor kick. He never goes lame, nor sickens, nor dies, nor needs a groom, nor —— "

"That's all bosh," said Lady Brandon impetuously. "It stumbles, and gives you the most awful tosses; and it goes lame by its treadles and thingamejigs coming off; and it wears out, and is twice as much trouble to keep clean and scrape the mud off as a horse; and all sorts of things. I think the most ridiculous sight in the world is a man on a velocipede, working away with his feet as hard as he possibly can, and believing that his horse is carrying him instead of, as anyone can see, he carrying the horse. You neednt tell me that it isnt easier to walk in the ordinary way than to drag a great dead iron thing along with you. It's not good sense."

"Nevertheless I can carry it a hundred miles further in a day than I can carry myself alone. Such are the marvels of machinery. But I know that we cut a very poor figure beside you and that magnificent creature — not that anyone will look at me whilst you are by to occupy their attention so much more worthily."

She darted a glance at him which clouded his vision and made his heart beat more strongly. This was an old habit of hers. She kept it up from love of fun, having no idea of the effect it produced on more ardent temperaments than her own. He continued hastily,

"Is Sir Charles within doors?"

"Oh, it's the most ridiculous thing I ever heard of in my life," she exclaimed. "A man that lives by himself in a place down by the Riverside Road like a toy savings bank — dont you know the things I mean? — called Sallust's House, says there is a right of way through our new pleasure ground. As if anyone could have any right there after all the money we have spent fencing it on three sides, and building up the wall by the road, and levelling, and planting, and draining, and goodness knows what else! And now the man says that all the common people and tramps in the neighbourhood have a right to walk across it because they are too lazy to go round by the road. Sir Charles has gone to see the man about it. Of course he wouldnt do as I wanted him."

"What was that?"

"Write to tell the man to mind his own business, and to say that the first person we found attempting to trespass on our property should be given to the police."

"Then I shall find no one at home. I beg your pardon for calling it so; but it is the only place like home to me."

"Yes: it is so comfortable since we built the billiard room, and took away those nasty hangings in the hall. I was ever so long trying to pers —— "

She was interrupted by an old labourer, who hobbled up as fast as his rheumatism would allow him, and began to speak without further ceremony than snatching off his cap.

"Th'ave coom to the noo grouns, my lady: crowds of 'em. An' a parson with 'em, an' a flag! Sur Chorles he dont know what to say; an' sooch doins never was."

Lady Brandon turned pale, and pulled at her horse as if to back him out of some danger. Her visitor, puzzled, asked the old man what he meant.

"There's goin' to be a proceyshon through the noo grouns," he replied; "an' the master cant stop 'em. Th'ave throon down the wall: three yards of it is lyin' on Riverside Road. An' there's a parson with 'em, and a flag. An' him that lives in Sallust's Hoos, he's there, hoddin' 'em on."

"Thrown down the wall!" exclaimed Lady Brandon, scarlet with indignation and pale with apprehension by turns. "What a disgraceful thing! Where are the police? Chester: will you come with me and see what they are doing: Sir Charles is no use. Do you think there is any danger?"

"There's two police," said the old man; "an' him that lives at Sallust's dar'd them stop him. They're lookin' on. An' there's a parson among 'em. I see him pullin' away at the wall with his own han's."

"I will go and see the fun," said Chester.

Lady Brandon hesitated. But her anger and curiosity vanquished her fears. She overtook the bicycle; and they went together through the gates and by the high-road to the scene the old man had described. A heap of bricks and mortar lay in the roadway on each side of a breach in the newly built wall, over which Lady Brandon, from her eminence on horseback, could see, coming towards her across the pleasure ground, a column of about thirty persons. They marched three abreast in good order and in silence: the expression of all except a few mirthful faces being that of devotees fulfilling a rite. The gravity of the procession was deepened by the appearance of a clergyman in its ranks, which were composed of men of the middle class, and a few workmen carrying a banner inscribed THE SOIL OF ENGLAND THE BIRTHRIGHT OF ALL HER PEOPLE. There were also four women, upon whom Lady Brandon looked with intense indignation and contempt. None of the men of the neighbourhood had dared to join: they stood in the road whispering, and occasionally venturing to laugh at the jests of a couple of tramps who had stopped to see the fun, and who cared nothing for Sir Charles.

He, standing a little way within the field, was remonstrating angrily with a man of his own class, who stood with his back to the breach and his hands in the pockets of his snuff-coloured clothes, contemplating the procession with elate satisfaction. Lady Brandon, at once suspecting that this was the man from Sallust's House, and encouraged by the loyalty of the crowd, most of whom made way for her and touched their hats, hit the bay horse smartly with her whip, and rode him, with a clatter of hoofs and scattering of clods, right at the snuff-coloured enemy, who had to spring hastily aside to avoid her. There was a roar of laughter from the roadway; and the man turned sharply on her. But he suddenly smiled affably; replaced his hands in his pockets after raising his hat; and said,

"How do you do, Miss Carpenter? I thought you were a charge of cavalry."

"I am not Miss Carpenter: I am Lady Brandon; and you ought to be ashamed of yourself, Mr. Smilash, if it is you that have brought these disgraceful people here."

His eyes as he replied were eloquent with reproach to her for being no longer Miss Carpenter. "I am not Smilash," he said: "I am Sidney Trefusis. I have just had the pleasure of meeting Sir Charles for the first time; and we shall be the best friends possible when I have convinced him that it is hardly fair to seize on a path belonging to the people, and compel them to walk a mile and a half round his estate instead of four hundred yards between two portions of it."

"I have already told you, sir," said Sir Charles, "that I intend to open a still shorter path, and to allow all the well-conducted work-people to pass through twice a day. This will enable them to go to their work and return from it; and I will be at the cost of keeping the path in repair."

"Thank you," said Trefusis drily; "but why should we trouble you when we have a path of our own to use fifty times a day if we choose, without any man barring our way until our conduct happens to please him. Besides, your next heir would probably shut the path up the moment he came into possession."

"Offering them a path is just what makes them impudent," said Lady Brandon to her husband. "Why did you promise them anything? They would not think it a hardship to walk a mile and a half, or twenty miles, to a public-house; but when they go to their work they think it dreadful to have to walk a yard. Perhaps they would like us to lend them the waggonette to drive in."

"I have no doubt they would," said Trefusis, beaming at her.

"Pray leave me to manage here, Jane: this is no place for you. Bring Erskine to the house. He must be ——"

"Why dont the police make them go away?" said Lady Brandon, too excited to listen to her husband.

"Hush, Jane, pray. What can three men do against thirty or forty?"

"They ought to take up somebody, as an example to the rest."

"They have offered, in the handsomest manner, to arrest me if Sir Charles will give me in charge," said Trefusis.

"There!" said Lady Jane, turning to her husband. "Why dont you give him — or someone — in charge?"

"You know nothing about it," said Sir Charles, vexed by a sense that she was publicly making him ridiculous.

"If you dont, I will," she persisted. "The idea of having our ground broken into, and our new wall knocked down! A nice state of things it would be if people were allowed to do as they liked with other peoples' property. I will give every one of them in charge."

"Would you consign me to a dungeon?" said Trefusis, in melancholy tones.

"I dont mean you exactly," she said, relenting. "But I will give that clergyman into charge, because he ought to know better. He is the ringleader of the whole thing."

"He will be delighted, Lady Brandon: he pines for martyrdom. But will you really give him into custody?"

"I will," she said vehemently, emphasizing the assurance by a plunge in the saddle that made the bay stagger.

"On what charge?" he said, patting the horse, and looking up at her.

"I dont care what charge," she replied, conscious that she was being admired, and not displeased. "Let them take him up: that's all."

Human beings on horseback are so far centaurs that liberties taken with their horses are almost as personal as liberties taken with themselves. When Sir Charles saw Trefusis patting the bay, he felt as much outraged as if Lady Brandon herself were being patted; and he felt bitterly towards her for permitting the familiarity. He was relieved by the arrival of the procession. It halted as the leaders came up to Trefusis, who said gravely,

"Gentlemen: I congratulate you on the firmness with which you have this day asserted the rights of the people of this place to the use of one of the few scraps of mother earth of which they have not been despoiled."

"Gentlemen," shouted an excited member of the procession: "three cheers for the resumption of the land of England by the people of England! Hip, hip, hurrah!"

The cheers were given with much spirit, Sir Charles's cheeks becoming redder at each repetition. He looked angrily at the clergyman, now distracted by the charms of Lady Brandon, whose scorn, as she surveyed the crowd, expressed itself by a pout which became her pretty lips extremely.

Then a middle-aged labourer stepped from the road into the field, hat in hand; ducked respectfully; and said, "Look 'e here, Sir Charles. Dont 'e mind them fellers. There aint a man belonging to this neighbourhood among 'em: not one in your employ or on your land. Our dooty to you and your ladyship; and we will trust to you to do what is fair by us. We want no interlopers from Lunnon to get us into trouble with your honour; and ——"

"You unmitigated cur," exclaimed Trefusis fiercely: "what right have you to give away to his unborn children the liberty of your own?"

"They're not unborn," said Lady Brandon indignantly. "That just shows how little you know about it."

"No, nor mine either," said the man, emboldened by her ladyship's support. "And who are you that call me a cur?"

"Who am I! I am a rich man — one of your masters, and privileged to call you what I please. You are a grovelling famine-broken slave. Now go and seek redress against me from the law. I can buy law enough to ruin you for less money than it would cost me to shoot deer in Scotland or vermin here. How do you like that state of things? Eh?"

The man was taken aback. "Sir Charles will stand by me," he said, after a pause, with assumed confidence, but with an anxious glance at the baronet.

"If he does, after witnessing the return you have made me for standing by you, he is a greater fool than I take him to be."

"Gently, gently," said the clergyman. "There is much excuse to be made for the poor fellow."

"As gently as you please with any man that is a free man at heart," said Trefusis; "but slaves must be driven; and this fellow is a slave to the marrow."

"Still, we must be patient. He does not know ——"

"He knows a great deal better than you do," said Lady Brandon, interrupting. "And the more shame for you, because you ought to know best: I suppose you were educated somewhere. You will not be so satisfied with yourself when your bishop hears of this. Yes," she added, turning to Trefusis with an infantile air of wanting to cry and being forced to laugh against her will: "you may laugh as much as you please — dont trouble to pretend it's only coughing —; but we will write to his bishop, as he shall find to his cost."

"Hold your tongue, Jane, for God's sake," said Sir Charles, taking her horse by the bridle, and backing him from Trefusis.

"I will not. If you choose to stand here and allow them to walk away with the walls in their pockets, I dont and wont. Why cannot you make the police do something?"

"They can do nothing," said Sir Charles, almost beside himself with humiliation. "I cannot do anything until I see my solicitor. How can you bear to stay here wrangling with these fellows? It is so undignified!"

"It's all very well to talk of dignity; but I dont see the dignity of letting people trample on our grounds without leave. Mr. Smilash: will you make them all go away, and tell them that they shall all be prosecuted and put in prison."

"They are going to the cross roads, to hold a public meeting and —
of course — make speeches. I am desired to say that they deeply regret that their demonstration should have disturbed you personally,
Lady Brandon."

"So they ought," she replied. "They dont look very sorry. They are
getting frightened at what they have done; and they would be glad to
escape the consequences by apologizing, most likely. But they shant.
I am not such a fool as they think."

"They dont think so. You have proved the contrary."

"Jane," said Sir Charles pettishly: "do you know this gentleman?"

"I should think I do," said Lady Brandon emphatically.

Trefusis bowed as if he had just been formally introduced to the
baronet, who, against his will, returned the salutation stiffly, unable
to ignore an older, firmer and quicker man under the circumstances.

"This seems an unneighbourly business, Sir Charles," said Trefusis,
quite at his ease; "but as it is a public question, it need not prejudice
our private relations. At least I hope not."

Sir Charles bowed again, more stiffly than before.

"I am, like you, a capitalist and landlord ——"

"— which it seems to me you have no right to be, if you are in
earnest," struck in Chester, who had been watching the scene in
silence by Sir Charles's side.

"Which, as you say, I have undoubtedly no right to be," said Trefusis, surveying him with interest; "but which I nevertheless cannot
help being. Have I the pleasure of speaking to Mr. Chichester Erskine,
author of a tragedy entitled 'The Patriot Martyrs,' dedicated with enthusiastic devotion to the Spirit of Liberty and half a dozen famous
upholders of that principle, and denouncing in forcible language the
tyranny of the late Tsar of Russia, Bomba of Naples, and Napoleon
the Third?"

"Yes, sir," said Erskine, reddening; for he felt that this description
might make his drama seem ridiculous to those present who had not
read it.

"Then," said Trefusis, extending his hand — Erskine at first thought
for a hearty shake — "give me half-a-crown towards the cost of our
expedition here to-day to assert the right of the people to tread the
soil we are standing upon."

"You shall do nothing of the sort, Chester," cried Lady Brandon.
"I never heard of such a thing in my life! Do *you* pay us for the wall
and fence your people have broken, Mr. Smilash: that would be more
to the purpose."

"If I could find a thousand men as practical as you, Lady Brandon, I might accomplish the next great revolution before the end of this season." He looked at her for a moment curiously, as if trying to remember; and then added inconsequently, "How are your friends? There was a Miss — Miss — I am afraid I have forgotten all the names except your own."

"Gertrude Lindsay is staying with us. Do you remember her?"

"I think — no, I am afraid I do not. Let me see. Was she a haughty young lady?"

"Yes," said Lady Brandon eagerly, forgetting the wall and fence. "But who do you think is coming next Thursday? — I met her accidentally the last time I was in town. She's not a bit changed. You cant forget her; so dont pretend to be puzzled."

"You have not told me who she is yet. And I shall probably not remember her. You must not expect me to recognize everyone instantaneously, as I recognized you."

"What stuff! You will know Agatha fast enough."

"Agatha Wylie!" he said, with sudden gravity.

"Yes. She is coming on Thursday. Are you glad?"

"I fear I shall have no opportunity of seeing her."

"Oh, of course you must see her. It will be so jolly for us all to meet again just as we used. Why cant you come to luncheon on Thursday?"

"I shall be delighted, if you will really allow me to come after my conduct here."

"The lawyers will settle that. Now that you have found out who we are, you will stop pulling down our walls, of course."

"Of course," said Trefusis, smiling, as he took out a pocket diary and entered the engagement. "I must hurry away to the cross roads. They have probably voted me into the chair by this time, and are waiting for me to open their meeting. Good-bye. You have made this place, which I was growing tired of, unexpectedly interesting to me."

They exchanged glances of the old college pattern. Then he nodded to Sir Charles; waved his hand familiarly to Erskine; and followed the procession, which was by this time out of sight.

Sir Charles, who, waiting to speak, had been repeatedly baffled by the hasty speeches of his wife and the unhesitating replies of Trefusis, now turned angrily upon her, saying,

"What do you mean by inviting that fellow to my house?"

"*Your* house, indeed! I will invite whom I please. You are getting into one of your tempers."

Sir Charles looked about him. Erskine had discreetly slipped away, and was in the road, tightening a screw in his velocipede. The few persons who remained were out of earshot.

"Who and what the devil is he; and how do you come to know him?" he demanded. He never swore in the presence of any lady except his wife, and then only when they were alone.

"He is a gentleman, which is more than you are," she retorted, and, with a cut of her whip that narrowly missed her husband's shoulder, sent the bay plunging through the gap.

"Come along," she said to Erskine. "We shall be late for luncheon."

"Had we not better wait for Sir Charles?" he asked, injudiciously.

"Never mind Sir Charles: he is in the sulks," she said, without abating her voice. "Come along." And she went off at a canter: Erskine following her with a misgiving that his visit was unfortunately timed.

CHAPTER XII.

On the following Thursday, Gertrude, Agatha and Jane met for the first time since they had parted at Alton College. Agatha was the shyest of the three, and externally the least changed. She fancied herself very different from the Agatha of Alton; but it was her opinion of herself that had altered, not her person. Expecting to find a corresponding alteration in her friends, she had looked forward to the meeting with much doubt, and little hope of its proving pleasant.

She was more anxious about Gertrude than about Jane, concerning whom, at a brief interview in London, she had already discovered that Lady Brandon's manner, mind and speech were just what Miss Carpenter's had been. But, even from Agatha, Jane commanded more respect than before, having changed from an overgrown girl into a fine woman, and made a brilliant match in her first season, whilst many of her pretty, proud and clever contemporaries, whom she had envied at school, were still unmarried, and were having their homes made uncomfortable by parents anxious to get rid of the burthen of supporting them, and to profit in purse or position by their marriages.

This was Gertrude's case. Like Agatha, she had thrown away her matrimonial opportunities. Proud of her rank and exclusiveness, she had resolved to have as little as possible to do with persons who did not share both with her. She began by repulsing the proffered acquaintance of many families of great wealth and fashion, who either did not know their grandparents or were ashamed of them. Having shut herself out of their circle, she was presented at court, and thenceforth accepted the invitations of those only who had, in her opinion, a right to the same honour. And she was far stricter on that point than the Lord Chamberlain, who had, she held, betrayed his trust by practically turning Leveller. She was well educated; refined in her manners and habits; skilled in etiquette to an extent irritating to the ignorant; and gifted with a delicate complexion, pearly teeth, and a face that would have been Grecian but for a slight upward tilt of the nose, and traces of a square, heavy type in the jaw. Her father was a retired admiral, with sufficient influence to have had a sinecure made by a Conservative government expressly for the maintenance of his son pending alliance with some heiress. Yet Gertrude remained single; and the admiral, who had formerly spent more money than he could comfortably afford on her education, and was still doing so upon her state and personal adornment, was complaining so unpleasantly of her failure to get taken off his hands, that she could hardly bear to live at home, and was ready to marry any thoroughbred gentleman, however unsuitable his age or character, who would relieve her from her humiliating dependence. She was prepared to sacrifice her natural desire for youth, beauty and virtue in a husband if she could escape from her parents on no easier terms; but she was resolved to die an old maid sooner than marry an upstart.

The difficulty in her way was pecuniary. The admiral was poor. He had not quite six thousand a year; and though he practised the utmost economy in order to keep up the most expensive habits, he could not afford to give his daughter a dowry. Now the well born bachelors of her set, having more blue blood, but much less wealth, than they needed, admired her; paid her compliments; danced with her; but could not afford to marry her. Some of them even told her so; married rich daughters of tea merchants, ironfounders, or successful stockbrokers; and then tried to make matches between her and their lowly born brothers-in-law.

So, when Gertrude met Lady Brandon, her lot was secretly wretched; and she was glad to accept an invitation to Brandon Beeches in order to escape for a while from the Admiral's daily sarcasms on the marriage list in the *Times*. The invitation was the more acceptable because Sir Charles was no mushroom noble; and, in the schooldays which Gertrude now remembered as the happiest of her life, she had acknowledged that Jane's family and connexions were more aristocratic than those of any other student then at Alton, herself excepted. To Agatha, whose grandfather had amassed wealth as a proprietor of gasworks (novelties in his time), she had never offered her intimacy. Agatha had taken it by force, partly moral, partly physical. But the gasworks were never forgotten; and when Lady Brandon mentioned, as a piece of delightful news, that she had found out their old school companion, and had asked her to join them, Gertrude was not quite pleased. Yet, when they met, her eyes were the only wet ones there; for she was the least happy of the three; and, though she did not know it, her spirit was somewhat broken. Agatha, she thought, had lost the bloom of girlhood, but was bolder, stronger and cleverer than before. Agatha had, in fact, summoned all her self-possession to hide her shyness. She detected the emotion of Gertrude, who at the last moment did not try to conceal it. It would have been poured out freely in words, had Gertrude's social training taught her to express her feelings as well as it had accustomed her to dissemble them.

"Do you remember Miss Wilson?" said Jane, as the three drove from the railway station to Brandon Beeches. "Do you remember Mrs. Miller, and her cat? Do you remember the Recording Angel? Do you remember how I fell into the canal?"

These reminiscences lasted until they reached the house and went together to Agatha's room. Here Jane, having some orders to give in the household, had to leave them — reluctantly; for she was jealous lest Gertrude should get the start of her in the renewal of Agatha's affection. She even tried to take her rival away with her; but in vain: Gertrude would not budge.

"What a beautiful house and splendid place!" said Agatha, when Jane was gone. "And what a nice fellow Sir Charles is! We used to laugh at Jane; but she can afford to laugh at the luckiest of us now. I always said she would blunder into the best of everything. Is it true that she married in her first season?"

"Yes. And Sir Charles is a man of great culture. I cannot understand it. Her size is really beyond everything; and her manners are bad."

"Hm!" said Agatha, with a wise air. "There was always something about Jane that attracted men. And she is more knave than fool. But she is certainly a great ass."

Gertrude looked serious, to imply that she had grown out of the habit of using or listening to such language. Agatha, stimulated by this, continued,

"Here are you and I, who consider ourselves twice as presentable and conversable as she, two old maids." Gertrude winced; and Agatha hastened to add, "Why, as for you, you are perfectly lovely! And she has asked us down expressly to marry us."

"She would not presume ——"

"Nonsense, my dear Gertrude. She thinks that we are a couple of fools who have mismanaged our own business; and that she, having managed so well for herself, can settle us in a jiffy. Come: did she not say to you, before I came, that it was time for me to be getting married?"

"Well, she did. But ——"

"She said exactly the same thing to me about you when she invited me."

"I would leave her house this moment," said Gertrude, "if I thought she dared meddle in my affairs. What is it to her whether I am married or not?"

"Where have you been living all these years, if you do not know that the very first thing a woman wants to do when she has made a good match, is to make ones for all her spinster friends. Jane does not mean any harm. She does it out of pure benevolence."

"I do not need Jane's benevolence."

"Neither do I; but it doesnt do any harm; and she is welcome to amuse herself by trotting out her male acquaintances for my approval. Hush! Here she comes."

Gertrude subsided. She could not quarrel with Lady Brandon without leaving the house; and she could not leave the house without returning to her home. But she privately resolved to discourage the attentions of Erskine, suspecting that instead of being in love with her as he pretended, he had merely been recommended by Jane to marry her.

Chichester Erskine had made sketches in Palestine with Sir Charles, and had tramped with him through many European picture galleries. He was a young man of gentle birth, and had inherited fifteen hundred a year from his mother: the bulk of the family property being his elder brother's. Having no profession, and being fond of books and pictures, he had devoted himself to fine art, a pursuit which offered him on the cheapest terms a high opinion of the beauty and capacity of his own nature. He had published a tragedy entitled, "The Patriot Martyrs," with an etched frontispiece by Sir Charles; and an edition of it had been speedily disposed of in presentations to the friends of the artist and poet, and to the reviews and newspapers. Sir Charles had asked an eminent tragedian of his acquaintance to place the work on the stage and to enact one of the patriot martyrs. But the tragedian had objected that the other patriot martyrs had parts of equal importance to that proposed for him. Erskine had indignantly refused to cut these parts down or out; and so the project had fallen through.

Since then, Erskine had been bent on writing another drama, without regard to the exigencies of the stage; but he had not yet begun it, in consequence of his inspiration coming upon him at inconvenient hours, chiefly late at night, when he had been drinking, and had leisure for sonnets only. The morning air and bicycle riding were fatal to the vein in which his poetry struck him as being worth writing. In spite of the bicycle, however, the drama, which was to be entitled "Hypatia," was now in a fair way to be written; for the poet had met and fallen in love with Gertrude Lindsay, whose almost Grecian features, and some knowledge of the differential calculus which she had acquired at Alton, helped him to believe that she was a fit model for his heroine.

When the ladies came downstairs, they found their host and Erskine in the picture gallery, famous in the neighbourhood for the sum it had cost Sir Charles. There was a new etching to be admired; and they were called on to observe what the baronet called its tones, and what Agatha would have called its degrees of smudginess. Sir Charles's attention often wandered from this work of art. He looked at his watch twice, and said to his wife,

"I have ordered them to be punctual with the luncheon."

"Oh yes: it's all right," said Lady Brandon, who had given orders that luncheon was not to be served until the arrival of another gentleman. "Show Agatha the picture of the man in the ——"

"Mr. Trefusis," said a servant.

Mr. Trefusis, still in snuff colour, entered: coat unbuttoned and attention unconstrained: exasperatingly unconscious of any occasion for ceremony.

"Here you are at last," said Lady Brandon. "You know everybody, dont you?"

"How do you do?" said Sir Charles, offering his hand as a severe expression of his duty to his wife's guest, who took it cordially; nodded to Erskine; looked without recognition at Gertrude, whose frosty stillness repudiated Lady Brandon's implication that the stranger was acquainted with her; and turned to Agatha, to whom he bowed. She made no sign: she was paralyzed. Lady Brandon reddened with anger. Sir Charles noted his guest's reception with secret satisfaction, but shared the embarrassment which oppressed all present except Trefusis, who seemed quite indifferent and assured, and unconsciously produced an impression that the others had not been equal to the occasion, as indeed they had not.

"We were looking at some etchings when you came in," said Sir Charles, hastening to break the silence. "Do you care for such things?" And he handed him a proof.

Trefusis looked at it as if he had never seen such a thing before, and did not quite know what to make of it. "All these scratches seem to me to have no meaning," he said dubiously.

Sir Charles stole a contemptuous smile and significant glance at Erskine. He, seized already with an instinctive antipathy to Trefusis, said emphatically,

"There is not one of those scratches that has not a meaning."

"That one, for instance, like the limb of a daddy-long-legs: what does that mean?"

Erskine hesitated a moment; recovered himself; and said, "Obviously enough — to me at least — it indicates the marking of the roadway."

"Not a bit of it," said Trefusis. "There never was such a mark as that on a road. It may be a very bad attempt at a briar; but briars dont straggle into the middle of roads frequented as that one seems to be — judging by those overdone ruts." He put the etching away, showing no disposition to look further into the portfolio; and remarked, "The only art that interests me is photography."

Erskine and Sir Charles again exchanged glances; and the former said,

"Photography is not an art in the sense in which I understand the term. It is a process."

"And a much less troublesome and more perfect process than that," said Trefusis, pointing to the etching. "The artists are sticking to the old barbarous, difficult, and imperfect processes of etching and portrait painting merely to keep up the value of their monopoly of the required skill. They have left the new, more complexly organized, and more perfect, yet simple and beautiful method of photography in the hands of tradesmen, sneering at it publicly, and resorting to its aid surreptitiously. The result is that the tradesmen are becoming better artists than they, and naturally so; for where, as in photography, the drawing counts for nothing, the thought and judgment count for everything; whereas in the etching and daubing processes, where great manual skill is needed to produce anything that the eye can endure, the execution counts for more than the thought; and if a fellow only fit to carry bricks up a ladder or the like has ambition and perseverance enough to train his hand and push into the van, you cannot afford to put him back into his proper place, because thoroughly trained hands are so scarce. Consider the proof of this that you have in literature. Our books are manually the work of printers and paper-makers: you may cut an author's hand off, and he is as good an author as before. What is the result? There is more imagination in any number of a penny journal than in half-a-dozen of the Royal Academy rooms in the season. No author can live by his work and be as empty-headed as an average successful painter. Again, consider our implements of music — our pianofortes, for example. Nobody but an acrobat will voluntarily spend years at such a difficult mechanical puzzle as the keyboard; and so we have to take our impressions of Beethoven's sonatas from acrobats who vie with each other in the rapidity of their *prestos,* or the staying power of their left wrists. Thoughtful men will not spend their lives acquiring sleight-of-hand. Invent a piano which will respond as delicately to the turning of a handle as our present ones do to the pressure of the fingers, and the acrobats will be driven back to their carpets and trapezes, because the sole faculty necessary to the executant musician will be the musical faculty, and no other will enable him to obtain a hearing."

The company were somewhat overcome by this unexpected lecture. Sir Charles, feeling that such views bore adversely on him, and were somehow iconoclastic and low-lived, was about to make a peevish retort, when Erskine forestalled him by asking Trefusis what idea he had formed of the future of the arts. He replied promptly,

"Photography perfected in its recently discovered power of reproducing colour as well as form! Historical pictures replaced by photographs of *tableaux vivants* formed and arranged by trained actors and artists, and used chiefly for the instruction of children. Nine-tenths of painting as we understand it at present extinguished by the competition of these photographs; and the remaining tenth only holding its own against them by dint of extraordinary excellence! Our mistuned and unplayable organs and pianofortes replaced by harmonious instruments, as manageable as barrel organs! Works of fiction superseded by interesting company and conversation, and made obsolete by the human mind outgrowing the childishness that delights in the tales told by grown-up children such as novelists and their like! An end to the silly confusion, under the one name of Art, of the tomfoolery and make-believe of our playhours with the higher methods of teaching men to know themselves! Every artist an amateur; and a consequent return to the healthy old disposition to look on every man who makes art a means of money-getting as a vagabond not to be entertained as an equal by honest men!"

"In which case artists will starve! and there will be no more art."

"Sir," said Trefusis, excited by the word, "I, as a Socialist, can tell you that starvation is now impossible, except where, as in England, masterless men are forcibly prevented from producing the food they need. And you, as an artist, can tell me that at present great artists invariably do starve, except when they are kept alive by charity, private fortune, or some drudgery which hinders them in the pursuit of their vocation."

"Oh!" said Erskine. "Then Socialists have some little sympathy with artists after all."

"I fear," said Trefusis, repressing himself and speaking quietly again, "that when a Socialist hears of a hundred pounds paid for a drawing which Andrea del Sarto was glad to sell for tenpence, his heart is not wrung with pity for the artist's imaginary loss, as that of a modern capitalist is. Yet that is the only way nowadays of enlisting sympathy for the old masters. Frightful disability, to be out of reach of the dearest market when you want to sell your drawings! But," he added, giving himself a shake, and turning round gaily, "I did not come here to talk shop. So — pending the deluge — let us enjoy ourselves after our manner."

"No," said Jane. "Please go on about Art. It's such a relief to hear any one talking sensibly about it. I hate etching. It makes your eyes sore — at least the acid gets into Sir Charles's; and the difference between the first and second states is nothing but imagination, except that the last state is worse than the — here's luncheon!"

They went downstairs then. Trefusis sat between Agatha and Lady Brandon, to whom he addressed all his conversation. They chatted without much interruption from the business of the table; for Jane, despite her amplitude, had a small appetite, and was fearful of growing fat; whilst Trefusis was systematically abstemious. Sir Charles was unusually silent. He was afraid to talk about art, lest he should be contradicted by Trefusis, who, he already felt, cared less and perhaps knew more about it than he. Having previously commented to Agatha on the beauty of the ripening spring, and inquired whether her journey had fatigued her, he had said as much as he could think of at a first meeting. For her part, she was intent on Trefusis, who, though he must know, she thought, that they were all hostile to him except Jane, seemed as confident now as when he had befooled her long ago. That thought set her teeth on edge. She did not doubt the sincerity of her antipathy to him even when she detected herself in the act of protesting inwardly that she was not glad to meet him again, and that she would not speak to him. Gertrude, meanwhile, was giving short answers to Erskine, and listening to Trefusis. She had gathered from the domestic squabbles of the last few days that Lady Brandon, against her husband's will, had invited a notorious demagogue, the rich son of a successful cotton-spinner, to visit the Beeches. She had made up her mind to snub any such man. But on recognizing the long-forgotten Smilash, she had been astonished, and had not known what to do. So, to avoid doing anything improper, she had stood stiffly silent and done nothing, as the custom of English ladies in such cases is. Subsequently, his unconscious self-assertion had wrought with her as with the others; and her intention of snubbing him had faded into the limbo of projects abandoned without trial. Erskine alone was free from the influence of the intruder. He wished him elsewhere; but beside Gertrude the presence or absence of any other person troubled him very little.

"How are the Janseniuses?" said Trefusis, suddenly turning to Agatha.

"They are quite well, thank you," she said in measured tones.

"I met John Jansenius in the city lately. You know Jansenius?" he added parenthetically to Sir Charles. "Cotman's bank — the last Cotman died out of the firm before we were born. The Chairman of the Transcanadian Railway Company."

"I know the name. I am seldom in the city."

"Naturally," assented Trefusis; "for who would sadden himself by pushing his way through a crowd of such slaves, if he could help it? I mean slaves of Mammon, of course. To run the gauntlet of their faces in Cornhill is enough to discourage a thoughtful man for hours. Well, Jansenius, being high in the court of Mammon, is looking out for a good post in the household for his son. Jansenius, by-the-bye, is Miss Wylie's guardian, and the father of my late wife."

Agatha felt inclined to deny this; but, as it was true, she had to forbear. Resolved to show that the relations between her family and Trefusis were not cordial ones, she asked, deliberately, "Did Mr. Jansenius speak to you?"

Gertrude looked up, as if she thought this scarcely ladylike.

"Yes," said Trefusis. "We are the best friends in the world — as good as possible, at any rate. He wanted me to subscribe to a fund for relieving the poor at the east end of London by assisting them to emigrate."

"I presume you subscribed liberally," said Erskine. "It was an opportunity of doing some *practical* good."

"I did not," said Trefusis, grinning at the sarcasm. "This Transcanadian Railway Company, having got a great deal of spare land from the Canadian government for nothing, thought it would be a good idea to settle British workmen on it and screw rent out of them. Plenty of British workmen, supplanted in their employment by machinery, or cheap foreign labour, or one thing or another, were quite willing to go; but as they couldnt afford to pay their passages to Canada, the Company appealed to the benevolent to pay for them by subscription, as the change would improve their miserable condition. I did not see why I should pay to provide a rich company with tenant farmers; and I told Jansenius so. He remarked that when money and not talk was required, the workmen of England soon found out who were their real friends."

"I know nothing about these questions," said Sir Charles, with an air of conclusiveness; "but I see no objection to emigration."

"The fact is," said Trefusis, "the idea of emigration is a dangerous one for us. Familiarize the workman with it, and some day he may come to see what a capital thing it would be to pack off me, and you, with the peerage, and the whole tribe of unprofitable proprietors such as we are, to St. Helena: making us a handsome present of the island by way of indemnity! We are such a restless, unhappy lot, that I doubt whether it would not prove a good thing for us too.

The workmen would lose nothing but the contemplation of our elegant persons, exquisite manners, and refined tastes. They might provide against that loss by picking out a few of us to keep for ornament's sake. No nation with a sense of beauty would banish Lady Brandon, or Miss Lindsay, or Miss Wylie."

"Such nonsense!" said Jane.

"You would hardly believe how much I have spent in sending workmen out of the country against my own view of the country's interest," continued Trefusis, addressing Erskine. "When I make a convert among the working classes, the first thing he does is to make a speech somewhere declaring his new convictions. His employer immediately discharges him — 'gives him the sack' is the technical phrase. The sack is the sword of the capitalist; and hunger keeps it sharp for him. His shield is the law, made for the purpose by his own class. Thus equipped, he gives the worst of it to my poor convert, who comes ruined to me for assistance. As I cannot afford to pension him for life, I get rid of him by assisting him to emigrate. Sometimes he prospers and repays me: sometimes I hear no more of him: sometimes he comes back with his habits unsettled. One man whom I sent to America made his fortune; but he was not a social democrat: he was a clerk who had embezzled, and who applied to me for assistance under the impression that I considered it rather meritorious to rob the till of a capitalist."

"He was a practical Socialist, in fact," said Erskine.

"On the contrary, he was a somewhat too grasping Individualist. Howbeit, I enabled him to make good his defalcation — in the city they consider a defalcation *made good* when the money is replaced — and to go to New York. I recommended him not to go there; but he knew better than I; for he made a fortune by speculating with money that existed only in the imagination of those with whom he dealt. *He* never repaid me: he is probably far too good a man of business to pay money that cannot be extracted from him by an appeal to the law or to his commercial credit. Mr. Erskine," added Trefusis, lowering his voice, and turning to the poet: "you are wrong to take part with hucksters and money-hunters against your own nature, even though the attack upon them is led by a man who prefers photography to etching."

"But I assure you — You quite mistake me," said Erskine, taken aback. "I —— " He stopped; looked to Sir Charles for support; and then said airily, "I dont doubt that you are quite right. I hate business and men of business; and as to social questions, I have only one article of belief, which is, that the sole refiner of human nature is fine art."

"Whereas I believe that the sole refiner of art is human nature. Art rises when men rise, and grovels when men grovel. What is your opinion?"

"I agree with you in many ways," replied Sir Charles nervously; for a lack of interest in his fellow-creatures, and an excess of interest in himself, had prevented him from obtaining that power of dealing with social questions which, he felt, a baronet ought to possess; and he was consequently afraid to differ from any one who alluded to them with confidence. "If you take an interest in art, I believe I can show you a few things worth seeing."

"Thank you. In return I will some day shew you a remarkable collection of photographs I possess: many of them taken by me. I venture to think they will teach you something."

"No doubt," said Sir Charles. "Shall we return to the gallery? I have a few treasures there that photography is not likely to surpass for some time yet."

"Let's go through the conservatory," said Jane. "Dont you like flowers, Mr. Smi —— I never can remember your proper name."

"Extremely," said Trefusis.

They rose, and went out into a long hothouse. Here Lady Brandon, finding Erskine at her side, and Sir Charles before her with Gertrude, looked round for Trefusis, with whom she intended to enjoy a trifling flirtation under cover of showing him the flowers. He was out of sight; but she heard his footsteps in the passage on the opposite side of the greenhouse. Agatha was also invisible. Jane, not daring to rearrange their procession lest her design should become obvious, had to walk on with Erskine.

Agatha had turned unintentionally into the opposite alley to that which the others had chosen. When she saw what she had done, and found herself virtually alone with Trefusis, who had followed her, she blamed him for it, and was about to retrace her steps when he said coolly,

"Were you shocked when you heard of Henrietta's sudden death?"

Agatha struggled with herself for a moment, and then said in a suppressed voice, "How dare you speak to me?"

"Why not?" said he, astonished.

"I am not going to enter into a discussion with you. You know what I mean very well."

"You mean that you are offended with me: that is plain enough. But when I part from a young lady on good terms; and after a lapse of years, during which we neither meet nor correspond, she asks me how I dare speak to her, I am naturally startled."

"We did not part on good terms."

Trefusis stretched his eyebrows, as if to stretch his memory. "If not," he said, "I have forgotten it, on my honour. When did we part, and what happened? It cannot have been anything very serious, or I should remember it."

His forgetfulness wounded Agatha. "No doubt you are well accustomed to —— " She checked herself, and made a successful snatch at her normal manner with gentlemen. "I scarcely remember what it was, now that I begin to think. Some trifle, I suppose. Do you like orchids?"

"They have nothing to do with our affairs at present. You are not in earnest about the orchids; and you are trying to run away from a mistake instead of clearing it up. That is a short-sighted policy, always."

Agatha grew alarmed; for she felt his old influence over her returning. "I do not wish to speak of it," she said firmly.

Her firmness was lost on him. "I do not even know what *it* means yet," he said; "and I want to know; for I believe there is some misunderstanding between us; and it is the trick of your sex to perpetuate misunderstandings by forbidding all allusions to them. Perhaps, leaving Lyvern so hastily, I forgot to fulfil some promise, or to say farewell, or something of that sort. But do you know how suddenly I was called away? I got a telegram to say that Henrietta was dying; and I had only time to change my clothes — you remember my disguise — and catch the express. And, after all, she was dead when I arrived."

"I know that," said Agatha uneasily. "Please say no more about it."

"Not if it distresses you. Just let me hope that you did not suppose I blamed you for your share in the matter, or that I told the Janseniuses of it. I did not. Yes: I like orchids. A plant that can subsist on a scrap of board is an instance of natural econ —— "

"*You* blame *me!*" cried Agatha. "*I* never told the Janseniuses. What would they have thought of you if I had?"

"Far worse of you than of me, however unjustly. You were the immediate cause of the tragedy; I only the remote one. Jansenius is not far-seeing when his feelings are touched. Few men are."

"I dont understand you in the least. What tragedy do you mean?"

"Henrietta's death. I call it a tragedy conventionally. Seriously, of course, it was commonplace enough."

Agatha stopped and faced him. "What do you mean by what you said just now? You said that I was the immediate cause of the tragedy; and you say that you were talking of Henrietta's — of Henrietta. I had nothing to do with her illness."

Trefusis looked at her as if considering whether he would go any further. Then, watching her with the curiosity of a vivisector, he said, "Strange to say, Agatha" (she shrank proudly at the word), "Henrietta might have been alive now, but for you. I am very glad she is not; so you need not reproach yourself on my account. She died of a journey she made to Lyvern in great excitement and distress, and in intensely cold weather. You caused her to make that journey by writing her a letter which made her jealous."

"Do you mean to accuse me —— "

"No: stop!" he said hastily, the vivisecting spirit in him exorcised by her shaking voice: "I accuse you of nothing. Why do you not speak honestly to me when you are at your ease? If you confess your real thoughts only under torture, who can resist the temptation to torture you? One must charge you with homicide to make you speak of anything but orchids."

But Agatha had drawn the new inference from the old facts, and would not be talked out of repudiating it. "It was not my fault," she said. "It was yours — altogether yours."

"Altogether," he assented, relieved to find her indignant instead of remorseful.

She was not to be soothed by a verbal acquiescence. "Your behaviour was most unmanly; and I told you so; and you could not deny it. You pretended that you —— You pretended to have feelings —— You tried to make me believe that —— Oh, I am a fool to talk to you: you know perfectly well what I mean."

"Perfectly. I tried to make you believe that I was in love with you. How do you know I was not?"

She disdained to answer; but as he waited calmly she said, "You had no right to be."

"That does not prove that I was not. Come, Agatha: you pretended to like me when you did not care two straws about me. You confessed as much in that fatal letter, which I have somewhere at home. It has a great rent right across it; and the mark of her heel: she must have stamped on it in her rage, poor girl! So that I can shew your own hand for the very deception you accused me — without proof — of having practised on you."

"You are clever, and can twist things. What pleasure does it give you to make me miserable?"

"Ha!" he exclaimed, in an abrupt, sardonic laugh. "I dont know: you bewitch me, I think."

Agatha made no reply, but walked on quickly to the end of the conservatory, where the others were waiting for them.

"Where have you been; and what have you been doing all this time?"

said Jane, as Trefusis came up, hurrying after Agatha. "I dont know what you call it; but I call it perfectly disgraceful!"

Sir Charles reddened at his wife's bad taste; and Trefusis replied gravely, "We have been admiring the orchids, and talking about them. Miss Wylie takes an interest in them."

CHAPTER XIII.

One morning Gertrude got a letter from her father.

MY DEAR GERTY: *I have just received a bill for £110 from Madame Smith for your dresses. May I ask you how long this sort of thing is to go on? I need not tell you that I have not the means to support you in such extravagance. I am, as you know, always anxious that you should go about in a style worthy of your position; but unless you can manage without calling on me to pay away hundreds of pounds every season to Madame Smith, you had better give up society and stay at home. I positively cannot afford it. As far as I can see, going into society has not done you much good. I had to raise £500 last month on Franklands; and it is too bad if I must raise more to pay your dressmaker. You might at least employ some civil person, or one whose charges are moderate. Madame Smith tells me that she will not wait any longer, and charges £60 for a single dress. I hope you fully understand that there must be an end to this.*

I hear from your mother that young Erskine is with you at Brandon's. I do not think much of him. He is not well off, nor likely to get on, as he has taken to poetry and so forth. I am told also that a man named Trefusis visits at the Beeches a good deal now. He must be a fool; for he contested the last Birmingham election, and came out at the foot of the poll with thirty-two votes through calling himself a Social Democrat or some such foreign rubbish, instead of saying out like a man that he was a Radical. I suppose the name stuck in his throat; for his mother was one of the Howards of Breconcastle; so he has good blood in him, though his father was nobody. I wish he had your bills to pay: he could buy and sell me ten times over, after all my twenty-five years service.

As I am thinking of getting something done to the house, I had rather you did not come back this month, if you can possibly hold

on at Brandon's. *Remember me to him, and give our kind regards
to his wife. I should be obliged if you would gather some hemlock leaves and send them to me. I want them for my ointment:
the stuff the chemists sell is no good. Your mother's eyes are bad
again; and your brother Berkeley has been gambling, and seems
to think I ought to pay his debts for him. I am greatly worried
over it all; and I hope that, until you have settled yourself, you
will be more reasonable, and not run these everlasting bills upon
me. You are enjoying yourself out of reach of all the unpleasant-
ness; but it bears hardly upon*

> *your affectionate father,*
> C. B. LINDSAY.

A faint sketch of the lines Time intended to engrave on Gertrude's
brow appeared there as she read the letter; but she hastened to give
the admiral's kind regards to her host and hostess, and discussed her
mother's health feelingly with them. After breakfast she went to the
library, and wrote her reply.

> BRANDON BEECHES.
> *Tuesday.*

DEAR PAPA: *Considering that it is more than three years since
you paid Madame Smith last, and that then her bill, which included my court dress, was only £150, I cannot see how I could
possibly have been more economical, unless you expect me to go
in rags. I am sorry that Madame Smith has asked for the money
at such an inconvenient time; but when I begged you to pay her
something in March last year you told me to keep her quiet by
giving her a good order. I am not surprised at her not being very
civil, as she has plenty of tradesmen's daughters among her customers who pay her more than £300 a year for their dresses. I
am wearing a skirt at present which I got two years ago.*

*Sir Charles is going to town on Thursday: he will bring you the
hemlock. Tell mamma that there is an old woman here who
knows some wonderful cure for sore eyes. She will not tell what
the ingredients are; but it cures everyone; and there is no use in
giving an oculist two guineas for telling us that reading in bed is
bad for the eyes, when we know perfectly well that mamma will
not give up doing it. If you pay Berkeley's debts, do not forget
that he owes me £3.*

*Another schoolfellow of mine is staying here now; and I think
that Mr. Trefusis will have the pleasure of paying her bills some*

*day. He is a great pet of Lady Brandon's. Sir Charles was angry
at first because she invited him here; and we were all surprised
at it. The man has a bad reputation, and headed a mob that threw
down the walls of the park; and we hardly thought he would be
cool enough to come after that. But he does not seem to care
whether we want him or not; and he comes when he likes. As he
talks cleverly, we find him a godsend in this dull place. It is really
not such a paradise as you seem to think; but you need not be
afraid of my returning any sooner than I can help.*

Your affectionate daughter,

GERTRUDE LINDSAY.

When Gertrude had closed this letter, and torn up her father's, she
thought little more about either. They might have made her unhappy had they found her happy; but as hopeless discontent was her
normal state, and enjoyment but a rare accident, recriminatory passages with her father only put her into a bad humour, and did not in
the least disappoint or humiliate her.

For the sake of exercise, she resolved to carry her letter to the village post office, and return along the Riverside Road, whereby she had
seen hemlock growing. She took care to go out unobserved, lest
Agatha should volunteer to walk with her, or Jane declare her intention of driving to the post office in the afternoon, and sulk for the
rest of the day unless the trip to the village were postponed until then.
She took with her, as a protection against tramps, a big St. Bernard
dog named Max. This animal, which was young and enthusiastic, had
taken a strong fancy to her, and had expressed it frankly and bois-
terously; and she, whose affections had been starved in her home and
in society, had encouraged him with more kindness than she had ever
shown to any human being.

In the village, having posted her letter, she turned towards a lane
that led to the Riverside Road. Max, unaware of her reason for choos-
ing the longest way home, remonstrated by halting in the middle of
the lane, wagging his tail rapidly and uttering gruff barks.

"Dont be stupid, sir," said Gertrude impatiently. "I am going this
way."

Max, apparently understanding, rushed after her; passed her; and
disappeared in a cloud of dust raised by his effort to check himself
when he had left her far enough behind. When he came back she
kissed his nose, and ran a race with him until she too was panting, and
had to stand still to recover her breath, whilst he bounded about, barking ferociously. She had not for many years enjoyed such a frolic;
and the thought of this presently brought tears to her eyes. Rather

peevishly she bade Max be quiet; walked slowly to cool herself; and put up her sunshade to avert freckles.

The sun was now at the meridian. On a slope to Gertrude's right hand, Sallust's House, with its cinnamon coloured walls and yellow frieze, gave a foreign air to the otherwise very English landscape. She passed by without remembering who lived there. Further down, on some waste land separated from the road by a dry ditch and a low mud wall, a cluster of hemlocks, nearly six feet high, poisoned the air with their odour. She crossed the ditch; took a pair of gardening gloves from her plaited straw handbasket; and busied herself with the hemlock leaves, pulling the tender ones, separating them from the stalk, and filling her basket with the web. She forgot Max until an impression of dead silence, as if the earth had stopped, caused her to look round in vague dread. Trefusis, with his hand abandoned to the dog, who was trying how much of it he could cram into his mouth, was standing within a few yards of her, watching her intently. Gertrude turned pale, and came out hastily from among the bushes. Then she had a strange sensation as if something had happened high above her head. There was a threatening growl, a commanding exclamation, and an unaccountable pause, at the expiration of which she found herself supine on the sward, with her parasol between her eyes and the sun. A sudden scoop of Max's wet warm tongue in her right ear startled her into activity. She sat up, and saw Trefusis on his knees at her side, holding the parasol with an unconcerned expression, whilst Max was snuffing at her in restless anxiety opposite.

"I must go home," she said. "I must go home instantly."

"Not at all," said Trefusis, soothingly. "They have just sent word to say that everything is settled satisfactorily, and that you need not come."

"Have they?" she said faintly. Then she lay down again; and it seemed to her that a very long time elapsed. Suddenly recollecting that Trefusis had supported her gently with his hand to prevent her falling back too rudely, she rose again, and this time got upon her feet with his help.

"I must go home," she said again. "It is a matter of life or death."

"No, no," he said softly. "It is all right. You may depend on me."

She looked at him earnestly. He had taken her hand to steady her; for she was swaying a little. "Are you sure," she said, grasping his arm. "Are you quite sure?"

"Absolutely certain. You know I am always right, do you not?"

"Yes, oh yes: you have always been true to me. You —— " Here her senses came back with a rush. Dropping his hand as if it had become red hot, she said sharply, "What are you talking about?"

"I dont know," he said, resuming his indifferent manner with a laugh. "Are you better? Let me drive you to the Beeches. My stable is within a stone's throw: I can get a trap out in ten minutes."

"No, thank you," said Gertrude haughtily. "I do not wish to drive." She paused, and added in some bewilderment, "What has happened?"

"You fainted; and —— "

"I did not faint," said Gertrude indignantly. "I never fainted in my life."

"Yes, you did."

"Pardon me, Mr. Trefusis. I did not."

"You shall judge for yourself. I was coming through this field when I saw you gathering hemlock. Hemlock is interesting on account of Socrates; and you were interesting as a young lady gathering poison. So I stopped to look on. Presently you came out from among the bushes as if you had seen a snake there. Then you fell into my arms — which led me to suppose that you had fainted — ; and Max, concluding that it was all my fault, nearly sprang at my throat. You were overpowered by the scent of the water-hemlock, which you must have been inhaling for ten minutes or more."

"I did not know that there was any danger," said Gertrude, crestfallen. "I felt very tired when I came to. That was why I lay so long the second time. I really could not help it."

"You did not lie very long."

"Not when I first fell: that was only a few seconds, I know. But I must have lain there nearly ten minutes after I recovered."

"You were nearly a minute insensible when you first fell; and when you recovered you only rested for about one second. After that you raved; and I invented suitable answers until you suddenly asked me what I was talking about."

Gertrude reddened a little as the possibility of her having raved indiscreetly occurred to her. "It was very silly of me to faint," she said.

"You could not help it: you are only human. I shall walk with you to the Beeches."

"Thank you: I will not trouble you," she said quickly.

He shook his head. "I do not know how long the effect of that abominable water-weed may last," he said; "and I dare not leave you to walk alone. If you prefer it I can send you in a trap with my gardener; but I had rather accompany you myself."

"You are giving yourself a great deal of unnecessary trouble. I will walk. I am quite well again, and need no assistance."

They started without another word. Gertrude had to concentrate all her energy to conceal from him that she was giddy. Numbness and lassitude crept upon her; and she was beginning to hope that she was only dreaming it all when he roused her by saying,

"Take my arm."

"No, thank you."

"Do not be so senselessly obstinate. You will have to lean on the hedge for support if you refuse my help. I am sorry I did not insist on getting the trap."

Gertrude had not been spoken to in this tone since her childhood. "I am perfectly well," she said sharply. "You are really very officious."

"You are not perfectly well; and you know it. However, if you make a brave struggle, you will probably be able to walk home without my assistance; and the effort may do you good."

"You are very rude," she said peremptorily.

"I know it," he replied calmly. "You will find three classes of men polite to you: slaves; men who think much of their manners and nothing of you; and your lovers. I am none of these, and therefore give you back your ill manners with interest. Why do you resist your good angel by suppressing those natural and sincere impulses which come to you often enough, and sometimes bring a look into your face that might tame a bear — a look which you hasten to extinguish as a thief darkens his lantern at the sound of a footstep."

"Mr. Trefusis: I am not accustomed to be lectured."

"That is why I lecture you. I felt curious to see how your good breeding, by which I think you set some store, would serve you in entirely novel circumstances — those of a man speaking his mind to you, for instance. What is the result of my experiment? Instead of rebuking me with the sweetness and dignity which I could not, in spite of my past observation, help expecting from you, you churlishly repel my offer of the assistance you need; tell me that I am very rude, very officious; and, in short, do what you can to make my position disagreeable and humiliating."

She looked at him haughtily; but his expression was void of offence or fear; and he continued, unanswered,

"I would bear all this from a working woman without remonstrance; for she would owe me no graces of manner or morals. But you are a lady. That means that many have starved and drudged in uncleanly discomfort in order that you may have white and unbroken hands, fine garments, and exquisite manners — that you may be a living fountain of those influences that soften our natures and lives. When such a costly thing as a lady breaks down at the first touch of a firm hand, I feel justified in complaining."

Gertrude walked on quickly, and said between her teeth, "I dont want to hear any of your absurd views, Mr. Trefusis."

He laughed. "My unfortunate views!" he said. "Whenever I make an inconvenient remark, it is always set aside as an expression of certain dangerous crazes with which I am supposed to be afflicted. When I point out to Sir Charles that one of his favourite artists has not accurately observed something before attempting to draw it, he replies, 'You know our views differ on these things, Trefusis.' When I told Miss Wylie's guardian that his emigration scheme was little better than a fraud, he said, 'You must excuse me; but I cannot enter into your peculiar views.' One of my views at present is that Miss Lindsay is more amiable under the influence of hemlock than under that of the social system which has made her so unhappy."

"Well!" exclaimed Gertrude, outraged. Then, after a pause, "I was under the impression that I had accepted the escort of a gentleman." Then, after another pause, Trefusis being quite undisturbed, "How do you know that I am unhappy?"

"By a certain defect in your countenance, which lacks the crowning beauty of happiness; and a certain defect in your voice which will never disappear until you learn to love or pity those to whom you speak."

"You are wrong," said Gertrude, with calm disdain. "You do not understand me in the least. I am particularly attached to my friends."

"Then I have never seen you in their company."

"You are still wrong."

"Then how can you speak as you do, look as you do, act as you do?"

"What do you mean? How do I look and act?"

"Like one of the railings of Belgrave Square, cursed with consciousness of itself, fears of the judgment of the other railings, and doubts of their fitness to stand in the same row with it. You are cold, mistrustful, cruel to nervous or clumsy people, and more afraid of the criticisms of those with whom you dance and dine than of your conscience. All of which prevents you from looking like an angel."

"Thank you. Do you consider paying compliments the perfection of gentlemanly behaviour?"

"Have I been paying you many? That last remark of mine was not meant as one. On my honour, the angels will not disappoint me if they are no lovelier than you should be if you had that look in your face and that tone in your voice I spoke of just now. It can hardly displease you to hear that. If I were particularly handsome myself, I should like to be told so."

"I am sorry I cannot tell you so."

"Oh! Ha! ha! What a retort, Miss Lindsay! You are not sorry either: you are rather glad."

Gertrude knew it, and was angry with herself, not because her retort was false, but because she thought it unladylike. "You have no right to annoy me," she exclaimed, in spite of herself.

"None whatever," he said, humbly. "If I have done so, forgive me before we part. I will go no further with you: Max will give the alarm if you faint in the avenue, which I dont think you are likely to do, as you have forgotten all about the hemlock."

"Oh, how maddening!" she cried. "I have left my basket behind."

"Never mind: I will find it and have it filled and sent to you."

"Thank you. I am sorry to trouble you."

"Not at all. I hope you do not want the hemlock to help you to get rid of the burden of life."

"Nonsense. I want it for my father, who uses it for medicine."

"I will bring it myself to-morrow. Is that soon enough?"

"Quite. I am in no hurry. Thank you, Mr. Trefusis. Good-bye."

She gave him her hand, and even smiled a little; and then hurried away. He stood watching her as she passed along the avenue under the beeches. Once, when she came into a band of sunlight at a gap in the trees, she made so pretty a figure in her spring dress of violet and white that his eyes kindled as he gazed. He took out his note-book, and entered her name and the date, with a brief memorandum.

"I have thawed her," he said to himself as he put up his book. "She shall learn a lesson or two to hand on to her children before I have done with her. A trifle underbred, too, or she would not insist so much on her breeding. Henrietta used to wear a dress like that. I am glad to see that there is no danger of her taking to me personally."

He turned away, and saw a crone passing, bending beneath a bundle of sticks. He eyed it curiously; and she scowled at him, and hurried on.

"Hallo," he said.

She continued for a few steps; but her courage failed her, and she stopped.

"You are Mrs. Hickling, I think?"

"Yes, please your worship."

"You are the woman who carried away an old wooden gate that lay on Sir Charles Brandon's land last winter, and used it for fire-wood. You were imprisoned for seven days for it."

"You may send me there again if you like," she retorted, in a cracked voice, as she turned at bay. "But the Lord will make me even with you some day. Cursed be them that oppress the poor and needy: it is one of the seven deadly sins."

"Those green laths on your back are the remainder of my garden gate," he said. "You took the first half last Saturday. Next time you want fuel, come to the house and ask for coals; and let my gates alone: I suppose you can enjoy a fire without stealing the combustibles. Now pay me for my gate by telling me something I want to know."

"And a kind gentleman too, sir: blessings —— "

"What is the hemlock good for?"

"The hemlock, kind gentleman? For the evil, sir, to be sure."

"Scrofulous ulcers!" he exclaimed, recoiling. "The father of that beautiful girl!" He turned homeward, and trudged along with his head bent, muttering, "All rotten to the bone. Oh civilization! civilization! civilization!"

CHAPTER XIV.

"What has come over Gertrude?" said Agatha one day to Lady Brandon.

"Why? Is anything the matter with her?"

"I dont know: she has not been the same since she poisoned herself. And why did she not tell about it? But for Trefusis we should never have known."

"Gertrude always made secrets of things."

"She was in a vile temper for two days after; and now she is quite changed. She falls into long reveries, and does not hear a word of what is going on around. Then she starts into life again, and begs your pardon with the greatest sweetness for not catching what you have said."

"I hate her when she is polite: it is not natural to her. As to her going to sleep, that is the effect of the hemlock. We know a man who took a spoonful of strychnine in a bath; and he never was the same afterwards."

"I think she is making up her mind to encourage Erskine," said Agatha. "When I came here he hardly dared speak to her — at least, she always snubbed him. Now she lets him talk as much as he likes, and actually sends him on messages and allows him to carry things for her."

"Yes. I never saw anybody like Gertrude in my life. In London, if men were attentive to her, she sat on them for being officious; and if they let her alone she was angry at being neglected. Erskine is quite good enough for her, *I* think."

Here Erskine appeared at the door, and looked round the room.

"She's not here," said Jane.

"I am seeking Sir Charles," he said, withdrawing somewhat stiffly.

"What a lie!" said Jane, discomfited by his reception of her jest.

"He was talking to Sir Charles ten minutes ago in the billiard room. Men are such conceited fools!"

Agatha had strolled to the window, and was looking discontentedly at the prospect, as she had often done at school when alone, and sometimes did now in society. The door opened again; and Sir Charles appeared. He, too, looked round; but when his roving glance reached Agatha, it cast anchor; and he came in.

"Are you busy just now, Miss Wylie?" he asked.

"Yes," said Jane hastily. "She is going to write a letter for me."

"Really, Jane," he said, "I think you are old enough to write your letters without troubling Miss Wylie."

"When I do write my own letters, you always find fault with them," she retorted.

"I thought perhaps you might have leisure to try over a duet with me," he said, turning to Agatha.

"Certainly," she replied, hoping to smooth matters by humouring him. "The letter will do any time before post hour."

Jane reddened, and said shortly, "I will write it myself, if you will not."

Sir Charles quite lost his temper. "How can you be so damnably rude?" he said, turning upon his wife. "What objection have you to my singing duets with Miss Wylie?"

"Nice language that!' said Jane. "I never said I objected; and you have no right to drag her away to the piano just when she is going to write a letter for me."

"I do not wish Miss Wylie to do anything except what pleases her best. It seems to me that writing letters to your tradespeople cannot be a very pleasant occupation."

"Pray dont mind me," said Agatha, "It is not the least trouble to me. I used to write all Jane's letters for her at school. Suppose I write the letter first; and then we can have the duet. You will not mind waiting five minutes?"

"I can wait as long as you please, of course. But it seems such an absurd abuse of your good nature, that I cannot help protesti——"

"Oh, let it wait!" exclaimed Jane. "Such a ridiculous fuss to make about asking Agatha to write a letter, just because you happen to want her to play you your duets! I am certain she is heartily sick and tired of them."

Agatha, to escape the altercation, went to the library, and wrote the letter. When she returned to the drawing-room, she found no one there; but Sir Charles came in presently.

"I am so sorry, Miss Wylie," he said, as he opened the piano for her, "that you should be incommoded because my wife is silly enough to be jealous."

"Jealous!"

"Of course. Idiocy!"

"Oh, you are mistaken," said Agatha, incredulously. "How could she possibly be jealous of *me?*"

"She is jealous of everybody and everything," he replied bitterly; "and she cares for nobody and for nothing. You do not know what I have to endure sometimes from her."

Agatha thought her most discreet course was to sit down immediately, and begin "I would that my love." Whilst she played and sang, she thought over what Sir Charles had just let slip. She had found him a pleasant companion, light-hearted, fond of music and fun, polite and considerate, appreciative of her talents, quickwitted without being oppressively clever, and, as a married man, disinterested in his attentions. But it now occurred to her that perhaps they had been a good deal together of late.

Sir Charles had by this time wandered from his part into hers; and he now recalled her to the music by stopping to ask whether he was right. Knowing by experience what his difficulty was likely to be, she gave him his note, and went on. They had not been singing long when Jane came back and sat down, expressing a hope that her presence would not disturb them. It did disturb them. Agatha suspected that she had come there to watch them; and Sir Charles knew it. Besides, Lady Brandon, even when her mind was tranquil, was habitually restless. She could not speak because of the music; and, though she held an open book in her hand, she could not read and watch simultaneously. She gaped, and leaned to one end of the sofa until, on the point of overbalancing, she recovered herself with a prodigious bounce. The floor vibrated at her every movement. At last she could keep silence no longer.

"Oh dear!" she said, yawning audibly. "It must be five o'clock at the very earliest."

Agatha turned round upon the piano-stool, feeling that music and Lady Brandon were incompatible. Sir Charles, for his guest's sake, tried hard to restrain his exasperation.

"Probably your watch will tell you," he said.

"Thank you for nothing," said Jane. "Agatha: where is Gertrude?"

"How can Miss Wylie possibly tell you where she is, Jane? I think you have gone mad to-day."

"She is most likely playing billiards with Mr. Erskine," said Agatha, interposing quickly to forestall a retort from Jane, with its usual sequel of a domestic squabble.

"I think it is very strange of Gertrude to pass the whole day with Chester in the billiard room," said Jane discontentedly.

"There is not the slightest impropriety in her doing so," said Sir

Charles. "If our hospitality does not place Miss Lindsay above suspicion, the more shame for us. How would you feel if any one else made such a remark?"

"Oh, stuff!" said Jane peevishly. "You are always preaching long rigmaroles about nothing at all. I did not say that there was any impropriety about Gertrude. She is too proper to be pleasant, in my opinion."

Sir Charles, unable to trust himself further, frowned and left the room: Jane speeding him with a contemptuous laugh.

"Dont ever be such a fool as to get married," she said, when he was gone. She looked up as she spoke, and was alarmed to see Agatha seated on the pianoforte, with her ankles swinging in the old school fashion.

"Jane," she said, surveying her hostess coolly: "do you know what I would do if I were Sir Charles?"

Jane did not know.

"I would get a big stick; beat you black and blue; and then lock you up on bread and water for a week."

Jane half rose, red and angry. "Wh —— why?" she said, relapsing upon the sofa.

"If I were a man, I would not, for mere chivalry's sake, let a woman treat me like a troublesome dog. You want a sound thrashing."

"I'd like to see anybody thrash *me*," said Jane, rising again and displaying her formidable person erect. Then she burst into tears, and said, "I wont have such things said to me in my own house. How dare you?"

"You deserve it for being jealous of me," said Agatha.

Jane's eyes dilated angrily. "I! — I! — I jealous of you!" She looked round, as if for a missile. Not finding one, she sat down again, and said in a voice stifled with tears, "J — Jealous of *you,* indeed!"

"You have good reason to be; for he is fonder of me than of you."

Jane opened her mouth and eyes convulsively, but only uttered a gasp; and Agatha proceeded calmly, "I am polite to him, which you never are. When he speaks to me, I allow him to finish his sentence without expressing, as you do, a foregone conclusion that it is not worth attending to. I do not yawn and talk whilst he is singing. When he converses with me on art or literature, about which he knows twice as much as I do, and at least ten times as much as you" (Jane gasped again) "I do not make a silly answer and turn to my neighbour at the other side with a remark about the stables or the weather. When he is willing to be pleased, as he always is, I am willing to be pleasant. And that is why he likes me."

"He does *not* like you. He is the same to every one."

"Except his wife. He likes me so much, that you, like a great goose as you are, came up here to watch us at our duets, and made yourself as disagreeable as you possibly could whilst I was making myself charming. The poor man was ashamed of you."

"He wasnt," said Jane, sobbing. "I didnt do anything. I didnt say anything. I wont bear it. I will get a divorce. I will ———"

"You will mend your ways, if you have any sense left," said Agatha remorselessly. "Do not make such a noise, or some one will come to see what is the matter; and I shall have to get down from the piano, where I am very comfortable."

"It is you who are jealous."

"Oh, is it, Jane? I have not allowed Sir Charles to fall in love with me yet; but I can do so very easily. What will you wager that he will not kiss me before to-morrow evening?"

"It will be very mean and nasty of you if he does. You seem to think that I can be treated like a child."

"So you are a child," said Agatha, descending from her perch, and preparing to go. "An occasional slapping does you good."

"It is nothing to you whether I agree with my husband or not," said Jane with sudden fierceness.

"Not if you quarrel with him in private, as well bred couples do. But when it occurs in my presence, it makes me uncomfortable; and I object to being made uncomfortable."

"You would not be here at all if I had not asked you."

"Just think how dull the house would be without me, Jane!"

"Indeed! It was not dull before you came. Gertrude always behaved like a lady, at least."

"I am sorry that her example was so utterly lost on you."

"I wont bear it," said Jane with a sob, and a plunge upon the sofa that made the lustres of the chandeliers rattle. "I wouldnt have asked you if I had thought you could be so hateful. I will never ask you again."

"I will make Sir Charles divorce you for incompatibility of temper and marry me. Then I shall have the place to myself."

"He cant divorce me for that, thank goodness. You dont know what you're talking about."

Agatha laughed. "Come," she said good-humouredly: "dont be an old ass, Jane. Wash your face before any one sees it; and remember what I have told you about Sir Charles."

"It is very hard to be called an ass in one's own house."

"It is harder to be treated as one, like your husband. I am going to look for him in the billiard room."

Jane ran after her, and caught her by the sleeve. "Agatha," she pleaded: "promise me that you wont be mean. Say that you wont make love to him."

"I will consider about it," replied Agatha gravely.

Jane uttered a groan, and sank into a chair, which creaked at the shock. Agatha turned on the threshold, and seeing her shaking her head, pressing her eyes, and tapping with her heel in a restrained frenzy, said quickly,

"Here are the Waltons, and the Fitzgeorges, and Mr. Trefusis coming upstairs. How do you do, Mrs. Walton? Lady Brandon will be *so* glad to see you. Good-evening, Mr. Fitzgeorge."

Jane sprang up; wiped her eyes; and, with her hands on her hair, smoothing it, rushed to a mirror. No visitors appearing, she perceived that she was, for perhaps the hundredth time in her life, the victim of an imposture devised by Agatha. She, gratified by the success of her attempt to regain her old ascendency over Jane — she had made it with misgiving, notwithstanding her apparent confidence — went downstairs to the library, where she found Sir Charles gloomily trying to drown his domestic troubles in art criticism.

"I thought you were in the billiard room," said Agatha.

"I only peeped in," he replied; "but as I saw something particular going on, I thought it best to slip away; and I have been alone ever since."

The something particular which Sir Charles had not wished to interrupt was only a game of billiards. It was the first opportunity Erskine had ever enjoyed of speaking to Gertrude at leisure and alone. Yet their conversation had never been so commonplace. She, liking the game, played very well and chatted indifferently: he played badly, and broached trivial topics in spite of himself. After an hour-and-a-half's play, Gertrude had announced that this game must be their last. He thought desperately that if he were to miss many more strokes the game must presently end, and an opportunity which might never recur pass beyond recall. He determined to tell her without preface that he adored her; but when he opened his lips a question came forth of its own accord relating to the Persian way of playing billiards. Gertrude had never been in Persia, but had seen some Eastern billiard cues in the India Museum. Were not the Hindoos wonderful people for filagree work, and carpets, and such things? Did he not think the crookedness of their carpet patterns a blemish? Some people pretended to admire them; but was not that all nonsense? Was not the modern polished floor, with a rug in the middle, much superior to the old carpet fitted into the corners of the room? Yes. Enormously superior. Immensely ——

"Why, what are you thinking of to-day, Mr. Erskine? You have played with my ball."

"I am thinking of you."

"What did you say?" said Gertrude, not catching the serious turn he had given to the conversation, and poising her cue for a stroke. "Oh! I am as bad as you: that was the worst stroke I ever made, I think. — I beg your pardon: you said something just now."

"I forget. Nothing of any consequence." And he groaned at his own cowardice.

"Suppose we stop," she said. "There is no use in finishing the game if our hands are out. I am rather tired of it."

"I will finish if you like."

"Not at all. What pleases you, pleases me."

Gertrude made him a little bow, and idly knocked the balls about with her cue. Erskine's eyes wandered; and his lip moved irresolutely. He had settled with himself that his declaration should be a frank one — heart to heart. He had pictured himself in the act of taking her hand delicately, and saying, "Gertrude: I love you. May I tell you so again?" But this scheme did not now seem practicable.

"Miss Lindsay."

Gertrude, bending over the table, looked up in alarm.

"The present is as good an opportunity as I will — as I shall — as I will ——"

"Shall," said Gertrude.

"I beg your pardon?"

"*Shall*," repeated Gertrude. "Did you ever study the doctrine of necessity?"

"The doctrine of necessity?" he said, bewildered.

Gertrude went to the other side of the table in pursuit of a ball. She now guessed what was coming, and was willing that it should come; not because she intended to accept, but because, like other young ladies experienced in such scenes, she counted the proposals of marriage she received as a Red Indian counts the scalps he takes.

"We have had a very pleasant time of it here," he said, giving up as inexplicable the relevance of the doctrine of necessity. "At least, I have."

"Well," said Gertrude, quick to resent a fancied allusion to her private discontent: "so have I."

"I am glad of that — more so than I can convey by words."

"Is it any business of yours?" she said, following the disagreeable vein he had unconsciously struck upon, and suspecting pity in his efforts to be sympathetic.

"I wish I dared hope so. The happiness of my visit has been due to you entirely."

"Indeed," said Gertrude, wincing as all the hard things Trefusis had told her of herself came into her mind at the heels of Erskine's unfortunate allusion to her power of enjoying herself.

"I hope I am not paining you," he said earnestly.

"I dont know what you are talking about," she said, standing erect with sudden impatience. "You seem to think that it is very easy to pain me."

"No," he said timidly, puzzled by the effect he had produced. "I fear you misunderstand me. I am very awkward. Perhaps I had better say no more."

Gertrude, by turning away to put up her cue, signified that that was a point for him to consider: she not intending to trouble herself about it. When she faced him again, he was motionless and dejected, with a wistful expression like that of a dog that has proffered a caress and received a kick. Remorse, and a vague sense that there was something base in her attitude towards him, overcame her. She looked at him for an instant, and left the room.

The look excited him. He did not understand it, nor attempt to understand it; but it was a look that he had never before seen in her face or in that of any other woman. It struck him as a momentary revelation of what he had written of in "The Patriot Martyrs" as

"The glorious mystery of a woman's heart,"

and it made him feel unfit for ordinary social intercourse. He hastened from the house; walked swiftly down the avenue to the lodge, where he kept his velocipede; left word there that he was going for an excursion and should probably not return in time for dinner; mounted; and sped away recklessly along the Riverside Road. In less than two minutes he passed the gate of Sallust's House, where he nearly ran over an old woman laden with a basket of coals, who put down her burthen to scream curses after him. Warned by this that his headlong pace was dangerous, he slackened it a little, and presently saw Trefusis lying prone on the river bank, with his cheeks propped on his elbows, reading intently. Erskine, who had presented him, a few days before, with a copy of "The Patriot Martyrs and other Poems," tried to catch a glimpse of the book over which Trefusis was so serious. It was a Blue Book, full of figures. Erskine rode on in disgust, consoling himself with the recollection of Gertrude's face.

The highway now swerved inland from the river, and rose to a steep acclivity, at the brow of which he turned and looked back. The light was growing ruddy; and the shadows were lengthening. Trefusis was still prostrate in the meadow; and the old woman was in a field, gathering hemlock.

Erskine raced down the hill at full speed, and did not look behind him again until he found himself at nightfall on the skirts of a town, where he purchased some beer and a sandwich, which he ate with little appetite. Gertrude had set up a disturbance within him which made him impatient of eating.

It was now dark. He was many miles from Brandon Beeches, and not sure of the way back. Suddenly he resolved to complete his unfinished declaration that evening. He now could not ride back fast enough to satisfy his impatience. He tried a short cut; lost himself; spent nearly an hour seeking the high road; and at last came upon a railway station just in time to catch a train that brought him within a mile of his destination.

When he rose from the cushions of the railway-carriage, he found himself somewhat fatigued; and he mounted the bicycle stiffly. But his resolution was as ardent as ever; and his heart beat strongly as, after leaving his velocipede at the lodge, he walked up the avenue through the deep gloom beneath the beeches. Near the house, the first notes of *"Crudel perche finora"* reached him; and he stepped softly on to the turf lest his footsteps on the gravel should rouse the dogs and make them mar the harmony by barking. A rustle made him stop and listen. Then Gertrude's voice whispered through the darkness.

"What did you mean by what you said to me within?"

An extraordinary sensation shook Erskine: confused ideas of fairyland ran through his imagination. A bitter disappointment, like that of waking from a happy dream, followed as Trefusis's voice, more finely tuned than he had ever heard it before, answered,

"Merely that the expanse of stars above us is not more illimitable than my contempt for Miss Lindsay, nor brighter than my hopes of Gertrude."

"Miss Lindsay always to you, if you please, Mr. Trefusis."

"Miss Lindsay never to me, but only to those who cannot see through her to the soul within, which is Gertrude. There are a thousand Miss Lindsays in the world, formal and false. There is but one Gertrude."

"I am an unprotected girl, Mr. Trefusis; and you can call me what you please."

It occurred to Erskine that this was a fit occasion to rush forward and give Trefusis, whose figure he could now dimly discern, a black eye. But he hesitated; and the opportunity passed.

"Unprotected!" said Trefusis. "Why, you are fenced round and barred in with conventions, laws, and lies that would frighten the truth from the lips of any man whose faith in Gertrude was less strong than mine. Go to Sir Charles and tell him what I have said to Miss Lindsay; and within ten minutes I shall have passed these gates with a warning never to approach them again. I am in your power; and were I in Miss Lindsay's power alone, my shrift would be short. Happily, Gertrude, though she sees as yet but darkly, feels that Miss Lindsay is her bitterest foe."

"It is ridiculous: I am not two persons: I am only one. What does it matter to me if your contempt for me is as illimitable as the stars?"

"Ah: you remember that, do you? Whenever you hear a man talking about the stars, you may conclude that he is either an astronomer or a fool. But you and a fine starry night would make a fool of any man."

"I dont understand you. I try to; but I cannot: or, if I guess, I cannot tell whether you are in earnest or not."

"I am very much in earnest. Abandon at once and for ever all misgivings that I am trifling with you, or passing an idle hour as men do when they find themselves in the company of beautiful women. I mean what I say literally, and in the deepest sense. You doubt me: we have brought society to such a state that we all suspect one another. But whatever is true will command belief sooner or later from those who have wit enough to comprehend truth. Now let me recall Miss Lindsay to consciousness by remarking that we have been out for ten minutes, and that our hostess is not the woman to allow our absence to pass without comment."

"Let us go in. Thank you for reminding me."

"Thank you for forgetting."

Erskine heard their footsteps retreating, and presently saw the two enter the glow of light that shone from the open window of the billiard room, through which they went indoors. Trefusis, a man whom he had seen that day in a beautiful landscape, blind to everything except a row of figures in a Blue Book, was his successful rival, although it was plain from the very sound of his voice that he did not — could not — love Gertrude. Only a poet could do that. Trefusis was no poet, but a sordid brute unlikely to inspire interest in anything more human than a public meeting, much less in a woman, much less again in a woman so ethereal as Gertrude. She was proud too: yet she had allowed the fellow to insult her — had forgiven him for the sake of a few broad compliments. Erskine grew angry and cynical. The situation did not suit his poetry. Instead of being stricken to the heart with a solemn sorrow, as a Patriot Martyr would have been under similar circumstances, he felt slighted and ridiculous. He was hardly convinced of what had seemed at first the most obvious feature of the case, Trefusis's inferiority to himself.

He stood under the trees until Trefusis reappeared on his way home, making, Erskine thought, as much noise with his heels on the gravel as a regiment of delicately bred men would have done. He stopped for a moment to make inquiry at the lodge as he went out: then his footsteps died away in the distance.

Erskine, chilled, stiff, and with a sensation of a bad cold coming on, went into the house, and was relieved to find that Gertrude had retired, and that Lady Brandon, though she had been sure that he had ridden into the river in the dark, had nevertheless provided a warm supper for him.

CHAPTER XV.

Erskine soon found plenty of themes for his newly begotten cynicism. Gertrude's manner towards him softened so much that he, believing her heart given to his rival, concluded that she was tempting him to make a proposal which she had no intention of accepting. Sir Charles, to whom he told what he had overheard in the avenue, professed sympathy, but was evidently pleased to learn that there was nothing serious in the attentions Trefusis paid to Agatha. Erskine wrote three bitter sonnets on hollow friendship, and showed them to Sir Charles, who, failing to apply them to himself, praised them highly, and showed them to Trefusis without asking the author's permission. Trefusis remarked that in a corrupt society expressions of dissatisfaction were always creditable to a writer's sensibility; but he did not say much in praise of the verse.

"Why has he taken to writing in this vein?" he said. "Has he been disappointed in any way of late? Has he proposed to Miss Lindsay and been rejected?"

"No," said Sir Charles, surprised by this blunt reference to a subject they had never before discussed. "He does not intend to propose to Miss Lindsay."

"But he did intend to."

"He certainly did; but he has given up the idea."

"Why?" said Trefusis, apparently disapproving strongly of the renunciation.

Sir Charles shrugged his shoulders, and did not reply.

"I am sorry to hear it. I wish you could induce him to change his mind. He is a nice fellow, with enough to live on comfortably;

whilst he is yet what is called a poor man, so that she could feel perfectly disinterested in marrying him. It will do her good to marry without making a pecuniary profit by it: she will respect herself the more afterwards, and will neither want bread and butter nor be ashamed of her husband's origin, in spite of having married for love alone. Make a match of it if you can. I take an interest in the girl: she has good instincts."

Sir Charles's suspicion that Trefusis was really paying court to Agatha returned after this conversation, which he repeated to Erskine, who, much annoyed because his poems had been shown to a reader of Blue Books, thought it only a blind for Trefusis's design upon Gertrude. Sir Charles pooh-poohed this view; and the two friends were sharp with one another in discussing it. After dinner, when the ladies had left them, Sir Charles, repentant and cordial, urged Erskine to speak to Gertrude without troubling himself as to the sincerity of Trefusis. But Erskine, knowing himself ill able to brook a refusal, was loth to expose himself to one.

"If you had heard the tone of her voice when she asked him whether he was in earnest, you would not talk to me like this," he said despondently. "I wish he had never come here."

"Well, that, at least, was no fault of mine, my dear fellow," said Sir Charles. "He came among us against my will. And now that he appears to have been in the right — legally — about the field, it would look like spite if I cut him. Besides, he really isnt a bad man if he would only let the women alone."

"If he trifles with Miss Lindsay, I shall ask him to cross the Channel, and have a shot at him."

"I dont think he'd go," said Sir Charles dubiously. "If I were you, I would try my luck with Gertrude at once. In spite of what you heard, I dont believe she would marry a man of his origin. His money gives him an advantage, certainly; but Gertrude has sent richer men to the rightabout."

"Let the fellow have fair play," said Erskine. "I may be wrong, of course: all men are liable to err in judging themselves; but I think I could make her happier than he can."

Sir Charles was not so sure of that; but he cheerfully responded, "Certainly. He is not the man for her at all; and you are. He knows it, too."

"Hmf!" muttered Erskine, rising dejectedly. "Let's go upstairs."

"By-the-bye, we are to call on him to-morrow, to go through his house, and his collection of photographs. Photographs! Ha, ha!"

"Damn his house!" said Erskine.

Next day they went together to Sallust's House. It stood in the midst of an acre of land, waste except a little kitchen garden at the rear. The lodge at the entrance was uninhabited; and the gates stood open, with dust and fallen leaves heaped up against them. Free ingress had thus been afforded to two stray ponies, a goat, and a tramp, who lay asleep in the grass. His wife sat near, watching him.

"I have a mind to turn back," said Sir Charles, looking about him in disgust. "The place is scandalously neglected. Look at that rascal asleep within full view of the windows."

"I admire his cheek," said Erskine. "Nice pair of ponies, too."

Sallust's House was square and painted cinnamon colour. Beneath the cornice was a yellow frieze with figures of dancing children, imitated from the works of Donatello, and very unskilfully executed. There was a meagre portico of four columns, painted red; and a plain pediment, painted yellow. The colours, meant to match those of the walls, contrasted disagreeably with them, having been applied more recently, apparently by a colour-blind artist. The door beneath the portico stood open. Sir Charles rang the bell; and an elderly woman answered it; but before they could address her, Trefusis appeared, clad in a painter's jacket of white jean. Following him in, they found that the house was a hollow square, enclosing a courtyard with a bath sunk in the middle, and a fountain in the centre of the bath. The courtyard, formerly open to the sky, was now roofed in with dusty glass; the nymph that had once poured out the water of the fountain was barren and mutilated; and the bath was partly covered in with loose boards: the exposed part accommodating a heap of coals in one corner, a heap of potatoes in another, a beer barrel, some old carpets, a tarpaulin, and a broken canoe. The marble pavement extended to the outer walls of the house, and was roofed in at the sides by the upper stories, which were supported by fluted stone columns, much stained and chipped. The staircase, towards which Trefusis led his visitors, was a broad one at the end opposite the door, and gave access to a gallery leading to the upper rooms.

"This house was built in 1780 by an ancestor of my mother," said Trefusis. "He passed for a man of exquisite taste. He wished the place to be maintained for ever — he actually used that expression in his will — as the family seat; and he collected a fine library here, which I found useful, as all the books came into my hands in good condition, most of them with the leaves uncut. Some people prize uncut copies of old editions: a dealer gave me three hundred and fifty pounds for a lot of them. I came into possession of a number of family fetishes — heirlooms, as they are called. There was a sword that one of my forbears wore at Edgehill and other battles in Charles the First's time. We fought on the wrong side, of course; but the sword fetched thirty-five shillings nevertheless. You will hardly believe that I was offered one hundred and fifty pounds for a gold cup worth about twenty-five, merely because Queen Elizabeth once drank from it. This is my study. It was designed for a banqueting hall."

They entered a room as long as the wall of the house, pierced on one side by four tall windows, between which, square pillars, with Corinthian capitals supporting the cornice, were half sunk in the wall. There were similar pillars on the opposite side; but between them, instead of windows, were arched niches in which stood life-size plaster statues, chipped, broken, and defaced in an extraordinary fashion. The flooring, of diagonally set narrow boards, was uncarpeted and unpolished. The ceiling was adorned with frescoes, which at once excited Sir Charles's interest; and he noted with indignation that a large portion of the painting at the northern end had been destroyed, and some glass roofing inserted. In another place, bolts had been driven in to support the ropes of a trapeze and a few other pieces of gymnastic apparatus. The walls were white-washed; and at about four feet from the ground a dark band appeared, produced by pencil memoranda and little sketches scribbled on the whitewash. One end of the apartment was unfurnished, except by the gymnastic apparatus, a photographer's camera, a ladder in the corner, and a common deal table with oil cans and paint pots upon it. At the other end a comparatively luxurious show was made by a large bookcase; an elaborate combination of bureau and writing desk; a rack with a rifle, a set of foils, and an umbrella in it; several folio albums on a table; some comfortable chairs and sofas; and a thick carpet under foot. Close by, and seeming much out of place, was a carpenter's bench with the usual implements, and a number of boards of various thicknesses.

"This is a sort of comfort beyond the reach of any but a rich man," said Trefusis, turning and surprising his visitors in the act of exchanging glances of astonishment at his taste. "I keep a drawing room of the usual kind for receiving strangers with whom it is necessary to be conventional; but I never enter it except on such occasions. What do you think of this for a study?"

"On my soul, Trefusis, I think you are mad," said Sir Charles. "The place looks as if it had stood a siege. How did you manage to break the statues and chip the walls so outrageously?"

Trefusis took a newspaper from the table, and said, "Listen to this.

'In spite of the unfavourable nature of the weather, the sport of the Emperor and his guests in Styria has been successful. In three days 52 chamois and 79 stags and deer fell to 19 single barrelled rifles, the Emperor allowing no more on this occasion.'

"I share the Emperor's delight in shooting; but I am no butcher, and do not need the royal relish of blood to my sport. And I do not share my ancestor's taste in statuary. Hence —— " Here Trefusis opened a drawer, took out a pistol, and fired at the Hebe in the farthest niche.

"Well done!" said Erskine coolly, as the last fragment of Hebe's head crumbled at the touch of the bullet.

"Very fruitlessly done," said Trefusis. "I am a good shot; but of what use is it to me? None. I once met a gamekeeper who was a Methodist. He was a most eloquent speaker, but a bad shot. If he could have swapped talents with me I would have given him ten thousand pounds to boot willingly, although he would have profited as much as I by the exchange alone. I have no more desire or need to be a good shot than to be king of England, or owner of a Derby winner, or anything else equally ridiculous; and yet I never missed my aim in my life — thank blind fortune for nothing!"

"King of England!" said Erskine with a scornful laugh, to show Trefusis that other people were as liberty-loving as he. "Is it not absurd to hear a nation boasting of its freedom and tolerating a king?"

"Oh, hang your republicanism, Chester!" said Sir Charles, who privately held a low opinion of the political side of the Patriot Martyrs.

"I wont be put down on that point," said Erskine. "I admire a man that kills a king. You will agree with me there, Trefusis, wont you?"

"Certainly not," said Trefusis. "A king nowadays is only a dummy put up to draw your fire off the real oppressors of society; and the fraction of his salary that he can spend as he likes is usually far too small for his risk, his trouble, and the condition of personal slavery to which he is reduced. What private man in England is worse off than the constitutional monarch? We deny him all privacy: he may not marry whom he chooses, consort with whom he prefers, dress according to his taste, or live where he pleases. I dont believe he may even eat or drink what he likes best: a taste for tripe and onions on his part would provoke a remonstrance from the Privy Council. We dictate everything except his thoughts and dreams; and even these he must keep to himself if they are not suitable, in our opinion, to his condition. The work we impose on him has all the hardship of mere task work: it is unfruitful, incessant, monotonous, and has to be transacted for the most part with nervous bores. We make his kingdom a treadmill to him, and drive him to and fro on the face of it. Finally, having taken everything else that men prize from him, we fall upon his character, and that of every person to whom he ventures to show favour. We impose enormous expenses on him; stint him;

and then rail at his parsimony. We use him as I use those statues — stick him up in the place of honour for our greater convenience in disfiguring and abusing him. We send him forth through our crowded cities, proclaiming that he is the source of all good and evil in the nation; and he, knowing that many people believe it; knowing that it is a lie, and that he is powerless to shorten the working day by one hour, raise wages one penny, or annul the smallest criminal sentence, however unjust it may seem to him; knowing that every miner in the kingdom can manufacture dynamite, and that revolvers are sold for seven and sixpence apiece; knowing that he is not bullet proof, and that every king in Europe has been shot at in the streets; he must smile and bow, and maintain an expression of gracious enjoyment whilst the mayor and corporation inflict upon him the twaddling address he has heard a thousand times before. I do not ask you to be loyal, Erskine; but I expect you, in common humanity, to sympathize with the chief figure in the pageant, who is no more accountable for the manifold evils and abominations that exist in his realm than the Lord Mayor is accountable for the thefts of the pickpockets who follow his show on the ninth of November."

Sir Charles laughed at the trouble Trefusis took to prove his case, and said soothingly, "My dear fellow, kings are used to it, and expect it, and like it."

"And probably do not see themselves as I see them, any more than common people do," assented Trefusis.

"What an exquisite face!" exclaimed Erskine suddenly, catching sight of a photograph in a rich gold and coral frame on a miniature easel draped with ruby velvet. Trefusis turned quickly, so evidently gratified that Sir Charles hastened to say, "Charming!" Then, looking at the portrait, he added, as if a little startled, "It certainly is an extraordinarily attractive face."

"Years ago," said Trefusis, "when I saw that face for the first time, I felt as you feel now."

Silence ensued: the two visitors looking at the portrait: Trefusis looking at them.

"Curious style of beauty," said Sir Charles at last, not quite so assuredly as before.

Trefusis laughed unpleasantly. "Do you recognize the artist — the enthusiastic amateur — in her?" he said, opening another drawer and taking out a bundle of drawings, which he handed to be examined.

"Very clever. Very clever indeed," said Sir Charles. "I should like to meet the lady."

"I have often been on the point of burning them," said Trefusis;

"but there they are; and there they are likely to remain. The portrait has been much admired."

"Can you give us an introduction to the original, old fellow?" said Erskine.

"No, happily. She is dead."

Disagreeably shocked, they looked at him for a moment with aversion. Then Erskine, turning with pity and disappointment to the picture, said, "Poor girl! Was she married?"

"Yes. To me."

"Mrs. Trefusis!" exclaimed Sir Charles, "Ah! Dear me!"

Erskine, with proof before him that it was possible for a beautiful girl to accept Trefusis, said nothing.

"I keep her portrait constantly before me to correct my natural amativeness. I fell in love with her, and married her. I have fallen in love once or twice since; but a glance at my lost Hetty has cured me of the slightest inclination to marry."

Sir Charles did not reply. It occurred to him that Lady Brandon's portrait, if nothing else were left of her, might be useful in the same way.

"Come: you will marry again one of these days," said Erskine, in a forced tone of encouragement.

"It is possible. Men should marry, especially rich men. But I assure you I have no present intention of doing so."

Erskine's colour deepened; and he moved away to the table where the albums lay.

"This is the collection of photographs I spoke of," said Trefusis, following him and opening one of the books. "I took many of them myself under great difficulties with regard to light — the only difficulty that money could not always remove. This is a view of my father's house — or rather one of his houses. It cost seventy-five thousand pounds."

"Very handsome indeed," said Sir Charles, secretly disgusted at being invited to admire a photograph, such as house agents exhibit, of a vulgarly designed country house, merely because it had cost seventy-five thousand pounds. The figures were actually written beneath the picture.

"This is the drawing-room; and this one of the best bedrooms. In the right hand corner of the mount you will see a note of the cost of the furniture, fittings, napery, and so forth. They were of the most luxurious description."

"Very interesting," said Sir Charles, hardly disguising the irony of the comment.

"Here is a view — this is the first of my own attempts — of the apartment of one of the under servants. It is comfortable and spacious, and solidly furnished."

"So I perceive."

"These are the stables. Are they not handsome?"

"Palatial. Quite palatial."

"There is every luxury that a horse could desire, including plenty of valets to wait on him. You are noting the figures, I hope. There is the cost of the building, and the expenditure per horse per annum."

"I see."

"Here is the exterior of a house. What do you think of it?"

"It is rather picturesque in its dilapidation."

"Picturesque! Would you like to live in it?"

"No," said Erskine. "*I* dont see anything very picturesque about it. What induced you to photograph such a wretched old rookery?"

"Here is a view of the best room in it. Photography gives you a fair idea of the broken flooring and patched windows; but you must imagine the dirt and the odour of the place. Some of the stains are weather stains: others came from smoke and filth. The landlord of the house holds it from a peer, and lets it out in tenements. Three families occupied that room when I photographed it. You will see by the figures in the corner that it is more profitable to the landlord than an average house in Mayfair. Here is the cellar, let to a family for one and sixpence a week, and considered a bargain. The sun never shines there, of course: I took it by artificial light. You may add to the rent the cost of enough bad beer to make the tenant insensible to the filth of the place. Beer is the chloroform that enables the labourer to endure the severe operation of living: that is why we can always assure one another over our wine that the rascal's misery is due to his habit of drinking. We are down on him for it, because, if he could bear his life without beer, we should save his beer-money — get him for lower wages. In short, we should be richer and he soberer. Here is the yard: the arrangements are indescribable. Seven of the inhabitants of that house had worked for years in my father's mill. That is, they had created a considerable part of the vast sums of money for drawing your attention to which you were disgusted with me just now."

"Not at all," said Sir Charles faintly.

"You can see how their condition contrasts with that of my father's horses. The seven men to whom I have alluded, with three hundred others, were thrown destitute upon the streets by this." (Here he turned over a leaf and displayed a photograph of an elaborate machine.) "It enabled my father to dispense with their services, and to replace them by a handful of women and children. He had bought the patent of the machine for fifty pounds from the inventor, who was almost ruined by the expenses of his ingenuity, and would have sacrificed anything for a handful of ready money. Here is a portrait of my father in his masonic insignia. He believed that freemasons generally get on in the world; and as the main object of his life was to get on, he joined them, and wanted me to do the same. But I object to pretended secret societies and hocus pocus, and would not. You see what he was — a portly, pushing, egotistical tradesman. Mark the successful man, the merchant prince with argosies on every sea, the employer of thousands of hands, the munificent contributor to public charities, the churchwarden, the member of parliament, and the generous patron of his relatives: his self-approbation struggling with the instinctive sense of baseness in the money-hunter, the ignorant and greedy filcher of the labour of others, the seller of his own mind and manhood for luxuries and delicacies that he was too lowlived to enjoy, and for the society of people who made him feel his inferiority at every turn —— "

"And the man to whom you owe everything you possess," said Erskine boldly.

"I possess very little. Everything he left me, except a few pictures, I spent long ago; and even that was made by his slaves, and not by him. My wealth comes day by day fresh from the labour of the wretches who live in the dens I have just shown you, or of a few aristocrats of labour who are within ten shillings a week of being worse off. However, there is some excuse for my father. Once, at an election riot, I got into a free fight. I am a peaceful man; but as I had either to fight or be knocked down and trampled upon, I exchanged blows with men who were perhaps as peacefully disposed as I. My father, launched into a free competition (free in the sense that the fight is free: that is, lawless) — my father had to choose between being a slave himself and enslaving others. He chose the latter; and as he was applauded and made much of for succeeding, who dare blame him? Not I. Besides, he did something to destroy the anarchy that enabled him to plunder society with impunity. He furnished me, its enemy, with the powerful weapon of a large fortune. Thus our system of organizing industry sometimes hatches the eggs from which its destroyers break. Does Lady Brandon wear much lace?"

"I —— No: that is —— How the deuce do I know, Trefusis? What an extraordinary question!"

"This is a photograph of a lace school. It was a filthy room, twelve feet square. It was paved with brick; and the children were not allowed to wear their boots, lest the lace should get muddy. However, as there were twenty of them working there for fifteen hours a day ——

all girls — they did not suffer much from cold. They were pretty tightly packed — may be still, for aught I know. They brought three or four shillings a week sometimes to their fond parents; and they were very quick-fingered little creatures, and stuck intensely to their work, as the overseer always hit them when they looked up or —— "

"Trefusis," said Sir Charles, turning away from the table: "I beg your pardon; but I have no appetite for horrors. You really must not ask me to go through your collection. It is no doubt very interesting; but I cant stand it. Have you nothing pleasant to entertain me with?"

"Pooh! you are squeamish. However, as you are a novice, let us put off the rest until you are seasoned. The pictures are not all horrible. Each book refers to a different country. That one contains illustrations of modern civilization in Germany, for instance. That one is France: that, British India. Here you have the United States of America; home of liberty; theatre of manhood suffrage; kingless and lordless land of Protection, Republicanism and the realized Radical Programme, where all the black chattel slaves were turned into wage-slaves (like my father's white fellows) at a cost of 800,000 lives and wealth incalculable. You and I are paupers in comparison with the great capitalists of that country, where the labourers fight for bones with the Chinamen, like dogs. Some of these great men presented me with photographs of their yachts and palaces, not anticipating the use to which I would put them. Here are some portraits that will not harrow your feelings. This is my mother, a woman of good family, every inch a lady. Here is a Lancashire lass, the daughter of a common pitman. She has exactly the same physical characteristics as my well-born mother — the same small head, delicate features, and so forth: they might be sisters. This villainous-looking pair might be twin brothers, except that there is a trace of good humour about the one to the right. The good-humoured one is a bargee on the Lyvern Canal. The other is one of the senior noblemen of the British Peerage. They illustrate the fact that Nature, even when perverted by generations of famine fever, ignores the distinctions we set up between men. This group of men and women, all tolerably intelligent and thoughtful looking, are so-called enemies of society — Nihilists, Anarchists, Communards, members of the International and so on. These other poor devils, worried, stiff, strumous, awkward, vapid, and rather coarse, with here and there a passably pretty woman, are European kings, queens, grand-dukes and the like. Here are ship-captains, criminals, poets, men of science, peers, peasants, political economists and representatives of dozens of degrees. The object of the collection is to illustrate the natural inequality of man, and the failure of our artificial inequality to correspond with it."

"It seems to me a sort of infernal collection for the upsetting of people's ideas," said Erskine. "You ought to label it 'A Portfolio of Paradoxes.' "

"In a rational state of society they would be paradoxes; but now the time gives them proof — like Hamlet's paradox. It is, however, a collection of facts; and I will give no fanciful name to it. You dislike figures, dont you?"

"Unless they are by Phidias, yes."

"Here are a few, not by Phidias. This is the balance sheet of an attempt I made some years ago to carry out the idea of an International Association of Labourers — commonly known as *The* International — or union of all workmen throughout the world in defence of the interests of labour. You see the result. Expenditure, four thousand five hundred pounds. Subscriptions received from working men, twenty-two pounds, seven and tenpence halfpenny. The British workmen showed their sense of my efforts to emancipate them by accusing me of making a good thing out of the Association for my own pocket, and by mobbing and stoning me twice. I now help them only when they show some disposition to help themselves. I occupy myself partly in working out a scheme for the reorganization of industry, and partly in attacking my own class, women and all, as I am attacking you."

"There is little use in attacking us, I fear," said Sir Charles.

"Great use," said Trefusis confidently. "You have a very different opinion of our boasted civilization now from that which you held when I broke your wall down, and invited those Land Nationalization zealots to march across your pleasure ground. You have seen in my album something you had not seen an hour ago; and you are consequently not quite the same man you were an hour ago. My pictures stick in the mind longer than your scratchy etchings, or the leaden things in which you fancy you see tender harmonies in grey. Erskine's next drama may be about liberty; but its Patriot Martyrs will have something better to do than spout balderdash against figure-head kings who in all their lives never secretly plotted as much dastardly meanness, greed, cruelty, and tyranny as is openly voted for in London by every half-yearly meeting of dividend-consuming vermin whose miserable wage-slaves drudge sixteen hours out of the twenty-four."

"What is going to be the end of it all?" said Sir Charles, a little dazed.

"Socialism, or Smash. Socialism if the race has at last evolved the faculty of co-ordinating the functions of a society too crowded and complex to be worked any longer on the old haphazard private property system. Unless we reorganize our society socialistically —

humanly a most arduous and magnificent enterprise: economically a most simple and sound one — Free Trade by itself will ruin England; and I will tell you exactly how. When my father made his fortune, we had the start of all other nations in the organization of our industry and in our access to iron and coal. Other nations bought our products for less than they must have spent to raise them at home, and yet for so much more than they cost us, that profits rolled in Atlantic waves upon our capitalists. When the workers, by their trades-unions, demanded a share of the luck in the form of advanced wages, it paid better to give them the little they dared to ask than to stop gold-gathering to fight and crush them. But now our customers have set up in their own countries improved copies of our industrial organization, and have discovered places where iron and coal are even handier than they are by this time in England. They produce for themselves, or buy elsewhere, what they formerly bought from us. Our profits are vanishing: our machinery is standing idle: our workmen are locked out. It pays now to stop the mills and fight and crush the unions when the men strike, no longer for an advance, but against a reduction. Now that these unions are beaten, helpless, and drifting to bankruptcy as the proportion of unemployed men in their ranks becomes greater, they are being petted and made much of by our class: an infallible sign that they are making no further progress in their duty of destroying us. The small capitalists are left stranded by the ebb: the big ones will follow the tide across the water, and rebuild their factories where steam power, water power, labour power, and transport are now cheaper than in England, where they used to be cheapest. The workers will emigrate in pursuit of the factory; but they will multiply faster than they emigrate, and be told that their own exorbitant demand for wages is driving capital abroad, and must continue to do so whilst there is a Chinaman or a Hindoo unemployed to underbid them. As the British factories are shut up, they will be replaced by villas: the manufacturing districts will become fashionable resorts for capitalists living on the interest of foreign investments: the farms and sheep runs will be cleared for deer forests. All products that can in the nature of things be manufactured elsewhere than where they are consumed, will be imported in payment of deer-forest rents from foreign sportsmen, or of dividends due to shareholders resident in England, but holding shares in companies abroad; and these imports will not be paid for by exports, because rent and interest are not paid for at all — a fact which the Free Traders do not yet see, or at any rate do not mention, although it is the key to the whole mystery of their opponents. The cry for Protection will become wild; but no one will dare resort to a demonstrably absurd measure that must raise

prices before it raises wages, and that has everywhere failed to benefit the worker. There will be no employment for any one except in
doing things that must be done on the spot, such as unpacking and
distributing the imports, ministering to the proprietors as domestic
servants, or by acting, preaching, paving, lighting, housebuilding and
the rest; and some of these, as the capitalist comes to regard ostentation as vulgar, and to enjoy a simpler life, will employ fewer and
fewer people. A vast proletariat, beginning with a nucleus of those
formerly employed in export trades, with their multiplying progeny,
will be out of employment permanently. They will demand access to
the land and machinery to produce for themselves. They will be refused. They will break a few windows, and be dispersed with a
warning to their leaders. They will burn a few houses and murder
a policeman or two; and then an example will be made of the warned.
They will revolt, and be shot down with machine guns — emigrated
— exterminated anyhow and everyhow; for the proprietary classes
have no idea of any other means of dealing with the full claims of
labour. You yourself, though you would give fifty pounds to Jansenius's emigration fund readily enough, would call for the police, the
military, and the Riot Act, if the people came to Brandon Beeches and
bade you turn out and work for your living with the rest. Well: the
superfluous proletariat destroyed, there will remain a population of
capitalists living on gratuitous imports, and served by a disaffected
retinue. One day, the gratuitous imports will stop in consequence of
the occurrence abroad of revolution and repudiation, fall in the rate
of interest, purchase of industries by governments for lump sums, not
reinvestable, or what not. Our capitalist community is then thrown on
the remains of the last dividend, which it consumes long before it can
rehabilitate its extinct machinery of production in order to support
itself with its own hands. Horses, dogs, cats, rats, blackberries, mush-
rooms, and cannibalism only postpone —— "

"Ha! ha! ha!" shouted Sir Charles. "On my honour, I thought you
were serious at first, Trefusis. Come: confess, old chap: it's all a fad
of yours. I half suspected you of being a bit of a crank." And he
winked at Erskine.

"What I have described to you is the inevitable outcome of our
present Free Trade policy without Socialism. The theory of Free
Trade is only applicable to systems of exchange, not to systems of
spoliation. Our system is one of spoliation; and if we dont abandon
it, we must either return to Protection or go to smash by the road I
have just mapped. Now, sooner than let the Protectionists triumph,
the Codben Club itself would blow the gaff, and point out to the
workers that Protection only means compelling the proprietors of Eng-

land to employ slaves resident in England, and therefore presumably
— though by no means necessarily — Englishmen. This would open
the eyes of the nation at last to the fact that England is not their
property. Once let them understand that, and they would soon make
it so. When England is made the property of its inhabitants collec-
tively, England becomes socialistic. Artificial inequality will vanish
then before real freedom of contract; freedom of competition, or
unhampered emulation, will keep us moving ahead; and Free Trade
will fulfil its promises at last."

"And the idlers and loafers," said Erskine. "What of them?"

"You and I, in fact," said Trefusis. "Die of starvation, I suppose,
unless we choose to work; or unless they give us a little outdoor relief
in consideration of our bad bringing-up."

"Do you mean that they will plunder us?" said Sir Charles.

"I mean that they will make us stop plundering them. If they
hesitate to strip us naked, or to cut our throats if we offer them the
smallest resistance, they will shew us more mercy than we ever
shewed them. Consider what we have done to get our rents in Ireland
and Scotland, and our dividends in Egypt, if you have already forgotten my photographs and their lesson in our atrocities at home. Why,
man, we *murder* the great mass of these toilers with overwork and
hardship: their average lifetime is not half as long as ours. Human
nature is the same in them as in us. If we resist them, and succeed
in restoring order, as we call it, we will punish them mercilessly for
their insubordination, as we did in Paris in 1871, where, by-the-bye,
we taught them the folly of giving their enemies quarter. If they
beat us, we shall catch it; and serve us right. Far better turn honest
at once, and avert bloodshed. Eh, Erskine?"

Erskine was considering what reply he should make, when Trefusis
disconcerted him by ringing a bell. Presently the elderly woman appeared, pushing before her an oblong table mounted on wheels, like
a barrow.

"Thank you," said Trefusis, and dismissed her. "Here is some
good wine, some good water, some good fruit, and some good bread.
I know that you cling to wine as to a good familiar creature. As for
me, I make no distinction between it and other vegetable poisons: I
abstain from them all. Water for serenity: wine for excitement. I,
having boiling springs of excitement within myself, am never at a loss
for it, and have only to seek serenity. However" (here he drew a
cork), "a generous goblet of this will make you feel like gods for half
an hour at least. Shall we drink to your conversion to Socialism?"

Sir Charles shook his head.

"Come: Mr. Donovan Brown, the great artist, is a Socialist; and
why should not you be one?"

"Donovan Brown!" exclaimed Sir Charles with interest. "Is it possible? Do you know him personally?"

"Here are several letters from him. You may read them: the mere autograph of such a man is interesting."

Sir Charles took the letters, and read them earnestly: Erskine reading over his shoulder.

"I most cordially agree with everything he says here," said Sir Charles. "It is quite true, quite true."

"Of course you agree with us. Donovan Brown's eminence as an artist has gained me one recruit; and yours as a baronet will gain me some more."

"But —— "

"But what?" said Trefusis, deftly opening one of the albums at a photograph of a loathsome room. "You are against that, are you not? Donovan Brown is against it; and I am against it. You may disagree with us in everything else; but there you are at one with us. Is it not so?"

"But that may be the result of drunkenness, improvidence, or —— "

"My father's income was fifty times as great as that of Donovan Brown. Do you believe that Donovan Brown is fifty times as drunken and improvident as my father was?"

"Certainly not. I do not deny that there is much in what you urge. Still, you ask me to take a rather important step."

"Not a bit of it. I dont ask you to subscribe to, join, or in any way pledge yourself to any society or conspiracy whatsoever. I only want your name for private mention to cowards who think Socialism right, but will not say so because they do not think it respectable. They will not be ashamed of their convictions when they learn that a baronet shares them. Socialism offers you something already, you see: a good use for your hitherto useless title."

Sir Charles coloured a little, conscious that the example of his favourite painter had influenced him more than his own conviction or the arguments of Trefusis. "What do you think, Chester?" he said. "Will you join?"

"Erskine is already committed to the cause of liberty by his published writings," said Trefusis. "Three of the pamphlets on that shelf contain quotations from the Patriot Martyrs."

Erskine blushed, flattered by being quoted: an attention that had been shewn him only once before, and then by a reviewer with the object of proving that the Patriot Martyrs were slovenly in their grammar.

"Come!" said Trefusis. "Shall I write to Donovan Brown that his letters have gained the cordial assent and sympathy of Sir Charles Brandon?"

"Certainly, certainly. That is, if my unknown name would be of the least interest to him."

"Good," said Trefusis, filling his glass with water. "Erskine: let us drink to our brother Social Democrat."

Erskine laughed loudly, but not heartily. "What an ass you are, Brandon!" he said. "You, with a large landed estate, and bags of gold invested in railways, calling yourself a Social Democrat! Are you going to sell out and distribute? — to sell all that thou hast and give to the poor?"

"Not a penny," replied Trefusis for him promptly. "A man cannot be a Christian in this country: I have tried it, and found it impossible both in law and in fact. I am a capitalist and a landholder. I have railway shares, mining shares, building shares, bank shares, and stock of most kinds; and a great trouble they are to me. But these shares do not represent wealth actually in existence: they are a mortgage on the labour of unborn generations of labourers, who must work to keep me and mine in idleness and luxury. If I sold them, would the mortgage be cancelled and the unborn generations released from its thrall? No. It would only pass into the hands of some other capitalist; and the working class would be no better off for my self-sacrifice. Sir Charles cannot obey the command of Christ: I defy him to do it. Let him give his land for a public park: only the richer classes will have leisure to enjoy it. Plant it at the very doors of the poor, so that they may at least breathe its air; and it will raise the value of the neighbouring houses and drive the poor away. Let him endow a school for the poor, like Eton or Christ's Hospital; and the rich will take it for their own children as they do in the two instances I have named. Sir Charles does not want to minister to poverty, but to abolish it. No matter how much you give to the poor, everything except a bare subsistence wage will be taken from them again by force. All talk of practising Christianity, or even bare justice, is at present mere waste of words. How can you justly reward the labourer when you cannot ascertain the value of what he makes, owing to the prevalent custom of stealing it? I know this by experience: I wanted to pay a just price for my wife's tomb; but I could not find out its value, and never shall. The principle on which we farm out our national industry to private marauders, who recompense themselves by black mail, so corrupts and paralyzes us that we cannot be honest even when we want to. And the reason we bear it so calmly is that very few of us really want to."

"I must study this question of value," said Sir Charles dubiously, refilling his goblet. "Can you recommend me a good book on the subject?"

"Any good treatise on political economy will do," said Trefusis. "In economics all roads lead to Socialism; although in nine cases out of ten, so far, the economist doesnt recognize his destination, and incurs the malediction pronounced by Jeremiah on those who justify the wicked for reward. I will look you out a book or two. And if you will call on Donovan Brown the next time you are in London, he will be delighted, I know. He meets with very few who are capable of sympathizing with him from both his points of view — social and artistic."

Sir Charles brightened on being reminded of Donovan Brown. "I shall esteem an introduction to him a great honour," he said. "I had no idea that he was a friend of yours."

"I was a very practical young Socialist when I first met him," said Trefusis. "When Brown was an unknown and wretchedly poor man, my mother, at the petition of a friend of his, charitably bought one of his pictures for thirty pounds, which he was very glad to get. Years afterwards, when my mother was dead, and Brown famous, I was offered eight hundred pounds for this picture, which was, by-the-bye, a very bad one in my opinion. Now, after making the usual unjust allowance for interest on thirty pounds for twelve years or so that had elapsed, the sale of the picture would have brought me in a profit of over seven hundred and fifty pounds, an unearned increment to which I had no righteous claim. My solicitor, to whom I mentioned the matter, was of opinion that I might justifiably pocket the seven hundred and fifty pounds as reward for my mother's benevolence in buying a presumably worthless picture from an obscure painter. But he failed to convince me that I ought to be paid for my mother's virtues, though we agreed that neither I nor my mother had received any return in the shape of pleasure in contemplating the work, which had deteriorated considerably by the fading of the colours since its purchase. At last I went to Brown's studio with the picture, and told him that it was worth nothing to me, as I thought it a particularly bad one; and that he might have it back again for fifteen pounds, half the first price. He at once told me that I could get from any dealer more for it than he could afford to give me; but he told me too that I had no right to make a profit out of his work, and that he would give me the original price of thirty pounds. I took it, and then sent him the man who had offered me the eight hundred. To my discomfiture, Brown refused to sell it on any terms, because he considered it unworthy of his reputation. The man bid up to fifteen hundred; but Brown held out; and I found that instead of putting seven hundred and seventy pounds into his pocket, I had taken thirty out of it. I accordingly offered to return the thirty pieces. Brown, taking the offer as an insult, declined all further communication with me. I then insisted on the matter being submitted to arbitration, and demanded fifteen hundred pounds as the full exchange value of the picture. All the arbitrators agreed that this was monstrous; whereupon I contended that if they denied my right to the value in exchange, they must admit my right to the value in use. They assented to this after putting off their decision for a fortnight in order to read Adam Smith and discover what on earth I meant by my values in use and exchange. I now shewed that the picture had no value in use to me, as I disliked it; and that therefore I was entitled to nothing, and that Brown must take back the thirty pounds. They were glad to concede this also to me, as they were all artist friends of Brown, and wished him not to lose money by the transaction; though they of course privately thought that the picture was, as I described it, a bad one. After that Brown and I became very good friends. He tolerated my advances, at first lest it should seem that he was annoyed by my disparagement of his work. Subsequently he fell into my views much as you have done."

"That is very interesting," said Sir Charles. "What a noble thing — refusing fifteen hundred pounds! He could ill afford it, probably."

"Heroic — according to nineteenth century notions of heroism. Voluntarily to throw away a chance of making money! that is the *ne plus ultra* of martyrdom. Brown's wife was extremely angry with him for doing it."

"It is an interesting story — or might be made so," said Erskine. "But you make my head spin with your confounded exchange values and stuff. Everything is a question of figures with you."

"That comes of my not being a poet," said Trefusis. "But we Socialists need to study the romantic side of our movement to interest women in it. If you want to make a cause grow, instruct every woman you meet in it. She is or will one day be a wife, and will contradict her husband with scraps of your arguments. A squabble will follow. The son will listen, and will be set thinking if he be capable of thought. And so the mind of the people gets leavened. I have converted many young women. Most of them know no more of the economic theory of Socialism than they know of Chaldee; but they no longer fear or condemn its name. Oh! I assure you that much can be done in that way by men who are not afraid of women, and who are not in too great a hurry to see the harvest they have sown for."

"Take care. Some of your lady proselytes may get the better of you some day. The future husband to be contradicted may be Sidney Trefusis. Ha! ha! ha!" Sir Charles had emptied a second large goblet of wine, and was a little flushed and boisterous.

"No," said Trefusis: "I have had enough of love myself, and am not likely to inspire it. Women do not care for men to whom, as Erskine says, everything is a question of figures. I used to flirt with women: now I lecture them, and abhor a man-flirt worse than I do a woman one. Some more wine? Oh, you must not waste the remainder of this bottle."

"I think we had better go, Brandon," said Erskine, his mistrust of Trefusis growing. "We promised to be back before two."

"So you shall," said Trefusis. "It is not yet a quarter past one. By-the-bye, I have not shewn you Donovan Brown's pet instrument for the regeneration of society. Here it is. A monster petition praying that the holding back from the labourer of any portion of the net value produced by his labour be declared a felony. That is all."

Erskine nudged Sir Charles, who said hastily, "Thank you; but I had rather not sign anything."

"A baronet sign such a petition!" exclaimed Trefusis. "I did not think of asking you. I only shew it to you as an interesting historical document, containing the autographs of a few artists and poets. There is Donovan Brown's for example. It was he who suggested the petition, which is not likely to do much good, as the thing cannot be done in any such fashion. However, I have promised Brown to get as many signatures as I can; so you may as well sign it, Erskine. It says nothing in blank verse about the holiness of slaying a tyrant; but it is a step in the right direction. You will not stick at such a trifle — unless the reviews have frightened you. Come: your name and address."

Erskine shook his head.

"Do you then only commit yourself to revolutionary sentiments when there is a chance of winning fame as a poet by them?"

"I will not sign, simply because I do not choose to," said Erskine warmly.

"My dear fellow," said Trefusis, almost affectionately, "if a man has a conscience he can have no choice in matters of conviction. I have read somewhere in your book that the man who will not shed his blood for the liberty of his brothers is a coward and a slave. Will you not shed a drop of ink — my ink, too — for the right of your brothers to the work of their hands? I at first sight did not care to sign this petition, because I would as soon petition a tiger to share his prey with me, as our rulers to relax their grip of the stolen labour they live on. But Donovan Brown said to me, 'You have no choice. Either you believe that the labourer should have the fruit of his labour or you do not. If you do, put your conviction on record, even if it should be as useless as Pilate's washing his hands.' So I signed."

"Donovan Brown was right," said Sir Charles. "*I* will sign." And he did so with a flourish.

"Brown will be delighted," said Trefusis. "I will write to him to-day that I have got another good signature for him."

"Two more," said Sir Charles. "You shall sign, Erskine: hang me if you shant! It is only against rascals that run away without paying their men their wages."

"Or that dont pay them in full," observed Trefusis, with a curious smile. "But do not sign if you feel uncomfortable about it."

"If you dont sign after me, you are a sneak, Chester," said Sir Charles.

"I dont know what it means," said Erskine, wavering. "I dont understand petitions."

"It means what it says: you cannot be held responsible for any meaning that is not expressed in it," said Trefusis. "But never mind. You mistrust me a little, I fancy, and would rather not meddle with my petitions; but you will think better of that as you grow used to me. Meanwhile, there is no hurry. Dont sign yet."

"Nonsense! I dont doubt your good faith," said Erskine, hastily disavowing suspicions which he felt but could not account for. "Here goes!" And he signed.

"Well done!" said Trefusis. "This will make Brown happy for the rest of the month."

"It is time for us to go now," said Erskine gloomily.

"Look in upon me at any time: you shall be welcome," said Trefusis. "You need not stand upon any sort of ceremony."

Then they parted: Sir Charles assuring Trefusis that he had never spent a more interesting morning, and shaking hands with him at considerable length three times. Erskine said little until he was in the Riverside Road with his friend, when he suddenly burst out,

"What the devil do you mean by drinking two tumblers of such staggering stuff at one o'clock in the day in the house of a dangerous man like that? I am very sorry I went into the fellow's place. I had misgivings about it; and they have been fully borne out."

"How so?" said Sir Charles, taken aback.

"He has overreached us. I was a deuced fool to sign that paper; and so were you. It was for that that he invited us."

"Rubbish, my dear boy. It was not his paper, but Donovan Brown's."

"I doubt it. Most likely he talked Brown into signing it just as he talked us. I tell you his ways are all crooked, like his ideas. Did you hear how he lied about Miss Lindsay?"

"Oh, you are mistaken about that. He does not care two straws for her or for any one."

"Well, if you are satisfied, I am not. You would not be in such high spirits over it if you had taken as little wine as I."

"Pshaw! you're too ridiculous. It was capital wine. Do you mean to say I am drunk?"

"No. But you would not have signed if you had not taken that second goblet. If you had not forced me — I could not get out of it after you set the example — I would have seen him d——d sooner than have anything do with his petition."

"I dont see what harm can come of it," said Sir Charles, braving out some secret disquietude.

"I will never go into his house again," said Erskine moodily. "We were just like two flies in a spider's web."

Meanwhile, Trefusis was fulfilling his promise to write to Donovan Brown.

SALLUST'S HOUSE.

DEAR BROWN: *I have spent the forenoon angling for a couple of very young fish, and have landed them with more trouble than they are worth. One has gaudy scales: he is a baronet, and an amateur artist, save the mark. All my arguments and my little museum of photographs were lost on him; but when I mentioned your name, and promised him an introduction to you, he gorged the bait greedily. He was half drunk when he signed; and I should not have let him touch the paper if I had not convinced myself beforehand that he means well, and that my wine had only freed his natural generosity from his conventional cowardice and prejudice. We must get his name published in as many journals as possible as a signatory to the great petition: it will draw on others as your name drew him. The second novice, Chichester Erskine, is a young poet. He will not be of much use to us, though he is a devoted champion of liberty in blank verse, and dedicates his works to Mazzini, etc. He signed reluctantly. All this hesitation is the uncertainty that comes of ignorance: they have not found out the truth for themselves, and are afraid to trust me, matters having come to the pass at which no man dares trust his fellow.*

I have met a pretty young lady here who might serve you as a model for Hypatia. She is crammed with all the prejudices of the peerage; but I am effecting a cure. I have set my heart on marrying her to Erskine, who, thinking that I am making love to her on my own account, is jealous. The weather is pleasant here; and I am having a merry life of it; but I find myself too idle. Etc., etc., etc.

CHAPTER XVI.

One sunny forenoon, as Agatha sat reading on the doorstep of the conservatory, the shadow of her parasol deepened; and she, looking up for something denser than the silk of it, saw Trefusis.

"Oh!"

She offered him no further greeting, having fallen in with his habit of dispensing, as far as possible, with salutations and ceremonies. He seemed in no hurry to speak; and so, after a pause, she began, "Sir Charles ——"

"— is gone to town," he said. "Erskine is out on his bicycle. Lady Brandon and Miss Lindsay have gone to the village in the waggonette; and you have come out here to enjoy the summer sun and read rubbish. I know all your news already."

"You are very clever, and, as usual, wrong. Sir Charles has not gone to town. He has only gone to the railway station for some papers: he will be back for luncheon. How do you know so much of our affairs?"

"I was on the roof of my house with a field-glass. I saw you come out and sit down here. Then Sir Charles passed. Then Erskine. Then Lady Brandon, driving with great energy, and presenting a remarkable contrast to the disdainful repose of Gertrude."

"Gertrude! I like your cheek."

"You mean that you dislike my presumption."

"No: I think cheek a more expressive word than presumption; and I mean that I like it — that it amuses me."

"Really! What are you reading?"

"Rubbish, you said just now. A novel."

"That is, a lying story of two people who never existed, and who would have acted very differently if they had existed."

"Just so."

"Could you not imagine something just as amusing for yourself?"

"Perhaps so; but it would be too much trouble. Besides, cooking takes away one's appetite for eating. I should not relish stories of my own confection."

"Which volume are you at?"

"The third."

"Then the hero and heroine are on the point of being united?"

"I really dont know. This is one of your clever novels. I wish the characters would not talk so much."

"No matter. Two of them are in love with one another, are they not?"

"Yes. It would not be a novel without that."

"Do you believe, in your secret soul, Agatha — I take the liberty of using your Christian name because I wish to be very solemn — do you really believe that any human being was ever unselfish enough to love another in the story-book fashion?"

"Of course. At least I suppose so. I have never thought much about it."

"I doubt it. My own belief is that no latter-day man has any faith in the thoroughness or permanence of his affection for his mate. Yet he does not doubt the sincerity of her professions; and he conceals the hollowness of his own from her, partly because he is ashamed of it, and partly out of pity for her. And she, on her side, is playing exactly the same comedy."

"I believe that is what men do, but not women."

"Indeed! Pray do you remember pretending to be very much in love with me once when ——"

Agatha reddened, and placed her palm on the step as if about to spring up. But she checked herself, and said, "Stop, Mr. Trefusis. If you talk about that I shall go away. I wonder at you! Have you no taste?"

"None whatever. And as I was the aggrieved party on that — stay: dont go. I will never allude to it again. I am growing afraid of you. You used to be afraid of me."

"Yes; and you used to bully me. You have a habit of bullying women who are weak enough to fear you. You are a great deal cleverer than I, and know much more, I daresay; but I am not in the least afraid of you now."

"You have no reason to be, and never had any. Henrietta, if she were alive, could testify that if there is a defect in my relations with women, it arises from my excessive amiability. I could not refuse a woman anything she had set her heart upon — except my hand in marriage. As long as your sex are content to stop short of that, they can do as they please with me."

"How cruel! I thought you were nearly engaged to Gertrude."

"The usual interpretation of a friendship between a man and a woman! I have never thought of such a thing; and I am sure she never has. We are not half so intimate as you and Sir Charles."

"Oh, Sir Charles is married. And I advise you to get married if you wish to avoid creating misunderstandings by your friendships."

Trefusis was struck. Instead of answering, he stood, after one startled glance at her, looking intently at the knuckle of his forefinger.

"Do take pity on our poor sex," said Agatha maliciously. "You are so rich, and so very clever, and really so nice looking, that you ought to share yourself with somebody. Gertrude would be only too happy."

Trefusis grinned, and shook his head, slowly but emphatically.

"I suppose *I* should have no chance," continued Agatha pathetically.

"I should be delighted, of course," he replied with simulated confusion, but with a lurking gleam in his eye that might have checked her, had she noticed it.

"Do marry me, Mr. Trefusis," she pleaded, clasping her hands in a rapture of mischievous raillery. "Pray do."

"Thank you," said Trefusis determinedly: "I will."

"I am very sure you shant," said Agatha, after an incredulous pause, springing up and gathering her skirt as if to run away. "You do not suppose I was in earnest, do you?"

"Undoubtedly I do. *I* am in earnest."

Agatha hesitated, uncertain whether he might not be playing with her as she had just been playing with him. "Take care," she said. "I may change my mind and be in earnest too; and then how will you feel, Mr. Trefusis?"

"I think, under our altered relations, you had better call me Sidney."

"I think we had better drop the joke. It was in rather bad taste; and I should not have made it, perhaps."

"It would be an execrable joke: therefore I have no intention of regarding it as one. You shall be held to your offer, Agatha. Are you in love with me?"

"Not in the least. Not the very smallest bit in the world. I do not know anybody with whom I am less in love or less likely to be in love."

"Then you must marry me. If you were in love with me, I should run away. My sainted Henrietta adored me; and I proved unworthy of adoration — though I was immensely flattered."

"Yes: exactly! The way you treated your first wife ought to be sufficient to warn any woman against becoming your second."

"Any woman who loved me, you mean. But you do not love me; and if I run away you will have the advantage of being rid of me. Our settlements can be drawn so as to secure you half my fortune in such an event."

"You will never have a chance of running away from me."

"I shall not want to. I am not so squeamish as I was. No: I do not think I shall run away from you."

"I do not think so either."

"Well: when shall we be married?"

"Never," said Agatha, and fled. But before she had gone a step he caught her.

"Dont," she said breathlessly. "Take your arm away. How dare you?"

He released her and shut the door of the conservatory. "Now," he said, "if you want to run away, you will have to run in the open."

"You are very impertinent. Let me go in immediately."

"Do you want me to beg you to marry me after you have offered to do it freely?"

"But I was only joking: I dont care for you," she said, looking round for an outlet.

"Agatha," he said, with grim patience: "half an hour ago I had no more intention of marrying you than of making a voyage to the moon. But when you made the suggestion, I felt all its force in an instant; and now nothing will satisfy me but your keeping your word. Of all the women I know, you are the only one not quite a fool."

"I should be a great fool if —— "

"If you married me, you were going to say; but I dont think so. I am the only man, not quite an ass, of your acquaintance. I know my value, and yours. And I loved you long ago, when I had no right to."

Agatha frowned. "No," she said. "There is no use in saying anything more about it. It is out of the question."

"Come: dont be vindictive. I was more sincere then than you were. But that has nothing to do with the present. You have spent our renewed acquaintance on the defensive against me, retorting upon me, teasing and tempting me. Be generous for once; and say Yes with a good will."

"Oh, I *never* tempted you," cried Agatha. "I did not. It is not true." He said nothing, but offered his hand. "No: go away: I will not." He persisted; and she felt her power of resistance suddenly wane. Terror-stricken, she said hastily, "There is not the least use in bothering me: I will tell you nothing to-day."

"Promise me on your honour that you will say Yes to-morrow; and I will leave you in peace until then."

"I will not."

"The deuce take your sex," he said plaintively. "You know my mind now; and I have to stand here coquetting because you dont know your own. If I cared for my comfort I should remain a bachelor."

"I advise you to do so," she said, stealing backward towards the door. "You are a very interesting widower. A wife would spoil you. Consider the troubles of domesticity, too."

"I like troubles. They strengthen — Aha!" (she had snatched at the knob of the door; and he swiftly put his hand on hers and stayed her). "Not yet, if you please. Can you not speak out like a woman — like a man, I mean? You may withhold a bone from Max until he stands on his hind legs to beg for it; but you should not treat me like a dog. Say Yes frankly, and do not keep me begging."

"What in the world do you want to marry me for?"

"Because I was made to carry a house on my shoulders, and will do so. I want to do the best I can for myself; and I shall never have such a chance again. And I cannot help myself, and dont know why: that is the plain truth of the matter. You will marry someone some-day." She shook her head. "Yes, you will. Why not marry me?"

Agatha bit her nether lip; looked ruefully at the ground; and, after a long pause, said reluctantly, "Very well. But mind, I think you are acting very foolishly; and if you are disappointed afterwards, you must not blame *me*."

"I take the risk of my bargain," he said, releasing her hand, and leaning against the door as he took out his pocket diary. "You will have to take the risk of yours, which I hope may not prove the worse of the two. This is the seventeenth of June. What date before the twenty-fourth of July will suit you?"

"You mean the twenty-fourth of July next year, I presume."

"No: I mean this year. I am going abroad on that date, married or not, to attend a conference at Geneva; and I want you to come with me. I will show you a lot of places and things that you have never seen before. It is your right to name the day; but you have no serious business to provide for; and I have."

"But you dont know all the things I shall — I should have to provide. You had better wait until you come back from the continent."

"There is nothing to be provided on your part but settlements and your trousseau. The trousseau is all nonsense; and Jansenius knows me of old in the matter of settlements. I got married in six weeks before."

"Yes," said Agatha sharply; "but I am not Henrietta."

"No, thank Heaven," he assented placidly.

Agatha was struck with remorse. "That was a vile thing for me to say," she said; "and for you too."

"Whatever is true is to the purpose, vile or not. Will you come to Geneva on the twenty-fourth?"

"But —— I really was not thinking when I —— I did not intend to say that I would —— I —— "

"I know. You will come if we are married."

"Yes. *If* we are married."

"We shall be married. Do not write either to your mother or Jansenius until I ask you."

"I dont intend to. I have nothing to write about."

"Wretch that you are! And do not be jealous if you catch me making love to Lady Brandon. I always do so: she expects it."

"You may make love to whom you please. It is no concern of mine."

"Here comes the waggonette with Lady Brandon and Ger —— and Miss Lindsay. I mustnt call her Gertrude now except when you are not by. Before they interrupt us, let me remind you of the three points we are agreed upon. I love you. You do not love me. We are to be married before the twenty-fourth of next month. Now I must fly to help her ladyship to alight."

He hastened to the house door, at which the waggonette had just stopped. Agatha, bewildered, and ashamed to face her friends, went in through the conservatory, and locked herself into her room.

Trefusis went into the library with Gertrude whilst Lady Brandon loitered in the hall to take off her gloves and ask questions of the servants. When she followed, she found the two standing together at the window. Gertrude was listening to him with the patient expression she now often wore when he talked. He was smiling; but it struck Jane that he was not quite at ease.

"I was just beginning to tell Miss Lindsay," he said, "of an extraordinary thing that has happened during your absence."

"I know," exclaimed Jane, with sudden conviction. "The heater in the conservatory has cracked."

"Possibly," said Trefusis; "but, if so, I have not heard of it."

"If it hasnt cracked, it will," said Jane gloomily. Then, assuming with some effort an interest in Trefusis's news, she added, "Well: what has happened?"

"I was chatting with Miss Wylie just now, when a singular idea occurred to us. We discussed it for some time; and the upshot is that we are to be married before the end of next month."

Jane reddened and stared at him; and he looked keenly back at her. Gertrude, though unobserved, did not suffer her expression of patient happiness to change in the least; but a greenish white colour suddenly appeared in her face, and only gave place very slowly to her usual complexion.

"Do you mean to say that you are going to marry *Agatha?*" said Lady Brandon incredulously, after a pause.

"Yes. I had no intention of doing so when I last saw you, or I should have told you."

"I never heard of such a thing in my life! You fell in love with one another in five minutes, I suppose."

"Good Heavens, no! we are not in love with one another. Can you believe that I would marry for such a frivolous reason? No. The subject turned up accidentally; and the advantages of a match between us struck me forcibly. I was fortunate enough to convert her to my opinion."

"Yes: she wanted a lot of pressing, I dare say," said Jane, glancing at Gertrude, who was smiling unmeaningly.

"As you imply," said Trefusis coolly, "her reluctance may have been affected, and she only too glad to get such a charming husband. Assuming that to be the case, she dissembled remarkably well."

Gertrude took off her bonnet, and left the room without speaking.

"This is my revenge upon you for marrying Brandon," he said then, approaching Jane.

"Oh yes," she retorted ironically. "I believe all that, of course."

"You have the same security for its truth as for that of all the foolish things I confess to you. There!" He pointed to a panel of looking glass, in which Jane's figure was reflected at full length.

"I dont see anything to admire," said Jane, looking at herself with no great favour. "There is plenty of me, if you admire that."

"It is impossible to have too much of a good thing. But I must not look any more. Though Agatha says she does not love me, I am not sure that she would be pleased if I were to look for love from anyone else."

"Says she does not love you! Dont believe her: she has taken trouble enough to catch you."

"I am flattered. You caught me without any trouble; and yet you would not have me."

"It is manners to wait to be asked. I think you have treated Gertrude shamefully — I hope you wont be offended with me for saying so. I blame Agatha most. She is an awfully double-faced girl."

"How so?" said Trefusis, surprised. "What has Miss Lindsay to do with it?"

"You know very well."

"I assure you I do not. If you were speaking of yourself, I could understand you."

"Oh, you can get out of it very cleverly, like all men; but you cant hoodwink me. You shouldnt have pretended to like Gertrude when you were really pulling a cord with Agatha. And she, too, pretending to flirt with Sir Charles — as if he would care twopence for her!"

Trefusis seemed a little disturbed. "I hope Miss Lindsay had no such — but she could not."

"Oh, couldnt she? You will soon see whether she had or not."

"You misunderstood us, Lady Brandon: Miss Lindsay knows better. Remember, too, that this proposal of mine was quite unpremeditated. This morning I had no tender thoughts of anyone — except one whom it would be improper to name."

"Oh, that is all talk. It wont do *now*."

"I will talk no more at present: I must be off to the village to telegraph to my solicitor. If I meet Erskine, I will tell him the good news."

"He will be delighted. He thought, as we all did, that you were cutting him out with Gertrude."

Trefusis smiled; shook his head; and, with a glance of admiring homage to Jane's charms, went out. Jane was contemplating herself in the glass when a servant begged her to come and speak to Master Charles and Miss Fanny. She hurried upstairs to the nursery, where her boy and girl, disputing each other's prior right to torture the baby, had come to blows. They were somewhat frightened, but not at all appeased, by Jane's entrance. She scolded, coaxed, threatened, bribed, quoted Dr. Watts, appealed to the nurse and then insulted her, demanded of the children whether they loved one another, whether they loved mamma, and whether they wanted a right good whipping. At last, exasperated by her own inability to restore order, she seized the baby, which had cried incessantly throughout; and, declaring that it was doing it on purpose and should have something real to cry for, gave it an exemplary smacking, and ordered the others to bed. The boy, awed by the fate of his infant brother, offered, by way of compromise, to be good if Miss Wylie would come and play with him: a proposal which provoked from his jealous mother a box on the ear that sent him howling to his cot. Then she left the room, pausing on the threshold to remark that if she heard another sound from them that day, they might expect the worst from her. On descending, heated and angry, to the drawing-room, she found Agatha there alone, looking out of window as if the landscape were especially unsatisfactory this time.

"Selfish little beasts!" exclaimed Jane, making a miniature whirlwind with her skirts as she came in. "Charlie is a perfect little fiend. He spends all his time thinking how he can annoy me. Ugh! He's just like his father."

"Thank you, my dear," said Sir Charles, from the doorway.

Jane laughed. "I knew you were there," she said. "Where's Gertrude?"

"She has gone out," said Sir Charles.

"Nonsense! She has only just come in from driving with me."

"I do not know what you mean by nonsense," said Sir Charles, chafing. "I saw her walking along the Riverside Road. I was in the village road; and she did not see me. She seemed in a hurry."

"I met her on the stairs, and spoke to her," said Agatha; "but she didnt hear me."

"I hope she is not going to throw herself into the river," said Jane. Then, turning to her husband, she added, "Have you heard the news?"

"The only news I have heard is from this paper," said Sir Charles, taking out a journal, and flinging it on the table. "There is a paragraph in it stating that I have joined some infernal Socialistic league; and I am told that there is an article in the *Times* on the spread of Socialism, in which my name is mentioned. This is all due to Trefusis; and I think he has played me a most dishonourable trick. I will tell him so, too, when next I see him."

"You had better be careful what you say of him before Agatha," said Jane. "Oh, you need not be alarmed, Agatha: I know all about it. He told us in the library. We went out this morning — Gertrude and I; and when we came back we found Mr. Trefusis and Agatha talking very lovingly to one another on the conservatory steps, newly engaged."

"Indeed!" said Sir Charles, disconcerted and displeased, but trying to smile. "I may then congratulate you, Miss Wylie?"

"You need not," said Agatha, keeping her countenance as well as she could. "It was only a joke. At least it came about quite in jest. He has no right to say that we are engaged."

"Stuff and nonsense," said Jane. "That wont do, Agatha. He has gone off to telegraph to his solicitor. He is quite in earnest."

"I am a great fool," said Agatha, sitting down and twisting her hands perplexedly. "I believe I said something; but I really did not intend to. He surprised me into speaking before I knew what I was saying. A pretty mess I have got myself into!"

"I am glad you have been outwitted at last," said Jane, laughing spitefully. "You never had any pity for me when I could not think of the proper thing to say at a moment's notice."

Agatha let the taunt pass unheeded. Her gaze wandered anxiously, and at last settled appealingly upon Sir Charles. "What shall I do?" she said to him.

"Well, Miss Wylie," he said gravely: "if you did not mean to marry him, you should not have promised. I dont wish to be unsympathetic; and I know that it is very hard to get rid of Trefusis when he makes up his mind to get something out of you; but still —— "

"Never mind her," said Jane, interrupting him. "She wants to marry him just as badly as he wants to marry her. You would be preciously disappointed if he cried off, Agatha; for all your interesting reluctance."

"That is not so, really," said Agatha, earnestly. "I wish I had taken time to think about it. I suppose he has told everybody by this time."

"May we then regard it as settled?" said Sir Charles.

"Of course you may," said Jane contemptuously.

"Pray allow Miss Wylie to speak for herself, Jane. I confess I do not understand why you are still in doubt — if you have really engaged yourself to him."

"I suppose I am in for it," said Agatha. "I feel as if there were some fatal objection, if I could only remember what it is. I wish I had never seen him."

Sir Charles was puzzled. "I do not understand ladies' ways in these matters," he said. "However, as there seems to be no doubt that you and Trefusis are engaged, I shall of course say nothing that would make it unpleasant for him to visit here; but I must say that he has — to say the least — been inconsiderate to me personally. I signed a paper at his house on the implicit understanding that it was strictly private; and now he has trumpeted it forth to the whole world, and publicly associated my name not only with his own, but with those of persons of whom I know nothing except that I would rather not be connected with them in any way."

"What does it matter?" said Jane. "Nobody cares twopence."

"*I* care," said Sir Charles angrily. "No sensible person can accuse me of exaggerating my own importance because I value my reputation sufficiently to object to my approval being publicly cited in support of a cause with which I have no sympathy."

"Perhaps Mr. Trefusis has had nothing to do with it," said Agatha. "The papers publish whatever they please, dont they?"

"That's right, Agatha," said Jane maliciously. "Dont let anyone speak ill of him."

"I am not speaking ill of him," said Sir Charles, before Agatha could retort. "It is a mere matter of feeling; and I should not have mentioned it had I known the altered relations between him and Miss Wylie."

"Pray dont speak of them," said Agatha. "I have a mind to run away by the next train."

Sir Charles, to change the subject, suggested a duet.

Meanwhile, Erskine, returning through the village from his morning ride, had met Trefusis, and attempted to pass him with a nod. But Trefusis called to him to stop; and he dismounted reluctantly.

"Just a word to say that I am going to be married," said Trefusis.

"To —— ?" Erskine could not add Gertrude's name.

"To one of our friends at the Beeches. Guess to which."

"To Miss Lindsay, I presume."

"What in the fiend's name has put it into all your heads that Miss Lindsay and I are particularly attached to one another?" exclaimed Trefusis. *"You* have always appeared to me to be the man for Miss Lindsay. I am going to marry Miss Wylie."

"Really!" exclaimed Erskine, with a sensation of suddenly thawing after a bitter frost.

"Of course. And now, Erskine, you have the advantage of being a poor man. Do not let that splendid girl marry for money. If you go further you are likely to fare worse; and so is she." Then he nodded and walked away, leaving the other staring after him.

"If he has jilted her, he is a scoundrel," said Erskine. "I am sorry I didnt tell him so."

He mounted, and rode slowly along the Riverside Road, partly suspecting Trefusis of some mystification, but inclining to believe in him, and, in any case, to take his advice as to Gertrude. The conversation he had overheard in the avenue still perplexed him. He could not reconcile it with Trefusis's profession of disinterestedness towards her.

His bicycle carried him noiselessly on its indiarubber tires to the place by which the hemlock grew; and there he saw Gertrude sitting on the low earthen wall that separated the field from the road. Her straw bag, with her scissors in it, lay beside her. Her fingers were interlaced; and her hands rested, palms downwards, on her knee. Her expression was rather vacant, and so little suggestive of any serious emotion that Erskine laughed as he alighted close to her.

"Are you tired?" he said.

"No," she replied, not startled, and smiling mechanically — an unusual condescension on her part.

"Indulging in a day-dream?"

"No." She moved a little to one side, and concealed the basket with her dress.

He began to fear that something was wrong. "Is it possible that you have ventured among those poisonous plants again?" he said. "Are you ill?"

"Not at all," she replied, rousing herself a little. "Your solicitude is quite thrown away. I am perfectly well."

"I beg your pardon," he said, snubbed. "I thought —— Dont you think it dangerous to sit on that damp wall?"

"It is not damp. It is crumbling into dust with dryness." An unnatural laugh, with which she concluded, intensified his uneasiness.

He began a sentence; stopped; and, to gain time to recover himself, placed his velocipede in the opposite ditch: a proceeding which she witnessed with impatience, as it indicated his intention to stay and talk. She, however, was the first to speak; and she did so with a callousness that shocked him.

"Have you heard the news?"

"What news?"

"About Mr. Trefusis and Agatha. They are engaged."

"So Trefusis told me. I met him just now in the village. I was very glad to hear it."

"Of course."

"But I had a special reason for being glad."

"Indeed?"

"I was desperately afraid, before he told me the truth, that he had other views — views that might have proved fatal to my dearest hopes."

Gertrude frowned at him; and the frown roused him to brave her. He lost his self-command, already shaken by her strange behaviour. "You know that I love you, Miss Lindsay," he said. "It may not be a perfect love; but, humanly speaking, it is a true one. I almost told you so that day when we were in the billiard room together; and I did a very dishonourable thing the same evening. When you were speaking to Trefusis in the avenue, I was close to you; and I listened."

"Then you heard him," cried Gertrude vehemently. "You heard him swear that he was in earnest."

"Yes," said Erskine, trembling; "and I thought he meant in earnest in loving you. You can hardly blame me for that: I was in love myself; and love is blind and jealous. I never hoped again until he told me that he was to be married to Miss Wylie. May I speak to you, now that I know I was mistaken, or that you have changed your mind?"

"Or that *he* has changed his mind," said Gertrude scornfully.

Erskine, with a new anxiety for her sake, checked himself. Her dignity was dear to him; and he saw that her disappointment had made her reckless of it. "Do not say anything to me now, Miss Lindsay, lest —— "

"What have I said? What have I to say?"

"Nothing, except on my own affairs. I love you dearly."

She made an impatient movement, as if that were a very insignificant matter.

"You believe me, I hope," he said, timidly.

Gertrude made an effort to recover her habitual ladylike reserve; but her energy failed before she had done more than raise her head. She relapsed into her listless attitude, and made a faint gesture of intolerance.

"You cannot be quite indifferent to being loved," he said, becoming more nervous and more urgent. "Your existence constitutes all my happiness. I offer you my services and devotion. I do not ask any reward." (He was now speaking very quickly and almost inaudibly.) "You may accept my love without returning it. I do not want — seek to make a bargain. If you need a friend, you may be able to rely on me more confidently because you know I love you."

"Oh, you think so," said Gertrude, interrupting him; "but you will get over it. I am not the sort of person that men fall in love with. You will soon change your mind."

"Not the sort! Oh, how little you know!" he said, becoming eloquent. "I have had plenty of time to change; but I am as fixed as ever. If you doubt, wait and try me. But do not be rough with me. You pain me more than you can imagine, when you are hasty or indifferent. I am in earnest."

"Ha, ha! That is easily said."

"Not by me. I change in my judgment of other people according to my humour; but I believe steadfastly in your goodness and beauty — as if you were an angel. I am in earnest in my love for you as I am in earnest for my own life, which can only be perfected by your aid and influence."

"You are greatly mistaken if you suppose that I am an angel."

"You are wrong to mistrust yourself; but it is what I owe to you and not what I expect from you that I try to express by speaking of you as an angel. I know that you are not an angel to yourself. But you are to me."

She sat stubbornly silent.

"I will not press you for an answer now. I am content that you know my mind at last. Shall we return together?"

She looked round slowly at the hemlock, and from that to the river. Then she took up her basket; rose; and prepared to go, as if under compulsion.

"Do you want any more hemlock?" he said. "If so, I will pluck some for you."

"I wish you would let me alone," she said, with sudden anger. She added, a little ashamed of herself, "I have a headache."

"I am very sorry," he said, crestfallen.

"It is only that I do not wish to be spoken to. It hurts my head to listen."

He meekly took his bicycle from the ditch, and wheeled it along beside her to the Beeches without another word. They went in through the conservatory, and parted in the dining-room. Before leaving him she said, with some remorse, "I did not mean to be rude, Mr. Erskine."

He flushed; murmured something; and attempted to kiss her hand.

But she snatched it away and went out quickly. He was stung by this repulse, and stood mortifying himself by thinking of it until he was disturbed by the entrance of a maid-servant. Learning from her that Sir Charles was in the billiard-room, he joined him there, and asked him carelessly if he had heard the news.

"About Miss Wylie?" said Sir Charles. "Yes, I should think so. I believe the whole country knows it, though they have not been engaged three hours. Have you seen these?" And he pushed a couple of newspapers across the table.

Erskine had to make several efforts before he could read. "You were a fool to sign that document," he said. "I told you so at the time."

"I relied on the fellow being a gentleman," said Sir Charles warmly. "I do not see that I was a fool. I see that he is a cad; and but for this business of Miss Wylie's I would let him know my opinion. Let me tell you, Chester, that he has played fast and loose with Miss Lindsay. There is a deuce of a row upstairs. She has just told Jane that she must go home at once; Miss Wylie declares that she will have nothing to do with Trefusis if Miss Lindsay has a prior claim to him; and Jane is annoyed at his admiring anybody except herself. It serves me right: my instinct warned me against the fellow from the first."

Just then luncheon was announced. Gertrude did not come down. Agatha was silent and moody. Jane tried to make Erskine describe his walk with Gertrude; but he baffled her curiosity by omitting from his account everything except its commonplaces.

"I think her conduct very strange," said Jane. "She insists on going to town by the four o'clock train. I consider that it's not polite to me, although she always made a point of her perfect manners. I never heard of such a thing!"

When they had risen from table, they went together to the drawing-room. They had hardly arrived there when Trefusis was announced; and he was in their presence before they had time to conceal the expression of consternation his name brought into their faces.

"I have come to say good-bye," he said. "I find that I must go to town by the four o'clock train to push my arrangements in person: the telegrams I have received breathe nothing but delay. Have you seen the *Times?*"

"I have indeed," said Sir Charles, emphatically.

"You are in some other paper too, and will be in half-a-dozen more in the course of the next fortnight. Men who have committed themselves to an opinion are always in trouble with the newspapers: some because they cannot get into them: others because they cannot keep out. If you had put forward a thundering revolutionary manifesto, not a daily paper would have dared allude to it: there is no cowardice like Fleet Street cowardice! I must run off: I have much to do before I start; and it is getting on for three. Good-bye, Lady Brandon, and everybody."

He shook Jane's hand; dealt nods to the rest rapidly, making no distinction in favour of Agatha; and hurried away. They stared after him for a moment; and then Erskine ran out and went downstairs two steps at a time. Nevertheless he had to run as far as the avenue before he overtook his man.

"Trefusis," he said breathlessly: "you must not go by the four o'clock train."

"Why not?"

"Miss Lindsay is going to town by it."

"So much the better, my dear boy; so much the better. You are not jealous of me now, are you?"

"Look here, Trefusis. I dont know and I dont ask what there has been between you and Miss Lindsay; but your engagement has quite upset her; and she is running away to London in consequence. If she hears that you are going by the same train, she will wait until to-morrow; and I believe the delay would be very disagreeable. Will you inflict that additional pain upon her?"

Trefusis, evidently concerned, looking doubtfully at Erskine, and pondered for a moment. "I think you are on a wrong scent about this," he said. "My relations with Miss Lindsay were not of a senti- mental kind. Have you said anything to her? — on your own ac- count, I mean."

"I have spoken to her on both accounts; and I know from her own lips that I am right."

Trefusis uttered a low whistle.

"It is not the first time I have had the evidence of my senses in the matter," said Erskine significantly. "Pray think of it seriously, Trefusis. Forgive my telling you frankly that nothing but your own utter want of feeling could excuse you for the way in which you have acted towards her."

Trefusis smiled. "Forgive me in turn for my inquisitiveness," he said. "What does she say to your suit?"

Erskine hesitated, shewing by his manner that he thought Trefusis had no right to ask the question. "She says nothing," he answered.

"Hm!" said Trefusis. "Well, you may rely on me as to the train. There is my hand upon it."

"Thank you," said Erskine fervently. They shook hands and parted: Trefusis walking away with a grin suggestive of anything but good faith.

CHAPTER XVII.

Gertrude, unaware of the extent to which she had already betrayed her disappointment, believed that anxiety for her father's health, which she alleged as the motive of her sudden departure, was an excuse plausible enough to blind her friends to her overpowering reluctance to speak to Agatha or endure her presence; to her fierce shrinking from the sort of pity usually accorded to a jilted woman; and, above all, to her dread of meeting Trefusis. She had for some time past thought of him as an upright and perfect man deeply interested in her. Yet, comparatively liberal as her education had been, she had no idea of any interest of man in woman existing apart from a desire to marry. He had, in his serious moments, striven to make her sensible of the baseness he saw in her worldliness, flattering her by his apparent conviction — which she shared — that she was capable of a higher life. Almost in the same breath, a strain of gallantry which was incorrigible in him, and to which his humour and his tenderness to women whom he liked gave variety and charm, would supervene upon his seriousness with a rapidity which her far less flexible temperament could not follow. Hence she, thinking him still in earnest when he had swerved into florid romance, had been dangerously misled. He had no conscientious scruples in his love-making, because he was unaccustomed to consider himself as likely to inspire love in women; and Gertrude did not know that her beauty gave to an hour spent alone with her a transient charm which few men of imagination and address could resist. She, who had lived in the marriage market since she had left school, looked upon love-making as the most serious business of life. To him it was only a pleasant sort of trifling, enhanced by a dash of sadness in the reflection that it meant so little.

Of the ceremonies attending her departure, the one that cost her most was the kiss she felt bound to offer Agatha. She had been jealous of her at college, where she had esteemed herself the better bred of the two; but that opinion had hardly consoled her for Agatha's superior quickness of wit, dexterity of hand, audacity, aptness of resource, capacity for forming or following intricate associations of ideas, and consequent power to dazzle others. Her jealousy of these qualities was now barbed by the knowledge that they were much nearer akin than her own to those of Trefusis. It mattered little to her how she appeared to herself in comparison with Agatha. But it mattered the whole world (she thought) that she must appear to Trefusis so slow, stiff, cold, and studied, and that she had no means to make him understand that she was not really so. For she would not admit the justice of impressions made by what she did not intend to do, however habitually she did it. She had a theory that she was not herself, but what she would have liked to be. As to the one quality in which she had always felt superior to Agatha, and which she called "good breeding," Trefusis had so far destroyed her conceit in that, that she was beginning to doubt whether it was not her cardinal defect.

She could not bring herself to utter a word as she embraced her schoolfellow; and Agatha was tongue-tied too. But there was much remorseful tenderness in the feelings that choked them. Their silence would have been awkward but for the loquacity of Jane, who talked enough for all three. Sir Charles was without, in the trap, waiting to drive Gertrude to the station. Erskine intercepted her in the hall as she passed out; told her that he should be desolate when she was gone; and begged her to remember him: a simple petition which moved her a little, and caused her to note that his dark eyes had a pleading eloquence which she had observed before in the kangaroos at the Zoological Society's gardens.

On the way to the train, Sir Charles worried the horse in order to be excused from conversation on the sore subject of his guest's sudden departure. He made a few remarks on the skittishness of young ponies, and on the weather; and that was all until they reached the station, a pretty building standing in the open country, with a view of the river from the platform. There were two flies waiting, two porters, a bookstall, and a refreshment room with a neglected beauty pining behind the bar. Sir Charles waited in the booking office to purchase a ticket for Gertrude, who went through to the platform. The first person she saw there was Trefusis, close beside her.

"I am going to town by this train, Gertrude," he said quickly. "Let me take charge of you. I have something to say; for I hear that some mischief has been made between us which must be stopped at once. You —— "

Just then Sir Charles came out, and stood amazed to see them in conversation.

"It happens that I am going by this train," said Trefusis. "I will see after Miss Lindsay."

"Miss Lindsay has her maid with her," said Sir Charles, almost stammering, and looking at Gertrude, whose expression was inscrutable.

"We can get into the Pullman car," said Trefusis. "There we shall be as private as in a corner of a crowded drawing-room. I may travel with you, may I not?" he said, seeing Sir Charles's disturbed look, and turning to her for express permission.

She felt that to deny him would be to throw away her last chance of happiness. Nevertheless she resolved to do it, though she should die of grief on the way to London. As she raised her head to forbid him the more emphatically, she met his gaze, which was grave and expectant. For an instant she lost her presence of mind, and in that instant said, "Yes. I shall be very glad."

"Well, if that is the case," said Sir Charles, in the tone of one whose sympathy had been alienated by an unpardonable outrage, "there can be no use in my waiting. I leave you in the hands of Mr. Trefusis. Good-bye, Miss Lindsay."

Gertrude winced. Unkindness from a man usually kind proved hard to bear at parting. She was offering him her hand in silence when Trefusis said,

"Wait and see us off. If we chance to be killed on the journey — which is always probable on an English railway — you will reproach yourself afterwards if you do not see the last of us. Here is the train: it will not delay you a minute. Tell Erskine that you saw me here; that I have not forgotten my promise; and that he may rely on me. Get in at this end, Miss Lindsay."

"My maid," said Gertrude hesitating; for she had not intended to travel so expensively. "She —— "

"She comes with us to take care of me: I have tickets for everybody," said Trefusis, handing the woman in.

"But —— "

"Take your seats, please," said the guard. "Going by the train, sir?"

"Good-bye, Sir Charles. Give my love to Lady Brandon, and Agatha, and the dear children; and thanks so much for a very pleasant —— " Here the train moved off; and Sir Charles, melting, smiled and waved his hat until he caught sight of Trefusis looking back at him with a grin which seemed, under the circumstances, so Satanic, that he stopped as if petrified in the midst of his gesticulations, and stood with his arm out like a semaphore.

The drive home restored him somewhat; but he was still full of his surprise when he rejoined Agatha, his wife, and Erskine, in the drawing-room at the Beeches. The moment he entered, he said without preface, "She has gone off with Trefusis."

Erskine, who had been reading, started up, clutching his book as if about to hurl it at some one; and cried, "Was he at the train?"

"Yes, and has gone to town by it."

"Then," said Erskine, flinging the book violently on the floor, "he is a scoundrel and a liar."

"What is the matter?" said Agatha rising, whilst Jane stared open-mouthed at him.

"I beg your pardon, Miss Wylie: I forgot you. He pledged me his honour that he would not go by that train. I will —— " He hurried from the room. Sir Charles rushed after him, and overtook him at the foot of the stairs.

"Where are you going? What do you want to do?"

"I will follow the train and catch it at the next station. I can do it on my bicycle."

"Nonsense! you're mad. They have thirty-five minutes start; and the train travels forty-five miles an hour."

Erskine sat down on the stairs, and gazed blankly at the opposite wall.

"You must have mistaken him," said Sir Charles. "He told me to tell you that he had not forgotten his promise, and that you may rely on him."

"What *is* the matter?" said Agatha, coming down, followed by Lady Brandon.

"Miss Wylie," said Erskine, springing up: "he gave me his word that he would not go by that train when I told him Miss Lindsay was going by it. He has broken his word and seized the opportunity I was mad and credulous enough to tell him of. If I had been in your place, Brandon, I would have strangled him or thrown him under the wheels sooner than let him go. He has shewn himself in this as in everything else, a cheat, a conspirator, a man of crooked ways, shifts, tricks, lying sophistries, heartless selfishness, cruel cynicism —— " He stopped to catch his breath; and Sir Charles interposed a remonstrance.

"You are exciting yourself about nothing, Chester. They are in a Pullman, with her maid and plenty of people; and she expressly gave him leave to go with her. He asked her the question flatly before my face; and I must say I thought it a strange thing for her to consent to. However, she did consent; and of course I was not in a position to prevent him from going to London if he pleased. Dont let us have a scene, old man. It cant be helped."

"I am very sorry," said Erskine, hanging his head. "I did not mean to make a scene. I beg your pardon."

He went away to his room without another word. Sir Charles followed and attempted to console him; but Erskine caught his hand, and asked to be left to himself. So Sir Charles returned to the drawing-room, where his wife, at a loss for once, hardly ventured to remark that she had never heard of such a thing in her life.

Agatha kept silence. She had long ago come unconsciously to the conclusion that Trefusis and she were the only members of the party at the Beeches who had much common sense; and this made her slow to believe that he could be in the wrong and Erskine in the right in any misunderstanding between them. She had a slovenly way of summing up as "asses" people whose habits of thought differed from hers. Of all varieties of man, the minor poet realized her conception of the human ass most completely; and Erskine, though a very nice fellow indeed, thoroughly good and gentlemanly, in her opinion, was yet a minor poet, and therefore a pronounced ass. Trefusis, on the contrary, was the last man of her acquaintance whom she would have thought of as a very nice fellow or a virtuous gentleman; but he was not an ass, although he was obstinate in his socialistic fads. She had indeed suspected him of weakness almost asinine with respect to Gertrude; but then all men were asses in their dealings with women; and since he had transferred his weakness to her own account it no longer seemed to need justification. And now, as her concern for Erskine, whom she pitied, wore off, she began to resent Trefusis's journey with Gertrude as an attack on her recently acquired monopoly of him. There was an air of aristocratic pride about Gertrude which Agatha had formerly envied, and which she still feared Trefusis might mistake for an index of dignity and refinement. Agatha did not believe that her resentment was the common feeling called jealousy; for she still deemed herself unique; but it gave her a sense of meanness that did not improve her spirits.

The dinner was dull. Lady Brandon spoke in an undertone, as if someone lay dead in the next room. Erskine was depressed by the consciousness of having lost his head and acted foolishly in the afternoon. Sir Charles did not pretend to ignore the suspense they were all in pending intelligence of the journey to London: he ate and drank and said nothing. Agatha, disgusted with herself and with Gertrude, and undecided whether to be disgusted with Trefusis or to trust him affectionately, followed the example of her host. After dinner she accompanied him in a series of songs by Schubert. This proved an aggravation instead of a relief. Sir Charles, excelling in the expression of melancholy, preferred songs of that character; and as his musical ideas, like those of most Englishmen, were founded on what he had heard in church in his childhood, his style was oppressively monotonous. Agatha took the first excuse that presented itself to leave the piano. Sir Charles felt that his performance had been a failure, and remarked, after a cough or two, that he had caught a touch of cold returning from the station. Erskine sat on a sofa with his head drooping, and his palms joined and hanging downward between his knees. Agatha stood at the window, looking at the late summer afterglow. Jane yawned, and presently broke the silence.

"You look exactly as you used at school, Agatha. I could almost fancy us back again in number six."

Agatha shook her head.

"Do I ever look like that? — like myself, as I used to be."

"Never," said Agatha emphatically, turning and surveying the figure of which Miss Carpenter had been the unripe antecedent.

"But why?" said Jane querulously. "I dont see why I shouldnt. I am not so changed."

"You have become an exceedingly fine woman, Jane," said Agatha gravely, and then, without knowing why, turned her attentive gaze upon Sir Charles, who bore it uneasily, and left the room. A minute later he returned with two buff envelopes in his hand.

"A telegram for you, Miss Wylie; and one for Chester." Erskine started up, white with vague fears. Agatha's colour went, and came again with increased richness as she read,

I have arrived safe and ridiculously happy. Read a thousand things between the lines. I will write tomorrow. Good night.

"You may read it," said Agatha, handing it to Jane.

"Very pretty," said Jane. "A shillingsworth of attention — exactly twenty words! He may well call himself an economist."

Suddenly a crowing laugh from Erskine caused them to turn and stare at him. "What nonsense!" he said, blushing. "What a fellow he is! I dont attach the slightest importance to this."

Agatha took a corner of his telegram and pulled it gently.

"No, no," he said, holding it tightly. "It is too absurd. I dont think I ought —— "

Agatha gave a decisive pull, and read the message aloud. It was from Trefusis, thus,

I forgive your thoughts since Brandon's return. Write to her to-night; and follow your letter to receive an affirmative answer in person. I promised that you might rely on me. She loves you.

"I never heard of such a thing in my life," said Jane. "Never!"

"He is certainly a most unaccountable man," said Sir Charles.

"I am glad, for my own sake, that he is not so black as he is painted," said Agatha. "You may believe every word of it, Mr. Erskine. Be sure to do as he tells you. He is quite certain to be right."

"Pooh!" said Erskine, crumpling the telegram and thrusting it into his pocket as if it were not worth a second thought. Presently he slipped away, and did not reappear. When they were about to retire, Sir Charles asked a servant where he was.

"In the library, Sir Charles; writing."

They looked significantly at one another, and went to bed without disturbing him.

CHAPTER XVIII.

When Gertrude found herself beside Trefusis in the Pullman, she wondered how she came to be travelling with him against her resolution, if not against her will. In the presence of two women scrutinizing her as if they suspected her of being there with no good purpose, a male passenger admiring her a little further off, her maid reading Trefusis's newspapers just out of earshot, an uninterested country gentleman looking glumly out of window, a city man preoccupied with the *Economist,* and a polite lady who refrained from staring but not from observing, she felt that she must not make a scene: yet she knew he had not come there to hold an ordinary conversation. Her doubt did not last long. He began promptly, and went to the point at once.

"What do you think of this engagement of mine?"

This was more than she could bear calmly. "What is it to me?" she said indignantly. "I have nothing to do with it."

"Nothing! You are a cold friend to me then. I thought you one of the surest I possessed."

She moved as if about to look at him, but checked herself; closed her lips; and fixed her eyes on the vacant seat before her. The reproach he deserved was beyond her power of expression.

"I cling to that conviction still, in spite of Miss Lindsay's indifference to my affairs. But I confess I hardly know how to bring you into sympathy with me in this matter. In the first place, you have never been married: I have. In the next, you are much younger than I, in more respects than that of years. Very likely half your ideas on the subject are derived from fictions in which happy results are tacked on to conditions very ill-calculated to produce them — which in real life hardly ever do produce them. If our friendship were a chapter in a novel, what would be the upshot of it? Why, I should marry you; or you break your heart at my treachery."

Gertrude moved her eyes as if she had some intention of taking to flight.

"But our relations being those of real life — far sweeter, after all — I never dream of marrying you, having gained and enjoyed your friendship without that eye to business which our nineteenth century keeps open even whilst it sleeps. You, being equally disinterested in your regard for me, do not think of breaking your heart; but you are, I suppose, a little hurt at my apparently meditating and resolving on such a serious step as marriage with Agatha without confiding my intention to you. And you punish me by telling me that you have nothing to do with it — that it is nothing to you. But I never meditated the step, and so had nothing to conceal from you. It was conceived and executed in less than a minute. Although my first marriage was a silly love match and a failure, I have always admitted to myself that I should marry again. A bachelor is a man who shirks responsibilities and duties: I seek them, and consider it my duty, with my monstrous superfluity of means, not to let the individualists outbreed me. Still, I was in no hurry, having other things to occupy me, and being fond of my bachelor freedom, and doubtful sometimes whether I had any right to bring more idlers into the world for the workers to feed. Then came the usual difficulty about the lady. I did not want a helpmeet: I can help myself. Nor did I expect to be loved devotedly; for the race has not yet evolved a man lovable on thorough acquaintance: even my self-love is neither thorough nor constant. I wanted a genial partner for domestic business; and Agatha struck me quite suddenly as being the nearest approach to what I desired that I was likely to find in the marriage market, where it is extremely hard to suit oneself, and where the likeliest bargains are apt to be snapped up by others if one hesitates too long in the hope of finding something better. I admire Agatha's courage and capability, and believe I shall be able to make her like me, and that the attachment so begun may turn into as close a union as is either healthy or necessary between two separate individuals. I may mistake her character; for I do not know her as I know you, and have scarcely enough faith in her as yet to tell her such things as I have told you. Still, there is a consoling dash of romance in the transaction. Agatha has charm. Do you not think so?"

Gertrude's emotion was gone. She replied with cool scorn, "Very romantic indeed. She is very fortunate."

Trefusis half laughed, half sighed with relief to find her so self-possessed. "It sounds like — and indeed is — the selfish calculation of a disilluded widower. You would not value such an offer, or envy the recipient of it?"

"No," said Gertrude with quiet contempt.

"Yet there is some calculation behind every such offer. We marry to satisfy our needs; and the more reasonable our needs are, the more likely are we to get them satisfied. I see you are disgusted with me: I feared as much. You are the sort of woman to admit no excuse for my marriage except love — pure emotional love, blindfolding reason."

"I really do not concern myself —— "

"Do not say so, Gertrude. I watch every step you take with anxiety; and I do not believe you are indifferent to the worthiness of my conduct. Believe me, love is an overrated passion; it would be irremediably discredited but that young people, and the romancers who live upon their follies, have a perpetual interest in rehabilitating it. No relation involving divided duties and continual intercourse between two people can subsist permanently on love alone. Yet love is not to be despised when it comes from a fine nature. There is a man who loves you exactly as you think I ought to love Agatha — and as I dont love her."

Gertrude's emotion stirred again; and her colour rose. "You have no right to say these things now," she said.

"Why may I not plead the cause of another? I speak of Erskine." Her colour vanished; and he continued, "I want you to marry him. When you are married you will understand me better; and our friendship, shaken just now, will be deepened; for I dare assure you, now that you can no longer misunderstand me, that no living woman is dearer to me than you. So much for the inevitable selfish reason. Erskine is a poor man; and in his comfortable poverty — save the mark — lies your salvation from the baseness of marrying for wealth and position: a baseness of which women of your class stand in constant peril. They court it: you must shun it. The man is honourable and loves you: he is young, healthy, and suitable. What more do you think the world has to offer you?"

"Much more, I hope. Very much more."

"I fear that the names I give things are not romantic enough. He is a poet. Perhaps he would be a hero if it were possible for a man to be a hero in this nineteenth century, which will be infamous in history as a time when the greatest advances in the power of man over nature only served to sharpen his greed and make famine its avowed minister. Erskine is at least neither a gambler nor a slavedriver at first hand: if he lives upon plundered labour, he can no more help himself than I. Do not say that you hope for much more; but tell me, if you can, what more you have any chance of getting. Mind: I do not ask what more you desire: we all desire unutterable things. I ask you what more you can obtain!"

"I have not found Mr. Erskine such a wonderful person as you seem to think him."

"He is only a man. Do you know anybody more wonderful?"

"Besides, my family might not approve."

"They most certainly will not. If you wish to please them, you must sell yourself to some rich vampire of the factories or great landlord. If you give yourself away to a poor poet who loves you, their disgust will be unbounded. If a woman wishes to honour her father and mother to their own satisfaction nowadays, she must dishonour herself."

"I do not understand why you should be so anxious for me to marry someone else?"

"Someone else?" said Trefusis, puzzled.

"I do not mean someone else," said Gertrude hastily, reddening. "Why should I marry at all?"

"Why do any of us marry? Why do I marry? It is a function craving fulfilment. If you do not marry betimes from choice, you will be driven to do so later on by the importunity of your suitors and of your family, and by weariness of the suspense that precedes a definite settlement of oneself. Marry generously. Do not throw yourself away or sell yourself: give yourself away. Erskine has as much at stake as you; and yet he offers himself fearlessly."

Gertrude raised her head proudly.

"It is true," continued Trefusis, observing the gesture with some anger, "that he thinks more highly of you than you deserve; but you, on the other hand, think too lowly of him. When you marry him you must save him from a cruel disenchantment by raising yourself to the level he fancies you have attained. This will cost you an effort; and the effort will do you good, whether it fail or succeed. As for him, he will find his just level in your estimation if your thoughts reach high enough to comprehend him at that level."

Gertrude moved impatiently.

"What!" he said quickly. "Are my long-winded sacrifices to the god of reason distasteful? I believe I am involuntarily making them so because I am jealous of the fellow after all. Nevertheless I am serious: I want you to get married; though I shall always have a secret grudge against the man who marries you. Agatha will suspect me of treason if you dont. Erskine will be a disappointed man if you dont. You will be moody, wretched, and — and unmarried if you dont."

Gertrude's cheeks flushed at the word jealous, and again at his mention of Agatha. "And if I do," she said bitterly: "what then?"

"If you do, Agatha's mind will be at ease; Erskine will be happy; and you! You will have sacrificed yourself, and will have the happiness which follows that when it is worthily done."

"It is you who have sacrificed me," she said, casting away her reticence, and looking at him for the first time during the conversation.

"I know it," he said, leaning towards her and half whispering the words. "Is not renunciation the beginning and the end of wisdom? I have sacrificed you rather than profane our friendship by asking you to share my whole life with me. You are unfit for that; and I have committed myself to another union, and am begging you to follow my example, lest we should tempt one another to a step which would soon prove to you how truly I tell you that you are unfit. I have never allowed you to roam through all the chambers of my consciousness; but I keep a sanctuary there for you alone, and will keep it inviolate for you always. Not even Agatha shall have the key: she must be content with the other rooms — the drawing-room, the working-room, the dining-room, and so forth. They would not suit you: you would not like the furniture or the guests: after a time you would not like the master. Will you be content with the sanctuary?"

Gertrude bit her lip: tears came into her eyes. She looked imploringly at him. Had they been alone, she would have thrown herself into his arms and entreated him to disregard everything except their strong cleaving to one another.

"And will you keep a corner of your heart for me?"

She slowly gave him a painful look of acquiescence.

"Will you be brave, and sacrifice yourself to the poor man who loves you? He will save you from useless solitude, or from a worldly marriage — I cannot bear to think of either as your fate."

"I do not care for Mr. Erskine," she said, hardly able to control her voice; "but I will marry him if you wish it."

"I do wish it earnestly, Gertrude."

"Then you have my promise," she said, again with some bitterness.

"But you will not forget me? Erskine will have all but that — a tender recollection — nothing."

"Can I do more than I have just promised?"

"Perhaps so; but I am too selfish to be able to conceive anything more generous. Our renunciation will bind us to one another as our union could never have done."

They exchanged a long look. Then he took out his watch, and began to speak of the length of their journey, now nearly at an end. When they arrived in London, the first person they recognized on the platform was Mr. Jansenius.

"Ah! you got my telegram, I see," said Trefusis. "Many thanks for coming. Wait for me whilst I put this lady into a cab."

When the cab was engaged, and Gertrude, with her maid, stowed within, he whispered to her hurriedly,

"In spite of all, I have a leaden pain here" (indicating his heart). "You have been brave; and I have been wise. Do not speak to me; but remember that we are friends always and deeply."

He touched her hand, and turned to the cabman, directing him whither to drive. Gertrude shrank back into a corner of the vehicle

as it departed. Then Trefusis, expanding his chest like a man just released from some cramping drudgery, rejoined Mr. Jansenius.

"There goes a true woman," he said. "I have been persuading her
to take the very best step open to her. I began by talking sense, like
a man of honour, and kept at it for half an hour; but she would not
listen to me. Then I talked romantic nonsense of the cheapest sort
for five minutes; and she consented with tears in her eyes. Let us
take this hansom. Hi! Belsize Avenue. Yes: you sometimes have to
answer a woman according to her womanishness, just as you have
to answer a fool according to his folly. Have you ever made up your
mind, Jansenius, whether I am an unusually honest man, or one of the
worst products of the social organization I spend all my energies in
assailing — an infernal scoundrel, in short?"

"Now pray do not be absurd," said Mr. Jansenius. "I wonder at a
man of your ability behaving and speaking as you sometimes do."

"I hope a little insincerity, when meant to act as chloroform —to
save a woman from feeling a wound to her vanity — is excusable.
By-the-bye, I must send a couple of telegrams from the first post
office we pass. Well, sir, I am going to marry Agatha, as I sent you
word. There was only one other single man, and one other virgin
down at Brandon Beeches; and they are as good as engaged. And
so ——

> 'Jack shall have Jill;
> Nought shall go ill;
> The man shall have his mare again;
> And all shall be well.' "

APPENDIX

LETTER TO THE AUTHOR FROM MR. SIDNEY TREFUSIS

My Dear Sir: I find that my friends are not quite satisfied with the account you have given of them in your clever novel entitled, "An Unsocial Socialist." You already understand that I consider it my duty to communicate my whole history, without reserve, to whoever may desire to be guided or warned by my experience, and that I have no sympathy whatever with the spirit in which one of the ladies concerned recently told you that her affairs were no business of yours or of the people who read your books. When you asked my permission some years ago to make use of my story, I at once said that you would be perfectly justified in giving it the fullest publicity whether I consented or not, provided only that you were careful not to falsify it for the sake of artistic effect. Now, whilst cheerfully admitting that you have done your best to fulfil that condition, I cannot help feeling that, in presenting the facts in the guise of fiction, you have, in spite of yourself, shewn them in a false light. Actions described in novels are judged by a romantic system of morals as fictitious as the actions themselves. The traditional parts of this system are, as Cervantes tried to show, for the chief part, barbarous and obsolete: the modern additions are largely due to the novel readers and writers of our own century — most of them half educated women, rebelliously slavish, superstitious, sentimental, full of the intense egotism fostered by their struggle for personal liberty, and, outside their families, with absolutely no social sentiment except love. Meanwhile, man, having fought and won his fight for this personal liberty, only to find himself a more abject slave than before, is turning with loathing from his egotist's dream of independence to the collective interests of society, with the welfare of which he now perceives his own happiness to be inextricably bound up. But man in this phase (would that all had reached it!) has not yet leisure to write or read novels. In noveldom woman still sets the moral standard; and to her the males, who are in full revolt against the acceptance of the infatuation of a pair of lovers as the highest manifestation of the social instinct, and against the restriction of the affections within the narrow circle of blood relationship, and of the political sympathies within frontiers, are to her what she calls heartless brutes. That is exactly what I have been called by readers of your novel; and that, indeed, is exactly what I am, judged by the fictitious and feminine standard of morality. Hence some critics have been able plausibly to pretend to take the book as a satire on Socialism. It may, for what I know, have been so intended by you. Whether or no, I am sorry you made a novel of my story; for the effect has been almost as if you had misrepresented me from beginning to end.

At the same time, I acknowledge that you have stated the facts, on the whole, with scrupulous fairness. You have, indeed, flattered me very strongly by representing me as constantly thinking of and for other people, whereas the rest think of themselves alone; but on the other hand you have contradictorily called me "unsocial," which is certainly the last adjective I should have expected to find in the neighbourhood of my name. I deny, it is true, that what is now called "society" is society in any real sense; and my best wish for it is that it may dissolve too rapidly to make it worth the while of those who are "not in society" to facilitate its dissolution by violently pounding it into small pieces. But no reader of "An Unsocial Socialist" needs to be told how, by the exercise of a certain considerate tact (which on the outside, perhaps, seems the opposite of tact), I have contrived to maintain genial terms with men and women of all classes, even those whose opinions and political conduct seemed to me most dangerous.

However, I do not here propose to go fully into my own position, lest I should seem tedious, and be accused, not for the first time, of a propensity to lecture — a reproach which comes naturally enough from persons whose conceptions are never too wide to be expressed within the limits of a sixpenny telegram. I shall confine myself to correcting a few misapprehensions which have, I am told, arisen among readers who from inveterate habit cannot bring the persons and events of a novel into any relation with the actual conditions of life.

In the first place, then, I desire to say that Mrs. Erskine is not dead of a broken heart. Erskine and I and our wives are very much in and out at one another's houses; and I am therefore in a position to declare that Mrs. Erskine, having escaped by her marriage from the vile caste in which she was relatively poor and artificially unhappy and ill conditioned, is now, as the pretty wife of an art-critic, relatively rich, as well as pleasant, active, and in sound health. Her chief trouble, as far as I can judge, is the impossibility of shaking off her distinguished relatives, who furtively quit their abject splendour to drop in upon her for dinner and a little genuine human society much oftener than is convenient to poor Erskine. She has taken a patronizing fancy to her father, the Admiral, who accepts her condescension gratefully as age brings more and more home to him the futility of his social position. She has also, as might have been expected, become an extreme advocate of socialism; and indeed, being in a great hurry for the new order of things, looks on me as a lukewarm disciple because I do not propose to interfere with the slowly-grinding mill of Evolution, and effect the change by one tremendous stroke from the united and awakened people (for such she — vainly, alas! — believes the proletariat already to be).

As to my own marriage, some have asked sarcastically whether I ran away again or not; others, whether it has been a success. These are foolish questions. My marriage has turned out much as I expected it would. I find that my wife's views on the subject vary with the circumstances under which they are expressed.

I have now to make one or two comments on the impressions conveyed by the style of your narrative. Sufficient prominence has not, in my opinion, been given to the extraordinary destiny of my father, the true hero of a nineteenth century romance. I, who have seen society reluctantly accepting works of genius for nothing from men of extraordinary gifts, and at the same time helplessly paying my father millions, and submitting to monstrous mortgages of its future production, for a few directions as to the most business-like way of manufacturing and selling cotton, cannot but wonder, as I prepare my income-tax returns, whether society was mad to sacrifice thus to him and to me. He was the man with power to buy, to build, to choose, to endow, to sit on committees and adjudicate upon designs, to make his own terms for placing anything on a sound business footing. He was hated, envied, sneered at for his low origin, reproached for his ignorance; yet nothing would pay unless he liked or pretended to like it. I look round at our buildings, our statues, our pictures, our newspapers, our domestic interiors, our books, our vehicles, our morals, our manners, our statutes, and our religion; and I see his hand everywhere, for they were all made or modified to please him. Those which did not please him failed commercially: he would not buy them, or sell them, or countenance them; and except through him, as "master of the industrial situation," nothing could be bought, or sold, or countenanced. The landlord could do nothing with his acres except let them to him; the capitalist's hoard rotted and dwindled until it was lent to him; the worker's muscles and brain were impotent until sold to him. What king's son would not exchange with me — the son of the Great Employer — the Merchant Prince? No wonder they proposed to imprison me for treason when, by applying my inherited business talent, I put forward a plan for securing his full services to society for a few hundreds a year. But pending the adoption of my plan, do not describe him contemptuously as a vulgar tradesman. Industrial kingship, the only real kingship of our century, was his by divine right of his turn for business; and I, his son, bid you respect the crown whose revenues I inherit. If you dont, my friend, your book wont pay.

I hear, with some surprise, that the kindness of my conduct to Henrietta (my first wife, you recollect) has been called in question: why, I do not exactly know. Undoubtedly I should not have married her; but it is waste of time to criticise the judgment of a young man in love. Since I do not approve of the usual plan of neglecting and avoiding a spouse without ceasing to keep up appearances, I cannot for the life of me see what else I could have done than vanish when I found out my mistake. It is but a short-sighted policy to wait for the mending of matters that are bound to get worse. The notion that her death was my fault is sheer unreason on the face of it; and I need no exculpation on that score; but I must disclaim the credit of having borne her death like a philosopher. I ought to have done so; but the truth is that I was greatly affected at the moment; and the proof of it is that I and Jansenius (the only other person who cared) behaved in a most unbecoming fashion, as men invariably do when they are really upset. Perfect propriety at a death is seldom achieved except by the undertaker, who has the advantage of being free from emotion.

Your rigmarole (if you will excuse the word) about the tombstone gives quite a wrong idea of my attitude on that occasion. I stayed away from the funeral for reasons which are, I should think, sufficiently obvious and natural, but which you somehow seem to have missed. Granted that my fancy for Hetty was only a cloud of illusions, still I could not, within a few days of her sudden death, go in cold blood to take part in a grotesque and heathenish mummery over her coffin. I should have broken out and strangled somebody. But on every other point I — weakly enough — sacrificed my own feelings to those of Jansenius. I let him have his funeral, though I object to funerals and to the practice of sepulture. I consented to a monument, although there is, to me, no more bitterly ridiculous outcome of human vanity than the blocks raised to tell posterity that John Smith, or Jane Jackson, late of this parish, was born, lived, and died worth enough money to pay a mason to distinguish their bones from those of the unrecorded millions. To gratify Jansenius I waived this objection, and only interfered to save him from being fleeced and fooled by an unnecessary West End middleman, who, as likely as not, would have eventually employed the very man to whom I gave the job. Even the epitaph was not mine. If I had had my way I should have written: "HENRIETTA JANSENIUS WAS BORN ON SUCH A DATE, MARRIED A MAN NAMED TREFUSIS, AND DIED ON SUCH ANOTHER DATE; AND NOW WHAT DOES IT MATTER WHETHER SHE DID OR NOT?" The whole notion conveyed in the book that I rode roughshod over everybody in the affair, and only consulted my own feelings, is the very reverse of the truth.

As to the tomfoolery down at Brandon's, which ended in Erskine and myself marrying the young lady visitors there, I can only congratulate you on the determination with which you have striven to make something like a romance out of such very thin material. I cannot say that I remember it all exactly as you have described it; my wife declares flatly there is not a word of truth in it as far as she is concerned; and Mrs. Erskine steadily refuses to read the book.

On one point I must acknowledge that you have proved yourself a master of the art of fiction. What Hetty and I said to one another that day when she came upon me in the shrubbery at Alton College, was known only to us two. She never told it to anyone, and I soon forgot it. All due honor, therefore, to the ingenuity with which you have filled the hiatus, and shewn the state of affairs between us by a discourse on "surplus value," cribbed from an imperfect report of one of my public lectures, and from the pages of Karl Marx! If you were an economist, I should condemn you for confusing economic with ethical considerations, and for your uncertainty as to the function which my father got his start by performing. But as you are only a novelist, I compliment you heartily on your clever little *pasticcio,* adding, however, that as an account of what actually passed between myself and Hetty, it is the wildest romance ever penned. Wickens's boy was far nearer the mark.

In conclusion, allow me to express my regret that you can find no better employment for your talent than the writing of novels. The first literary result of the foundation of our industrial system upon the profits of piracy and slave-trading was Shakspere. It is our misfortune that the sordid misery and hopeless horror of his view of man's destiny is still so appropriate to English society that we even to-day regard him as not for an age, but for all time. But the poetry of despair will not outlive despair itself. Your nineteenth century novelists are only the tail of Shakspere. Dont tie yourself to it: it is fast wriggling into oblivion.

I am, dear sir, yours truly,
SIDNEY TREFUSIS.

London, *Christmas,* 1887.

The Quintessence
of Ibsenism

The Quintessence of Ibsenism, which had its inception in a paper on Ibsen read by Shaw on 18 July 1890, as part of a Fabian Society series of lectures on "Socialism in Contemporary Literature," was first published in London in 1891, and, later in the same year, in an unauthorized edition in Boston. An enlarged edition, "Now Completed to the Death of Ibsen," was issued in 1913; this edition, however, lacked the important Appendix to the first edition. A new preface was added, in 1922, to the third edition, but the text was unaltered. All subsequent settings have followed the third edition.

The section titled "The Last Four Plays," written by Shaw for the 1913 edition, is here reprinted by permission of the Public Trustee and The Society of Authors, London.

PREFACE

In the spring of 1890, the Fabian Society, finding itself at a loss for a course of lectures to occupy its summer meetings, was compelled to make shift with a series of papers put forward under the general heading "Socialism in Contemporary Literature." The Fabian Essayists, strongly pressed to do "something or other," for the most part shook their heads; but in the end Sydney Olivier consented to "take Zola"; I consented to "take Ibsen"; and Hubert Bland undertook to read all the Socialist novels of the day, an enterprise the desperate failure of which resulted in the most amusing paper of the series. William Morris, asked to read a paper on himself, flatly declined, but gave us one on Gothic Architecture. Stepniak also came to the rescue with a lecture on modern Russian fiction; and so the Society tided over the summer without having to close its doors, but also without having added anything whatever to the general stock of information on Socialism in Contemporary Literature. After this I cannot claim that my paper on Ibsen, which was duly read at the St James's Restaurant on the 18th July 1890, under the presidency of Mrs Annie Besant, and which was the first form of this little book, is an original work in the sense of being the result of a spontaneous internal impulse on my part. Having purposely couched it in the most provocative terms (of which traces may be found by the curious in its present state), I did not attach much importance to the somewhat lively debate that arose upon it; and I had laid it aside as a *pièce d'occasion* which had served its turn, when the production of *Rosmersholm* at the Vaudeville Theatre by Miss Farr, the inauguration of the Independent Theatre by Mr J. T. Grein with a performance of *Ghosts,* and the sensation created by the experiment of Miss Robins and Miss Lea with *Hedda Gabler,* started a frantic newspaper controversy, in which I could see no sign of any of the disputants having ever been forced by circumstances, as I had, to make up his mind definitely as to what Ibsen's plays meant, and to defend his view face to face with some of the keenest debaters in London. I allow due weight to the fact that Ibsen himself has not enjoyed this advantage (see page 236); but I have also shewn that the existence of a discoverable and perfectly definite thesis in a poet's work by no means depends on the completeness of his own intellectual consciousness of it. At any rate, the controversialists, whether in the abusive stage, or the apologetic stage, or the hero worshipping stage,

207

by no means made clear what they were abusing, or apologizing for, or going into ecstasies about; and I came to the conclusion that my explanation might as well be placed in the field until a better could be found.

With this account of the origin of the book, and a reminder that it is not a critical essay on the poetic beauties of Ibsen, but simply an exposition of Ibsenism, I offer it to the public to make what they can of.

LONDON, *June* 1891.

The
Quintessence of Ibsenism

I
The Two Pioneers

That is, pioneers of the march to the plains of heaven (so to speak).

The second, whose eyes are in the back of his head, is the man who declares that it is wrong to do something that no one has hitherto seen any harm in.

The first, whose eyes are very longsighted and in the usual place, is the man who declares that it is right to do something hitherto regarded as infamous.

The second is treated with great respect by the army. They give him testimonials; name him the Good Man; and hate him like the devil.

The first is stoned and shrieked at by the whole army. They call him all manner of opprobrious names; grudge him his bare bread and water; and secretly adore him as their saviour from utter despair.

Let me take an example from life of my pioneer. Shelley was a pioneer and nothing else: he did both first and second pioneer's work.

Now compare the effect produced by Shelley as abstinence preacher or second pioneer with that which he produced as indulgence preacher or first pioneer. For example:

SECOND PIONEER PROPOSITION. — It is wrong to kill animals and eat them.

FIRST PIONEER PROPOSITION. — It is not wrong to take your sister as your wife.

Here the second pioneer appears as a gentle humanitarian, and the first as an unnatural corrupter of public morals and family life. So much easier is it to declare the right wrong than the wrong right in a society with a guilty conscience, to which, as to Dickens's detective, "Any possible move is a probable move provided it's in a wrong direction." Just as the liar's punishment is, not in the least that he is not believed, but that he cannot believe any one else, so a guilty society can more easily be persuaded that any apparently innocent act is guilty than that any apparently guilty act is innocent.

The English newspaper which best represents the guilty conscience of the middle class, or dominant factor in society to-day, is the *Daily Telegraph*. If we can find the *Daily Telegraph* speaking of Ibsen as the *Quarterly Review* used to speak of Shelley, it will occur to us at once that there must be something of the first pioneer about Ibsen.

Mr Clement Scott, dramatic critic to the *Daily Telegraph,* a good-natured gentleman, not a pioneer, but emotional, impressionable, zealous, and sincere, accuses Ibsen of dramatic impotence, ludicrous amateurishness, nastiness, vulgarity, egotism, coarseness, absurdity, uninteresting verbosity, and suburbanity, declaring that he has taken ideas that would have inspired a great tragic poet, and vulgarized and debased them in dull, hateful, loathsome, horrible plays. This criticism, which occurs in a notice of the first performance of *Ghosts* in England, is to be found in the *Daily Telegraph* for the 14th March 1891, and is supplemented by a leading article which compares the play to an open drain, a loathsome sore unbandaged, a dirty act done publicly, or a lazar house with all its doors and windows open. Bestial, cynical, disgusting, poisonous, sickly, delirious, indecent, loathsome, fetid, literary carrion, crapulous stuff, clinical confessions: all these epithets are used in the article as descriptive of Ibsen's work. "Realism," says the writer, "is one thing; but the nostrils of the audience must not be visibly held before a play can be stamped as true to nature. It is difficult to expose in decorous words — the gross, and almost putrid indecorum of this play." As the performance of *Ghosts* took place on the evening of the 13th March, and the criticism appeared next morning, it is evident that Mr Scott must have gone straight from the theatre to the newspaper office, and there, in an almost hysterical condition, penned his share of this extraordinary protest. The literary workmanship bears marks of haste and disorder, which, however, only heighten the expression of the passionate horror produced in the writer by seeing *Ghosts* on the stage. He calls on the authorities to cancel the license of the theatre, and declares that he has been exhorted to laugh at honour, to disbelieve in love, to mock virtue, to distrust friendship, and to deride fidelity. If this document were at all singular, it would rank as one of the curiosities of criticism, exhibiting, as it does, the most seasoned play-goer in the world thrown into convulsions by a performance which was witnessed with approval, and even with enthusiasm, by many persons of approved moral and artistic conscientiousness. But Mr Scott's criticism was hardly distinguishable in tone from hundreds of others which appeared simultaneously. His opinion was the vulgar opinion. Mr Alfred Watson, critic to the *Standard*, the leading Tory daily paper, proposed that proceedings should be taken against the theatre under Lord Campbell's Act for the suppression of disorderly houses. Clearly Mr Scott and his editor Sir Edwin Arnold, with whom rests the responsibility for the article which accompanied the criticism, may claim to represent a considerable party. How then is it that Ibsen, a Norwegian playwright of European celebrity, attracts one section of the English people so strongly that they hail him as the greatest living dramatic poet and moral teacher, whilst another section is so revolted by his works that they describe him in terms which they themselves admit are, by the necessities of the case, all but obscene? This phenomenon, which has occurred throughout Europe wherever Ibsen's plays have been acted, as well as in America and Australia, must be exhaustively explained before the plays can be described without danger of reproducing the same confusion in the reader's own mind. Such an explanation, therefore, must be my first business.

Understand, at the outset, that the explanation will not be an explaining away. Mr Clement Scott's judgment has not misled him in the least as to Ibsen's meaning. Ibsen means all that most revolts his critic. For example, in *Ghosts*, the play in question, a clergyman and a married woman fall in love with one another. The woman proposes to abandon her husband and live with the clergyman. He recalls her to her duty, and makes her behave as a virtuous woman. She afterwards tells him that this was a crime on his part. Ibsen agrees with her, and has written the play to bring you round to his opinion. Mr Clement Scott does not agree with her, and believes that when you are brought round to her opinion you will be morally corrupted. By this conviction he is impelled to denounce Ibsen as he does, Ibsen being equally impelled to propagate the convictions which provoke the attack. Which of the two is right cannot be decided until it is ascertained whether a society of persons holding Ibsen's opinions would be higher or lower than a society holding Mr Clement Scott's.

There are many people who cannot conceive this as an open question. To them a denunciation of any of the recognized virtues is an incitement to unsocial conduct; and every utterance in which an assumption of the eternal validity of these virtues is not implicit, is a paradox. Yet all progress involves the beating of them from that position. By way of illustration, one may rake up the case of Proudhon, who nearly half a century ago denounced "property" as theft. This was thought the very maddest paradox that ever man hazarded: it seemed obvious that a society which countenanced such a proposition would speedily be reduced to the condition of a sacked city. To-day schemes for the confiscation by taxation of mining royalties and ground rents are commonplaces of social reform; and the honesty of the relation of our big property holders to the rest of the community is challenged on all hands. It would be easy to multiply instances, though the most complete are now ineffective through the triumph of the original "paradox" having obliterated all memory of the opposition it first had to encounter. The point to seize is that social progress takes effect through the replacement of old institutions by new ones; and since every institution involves the recognition of the duty of conforming to it, progress must involve the repudiation of an established duty at every step. If the Englishman had not repudiated the duty of absolute obedience to his king, his political progress would have been impossible. If women had not repudiated the duty of absolute submission to their husbands, and defied public opinion as to the limits set by modesty to their education, they would never have gained the protection of the Married Women's Property Act or the power to qualify themselves as medical practitioners. If Luther had not trampled on his duty to the head of his Church and on his vow of chastity, our priests would still have to choose between celibacy and profligacy. There is nothing new, then, in the defiance of duty by the reformer: every step of progress means a duty repudiated, and a scripture torn up. And every reformer is denounced accordingly, Luther as an apostate, Cromwell as a traitor, Mary Wollestonecraft as an unwomanly virago, Shelley as a libertine, and Ibsen as all the things enumerated in the *Daily Telegraph*.

This crablike progress of social evolution, in which the individual advances by seeming to go backward, continues to illude us in spite of all the lessons of history. To the pious man the newly made freethinker, suddenly renouncing supernatural revelation, and denying all obligation to believe the Bible and obey the commandments as such, appears to be claiming the right to rob and murder at large. But the freethinker soon finds reasons for not doing what he does not want to do; and these reasons seem to him to be far more binding on the conscience than the precepts of a book of which the divine inspiration cannot be rationally proved. The pious man is at last forced to admit — as he was in the case of the late Charles Bradlaugh, for instance — that the disciples of Voltaire and Tom Paine do not pick pockets or cut throats oftener than your even Christian: he actually is driven to doubt whether Voltaire himself really screamed and saw the devil on his deathbed.

This experience by no means saves the rationalist* from falling into the same conservatism when the time comes for his own belief to be questioned. No sooner has he triumphed over the theologian than he forthwith sets up as binding on all men the duty of acting logically with the object of securing the greatest good of the greatest number, with the result that he is presently landed in vivisection, Contagious Diseases Acts, dynamite conspiracies, and other grotesque but strictly reasonable abominations. Reason becomes Dagon, Moloch, and Jehovah rolled into one. Its devotees exult in having freed themselves from the old slavery to a collection of books written by Jewish men of letters. To worship such books was, they can prove, manifestly as absurd as to worship sonatas composed by German musicians, as was done by the hero of Wagner's novelette, who sat up on his deathbed to say his creed, beginning, "I believe in God, Mozart, and Beethoven." The Voltairian freethinker despises such a piece of sentiment; but is it not much more sensible to worship a sonata constructed by a musician than to worship a syllogism constructed by a logician, since the sonata may at least inspire feelings of awe and devotion? This does not occur to the votary of reason; and rationalist "free-thinking" soon comes to mean syllogism worship with rites of human sacrifice; for just as the rationalist's pious predecessor thought that the man who scoffed at the Bible must infallibly yield without resistance to all his criminal propensities, so the rationalist in turn becomes convinced that when a man once loses his faith in Mr Herbert Spencer's *Data of Ethics,* he is no longer to be trusted to keep his hands off his neighbour's person, purse, or wife.

In process of time the age of reason had to go its way after the age of faith. In actual experience, the first shock to rationalism came from the observation that though nothing could persuade women to adopt it, their inaptitude for reasoning no more prevented them from arriving at right conclusions than the masculine aptitude for it saved men from arriving at wrong ones. When this generalization had to be modified in view of the fact that some women did at last begin to try their skill at ratiocination, reason was not re-established on the throne; because the result of Woman's reasoning was that she began to fall into all the errors which men are just learning to mistrust. From the moment she set about doing things for reasons instead of merely finding reasons for what she wanted to do, there was no saying what mischief she would be at next; since there are just as good reasons for burning a heretic at the stake as for rescuing a shipwrecked crew from drowning — in fact, there are better. One of the first and most famous utterances of rationalism would have condemned it without

* I had better here warn students of philosophy that I am speaking of rationalism, not as classified in the books, but as apparent in men.

further hearing had its full significance been seen at the time. Voltaire, taking exception to the trash of some poetaster, was met with the plea "One must live." "I dont see the necessity," replied Voltaire. The evasion was worthy of the Father of Lies himself; for Voltaire was face to face with the very necessity he was denying — must have known, consciously or not, that it was the universal postulate — would have understood, if he had lived to-day, that since all human institutions are constructed to fulfil man's will, and that his will is to live even when his reason teaches him to die, logical necessity, which was the sort Voltaire meant (the other sort being visible enough) can never be a motor in human action, and is, in short, not necessity at all. But that was not brought to light in Voltaire's time; and he died impenitent, bequeathing to his disciples that most logical of agents, the guillotine, which also "did not see the necessity." In our own century the recognition of the will as distinct from the reasoning machinery began to spread. Schopenhauer was the first among the moderns* to appreciate the enormous practical importance of the distinction, and to make it clear to amateur metaphysicians by concrete instances. Out of his teaching came the formulation of the dilemma that Voltaire shut his eyes to. Here it is. Rationally considered, life is only worth living when its pleasures are greater than its pains. Now to a generation which has ceased to believe in heaven, and has not yet learned that the degradation by poverty of four out of every five of its number is artificial and remediable, the fact that life is not worth living is obvious. It is useless to pretend that the pessimism of Koheleth, Shakspere, Dryden, and Swift can be refuted if the world progresses solely by the destruction of the unfit, and yet can only maintain its civilization by manufacturing the unfit in swarms of which that appalling proportion of four to one represents but the comparatively fit survivors. Plainly then, the reasonable thing for the rationalists to do is to refuse to live. But as none of them will com-

---

* I say the moderns, because the will is our old friend the soul or spirit of man; and the doctrine of justification, not by works, but by faith, clearly derives its validity from the consideration that no action, taken apart from the will behind it, has any moral character: for example, the acts which make the murderer and incendiary infamous are exactly similar to those which make the patriotic hero famous. "Original sin" is the will doing mischief. "Divine grace" is the will doing good. Our fathers, unversed in the Hegelian dialectic, could not conceive that these two, each the negation of the other, were the same. Schopenhauer's philosophy, like that of all pessimists, is really based on the old view of the will as original sin, and on the 1750–1850 view that the intellect is the divine grace that is to save us from it. It is as well to warn those who fancy that Schopenhauerism is one and indivisible, that acceptance of its metaphysics by no means involves endorsement of its philosophy.

mit suicide in obedience to this demonstration of "the necessity" for it, there is an end of the notion that we live for reasons instead of in fulfilment of our will to live. Thus we are landed afresh in mystery; for positive science gives no account whatever of this will to live. Indeed the utmost light that positive science throws is but feeble in comparison with the illumination that was looked forward to when it first began to dazzle us with its analyses of the machinery of sensation — its researches into the nature of sound and the construction of the ear, the nature of light and the construction of the eye, its measurement of the speed of sensation, its localization of the functions of the brain, and its hints as to the possibility of producing a homunculus presently as the fruit of its chemical investigation of protoplasm. The fact remains that when Darwin, Haeckel, Helmholtz, Young, and the rest, popularized here among the middle class by Tyndall and Huxley, and among the proletariat by the lectures of the National Secular Society, have taught you all they know, you are still as utterly at a loss to explain the fact of consciousness as you would have been in the days when you were satisfied with Chambers' *Vestiges of Creation*. Materialism, in short, only isolated the great mystery of consciousness by clearing away several petty mysteries with which we had confused it; just as rationalism isolated the great mystery of the will to live. The isolation made both more conspicuous than before. We thought we had escaped for ever from the cloudy region of metaphysics; and we were only carried further into the heart of them.*

We have not yet worn off the strangeness of the position to which we have now been led. Only the other day our highest boast was that we were reasonable human beings. To-day we laugh at that conceit, and see ourselves as wilful creatures. Ability to reason accurately is as desirable as ever, since it is only by accurate reasoning that we can calculate our actions so as to do what we intend to do — that is, to fulfil our will; but faith in reason as a prime motor is no longer the criterion of the sound mind, any more than faith in the Bible is the criterion of righteous intention.

At this point, accordingly, the illusion as to the retrogressive movement of progress recurs as strongly as ever. Just as the beneficent step

* The correlation between rationalism and materialism in this process has some immediate practical importance. Those who give up materialism whilst clinging to rationalism generally either relapse into abject submission to the most paternal of the Churches, or are caught by the attempts, constantly renewed, of mystics to found a new faith by rationalizing on the hollowness of materialism. The hollowness has nothing in it; and if you have come to grief as a materialist by reasoning about something, you are not likely, as a mystic, to improve matters by reasoning about nothing.

from theology to rationalism seems to the theologist a growth of impiety, does the step from rationalism to the recognition of the will as
the prime motor strike the rationalist as a lapse of common sanity, so
that to both theologist and rationalist progress at last appears alarming, threatening, hideous, because it seems to tend towards chaos.
The deists Voltaire and Tom Paine were, to the divines of their day,
predestined devils, tempting mankind hellward. To deists and divines
alike Ferdinand Lassalle, the godless self-worshipper and man-wor-
shipper would have been a monster. Yet many who to-day echo
Lassalle's demand that economic and political institutions should be
adapted to the poor man's will to eat and drink his fill out of the
product of his own labour, are revolted by Ibsen's acceptance of the
impulse towards greater freedom as sufficient ground for the repudiation of any customary duty, however sacred, that conflicts with it.
Society — were it even as free as Lassalle's Social-Democratic republic — *must,* it seems to them, go to pieces when conduct is no longer
regulated by inviolable covenants.

For what, during all these overthrowings of things sacred and things
infallible, has been happening to that pre-eminently sanctified thing,
Duty? Evidently it cannot have come off scatheless. First there was
man's duty to God, with the priest as assessor. That was repudiated;
and then came Man's duty to his neighbour, with Society as the assessor. Will this too be repudiated, and be succeeded by Man's duty to
himself, assessed by himself? And if so, what will be the effect on
the conception of Duty in the abstract? Let us see.

I have just called Lassalle a self-worshipper. In doing so I cast no
reproach on him; for this is the last step in the evolution of the conception of duty. Duty arises at first, a gloomy tyranny, out of man's
helplessness, his self-mistrust, in a word, his abstract fear. He personifies all that he abstractly fears as God, and straightway becomes
the slave of his duty to God. He imposes that slavery fiercely on his
children, threatening them with hell, and punishing them for their
attempts to be happy. When, becoming bolder, he ceases to fear
everything, and dares to love something, this duty of his to what he
fears evolves into a sense of duty to what he loves. Sometimes he
again personifies what he loves as God; and the God of Wrath becomes the God of Love: sometimes he at once becomes a humanitarian, an altruist, acknowledging only his duty to his neighbour. This
stage is correlative to the rationalist stage in the evolution of philosophy
and the capitalist phase in the evolution of industry. But in it the
emancipated slave of God falls under the dominion of Society, which,
having just reached a phase in which all the love is ground out of it
by the competitive struggle for money, remorselessly crushes him until,

in due course of the further growth of his spirit or will, a sense at last arises in him of his duty to himself. And when this sense is fully grown, which it hardly is yet, the tyranny of duty is broken; for now the man's God is himself; and he, self-satisfied at last, ceases to be selfish. The evangelist of this last step must therefore preach the repudiation of duty. This, to the unprepared of his generation, is indeed the wanton masterpiece of paradox. What! after all that has been said by men of noble life as to the secret of all right conduct being only "Duty, duty, duty," is he to be told now that duty is the primal curse from which we must redeem ourselves before we can advance another step on the road along which, as we imagine — having forgotten the repudiations made by our fathers — duty and duty alone has brought us thus far? But why not? God was once the most sacred of our conceptions; and he had to be denied. Then Reason became the Infallible Pope, only to be deposed in turn. Is Duty more sacred than God or Reason?

Having now arrived at the prospect of the repudiation of duty by Man, I shall make a digression on the subject of ideals and idealists, as treated by Ibsen. I shall go round in a loop, and come back to the same point by way of the repudiation of duty by Woman; and then at last I shall be in a position to describe the plays without risk of misunderstanding.

II
Ideals and Idealists

We have seen that as Man grows through the ages, he finds himself bolder by the growth of his spirit (if I may so name the unknown) and dares more and more to love and trust instead of to fear and fight. But his courage has other effects: he also raises himself from mere consciousness to knowledge by daring more and more to face facts and tell himself the truth. For in his infancy of helplessness and terror he could not face the inexorable; and facts being of all things the most inexorable, he masked all the threatening ones as fast as he discovered them; so that now every mask requires a hero to tear it off. The king of terrors, Death, was the Arch-Inexorable: Man could not bear the dread of that thought. He must persuade himself that Death could be propitiated, circumvented, abolished. How he fixed the mask of immortality on the face of Death for this purpose we all know. And he did the like with all disagreeables as long as they remained inevitable. Otherwise he must have gone mad with terror of the grim shapes around him, headed by the skeleton with the scythe and hourglass. The masks were his ideals, as he called them; and what, he would ask, would life be without ideals? Thus he became an idealist, and remained so until he dared to begin pulling the masks off and looking the spectres in the face — dared, that is, to be more and more a realist. But all men are not equally brave; and the greatest terror prevailed whenever some realist bolder than the rest laid hands on a mask which they did not yet dare to do without.

We have plenty of these masks around us still — some of them more fantastic than any of the Sandwich islanders' masks in the British Museum. In our novels and romances especially we see the most beautiful of all the masks — those devised to disguise the brutalities of the sexual instinct in the earlier stages of its development, and to soften the rigorous aspect of the iron laws by which Society regulates its gratification. When the social organism becomes bent on civilization, it has to force marriage and family life on the individual, because it can perpetuate itself in no other way whilst love is still known only by fitful glimpses, the basis of sexual relationship being in the main mere physical appetite. Under these circumstances men try to graft pleasure on necessity by desperately pretending that the institution forced upon them is a congenial one, making it a point of public decency to assume always that men spontaneously love their kindred better than their chance acquaintances, and that the woman once desired is always desired: also that the family is woman's proper sphere, and that no really womanly woman ever forms an attachment, or even knows what it means, until she is requested to do so by a man. Now if anyone's childhood has been embittered by the dislike of his mother and the ill-temper of his father; if his wife has ceased to care for him and he is heartily tired of his wife; if his brother is going to law with him over the division of the family property, and his son acting in studied defiance of his plans and wishes, it is hard for him to persuade himself that passion is eternal and that blood is thicker than water. Yet if he tells himself the truth, all his life seems a waste and a failure by the light of it. It comes then to this, that his neighbours must either agree with him that the whole system is a mistake, and discard it for a new one, which cannot possibly happen until social organization so far outgrows the institution that Society can perpetuate itself without it; or else they must keep him in countenance by resolutely making believe that all the illusions with which it has been masked are realities.

For the sake of precision, let us imagine a community of a thousand persons, organized for the perpetuation of the species on the basis of the British family as we know it at present. Seven hundred of them, we will suppose, find the British family arrangement quite good enough for them. Two hundred and ninety-nine find it a failure, but must put up with it since they are in a minority. The remaining person occupies a position to be explained presently. The 299 failures will not have the courage to face the fact that they are failures — irremediable failures, since they cannot prevent the 700 satisfied ones from coercing them into conformity with the marriage law. They will accordingly try to persuade themselves that, whatever their own particular domestic arrangements may be, the family is a beautiful and holy natural institution. For the fox not only declares that the grapes he cannot get are sour: he also insists that the sloes he *can* get are sweet. Now observe what has happened. The family as it really is is a conventional arrangement, legally enforced, which the majority, because it happens to suit them, think good enough for the minority, whom it happens not to suit at all. The family as a beautiful and holy natural institution is only a fancy picture of what every family would have to be if everybody was to be suited, invented by the minority as a mask for the reality, which in its nakedness is intolerable to them. We call this sort of fancy picture an IDEAL; and the policy of forcing individuals to act on the assumption that all ideals are real, and to recognize and accept such action as standard moral conduct, absolutely valid under all circumstances, contrary conduct or any advocacy of it being discountenanced and punished as immoral, may therefore be described as the policy of IDEALISM. Our 299 domestic failures are therefore become idealists as to marriage; and in proclaiming the ideal in fiction, poetry, pulpit and platform oratory, and serious private conversation, they will far outdo the 700 who comfortably accept marriage as a matter of course, never dreaming of calling it an "institution," much less a holy and beautiful one, and being pretty plainly of opinion that idealism is a crackbrained fuss about nothing. The idealists, hurt by this, will retort by calling them Philistines. We then have our society classified as 700 Philistines and 299 idealists, leaving one man unclassified. He is the man who is strong enough to face the truth that the idealists are shirking. He says flatly of marriage, "This thing is a failure for many of us. It is insufferable that two human beings, having entered into relations which only warm affection can render tolerable, should be forced to maintain them after such affections have ceased to exist, or in spite of the fact that they have never arisen. The alleged natural attractions and repulsions upon which the family ideal is based do not exist; and it is historically false that the family was founded for the purpose of satisfying them. Let us provide otherwise for the social ends which the family subserves, and then abolish its compulsory character altogether." What will be the attitude of the rest to this outspoken man? The Philistines will simply think him mad. But the idealists will be terrified beyond measure at the proclamation of their hidden thought — at the presence of the traitor among the conspirators of silence — at the rending of the beautiful veil they and their poets have woven to hide the unbearable face of the truth. They will crucify him, burn him, violate their own ideals of family affection by taking his children away from him, ostracize him, brand him as immoral, profligate, filthy, and appeal against him to the despised Philistines, specially idealized for the occasion as SOCIETY. How far they will proceed against him depends on how far his courage exceeds theirs. At his worst, they call him cynic and paradoxer: at his best they do their utmost to ruin him if not to take his life. Thus, purblindly courageous moralists like Mandeville and Larochefoucauld, who merely state unpleasant facts without denying the validity of current ideals, and who indeed depend on those ideals to make their statements piquant, get off with nothing worse than this name of cynic, the free use of which is a familiar mark of the zealous idealist. But take the case of the man who has already served us as an example — Shelley. The idealists did not call Shelley a cynic: they called him a fiend until they in-

vented a new illusion to enable them to enjoy the beauty of his lyrics
— said illusion being nothing less than the pretence that since he was
at bottom an idealist himself, his ideals must be identical with those
of Tennyson and Longfellow, neither of whom ever wrote a line in
which some highly respectable ideal was not implicit.*

Here the admission that Shelley, the realist, was an idealist too,
seems to spoil the whole argument. And it certainly spoils its verbal
consistency. For we unfortunately use this word ideal indifferently to
denote both the institution which the ideal masks and the mask itself,
thereby producing desperate confusion of thought, since the institution may be an effete and poisonous one, whilst the mask may be, and
indeed generally is, an image of what we would fain have in its place.
If the existing facts, with their masks on, are to be called ideals, and
the future possibilities which the masks depict are also to be called
ideals — if, again, the man who is defending existing institutions by
maintaining their identity with their masks is to be confounded under
one name with the man who is striving to realize the future possibilities by tearing the mask and the thing masked asunder, then the
position cannot be intelligibly described by mortal pen: you and I,
reader, will be at cross purposes at every sentence unless you allow
me to distinguish pioneers like Shelley and Ibsen as realists from the
idealists of my imaginary community of one thousand. If you ask
why I have not allotted the terms the other way, and called Shelley and
Ibsen idealists and the conventionalists realists, I reply that Ibsen himself, though he has not formally made the distinction, has so repeatedly
harped on conventions and conventionalists as ideals and idealists that
if I were now perversely to call them realities and realists, I should
confuse readers of *The Wild Duck* and *Rosmersholm* more than I
should help them. Doubtless I shall be reproached for puzzling people by thus limiting the meaning of the term ideal. But what, I ask,

---

* The following are examples of the two stages of Shelley criticism:
"We feel as if one of the darkest of the fiends had been clothed with a
human body to enable him to gratify his enmity against the human race,
and as if the supernatural atrocity of his hate were only heightened by his
power to do injury. So strongly has this impression dwelt upon our minds
that we absolutely asked a friend, who had seen this individual, to describe
him to us — as if a cloven hoof, or horn, or flames from the mouth, must
have marked the external appearance of so bitter an enemy of mankind."
(*Literary Gazette,* 19th May 1821.)

"A beautiful and ineffectual angel, beating in the void his luminous wings
in vain." (MATTHEW ARNOLD, in his preface to the selection of poems by
Byron, dated 1881.)

The 1881 opinion is much sillier than the 1821 opinion. Further samples
will be found in the articles of Henry Salt, one of the few writers on Shelley
who understand his true position as a social pioneer.

is that inevitable passing perplexity compared to the inextricable tangle I must produce if I follow the custom, and use the word indiscriminately in its two violently incompatible senses? If the term realist is objected to on account of some of its modern associations, I can only recommend you, if you must associate it with something else than my own description of its meaning (I do not deal in definitions), to associate it, not with Zola and Maupassant, but with Plato.

Now let us return to our community of 700 Philistines, 299 idealists, and 1 realist. The mere verbal ambiguity against which I have just provided is as nothing beside that which comes of any attempt to express the relations of these three sections, simple as they are, in terms of the ordinary systems of reason and duty. The idealist, higher in the ascent of evolution than the Philistine, yet hates the highest and strike at him with a dread and rancour of which the easy going Philistine is guiltless. The man who has risen above the danger and the fear that his acquisitiveness will lead him to theft, his temper to murder, and his affections to debauchery: this is he who is denounced as an arch-scoundrel and libertine, and thus confounded with the lowest because he is the highest. And it is not the ignorant and stupid who maintain this error, but the literate and the cultured. When the true prophet speaks, he is proved to be both rascal and idiot, not by those who have never read of how foolishly such learned demonstrations have come off in the past, but by those who have themselves written volumes on the crucifixions, the burnings, the stonings, the headings and hangings, the Siberia transportations, the calumny and ostracism which have been the lot of the pioneer as well as of the camp follower. It is from men of established literary reputation that we learn that William Blake was mad, that Shelley was spoiled by living in a low set, that Robert Owen was a man who did not know the world, that Ruskin is incapable of comprehending political economy, that Zola is a mere blackguard, and that Ibsen is "a Zola with a wooden leg." The great musician, accepted by the unskilled listener, is vilified by his fellow-musicians: it was the musical culture of Europe that pronounced Wagner the inferior of Mendelssohn and Meyerbeer. The great artist finds his foes among the painters, and not among the men in the street: it is the Royal Academy which places Mr Marcus Stone — not to mention Mr [J. E.] Hodgson — above Mr Burne Jones. It is not rational that it should be so; but it is so, for all that. The realist at last loses patience with ideals altogether, and sees in them only something to blind us, something to numb us, something to murder self in us, something whereby, instead of resisting death, we can disarm it by committing suicide. The idealist, who has taken refuge with the ideals because he hates himself and is ashamed of himself, thinks that all this is so much the better. The realist, who has come to have a deep respect for himself and faith in the validity of his own will, thinks it so much the worse. To the one, human nature, naturally corrupt, is only held back from the excesses of the last years of the Roman empire by self-denying conformity to the ideals. To the other these ideals are only swaddling clothes which man has outgrown, and which insufferably impede his movements. No wonder the two cannot agree. The idealist says, "Realism means egotism; and egotism means depravity." The realist declares that when a man abnegates the will to live and be free in a world of the living and free, seeking only to conform to ideals for the sake of being, not himself, but "a good man," then he is morally dead and rotten, and must be left unheeded to abide his resurrection, if that by good luck arrive before his bodily death. Unfortunately, this is the sort of speech that nobody but a realist understands. It will be more amusing as well as more convincing to take an actual example of an idealist criticising a realist.

III

The Womanly Woman

Everybody remembers the "Diary of Marie Bashkirtseff." An outline of it, with a running commentary, was given in the *Review of Reviews* (June 1890) by the editor, Mr William Stead, a sort of modern Julian the Apostate, who, having gained an immense following by a public service in rendering which he had to perform a realistic feat of a somewhat scandalous character, entered upon a campaign with the object of establishing the ideal of sexual "purity" as a condition of public life. As he retains his best qualities — faith in himself, wilfulness, conscientious unscrupulousness — he can always make himself heard. Prominent among his ideals is an ideal of womanliness. In support of that ideal he will, like all idealists, make and believe any statement, however obviously and grotesquely unreal. When he found Marie Bashkirtseff's account of herself utterly incompatible with the account of a woman's mind given to him by his ideal, he was confronted with the dilemma that either Marie was not a woman or else his ideal did not correspond to nature. He actually accepted the former alternative. "Of the distinctively womanly," he says, "there is in her but little trace. She was the very antithesis of a true woman." Mr Stead's next difficulty was, that self-control, being a leading quality in his ideal, could not have been possessed by Marie: otherwise she would have been more like his ideal. Nevertheless he had to record that she, without any compulsion from circumstances, made herself a highly skilled artist by working ten hours a day for six years. Let anyone who thinks that this is no evidence of self-control just try it for six months. Mr Stead's verdict nevertheless, was "No self-control." However, his fundamental quarrel with Marie came out in the following lines. "Marie," he said, "was artist, musician, wit, philosopher, student — anything you like but a natural woman with a heart to love, and a soul to find its supreme satisfaction in sacrifice for lover or for child." Now of all the idealist abominations that make society pestiferous, I doubt if there be any so mean as that of forcing self-sacrifice on a woman under pretence that she likes it; and, if she ventures to contradict the pretence, declaring her no true woman. In India they carried this piece of idealism to the length of declaring that a wife could not bear to survive her husband, but would be prompted by her own faithful, loving, beautiful nature to offer up her life on the pyre which consumed his dead body. The astonishing thing is that women, sooner than be branded as unsexed wretches, allowed themselves to be stupefied with drink, and in that unwomanly condition burnt alive. British Philistinism put down widow idealizing with the strong hand; and suttee is abolished in India. The English form of it still survives; and Mr Stead, the rescuer of the children, is one of its high-priests. Imagine his feelings on coming across this entry in a woman's diary, "I love myself." Or this, "I swear solemnly — by the Gospels, by the passion of Christ, by MYSELF — that in four years I will be famous." The young woman was positively proposing to exercise for her own sake all the powers that were given her, in Mr Stead's opinion, solely that she might sacrifice them for her lover or child! No wonder he is driven to exclaim again, "She was very clever, no doubt; but woman she was not." Now observe this notable result. Marie Bashkirtseff, instead of being a less agreeable person than the ordinary female conformer to the ideal of womanliness, was conspicuously the reverse. Mr Stead himself wrote as one infatuated with her mere diary, and pleased himself by representing her as a person who fascinated everybody, and was a source of delight to all about her by the mere exhilaration and hope-giving atmosphere of her wilfulness. The truth is, that in real life a self-sacrificing woman, or, as Mr Stead would put it, a womanly woman, is not only taken advantage of, but disliked as well for her pains. No *man* pretends that his soul finds its supreme satisfaction in self-sacrifice: such an affectation would stamp him as a coward and weakling; the manly man is he who takes the Bashkirtseff view of himself. But men are not the less loved on this account. No one ever feels helpless by the side of the self-helper; whilst the self-sacrificer is always a drag, a responsibility, a reproach, an everlasting and unnatural trouble with whom no really strong soul can live. Only those who have helped themselves know how to help others, and to respect their right to help themselves.

Although romantic idealists generally insist on self-surrender as an indispensable element in true womanly love, its repulsive effect is well known and feared in practice by both sexes. The extreme instance is the reckless self-abandonment seen in the infatuation of passionate sexual desire. Everyone who becomes the object of that infatuation shrinks from it instinctively. Love loses its charm when it is not free; and whether the compulsion is that of custom and law, or of infatuation, the effect is the same: it becomes valueless. The desire to give inspires no affection unless there is also the power to withhold; and the successful wooer, in both sexes alike, is the one who can stand

out for honourable conditions, and, failing them, go without. Such
conditions are evidently not offered to either sex by the legal marriage
of to-day; for it is the intense repugnance inspired by the compulsory
character of the legalized conjugal relation that leads, first to the
idealization of marriage whilst it remains indispensable as a means
of perpetuating society; then to its modification by divorce and by the
abolition of penalties for refusal to comply with judicial orders for
restitution of conjugal rights; and finally to its disuse and disappearance as the responsibility for the maintenance and education of the
rising generation is shifted from the parent to the community.*

Although the growing repugnance to face the Church of England
marriage service has led many celebrants to omit those passages which
frankly explain the object of the institution, we are not likely to dispense with legal ties and obligations, and trust wholly to the permanence of love, until the continuity of society no longer depends on the
private nursery. Love, as a practical factor in society, is still a mere
appetite. That higher development of it which Ibsen shews us oc-
curring in the case of Rebecca West in *Rosmersholm* is only known
to most of us by the descriptions of great poets, who themselves, as
their biographies prove, have often known it, not by sustained experience, but only by brief glimpses. And it is never a first-fruit of
their love affairs. Tannhäuser may die in the conviction that one
moment of the emotion he felt with St Elizabeth was fuller and happier than all the hours of passion he spent with Venus; but that does
not alter the fact that love began for him with Venus, and that its
earlier tentatives towards the final goal were attended with relapses.
Now Tannhäuser's passion for Venus is a development of the hum-
drum fondness of the bourgeois Jack for his Gill, a development at

---

* A dissertation on the anomalies and impossibilities of the marriage law
at its present stage would be too far out of the main course of my argument to be introduced in the text above; but it may be well to point out in
passing to those who regard marriage as an inviolable and inviolate institution, that necessity has already forced us to tamper with it to such an
extent that at this moment the highest court in the kingdom is face to face
with a husband and wife, the one demanding whether a woman may saddle
him with all the responsibilities of a husband and then refuse to live with
him, and the other asking whether the law allows her husband to commit
abduction, imprisonment and rape upon her. If the court says Yes to the
husband, marriage is made intolerable for men; if it says Yes to the wife,
marriage is made intolerable for women; and as this exhausts the possible
alternatives, it is clear that provision must be made for the dissolution of
such marriages if the institution is to be maintained at all, which it must
be until its social function is otherwise provided for. Marriage is thus, by
force of circumstances, compelled to buy extension of life by extension of
divorce, much as if a fugitive should try to delay a pursuing wolf by throwing portions of his own heart to it.

once higher and more dangerous, just as idealism is at once higher and more dangerous than Philistinism. The fondness is the germ of the passion: the passion is the germ of the more perfect love. When Blake told men that through excess they would learn moderation, he knew that the way for the present lay through the Venusberg, and that the race would assuredly not perish there as some individuals have, and as the Puritan fears we all shall unless we find a way round. Also he no doubt foresaw the time when our children would be born on the other side of it, and so be spared that fiery purgation.

But the very facts that Blake is still commonly regarded as a crazy visionary, and that the current criticism of *Rosmersholm* entirely fails even to notice the evolution of Rebecca's passion for Rosmer into her love for him, much more to credit the moral transfiguration which accompanies it, shew how absurd it would be to pretend, for the sake of edification, that the ordinary marriage of to-day is a union between a William Blake and a Rebecca West, or that it would be possible, even if it were enlightened policy, to deny the satisfaction of the sexual appetite to persons who have not reached that stage. An overwhelming majority of such marriages as are not purely *de convenance,* are entered into for the gratification of that appetite either in its crudest form or veiled only by those idealistic illusions which the youthful imagination weaves so wonderfully under the stimulus of desire, and which older people indulgently laugh at. This being so, it is not surprising that our society, being directly dominated by men, comes to regard Woman, not as an end in herself like Man, but solely as a means of ministering to his appetite. The ideal wife is one who does everything that the ideal husband likes, and nothing else. Now to treat a person as a means instead of an end is to deny that person's right to live. And to be treated as a means to such an end as sexual intercourse with those who deny one's right to live is insufferable to any human being. Woman, if she dares face the fact that she is being so treated, must either loathe herself or else rebel. As a rule, when circumstances enable her to rebel successfully — for instance, when the accident of genius enables her to "lose her character" without losing her employment or cutting herself off from the society she values — she does rebel; but circumstances seldom do. Does she then loathe herself? By no means: she deceives herself in the idealist fashion by denying that the love which her suitor offers her is tainted with sexual appetite at all. It is, she declares, a beautiful, disinterested, pure, sublime devotion to another by which a man's life is exalted and purified, and a woman's rendered blest. And of all the cynics, the filthiest to her mind is the one who sees, in the man making honourable proposals to his future wife, nothing but the human male seeking his female. The man himself keeps her confirmed in her illusion; for the truth is unbearable to him too: he wants to form an affectionate tie, and not to drive a degrading bargain. After all, the germ of the highest love is in them both, though as yet it is no more than the appetite they are disguising so carefully from themselves. Consequently every stockbroker who has just brought his business up to marrying point woos in terms of the romantic illusion; and it is agreed between the two that their marriage shall realize the romantic ideal. Then comes the breakdown of the plan. The young wife finds that her husband is neglecting her for his business; that his interests, his activities, his whole life except that one part of it to which only a cynic ever referred before her marriage, lies away from home; and that her business is to sit there and mope until she is wanted. Then what can she do? If she complains, he, the self-helper, can do without her; whilst she is dependent on him for her position, her livelihood, her place in society, her home, her name, her very bread. All this is brought home to her by the first burst of displeasure her complaints provoke. Fortunately, things do not remain for ever at this point — perhaps the most wretched in a woman's life. The self-respect she has lost as a wife she regains as a mother, in which capacity her use and importance to the community compare favourably with those of most men of business. She is wanted in the house, wanted in the market, wanted by the children; and now, instead of weeping because her husband is away in the city, thinking of stocks and shares instead of his ideal woman, she would regard his presence in the house all day as an intolerable nuisance. And so, though she is completely disillusioned on the subject of ideal love, yet, since it has not turned out so badly after all, she countenances the illusion still from the point of view that it is a useful and harmless means of getting boys and girls to marry and settle down. And this conviction is the stronger in her because she feels that if she had known as much about marriage the day before her wedding as she did six months after, it would have been extremely hard to induce her to get married at all.

This prosaic solution is satisfactory only within certain limits. It depends altogether upon the accident of the woman having some natural vocation for domestic management and the care of children, as well as on the husband being fairly good-natured and livable-with. Hence arises the idealist illusion that a vocation for domestic management and the care of children is natural to women, and that women who lack them are not women at all, but members of the third, or Bashkirtseff sex. Even if this were true, it is obvious that if the Bashkirtseffs are to be allowed to live, they have a right to suitable institutions just as much as men and women. But it is not true. The domestic career is no more natural to all women than the military career is natural to all men; although it may be necessary that every able-bodied woman should be called on to risk her life in childbed just as it may be necessary that every man should be called on to risk his life in the battlefield. It is of course quite true that the majority of women are kind to children and prefer their own to other people's. But exactly the same thing is true of the majority of men, who nevertheless do not consider that their proper sphere is the nursery. The case may be illustrated more grotesquely by the fact that the majority of women who have dogs are kind to them, and prefer their own dogs to other people's; yet it is not proposed that women should restrict their activities to the rearing of puppies. If we have come to think that the nursery and the kitchen are the natural sphere of a woman, we have done so exactly as English children come to think that a cage is the natural sphere of a parrot — because they have never seen one anywhere else. No doubt there are Philistine parrots who agree with their owners that it is better to be in a cage than out, so long as there is plenty of hempseed and Indian corn there. There may even be idealist parrots who persuade themselves that the mission of a parrot is to minister to the happiness of a private family by whistling and saying "Pretty Polly," and that it is in the sacrifice of its liberty to this altruistic pursuit that a true parrot finds the supreme satisfaction of its soul. I will not go so far as to affirm that there are theological parrots who are convinced that imprisonment is the will of God because it is unpleasant; but I am confident that there are rationalist parrots who can demonstrate that it would be a cruel kindness to let a parrot out to fall a prey to cats, or at least to forget its accomplishments and coarsen its naturally delicate fibres in an unprotected struggle for existence. Still, the only parrot a free-souled person can sympathize with is the one that insists on being let out as the first condition of its making itself agreeable. A selfish bird, you may say: one that puts its own gratification before that of the family which is so fond of it — before even the greatest happiness of the greatest number: one that, in aping the independent spirit of a man, has unparroted itself and become a creature that has neither the home-loving nature of a bird nor the strength and enterprise of a mastiff. All the same, you respect that parrot in spite of your conclusive reasoning; and if it persists, you will have either to let it out or kill it.

The sum of the matter is that unless Woman repudiates her womanliness, her duty to her husband, to her children, to society, to the law, and to everyone but herself, she cannot emancipate herself. But her duty to herself is no duty at all, since a debt is cancelled when the debtor and creditor are the same person. Its payment is simply a fulfilment of the individual will, upon which all duty is a restriction, founded on the conception of the will as naturally malign and devilish. Therefore Woman has to repudiate duty altogether. In that repudiation lies her freedom; for it is false to say that Woman is now directly the slave of Man: she is the immediate slave of duty; and as man's path to freedom is strewn with the wreckage of the duties and ideals he has trampled on, so must hers be. She may indeed mask her inconoclasm by proving in rationalist fashion, as Man has often done for the sake of a quiet life, that all these discarded idealist conceptions will be fortified instead of shattered by her emancipation. To a person with a turn for logic, such proofs are as easy as playing the piano is to Paderewski. But it will not be true. A whole basketful of ideals of the most sacred quality will be smashed by the achievement of equality for women and men. Those who shrink from such a clatter and breakage may comfort themselves with the reflection that the replacement of the broken goods will be prompt and certain. It is always a case of "The ideal is dead: long live the ideal!" And the advantage of the work of destruction is, that every new ideal is less of an illusion than the one it has supplanted; so that the destroyer of ideals, though denounced as an enemy of society, is in fact sweeping the world clear of lies.

My digression is now over. Having traversed my loop as I promised, and come back to Man's repudiation of duty by way of Woman's, I may at last proceed to give some more particular account of Ibsen's work without further preoccupation with Mr Clement Scott's protest, or the many others of which it is the type. For we now see that the pioneer must necessarily provoke such outcry as he repudiates duties, tramples on ideals, profanes what was sacred, sanctifies what was infamous, always driving his plough through gardens of pretty weeds in spite of the laws made against trespassers for the protection of the worms which feed on the roots, letting in light and air to hasten the putrefaction of decaying matter, and everywhere proclaiming that "the old beauty is no longer beautiful, the new truth no longer true." He can do no less; and what more and what else he does it is not given to all of his generation to understand. And if any man does not understand, and cannot foresee the harvest, what can he do but cry out in all sincerity against such destruction, until at last we come to know the cry of the blind like any other street cry, and to bear with it as an honest cry, albeit a false alarm.

IV

The Plays

BRAND [1866]

We are now prepared to learn without misgiving that a typical Ibsen play is one in which the "leading lady" is an unwomanly woman, and the "villain" an idealist. It follows that the leading lady is not a heroine of the Drury Lane type; nor does the villain forge or assassinate, since he is a villain by virtue of his determination to do nothing wrong. Therefore readers of Ibsen — not playgoers — have sometimes so far misconceived him as to suppose that his villains are examples rather than warnings, and that the mischief and ruin which attend their actions are but the tribulations from which the soul comes out purified as gold from the furnace. In fact, the beginning of Ibsen's European reputation was the edification with which the pious of Scandinavia received his great dramatic poem *Brand*. Brand the priest is an idealist of heroic earnestness, strength, and courage. He declares himself the champion, not of things as they are, nor of things as they can be made, but of things as they ought to be. Things as they ought to be mean for him things as ordered by men conformed to his ideal of the perfect Adam, who, again, is not man as he is or can be, but man conformed to all the ideals — man as it is his duty to be. In insisting on this conformity, Brand spares neither himself nor anyone else. Life is nothing: self is nothing: the perfect Adam is everything. The imperfect Adam does not fall in with these views. A peasant whom he urges to cross a glacier in a fog because it is his duty to visit his dying daughter, not only flatly declines, but endeavours forcibly to prevent Brand from risking his own life. Brand knocks him down, and sermonizes him with fierce earnestness and scorn. Presently Brand has to cross a fiord in a storm to reach a dying man who, having committed a series of murders, wants "consolation" from a priest. Brand cannot go alone: someone must hold the rudder of his boat whilst he manages the sail. The fisher folk, in whom the old Adam is strong, do not adopt his estimate of the gravity of the situation, and refuse to go. A woman, fascinated by his heroism and idealism, goes. That ends in their marriage, and in the birth of a child to which they become deeply attached. Then Brand, aspiring from

231

height to height of devotion to his ideal, plunges from depth to depth of murderous cruelty. First the child must die from the severity of the climate because Brand must not flinch from the post of duty and leave his congregation exposed to the peril of getting an inferior preacher in his place. Then he forces his wife to give the clothes of the dead child to a gipsy whose baby needs them. The bereaved mother does not grudge the gift; but she wants to hold back only one little garment as a relic of her darling. But Brand sees in this reservation the imperfection of the imperfect Eve. He forces her to regard the situation as a choice between the relic and his ideal. She sacrifices the relic to the ideal, and then dies, broken-hearted. Having killed her, and thereby placed himself beyond ever daring to doubt the idealism upon whose altar he has immolated her — having also refused to go to his mother's death-bed because she compromises with his principles in disposing of her property, he is hailed by the people as a saint, and finds his newly built church too small for his congregation. So he calls upon them to follow him to worship God in His own temple, the mountains. After a brief practical experience of this arrangement, they change their minds, and stone him. The very mountains themselves stone him, indeed; for he is killed by an avalanche.

PEER GYNT [1867]

Brand dies a saint, having caused more intense suffering by his saintliness than the most talented sinner could possibly have done with twice his opportunities. Ibsen does not leave this to be inferred. In another dramatic poem he gives us an accomplished rascal named Peer Gynt, an idealist who avoids Brand's errors by setting up as his ideal the realization of himself by the utter satisfaction of his own will. In this he would seem to be on the path to which Ibsen himself points; and indeed all who know the two plays will agree that whether or no it was better to be Peer Gynt than Brand, it was beyond all question better to be the mother or the sweetheart of Peer, scapegrace and liar as he was, than mother or wife to the saintly Brand. Brand would force his ideal on all men and women: Peer Gynt keeps his ideal for himself alone: it is indeed implicit in the ideal itself that it should be unique — that he alone should have the force to realize it. For Peer's first boyish notion of the self-realized man is not the saint, but the demigod whose indomitable will is stronger than destiny, the fighter, the master, the man whom no woman can resist, the mighty hunter, the knight of a thousand adventures, — the model, in short, of the lover in a lady's novel, or the hero in a boy's romance. Now, no such person exists, or ever did exist, or ever can exist. The man who cultivates an indomitable will and refuses to make way for anything or anybody, soon finds that he cannot hold a street crossing against a tram car, much less a world against the whole human race. Only by plunging into illusions to which every fact gives the lie can he persuade himself that his will is a force that can overcome all other forces, or that it is less conditioned by circumstances than is a wheelbarrow. However, Peer Gynt, being imaginative enough to conceive his ideal, is also imaginative enough to find illusions to hide its unreality, and to persuade himself that Peer Gynt, the shabby countryside loafer, is Peer Gynt, Emperor of Himself, as he writes over the door of his hut in the mountains. His hunting feats are invented; his military genius has no solider foundation than a street fight with a smith; and his reputation as an adventurous daredevil he has to gain by the bravado of carrying off the bride from a wedding at which the guests snub him. Only in the mountains can he enjoy his illusions undisturbed by ridicule: yet even in the mountains he finds obstacles which he cannot force his way through, obstacles which withstand him as spirits with voices, telling him that he must go round. But he will not: he will go forward: he will cut his path sword in hand, in spite of fate. All the same, he has to go round; for the world-will is without Peer Gynt as well as within him. Then he tries the supernatural, only to find that it means nothing more than the transmogrifying of squalid realities by lies and pretences. Still, like our amateurs of thaumaturgy, he is willing to enter into a conspiracy of make-believe up to a certain point. When the Trold king's daughter appears as a repulsive ragged creature riding on a pig, he is ready to accept her as a beautiful princess on a noble steed, on condition that she accepts his mother's tumble-down farmhouse, with the broken window panes stopped up with old clouts, as a splendid castle. He will go with her among the Trolds, and pretend that the gruesome ravine in which they hold their orgies is a glorious palace; he will partake of their filthy food and declare it nectar and ambrosia; he will applaud their obscene antics as exquisite dancing, and their discordant din as divine music; but when they finally propose to slit his eyes so that he may see and hear these things, not as they are, but as he has been pretending to see and hear them, he draws back, resolved to be himself even in self-deception. He leaves the mountains and becomes a prosperous man of business in America, highly respectable and ready for any profitable speculation — slave trade, Bible trade, whisky trade, missionary trade, anything! In this phase he takes to piety, and persuades himself, like Mr Stanley, that he is under the special care of God. This opinion is shaken by an adventure in which he is marooned on the African coast; and it is not restored until the treacherous friends who marooned him are destroyed before his eyes by the blowing-up of the steam yacht they have just stolen from him, when he utters his celebrated exclamation, "Ah, God is a Father to me after all; but economical he certainly is not." He finds a white horse in the desert, and is accepted on its account as the Messiah by an Arab tribe, a success which moves him to declare that now at last he is really worshipped for himself, whereas in America people only respected his breast-pin, the symbol of his money. In commerce, too, he reflects, his eminence was a mere matter of chance, whilst as a prophet he is eminent by pure natural fitness for the post. This is ended by his falling in love with a dancing-girl, who, after leading him into every sort of undignified and ludicrous extravagance, ranging from his hailing her as the Eternal-Feminine of Goethe to the more practical folly of giving her his white horse and all his prophetic finery, runs away with the spoil, and leaves him once more helpless and alone in the desert. He wanders until he comes to the great Sphinx, beside which he finds a German gentleman in great perplexity as to who the Sphinx is. Peer Gynt, seeing in that impassive, immovable, majestic figure a symbol of his own ideal, is able to tell the German gentleman at once that the Sphinx is itself. This explanation dazzles the German, who, after some further discussion of the philosophy of self-realization, invites Peer Gynt to accompany him to a club of learned men in Cairo, who are ripe for enlightenment on this very question. Peer, delighted, accompanies the German to the club, which turns out to be a madhouse in which the lunatics have broken loose and locked up their keepers. It is in this madhouse, and by these madmen, that Peer Gynt is at last crowned Emperor of Himself. He receives their homage as he lies in the dust, fainting with terror.

As an old man, Peer Gynt, returning to the scenes of his early adventures, is troubled with the prospect of meeting a certain button moulder who threatens to make short work of his realized self by melting it down into buttons in his crucible with a heap of other button-material. Immediately the old exaltation of the self realizer is changed into an unspeakable dread of the button-moulder Death, to avoid whom Peer Gynt will commit any act, even to pushing a drowning man from the spar he is clinging to in a shipwreck lest it should not suffice to support two. At last he finds a deserted sweetheart of his youth still waiting for him and still believing in him. In the imagination of this old woman he finds the ideal Peer Gynt; whilst in himself, the loafer, the braggart, the confederate of sham magicians, the Charleston speculator, the false prophet, the dancing-girl's dupe, the bedlam emperor, the selfish thruster of the drowning man into the waves, there is nothing heroic — nothing but commonplace self-seeking and shirking, cowardice and sensuality, veiled only by the romantic fancies of the born liar. With this crowningly unreal realization he is left to face the button moulder as best he can.

Peer Gynt has puzzled a good many people by Ibsen's fantastic and subtle treatment of its thesis. It is so far a difficult play, that the ideal of unconditional self-realization, however familiar its suggestions may be to the ambitious reader, is not at all understood by him, much less formulated as a proposition in metaphysics. When it is stated to him by someone who does understand it, he unhesitatingly dismisses it as idiotic; and it is because he is perfectly right in doing so — because it is idiotic in the most accurate sense of the term — that he finds such difficulty in recognizing it as the common ideal of his own prototype, the pushing, competitive, success-loving man who is the hero of the modern world.

There is nothing novel in Ibsen's dramatic method of reducing these ideals to absurdity. Exactly as Cervantes took the old ideal of chivalry, and shewed what came of a man attempting to act as if it were real, so Ibsen takes the ideals of Brand and Peer Gynt, and treats them in the very same manner. Don Quixote acts as if he were a perfect knight in a world of giants and distressed damsels instead of a country gentleman in a land of innkeepers and farm wenches; Brand acts as if he were the perfect Adam in a world where, by resolute rejection of all compromise with imperfection, it was immediately possible to change the rainbow "bridge between flesh and spirit" into as enduring a structure as the tower of Babel was intended to be, thereby restoring man to the condition in which he walked with God in the garden; and Peer Gynt tries to act as if he had in him a special force that could be concentrated so as to prevail over all other forces. They ignore the real — ignore what they are and where they are, not only, like Nelson, shutting their eyes to the signals that a brave man may disregard, but insanely steering straight on the rocks that no resolution can prevail against. Observe that neither Cervantes nor Ibsen is incredulous, in the Philistine way, as to the power of ideals over men. Don Quixote, Brand, and Peer Gynt are, all three, men of action seeking to realize their ideals in deeds. However ridiculous Don Quixote makes himself, you cannot dislike or despise him, much less think that it would have been better for him to have been a Philistine like Sancho; and Peer Gynt, selfish rascal as he is, is not unlovable. Brand, made terrible by the consequences of his idealism to others, is heroic. Their castles in the air are more beautiful than castles of brick and mortar, but one cannot live in them; and they seduce men into pretending that every hovel is such a castle, just as Peer Gynt pretended that the Trold king's den was a palace.

EMPEROR AND GALILEAN [1873]

When Ibsen, by merely giving the rein to the creative impulse of his poetic nature, had produced *Brand* and *Peer Gynt,* he was nearly forty. His will, in setting his imagination to work, had produced a great puzzle for his intellect. In no case does the difference between the will and the intellect come out more clearly than in that of the poet, save only that of the lover. Had Ibsen died in 1867, he, like many another great poet, would have gone to his grave without having ever rationally understood his own meaning. Nay, if in that year an intellectual expert — a commentator, as we call him — had gone to Ibsen and offered him the explanation of *Brand* which he himself must have arrived at before he constructed *Ghosts* and *The Wild Duck,* he would perhaps have repudiated it with as much disgust as a maiden would feel if anyone were brutal enough to give her the physiological *rationale* of her dreams of meeting a fairy prince. It is only the naif who goes to the creative artist with absolute confidence in receiving an answer to his "What does this passage mean?" That is the very question which the poet's own intellect, which had no part in the conception of the poem, may be asking him. And this curiosity of the intellect — this restless life in it which differentiates it from dead machinery, and which troubles our lesser artists but little, is one of the marks of the greater sort. Shakespear, in *Hamlet,* made a drama of the self-questioning that came upon him when his intellect rose up in alarm, as well it might, against the vulgar optimism of his *Henry V.,* and yet could mend it to no better purpose than by the equally vulgar pessimism of *Troilus and Cressida.* Dante took pains to understand himself: so did Goethe. Richard Wagner, one of the greatest poets of our own day, has left us as many volumes of criticism of art and life as he has left musical scores; and he has expressly described how the intellectual activity which he brought to the analysis of his music dramas was in abeyance during their creation. Just so do we find Ibsen, after composing his two great dramatic poems, entering on a struggle to become intellectually conscious of what he had done.

We have seen that with Shakespear such an effort became itself creative and produced a drama of questioning. With Ibsen the same thing occurred: he harked back to an abandoned project of his, and wrote two huge dramas on the subject of the apostasy of the Emperor Julian. In this work we find him at first preoccupied with a piece of old-fashioned freethinking — the dilemma that moral responsibility presupposes free-will, and that free-will sets man above God. Cain, who slew because he willed, willed because he must, and must have willed to slay because he was himself, comes upon the stage to claim that murder is fertile, and death the ground of life, though he cannot say what is the ground of death. Judas, who betrayed under the same necessity, wants to know whether, since the Master chose him, he chose him foreknowingly. This part of the drama has no very deep significance. It is easy to invent conundrums which dogmatic evangelicalism cannot answer; and no doubt, whilst it was still a nine days' wonder that evangelicalism could not solve all enigmas, such invention seemed something much deeper than the mere intellectual chess-play which it is seen to be now that the nine days are past. In his occasional weakness for such conundrums, and later on in his harping on the hereditary transmission of disease, we see Ibsen's active intellect busy, not only with the problems peculiar to his own plays, but with the fatalism and pessimism of the middle of our century, when the typical advanced culture was attainable by reading Strauss's *Leben Jesu,* the popularizations of Helmholtz and Darwin by Tyndall and Huxley, and George Eliot's novels, vainly protested against by Ruskin as peopled with "the sweepings of a Pentonville omnibus." The traces of this period in Ibsen's writings show how well he knew the crushing weight with which the sordid cares of the ordinary struggle for money and respectability fell on the world when the romance of the creeds was discredited, and progress seemed for the moment to mean, not the growth of the spirit of man, but an effect of the survival of the fittest, brought about by the destruction of the unfit, all the most frightful examples of this systematic destruction being thrust into the utmost prominence by those who were fighting the Church with Mill's favourite dialectical weapon, the incompatibility of divine omnipotence with divine benevolence. His plays are full of evidence for his overwhelming sense of the necessity for rousing the individual into self-assertion against this numbing fatalism; and yet he never seems to have freed his intellect wholly from the acceptance of its scientific validity. That it only accounted for progress at all on the hypothesis of a continuous increase in the severity of the conditions of existence, — that is, on an assumption of just the reverse of what was actually taking place — appears to have escaped Ibsen as completely as it has escaped Professor Huxley himself. It is true that he did not allow himself to be stopped by this gloomy fortress of pessimism and materialism: his genius pushed him past it, but without intellectually reducing it; and the result is, that as far as one can guess, he believes to this day that it is impregnable, not dreaming that it has been demolished, and that too with ridiculous ease, by the mere march behind him of the working class, which, by its freedom from the characteristic bias of the middle classes, has escaped their characteristic illusions, and solved many of the enigmas which they found insoluble because they wished to find them so. His prophetic belief in the spontaneous growth of the will makes him a meliorist without reference to the operation of natural selection; but his impression of the light thrown by physical and biological science on the facts of life seems to be the gloomy one of the period at which he must have received his education in these departments. External nature often plays her most ruthless and destructive part in his works, which have an extraordinary fascination for the pessimists of that school, in spite of the incompatibility of his individualism with that mechanical utilitarian ethic of theirs which treats Man as the sport of every circumstance, and ignores his will altogether.

Another inessential but very prominent feature in Ibsen's dramas will be understood easily by anyone who has observed how a change of religious faith intensifies our concern about our own salvation. An ideal, pious or secular, is practically used as a standard of conduct; and whilst it remains unquestioned, the simple rule of right is to conform to it. In the theological stage, when the Bible is accepted as the revelation of God's will, the pious man, when in doubt as to whether he is acting rightly or wrongly, quiets his misgivings by searching the Scripture until he finds a text which endorses his action.* The rationalist, for whom the Bible has no authority, brings his conduct to such tests as asking himself, after Kant, how it would be if everyone did as he proposes to do; or by calculating the effect of his action on the greatest happiness of the greatest number; or by judging whether the liberty of action he is claiming infringes the equal liberty of others, &c. &c. Most men are ingenious enough to pass examinations of this kind successfully in respect to everything they really want to do. But in periods of transition, as, for instance, when faith in the infallibility of the Bible is shattered, and faith in that of reason not yet perfected, men's uncertainty as to the rightness and wrongness of their actions keeps them in a continual perplexity, amid which casuistry seems the most important branch of intellectual activity. Life, as depicted by Ibsen, is very full of it. We find the great double drama of *Emperor and Galilean* occupied at first with Julian's case regarded as a case of conscience. It is compared, in the manner already described, with the cases of Cain and Judas, the three men being introduced as "corner stones under the wrath of necessity," "great freedom under necessity," and so forth. The qualms of Julian are theatrically effective in producing the most exciting suspense as to whether he will dare to choose between Christ and the imperialist purple; but the mere exhibition of a

---

* As such misgivings seldom arise except when the conscience revolts against the contemplated action, an appeal to Scripture to justify a point of conduct is generally found in practice to be an attempt to excuse a crime.

man struggling between his ambition and his creed belongs to a phase of intellectual interest which Ibsen had passed even before the production of *Brand*, when he wrote his *Kongs Emnerne* or *The Pretenders*. *Emperor and Galilean* might have been appropriately, if prosaically, named *The Mistake of Maximus the Mystic*. It is Maximus who forces the choice on Julian, not as between ambition and principle — between Paganism and Christianity — between "the old beauty that is no longer beautiful and the new truth that is no longer true," but between Christ and Julian himself. Maximus knows that there is no going back to "the first empire" of pagan sensualism. "The second empire," Christian or self-abnegatory idealism, is already rotten at heart. "The third empire" is what he looks for — the empire of Man asserting the eternal validity of his own will. He who can see that not on Olympus, not nailed to the cross, but in himself is God: he is the man to build Brand's bridge between the flesh and the spirit, establishing this third empire in which the spirit shall not be unknown, nor the flesh starved, nor the will tortured and baffled. Thus throughout the first part of the double drama we have Julian prompted step by step to the stupendous conviction that he and not the Galilean is God. His final resolution to seize the throne is expressed in his interruption of the Lord's prayer, which he hears intoned by worshippers in church as he wrestles in the gloom of the catacombs with his own fears and the entreaties and threats of his soldiers urging him to take the final decisive step. At the cue "Lead us not into temptation; but deliver us from evil" he rushes to the church with his soldiers, exclaiming "For mine is the kingdom." Yet he halts on the threshold, dazzled by the light, as his follower Sallust points the declaration by adding, — "and the kingdom, and the power, and the glory."

Once on the throne Julian becomes a mere pedant-tyrant, trying to revive Paganism mechanically by cruel enforcement of external conformity to its rites. In his moments of exaltation he half grasps the meaning of Maximus, only to relapse presently and pervert it into a grotesque mixture of superstition and monstrous vanity. We have him making such speeches as this, worthy of Peer Gynt at his most ludicrous. "Has not Plato long ago enunciated the truth that only a god can rule over men? What did he mean by that saying? Answer me: what did he mean? Far be it from me to assert that Plato — incomparable sage though he was — had any individual, even the greatest, in his prophetic eye," &c. In this frame of mind Christ appears to him, not as the prototype of himself, as Maximus would have him feel, but as a rival god over whom he must prevail at all costs. It galls him to think that the Galilean still reigns in the hearts of men whilst the emperor can only extort lip honour from them by brute force; for in his wildest excesses of egotism he never so loses his saving sense of the realities of things as to mistake the trophies of persecution for the proofs of faith. "Tell me who shall conquer," he demands of Maximus, "— the emperor or the Galilean?"

"Both the emperor and the Galilean shall succumb," says Maximus. "Whether in our time or in hundreds of years I know not; but so it shall be when the right man comes."

"Who is the right man?" says Julian.

"He who shall swallow up both emperor and Galilean," replies the seer. "Both shall succumb; but you shall not therefore perish. Does not the child succumb in the youth and the youth in the man: yet neither child nor youth perishes. You know I have never approved of your policy as emperor. You have tried to make the youth a child again. The empire of the flesh is fallen a prey to the empire of the spirit. But the empire of the spirit is not final, any more than the youth is. You have tried to hinder the youth from growing — from becoming a man. Oh fool, who have drawn your sword against that which is to be — against the third empire, in which the twin-natured shall reign. For him the Jews have a name. They call him Messiah, and are waiting for him."

Still Julian stumbles on the threshold of the idea without entering into it. He is galled out of all comprehension by the rivalry of the Galilean, and asks despairingly who shall break his power. Then Maximus drives the lesson home.

> MAXIMUS. — Is it not written, "Thou shalt have none other gods but me"?
>
> JULIAN. — Yes — yes — yes.
>
> MAXIMUS. — The seer of Nazareth did not preach this god or that: he said "God is I: I am God."
>
> JULIAN. — And that is what makes the emperor powerless. The third empire? The Messiah? Not the Jews' Messiah, but the Messiah of the two empires, the spirit and the world — ?
>
> MAXIMUS. — The God-Emperor.
>
> JULIAN. — The Emperor-God.
>
> MAXIMUS. — Logos in Pan, Pan in Logos.
>
> JULIAN. — How is he begotten?
>
> MAXIMUS. — He is self-begotten in the man who wills.

But it is of no use. Maximus's idea is a synthesis of relations in which not only is Christ God in exactly the same sense as that in which Julian is God, but Julian is Christ as well. The persistence of Julian's jealousy of the Galilean shews that he has not comprehended the synthesis at all, but only seized on that part of it which flatters his own egotism. And since this part is only valid as a constituent of the synthesis, and has no reality when isolated from it, it cannot by itself convince Julian. In vain does Maximus repeat his lesson in every sort of parable, and in such pregnant questions as "How do you know, Julian, that you were not in him whom you now persecute?" He can only wreak him to utter commands to the winds, and to exclaim, in the excitement of burning his fleet on the borders of Persia, "The third empire is here, Maximus. I feel that the Messiah of the earth lives within me. The spirit has become flesh and the flesh spirit. All creation lies within my will and power. More than the fleet is burning. In that glowing, swirling pyre the crucified Galilean is burning to ashes; and the earthly emperor is burning with the Galilean. But from the ashes shall arise, phœnix-like, the God of earth and the Emperor of the spirit in one, in one, in one." At which point he is informed that the Persian refugee whose information has emboldened him to burn his ships, has fled from the camp and is a manifest spy. From that moment he is a broken man. In his next and last emergency, when the Persians fall upon his camp, his first desperate exclamation is a vow to sacrifice to the gods. "To what gods, oh fool?" cries Maximus. "Where are they; and what are they?" "I will sacrifice to this god and that god — I will sacrifice to many," he answers desperately. "One or other must surely hear me. *I must call on something without me and above me.*" A flash of lightning seems to him a response from above; and with this encouragement he throws himself into the fight, clinging, like Macbeth, to an ambiguous oracle which leads him to suppose that only in the Phrygian regions need he fear defeat. He imagines he sees the Nazarene in the ranks of the enemy; and in fighting madly to reach him he is struck down, in the name of Christ, by one of his own soldiers. Then his one Christian general, Jovian, calls on his "believing brethren" to give Cæsar what is Cæsar's. Declaring that the heavens are open and the angels coming to the rescue with their swords of fire, he rallies the Galileans of whom Julian has made slave-soldiers. The pagan free legions, crying out that the god of the Galileans is on the Roman side, and that he is the strongest, follow Jovian as he charges the enemy, who fly in all directions whilst Julian, sinking back from a vain effort to rise, exclaims, "Thou hast conquered, oh Galilean."

Julian dies quietly in his tent, averring, in reply to a Christian friend's inquiry, that he has nothing to repent of. "The power which circumstances placed in my hands," he says, "and which is an emanation of divinity, I am conscious of having used to the best of my skill. I have never wittingly wronged anyone. If some should think that

I have not fulfilled all expectations, they should in justice reflect that there is a mysterious power outside us, which in a great measure governs the issue of human undertakings." He still does not see eye to eye with Maximus, though there is a flash of insight in his remark to him, when he learns that the village where he fell is called the Phrygian region, that "the world-will has laid an ambush for him." It was something for Julian to have seen that the power which he found stronger than his individual will was itself will; but inasmuch as he conceived it, not as the whole of which his will was but a part, but as a rival will, he was not the man to found the third empire. He had felt the godhead in himself, but not in others. Being only able to say, with half conviction, "The kingdom of heaven is within ME," he had been utterly vanquished by the Galilean who had been able to say, "The kingdom of heaven is within YOU." But he was on the way to that full truth. A man cannot believe in others until he believes in himself; for his conviction of the equal worth of his fellows must be filled by the overflow of his conviction of his own worth. Against the spurious Christianity of asceticism, starving that indispensable prior conviction, Julian rightly rebelled; and Maximus rightly incited him to rebel. But Maximus could not fill the prior conviction even to fulness, much less to overflowing; for the third empire was not yet, and is not yet. Still the tyrant dies with a peaceful conscience; and Maximus is able to tell the priest at the bedside that the world-will shall answer for Julian's soul. What troubles the mystic is his having misled Julian by encouraging him to bring upon himself the fate of Cain and Judas. As water can be boiled by fire, man can be prompted and stimulated from without to assert his individuality; but just as no boiling can fill a half-empty well, no external stimulus can enlarge the spirit of man to the point at which he can self-beget the Emperor-God in himself by willing. At that point "to will is to have to will"; and it is with these words on his lips that Maximus leaves the stage, still sure that the third empire is to come.

It is not necessary to translate the scheme of *Emperor and Galilean* into terms of the antithesis between idealism and realism. Julian, in this respect, is a reincarnation of Peer Gynt. All the difference is that the subject which was instinctively projected in the earlier poem, is intellectually constructed as well in the later history, Julian plus Maximus the Mystic being Peer plus one who understands him better than Ibsen did when he created him. The current interest of Ibsen's interpretation of original Christianity is obvious. The deepest sayings recorded in the gospels are now nothing but eccentric paradoxes to most of those who reject the superstitious view of Christ's divinity. Those who accept that view often consider that such acceptance absolves them from attaching any sensible meaning to his words at all, and so might as well pin their faith to a stock or stone. Of these attitudes the first is superficial, and the second stupid. Ibsen's interpretation, whatever may be its validity, will certainly hold the field long after the current "Crosstianity," as it has been aptly called, becomes unthinkable.

Ibsen had now written three immense dramas, all dealing with the effect of idealism on individual egotists of exceptional imaginative excitability. This he was able to do whilst his intellectual consciousness of his theme was yet incomplete, by simply portraying sides of himself. He has put himself into the skin of Brand, of Peer Gynt, and of Julian; and these figures have accordingly a certain direct vitality which belongs to none of his subsequent creations of the male sex. There are flashes of it in Relling, in Lövborg, in Ellida's stranger from the sea; but they are only flashes: henceforth all his really vivid and solar figures are women. For, having at last completed his intellectual analysis of idealism, he could now construct methodical illustrations of its social working, instead of, as before, blindly projecting imaginary personal experiences which he himself had not yet succeeded in interpreting. Further, now that he understood the matter, he could see plainly the effect of idealism as a social force on people quite unlike himself: that is to say, on everyday people in everyday life — on shipbuilders, bank managers, parsons, and doctors, as well as on saints, romantic adventurers, and emperors. With his eyes thus opened, instances of the mischief of idealism crowded upon him so rapidly that he began deliberately to inculcate their moral by writing realistic prose plays of modern life, abandoning all production of art for art's sake. His skill as a playwright and his genius as an artist were thenceforth used only to secure attention and effectiveness for his detailed attack on idealism. No more verse, no more tragedy for the sake of tears or comedy for the sake of laughter, no more seeking to produce specimens of art forms in order that literary critics might fill the public belly with the east wind. The critics, it is true, soon declared that he had ceased to be an artist; but he, having something else to do with his talent than to fulfil critics' definitions, took no notice of them, not thinking their ideal sufficiently important to write a play about.

THE LEAGUE OF YOUTH [1869]

The first of the series of realistic prose plays is called *Pillars of Society;* but before describing this, a word must be said about a previous work which seems to have determined the form which the later series took. Between *Peer Gynt* and *Emperor and Galilean*, Ibsen had let fall an amusing comedy called *The League of Youth* (*De Unges Forbund*) in which the imaginative egotist reappears farcically as an ambitious young lawyer-politician who, smarting under a snub from a local landowner and county magnate, relieves his feelings with such a passionate explosion of Radical eloquence that he is cheered to the echo by the progressive party. Intoxicated with this success, he imagines himself a great leader of the people and a wielder of the mighty engine of democracy. He narrates to a friend a dream in which he saw kings swept helplessly over the surface of the earth by a mighty wind. He has hardly achieved this impromptu when he receives an invitation to dine with the local magnate, whose friends, to spare his feelings, have misled him as to the person aimed at in the new demagogue's speech. The invitation sets the egotist's imagination on the opposite tack: he is presently pouring forth his soul in the magnate's drawing-room to the very friend to whom he related the great dream.

> "My goal is this: in the course of time I shall get into Parliament, perhaps into the Ministry, and marry happily into a rich and honourable family. I intend to reach it by my own exertions. I must and shall reach it without help from anyone. Meanwhile I shall enjoy life here, drinking in beauty and sunshine. Here there are fine manners: life moves gracefully here: the very floors seem laid to be trodden only by lacquered shoes: the arm chairs are deep; and the ladies sink exquisitely into them. Here the conversation goes lightly and elegantly, like a game at battledore; and no blunders come plumping in to make an awkward silence. Here I feel for the first time what distinction means. Yes: we have indeed an aristocracy of culture; and to it I will belong. Dont you yourself feel the refining influence of the place," &c. &c.

For the rest, the play is an ingenious comedy of intrigue, clever enough in its mechanical construction to entitle the French to claim that Ibsen owes something to his technical education as a playwright in the school of Scribe, although it is hardly necessary to add that the difference between *The League of Youth* and the typical "well made play" of Scribe is like the difference between a human being and a marionette. One or two episodes in the last two acts contain the germs of later plays; and it was the suitability of the realistic prose comedy form to these episodes that no doubt confirmed Ibsen in his choice of it. Therefore *The League of Youth* would stand as the first of the realistic plays in any classification which referred to form alone. In a classification by content, with which we are here alone concerned, it must stand in its chronological place as a farcical member of the group of heroic plays beginning with *The Pretenders* and ending with *Emperor and Galilean*.

PILLARS OF SOCIETY [1877]

Pillars of Society, then, is the first play in which Ibsen writes as one who has intellectually mastered his own didactic purpose, and no longer needs to project himself into his characters. It is the history of one Karsten Bernick, a "pillar of society" who, in pursuance of the duty of maintaining the respectability of his father's famous firm of shipbuilders (to shatter which would be to shatter one of the ideals of commercial society and to bring abstract respectability into disrepute), has averted a disgraceful exposure by allowing another man to bear the discredit not only of a love affair in which he himself had been the sinner, but of a theft which was never committed at all, having been merely alleged as an excuse for the firm being out of funds at a critical period. Bernick is an abject slave to the idealizings of a certain schoolmaster Rörlund about respectability, duty to society, good example, social influence, health of the community, and so on. When he falls in love with a married actress, he feels that no man has a right to shock the feelings of Rörlund and the community for his own selfish gratification. However, a clandestine intrigue will shock nobody, since nobody need know of it. He accordingly adopts this method of satisfying himself and preserving the moral tone of the community at the same time. Unluckily, the intrigue is all but discovered; and Bernick has either to see the moral security of the community shaken to its foundations by the terrible scandal of his exposure, or else to deny what he did and put it on another man. As the other man happens to be going to America, where he can easily conceal his imputed shame, Bernick's conscience tells him that it would be little short of a crime against society to neglect such an opportunity; and he accordingly lies his way back into the good opinion of Rörlund and company at the emigrant's expense. There are three women in the play for whom the schoolmaster's ideals have no attractions. First, there is the actress's daughter, who wants to get to America because she hears that people there are not good; and she is heartily tired of good people, since it is part of their goodness to look down on her because of her mother's disgrace. The schoolmaster, to whom she is engaged, condescends to her for the same reason. The second has already sacrificed her happiness and wasted her life in conforming to Mr Stead's ideal of womanliness; and she earnestly advises the younger woman not to commit that folly, but to break her engagement with the schoolmaster, and elope promptly with the man she loves. The third is a naturally free woman who has snapped her fingers at the current ideals all her life; and it is her presence that at last encourages the liar to break with the ideals by telling the truth about himself. The comic personage of the piece is a useless hypochondriac whose function in life, as described by himself, is "to hold up the banner of the ideal." This he does by sneering at everything and everybody for not resembling the heroic incidents and characters he reads about in novels and tales of adventure. But in his obvious peevishness and folly, he is much less dangerous than the pious idealist, the earnest and respectable Rörlund. The play concludes with Bernick's admission that the spirits of Truth and Freedom are the true pillars of society, a phrase which sounds so like an idealistic commonplace that it is necessary to add that Truth in this passage does not mean the nursery convention of truth-telling satirized by Ibsen himself in a later play, as well as by Labiche and other comic dramatists. It means the unflinching recognition of facts, and the abandonment of the conspiracy to ignore such of them as do not bolster up the ideals. The idealist rule as to truth dictates the recognition only of those facts or idealistic masks of facts which have a respectable air, and the mentioning of these on all occasions and at all hazards. Ibsen urges the recognition of all facts; but as to mentioning them, he wrote a whole play, as we shall see presently, to shew that you must do that at your own peril, and that a truth-teller who cannot hold his tongue on occasion may do as much mischief as a whole university full of trained liars. The word Freedom, I need hardly say, means freedom from slavery to the Rörlund ideals.

A DOLL'S HOUSE [1879]

Unfortunately, *Pillars of Society,* as a propagandist play, is disabled by the circumstance that the hero, being a fraudulent hypocrite in the ordinary police-court sense of the phrase, is not accepted as a typical pillar of society by the class which he represents. Accordingly, Ibsen took care next time to make his idealist irreproachable from the standpoint of the ordinary idealist morality. In the famous *Doll's House,* the pillar of society who owns the doll is a model husband, father, and citizen. In his little household, with the three darling children and the affectionate little wife, all on the most loving terms with one another, we have the sweet home, the womanly woman, the happy family life of the idealist's dream. Mrs Nora Helmer is happy in the belief that she has attained a valid realization of all these illusions — that she is an ideal wife and mother, and that Helmer is an ideal husband who would, if the necessity arose, give his life to save her reputation. A few simply contrived incidents disabuse her effectually on all these points. One of her earliest acts of devotion to her husband has been the secret raising of a sum of money to enable him to make a tour which was necessary to restore his health. As he would have broken down sooner than go into debt, she has had to persuade him that the money was a gift from her father. It was really obtained from a moneylender, who refused to make her the loan unless she induced her father to endorse the promissory note. This being impossible, as her father was dying at the time, she took the shortest way out of the difficulty by writing the name herself, to the entire satisfaction of the moneylender, who, though not at all duped, knows that forged bills are often the surest to be paid. Then she slaves in secret at scrivener's work until she has nearly paid off the debt. At this point Helmer is made manager of the bank in which he is employed; and the moneylender, wishing to obtain a post there, uses the forged bill to force Nora to exert her influence with Helmer on his behalf. But she, having a hearty contempt for the man, cannot be persuaded by him that there was any harm in putting her father's name on the bill, and ridicules the suggestion that the law would not recognize that she was right under the circumstances. It is her husband's own contemptuous denunciation of a forgery formerly committed by the moneylender himself that destroys her self-satisfaction and opens her eyes to her ignorance of the serious business of the world to which her husband belongs — the world outside the home he shares with her. When he goes on to tell her that commercial dishonesty is generally to be traced to the influence of bad mothers, she begins to perceive that the happy way in which she plays with the children, and the care she takes to dress them nicely, are not sufficient to constitute her a fit person to train them. In order to redeem the forged bill, she resolves to borrow the balance due upon it from a friend of the family. She has learnt to coax her husband into giving her what she asks by appealing to his affection for her: that is, by playing all sorts of pretty tricks until he is wheedled into an amorous humour. This plan she has adopted without thinking about it, instinctively taking the line of least resistance with him. And now she naturally takes the same line with her husband's friend. An unexpected declaration of love from him is the result; and it at once explains to her the real nature of the domestic influence she has been so proud of. All her illusions about herself are now shattered: she sees herself as an ignorant and silly woman, a dangerous mother, and a wife kept for her husband's pleasure merely; but she only clings the harder to her illusion about him: he is still the ideal husband who would make any sacrifice to rescue her from ruin. She resolves to kill herself rather than allow him to destroy his own career by taking the forgery on himself to save her reputation. The final disillusion comes when he, instead of at once proposing to pursue this ideal line of conduct when he hears of the forgery, naturally enough flies into a vulgar rage and heaps invective on her for disgracing him. Then she sees that their whole family life has been a fiction — their home a mere doll's house in which they have been playing at ideal husband and father, wife and mother. So she leaves him then and there in order to find out the reality of things for herself, and to gain some position not fundamentally false, refusing to see her children again until she is fit to be in charge of them, or to live with him until she and he become capable of a more honourable relation to one another than that in which they have hitherto stood. He at first cannot understand what has happened, and flourishes the shattered ideals over her as if they were as potent as ever. He presents the course most agreeable to him — that of her staying at home and avoiding a scandal — as her duty to her husband, to her children, and to her religion; but the magic of these disguises is gone; and at last even he understands what has really happened, and sits down alone to wonder whether that more honourable relation can ever come to pass between them.

GHOSTS [1881]

In his next play, Ibsen returned to the charge with such an uncompromising and outspoken attack on marriage as a useless sacrifice of human beings to an ideal, that his meaning was obscured by its very obviousness. *Ghosts,* as it is called, is the story of a woman who has faithfully acted as a model wife and mother, sacrificing herself at every point with selfless thoroughness. Her husband is a man with a huge capacity and appetite for sensuous enjoyment. Society, prescribing ideal duties and not enjoyment for him, drives him to enjoy himself in underhand and illicit ways. When he marries his model wife, her devotion to duty only makes life harder for him; and he at last takes refuge in the caresses of an undutiful but pleasure-loving housemaid, and leaves his wife to satisfy her conscience by managing his business affairs whilst he satisfies his cravings as best he can by reading novels, drinking, and flirting, as aforesaid, with the servants. At this point even those who are most indignant with Nora Helmer for walking out of the doll's house, must admit that Mrs Alving would be justified in walking out of *her* house. But Ibsen is determined to show you what comes of the scrupulous line of conduct you were so angry with Nora for not pursuing. Mrs Alving feels that her place is by her husband for better for worse, and by her child. Now the ideal of wifely and womanly duty which demands this from her also demands that she should regard herself as an outraged wife, and her husband as a scoundrel. The family ideal again requires that she should suffer in silence, and, for her son's sake, never shatter his faith in the purity of home life by letting him know the truth about his father. It is her duty to conceal that truth from the world and from him. In this she only falters for one moment. Her marriage has not been a love match: she has, in pursuance of her duty as a daughter, contracted it for the sake of her family, although her heart inclined to a highly respectable clergyman, a professor of her own idealism, named Manders. In the humiliation of her first discovery of her husband's infidelity, she leaves the house and takes refuge with Manders; but he at once leads her back to the path of duty, from which she does not again swerve. With the utmost devotion she now carries out a tremendous scheme of lying and imposture. She so manages her husband's affairs and so shields his good name that everybody believes him to be a public-spirited citizen of the strictest conformity to current ideals of respectability and family life. She sits up of nights listening to his lewd and silly conversation, and even drinking with him, to keep him from going into the streets and betraying what she considers his vices. She provides for the servant he has seduced, and brings up his illegitimate daughter as a maid in her own houshold. And as a crowning sacrifice, she sends her son away to Paris to be educated there, knowing that if he stays at home the shattering of his ideals must come sooner or later. Her work is crowned with success. She gains the esteem of her old love the clergyman, who is never tired of holding up her household as a beautiful realization of the Christian ideal of marriage. Her own martyrdom is brought to an end at last by the death of her husband in the odour of a most sanctified reputation, leaving her free to recall her son from Paris and enjoy his society, and his love and gratitude, in the flower of his early manhood. But when he comes home, the facts refuse as obstinately as ever to correspond to her ideals. Oswald, the son, has inherited his father's love of enjoyment; and when, in dull rainy weather, he returns from Paris to the solemn, strictly ordered house, where virtue and duty have had their temple for so many years, his mother sees him first shew the unmistakable signs of boredom with which she is so miserably familiar from of old; then sit after dinner killing time over the bottle; and finally — the climax of anguish — begin to flirt with the maid who, as the mother alone knows, is his own father's daughter. But there is this worldwide difference in her insight to the cases of the father and the son. She did not love the father: she loves the son with the intensity of a heart-starved woman who has nothing else left to love. Instead of recoiling from him with pious disgust and Pharisaical consciousness of moral superiority, she sees at once that he has a right to be happy in his own way, and that she has no right to force him to be dutiful and wretched in hers. She sees, too, her injustice to the unfortunate father, and the iniquity of the monstrous fabric of lies and false appearances which she has wasted her life in manufacturing. She resolves that her son's life, at least, shall not be sacrificed to joyless and unnatural ideals. But she soon finds that the work of the ideals is not to be undone quite so easily. In driving the father to steal his pleasures in secrecy and squalor, they had brought upon him the diseases bred by such conditions; and her son now tells her that those diseases have left their mark on him, and that he carries poison in his pocket against the time, foretold to him by a Parisian surgeon, when he shall be struck down with softening of the brain. In desperation she turns to the task of rescuing him from this horrible apprehension by making his life happy. The house shall be made as bright as Paris for him; he shall have as much champagne as he wishes until he is no longer driven to that dangerous resource by the dulness of his life with her: if he loves the girl he shall marry her if she were fifty times his half-sister. But the half-sister, on learning the state of his health, leaves the house; for she, too, is her father's daughter, and is not going to sacrifice her life in devotion to an invalid. When the mother and son are left alone in their dreary home, with the rain still falling outside, all she can do for him is to promise that if his doom overtakes him before he can poison himself, she will make a final sacrifice of her natural feelings by performing that dreadful duty, the first of all her duties that has any real basis. Then the weather clears up at last; and the sun, which the young man has so longed to see, appears. He asks her to give it to him to play with; and a glance at him shews her that the ideals have claimed their victim, and that the time has come for her to save him from a real horror by sending him from her out of the world, just as she saved him from an imaginary one years before by sending him out of Norway.

This last scene of *Ghosts* is so appallingly tragic that the emotions it excites prevent the meaning of the play from being seized and discussed like that of *A Doll's House*. In England nobody, as far as I know, seems to have perceived that *Ghosts* is to *A Doll's House* what Mr Walter Besant intended his own "sequel"* to that play to be.

---

* An astonishing production, which will be found in the *English Illustrated Magazine* for January 1890. Mr Besant makes the moneylender, as a reformed man, and a pattern of all the virtues, repeat his old tactics

Mr Besant attempted to shew what might come of Nora's repudiation of that idealism of which he is one of the most popular professors. But the effect made on Mr Besant by *A Doll's House* was very faint compared to that produced on the English critics by the first perform-ance of *Ghosts* in this country. In the earlier part of this essay I have shewn that since Mrs Alving's early conceptions of duty are as valid to ordinary critics as to Pastor Manders, who must appear to them as an admirable man, endowed with Helmer's good sense without Helmer's selfishness, a pretty general disapproval of the "moral" of the play was inevitable. Fortunately, the newspaper press went to such bedlamite lengths on this occasion that Mr William Archer, the well-known dramatic critic and translator of Ibsen, was able to put the whole body of hostile criticism out of court by simply quoting its excesses in an article entitled *Ghosts and Gibberings,* which appeared in the *Pall Mall Gazette* of the 8th of April 1891. Mr Archer's extracts, which he offers as a nucleus for a Dictionary of Abuse modelled upon the Wagner "Schimpf-Lexicon," are worth reprinting here as samples of contemporary idealist criticism of the drama.

Descriptions of the Play

"Ibsen's positively abominable play entitled *Ghosts* . . . This dis-gusting representation . . . Reprobation due to such as aim at in-fecting the modern theatre with poison after desperately inoculating themselves and others . . . An open drain; a loathsome sore un-bandaged; a dirty act done publicly; a lazar-house with all its doors and windows open . . . Candid foulness . . . Kotzebue turned bestial and cynical. Offensive cynicism . . . Ibsen's melancholy and mal-

---

by holding a forged bill *in terrorem* over Nora's grown-up daughter, who is engaged to his son. The bill has been forged by her brother, who has inherited a tendency to this sort of offence from his mother. Helmer having taken to drink after the departure of his wife, and forfeited his social posi-tion, the moneylender tells the girl that if she persists in disgracing him by marrying his son, he will send her brother to gaol. She evades the dilemma by drowning herself. An exquisite absurdity is given to this *jeu d'esprit* by the moral, which is, that if Nora had never run away from her husband her daughter would never have drowned herself; and *also* by the writer's naïve unconsciousness of the fact that he has represented the moneylender as doing over again what he did in the play, with the difference that, having become eminently respectable, he has also become a remorseless scoundrel. Ibsen shows him as a good-natured fellow at bottom. [Besant's "After The Doll's House" stirred Shaw to respond with "Still after The Doll's House: A Sequel to Mr. Walter Besant's Sequel to Henrik Ibsen's Play." This appeared in *Time,* London, February 1890, and in *The Transatlantic,* Boston, 15 April 1890. It was reprinted in Shaw's *Short Stories, Scraps & Shavings,* 1932. — Ed.]

odorous word . . . Absolutely loathsome and fetid . . . Gross, almost putrid indecorum . . . Literary carrion . . . Crapulous stuff . . . Novel and perilous nuisance." — *Daily Telegraph* (leading article). "This mass of vulgarity, egotism, coarseness, and absurdity." — *Daily Telegraph* (criticism). "Unutterably offensive . . . Prosecution under Lord Campbell's Act . . . Abominable piece . . . Scandalous." — *Standard*. "Naked loathsomeness . . . Most dismal and repulsive production." — *Daily News*. "Revolting suggestive and blasphemous . . . Characters either contradictory in themselves, uninteresting or abhorrent." — *Daily Chronicle*. "A repulsive and degrading work." — *Queen*. "Morbid, unhealthy, unwholesome and disgusting story . . . A piece to bring the stage into disrepute and dishonour with every right-thinking man and woman." — *Lloyd's*. "Merely dull dirt long drawn out." — *Hawk*. "Morbid horrors of the hideous tale . . . Ponderous dulness of the didactic talk . . . If any repetition of this outrage be attempted, the authorities will doubtless wake from their lethargy." — *Sporting and Dramatic News*. "Just a wicked nightmare." — *The Gentlewoman*. "Lugubrious diagnosis of sordid impropriety . . . Characters are prigs, pedants, and profligates . . . Morbid caricatures . . . Maunderings of nookshotten Norwegians . . . It is no more of a play than an average Gaiety burlesque." — W. St. Leger in *Black and White*. "Most loathsome of all Ibsen's plays . . . Garbage and offal." — *Truth*. "Ibsen's putrid play called *Ghosts* . . . So loathsome an enterprise." — *Academy*. "As foul and filthy a concoction as has ever been allowed to disgrace the boards of an English theatre . . . Dull and disgusting . . . Nastiness and malodorousness laid on thickly as with a trowel." — *Era*. "Noisome corruption." — *Stage*.

Descriptions of Ibsen

"An egotist and a bungler." — *Daily Telegraph*. "A crazy fanatic . . . A crazy, cranky being . . . Not only consistently dirty but deplorably dull." — *Truth*. "The Norwegian pessimist *in petto*" [*sic*]. — W. St Leger in *Black and White*. "Ugly, nasty, discordant, and downright dull . . . A gloomy sort of ghoul, bent on groping for horrors by night, and blinking like a stupid owl when the warm sunlight of the best of life dances into his wrinkled eyes." — *Gentlewoman*. "A teacher of the æstheticism of the Lock Hospital." — *Saturday Review*.

Descriptions of Ibsen's Admirers

"Lovers of prurience and dabblers in impropriety who are eager to gratify their illicit tastes under the pretence of art." — *Evening Stand-*

ard. "Ninety-seven per cent. of the people who go to see *Ghosts* are nasty-minded people who find the discussion of nasty subjects to their taste in exact proportion to their nastiness." — *Sporting and Dramatic News.* "The sexless . . . The unwomanly woman, the unsexed females, the whole army of unprepossessing cranks in petticoats . . . Educated and muck-ferreting dogs . . . Effeminate men and male women . . . They all of them — men and women alike — know that they are doing not only a nasty but an illegal thing . . . The Lord Chamberlain left them alone to wallow in *Ghosts* . . . Outside a silly clique, there is not the slightest interest in the Scandinavian humbug or all his works . . . A wave of human folly." — *Truth.*

AN ENEMY OF THE PEOPLE [1882]

After this, the reader will understand the temper in which Ibsen set about his next play, *An Enemy of the People,* in which, having done sufficient execution among the ordinary social, domestic, and puritanic ideals, he puts his finger for a moment on political ideals. The play deals with a local majority of middle-class people who are pecuniarily interested in concealing the fact that the famous baths which attract visitors to their town and customers to their shops and hotels are contaminated by sewage. When an honest doctor insists on exposing this danger, the townspeople immediately disguise themselves ideally. Feeling the disadvantage of appearing in their true character as a conspiracy of interested rogues against an honest man, they pose as Society, as The People, as Democracy, as the solid Liberal Majority, and other imposing abstractions, the doctor, in attacking them, of course being thereby made an enemy of The People, a danger to Society, a traitor to Democracy, an apostate from the great Liberal party, and so on. Only those who take an active part in politics can appreciate the grim fun of the situation, which, though it has an intensely local Norwegian air, will be at once recognized as typical in England, not, perhaps, by the professional literary critics, who are for the most part, *fainéants* as far as political life is concerned, but certainly by everyone who has got as far as a seat on the committee of the most obscure caucus.

As *An Enemy of the People* contains one or two references to democracy which are anything but respectful, it is necessary to define Ibsen's criticism of it with precision. Democracy is really only an arrangement by which the whole people are given a certain share in the control of the government. It has never been proved that this is ideally the best arrangement: it became necessary because the people willed to have it; and it has been made effective only to the very limited extent short of which the dissatisfaction of the majority would have taken the form of actual violence. Now when men had to submit to kings, they consoled themselves by making it an article of faith that the king was always right — idealized him as a Pope, in fact. In the same way we who have to submit to majorities set up Voltaire's pope, "Monsieur Tout-le-monde," and make it blasphemy against Democracy to deny that the majority is always right, although that, as Ibsen says, is a lie. It is a scientific fact that the majority, however eager it may be for the reform of old abuses, is always wrong in its opinion of new developments, or rather is always unfit for them (for it can hardly be said to be wrong in opposing developments for which it is not yet fit). The pioneer is a tiny minority of the force he heads; and so, though it is easy to be in a minority and yet be wrong, it is absolutely impossible to be in the majority and yet be right as to the newest social prospects. We should never progress at all if it were possible for each of us to stand still on democratic principles until we saw whither all the rest were moving, as our statesmen declare themselves bound to do when they are called upon to lead. Whatever clatter we may make for a time with our filing through feudal serf collars and kicking off rusty capitalistic fetters, we shall never march a step forward except at the heels of "the strongest man, he who is able to stand alone" and to turn his back on "the damned compact Liberal majority." All of which is no disparagement of adult suffrage, payment of members, annual parliaments and so on, but simply a wholesome reduction of them to their real place in the social economy as pure machinery — machinery which has absolutely no principles except the principles of mechanics, and no motive power in itself whatsoever. The idealization of public organizations is as dangerous as that of kings or priests. We need to be reminded that though there is in the world a vast number of buildings in which a certain ritual is conducted before crowds called congregations by a functionary called a priest, who is subject to a central council controlling all such functionaries on a few points, there is not therefore any such thing in reality as the ideal Catholic Church, nor ever was, nor ever will be. There may, too, be a highly elaborate organization of public affairs; but there is no such thing as the ideal State. All abstractions invested with collective consciousness or collective authority, set above the individual, and exacting duty from him on pretence of acting or thinking with greater validity than he, are man-eating idols red with human sacrifices. This position must not be confounded with Anarchism, or the idealization of the repudiation of Governments. Ibsen does not refuse to pay the tax collector, but may be supposed to regard him, not as an emissary of something that does not exist and never did, called THE STATE, but simply as the man sent round by the committee of citizens (mostly fools as far as "the third empire" is concerned) to collect the money for the police or the paving and lighting of the streets.

THE WILD DUCK [1884]

After *An Enemy of the People*, Ibsen, as I have said, left the vulgar ideals for dead, and set about the exposure of those of the choicer spirits, beginning with the incorrigible idealists who had idealized his very self, and were becoming known as Ibsenites. His first move in this direction was such a tragi-comic slaughtering of sham Ibsenism that his astonished victims plaintively declared that *The Wild Duck*, as the new play was called, was a satire on his former works; whilst the pious, whom he had disappointed so severely by his interpretation of *Brand*, began to think that he had come back repentant to the fold. The household to which we are introduced in *The Wild Duck* is not, like Mrs Alving's, a handsome one made miserable by superstitious illusions, but a shabby one made happy by romantic illusions. The only member of it who sees it as it really is is the wife, a good-natured Philistine who desires nothing better. The husband, a vain, petted, spoilt dawdler, believes that he is a delicate and high-souled man, devoting his life to redeeming his old father's name from the disgrace brought on it by an imprisonment for breach of the forest laws. This redemption he proposes to effect by making himself famous as a great inventor some day when he has the necessary inspiration. Their daughter, a girl in her teens, believes intensely in her father and in the promised invention. The disgraced grandfather cheers himself by drink whenever he can get it; but his chief resource is a wonderful garret full of rabbits and pigeons. The old man has procured a number of second-hand Christmas trees; and with these he has turned the garret into a sort of toy forest, in which he can play at bear hunting, which was one of the sports of his youth and prosperity. The weapons employed in the hunting expeditions are a gun which will not go off, and a pistol which occasionally brings down a rabbit or a pigeon. A crowning touch is given to the illusion by a wild duck, which, however, must not be shot, as it is the special property of the girl, who reads and dreams whilst the woman cooks and washes, besides carrying on the photographic work which is supposed to be the business of her husband. She does not appreciate his highly strung sensitiveness of character, which is constantly suffering agonizing jars from her vulgarity; but then she does not appreciate that other fact that he is a lazy and idle impostor. Downstairs there is a disgraceful clergyman named Molvik, a hopeless drunkard; but even he respects himself and is tolerated because of a special illusion invented for him by another lodger, a doctor — the now famous Dr Relling — upon whom the lesson of the household above has not been thrown away. Molvik, says the doctor, must break out into drinking fits because he is daimonic, an interesting explanation which completely relieves the reverend gentleman from the imputation of vulgar tippling.

Into this domestic circle there comes a new lodger, an idealist of the most advanced type. He greedily swallows the daimonic theory of the clergyman's drunkenness, and enthusiastically accepts the photographer as the high-souled hero he supposes himself to be; but he is troubled because the relations of the man and his wife do not constitute an ideal marriage. He happens to know that the woman, before her marriage, was the cast-off mistress of his own father; and because she has not told her husband this, he conceives her life as founded on a lie, like that of Bernick in *Pillars of Society*. He accordingly sets himself to work out the woman's salvation for her, and establish ideally frank relations between the pair, by simply blurting out the truth, and then asking them, with fatuous self-satisfaction, whether they do not feel much the better for it. This wanton piece of mischief has more serious results than a mere domestic scene. The husband is too weak to act on his bluster about outraged honour and the impossibility of his ever living with his wife again; and the woman is merely annoyed with the idealist for telling on her; but the girl takes the matter to heart and shoots herself. The doubt cast on her parentage, with her father's theatrical repudiation of her, destroys her ideal place in the home, and makes her a source of discord there; so she sacrifices herself, thereby carrying out the teaching of the idealist mischief-maker, who has talked a good deal to her about the duty and beauty of self-sacrifice, without foreseeing that he might be taken in mortal earnest. The busybody thus finds that people cannot be freed from their failings from without. They must free themselves. When Nora is strong enough to live out of the doll's house, she will go out of it of her own accord if the door stands open; but if before that period you take her by the scruff of the neck and thrust her out, she will only take refuge in the next establishment of the kind that offers to receive her. Woman has thus two enemies to deal with: the old-fashioned one who wants to keep the door locked, and the new-fashioned one who wants to thrust her into the street before she is ready to go. In the cognate case of a hypocrite and liar like Bernick, exposing him is a mere police measure: he is none the less a liar and hypocrite when you have exposed him. If you want to make a sincere and truthful man of him, all that you can do is to remove what you can of the external obstacles to his exposing himself, and then wait for the operation of his internal impulse to confess. If he has no such impulse, then you must put up with him as he is. It is useless to make claims on him which he is not yet prepared to meet. Whether, like Brand, we make such claims because to refrain would be to compromise with evil, or, like Gregers Werle, because we think their moral beauty must recommend them at sight to every one, we shall alike incur Relling's impatient assurance that "life would be quite tolerable if we could only get rid of the confounded duns that keep on pestering us in our poverty with the claims of the ideal."

ROSMERSHOLM [1886]

Ibsen did not in *The Wild Duck* exhaust the subject of the danger of forming ideals for other people, and interfering in their lives with a view to enabling them to realize those ideals. Cases far more typical than that of the meddlesome lodger are those of the priest who regards the ennobling of mankind as a sort of trade process of which his cloth gives him a monopoly, and the clever woman who pictures a noble career for the man she loves, and devotes herself to helping him to achieve it. In *Rosmersholm,* the play with which Ibsen followed up *The Wild Duck,* there is an unpractical country parson, a gentleman of ancient stock, whose family has been for many years a centre of social influence. The tradition of that influence reinforces his priestly tendency to regard the ennoblement of the world as an external operation to be performed by himself; and the need of such ennoblement is very evident to him; for his nature is a fine one: he looks at the world with some dim prevision of "the third empire." He is married to a woman of passionately affectionate nature, who is very fond of him, but does not regard him as a regenerator of the human race. Indeed she does not share any of his dreams, and only acts as an extinguisher on the sacred fire of his idealism. He, she, her brother Kroll the headmaster, Kroll's wife, and their set form a select circle of the best people in the place, comfortably orbited in the social system, and quite planetary in ascertained position and unimpeachable respectability. Into the orbit comes presently a wandering star, one Rebecca Gamvik, an unpropertied orphan, who has been allowed to read advanced books, and is a Freethinker and a Radical — all things that disqualify a poor woman for admission to the Rosmer world. However, one must live somewhere; and as the Rosmer world is the only one in which an ambitious and cultivated woman can find powerful allies and educated companions, Rebecca, being both ambitious and cultivated, makes herself agreeable to the Rosmer circle with such success that the affectionate and impulsive but unintelligent Mrs

Rosmer becomes wildly fond of her, and is not content until she has persuaded her to come and live with them. Rebecca, then a mere adventuress fighting for a foothold in polite society (which has hitherto shown itself highly indignant at her thrusting herself in where nobody has thought of providing room for her), accepts the offer all the more readily because she has taken the measure of Parson Rosmer, and formed the idea of playing upon his aspirations, and making herself a leader in politics and society by using him as a figure-head.

But now two difficulties arise. First, there is Mrs Rosmer's extinguishing effect on her husband — an effect which convinces Rebecca that nothing can be done with him whilst his wife is in the way. Second — a contingency quite unallowed for in her provident calculations — she finds herself passionately enamoured of him. The poor parson, too, falls in love with her; but he does not know it. He turns to the woman who understands him like a sunflower to the sun, and makes her his real friend and companion. The wife feels this soon enough; and he, quite unconscious of it, begins to think that her mind must be affected, since she has become so intensely miserable and hysterical about nothing — nothing that he can see. The truth is that she has come under the curse of the ideal too: she sees herself standing, a useless obstacle, between her husband and the woman he really loves, the woman who can help him to a glorious career. She cannot even be the mother in the household; for she is childless. Then comes Rebecca, fortified with a finely reasoned theory that Rosmer's future is staked against his wife's life, and says that it is better for all their sakes that she should quit Rosmersholm. She even hints that she must go at once if a grave scandal is to be avoided. Mrs Rosmer, regarding a scandal in Rosmersholm as the most terrible thing that can happen, and seeing that it could be averted by the marriage of Rebecca and Rosmer if she were out of the way, writes a letter secretly to Rosmer's bitterest enemy, the editor of the local Radical paper, a man who has forfeited his moral reputation by an intrigue which Rosmer has pitilessly denounced. In this letter she implores him not to believe or publish any stories that he may hear about Rosmer, to the effect that he is in any way to blame for anything that may happen to her. Then she sets Rosmer free to marry Rebecca, and to realize his ideals, by going out into the garden and throwing herself into the millstream that runs there.

Now follows a period of quiet mourning at Rosmersholm. Everybody except Rosmer suspects that Mrs Rosmer was not mad, and guesses why she committed suicide. Only it would not do to compromise the aristocratic party by treating Rosmer as the Radical editor was treated. So the neighbours shut their eyes and condole with the bereaved clergyman; and the Radical editor holds his tongue because Radicalism is getting respectable, and he hopes, with Rebecca's help, to get Rosmer over to his side presently. Meanwhile the unexpected has again happened to Rebecca. Her passion is worn out; but in the long days of mourning she has found the higher love; and it is now for Rosmer's own sake that she urges him to become a man of action, and brood no more over the dead. When his friends start a Conservative paper and ask him to become editor, she induces him to reply by declaring himself a Radical and Freethinker. To his utter amazement, the result is, not an animated discussion of his views, but just such an attack on his home life and private conduct as he had formerly made on those of the Radical editor. His friends tell him plainly that the compact of silence is broken by his defection, and that there will be no mercy for the traitor to the party. Even the Radical editor not only refuses to publish the fact that his new ally is a Freethinker (which would destroy all his social weight as a Radical recruit), but brings up the dead woman's letter as a proof that the attack is sufficiently well-founded to make it unwise to go too far. Rosmer, who at first had been simply shocked that men whom he had always honoured as gentlemen should descend to such hideous calumny, now sees that he really did love Rebecca, and is indeed guilty of his wife's death. His first impulse is to shake off the spectre of the dead woman by marrying Rebecca; but she, knowing that the guilt is hers, puts that temptation behind her and refuses. Then, as he thinks it all over, his dream of ennobling the world slips away from him: such work can only be done by a man conscious of his own innocence. To save him from despair, Rebecca makes a great sacrifice. She "gives him back his innocence" by confessing how she drove his wife to kill herself; and, as the confession is made in the presence of Kroll, she ascribes the whole plot to her ambition, and says not a word of her passion. Rosmer, confounded as he realizes what helpless puppets they have all been in the hands of this clever woman, for the moment misses the point that unscrupulous ambition, though it explains her crime, does not account for her confession. He turns his back on her and leaves the house with Kroll. She quietly packs up her trunk, and is about to vanish from Rosmersholm without another word when he comes back alone to ask why she confessed. She tells him why, offering him her self-sacrifice as a proof that his power of ennobling others was no vain dream, since it is his companionship that has changed her from the selfish adventuress she was to the devoted woman she had just proved herself to be. But he has lost his faith in himself, and cannot believe her. The proof is too subtle, too artful: he cannot forget that she duped him by flattering this very weakness of his before.

Besides, he knows now that it is not true — that people are not ennobled from without. She has no more to say; for she can think of no further proof. But he has thought of an unanswerable one. Dare she make all doubt impossible by doing for his sake what the wife did? She asks what would happen if she had the heart and the will to do it. "Then," he replies, "I should have to believe in you. I should recover my faith in my mission. Faith in my power to ennoble human souls. Faith in the human soul's power to attain nobility." "You shall have your faith again," she answers. At this pass the inner truth of the situation comes out; and the thin veil of a demand for "proof," with its monstrous sequel of asking the woman to kill herself in order to restore the man's good opinion of himself, falls away. What has really seized Rosmer is the old fatal ideal of expiation by sacrifice. He sees that when Rebecca goes into the millstream he must go too. And he speaks his real mind in the words, "There is no judge over us: therefore we must do justice upon ourselves." But the woman's soul is free of this to the end; for when she says, "I am under the power of the Rosmersholm view of life *now*. What I have sinned it is fit I should expiate," we feel in that speech a protest against the Rosmersholm view of life — the view that denied her right to live and be happy from the first, and now at the end, even in denying its God, exacts her life as a vain blood-offering for its own blindness. The woman has the higher light: she goes to her death out of fellowship with the man who is driven thither by the superstition which has destroyed his will. The story ends with his taking her solemnly as his wife, and casting himself with her into the millstream.

It is unnecessary to repeat here what is said on pages 225–6 as to the vital part played in this drama by the evolution of the lower into the higher love. Peer Gynt, during the prophetic episode in his career, shocks the dancing girl Anitra into a remonstrance by comparing himself to a cat. He replies, with his wisest air, that from the standpoint of love there is perhaps not so much difference between a tomcat and a prophet as she may imagine. The number of critics who have entirely missed the point of Rebecca's transfiguration seems to indicate that the majority of men, even among critics of dramatic poetry, have not got beyond Peer Gynt's opinion in this matter. No doubt they would not endorse it as a definitely stated proposition, aware, as they are, that there is a poetic convention to the contrary. But if they fail to recognize the only possible alternative proposition when it is not only stated in so many words by Rebecca West, but when without it her conduct dramatically contradicts her character — when they even complain of the contradiction as a blemish on the play, I am afraid there can be no further doubt that the extreme perplexity into which the first performance of *Rosmersholm* in England plunged the Press was due entirely to the prevalence of Peer Gynt's view of love among the dramatic critics.

THE LADY FROM THE SEA [1888]

Ibsen's next play, though it deals with the old theme, does not insist on the power of ideals to kill, as the two previous plays do. It rather deals with the origin of ideals in unhappiness — in dissatisfaction with the real. The subject of *The Lady from the Sea* is the most poetic fancy imaginable. A young woman, brought up on the sea-coast, marries a respectable doctor, a widower, who idolizes her and places her in his household with nothing to do but dream and be made much of by everybody. Even the housekeeping is done by her stepdaughter: she has no responsibility, no care, and no trouble. In other words, she is an idle, helpless, utterly dependent article of luxury. A man turns red at the thought of being such a thing; but he thoughtlessly accepts a pretty and fragile-looking woman in the same position as a charming natural picture. The lady from the sea feels an indefinite want in her life. She reads her want into all other lives, and comes to the conclusion that man once had to choose whether he would be a land animal or a creature of the sea; and that having chosen the land, he has carried about with him ever since a secret sorrow for the element he has forsaken. The dissatisfaction that gnaws her is, as she interprets it, this desperate longing for the sea. When her only child dies and leaves her without the work of a mother to give her a valid place in the world, she yields wholly to her longing, and no longer cares for her husband, who, like Rosmer, begins to fear that she is going mad. At last a seaman appears and claims her as his wife on the ground that they went years before through a rite which consisted of their marrying the sea by throwing their rings into it. This man, who had to fly from her in the old time because he killed his captain, and who fills her with a sense of dread and mystery, seems to her to embody the attraction which the sea has for her. She tells her husband that she must go away with the seaman. Naturally the doctor expostulates — declares that he cannot for her own sake let her do so mad a thing. She replies that he can only prevent her by locking her up, and asks him what satisfaction it will be to him to have her body under lock and key whilst her heart is with the other man. In vain he urges that he will only keep her under restraint until the seaman goes — that he must not, dare not, allow her to ruin herself. Her argument remains unanswerable. The seaman openly declares that she will come; so that the distracted husband asks him does he suppose he can force her from her home. To this the seaman replies that, on the contrary, unless she comes of her own free will there is no satisfaction to him in her coming at all — the unanswerable argument again. She echoes it by demanding her freedom to choose. Her husband must cry off his law-made and Church-made bargain; renounce his claim to the fulfilment of her vows; and leave her free to go back to the sea with her old lover. Then the doctor, with a heavy heart, drops his prate about his heavy responsibility for her actions, and throws the responsibility on her by crying off as she demands. The moment she feels herself a free and responsible woman, all her childish fancies vanish: the seaman becomes simply an old acquaintance whom she no longer cares for; and the doctor's affection produces its natural effect. In short, she says No to the seaman, and takes over the housekeeping keys from her stepdaughter without any further speculations concerning that secret sorrow for the abandoned sea.

It should be noted here that Ellida, the Lady from the Sea, appears a much more fantastic person to English readers than to Norwegian ones. The same thing is true of many other characters drawn by Ibsen, notably Peer Gynt, who, if born in England, would certainly not have been a poet and metaphysician as well as a blackguard and a speculator. The extreme type of Norwegian, as depicted by Ibsen, imagines himself doing wonderful things, but does nothing. He dreams as no Englishman dreams, and drinks to make himself dream the more, until his effective will is destroyed, and he becomes a broken-down, disreputable sot, carrying about the tradition that he is a hero, and discussing himself on that assumption. Although the number of persons who dawdle their life away over fiction in England must be frightful, and is probably increasing, yet we have no Ulric Brendels, Rosmers, Ellidas, Peer Gynts, nor anything at all like them; and it is for this reason that I am disposed to fear that *Rosmersholm* and *The Lady from the Sea* will always be received much more incredulously by English audiences than *A Doll's House* and the plays in which the leading figures are men and women of action.

HEDDA GABLER [1890]

Hedda Gabler, the heroine after whom the last of Ibsen's plays (so far) is named, has no ideals at all. She is a pure sceptic, a typical nineteenth century figure, falling into the abyss between the ideals which do not impose on her and the realities which she has not yet discovered. The result is that she has no heart, no courage, no conviction: with great beauty and great energy she remains mean, envious, insolent, cruel in protest against others' happiness, a bully in reaction from her own cowardice. Hedda's father, a general, is a widower. She has the traditions of the military caste about her; and these narrow her activities to the customary hunt for a socially and pecuniarily eligible husband. She makes the acquaintance of a young man of genius who, prohibited by an ideal-ridden society from taking his pleasures except where there is nothing to restrain him from excess, is going to the bad in search of his good, with the usual consequences. Hedda is intensely curious about the side of life which is forbidden to her, and in which powerful instincts, absolutely ignored and condemned by the society with which intercourse is permitted to her, steal their satisfaction. An odd intimacy springs up between the inquisitive girl and the rake. Whilst the general reads the paper in the afternoon, Lövborg and Hedda have long conversations in which he describes to her all his disreputable adventures. Although she is the questioner, she never dares to trust him: all the questions are indirect; and the responsibility for his interpretations rests on him alone. Hedda has no conviction whatever that these conversations are disgraceful; but she will not risk a fight with society on the point: hypocrisy, the homage that truth pays to falsehood, is easier to face, as far as she can see, than ostracism. When he proceeds to make advances to her, Hedda has again no conviction that it would be wrong for her to gratify his instinct and her own; so that she is confronted with the alternative of sinning against herself and him, or sinning against social ideals in which she has no faith. Making the coward's choice, she carries it out with the utmost bravado, threatening Lövborg with one of her father's pistols, and driving him out of the house with all that ostentation of outraged purity which is the instinctive defence of women to whom chastity is not natural, much as libel actions are mostly brought by persons concerning whom libels are virtually, if not technically, justifiable.

Hedda, deprived of her lover, now finds that a life of conformity without faith involves something more terrible than the utmost ostracism: to wit, boredom. This scourge, unknown among revolutionists, is the curse which makes the security of respectability as dust in the balance against the unflagging interest of rebellion, and which forces society to eke out its harmless resources for killing time by licensing gambling, gluttony, hunting, shooting, coursing, and other vicious distractions for which even idealism has no disguise. These licenses, however, are only available for people who have more than enough money to keep up appearances with; and as Hedda's father is too poor to leave her much more than the case of pistols, her boredom is only mitigated by dancing, at which she gains much admiration, but no substantial offers of marriage. At last she has to find someone to support her. A good-natured mediocrity of a professor is all that is to be had; and though she regards him as a member of an inferior class, and despises almost to loathing his family circle of two affectionate old aunts and the inevitable general servant who has helped to bring him up, she marries him *faute de mieux,* and immediately proceeds to wreck this prudent provision for her livelihood by accommodating his income to her expenditure instead of accommodating her expenditure to his income. Her nature so rebels against the whole sordid transaction that the prospect of bearing a child to her husband drives her almost frantic, since it will not only expose her to the intimate solicitude of his aunts in the course of a derangement of her health in which she can see nothing that is not repulsive and humiliating, but will make her one of his family in earnest. To amuse herself in these galling circumstances, she forms an underhand alliance with a visitor who belongs to her old set, an elderly gallant who quite understands how little she cares for her husband, and proposes a *ménage à trois* to her. She consents to his coming there and talking to her as he pleases behind her husband's back; but she keeps her pistols in reserve in case he becomes seriously importunate. He, on the other hand, tries to get some hold over her by placing her husband under pecuniary obligations, as far as he can do it without being out of pocket. And so Hedda's married life begins, with only this gallant as a precaution against the most desperate tedium.

Meanwhile Lövborg is drifting to disgrace by the nearest way — through drink. In due time he descends from lecturing at the university on the history of civilization to taking a job in an out-of-the-way place as tutor to the little children of Sheriff Elvsted. This functionary, on being left a widower with a number of children, marries their governess, finding that she will cost him less and be bound to do more for him as his wife. As for her, she is too poor to dream of refusing such a settlement in life. When Lövborg comes, his society is heaven to her. He does not dare to tell her about his dissipations; but he tells her about his unwritten books. She does not dare to remonstrate with him for drinking; but he gives it up as soon as he sees that it shocks her. Just as Mr Fearing, in Bunyan's story, was in a way the bravest of the pilgrims, so this timid and unfortunate Mrs Elvsted trembles her way to a point at which Lövborg, quite reformed, publishes one book which makes him celebrated for the moment, and completes another, fair-copied in her handwriting, to which he looks for a solid position as an original thinker. But he cannot now stay tutoring Elvsted's children; so off he goes to town with his pockets full of the money the published book has brought him. Left once more in her old lonely plight, knowing that without her Lövborg will probably relapse into dissipation, and that without him her life will not be worth living, Mrs Elvsted is now confronted, on her own higher plane, with the same alternative which Hedda encountered. She must either sin against herself and him or against the institution of marriage under which Elvsted purchased his housekeeper. It never occurs to her even that she has any choice. She knows that her action will count as "a dreadful thing"; but she sees that she must go; and accordingly Elvsted finds himself without a wife and his children without a governess, and so disappears unpitied from the story.

Now it happens that Hedda's husband, Jörgen Tesman, is an old friend and competitor (for academic honours) of Lövborg, and also that Hedda was a schoolfellow of Mrs Elvsted, or Thea, as she had better now be called. Thea's first business is to find out where Lövborg is; for hers is no preconcerted elopement: she has hurried to town to keep Lövborg away from the bottle, a design which she dare not hint at to himself. Accordingly, the first thing she does is to call on the Tesmans, who have just returned from their honeymoon, to beg them to invite Lövborg to their house so as to keep him in good company. They consent, with the result that the two pairs are brought together under the same roof, and the tragedy begins to work itself out.

Hedda's attitude now demands a careful analysis. Lövborg's experience with Thea has enlightened his judgment of Hedda; and as he is, in his gifted way, an arrant *poseur* and male coquet, he immediately tries to get on romantic terms with her — for have they not "a past"? — by impressing her with the penetrating criticism that she is and always was a coward. She admits that the virtuous heroics with the pistol were pure cowardice; but she is still so void of any other standard of conduct than conformity to the conventional ideals, that she thinks her cowardice consisted in not daring to be wicked. That is, she thinks that what she actually did was the right thing; and since she despises herself for doing it, and feels that he also rightly despises her for doing it, she gets a passionate feeling that what is wanted is the courage to do wrong. This unlooked-for reaction of idealism — this monstrous but very common setting-up of wrong-doing as an ideal, and of the wrongdoer as a hero or heroine *qua* wrongdoer — leads Hedda to conceive that when Lövborg tried to seduce her he was a hero, and that in allowing Thea to reform him he has played the recreant. In acting on this misconception, she is restrained by no consideration for any of the rest. Like all people whose lives are valueless, she has no more sense of the value of Lövborg's or Tesman's or Thea's lives than a railway shareholder has of the value of a shunter's. She gratifies her intense jealousy of Thea by deliberately taunting Lövborg into breaking loose from her influence by joining a carouse at which he not only loses his manuscript, but finally gets into the hands of the police through behaving outrageously in the house of a disreputable woman whom he accuses of stealing it, not knowing that it has been picked up by Tesman and handed to Hedda for safe keeping. Now to Hedda this bundle of paper in another woman's handwriting is the fruit of Lövborg's union with Thea: he himself speaks of it as "their child." So when he turns his despair to romantic account by coming to the two women and making a tragic scene, telling Thea that he has cast the manuscript, torn into a thousand pieces, out upon the fiord; and then, when she is gone, telling Hedda that he has brought "the child" to a house of ill-fame and lost it there, she, deceived by his posing, and thirsting to gain faith in human nobility from a heroic deed of some sort, makes him a present of one of her pistols, only begging him to "do it beautifully," by which she means that he is to kill himself without spoiling his appearance. He takes it unblushingly, and leaves her with the air of a man who is looking his last on earth. But the moment he is out of sight of his audience, he goes back to the house where he still supposes that the manuscript was lost, and there renews the wrangle of the night before, using the pistol to threaten the woman, with the result that he gets shot in the abdomen, leaving the weapon to fall into the hands of the police. Meanwhile Hedda deliberately burns "the child." Then comes her elderly gallant to tell her the true story of the heroic deed which Lövborg promised her to do so beautifully, and to make her understand that he himself has now got her into his power by his ability to identify the pistol. She has either to be the slave of this man, or else to face the scandal of the connection of her name at the inquest with a squalid debauch ending in a murder. Thea, too, is not crushed by Lövborg's death. Ten minutes after she has received the news with a cry of heartfelt loss, she sits down with Tesman to reconstruct "the child" from the old notes which she has preserved. Over the congenial task of collecting and arranging another man's ideas Tesman is perfectly happy, and forgets his beautiful Hedda for the first time. Thea the trembler is still mistress of the situation, holding the dead Lövborg, gaining Tesman, and leaving Hedda to her elderly admirer, who smoothly remarks that he will answer for Mrs Tesman not being bored whilst her husband is occupied with Thea in putting the pieces of the book together. However, he has again reckoned without General Gabler's second pistol. She shoots herself then and there; and so the story ends.

The Last Four Plays *

DOWN AMONG THE DEAD MEN

Ibsen now lays down the completed task of warning the world against its idols and anti-idols, and passes into the shadow of death, or rather into the splendor of his sunset glory; for his magic is extraordinarily potent in these four plays, and his purpose more powerful. And yet the shadow of death is here; for all four, except Little Eyolf, are tragedies of the dead, deserted and mocked by the young who are still full of life. The Master Builder is a dead man before the curtain rises: the breaking of his body to pieces in the last act by its fall from the tower is rather the impatient destruction of a ghost of whose delirious whisperings Nature is tired than of one who still counts among the living. Borkman and the two women, his wife and her sister, are not merely dead: they are buried; and the creatures we hear and see are only their spirits in torment. "Never dream of life again," says Mrs. Borkman to her husband: "lie quiet where you are." And the last play of all is frankly called When We Dead Awaken. Here the quintessence of Ibsenism reaches its final distillation: morality and reformation give place to mortality and resurrection; and the next event is the death of Ibsen himself: he, too, creeping ghost-like through the blackening mental darkness until he reaches his actual grave, and can no longer make Europe cry with pity by sitting at a copybook, like a child, trying to learn again how to write, only to find that divine power gone for ever from his dead hand. He, the crustiest, grimmest hero since Beethoven, could not die like him, shaking his fist at the thunder and alive to the last: he must follow the path he had traced for Solness and Borkman, and survive himself. But as these two were dreamers to the last, and never so luminous in their dreams as when they could no longer put the least of them into action; so we may believe that when Ibsen could no longer remember the alphabet, or use a dictionary, his soul may have been fuller than ever before of the unspeakable. Do not snivel, reader, over the contrast he himself drew between the man who was once the greatest writer in the world, and the child of seventy-six trying to begin again at pothooks and hangers. Depend on it, whilst there was anything left of him at all there was enough of his

*This section was added by Shaw to the 1913 edition, "now completed to the death of Ibsen." — Ed.

iron humor to grin as widely as the skeleton with the hour-glass who was touching him on the shoulder.

THE MASTER BUILDER [1892]

Halvard Solness is a dead man who has been a brilliantly success-ful builder, and, like the greatest builders, his own architect. He is sometimes in the sublime delirium that precedes bodily death, and sometimes in the horror that varies the splendors of delirium. He is mortally afraid of young rivals; of the younger generation knocking at the door. He has built churches with high towers (much as Ibsen built great historical dramas in verse). He has come to the end of that and built "homes for human beings" (much as Ibsen took to writ-ing prose plays of modern life). He has come to the end of that too, as men do at the end of their lives; and now he must take to dead men's architecture, the building of castles in the air. Castles in the air are the residences not only of those who have finished their lives, but of those who have not yet begun them. Another peculiarity of castles in the air is that they are so beautiful and so wonderful that human beings are not good enough to live in them: therefore when you look round you for somebody to live with you in your castle in the air, you find nobody glorious enough for that sanctuary. So you resort to the most dangerous of all the varieties of idolization: the idolization of the person you are most in love with; and you take him or her to live with you in your castle. And as imaginative young people, because they are young, have no illusions about youth, whilst old people, be-cause they are old, have no illusions about age, elderly gentlemen very often idolize adolescent girls, and adolescent girls idolize elderly gentle-men. When the idolization is not reciprocal, the idolizer runs terrible risks if the idol is selfish and unscrupulous. Cases of girls enslaved by elderly gentlemen whose scrupulous respect for their maiden purity is nothing but an excuse for getting a quantity of secretarial or domestic service out of them that is limited only by their physical endurance, without giving them anything in return, are not at all so rare as they would be if the theft of a woman's youth and devotion were as severely condemned by public opinion as the comparatively amiable and negli-gible theft of a few silver spoons and forks. On the other hand doting old gentlemen are duped and ruined by designing young women who care no more for them than a Cornish fisherman cares for a conger eel. But sometimes, when the two natures are poetic, we have scenes of Bettina and Goethe, which are perhaps wholesome as well as pleasant for both parties when they are good enough and sensible enough to face the inexorable on the side of age and to recognize the impossible on the side of youth. On these conditions, old gentlemen are indulged in fancies for poetic little girls; and the poetic little girls have their emotions and imaginations satisfied harmlessly until they find a suitable mate.

But the master builder, though he gets into just such a situation, does not get out of it so cheaply, because he is not outwardly an old, or even a very elderly gentleman. "He is a man no longer young, but healthy and vigorous, with closely cut curly hair, dark moustache, and dark thick eyebrows." Also he is daimonic, not sham daimonic like Molvik in The Wild Duck, but really daimonic, with luck, a star, and mystic "helpers and servers" who find the way through the maze of life for him. In short, a very fascinating man, whom nobody, himself least of all, could suspect of having shot his bolt and being already dead. Therefore a man for whom a girl's castle in the air is a very dangerous place, as she may easily thrust upon him adventures that would tax the prime of an unexhausted man, and are mere delirious madness for a spent one.

Grasp this situation and you will be able to follow a performance of The Master Builder without being puzzled; though to the unprepared theatregoer it is a bewildering business. You see Solness in his office, ruthlessly exploiting the devotion of the girl secretary Kaia, who idolizes him, and giving her nothing in return but a mesmerizing word occasionally. You see him with equal ruthlessness apparently, but really with the secret terror of "the priest who slew the slayer and shall himself be slain," trying to suppress a young rival who is as yet only a draughtsman in his employment. To keep the door shut against the younger generation already knocking at it: that is all he can do now, except build castles in the air; for, as I have said, the effective part of the man is dead. Then there is his wife, who, knowing that he is failing in body and mind, can do nothing but look on in helpless terror. She cannot make a happy home for Solness, because her own happiness has been sacrificed to his. Or rather, her own genius, which is for "building up the souls of little children," has been sacrificed to his. For they began their family life in an old house that was part of her property: the sort of house that may be hallowed by old family associations and memories of childhood, but that it pays the speculative builder to pull down and replace by rows of villas. Now the ambitious Solness knows this but dares not propose such a thing to his wife, who cherishes all the hallowing associations, and even keeps her dolls: nine lovely dolls, feeling them "under her heart, like little unborn children." Everything in the house is precious to her: the old silk dresses, the lace, the portraits. Solness knows that to touch these would be tearing her heart up by the roots. So he says nothing; does nothing; only notes

a crack in the old chimney which should be repaired if the house is to
be safe against fire, and does not repair it. Instead, he pictures to
himself a fire, with his wife out in the sledge with his two children, and
nothing but charred ruins facing her when she returns; but what matter,
since the children have escaped and are still with her? He even calls
upon his helpers and servers to consider whether this vision might not
become a reality. And it does. The house is burnt; the villas rise on
its site and cover the park; and Halvard Solness becomes rich and
successful.

But the helpers and servers have not stuck to the program for all
that. The fire did not come from the crack in the chimney when
all the domestic fires were blazing. It came at night when the fires
were low, and began in a cupboard quite away from the chimney. It
came when Mrs. Solness and the children were in bed. It shattered
the mother's health; it killed the children she was nursing; it devoured
the portraits and the silk dresses and the old lace; it burnt the nine
lovely dolls; and it broke the heart under which the dolls had lain like
little unborn children. That was the price of the master builder's
success. He is married to a dead wman; and he is trying to atone by
building her a new villa: a new tomb to replace the old home; for he
is gnawed with remorse.

But the fire was not only a good building speculation: it also led
to his obtaining commissions to build churches. And one triumphant
day, when he was celebrating the completion of the giant tower he had
added to the old church at Lysanger, it suddenly flashed on him that
his house had been burnt, his wife's life laid waste, and his own happiness destroyed, so that he might become a builder of churches. Now
it happens that one of his difficulties as a builder is that he has a
bad head for heights, and cannot venture even on a second floor
balcony. Yet in the fury of that thought he mounts to the pinnacle
of his tower, and there, face to face with God, who has, he feels,
wasted the wife's gift of building up the souls of little children to make
the husband a builder of steeples, he declares that he will never set
hand to church-building again, and will henceforth build nothing but
homes for happier men than he. Which vow he keeps, only to find
that the home, too, is a devouring idol, and that men and women
have no longer any use for it.

In spite of his excitement, he very nearly breaks his neck after all;
for among the crowd below there is a little devil of a girl who waves a
white scarf and makes his head swim. This tiny animal is no other
than the younger stepdaughter of Ellida, The Lady from the Sea, Hilda
Wangel, of whose taste for "thrilling" sensations we had a glimpse in
that play. On the same evening Solness is entertained at a club ban-
quet, in consequence of which he is not in the most responsible con-

dition when he returns to sup at the house of Dr. Wangel, who is putting him up for the night. He meets the imp there; thinks her like a little princess in her white dress; kisses her; and promises her to come back in ten years and carry her off to the kingdom of Orangia. Perhaps it is only just to mention that he stoutly denies these indiscretions afterwards; though he admits that when he wishes something to happen between himself and somebody else, the somebody else always imagines it actually has happened.

The play begins ten years after the climbing of the tower. The younger generation knocks at the door with a vengeance. Hilda, now a vigorous young woman, and a great builder of castles in the air, bursts in on him and demands her kingdom; and very soon she sends him up to a tower again (the tower of the new house) and waves her scarf to him as madly as ever. This time he really does break his neck; and so the story ends.

LITTLE EYOLF *[1894]*

Though the most mischievous ideals are social ideals which have become institutions, laws, and creeds, yet their evil must come to a personal point before they can strike down the individual. Jones is not struck down by an ideal in the abstract, but by Smith making monstrous claims or inflicting monstrous injuries on him in the name of an ideal. And it is fair to add that the ideals are sometimes beneficent, and their repudiation sometimes cruel. For ideals are in practice not so much matters of conscience as excuses for doing what we like; and thus it happens that of two people worshipping the same ideals, one will be a detestable tyrant and the other a kindly and helpful friend of mankind. What makes the bad side of idealism so dangerous is that wicked people are allowed to commit crimes in the name of the ideal that would not be tolerated for a moment as open devilment. Perhaps the worst, because the commonest and most intimate cases, are to be found in family life. Even during the Reign of Terror, the chances of any particular Frenchman or Frenchwoman being guillotined were so small as to be negligible. Under Nero a Christian was far safer from being smeared with pitch and set on fire than he was from domestic trouble. If the private lives that have been wasted by idealistic persecution could be recorded and set against the public martyrdoms and slaughterings and torturings and imprisonments, our millions of private Neros and Torquemadas and Calvins, Bloody Maries and Cleopatras and Semiramises, would eclipse the few who have come to the surface of history by the accident of political or ecclesiastical conspicuousness.

Thus Ibsen, at the beginning of his greatness, shewed us Brand sacrificing his wife; and this was only the first of a series of similar exhibitions, ending, so far, in Solness sacrificing his wife and being himself sacrificed to a girl's enthusiasm. And he brings Solness to the point of rebelling furiously against the tyranny of his wife's ideal of home, and declaring that "building homes for happy human beings is not worth a rap: men are not happy in these homes: I should not have been happy in such a home if I had had one." It is not surprising to find that Little Eyolf is about such a home.

This home clearly cannot be a working-class home. And here let it be said that the comparative indifference of the working class to Ibsen's plays is neither Ibsen's fault nor that of the working class. To the man who works for his living in modern society home is not the place where he lives, nor his wife the woman he lives with. Home is the roof under which he sleeps and eats; and his wife is the woman who makes his bed, cooks his meals, and looks after their children when they are neither in school nor in the streets, or who at least sees that the servants do these things. The man's work keeps him from home from eight to twelve hours a day. He is unconscious through sleep for another eight hours. Then there is the public house and the club. There is eating, washing, dressing, playing with the children or the dog, entertaining or visiting friends, reading, and pursuing hobbies such as gardening and the like. Obviously the home ideal cannot be tested fully under these conditions, which enable a married pair to see less and know less of one another than they do of those who work side by side with them. It is in the propertied class only that two people can really live together and devote themselves to one another if they want to. There are certain businesses which men and women can conduct jointly, and certain professions which men can pursue at home; and in these the strain of idealism on marriage is more severe than when the two work separately. But the full strain comes on with the modern unearned income from investments, which does not involve even the management of an estate. And it is under this full strain that Ibsen tests it in Little Eyolf.

Shakespear, in a flash of insight which has puzzled many commentators, and even set them proposing alterations of a passage which they found unthinkable, has described one of his characters as "a fellow almost damned in a fair wife." There is no difficulty or obscurity about this phrase at all: you have only to look round at the men who have ventured to marry very fascinating women to see that most of them are not merely "almost damned" but wholly damned. Allmers, in Little Eyolf, is a fellow almost damned in a fair wife. She, Rita Allmers, has brought him "gold and green forests" (a reminiscence from an early play called The Feast at Solhoug), and not only troubles and uncentres him as only a woman can trouble and uncentre a man who is susceptible to her bodily attraction, but is herself furiously and jealously in love with him. In short, they form the ideal home of romance; and it would be hard to find a compacter or more effective formula for a small private hell. The "almost damned" are commonly saved by the fact that the devotion is usually on one side only, and that the lovely lady (or gentleman; for a woman almost damned in a fair husband is also a common object in domestic civilization), if she has only one husband, relieves the boredom of his devotion by having fifty courtiers. But Rita will neither share Allmers with anyone else nor be shared. He must be wholly and exclusively hers; and she must be wholly and exclusively his. By her gold and green forests she snatches him from his work as a schoolmaster and imprisons him in their house, where the poor wretch pretends to occupy himself by writing a book on Human Responsibility, and forming the character of their son, little Eyolf. For your male sultana takes himself very seriously indeed, as do most sultanas and others who are so closely shut up with their own vanities and appetites that they think the world a little thing to be moulded and arranged at their silly pleasure like a lump of plasticine. Rita is jealous of the book, and hates it not only because Allmers occupies himself with it instead of with her, but talks about it to his half-sister Asta, of whom she is of course also jealous. She is jealous of little Eyolf, and hates him too, because he comes between her and her prey.

One day, when the baby child is lying on the table, they have an amorous fit and forget all about him. He falls off the table and is crippled for life. He and his crutch become thenceforth a standing reproach to them. They hate themselves; they hate each other; they hate him; their atmosphere of ideal conjugal love breeds hate at every turn; hatred masquerading as a loving bond that has been drawn closer and sanctified by their common misfortune. After ten years of this hideous slavery the man breaks loose: actually insists on going for a short trip into the mountains by himself. It is true that he reassures Rita by coming back before his time; but her conclusion that this was because he could not abstain from her society is rudely shattered by his conduct on his return. She dresses herself beautifully to receive him, and makes the seraglio as delightful as possible for their reunion; but he purposely arrives tired out, and takes refuge in the sleep of exhaustion, without a caress. As she says, quoting a popular poem when reproaching him for this afterwards, "There stood your champagne and you tasted it not." It soon appears that he has come to loathe his champagne, and that the escape into the mountains has helped him to loathe his situation to some extent, even to discovering the absurdity of his book on Human Responsibility, and the cruelty of his educational experiments on Eyolf. In future he is going to make Eyolf "an open air little boy," which of course involves being a good deal in the open air with him, and out of the seraglio. Then the woman's hatred of the child unveils itself; and she openly declares what she really feels as to this little creature, with its "evil eyes," that has come between them.

At this point, very opportunely, comes the Rat Wife, who, like the Pied Piper, clears away rats for a consideration. Has Rita any little gnawing things she wants to get rid of? Here, it seems, is a helper and server for Rita. The Rat Wife's method is to bewitch the rats so that when she rows out to sea they follow her and are drowned. She describes this with a heart-breaking poetry that frightens Rita, who makes Allmers send her away. But a helper and server is not so easily exorcized. Rita's little gnawing thing, Eyolf, has come under the spell; and when the Rat Wife rows out to sea, he follows her and is drowned.

The family takes the event in a very proper spirit. Horror, lamentation, shrieks and tears, and all the customary homages to death and attestations of bereavement are duly and even sincerely gone through; for the shock of such an accident makes us all human for a moment. But next morning Allmers finds some difficulty in keeping it up, miserable as he is. He finds himself forgetting about Eyolf for several minutes, and thinking about other things, even about his breakfast; and in his idealistic self-devotion to artificial attitudes he reproaches himself and tries to force himself to keep thinking of Eyolf and being overwhelmed with grief about him. Besides, it is an excuse for avoiding his wife. The revulsion against his slavery to her has made her presence unbearable to him. He can bear nobody but his half-sister Asta, whose relation to him is a most blessed comfort and relief because their blood kinship excludes from it all the torment and slavery of his relation to Rita. But this consolation is presently withdrawn; for Asta has just discovered, in some old correspondence, convincing proofs that she is not related to him at all; and the effect of the discovery has been to remove the inhibition which has hitherto limited her strong affection for him; so that she now perceives that she must leave him. Hitherto, she has refused, for his sake, the offers of Borgheim, an engineer who wants to marry her, but who, like Rita, wants to take her away and make her exclusively his own; for he, too, cannot share with anyone. And though both Allmers and Rita implore her to stay, dreading now nothing so much as being left alone with one another, she knows that she cannot stay innocently, and accepts the engineer and vanishes lest a worse thing should befall.

And now Rita has her man all to herself. Eyolf dead, Asta gone, the book on Human Responsibility thrown into the waste paper basket: there are no more rivals now, no more distractions: the field is clear for the ideal union of "two souls with but a single thought, two hearts that beat as one." The result may be imagined.

The situation is insufferable from the beginning. Allmers' attempts to avoid seeing or speaking to Rita are of course impracticable. Equally impracticable are their efforts to behave kindly to one another. They are presently at it hammer and tongs, each tearing the mask from the other's grief for the child, and leaving it exposed as their remorse: hers for having jealously hated Eyolf: his for having sacrificed him to his passion for Rita, and to the schoolmasterly vanity and folly which sees in the child nothing more than the vivisector sees in a guinea-pig: something to experiment on with a view to rearranging the world to suit his own little ideas. If ever two cultivated souls of the propertied middle class were stripped naked and left bankrupt, these two are. They cannot bear to live; and yet they are forced to confess that they dare not kill themselves.

The solution of their problem, as far as it is solved, is, as coming from Ibsen, very remarkable. It is not, as might have been expected after his long propaganda of Individualism, that they should break up the seraglio and go out into the world until they have learnt to stand alone, and through that to accept companionship on honorable conditions only. Ibsen here explicitly insists for the first time that "we are members one of another," and that though the strongest man is he who stands alone, the man who is standing alone for his own sake solely is literally an idiot. It is indeed a staring fact in history and contemporary life that nothing is so gregarious as selfishness, and nothing so solitary as the selflessness that loathes the word Altruism because to it there are no "others": it sees and feels in every man's case the image of its own. "Inasmuch as ye have done it unto one of the least of these my brethren ye have done it unto me" is not Altruism or Othersism. It is an explicit repudiation of the patronizing notion that "the least of these" is *another* to whom you are invited to be very nice and kind: in short, it accepts entire identification of "me" with "the least of these." The fashionably sentimental version, which runs, in effect, "If you subscribe eighteenpence to give this little dear a day in the country I shall regard it as a loan of one-and-sixpence to myself" is really more conceitedly remote from the spirit of the famous Christian saying than even the sham political economy that took in Mr. Gradgrind. Accordingly, if you would see industrial sweating at its vilest, you must go, not to the sempstresses who work for commercial firms, but to the victims of pious Altruistic Ladies' Work Guilds and the like, in which ladies with gold and green forests offer to "others" their blouses to be stitched at prices that the most sordid East End slave-driver would recoil from offering.

Thus we see that in Ibsen's mind, as in the actual history of the nineteenth century, the way to Communism lies through the most resolute and uncompromising Individualism. James Mill, with an inhuman conceit and pedantry which leaves the fable of Allmers and Eyolf far behind, educated John Stuart Mill to be the arch Individualist of his time, with the result that John Stuart Mill became a Socialist quarter of a century before the rest of his set moved in that direction. Herbert Spencer lived to write despairing pamphlets against the Socialism of his ablest pupils. There is no hope in Individualism for egotism. When a man is at last brought face to face with himself by a brave Individualism, he finds himself face to face, not with an individual, but with a species, and knows that to save himself, he must save the race. He can have no life except a share in the life of the community; and if that life is unhappy and squalid, nothing that he can do to paint and paper and upholster and shut off his little corner of it can really rescue him from it.

It happens so to that bold Individualist Mrs. Rita Allmers. The Allmers are, of course, snobs, and have always been very determined that the common little children down at the pier should be taught their place as Eyolf's inferiors. They even go the length of discussing whether these dirty little wretches should not be punished for their cowardice in not rescuing Eyolf. Thereby they raise the terrible question whether they themselves, who are afraid to commit suicide in their misery, would have been any braver. There is nobody to comfort them; for the income from the gold and green forests, by enabling them to cut themselves off from all industry of the place, has led them into something like total isolation. They hate their neighbors as themselves. They are alone together with nothing to do but wear each other out and drive each other mad to an extent impossible under any other conditions. And Rita's plight is the more desperate of the two, because as she has been the more unscrupulous, the more exacting, she has left him something to look forward to: freedom from her. He is bent on that, at least: he will not live with her on any terms, not stay anywhere within reach of her: the one thing he craves is that he may never see her or speak to her again. That is the end of the "two souls with but a single thought," &c. But to her his release is only a supreme privation, the end of everything that gave life any meaning for her. She has not even egotism to fall back on.

At this pass, an annoyance of which she has often complained occurs again. The children down at the pier make a noise, playing and yelling as if Eyolf had never existed. It suddenly occurs to her that these are children too, just like Eyolf, and that they are suffering a good deal from neglect. After all, they too are little Eyolfs. Inasmuch as she can do it unto one of the least of these his brethren she can do it unto him. She determines to take the dirty little wretches in hand and look after them. It is at all events a more respectable plan than that of the day before, which was to throw herself away on the first man she met if Allmers dared to think of anybody but her. And it has the domestic advantage that Allmers has nothing to fear from a woman who has something else to do than torment him with passions that devour and jealousies that enslave him. The world and the home suddenly take on their natural aspect. Allmers offers to stay and help her. And so they are delivered from their evil dream, and, let us hope, live happily ever after.

JOHN GABRIEL BORKMAN [1896]

In Little Eyolf the shadow of death lifted for a moment; but now we enter it again. Here the persons of the drama are not only dead but buried. Borkman is a Napoleon of finance. He has the root of finance in him in a born love of money in its final reality: a love, that is, of precious metals. He does not dream of beautiful ladies calling to him for knightly rescue from dragons and tyrants, but of metals imprisoned in undiscovered mines, calling to him to release them and send them out into all lands fertilizing, encouraging, creating. Music to him means the ring of the miner's pick and hammer: the eternal night underground is as magical to him as the moonlit starlit night of the upper air to the romantic poet. This love of metal is common enough: no man feels towards a cheque for £20 as he does towards twenty gold sovereigns: he will part from the paper with less of a pang than from the coins. There are misers whose fingers tremble when they touch gold, but close steadily on banknotes. True love of money is, in fact, a passion based on a physical appetite for precious metals. It is not greed: you cannot call a man who starves himself sooner than part with one sovereign from his sack of sovereigns, greedy. If he did the same for the love of God, you would call him a saint: if for the love of a woman, a perfect gentle knight. Men grow rich according to the strength of their obsession by this passion: its great libertines become Napoleons of finance: its narrow debauchees become misers, petty moneylenders, and the like. It must not be looked for in all our millionaires, because most of these are rich by pure accident (our abandonment of industry to the haphazard scrambles of private adventurers necessarily produces occasional wind-falls which enrich the man who happens to be on the spot), as may be seen when the lucky ones are invited to display their supposed Napoleonic powers in spending their windfalls, when they reveal themselves as quite ordinary mortals, if not indeed sometimes as exceptionally resourceless ones. Besides, finance is one business, and industrial organization another: the man with a passion for altering the map by digging isthmuses never thinks of money save as a means to his end. But those who as financiers have passionately "made" money instead of merely holding their hats under an accidental shower of it, will be found to have a genuine disinterested love of it. It is not easy to say how common this passion is. Poverty is general, which would seem to indicate a general lack of it; but poverty is mainly the result of organized robbery and oppression (politely called Capitalism) starving the passion for gold as it starves all the passions. The evidence is further confused by the decorative instinct: some men will load their fingers and shirt-fronts with rings and studs, whilst others of equal means are ringless and fasten their shirts with sixpennorth of mother of pearl. But it is significant that Plato, and, following him, Sir Thomas More, saw with Ibsen, and made complete indifference to the precious metals, minted or not, a necessary qualification for aristocracy. This indifference is, as a matter of fact, so characteristic of our greatest non-industrial men that when they do not happen to inherit property they are generally poor and in difficulties. Therefore we who have never cared for money enough to do more than keep our heads above water, and are therefore tempted to regard ourselves as others regard us (that is, as failures, or, at best, as persons of no account) may console ourselves with the reflection that money-hunger is no more respectable than gluttony, and that unless its absence or feebleness is only a symptom of a general want of power to care for anything at all, it usually means that the soul has risen above it to higher concerns.

All this is necessary to the appreciation of Ibsen's presentment of the Napoleon of finance. Ibsen does not take him superficially: he goes to the poetic basis of the type: the love of gold — actual metallic gold — and the idealization of gold through that love.

Borkman meets the Misses Rentheim: two sisters: the elder richer than the younger. He falls in love with the younger; and she falls in love with him; but the love of gold is the master passion: he marries the elder. Yet he respects his secondary passion in the younger. When he speculates with other peoples' securities he spares hers. On the point of bringing off a great stroke of finance, the other securities are missed; and he is imprisoned for embezzlement. That is the end of him. He comes out of prison a ruined man and a dead man, and would not have even a tomb to sleep in but for the charity of Ella Rentheim, whose securities he spared when he broke her heart. She maintains his old home for him.

He now enters on the grimmest lying in state ever exposed to public view by mortal dramatist. His wife, a proud woman, must live in the same house with the convicted thief who has disgraced her, because she has nowhere else to lay her head; but she will not see him nor speak to him. She sits downstairs in the drawing-room eating the bitter bread of her sister's charity, and listening with loathing to her husband's steps as he paces to and fro in the long gallery upstairs "like a sick wolf." She listens not for days but for years. And her one hope is that her son Erhart will rehabilitate the family name; repay the embezzled money; and lead her from her tomb up again into honor and prosperity. To this task she has devoted *his* life.

Borkman has quite another plan. He is still Napoleon, and will return from his Elba to scatter his enemies and complete the stroke that ill-luck and the meddlesomeness of the law frustrated. But he is proud: prouder than Napoleon. He will not come back to the financial world until it finds out that it cannot do without him and comes to ask him to resume his place at the head of the board. He keeps himself in readiness for that deputation. He is always dressed for it; and when he hears steps on the threshold, he stands up by the table; puts one hand into the breast of his coat; and assumes the attitude of a conqueror receiving suppliants. And this also goes on not for days but for years, long after the world has forgotten him, and there is nobody likely to come for him except Peer Gynt's button moulder.

Borkman, like all madmen, cannot nourish his delusion without some response from without. One of the victims of his downfall is a clerk who once wrote a tragedy, and has lived ever since in his own imagination as a poet. His family ridicules his tragedy and his pretensions; and as he is a poor ineffectual little creature who has never lived enough to feel dignified among the dead, like Borkman, he too finds it hard to keep his illusion alive without help. Fortunately he has admired Borkman, the great financier; and Borkman, when he has ruined him and ruined himself, is quite willing to be admired by this humble victim, and even to reward him by a pretence of believing in his poetic genius. Thus the two form one of those Mutual Admiration Societies on which the world so largely subsists, and make the years in the long gallery tolerable by flattering each other. There are even moments when Borkman is nerved to the point of starting for his second advent as a great financial redeemer. On such occasions the woman downstairs hears the footsteps of the sick wolf on the stairs approaching the hat-stand where his hat and stick have waited unused all the years of his entombment; but they never reach that first stage of the journey. They always turn back into the gallery again.

This melancholy household of the dead crumbles to dust at the knock of the younger generation at the door. Erhart, dedicated by his mother to the task of paying his father's debts and retrieving his ruin, and by his aunt to the task of sweetening her last days with his grateful love, has dedicated himself to his own affairs — for the moment mostly love affairs — and has not the faintest intention of concerning himself with the bygone career of the crazy ex-felon upstairs or the sentimentalities of the old maid downstairs. He detests the house and the atmosphere, and associates his aunt's broken heart with nothing more important than the scent of stale lavender, which he dislikes. He spends his time happily in the house of a pretty lady in the neighborhood, who has been married and divorced, and knows how to form an adolescent youth. And as to the unpardonable enemy of the family, one Hinkel, who betrayed Borkman to the police and rose on his ruins, Erhart cares so little for that old story that he goes to Hinkel's parties and enjoys himself there very much. And when at last the pretty lady raises his standard of happiness to a point at which the old house and the old people become impossible, unthinkable, unbearable, he goes off with her to Italy and leaves the dead to bury their dead.

The details of this catastrophe make the play. The fresh air and the light of day break into the tomb; and its inhabitants crumble into dust. Foldal, the poet clerk, lets slip the fact that he has not the slightest belief in Borkman's triumphant return to the world; and Borkman retorts by telling him he is no poet. After this comedy comes the tragedy of the son's defection; and amid the recriminations of the broken heart, the baffled pride, and the shattered dreams, the castles in the air vanish and reveal the open grave they have hidden. Poor Foldal, limping home after being run over by a sledge in which his daughter is running away to act as "second string" and chaperone for Erhart and the pretty lady, is the only one who is wanted in the world, since he must still work for his derisive family. But Borkman returns to his dream, and ventures out of doors at last, not this time to resume his place as governor of the bank, but to release the imprisoned metal that rings and sings to him from the earth. In other words, to die in the open, mad but happy, whilst the two sisters, "we two shadows," end their strife over his body.

WHEN WE DEAD AWAKEN [1900]

This play, the last work of Ibsen, and at first the least esteemed, has had its prophecy so startlingly fulfilled in England that nobody will now question the intensity of its inspiration. With us the dead have awakened in the very manner prefigured in the play. The simplicity and brevity of the story is so obvious, and the enormous scope of the conception so difficult to comprehend, that many of Ibsen's most devoted admirers failed to do it justice. They knew that he was a man of seventy, and were prepossessed with the belief that at such an age his powers must be falling off. It certainly was easier at that time to give the play up as a bad job than to explain it. Now that the great awakening of women which we call the Militant Suffrage Movement is upon us, and you may hear our women publicly and passionately paraphrasing Ibsen's heroine without having read a word of the play, the matter is simpler. There is no falling-off here in Ibsen. It may be said that this is physically impossible; but those who say so forget that the natural decay of a writer's powers may shew itself in two ways. The inferiority of the work produced is only one way. The other is the production of equally good or even better work with much greater effort than it would have cost its author ten years earlier. Ibsen produced this play with great difficulty in twice as long a period as had before sufficed; and even at that the struggle left his mind a wreck; for he not only never wrote another play, but, like an overstrained athlete, lost even the normal mental capacity of an ordinary man. Yet it would be hard to say that the play was not worth the sacrifice. It shews no decay of Ibsen's highest qualities: his magic is nowhere more potent. It is shorter than usual: that is all. The extraordinarily elaborate private history, family and individual, of the personages, which lies behind the action of the other plays, is replaced by a much simpler history of a few people in their general human relations without any family history at all. And the characteristically conscientious fitting of the play to the mechanical conditions of old-fashioned stages has given way to demands that even the best equipped and largest modern stages cannot easily comply with; for the second act takes place in a valley; and though it is easy to represent a valley by a painted scene when the action is confined to one spot in the foreground, it is a different matter when the whole valley has to be practicable, and the movements of the figures cover distances which do not exist on the stage, and cannot, as far as my experience goes, be satisfactorily simulated by the stage carpenter, though they are easy enough for the painter. I should attach no importance at all to this in a writer less mindful of technical limitations, and less ingenious in circumventing them than Ibsen, who was for some years a professional stage manager; but in his case it is clear that in calling on the theatre to expand to his requirements instead of, as his custom was, limiting his scene of action to the possibilities of a modest provincial theatre, he knew quite well what he was doing. Here, then, we have three differences from the earlier plays. None of them are inferiorities. They are proper to the difference of subject, and in fact increased the difficulty of the playwright's task by throwing him back on sheer dramatic power, unaided by the cheaper interest that can be gained on the stage by mere ingenuity of construction. Ibsen, who has always before played on the spectator by a most elaborate gradual development which would have satisfied Dumas, here throws all his cards on the table as rapidly as possible, and proceeds to deal intensively with a situation that never alters.

This situation is simple enough in its general statement, though it is so complex in its content that it raises the whole question of domestic civilization. Take a man and a woman at the highest pitch of natural ability and charm yet attained, and enjoying all the culture that modern art and literature can offer them; and what does it all come to? Contrast them with an essentially uncivilized pair, with a man who lives for hunting and eating and ravishing, and whose morals are those of the bully with the strong hand: in short, a man from the stone age as we conceive it (such men are still common enough in the classes that can afford the huntsman's life); and couple him with a woman who has no interest or ambition in life except to be captured by such a man (and of these we have certainly no lack). Then face this question. What is there to choose between these two pairs? Is the cultured gifted man less hardened, less selfish towards the woman, than the paleolithic man? Is the woman less sacrificed, less enslaved, less dead spiritually in the one case than in the other? Modern culture, except when it has rotted into mere cynicism, shrieks that the question is an insult. The stone age, anticipating Ibsen's reply, guffaws heartily and says, "Bravo, Ibsen!" Ibsen's reply is that the sacrifice of the woman of the stone age to fruitful passions which she herself shares is as nothing compared to the wasting of the modern woman's soul to gratify the imagination and stimulate the genius of the modern artist, poet, and philosopher. He shews us that no degradation ever devized or permitted is as disastrous as this degradation; that through it women die into luxuries for men, and yet can kill them; that men and women are becoming conscious of this; and that what remains to be seen as perhaps the most interesting of all imminent social developments is what will happen "when we dead awaken."

Ibsen's greatest contemporary outside his own art was Rodin the French sculptor. Whether Ibsen knew this, or whether he was inspired to make his hero a sculptor just as Dickens was inspired to make Pecksniff an architect, is not known. At all events, having to take a type of the highest and ablest masculine genius, he made him a sculptor, and called his name, not Rodin, but Rubeck: a curious assonance, if it was not intentional. Rubeck is as able an individual as our civilization can produce. The difficulty of presenting such an individual in fiction is that it can be done only by a writer who occupies that position himself; for a dramatist cannot conceive anything higher than himself. No doubt he can invest an imaginary figure with all sorts of imaginary gifts. A drunken author may make his hero sober; an ugly, weak, puny, timid one may make him a Hyperion or a Hercules; a deaf mute may write novels in which the lover is an orator and his mistress a prima donna; but whatever ornaments and accomplishments he may pile up on his personages, he cannot give them greater souls than his own. Defoe could invent wilder adventures for Robinson Crusoe than Shakespear for Hamlet; but he could not make that mean adventurer, with his dull eulogies of the virtues of "the middle station of life," anything even remotely like Shakespear's prince.

For Ibsen this difficulty did not exist. He knew quite well that he was one of the greatest men living; so he simply said "Suppose ME to be a sculptor instead of a playwright," and the thing was done. Thus he came forward himself to plead to his his own worst indictment of modern culture. One of the touches by which he identifies himself has all the irony of his earliest work. Rubeck has to make money out of human vanity, as all sculptors must nowadays, by portrait busts; but he revenges himself by studying and bringing out in his sitters "the respectable pompous horse faces, and self-opinionated donkey-muzzles, and lop-eared low-browed dog-skulls, and fatted swine-snouts, and dull brutal bull fronts" that lurk in so many human faces. All artists who deal with humanity do this, more or less. Leonardo da Vinci ruled his notebook in columns headed fox, wolf, etc., and made notes of faces by ticking them off in these columns, finding this, apparently, as satisfactory a memorandum as a drawing. Domestic animals, terriers, pugs, poultry, parrots, and cockatoos, are specially valuable to the caricaturist, as giving the original types which explain many faces. Ibsen must have classified his acquaintances a good deal in this way, not without an occasional chuckle; and his attribution of the practice to Rubeck is a confession of it.

Rubeck makes his reputation, as sculptors often do, by a statue of a woman. Not, be it observed, of a dress and a pair of boots, with a head protruding from them, but of a woman from the hand of Nature. It is worth noting here that we have hardly any portraits, either painted or carved, of our famous men and women or even of our nearest and dearest friends. Charles Dickens is known to us as a guy with a human head and face on top. Shakespear is a laundry advertisement of a huge starched collar with his head sticking out of it. Dr. Johnson is a face looking through a wig perched on a snuffy suit of old clothes. All the great women of history are fashion plates of their period. Bereaved parents, orphans, and widows weep fondly over photographs of uniforms, frock coats, gowns, and hats, for the sake of the little scrap of humanity that is allowed to peep through these trappings. Women with noble figures and plain or elderly faces are outdressed and outfaced by rivals who, if revealed as they really are, would be hardly human. Carlyle staggers humanity by inviting the House of Commons to sit unclothed, so that we, and they themselves, shall know them for what they really are.

Hence it is that the artist who adores mankind as his highest subject, always comes back to the reality beneath the clothes. His claim to be allowed to do this is so irresistible that in every considerable city in England you will find, supported by the rates of prudish chapel goers, and even managed and inspected by committees of them, an art school where, in the "life class" (significant term!) young women posed in ridiculous and painful attitudes by a drawing master, and mostly under the ugliest circumstances of light, color, and surroundings, earn a laborious wage by allowing a crowd of art students to draw their undraped figures. It is a joylessly grotesque spectacle: one wonders whether anything can really be learnt from it; for never have I seen one of these school models in an attitude which any human being would, unless the alternative were starvation, voluntarily sustain for thirty seconds, or assume on any natural occasion or provocation whatever. Male models are somewhat less slavish; and the stalwart laborer or olive-skinned young Italian who poses before a crowd of easels with ludicrously earnest young ladies in blue or vermilion gowns and embroidered pinafores, drawing away at him for dear life, is usually much more comfortably and possibly posed. But Life will not yield up her more intimate secrets for eighteenpence an hour; and these earnest young ladies and artsome young men, when they have filled portfolios with such sordid life studies, know less about living humanity than they did before, and very much less about even the mechanism of the body and the shape of its muscles than they could learn less inhumanly from a series of modern kinematographs of figures in motion.

Rubeck does not make his statues in a class at a municipal art school by looking at a weary girl in a tortured attitude with a background of match-boarding, under a roof of girders, and with the ghastly light of a foggy, smoky manufacturing town making the light side of her flesh dirty yellow and the shadowed side putrid purple. He knows better than that. He finds a beautiful woman, and tells her his vision of a statue of The Resurrection Day in the form of a woman "filled with a sacred joy at finding herself unchanged in the higher, freer, happier region after the long dreamless sleep of death." And the woman, immediately seizing his inspiration and sharing it, devotes herself to the work, not merely as his model, but as his friend, his helper, fellow worker, comrade, all things, save one, that may be humanly natural and necessary between them for an unreserved co-operation in the great work. The one exception is that they are not lovers; for the sculptor's ideal is a virgin, or, as he calls it, a pure woman.

And her reward is that when the work is finished and the statue achieved, he says "Thank you for a priceless EPISODE," at which significant word, revealing as it does that she has, after all, been nothing to him but a means to his end, she leaves him and drops out of his life. To earn her living she must then pose, not to him, but before crowds in Variety Theatres in living pictures, gaining much money by her beauty, winning rich husbands, and driving them all to madness or to death by "a fine sharp dagger which she always has with her in bed," much as Rita Allmers nearly killed her husband. And she calls the statue her child and Rubeck's, as the book in Hedda Gabler was the child of Thea and Eilert Lövborg. But finally she too goes mad under the strain.

Rubeck presently meets a pretty Stone Age woman, and marries her. And as he is not a Stone Age man, and she is bored to distraction by his cultured interests, he disappoints her as thoroughly as she disgusts and wearies him: the symptoms being that though he builds her a splendid villa, full of works of art and so forth, neither he nor she can settle down quietly; and they take trips here, trips there, trips anywhere to escape being alone and at home together.

But the retribution for his egotism takes a much subtler form, and strikes at a much more vital place in him: namely, his artistic inspiration. Working with Irene, the lost model, he had achieved a perfect work of art; and, having achieved it, had supposed that he was done with her. But art is not so simple as that. The moment she forsakes him and leaves him to the Stone Age woman and to his egotism, he no longer sees the perfection of his work. He becomes dissatisfied with it. He sees that it can be improved: for instance, why should it consist of a figure of Irene alone? Why should he not be in it himself? Is he not a far more important factor in the conception? He changes the single figure design to a group. He adds a figure of himself. He finds that the woman's figure, with its wonderful expression of gladness, puts his own image out of countenance. He rearranges the group so as to give himself more prominence. Even so the gladness outshines him; and at last he "tones it down," striking the gladness out with his chisel, and making his own expression the main interest of the group. But he cannot stop there. Having destroyed the thing that was superior to him, he now wants to introduce things that are inferior. He carves clefts in the earth at the feet of his figure, and from these clefts he makes emerge the folk with the horse faces and the swine snouts that are nearer the beast than his own fine face. Then he is satisfied with his work; and it is in this form that it makes him famous and is finally placed in a public museum. In his days with Irene, they used to call these museums the prisons of works of art. Precisely what the Italian Futurist painters of today are calling them.

And now the play begins. Irene comes from her madhouse to a "health resort." Thither also comes Rubeck, wandering about with the Stone Age woman to avoid being left at home with her. Thither also comes the man of the Stone Age with his dogs and guns, and carries off the Stone Age woman, to her husband's great relief. Rubeck and Irene meet; and as they talk over old times, she learns, bit by bit, what has happened to the statue, and is about to kill him when she realizes, also bit by bit, that the history of its destruction is the history of his own, and that as he used her up and left her dead, so with her death the life went out of him. But, like Nora in A Doll's House, she sees the possibility of a miracle. The dead may awaken if only they can find an honest and natural relation in which they shall no longer sacrifice and slay one another. She asks him to climb to the top of a mountain with her and see that promised land. Half way up, they meet the Stone Age pair hunting. There is a storm coming. It is death to go up and danger to climb down. The Stone Age man faces the danger and carries his willing prey down. The others are beyond the fear of death, and go up. And that is the end of them and of the plays of Henrik Ibsen.

The end, too, let us hope, of the idols, domestic, moral, religious and political, in whose name we have been twaddled into misery and confusion and hypocrisy unspeakable. For Ibsen's dead hand still keeps the grip he laid on their masks when he first tore them off; and whilst that grip holds, all the King's horses and all the King's men will find it hard to set those Humpty-Dumpties up again.

The Moral of the Plays

In following this sketch of the plays written by Ibsen to illustrate his thesis that the real slavery of to-day is slavery to ideals of virtue, it may be that readers who have conned Ibsen through idealist spectacles have wondered that I could so pervert the utterances of a great poet. Indeed I know already that many of those who are most fascinated by the poetry of the plays will plead for any explanation of them rather than that given by Ibsen himself in the plainest terms through the mouths of Mrs Alving, Relling, and the rest. No great writer uses his skill to conceal his meaning. There is a tale by a famous Scotch story-teller which would have suited Ibsen exactly if he had hit on it first. Jeanie Deans sacrificing her sister's life on the scaffold to her own ideal of duty is far more horrible than the sacrifice in *Rosmersholm;* and the *deus ex machina* expedient by which Scott makes the end of his story agreeable is no solution of the moral problem raised, but only a puerile evasion of it. He undoubtedly believed that it was right that Effie should hang for the sake of Jeanie's ideals.* Consequently, if I were to pretend that Scott wrote *The Heart of Midlothian* to shew that people are led to do as mischievous, as unnatural, as murderous things by their religious and moral ideals as by their envy and ambition, it would be easy to confute me from the pages of the book itself. But Ibsen has made his meaning no less plain than Scott's. If any one attempts to maintain that *Ghosts* is a polemic in favour of indissoluble monogamic marriage, or that *The Wild Duck* was written to inculcate that truth should be told for its own sake, they must burn the text of the plays if their contention is to stand. The reason that Scott's story is tolerated by those who shrink from *Ghosts* is not that it is less terrible, but that Scott's views are familiar

* The common-sense solution of the moral problem has often been delivered by acclamation in the theatre. Some sixteen or seventeen years ago I witnessed a performance of a melodrama founded on this story. After the painful trial scene, in which Jeanie Deans condemns her sister to death by refusing to swear to a perfectly innocent fiction, came a scene in the prison. "If it had been me," said the jailor, "I wad ha' sworn a hole through an iron pot." The roar of applause which burst from the pit and gallery was thoroughly Ibsenite in sentiment. The speech, by the way, was a "gag" of the actor's, and is not to be found in the acting edition of the play.

to all well-brought-up ladies and gentlemen, whereas Ibsen's are for the moment so strange as to be almost unthinkable. He is so great a poet that the idealist finds himself in the dilemma of being unable to conceive that such a genius should have an ignoble meaning, and yet equally unable to conceive his real meaning as otherwise than ignoble. Consequently he misses the meaning altogether in spite of Ibsen's explicit and circumstantial insistence on it, and proceeds to interpolate a meaning which conforms to his own ideal of nobility. Ibsen's deep sympathy with his idealist figures seems to countenance this method of making confusion. Since it is on the weaknesses of the higher types of character that idealism seizes, his examples of vanity, selfishness, folly, and failure are not vulgar villains, but men who in an ordinary novel or melodrama would be heroes. His most tragic point is reached in the destinies of Brand and Rosmer, who drive those whom they love to death in its most wanton and cruel form. The ordinary Philistine commits no such atrocities: he marries the woman he likes and lives more or less happily ever after; but that is not because he is greater than Brand or Rosmer, but because he is less. The idealist is a more dangerous animal than the Philistine just as a man is a more dangerous animal than a sheep. Though Brand virtually murdered his wife, I can understand many a woman, comfortably married to an amiable Philistine, reading the play and envying the victim her husband. For when Brand's wife, having made the sacrifice he has exacted, tells him that he was right; that she is happy now; that she sees God face to face — but reminds him that "whoso sees Jehovah dies," he instinctively clasps his hands over her eyes; and that action raises him at once far above the criticism that sneers at idealism from beneath, instead of surveying it from the clear ether above, which can only be reached through its mists.

If, in my account of the plays, I have myself suggested false judgments by describing the errors of the idealists in the terms of the life they had risen above rather than in that of the life they fell short of, I can only plead, with but a moderate disrespect to a large section of my readers, that if I had done otherwise I should have failed wholly to make the matter understood. Indeed the terms of the realist morality have not yet appeared in our living language; and I have already, in this very distinction between idealism and realism, been forced to insist on a sense of these terms which, had not Ibsen forced my hand, I should perhaps have conveyed otherwise, so strongly does it conflict in many of its applications with the vernacular use of the words. This, however, was a trifle compared to the difficulty which arose, when personal characters had to be described, from our inveterate habit of labelling men with the names of their moral qualities without the slightest reference to the underlying will which sets these qualities in action. At a recent anniversary celebration of the Paris Commune of 1871, I was struck by the fact that no speaker could find a eulogy for the Federals which would not have been equally appropriate to the peasants of La Vendée who fought for their tyrants against the French revolutionists, or to the Irishmen and Highlanders who fought for the Stuarts at the Boyne or Culloden. Nor could the celebrators find any other adjectives for their favourite leaders of the Commune than those which had recently been liberally applied by all the journals to an African explorer whose achievements were just then held in the liveliest abhorrence by the whole meeting. The statements that the slain members of the Commune were heroes who died for a noble ideal would have left a stranger quite as much in the dark about them as the counter statements, once common enough in middle-class newspapers, that they were incendiaries and assassins. Our obituary notices are examples of the same ambiguity. Of all the public men lately deceased, none have been made more interesting by strongly marked personal characteristics than the late Charles Bradlaugh. He was not in the least like any other notable member of the House of Commons. Yet when the obituary notices appeared, with the usual string of qualities — eloquence, determination, integrity, strong common-sense, and so on, it would have been possible, by merely expunging all names and other external details from these notices, to leave the reader entirely unable to say whether the subject of them was Mr Gladstone, Mr Morley, Mr Stead, or any one else no more like Mr Bradlaugh than Garibaldi or the late Cardinal Newman, whose obituary certificates of morality might nevertheless have been reprinted almost verbatim for the occasion without any gross incongruity. Bradlaugh had been the subject of many sorts of newspaper notice in his time. Ten years ago, when the middle classes supposed him to be a revolutionist, the string of qualities which the press hung upon him were all evil ones, great stress being laid on the fact that as he was an atheist it would be an insult to God to admit him to Parliament. When it became apparent that he was a conservative force in politics, he, without any recantation of his atheism, at once had the string of evil qualities exchanged for a rosary of good ones; but it is hardly necessary to add that neither the old badge nor the new will ever give any inquirer the least clue to the sort of man he actually was: he might have been Oliver Cromwell or Wat Tyler or Jack Cade, Penn or Wilberforce or Wellington, the late Mr Hampden of flat-earth-theory notoriety or Proudhon or the Archbishop of Canterbury, for all the distinction that such labels could give him one way or the other. The worthlessness of these accounts of individuals is recognized in practice every day. Tax a stranger before a crowd with being a thief, a coward, and a liar; and the crowd will suspend its judgment until you answer the question, "What's he done?" Attempt to make a collection for him on the ground that he is an upright, fearless, high-principled hero; and the same question must be answered before a penny goes into the hat.

The reader must therefore discount those partialities which I have permitted myself to express in telling the stories of the plays. They are as much beside the mark as any other example of the sort of criticism which seeks to create an impression favourable or otherwise to Ibsen by simply pasting his characters all over with good or bad conduct marks. If any person cares to describe Hedda Gabler as a modern Lucretia who preferred death to dishonour, and Thea Elvsted as an abandoned, perjured strumpet who deserted the man she had sworn before her God to love, honour, and obey until her death, the play contains conclusive evidence establishing both points. If the critic goes on to argue that as Ibsen manifestly means to recommend Thea's conduct above Hedda's by making the end happier for her, the moral of the play is a vicious one, that, again, cannot be gainsaid. If, on the other hand, *Ghosts* be defended, as the dramatic critic of *Piccadilly* lately did defend it, because it throws into divine relief the beatiful figure of the simple and pious Pastor Manders, the fatal compliment cannot be parried. When you have called Mrs Alving an "emancipated woman" or an unprincipled one, Alving a debauchee or a "victim of society," Nora a fearless and noble-hearted woman or a shocking little liar and an unnatural mother, Helmer a selfish hound or a model husband and father, according to your bias, you have said something which is at once true and false, and in either case perfectly idle.

The statement that Ibsen's plays have an immoral tendency, is, in the sense in which it is used, quite true. Immorality does not necessarily imply mischievous conduct: it implies conduct, mischievous or not, which does not conform to current ideals. Since Ibsen has devoted himself almost entirely to shewing that the spirit or will of Man is constantly outgrowing his ideals, and that therefore conformity to them is constantly producing results no less tragic than those which follow the violation of ideals which are still valid, the main effect of his plays is to keep before the public the importance of being always prepared to act immorally, to remind men that they ought to be as careful how they yield to a temptation to tell the truth as to a temptation to hold their tongues, and to urge upon women that the desirability of their preserving their chastity depends just as much on circumstances as the desirability of taking a cab instead of walking. He protests against the ordinary assumption that there are certain supreme ends which justify all means used to attain them; and insists that every end shall be challenged to shew that it justifies the means. Our ideals, like the gods of old, are constantly demanding human sacrifices. Let none of them, says Ibsen, be placed above the obligation to prove that they are worth the sacrifices they demand; and let every one refuse to sacrifice himself and others from the moment he loses his faith in the reality of the ideal. Of course it will be said here by incorrigibly slipshod readers that this, so far from being immoral, is the highest morality; and so, in a sense, it is; but I really shall not waste any further explanation on those who will neither mean one thing or another by a word nor allow me to do so. In short, then, among those who are not ridden by current ideals no question as to the morality of Ibsen's plays will ever arise; and among those who are so ridden his plays will seem immoral, and cannot be defended against the accusation.

There can be no question as to the effect likely to be produced on an individual by his conversion from the ordinary acceptance of current ideals as safe standards of conduct, to the vigilant open-mindedness of Ibsen. It must at once greatly deepen the sense of moral responsibility. Before conversion the individual anticipates nothing worse in the way of examination at the judgment bar of his conscience than such questions as, Have you kept the commandments? Have you obeyed the law? Have you attended church regularly; paid your rates and taxes to Cæsar; and contributed, in reason, to charitable institutions? It may be hard to do all these things; but it is still harder not to do them, as our ninety-nine moral cowards in the hundred well know. And even a scoundrel can do them all and yet live a worse life than the smuggler or prostitute who must answer No all through the catechism. Substitute for such a technical examination one in which the whole point to be settled is, Guilty or Not Guilty? — one in which there is no more and no less respect for chastity than for incontinence, for subordination than for rebellion, for legality than for illegality, for piety than for blasphemy, in short, for the standard virtues than for the standard vices, and immediately, instead of lowering the moral standard by relaxing the tests of worth, you raise it by increasing their stringency to a point at which no mere Pharisaism or moral cowardice can pass them. Naturally this does not please the Pharisee. The respectable lady of the strictest Christian principles, who has brought up her children with such relentless regard to their ideal morality that if they have any spirit left in them by the time they arrive at years of independence they use their liberty to rush deliriously to the devil — this unimpeachable woman has always felt it unjust that the respect she wins should be accompanied by deep-seated detestation, whilst the latest spiritual heiress of Nell Gwynne, whom no respectable person dare bow to in the street, is a popular idol. The reason is — though the virtuous lady does not know it — that Nell Gwynne is a better woman than she; and the abolition of the idealist test which brings her out a worse one, and its replacement by the realist test which would shew the true relation between them, would be a most desirable step forward in public morals, especially as it would act impartially, and set the good side of the Pharisee above the bad side of the Bohemian as ruthlessly as it would set the good side of the Bohemian above the bad side of the Pharisee. For as long as convention goes counter to reality in these matters, people will be led into Hedda Gabler's error of making an ideal of vice. If we maintain the convention that the distinction between Catherine of Russia and Queen Victoria, between Nell Gwynne and Mrs Proudie, is the distinction between a bad woman and a good woman, we need not be surprised when those who sympathize with Catherine and Nell conclude that it is better to be a bad woman than a good one, and go on recklessly to conceive a prejudice against teetotallism and monogamy, and a prepossession in favour of alcoholic excitement and promiscuous amours. Ibsen himself is kinder to the man who has gone his own way as a rake and a drunkard than to the man who is respectable because he dare not be otherwise. We find that the franker and healthier a boy is, the more certain is he to prefer pirates and highwaymen, or Dumas musketeers, to "pillars of society" as his favourite heroes of romance. We have already seen both Ibsenites and anti-Ibsenites who seem to think that the cases of Nora and Mrs Elvsted are meant to establish a golden rule for women who wish to be "emancipated," the said golden rule being simply, Run away from your husband. But in Ibsen's view of life, that would come under the same condemnation as the conventional golden rule, Cleave to your husband until death do you part. Most people know of a case or two in which it would be wise for a wife to follow the example of Nora or even of Mrs Elvsted. But they must also know cases in which the results of such a course would be as tragic-comic as those of Gregers Werle's attempt in *The Wild Duck* to do for the Ekdal household what Lona Hessel did for the Bernick household. What Ibsen insists on is that there is no golden rule — that conduct must justify itself by its effect upon happiness and not by its conformity to any rule or ideal. And since happiness consists in the fulfilment of the will, which is constantly growing, and cannot be fulfilled to-day under the conditions which secured its fulfilment yesterday, he claims afresh the old Protestant right of private judgment in questions of conduct as against all institutions, the so-called Protestant Churches themselves included.

Here I must leave the matter, merely reminding those who may think that I have forgotten to reduce Ibsenism to a formula for them, that its quintessence is that there is no formula.

I have a word or two to add as to the difficulties which Ibsen's philosophy places in the way of those who are called on to impersonate his characters on the stage in England. His idealist figures, at once higher and more mischievous than ordinary Philistines, puzzle by their dual aspect the conventional actor, who persists in assuming that if he is to be selfish on the stage he must be villainous; that if he is to be self-sacrificing and scrupulous he must be a hero; and that if he is to satirize himself unconsciously he must be comic. He is constantly striving to get back to familiar ground by reducing his part to one of the stage types with which he is familiar, and which he has learnt to present by rule of thumb. The more experienced he is, the more certain is he to de-Ibsenize the play into a melodrama or a farcical comedy of the common sort. Give him Helmer to play, and he begins by declaring that the part is a mass of "inconsistencies," and ends by suddenly grasping the idea that it is only Joseph Surface over again. Give him Gregers Werle, the devotee of Truth, and he will first play him in the vein of George Washington, and then, when he finds that the audience laughs at him instead of taking him respectfully, rush to the conclusion that Gregers is only his old friend the truthful milkman in *A Phenomenon in a Smock Frock,* and begin to play for the laughs and relish them. That is, if there are only laughs enough to make the part completely comic. Otherwise he will want to omit the passages which provoke them. To be laughed at when playing a serious part is hard upon an actor, and still more upon an actress: it is derision, than which nothing is more terrible to those whose livelihood depends on public approbation, and whose calling produces an abnormal development of self-consciousness. Now Ibsen undoubtedly does freely require from his artists that they shall not only possess great skill and power on every plane of their art, but that they shall also be ready to make themselves acutely ridiculous sometimes at the very climax of their most deeply felt passages. It is not to be wondered at that they prefer to pick and choose among the lines of their parts, retaining the great professional opportunities afforded by the tragic scenes, and leaving out the touches which complete the portrait at the expense of the model's vanity. If an actress of established reputation were asked to play Hedda Gabler, her first impulse would probably be to not only turn Hedda into a

Brinvilliers, or a Borgia, or a "Forget-me-not," but to suppress all the meaner callosities and odiousnesses which detract from Hedda's dignity as dignity is estimated on the stage. The result would be about as satisfactory to a skilled critic as that of the retouching which has made shop window photography the most worthless of the arts. The whole point of an Ibsen play lies in the exposure of the very conventions upon which are based those by which the actor is ridden. Charles Surface or Tom Jones may be very effectively played by artists who fully accept the morality professed by Joseph Surface and Blifil. Neither Fielding nor Sheridan forces upon either actor or audience the dilemma that since Charles and Tom are lovable, there must be something hopelessly inadequate in the commercial and sexual morality which condemns them as a pair of blackguards. The ordinary actor will tell you that the authors "do not defend their heroes' conduct," not seeing that making them lovable is the most complete defence of their conduct that could possibly be made. How far Fielding and Sheridan saw it — how far Molière or Mozart were convinced that the statue had right on his side when he threw Don Juan into the bottomless pit — how far Milton went in his sympathy with Lucifer: all these are speculative points which no actor has hitherto been called upon to solve. But they are the very subjects of Ibsen's plays: those whose interest and curiosity are not excited by them find him the most puzzling and tedious of dramatists. He has not only made "lost" women lovable; but he has recognized and avowed that this is a vital justification for them, and has accordingly explicitly argued on their side and awarded them the sympathy which poetic justice grants only to the righteous. He has made the terms "lost" and "ruined" in this sense ridiculous by making women apply them to men with the most ludicrous effect. Hence Ibsen cannot be played from the conventional point of view: to make that practicable the plays would have to be rewritten. In the rewriting, the fascination of the parts would vanish, and with it their attraction for the performers. *A Doll's House* was adapted in this fashion, though not at the instigation of an actress; but the adaptation fortunately failed. Otherwise we might have to endure in Ibsen's case what we have already endured in that of Shakespear, many of whose plays were supplanted for centuries by incredibly debased versions, of which Cibber's *Richard III.* and Garrick's *Katharine and Petruchio* have lasted to our own time.

Taking Talma's estimate of eighteen years as the apprenticeship of a completely accomplished stage artist, there is little encouragement to offer Ibsen parts to our finished actors and actresses. They do not understand them, and would not play them in their integrity if they could be induced to attempt them. In England only two women in the full maturity of their talent have hitherto meddled with Ibsen. One of these, Miss Geneviève Ward, who "created" the part of Lona Hessel in the English version of *Pillars of Society,* had the advantage of exceptional enterprise and intelligence, and of a more varied culture and experience of life and art than are common in her profession. The other, Mrs Theodore Wright, the first English Mrs Alving, was hardly known to the dramatic critics, though her personality and her artistic talent as an amateur reciter and actress had been familiar to the members of most of the advanced social and political bodies in London since the days of the International. It was precisely because her record lay outside the beaten track of newspaper criticism that she was qualified to surprise its writers as she did. In every other instance, the women who first ventured upon playing Ibsen heroines were young actresses whose ability had not before been fully tested and whose technical apprenticeships were far from complete. Miss Janet Achurch, though she settled the then disputed question of the feasibility of Ibsen's plays on the English stage by her impersonation of Nora in 1889, which still remains the most complete artistic achievement in the new *genre,* had not been long enough on the stage to secure a unanimous admission of her genius, though it was of the most irresistible and irrepressible kind. Miss Florence Farr, who may claim the palm for artistic courage and intellectual conviction in selecting for her experiment *Rosmersholm,* incomparably the most difficult and dangerous, as it also the greatest, of Ibsen's later plays, had almost relinquished her profession from lack of interest in its routine, after spending a few years in acting farcical comedies. Miss Elizabeth Robins and Miss Marion Lea, to whose unaided enterprise we owe our early acquaintance with *Hedda Gabler* on the stage, were, like Miss Achurch and Miss Farr, juniors in their profession. All four were products of the modern movement for the higher education of women, literate, in touch with advanced thought, and coming by natural predilection on the stage from outside the theatrical class, in contradistinction to the senior generation of inveterately sentimental actresses, schooled in the old fashion if at all, born into their profession, quite out of the political and social movement around them — in short, intellectually *naïve* to the last degree. The new school says to the old, You cannot play Ibsen because you are ignoramuses. To which the old school retorts, You cannot play anything because you are amateurs. But taking amateur in its sense of unpractised executant, both schools are amateur as far as Ibsen's plays are concerned. The old technique breaks down in the new theatre; for though in theory it is a technique of general application, making the artist so plastic that he can mould himself to any shape designed by the dramatist, in practice it is but a stock of tones and attitudes out of which, by appropriate selection and combination, a certain limited number of conventional stage figures can be made up. It is no more possible to get an Ibsen character out of it than to contrive a Greek costume out of an English wardrobe; and some of the attempts already made have been so grotesque, that at present, when one of the more specifically Ibsenian parts has to be filled, it is actually safer to entrust it to a novice than to a competent and experienced actor.

A steady improvement may be expected in the performances of Ibsen's plays as the young players whom they interest gain the experience needed to make mature artists of them. They will gain this experience not only in plays by Ibsen himself, but in the works of dramatists who will have been largely influenced by Ibsen. Playwrights who formerly only compounded plays according to the received prescriptions for producing tears or laughter, are already taking their profession seriously to the full extent of their capacity, and venturing more and more to substitute the incidents and catastrophes of spiritual history for the swoons, surprises, discoveries, murders, duels, assassinations and intrigues which are the commonplaces of the theatre at present. Others, who have no such impulse, find themselves forced to raise the quality of their work by the fact that even those who witness Ibsen's plays with undisguised weariness and aversion, find, when they return to their accustomed theatrical fare, that they have suddenly become conscious of absurdities and artificialities in it which never troubled them before. In just the same way the painters of the Naturalist school reformed their opponents much more extensively than the number of their own direct admirers indicates: for example, it is still common to hear the most contemptuous abuse and ridicule of Monet and Whistler from persons who have nevertheless had their former tolerance of the unrealities of the worst type of conventional studio picture wholly destroyed by these painters. Until quite lately, too, musicians were to be heard extolling Donizetti in the same breath with which they vehemently decried Wagner. They would make wry faces at every chord in *Tristan und Isolde,* and never suspected that their old faith was shaken until they went back to *La Favorita,* and found that it had become as obsolete as the rhymed tragedies of Lee and Otway. In the drama then, we may depend on it that though we shall not have another Ibsen, yet nobody will write for the stage after him as most playwrights wrote before him. This will involve a corresponding change in the technical stock-in-trade of the actor, whose ordinary training will then cease to be a positive disadvantage to him when he is entrusted with an Ibsen part.

No one need fear on this account that Ibsen will gradually destroy melodrama. It might as well be assumed that Shakespear will destroy music hall entertainments, or the prose romances of William Morris supersede the *Illustrated Police News*. All forms of art rise with the culture and capacity of the human race; but the forms rise together: the higher forms do not return upon and submerge the lower. The wretch who finds his happiness in setting a leash of greyhounds on a hare or in watching a terrier killing rats in a pit, may evolve into the mere blockhead who would rather go to a "free-and-easy" and chuckle over a dull, silly, obscene song; but such a step will not raise him to the level of the frequenter of music halls of the better class, where, though the entertainment is administered in small separate doses or "turns," yet the turns have some artistic pretension. Above him again is the patron of that elementary form of sensational drama in which there is hardly any more connection between the incidents than the fact that the same people take part in them and call forth some very simple sort of moral judgment by being consistently villainous or virtuous throughout. As such a drama would be almost as enjoyable if the acts were played in the reverse of their appointed order, no inconvenience except that of a back seat is suffered by the playgoer who comes in for half price at nine o'clock. On a higher plane we have dramas with a rational sequence of incidents, the interest of any one of which depends on those which have preceded it; and as we go up from plane to plane we find this sequence becoming more and more organic until at last we come to a class of play in which nobody can understand the last act who has not seen the first also. Accordingly, the institution of half price at nine o'clock does not exist at theatres devoted to plays of this class. The highest type of play is completely homogeneous, often consisting of a single very complex incident; and not even the most exhaustive information as to the story enables a spectator to receive the full force of the impression aimed at it in any given passage if he enters the theatre for that passage alone. The success of such plays depends upon the exercise by the audience of powers of memory, imagination, insight, reasoning, and sympathy, which only a small minority of the playgoing public at present possesses. To the rest the higher drama is as disagreeably perplexing as the game of chess is to a man who has barely enough capacity to understand skittles. Consequently, just as we have the chess club and the skittle alley prospering side by side, we shall have the theatre of Shakespear, Molière, Goethe, and Ibsen prospering alongside that of Henry Arthur Jones and Gilbert; of Sardou, Grundy, and Pinero; of Buchanan and Ohnet, as naturally as these already prosper alongside that of Pettit and Sims, which again does no more harm to the music halls than the music halls do to the waxworks or even the ratpit, although this last is dropping into the limbo of discarded brutalities by the same progressive movement that has led the intellectual playgoer to discard Sardou and take to Ibsen. It has often been said that political parties progress serpent-wise, the tail being to-day where the head was formerly, yet never overtaking the head. The same figure may be applied to grades of playgoers, with the reminder that this sort of serpent grows at the head and drops off joints of his tail as he glides along. Therefore it is not only inevitable that new theatres should be built for the new first class of playgoers, but that the best of the existing theatres should be gradually converted to their use, even at the cost of ousting, in spite of much angry protest, the old patrons who are being left behind by the movement.

The resistance of the old playgoers to the new plays will be supported by the elder managers, the elder actors, and the elder critics. One manager pities Ibsen for his ignorance of effective playwriting, and declares that he can see exactly what ought to have been done to make a real play of *Hedda Gabler*. His case is parallel to that of Mr Henry Irving, who saw exactly what ought to have been done to make a real play of Goethe's *Faust*, and got Mr Wills to do it. A third manager, repelled and disgusted by Ibsen, condemns *Hedda* as totally deficient in elevating moral sentiment. One of the plays which he prefers is Sardou's *La Tosca!* Clearly these three representative gentlemen, all eminent both as actors and managers, will hold by the conventional drama until the commercial success of Ibsen forces them to recognize that in the course of nature they are falling behind the taste of the day. Mr Thorne, at the Vaudeville Theatre, was the first leading manager who ventured to put a play of Ibsen's into his evening bill; and he did not do so until Miss Elizabeth Robins and Miss Marion Lea had given ten experimental performances at his theatre at their own risk. Mr Charrington and Miss Janet Achurch, who, long before that, staked their capital and reputation on *A Doll's House,* had to take a theatre and go into management themselves for the purpose. The production of *Rosmersholm* was not a managerial enterprise in the ordinary sense at all: it was an experiment made by Miss Farr, who played Rebecca — an experiment, too, which was considerably hampered by the refusal of the London managers to allow members of their companies to take part in the performance. In short, the senior division would have nothing to say for themselves in the matter of the one really progressive theatrical movement of their time, but for the fact that Mr W. H. Vernon's effort to obtain a hearing for *Pillars of Society* in 1880 was the occasion of the first appearance of the name of Ibsen on an English playbill.

But it had long been obvious that the want of a playhouse at which the aims of the management should be unconditionally artistic was not likely to be supplied either at our purely commercial theatres or at those governed by actor-managers reigning absolutely over all the other actors, a power which a young man abuses to provide opportunities for himself, and which an older man uses in an old-fashioned way. Mr William Archer, in an article in the *Fortnightly Review,* invited private munificence to endow a National Theatre; and some time later a young Dutchman, Mr J. T. Grein, an enthusiast in theatrical art, came forward with a somewhat similar scheme. Private munificence remained irresponsive — fortunately, one must think, since it was a feature of both plans that the management of the endowed theatre should be handed over to committees of managers and actors of established reputation — in other words, to the very people whose deficiencies have created the whole difficulty. Mr Grein, however, being prepared to take any practicable scheme in hand himself, soon saw the realities of the situation well enough to understand that to wait for the floating of a fashionable Utopian enterprise, with the Prince of Wales as President and a capital of at least £20,000, would be to wait for ever. He accordingly hired a cheap public hall in Tottenham Court Road, and, though his resources fell far short of those with which an ambitious young professional man ventures upon giving a dance, made a bold start by announcing a performance of *Ghosts* to inaugurate "The Independent Theatre" on the lines of the *Théâtre Libre* of Paris. The result was that he received sufficient support both in money and gratuitous professional aid to enable him to give the performance at the Royalty Theatre; and throughout the following week he shared with Ibsen the distinction of being abusively discussed to an extent that must have amply convinced him that his efforts had not passed unheeded. Possibly he may have counted on being handled generously for the sake of his previous services in obtaining some consideration for the contemporary English drama on the continent, even to the extent of bringing about the translation and production in foreign theatres of some of the most popular of our recent plays; but if he had any such hope it was not fulfilled; for he received no quarter whatever. And at present it is clear that unless those who appreciate the service he has rendered to theatrical art in England support him as energetically as his opponents attack him, it will be impossible for him to maintain the performances of the Independent Theatre at the pitch of efficiency and frequency which will be needed if it is to have any wide effect on the taste and seriousness of the playgoing public. One of the most formidable and exasperating obstacles in his way is the detestable censorship exercised by the official licenser of plays, a public nuisance of which it seems impossible to rid ourselves under existing Parliamentary conditions. The licenser has the London theatres at his mercy through his power to revoke their licenses; and he is empowered to exact a fee for reading each play submitted to him, so that his income depends on his allowing no play to be produced without going through that ordeal. As these powers are granted to him in order that he may forbid the performance of plays which would have an injurious effect on public morals, the unfortunate gentleman is bound in honor to try to do his best to keep the stage in the right path — which he of course can set about in no other way than by making it a reflection of his individual views, which are necessarily dictated by his temperament and by the political and pecuniary interests of his class. This he does not dare to do: self-mistrust and the fear of public opinion paralyze him wherever either the strong hand or the open mind claims its golden opportunity; and the net result is that indecency and vulgarity are rampant on the London stage, from which flows the dramatic stream that irrigates the whole country; whilst Shelley's *Cenci* tragedy and Ibsen's *Ghosts* are forbidden, and have in fact only been performed once "in private": that is, before audiences of invited non-paying guests. It is now so well understood that only plays of the commonest idealist type can be sure of a license in London, that the novel and not the drama is the form adopted as a matter of course by thoughtful masters of fiction. The merits of the case ought to be too obvious to need restating: it is plain that every argument that supports a censorship of the stage supports with tenfold force a censorship of the press, which is admittedly an abomination. What is wanted is the entire abolition of the censorship and the establishment of Free Art in the sense in which we speak of Free Trade. There is not the slightest ground for protecting theatres against the competition of music halls, or for denying to Mr Grein as a theatrical *entrepreneur* the freedom he would enjoy as a member of a publishing firm. In the absence of a censorship a manager can be prosecuted for an offence against public morals, just as a publisher can. At present, though managers may not touch Shelley or *Ghosts,* they find no difficulty in obtaining official sanction, practically amounting to indemnity, for indecencies from which our uncensured novels are perfectly free. The truth is that the real support of the censorship comes from those Puritans who regard Art as a department of original sin. To them the theatre is an unmixed evil, and every restriction on it a gain to the cause of righteousness. Against them stand those who regard Art in all its forms as a department of religion. The Holy War between the two sides has played a considerable part in the history of England, and is just now being prosecuted with renewed vigour by the Puritans.

If their opponents do not display equal energy, it is quite possible that we shall presently have a reformed censorship ten times more odious than the existing one, the very absurdity of which causes it to be exercised with a halfheartedness that prevents the licenser from doing his worst as well as his best. The wise policy for the friends of Art just now is to use the Puritan agitation in order to bring the matter to an issue, and then to make a vigorous effort to secure that the upshot shall be the total abolition of the censorship.

As it is with the actors and managers, so it is with the critics: the supporters of Ibsen are the younger men. In the main, however, the Press follows the managers instead of leading them. The average newspaper dramatic critic is not a Lessing, a Lamb, or a Lewes: there was a time when he was not necessarily even an accustomed play-goer, but simply a member of the reporting or literary staff told off for theatre duty without any question as to his acquaintance with dramatic literature. At present, though the special nature of his function is so far beginning to be recognized that appointments of the kind usually fall now into the hands of inveterate frequenters of the theatre, yet he is still little more than the man who supplies accounts of what takes place in the playhouses just as his colleague supplies accounts of what takes place at the police court — an important difference, however, being that the editor, who generally cares little about Art and knows less, will himself occasionally criticise, or ask one of his best writers to criticise, a remarkable police case, whereas he never dreams of theatrical art as a subject upon which there could be any editorial policy. Sir Edwin Arnold's editorial attack on Ibsen was due to the accidental circumstance that he, like Richelieu, writes verses between whiles. In fact, the "dramatic critic" of a newspaper, in ordinary circumstances, is at his best a good descriptive reporter, and at his worst a mere theatrical newsman. As such he is a person of importance among actors and managers, and of no importance what-ever elsewhere. Naturally he frequents the circles in which alone he is made much of; and by the time he has seen so many performances that he has formed some critical standards in spite of himself, he has also enrolled among his personal acquaintances every actor and manager of a few years' standing, and become engaged in all the private likes and dislikes, the quarrels and friendships, in a word, in all the partialities which personal relations involve, at which point the value of his verdicts may be imagined. Add to this that if he has the misfortune to be attached to a paper to which theatrical advertise-ments are an object, or of which the editor and proprietors (or their wives) do not hesitate to incur obligations to managers by asking for complimentary admissions, he may often have to choose between making himself agreeable and forfeiting his post. So that he is not always to be relied on even as a newsman where the plain truth would give offence to any individual.

Behind all the suppressive forces with which the critic has to contend comes the law of libel. Every adverse criticism of a public performer is a libel; and any agreement among the critics to boycott artists who appeal to the law is a conspiracy. Of course the boycott does take place to a certain extent; for if an artist, manager, or agent shews any disposition to retort to what is called a "slating" by a lawyer's letter, the critic, who cannot for his own sake expose his employers to the expenses of an action or the anxiety attending the threat of one, will be tempted to shun the danger by simply never again referring to the litigiously disposed person. But although this at first sight seems to sufficiently guarantee the freedom of criticism (for most public persons would suffer more from being ignored by the papers than from being attacked in them, however abusively) its operation is really restricted on the one side to the comparatively few and powerful critics who are attached to important papers at a fixed salary, and on the other to those *entrepreneurs* and artists about whom the public is not imperatively curious. Most critics get paid for their notices at so much per column or per line, so that their incomes depend on the quantity they write. Under these conditions they fine themselves every time they ignore a performance. Again, a dramatist or a manager may attain such a position that his enterprises form an indispensable part of the news of the day. He can then safely intimidate a hostile critic by a threat of legal proceedings, knowing that the paper can afford neither to brave nor ignore him. The late Charles Reade, for example, was a most dangerous man to criticize adversely; but the very writers against whom he took actions found it impossible to boycott him; and what Reade did out of a natural overflow of indignant pugnacity, some of our more powerful artistic *entrepreneurs* occasionally threaten to do now after a deliberate calculation of the advantages of their position. If legal proceedings are actually taken, and the case is not, as usual, compromised behind the scenes, the uncertainty of the law receives its most extravagant illustration from a couple of lawyers arguing a question of fine art before a jury of men of business. Even if the critic were a capable speaker and pleader, which he is not in the least likely to be, he would be debarred from conducting his own case by the fact that his comparatively wealthy employer and not himself would be the defendant in the case. In short, the law is against straightforward criticism at the very points where it is most needed; and though it is true that an ingenious and witty writer can make any artist or performance acutely ridiculous in the eyes of ingenious and witty people without laying himself open to an action, and indeed with every appearance of good-humoured indulgence, such applications of wit and ingenuity do criticism no good; whilst in any case they offer no remedy to the plain critic writing for plain readers.

All this does not mean that the entire Press is hopelessly corrupt in its criticism of Art. But it certainly does mean that the odds against the independence of the Press critic are so heavy that no man can maintain it completely without a force of character and a personal authority which are rare in any profession, and which in most of them can command higher pecuniary terms and prospects than any which journalism can offer. The final degrees of thoroughness have no market value on the Press; for, other things being equal, a journal with a critic who is goodhumoured and compliant will have no fewer readers than one with a critic who is inflexible where the interests of Art and the public are concerned. I do not exaggerate or go beyond the warrant of my own experience when I say that unless a critic is prepared not only to do much more work than the public will pay him for, but to risk his livelihood every time he strikes a serious blow at the powerful interests vested in artistic abuses of all kinds (conditions which in the long run tire out the strongest man), he must submit to compromises which detract very considerably from the trustworthiness of his criticism. Even the critic who is himself in a position to brave these risks must find a sympathetic and courageous editor-proprietor who will stand by him without reference to the commercial advantage — or disadvantage — of his incessant warfare. As all the economic conditions of our society tend to throw our journals more and more into the hands of successful moneymakers, the exceeding scarcity of this lucky combination of resolute, capable, and incorruptible critic, sympathetic editor, and disinterested and courageous proprietor, can hardly be appreciated by those who only know the world of journalism through its black and white veil.

On the whole, though excellent criticisms are written every week by men who, either as writers distinguished in other branches of literature and journalism, or as civil servants, are practically independent of this or that particular appointment as dramatic critic (not to mention the few whom strong vocation and force of character have rendered incorruptible) there remains a great mass of newspaper reports of theatrical events which is only called dramatic criticism by courtesy. Among the critics properly so called opinions are divided about Ibsen in the inevitable way into Philistine, idealist, and realist (more or less). Just at present the cross firing between them is rather confusing. Without being necessarily an Ibsenist, a critic may see at a glance that abuse of the sort quoted on pages 251–2 is worthless; and he may for the credit of his cloth attack it on that ground. Thus we have Mr A. B. Walkley, of *The Speaker,* one of the most able and independent of our critics, provoking Mr Clement Scott beyond measure by alluding to the writers who had just been calling the admirers of Ibsen "muck-ferreting dogs," as "these gentry," with a goodhumoured but very perceptible contempt for their literary attainments. Thereupon Mr Scott publishes a vindication of the literateness of that school, of which Mr Walkley makes unmerciful fun. But Mr Walkley is by no means committed to Ibsenism by his appreciation of Ibsen's status as an artist, much less by his depreciation of the literary status of Ibsen's foes. On the other hand there is Mr Frederick Wedmore, a professed admirer of Balzac, conceiving such a violent antipathy to Ibsen that he almost echoes Sir Edwin Arnold, whose denunciations are at least as applicable to the author of *Vautrin* as to the author of *Ghosts.* Mr George Moore, accustomed to fight on behalf of Zola against the men who are now attacking Ibsen, takes the field promptly against his old enemies in defence, not of Ibsenism, but of Free Art. Even Mr William Archer expressly guards himself against being taken as an Ibsenist doctrinaire. In the face of all this, it is little to the point that some of the critics who have attacked Ibsen have undoubtedly done so because — to put it bluntly — they are too illiterate and incompetent in the sphere of dramatic poetry to conceive or relish anything more substantial than the theatrical fare to which they are accustomed; or that others, intimidated by the outcry raised by Sir Edwin Arnold and the section of the public typified by Pastor Manders (not to mention Mr Pecksniff), against their own conviction join the chorus of disparagement from modesty, caution, compliance — in short, from want of the courage of their profession. There is no reason to suppose that if the whole body of critics had been endowed with a liberal education and an independent income, the number of Ibsenists among them would be much greater than at present, however the tone of their adverse criticism might have been improved. Ibsen, as a pioneer in stage progress no less than in morals, is bound to have the majority of his contemporaries against him, whether as actors, managers, or critics.

Finally, it is necessary to say, by way of warning, that many of the minor combatants on both sides have either not studied the plays at all, or else have been so puzzled that they have allowed themselves to be misled by the attacks of the idealists into reading extravagant immoralities between the lines, as, for instance, that Oswald in *Ghosts* is really the son of Pastor Manders, or that Lövborg is the father of Hedda Tesman's child. It has ever been asserted that horrible exhibitions of death and disease occur in almost every scene of Ibsen's plays, which, for tragedies, are exceptionally free from visible physical horrors. It is not too much to say that very few of the critics have yet got so far as to be able to narrate accurately the stories of the plays they have witnessed. No wonder, then, that they have not yet made up their minds on the more difficult point of Ibsen's philosophic drift — though I do not myself see how performances of his plays can be quite adequately judged without reference to it. One consequence of this is that those who are interested, fascinated, and refreshed by Ibsen's art misrepresent his meaning benevolently quite as often as those who are perplexed and disgusted misrepresent it maliciously; and it already looks as if Ibsen might attain undisputed supremacy as a modern playwright without necessarily converting a single critic to Ibsenism. Indeed it is not possible that his meaning should be fully recognized, much less assented to, until Society as we now know it loses its self-complacency through the growth of the conviction foretold by Richard Wagner when he declared that "Man will never be that which he can and should be until, by a conscious following of that inner natural necessity which is the only true necessity, he makes his life a mirror of nature, and frees himself from his thraldom to outer artificial counterfeits. Then will he first become a living man, who now is a mere wheel in the mechanism of this or that Religion, Nationality, or State."

Essays and Reviews

Mr. Bernard Shaw's Works of Fiction: Reviewed by Himself

(*The Novel Review*, London, February 1892)

The need for getting me to review my own works of fiction has arisen through the extreme difficulty of finding anyone else who has read them. This is not to be wondered at, as one of my novels has never been published at all; two others are buried in the pages of an extinct magazine; and of the two which enjoy a separate public existence only one has as yet shown any serious symptoms of immortality. I need hardly add that this one, "Cashel Byron's Profession," is, at bottom, a mere boy's romance. It has a sort of cleverness which has always been a cheap quality in me; and it is interesting, amusing, and at one point — unique in my works — actually exciting. The excitement is produced by the brutal expedient of describing a fight. It is not, as usual in novels, a case in which the hero fights a villain in defence of the heroine, or in the satisfaction of a righteous indignation. The two men are paid to fight for the amusement of the spectators. They set to for the sake of the money, and strive to beat each other out of pure ferocity. The success of this incident is a conclusive proof of the superfluity of the conventional hypocrisies of fiction. I guarantee to every purchaser of "Cashel Byron's Profession" a first class fight for his money. At the same time he will not be depraved by any attempt to persuade him that his relish for blood and violence is the sympathy of a generous soul for virtue in its eternal struggle with vice. I claim that from the first upper cut with which Cashel Byron stops his opponent's lead-off and draws his cork (I here use the accredited terminology of pugilism) to the cross-buttock with which he finally disables him, there is not a single incident which can be enjoyed on any other ground than that upon which the admittedly brutalized frequenter of prize-fights enjoys his favourite sport. Out of the savagery of my imagination I wrote the scene; and out of the savagery of your tastes you delight in it. My other novels contain nothing of the kind. And none of them have succeeded as well as "Cashel Byron's Profession."

The late James Runciman, himself, I understand, an amateur boxer of some distinction, wanted to dramatise "Cashel Byron's Profession," an enterprise from which I strongly dissuaded him on the ground that the means by which I had individualised the characters in the novel would prove quite ineffective on the stage; so that all that could be done was, not to dramatise the novel, but to take the persons out of it, and use them over again on the stage in an otherwise original play. Lest there should be any heir to Runciman's design, I may as well point out that the two incidents in the story which have dramatic potency in them have already been used prominently on the stage. All the essentials of the glove fight in which the hero vanquishes an antagonist personally much less attractive than himself in the presence of a fashionable audience which includes the heroine, are to be found in a play of Shakespere's called "As You Like it." Rosalind, Orlando, Charles the Wrestler, and Le Beau are sufficiently close copies of Lydia, Cashel, Paradise and Lord Worthington. The second instance is the episode of Bashville, the footman who loves his mistress. His place on the stage is already occupied by Victor Hugo's Ruy Blas, the valet who loves the Queen of Spain. And Bulwer Lytton disputed the novelty of "Ruy Blas" on the ground that the central idea was to be found in Claude Melnotte's passion for the Lady of Lyons. But as the only unusual feature in Victor Hugo's play springs from his perception that a domestic servant is a human being, Fielding's Joseph Andrews is more nearly related to Ruy Blas and Bashville than Claude, who was a gardener. If I had not seen quite clearly that the fact of my not being a footman myself was the merest accident (a proposition which most of our novelists would undoubtedly repudiate with the greatest indignation) I could not have created Bashville. Such romances, by the bye, are probably common enough in real life. One of my own relations, an elderly lady, was, in her teens, cautiously approached by her father's gardener with honorable overtures on the part of his son, who was enamoured of the young lady of the house. Unlike Lydia Carew, however, she did not take a democratic view of the offer: she regarded it rather as an act of insane presumption on the part of a being of another and inferior order. And though she has long since been to a great extent cured of this crude class feeling, and has even speculated once or twice as to whether she did not then throw away a more valuable opportunity than that of which she subsequently availed herself, she has not quite lost the old sense that the proposal was, relatively to the ideas of the current epoch, somewhat too Radical. Pauline Deschapelles, and not Lydia Carew, is still the representative of the common feeling among the footman-keeping classes on the subject of matrimonial overtures from the kitchen to the drawing-room.

This brings me to another point. Lydia's reply to Bashville's declaration is superhumanly reasonable. But Lydia is superhuman all through. On the high authority of William Morris (privately imparted) she is a "prig-ess." Other critics, of a more rationalistic turn, revere her as one of the noblest creations of modern fiction. I have no doubt that the latter view is defensible; but I must admit that, for a man of Morris's turn, her intellectual perfections are rather too obviously machine-made. If Babbage's calculator is ever finished, I believe it will be found quite possible, by putting an extra wheel or two in, to extend its uses to the manufacture of heroines of the Lydia Carew type. Doubtless the superior mechanical accuracy of Lydia's ratiocinative action is calculated to strike awe into the average superstitious bungler, just as the unfinished machine of Babbage strikes awe into me — awe born of my own incapacity for numerical calculation, which is so marked that I reached my fourteenth year before I solved the problem of how many herrings one could buy for elevenpence in a market where a herring and a half fetched three halfpence. Babbage seems to have been even worse off in that respect than I, since he could not get on at all without a machine; and of course I, too, fall far short of Lydia Carew in the reasonableness of my private conduct. Let me not deny, then, without at all wishing to go back on my admirers and Lydia's, that a post-mortem examination by a capable critical anatomist — probably my biographer — will reveal the fact that her inside is full of wheels and springs. At the same time it must be distinctly understood that this is no disparagement to her. There is nothing one gets so tired of in fiction as what is called "flesh and blood." The business of a novelist is largely to provide working models of improved types of humanity; and I designed Lydia as a suggestion for a high-class modern woman, not to gratify my own taste in womanhood, but for purposes of general utility. And I still think she is a vast improvement on the current female type.

My first working model of this kind was the hero of my second novel ("Cashel Byron" was my fourth), a huge work called "The Irrational Knot." This was really an extraordinary book for a youth of twenty-four to write; but, from the point of view of the people who think that an author has nothing better to do with his genius than to amuse them, it was a failure, because the characters, though life-like, were a dreary company, all undesirable as personal acquaintances; whilst the scenes and incidents were of the most commonplace and sordid kind. My model man, named Conolly, was a skilled workman who became rich and famous by inventing an electro-motor. He married a woman whom I took no end of trouble to make as "nice" as the very nicest woman can be according to conventional ideas. The point of the story was that though Conolly was a model of sound sense, intelligence, reasonableness, good temper, and everything that a thoroughly nice woman could desire and deserve, the most hopeless incompatibility developed itself between them; and finally she ran away with a man whose deficiency in every desirable quality made him as unlike her husband as it is possible for one man to be unlike another. Eventually she got rid of her lover, and met her husband again; but after a survey of the situation, Conolly decided, like Nora in "A Doll's House," that the matrimonial relation between them had no prospect of success under the circumstances, and walked out of the house, his exit ending the book. This anticipation of Ibsen, of whom at that time I had never heard, seems to me to prove that he is a representative writer, marching with the world and not against it, or by himself, as some people suppose.

I hardly know anybody who has got through "The Irrational Knot." Something was wanting in the book — perhaps a glovefight — which was not supplied even by the attraction of a subsidiary plot in which a fascinating but drunken actress threw a High Church clergyman into transports which he mistook for religious ecstasy. However, I suspect that the model Conolly was as incompatible with the public as with his wife. Long before I got to the writing of the last chapter I could hardly stand him myself.

A third novel, "Love Among the Artists," was written in 1881, and was interrupted by an attack of smallpox, my share of the epidemic of that year. Whether this enfeebled my intellectual convictions or not I cannot say; but it is a fact that the story exalts the wilful characters to the utter disparagement of the reasonable ones. As in most of my works, my aim throughout was to instruct rather than to entertain. I desired to shew our numerous amateurs of the fine arts, who would never have fallen in love with music or painting if they had not read books about them, the difference between their factitious enthusiasm and the creative energy of real genius. Some of the character studies are admirable, notably that of the musical composer Owen Jack, who is partly founded on Beethoven. I have a much higher opinion of this work than is as yet generally entertained; and, granting that it is perhaps hardly possible for an ordinary reader to persevere to the end without skipping, yet I think that he who reads as much of it as he finds he can bear, will be able to lay it down unfinished without any sense of having wasted his time provided always that it is worth his while to read fiction at all.

After "Love among the Artists" came "Cashel Byron's Profession," which I confess I wrote mainly to amuse myself. The glove fight and the conventional lived-happily-ever-afterwards ending, to which I had never previously condescended, exposed me for the first time to the humiliation of extravagantly favorable reviewing, and of numbering my readers by some thousands. But long before this happened my self-respect took alarm at the contemplation of the things I had made. I resolved to give up mere character sketching and the construction of models for improved types of individual, and at once to produce a novel which should be a gigantic grapple with the whole social problem. But, alas! at twenty-seven one does not know everything. When I had finished two chapters of this enterprise — chapters of colossal length, but containing the merest preliminary matter — I broke down in sheer ignorance and incapacity. Few novelists would have had their perseverance shaken by a consideration of this nature; but it must be remembered that at this time all my works were in manuscript: the complete unanimity of the publishers in their conviction that there were more remunerative enterprises open to them than the publication of my works, had saved me from becoming pecuniarily dependent on fiction. Anyhow, I have written no more novels; and as, since then, eight years have passed, during which I have done enough gratuitous work to produce half a dozen novels had I been so minded, my abstention may be taken as perhaps the most significant of my criticisms on myself as a writer of fiction.

Eventually the two prodigious chapters of my aborted *magnum opus* were published as a complete novel, in two "books," under the title, "An Unsocial Socialist." Though to me they are a monument of my failure, I unhesitatingly challenge any living writer of fiction to produce anything comparable in vivacity and originality to the few early scenes in which the hero, Trefusis, introduces himself by masquerading as Jefferson Smilash at the girls' school. It is true that a moderately intelligent poodle, once started, could have done a good deal of the rest; but this is true of all works of art, more or less. The hero is remarkable because, without losing his pre-eminence as hero, he not only violates every canon of propriety, like Tom Jones or Des Grieux, but every canon of sentiment as well. In an age when the average man's character is rotted at the core by the lust to be a true gentleman, the moral value of such an example as Trefusis is incalculable.

On the whole, after having more than once considered the advisability of consigning the four novels I have mentioned to the oblivion which shrouds that desperate first attempt which has never seen the light, I have come to the conclusion, based on some experience as a reviewer of contemporary fiction, that Mr Mudie's subscribers are very far from having reached that pitch of common sense at which they can decently pretend that my novels are not good enough for them. From their point of view the business of the fictionist is to tell lies for their amusement. Middle class respectability, out of the depths of the unspeakable dulness of its life, craves for scenes of love and adventure. Any book which conjures up some miserable ghost of either or both will go its circulating library round. Strenuous imaginings of muscle and pluck written by sedentary cowards for sedentary cowards, and passionate descriptions beginning "Their lips met" which almost make one cry, so obvious is it that nothing but the most ghastly and widespread starvation of the affections could make such poor fare marketable: these form the staple of nine novels out of ten. But there are readers who have sufficient experience and sense of reality to require a much higher degree of verisimilitude from fiction if it is to produce any illusion for them. Others, especially in the numerous class of tolerably educated persons occupied daily in routine work which does not half employ their intellects, are speculative, restlessly cerebrative, and cannot be interested except by exhibitions of character or suggestions of social problems. To such I recommend the works of my youth, in spite of their occasional vulgarity, puerility and folly. Indeed, to the vulgar my vulgarity, to the puerile my puerility, and to the foolish my folly will be a delight instead of a drawback. For the merely inane there is twaddle about Art and even a certain vein of philandering and flirtation. As to the literary execution of the books, I suppose it will not now be questioned that I am no mere man of genius, but a conscientious workman as well. What more can reasonably be claimed?

The best way to procure copies of "The Irrational Knot," and "Love among the Artists" is, I imagine, to advertise in the Sunday papers for old sets of the magazines which died of them, offering a suitable pecuniary inducement. "Cashel Byron's Profession" is still extant, and is retailed at ninepence by the London discount book-sellers. An extraordinary increase in the popularity of "An Unsocial Socialist" is indicated by the fact that my royalties upon it in the year 1891 were 170 per cent. greater then those received in 1889. I doubt if any other living novelist can shew such a record. In fact 170 is an understatement; for the exact figures were two and tenpence for 1889 and seven and tenpence for the year 1891. If any publisher is in search of a novelist whose popularity is advancing by leaps and bounds, it is possible that a handsome offer might tempt me back to the branch of literature which I originally cultivated.

Shaming the Devil about Shelley

(The Albemarle, London, September 1892. Reprinted in Shaw's *Pen Portraits and Reviews*, 1931)

When I first saw the proposal that Shelley's native county should celebrate the centenary of his birth by founding a Shelley Library and Museum at Horsham, I laughed — not publicly, because that would have been the act of a spoil-sport, but in my sleeve. The native county in question was Sussex, which had just distinguished itself at the General Election by a gloriously solid Conservative vote which had sent to Parliament a lord (son of a duke), an admiral, two baronets (one of them ex-Groom-in-Waiting to the Queen, and the other an ex-Dragoon officer), and two distinguished commoners (one of them son to a lord and the other to a Canon, once Her Majesty's chaplain): all of them high Tories. Now the difficulty of inducing so true-blue a corner of England to express any feeling towards Shelley but one of indignant abhorrence, can only be appreciated by those who are in possession of a complete and unexpurgated statement of what Shelley taught. Let me, therefore, draw up such a statement, as compendiously as may be.

In politics Shelley was a Republican, a Leveller, a Radical of the most extreme type. He was even an Anarchist of the old-fashioned Godwinian school, up to the point at which he perceived Anarchism to be impracticable. He publicly ranged himself with demagogues and gaol-birds like Cobbett and Henry Hunt (the original "Man in the White Hat"), and not only advocated the "Plan of Radical Reform" which was afterwards embodied in the proposals of the Chartists, but denounced the rent-roll of the landed aristocracy as "the true pension list," thereby classing himself as what we now call a Land Nationalizer. He echoed Cobbett's attacks on the National Debt and the Funding System in such a manner as to leave no reasonable doubt that if he had been born half a century later he would have been advocating Social-Democracy with a view to its development into the most democratic form of Communism practically attainable and maintainable. At the late election he would certainly have vehemently urged the agricultural laborers of Sussex to procure a candidate of the type of John Burns and to vote for him against the admiral, the lord, the two baronets, and against Messrs. Gathorne Hardy and Brookfield.

315

In religion, Shelley was an Atheist. There is nothing uncommon in that; but he actually called himself one, and urged others to follow his example. He never trifled with the word God: he knew that it meant a personal First Cause, Almighty Creator, and Supreme Judge and Ruler of the Universe, and that it did not mean anything else, never had meant anything else, and never whilst the English language lasted would mean anything else. Knowing perfectly well that there was no such person, he did not pretend that the question was an open one, or imply, by calling himself an Agnostic, that there might be such a person for all he knew to the contrary. He did know to the contrary; and he said so. Further, though there never was a man with so abiding and full a consciousness of the omnipresence of a living force, manifesting itself here in the germination and growth of a tree, there in the organization of a poet's brain, and elsewhere in the putrefaction of a dead dog, he never condescended to beg off being an Atheist by calling this omnipresent energy God, or even Pan. He lived and died professedly, almost boastfully, godless. In his time, however, as at present, God was little more than a word to the English people. What they really worshipped was the Bible; and our modern Church movement to get away from Bible fetishism and back to some presentable sort of Christianity (*vide* Mr. Horton's speech at Grindelwald the other day, for example) had not then come to the surface. The preliminary pick-axing work of Bible smashing had yet to be done; and Shelley, who found the moral atmosphere of the Old Testament murderous and abominable, and the asceticism of the New suicidal and pessimistic, smashed away at the Bible with all his might and main.

But all this, horrifying as it is from the Sussex point of view, was mere eccentricity compared to Shelley's teaching on the subject of the family. He would not draw any distinction between the privilege of the king or priest and that of the father. He pushed to its extremest consequences his denial that blood relationship altered by one jot or tittle the relations which should exist between human beings. One of his most popular performances at Eton and Oxford was an elaborate curse on his own father, who had thwarted and oppressed him; and the entirely serious intention of Shelley's curses may be seen in his solemn imprecation against Lord Eldon, ending with the words:

"I curse thee, though I hate thee not."

His determination to impress on us that our fathers should be no more and no less to us than other men, is evident in every allusion of his to the subject, from the school curse to *The Cenci,* which to this day is refused a licence for performance on the stage.

But Shelley was not the man to claim freedom of enmity, and say nothing about freedom of love. If father and son are to be as free in their relation to one another as hundredth cousins are, so must sister and brother. The freedom to curse a tyrannical father is not more sacred than the freedom to love an amiable sister. In a word, if filial duty is no duty, then incest is no crime. This sounds startling even now, disillusioned as we are by Herbert Spencer, Elie Réclus, and other writers as to there being anything "natural" in our code of prohibited degrees; but in Shelley's time it seemed the summit of impious vice, just as it would to the Sussexers to-day, if they only knew. Nevertheless, he did not shrink from it in the least: the hero and heroine of *Laon and Cythna* are brother and sister; and the notion that the bowdlerization of this great poem as *The Revolt of Islam* represents any repentance or withdrawal on Shelley's part, cannot be sustained for a moment in the face of the facts. No person who is well acquainted with Shelley's work can suppose that he would have thought any the worse of Byron if he had known and believed everything that Mrs. Beecher Stowe alleged concerning him. And no one who has ever reasoned out the consequences of such views can doubt for a moment that Shelley regarded the family, in its legal aspect, as a doomed institution.

So much for the opinions which Shelley held and sedulously propagated. Could Sussex be reconciled to them on the ground that they were mere "views" which did not affect his conduct? Not a bit of it. Although Shelley was the son of a prosperous country gentleman, his life was consistently disreputable except at one fatal moment of his boyhood, when he chivalrously married a girl who had run away from school and thrown herself on his protection. At this time he had been expelled from Oxford for writing and circulating a tract called "The Necessity of Atheism." His marriage, as might have been expected, was a hopeless failure; and when this fact was fully established the two parted; and Shelley was fallen in love with by the daughter of Mary Wollstonecraft and Godwin. Shelley took young Mary Godwin abroad, and started housekeeping with her without the least scruple; and he suggested that his wife should come and make one of the household, a notion which did not recommend itself to either of the ladies. The courts then deprived him of the custody of his children, on the ground that he was unfit to have charge of them; and his wife eventually committed suicide. Shelley then married his mistress, solely, as he explained, because the law forced him to do so in the interest of his son. The rest of his life was quite consistent with the beginning of it; and it is not improbable that he would have separated from his second wife as from his first, if he had not been drowned when he was twenty-nine.

It only remains to point out that Shelley was not a hotheaded nor an unpractical person. All his writings, whether in prose or verse, have a peculiarly deliberate quality. His political pamphlets are unique in their freedom from all appeal to the destructive passions: there is neither anger, sarcasm, nor frivolity in them; and in this respect his poems exactly resemble his political pamphlets. Other poets, from Shakespere to Tennyson, have let the tiger in them loose under pretext of patriotism, righteous indignation, or what not: he never did. His horror of violence, cruelty, injustice, and bravery was proof against their infection. Hence it cannot for a moment be argued that his opinions and his conduct were merely his wild oats. His seriousness, his anxious carefulness, are just as obvious in the writings which still expose their publishers to the possibility of a prosecution for sedition or blasphemy as in his writings on Catholic Emancipation, the propriety and practical sagacity of which are not now disputed. And he did not go back upon his opinions in the least as he grew older. By the time he had begun *The Triumph of Life,* he had naturally come to think *Queen Mab* a boyish piece of work, not that what it affirmed seemed false to him or what it denied true, but because it did not affirm and deny enough. Thus there is no excuse for Shelley on the ground of his youth or rashness. If he was a sinner, he was a hardened sinner and a deliberate one.

The delicate position of the gentlemen who invited Sussex to honor Shelley on the 4th of last month will now be apparent, especially when it is added that the facts are undeniable, accessible to all inquirers, and familiar to most fanciers of fine literature. The success of the celebration evidently depended wholly on the chances of inducing the aforesaid fanciers to wink and say nothing in as many words as possible. A conspiracy to keep an open secret of so scandalous a character seems extravagant; and yet it almost succeeded. The practical question was not whether Shelley could be shewn to be infamous, but whether anyone wished to undertake that demonstration. In Shelley's case it appeared that everybody — that is, everybody whose desire weighed two straws with the public — was anxious to make Shelley a saint. Mr. Cordy Jeaffreson's attempt to prove him the meanest of sinners had been taken in such uncommonly bad part that no literary man with any regard for his own popularity cared to follow up Mr. Jeaffreson's line. The feeblest excuses for Shelley had been allowed to pass. Matthew Arnold had explained how poor Percy had the misfortune to live in a low set, as if he had not been more free to choose his own set than most other men in England. Others had pleaded that he was young; that he was a poet; that you would find his works full of true piety if you only read them in a proper spirit; and — most exquisite of all —

that the people who persisted in raking up the story of Harriet must be low-minded gossips to allude to so improper a story. On all sides there went up the cry, "We want our great Shelley, our darling Shelley, our best, noblest, highest of poets. We will not have it said that he was a Leveller, an Atheist, a foe to marriage, an advocate of incest. He was a little unfortunate in his first marriage; and we pity him for it. He was a little eccentric in his vegetarianism; but we are not ashamed of that: we glory in the humanity of it [with morsels of beefsteak, fresh from the slaughter house, sticking between our teeth]. We ask the public to be generous — to read his really great works, such as the *Ode to a Skylark*, and not to gloat over those boyish indiscretions known as *Laon and Cythna, Prometheus, Rosalind and Helen, The Cenci, The Masque of Anarchy,* &c., &c. Take no notice of the Church papers; for our Shelley was a true Christian at heart. Away with Jeaffreson; for our Shelley was a gentleman if ever there was one. If you doubt it, ask — "

That was just the difficulty: who were we to ask when the Centenary came round? On reflection, the Horsham Committee decided that we had better ask Mr. Gosse. It was a wise choice. The job was one which required a certain gift of what is popularly called cheek; and Mr. Gosse's cheek is beyond that of any man of my acquaintance. I went down to Horsham expressly to hear him; and I can certify that he surpassed himself. I confess I thought he was going to overdo it when, extolling the poet's patriotism in selecting England for his birth-place, he applied to Shelley a brilliant paraphrase of Mr. Gilbert's

"For he might have been a Rooshan," &c.

but no: it came off perfectly. A subsequent fearless assertion that there was surprisingly little slime — he said slime — on Shelley's reputation, and that the "sordid" details of his career were really not so very numerous after all, hit off to a nicety the requirements of the occasion; and when he handsomely remarked that for his part he thought that far too much talk had already been made about Harriet, we all felt that a gentleman could say no less. It was a happy thought also to chaff Shelley as an eater of buns and raisins, the satirist being no doubt stoked up for the occasion with gobbets of cow or sheep, and perhaps a slice or two of pig. But what fairly banged everything in his address was his demonstration that Shelley was so fragile, so irresponsible, so ethereally tender, so passionate a creature that the wonder was that he was not a much greater rascal. The dodge of making allowances for a great man's differences with small men on the plea of his being a privileged weakling is one which I have of course often seen worked; but I never saw it brought to such perfection as by Mr. Gosse at Horsham. It was a triumph not only of audacity but of platform manner. At the stiffest parts of the game Mr. Gosse contrived to get on a sort of infatuated pomposity which is quite indescribable. Whilst it completely imposed on the innocents, there was yet lurking behind it a sly relish for the fun of the situation which disarmed those out-and-out Shelleyans who half expected to see Mr. Gosse struck by lightning for his presumption. For my own part, I have seldom been worse misunderstood than by the gentleman who wrote to a daily paper alleging, in proof of my sympathy with his own outraged feelings, that I walked out of the room in disgust. I protest I only went to catch the 5.17 train to London, where I had to act as the best available substitute for Mr. Gosse at the proletarian celebration of Shelley in the easterly parish of St. Luke's.

In a rougher, homelier, style, the chairman, Mr. Hurst, Justice of the Peace and Deputy Lieutenant for the county, gave Mr. Gosse an admirable lead. The judicious way in which he dwelt on the central fact that Shelley had been born in the neighbourhood; his remarks on the intellectual value of a free public library to the working classes, and his declaration that if Shelley were alive he would be the first to support a free library; his happy comparison of Horsham to Stratford-on-Avon (which brought the house down at once); his deprecation of the harshness of Oxford University in expelling Shelley for a "mere dialectical view" (meaning *The Necessity of Atheism*); and his genial peroration on the theme of "boys will be boys", pitched so as to half confess that he himself had held quite desperate views when he was young and foolish: all this was so ingenious that when I described it in the evening at the Hall of Science it established my reputation in St. Luke's as a platform humorist of the first order. But his point about the free library was really the essential one. It was for the sake of the library that I refused to blow the gaff by speaking at Horsham when Mr. Stanley Little, with characteristic intrepidity, invited me to do so. It was presumably for the sake of the library that Mr. Hurst, Mr. Gosse, and Mr. Frederic Harrison deliberately talked bogus Shelleyism to the reporters. Miss Alma Murray and Mr. Herbert Sims Reeves may have recited and sung for the sake of the real Shelley; and Professor Nicholl, as I gather, shewed an alarming disposition to let the cat out of the bag in moving a vote of thanks to the chair; but the rest were solid for the library, even if the front were to be decorated with a relief representing Shelley in a tall hat, Bible in hand, leading his children on Sunday morning to the church of his native parish.

Of the meeting in the evening at the Hall of Science I need say but little. It consisted for the most part of working men who took Shelley quite seriously, and were much more conscious of his opinions and of his spirit than of his dexterity as a versifier. It was summoned without the intervention of any committee by Mr. G. W. Foote, the President of the National Secular Society, who, by his own personal announcement and a few handbills, got a meeting which beat Horsham hollow. The task of the speakers was so easy that Mr. Gosse and Mr. Frederic Harrison might well have envied us. Mr. Foote, a militant Atheist like Shelley himself, and one who has suffered imprisonment under the outrageous Blasphemy Laws which some people suppose to be obsolete, was able to speak with all the freedom and force of a man who not only talks Shelley but lives him. Dr. Furnivall, incorrigible in the matter of speaking his mind, frankly stated how far he went with Shelley, which was far enough to explain why he was not one of the Horsham orators. As for me, my quotations from the Horsham proceedings came off so immensely that I could not but feel jealous of Mr. Hurst. For the rest, I had nothing to do but give a faithful account of Shelley's real opinions, with every one of which I unreservedly agree. Finally Mr. Foote recited "Men of England," which brought the meeting to an end amid thunders of applause. What would have happened had anyone recited it at Horsham is more than I can guess. Possibly the police would have been sent for.

Mr. Foote's meeting, which was as spontaneous as the absence of committee and advertisement could make it, was composed for the most part of people whose lives had been considerably influenced by Shelley. Some time ago Mr. H. S. Salt, in the course of a lecture on Shelley, mentioned on the authority of Mrs. Marx Axeling, who had it from her father, Karl Marx, that Shelley had inspired a good deal of that huge but badly-managed popular effort called the Chartist movement. An old Chartist who was present, and who seemed at first much surprised by this statement, rose to confess that, "now he came to think of it," (apparently for the first time), it was through reading Shelley that he got the ideas that led him to join the Chartists. A little further inquiry elicited that *Queen Mab* was known as The Chartists' Bible; and Mr. Buxton Forman's collection of small, cheap copies, blackened with the finger-marks of many heavy-handed trades, are the proofs that Shelley became a power — a power that is still growing. He made and is still making men and women join political societies, Secular societies, Vegetarian societies, societies for the loosening of the marriage contract, and Humanitarian societies of all sorts. There is at every election a Shelleyan vote, though there is no means of counting it. The discussion of his life, which makes our literary *dilettanti* so horribly uneasy, cannot be checked, no matter how exquisitely they protest. He is still forcing us to make up our minds whether the conventional judgment of his life as that of a scoundrel is the truth or only a *reductio-ad-absurdum* of the conventional morality. That is a vital question; and it is pitifully useless for the exponents of the fashionable culture to deprecate it as "chatter about Harriet", when no sensible man can hear any chattering except that of their own teeth at the prospect of having to face Shelley's ideas seriously.

Without any ill-conditioned desire to rub the situation into those who have offered Shelley a carnival of humbug as a centenary offering, I think no reasonable man can deny the right of those who appreciate the scope and importance of Shelley's views to refuse to allow the present occasion to be monopolized by triflers to whom he was nothing more than a word-jeweller. Besides, the Horsham affair has been a failure: nobody has been taken in by it. Mr. Foote scores heavily; and Mr. Gosse and Mr. Frederic Harrison are left sitting down, rather pensively, even though no newspaper except the *Pall Mall Gazette* and the *Daily Chronicle* dared to prick the bubble. I now venture to suggest that in future the bogus Shelley be buried and done with. I make all allowances for the fact that we are passing through an epidemic of cowardice on the part of literary men and politicians which will certainly make us appear to the historians of 1992 the most dastardly crew that has ever disgraced the platform and the press. It seems that as the march of liberty removes concrete terrors from our path, we become the prey of abstract fear, and are more and more persuaded that society is only held together by the closest trade unionism in senseless lying and make-believe. But it is vain to lie about Shelley: it is clear as day that if he were nothing more than what we try to make him out, his Centenary would be as little remembered as that of Southey. Why not be content to say, "I abhor Shelley's opinions; but my abhorrence is overwhelmed by my admiration of the exquisite artistic quality of his work", or "I am neither an Atheist nor a believer in Equality nor a Free Lover; and yet I am willing to celebrate Shelley because I feel that he was somehow a good sort", or even "I think Shelley's poetry slovenly and unsubstantial, and his ideas simply rot; but I will celebrate him because he said what he thought, and not what he was expected to say he thought." Instead of this, each of us gets up and says, "I am forced for the sake of my wife and family and social position to be a piffler and a trimmer; and as all you fellows are in the same predicament, I ask you to back me up in trying to make out that Shelley was a piffler and a trimmer too." As one of the literary brotherhood myself, I hope I am clubbable enough to stand in with any reasonable movement in my trade; but this is altogether too hollow. It will not do: the meanest Shelley reader knows better. If it were only to keep ourselves from premature putrefaction, we must tell the truth about somebody; and I submit that Shelley has pre-eminent claims to be that somebody. Hence this article.

A Dramatic Realist to His Critics

(*The New Review,* London, July 1894, and, unauthorized, in
Eclectic Magazine, New York, September 1894. Reprinted in
Shaw on Theatre, ed. E. J. West, 1958)

I think very few people know how troublesome dramatic critics are.
It is not that they are morally worse than other people; but they know
nothing. Or, rather, it is a good deal worse than that: they know everything wrong. Put a thing on the stage for them as it is in real life, and
instead of receiving it with the blank wonder of plain ignorance, they
reject it with scorn as an imposture, on the ground that the real thing
is known to the whole world to be quite different. Offer them Mr
Crummles's real pump and tubs, and they will denounce both as
spurious on the ground that tubs have no handles, and the pump
no bung-hole.

I am, among other things, a dramatist; but I am not an original one,
and so have to take all my dramatic material either from real life at
first hand, or from authentic documents. The more usual course is to
take it out of other dramas, in which case, on tracing it back from one
drama to another, you finally come to its origin in the inventive imagination of some original dramatist. Now a fact as invented by a
dramatist differs widely from the fact of the same name as it exists or
occurs objectively in real life. Not only stage pumps and tubs, but
(much more) stage morality and stage human nature differ from the
realities of these things. Consequently to a man who derives all his
knowledge of life from witnessing plays, nothing appears more unreal
than objective life. A dramatic critic is generally such a man; and the
more exactly I reproduce objective life for him on the stage, the more
certain he is to call my play an extravaganza.

It may be asked here whether it is possible for one who every day
contemplates the real world for fourteen of his waking hours, and the
stage for only two, to know more of the stage world than the real
world. As well might it be argued that a farmer's wife, churning for
only two hours a week, and contemplating nature almost constantly,
must know more about geology, forestry, and botany than about butter.
A man knows what he works at, not what he idly stares at. A dramatic critic works at the stage, writes about the stage, thinks about the

stage, and understands nothing of the real life he idly stares at until he has translated it into stage terms. For the rest, seeing men daily building houses, driving engines, marching to the band, making political speeches, and what not, he is stimulated by these spectacles to *imagine* what it is to be a builder, an engine driver, a soldier, or a statesman. Of course, he imagines a stage builder, engine driver, soldier, and so on, not a real one. Simple as this is, few dramatic critics are intelligent enough to discover it for themselves. No class is more idiotically confident of the reality of its own unreal knowledge than the literary class in general and dramatic critics in particular.

We have, then, two sorts of life to deal with: one subjective or stagey, the other objective or real. What are the comparative advantages of the two for the purposes of the dramatist? Stage life is artificially simple and well understood by the masses; but it is very stale; its feeling is conventional; it is totally unsuggestive of thought because all its conclusions are foregone; and it is constantly in conflict with the real knowledge which the separate members of the audience derive from their own daily occupations. For instance, a naval or military melodrama only goes down with civilians. Real life, on the other hand, is so ill understood, even by its clearest observers, that no sort of consistency is discoverable in it; there is no "natural justice" corresponding to that simple and pleasant concept, "poetic justice"; and, as a whole, it is unthinkable. But, on the other hand, it is credible, stimulating, suggestive, various, free from creeds and systems — in short, it is real.

This rough contrast will suffice to show that the two sorts of life, each presenting dramatic potentialities to the author, will, when reproduced on the stage, affect different men differently. The stage world is for the people who cannot bear to look facts in the face, because they dare not be pessimists, and yet cannot see real life otherwise than as the pessimist sees it. It might be supposed that those who conceive all the operations of our bodies as repulsive, and of our minds as sinful, would take refuge in the sects which abstain from playgoing on principle. But this is by no means what happens. If such a man has an artistic or romantic turn, he takes refuge, not in the conventicle, but in the theatre, where, in the contemplation of the idealised, or stage life, he finds some relief from his haunting conviction of omnipresent foulness and baseness. Confront him with anything like reality, and his chronic pain is aggravated instead of relieved: he raises a terrible outcry against the spectacle of cowardice, selfishness, faithlessness, sensuality — in short, everything that he went to the theatre to escape from. This is not the effect on those pessimists who dare face facts and

profess their own faith. They are great admirers of the realist playwright, whom they embarrass greatly by their applause. Their cry is
"Quite right: strip off the whitewash from the sepulchre; expose human
nature in all its tragi-comic baseness; tear the mask of respectability
from the smug bourgeois, and show the liar, the thief, the coward, the
libertine beneath."

Now to me, as a realist playwright, the applause of the conscious,
hardy pessimist is more exasperating than the abuse of the unconscious, fearful one. I am not a pessimist at all. It does not concern
me that, according to certain ethical systems, all human beings fall into
classes labelled liar, coward, thief, and so on. I am myself, according
to these systems, a liar, a coward, a thief, and a sensualist; and it is
my deliberate, cheerful, and entirely self-respecting intention to continue to the end of my life deceiving people, avoiding danger, making
my bargains with publishers and managers on principles of supply and
demand instead of abstract justice, and indulging all my appetites,
whenever circumstances commend such actions to my judgment. If
any creed or system deduces from this that I am a rascal incapable
on occasion of telling the truth, facing a risk, foregoing a commercial
advantage, or resisting an intemperate impulse of any sort, then so
much the worse for the creed or system, since I have done all these
things, and will probably do them again. The saying "All have sinned,"
is, in the sense in which it was written, certainly true of all the people
I have ever known. But the sinfulness of my friends is not unmixed
with saintliness: some of their actions are sinful, others saintly. And
here, again, if the ethical system to which the classifications of saint
and sinner belong, involves the conclusion that a line of cleavage drawn
between my friends' sinful actions and their saintly ones will coincide
exactly with one drawn between their mistakes and their successes
(I include the highest and widest sense of the two terms), then so much
the worse for the system; for the facts contradict it. Persons obsessed
by systems may retort: "No; so much the worse for your friends" —
implying that I must move in a circle of rare blackguards; but I am
quite prepared not only to publish a list of friends of mine whose names
would put such a retort to open shame, but to take any human being,
alive or dead, of whose actions a genuinely miscellaneous unselected
dozen can be brought to light, to show that none of the ethical systems
habitually applied by dramatic critics (not to mention other people)
can verify their inferences. As a realist dramatist, therefore, it is my
business to get outside these systems. For instance, in the play of
mine which is most in evidence in London just now, the heroine has
been classified by critics as a minx, a liar, and a *poseuse*. I have nothing

to do with that: the only moral question for me is, does she do good or harm? If you admit that she does good, that she generously saves a man's life and wisely extricates herself from a false position with another man, then you may classify her as you please — brave, generous, and affectionate; or artful, dangerous, faithless — it is all one to me: you can no more prejudice me for or against her by such artificial categorising than you could have made Molière dislike Monsieur Jourdain by a lecture on the vanity and pretentiousness of that amiable "bourgeois gentilhomme." The fact is, though I am willing and anxious to see the human race improved, if possible, still I find that, with reasonably sound specimens, the more intimately I know people the better I like them; and when a man concludes from this that I am a cynic, and that he, who prefers stage monsters — walking catalogues of the systematised virtues — to his own species, is a person of wholesome philanthropic tastes, why, how can I feel towards him except as an Englishwoman feels towards the Arab who, faithful to *his* system, denounces her indecency in appearing in public with her mouth uncovered.

The production of "Arms and the Man" at the Avenue Theatre, about nine weeks ago, brought the misunderstanding between my real world and the stage world of the critics to a climax, because the misunderstanding was itself, in a sense, the subject of the play. I need not describe the action of the piece in any detail: suffice it to say that the scene is laid in Bulgaria in 1885–6, at a moment when the need for repelling the onslaught of the Servians made the Bulgarians for six months a nation of heroes. But as they had only just been redeemed from centuries of miserable bondage to the Turks, and were, therefore, but beginning to work out their own redemption from barbarism — or, if you prefer it, beginning to contract the disease of civilisation — they were very ignorant heroes, with boundless courage and patriotic enthusiasm, but with so little military skill that they had to place themselves under the command of Russian officers. And their attempts at Western civilisation were much the same as their attempts at war — instructive, romantic, ignorant. They were a nation of plucky beginners in every department. Into their country comes, in the play, a professional officer from the high democratic civilisation of Switzerland — a man completely acquainted by long, practical experience with the realities of war. The comedy arises, of course, from the collision of the knowledge of the Swiss with the illusions of the Bulgarians. In this dramatic scheme Bulgaria may be taken as symbolic of the stalls on the first night of a play. The Bulgarians are dramatic critics; the Swiss is the realist playwright invading their realm; and the comedy is the comedy of the collision of the realities represented by the realist playwright with the preconceptions of stageland. Let us follow this comedy a little into particulars.

War, as we all know, appeals very strongly to the romantic imagination. We owe the greatest realistic novel in the world, "Don Quixote," to the awakening lesson which a romantically imaginative man received from some practical experience of real soldiering. Nobody is now foolish enough to call Cervantes a cynic because he laughed at Amadis de Gaul, or Don Quixote a worthless creature because he charged windmills and flocks of sheep. But I have been plentifully denounced as a cynic, my Swiss soldier as a coward, and my Bulgarian Don Quixote as a humbug, because I have acted on the same impulse and pursued the same method as Cervantes. Not being myself a soldier like Cervantes, I had to take my facts at second hand; but the difficulties were not very great, as such wars as the Franco-Prussian and Russo-Turkish have left a considerable number of experienced soldiers who may occasionally be met and consulted even in England; whilst the publication of such long-delayed works as Marbot's Memoirs, and the success with which magazine editors have drawn some of our generals, both here and in America, on the enthralling subject of military courage, has placed a mass of documentary evidence at the disposal of the realist. Even realistic fiction has become valuable in this way: for instance, it is clear that Zola, in his "Débâcle," has gone into the evidence carefully enough to give high authority to his description of what a battle is really like.

The extent to which this method brought me into conflict with the martial imaginings of the critics is hardly to be conveyed by language. The notion that there could be any limit to a soldier's courage, or any preference on his part for life and a whole skin over a glorious death in the service of his country, was inexpressibly revolting to them. Their view was simple, manly, and straightforward, like most impracticable views. A man is either a coward or he is not. If a brave man, then he is afraid of nothing. If a coward, then he is no true soldier; and to represent him as such is to libel a noble profession.

The tone of men who know what they are talking about is remarkably different. Compare, for instance, this significant little passage from no less an authority than Lord Wolseley, who far from being a cynic, writes about war with an almost schoolboyish enthusiasm, considering that he has seen so much of it: —

> "One of the most trying things for the captain or subaltern is to make their men who have found some temporary haven of

refuge from the enemy's fire, leave it and spring forward in a body to advance over the open upon a position to be attacked. It is even difficult to make a line of men who have lain down, perhaps to take breath after a long advance at a running pace, rise up together." — *Fortnightly Review,* Aug., 1888.

This, you will observe, is your British soldier, who is quite as brave as any soldier in the world. It may be objected, however, by believers in the gameness of blue blood, that it is the British officer who wins our battles, on the playing fields of Eton and elsewhere. Let me, therefore, quote another passage from our veteran commander: —

"I have seen a whole division literally crazy with terror when suddenly aroused in the dark by some senseless alarm. I have known even officers to tackle and wound their own comrades upon such occasions. Reasoning men are for the time reduced to the condition of unreasoning animals who, stricken with terror, will charge walls or houses, unconscious of what they do. . . . [Here Lord Wolseley describes a scare which took place on a certain occasion.] In that night's panic several lost their lives; and many still bear the marks of wounds then received." *Ib.,* pp. 284–5.

Now let us hear General Horace Porter, a veteran of the American War, which had the advantage of being a civil war, the most respectable sort of war, since there is generally a valuable idea of some kind at stake in it. General Porter, a cooler writer than our General, having evidently been trained in the world, and not in the army, delivers himself as follows: —

"The question most frequently asked of soldiers is 'How does a man feel in battle?' There is a belief, among some who have never indulged in the pastime of setting themselves up as targets to be shot at, that there is a delicious sort of exhilaration experienced in battle, which arouses a romantic enthusiasm; surfeits the mind with delightful sensations; makes one yearn for a lifetime of fighting, and feel that peace is a pusillanimous sort of thing at best. Others suppose, on the contrary, that one's knees rattle like a Spanish ballerina's castanets, and that one's mind dwells on little else than the most approved means of running away.

"A happy mean between these two extremes would doubtless define the condition of the average man when he finds that, as a soldier, he is compelled to devote himself to stopping bullets as well as directing them. He stands his ground and faces the dangers into which his profession leads him, under a sense of duty and a regard for his self-respect, but often feels that the sooner the firing ceases, the better it would accord with his notion of the general fitness of things, and that if the enemy is going to fall back, the present moment would be as good a time as any at which to begin such a highly judicious and commendable movement. Braving danger, of course, has its compensations. 'The blood more stirs to rouse a lion than to start a hare.' In the excitement of a charge, or in the enthusiasm of approaching victory, there is a sense of pleasure which no one should attempt to underrate. It is the gratification which is always born of success, and, coming to one at the supreme moment of a favourable crisis in battle, rewards the soldier for many severe trials and perilous tasks." — (Article in *The Century*, June, 1888, p. 251.)

Probably nothing could convey a more sickening sense of abandoned pusillanimity to the dramatic critic than the ignoble spectacle of a soldier dodging a bullet. [Alfred] Bunn's sublime conception of Don Cæsar de Bazan, with his breast "expanding to the ball," has fixed for ever the stage ideal of the soldier under fire. General Porter falls far beneath Bunn in this passage: —

"I can recall only two persons who, throughout a rattling musketry fire, always sat in their saddles without moving a muscle or even winking an eye. One was a bugler in the regular cavalry, and the other was General Grant."

It may be urged against me here that in my play I have represented a soldier as shying like a nervous horse, not at bullets, but at such trifles as a young lady snatching a box of sweets from him and throwing it away. But my soldier explains that he has been three days under fire; and though that would, of course, make no difference to the ideal soldier, it makes a considerable difference to the real one, according to General Porter.

"Courage, like everything else, wears out. Troops used to go into action during our late war, displaying a coolness and steadiness the first day that made them seem as if the screeching of shot and shell was the music on which they had been brought up. After fighting a couple of days their nerves gradually lost their tension; their buoyancy of spirits gave way; and dangers they would have laughed at the first day, often sent them panic-stricken to the rear on the third. It was always a curious sight in camp after a three days' fight to watch the effect of the sensitiveness of the nerves: men would start at the slightest sound, and dodge the flight of a bird or a pebble tossed at them. One of the chief amusements on such occasions used to be to throw stones and chips past one another's heads to see the active dodging that would follow."

A simple dramatic paraphrase of that matter-of-fact statement in the first act of "Arms and the Man" has been received as a wild topsy-turvyist invention; and when Captain Bluntschli said to the young lady, "If I were in camp now they'd play all sorts of tricks on me," he was supposed to be confessing himself the champion coward of the Servian army. But the truth is that he was rather showing off, in the style characteristic of the old military hand. When an officer gets over the youthful vanity of cutting a figure as a hero, and comes to understand that courage is a quality for use and not for display, and that the soldier who wins with the least risk is the best soldier, his vanity takes another turn; and, if he is a bit of a humorist, he begins to appreciate the comedy latent in the incongruity between himself and the stage soldier which civilians suppose him. General Porter puts this characteristic of the veteran before us with perfect clearness: —

"At the beginning of the war officers felt that, as untested men, they ought to do many things for the sake of appearance that were wholly unnecessary. This at times led to a great deal of posing for effect and useless exposure of life. Officers used to accompany assaulting columns over causeways on horseback, and occupy the most exposed positions that could be found. They were not playing the bravo: they were confirming their own belief in their courage, and acting under the impression that bravery ought not only to be undoubted, but conspicuous. They were simply putting their courage beyond suspicion.

"At a later period of the war, *when men began to plume themselves as veterans,* they could afford to be more conservative: they had won their spurs; their reputations were established; they were beyond reproach. Officers then dismounted to lead close assaults, dodged shots to their hearts' content, did not hesitate to avail themselves of the cover of earthworks when it was wise to seek such shelter, and resorted to many acts which conserved human life and in no wise detracted from their efficiency as soldiers. There was no longer anything done for buncombe: they had settled down to practical business." — *Ib.,* p. 249.

In Arms and the Man, this very simple and intelligible picture is dramatized by the contrast between the experienced Swiss officer, with a high record for distinguished services, and the Bulgarian hero who wins the battle by an insanely courageous charge for which the Swiss thinks he ought to be court-martialled. Result: the dramatic critics pronounce the Swiss "a poltroon." I again appeal to General Porter for a precedent both for the Swiss's opinion of the heroic Bulgarian, and the possibility of a novice, in "sheer ignorance of the art of war" (as the Swiss puts it), achieving just such a success as I have attributed to Sergius Saranoff: —

> "Recruits sometimes rush into dangers from which veterans would shrink. When Thomas was holding on to his position at Chickamauga on the afternoon of the second day, and resisting charge after charge of an enemy flushed with success, General Granger came up with a division of troops, many of whom had never before been under fire. As soon as they were deployed in front of the enemy, they set up a yell, sprang over the earthworks, charged into the ranks, and created such consternation that the Confederate veterans were paralysed by the very audacity of such conduct. Granger said, as he watched their movements, 'Just look at them: they don't know any better; they think that's the way it ought to be done. I'll bet they'll never do it again.' "

According to the critics, Granger was a cynic and a worldling, incapable of appreciating true courage.

I shall perhaps here be reminded by some of my critics that the charge in "Arms and the Man" was a cavalry charge; and that I am suppressing the damning sneer at military courage implied in Captain Bluntschli's reply to Raïna Petkoff's demand to have a cavalry charge described to her: —

> "Bluntschli — You never saw a cavalry charge, did you?
> "Raïna — No: how could I?
> "Bluntschli — Of course not. Well, it's a funny sight. It's like slinging a handful of peas against a window-pane — first one comes, then two or three close behind them, and then all the rest in a lump.
> "Raïna (*thinking of her lover, who has just covered himself with glory in a cavalry charge*) — Yes; first one, the bravest of the brave!
> "Bluntschli — Hm! you should see the poor devil pulling at his horse.

"Raïna — Why should he pull at his horse?

"Bluntschli — It's running away with him, of course: do you suppose the fellow wants to get there before the others and be killed?"

Imagine the feelings of the critics — countrymen of the heroes of Balaclava, and trained in warfare by repeated contemplation of the reproduction of Miss Elizabeth Thompson's pictures in the Regent Street shop windows, not to mention the recitations of Tennyson's "Charge of the Light Brigade," which they have criticised — on hearing this speech from a mere Swiss! I ask them now to put aside these authorities for a moment and tell me whether they have ever seen a horse bolt in Piccadilly or the Row. If so, I would then ask them to consider whether it is not rather likely that in a battlefield, which is, on the whole, rather a startling place, it is not conceivable and even likely that at least one horse out of a squadron may bolt in a charge. Having gently led them to this point, I further ask them how they think they would feel if they happened to be on the back of that horse, with the danger that has so often ended in death in Rotten Row complicated with the glory of charging a regiment practically single-handed. If we are to believe their criticisms, they would be delighted at the distinction. The Swiss captain in my play takes it for granted that they would pull the horse's head off. Leaving the difference of opinion unsettled, there can be no doubt as to what their duty would be if they were soldiers. A cavalry charge attains its maximum effect only when it strikes the enemy solid. This fact ought to be particularly well known to Balaclava amateurs; for Kinglake, the popular authority on the subject, gives us specimens of the orders that were heard during the frightful advance down "the valley of death." The dramatic-critical formula on that occasion would undoubtedly have been, "Charge, Chester, charge! on, Stanley, on!" Here is the reality: —

> "The crash of dragoons overthrown by round shot, by grape and by rifle-ball, was alternate with dry technical precepts: 'Back, right flank!' 'Keep back, private This,' 'Keep back, private That!' 'Close in to your centre!' 'Do look to your dressing!' 'Right squadron, right squadron, keep back!' "

There is cynicism for you! Nothing but "keep back!" Then consider the conduct of Lord Cardigan, who rode at the head of the Light Brigade. Though he, too, said "Keep back," when Captain White tried to force the pace, he charged the centre gun of the battery just like a dramatic critic, and was the first man to sweep through the Russian gunners. In fact, he got clean out at the other side of the battery, happening to hit on a narrow opening by chance. The result was that he found himself presently riding down, quite alone, upon a mass of Russian cavalry. Here was a chance to cut them all down single-handed and plant the British flag on a mountain of Muscovite corpses. By refusing it, he flinched from the first-nighter's ideal. Realising the situation when he was twenty yards from the foe, he pulled up and converted that twenty yards into 200 as quickly as was consistent with his dignity as an officer. The stage hero finds in death the supreme consolation of being able to get up and go home when the curtain falls; but the real soldier, even when he leads Balaclava charges under conditions of appalling and pro-longed danger, does not commit suicide for nothing. The fact is, Captain Bluntschli's description of the cavalry charge is taken almost verbatim from an account given privately to a friend of mine by an officer who served in the Franco-Prussian war. I am well aware that if I choose to be guided by men grossly ignorant of dramatic criticism, whose sole qualification is that they have seen cavalry charges on stricken fields, I must take the consequences. Happily, as between myself and the public, the consequences have not been unpleasant; and I recommend the experiment to my fellow dramatists with every confidence.

But great as has been the offence taken at my treating a soldier as a man with no stomach for unnecessary danger, I have given still greater by treating him as a man with a stomach for necessary food. Nature provides the defenders of our country with regular and efficient ap-petites. The taxpayer provides, at considerable cost to himself, rations for the soldier which are insufficient in time of peace and occasionally irregular in time of war. The result is that our young, growing soldiers sometimes go for months without once experiencing the sensation of having had enough to eat, and will often, under stress of famine, con-descend to borrow florins and other trifles in silver from the young ladies who walk out with them, in order to eke out "the living wage." Let me quote a passage from Cobbett's description of his soldiering days in his "Advice to Young Men," which nobody who has read the book ever forgets: —

"I remember, and well I may! that, upon occasion, I, after all absolutely necessary expenses, had, on Friday, made shift to have a halfpenny in reserve, which I had destined for the purchase of a *red herring* in the morning; but, when I pulled off my clothes at night, so hungry then as to be hardly able to endure life, I found that I had *lost my halfpenny*. I buried my head under the miserable sheet and rug and cried like a child."

I am by no means convinced that the hidden tears still shed by young soldiers (who would rather die than confess to them) on similar provocation would not fill a larger cask than those shed over lost comrades or wounds to the national honour of England. In the field the matter is more serious. It is a mistake to suppose that in a battle the waiters come round regularly with soup, fish, an entrée, a snack of game, a cut from the joint, ice pudding, coffee and cigarettes, with drinks at discretion. When battles last for several days, as modern battles often do, the service of food and ammunition may get disorganised or cut off at any point; and the soldier may suffer exceedingly from hunger in consequence. To guard against this the veteran would add a picnic hamper to his equipment if it were portable enough and he could afford it, or if Fortnum and Mason would open a shop on the field. As it is, he falls back on the cheapest, most portable and most easily purchased sort of stomach-stayer, which, as every cyclist knows, is chocolate. This chocolate, which so shocks Raïna in the play — for she, poor innocent, classes it as "sweets" — and which seems to so many of my critics to be the climax of my audacious extravagances, is a commonplace of modern warfare. I know of a man who lived on it for two days in the Shipka Pass.

By the way, I have been laughed at in this connection for making my officer carry an empty pistol, preferring chocolate to cartridges. But I might have gone further and represented him as going without any pistol at all. Lord Wolseley mentions two officers who seldom carried any weapons. One of them had to defend himself by shying stones when the Russians broke into his battery at Sebastopol. The other was Gordon.

The report that my military realism is a huge joke has once or twice led audiences at the Avenue Theatre to laugh at certain grim touches which form no part of the comedy of disillusionment elsewhere so constant between the young lady and the Swiss. Readers of General Marbot's Memoirs will remember his description of how, at the battle of Wagram, the standing corn was set on fire by the shells and many of the wounded were roasted alive. "This often happens," says Marbot, coolly, "in battles fought in summer." The Servo-Bulgarian war was fought in winter; but Marbot will be readily recognised as the source of the incident of Bluntschli's friend Stolz, who is shot in the hip in a wood-yard and burnt in the conflagration of the timber caused by the Servian shells. There is, no doubt, a certain barbarous humour in the situation — enough to explain why the Bul-

garian, on hearing Raïna exclaim, "How horrible!" adds bitterly, "And
how ridiculous!" but I can assure those who are anxious to fully appreciate the fun of the travesty of war discovered in my work by the
critics, and whose rule is, "When in doubt, laugh," that I should not
laugh at that passage myself were I looking at my own play. Marbot's
picture of the fire-eaters fire-eaten is one which I recommend to our
music-hall tableauists when they are in need of a change. Who that
has read that Wagram chapter does not remember Marbot forcing his
wretched horse to gallop through the red-hot straw embers on his way
to Massena; finding that general with no *aide-de-camp* left to send
on a probably fatal errand except his only son; being sent in the son's
place as soon as he had changed the roasted horse for a fresh one;
being followed into the danger by the indignant son; and, finally —
Nature seldom fails with her touch of farce — discovering that the son
could not handle his sabre, and having to defend him against the
pursuing cavalry of the enemy, who, as Bluntschli would have prophesied, no sooner found that they had to choose between two men
who stood to fight and hundreds who were running away and allowing
themselves to be slaughtered like sheep, [than they] devoted themselves
entirely to the sheep, and left Marbot to come out of the battle of
Wagram with a whole skin?

I might considerably multiply my citations of documents; but the
above will, I hope, suffice to show that what struck my critics as topsy-
turvy extravaganza, having no more relation to real soldiering than
Mr. Gilbert's "Pinafore" has to real sailoring, is the plainest matter-of-
fact. There is no burlesque: I have stuck to the routine of war, as
described by real warriors, and avoided such farcical incidents as Sir
William Gordon defending his battery by throwing stones, or General
Porter's story of the two generals who, though brave and capable men,
always got sick under fire, to their own great mortification. I claim
that the dramatic effect produced by the shock which these realities
give to the notions of romantic young ladies and fierce civilians is not
burlesque, but legitimate comedy, none the less pungent because, on
the first night at least, the romantic young lady was on the stage and
the fierce civilians in the stalls. And since my authorities, who record
many acts almost too brave to make pleasant reading, are beyond
suspicion of that cynical disbelief in courage which has been freely
attributed to me, I would ask whether it is not plain that the difference
between my authenticated conception of real warfare and the stage
conception lies in the fact that in real warfare there is real personal
danger, the sense of which is constantly present to the mind of the
soldier, whereas in stage warfare there is nothing but glory? Hence
Captain Bluntschli, who thinks of a battlefield as a very busy and very

dangerous place, is incredible to the critic who thinks of it only as a theatre in which to enjoy the luxurious excitements of patriotism, victory, and bloodshed without risk or retribution.

There are one or two general points in the play on which I may as well say a word whilst I have the opportunity. It is a common practice in England to speak of the courage of the common soldier as "bulldog pluck." I grant that it is an insulting practice — who would dream of comparing the spirit in which an ancient Greek went to battle with the ferocity of an animal? — though it is not so intended, as it generally comes from people who are thoughtless enough to suppose that they are paying the army a compliment. A passage in the play which drove home the true significance of the comparison greatly startled these same thoughtless ones. Can we reasonably apply such a word as valour to the quality exhibited in the field by, for instance, the armies of Frederick the Great, consisting of kidnapped men, drilled, caned, and flogged to the verge of suicide, and sometimes over it? Flogging, sickeningly common in English barracks all through the most "glorious" periods of our military history, was not abolished here by any revolt of the English soldier against it: our warriors would be flogging one another to-day as abjectly as ever but for the interference of humanitarians who hated the whole conception of military glory. We still hear of soldiers severely punished for posting up in the barrack stables a newspaper paragraph on the subject of an army grievance. Such absurd tyranny would, in a dockyard or a factory full of matchgirls, produce a strike; but it cows a whole regiment of soldiers. The fact is, armies as we know them are made possible, not by valour in the rank and file, but by the lack of it; not by physical courage (we test the eyes and lungs of our recruits, never their courage), but by civic impotence and moral cowardice. I am afraid of a soldier, not because he is a brave man, but because he is so utterly unmanned by discipline that he will kill me if he is told, even when he knows that the order is given because I am trying to overthrow the oppression which he fears and hates. I respect a regiment for a mutiny more than for a hundred victories; and I confess to the heartiest contempt for the warlike civilian who pays poor men a pittance to induce them to submit to be used as pawns on a battlefield in time of war, he himself, meanwhile, sitting at home talking impudent nonsense about patriotism, heroism, devotion to duty, the inspiring sound of the British cheer, and so on. "Bulldog pluck" is much more sensible and candid. And so the idealist in my play continues to admit nightly that his bull terrier, which will fight as fiercely as a soldier, will let himself be thrashed as helplessly by the man in authority over him. One critic seems to think that it requires so much courage to say such things that he describes me as "protecting" myself by "ostensibly throwing the burden of my attack upon a couple of small and unimportant nationalities," since "there would have been a certain danger in bringing my malevolent mockery too near home." I can assure the gentleman that I meant no mockery at all. The observation is made in the play in a manner dramatically appropriate to the character of an idealist who is made a pessimist by the shattering of his illusions. His conclusion is that "life is a farce." My conclusion is that a soldier ought to be made a citizen and treated like any other citizen. And I am not conscious of running any risk in making that proposal, except the risk of being foolishly criticised.

I have been much lectured for my vulgarity in introducing certain references to soap and water in Bulgaria. I did so as the shortest and most effective way of bringing home to the audience the stage of civilisation in which the Bulgarians were in 1885, when, having clean air and clean clothes, which made them much cleaner than any frequency of ablution can make us in the dirty air of London, they were adopting the washing habits of big western cities as pure ceremonies of culture and civilisation, and not on hygienic grounds. I had not the slightest intention of suggesting that my Bulgarian major, who submits to a good wash for the sake of his social position, or his father, who never had a bath in his life, are uncleanly people, though a cockney, who by simple exposure to the atmosphere becomes more unpresentable in three hours than a Balkan mountaineer in three years, may feel bound to pretend to be shocked at them, and to shrink with disgust from even a single omission of the daily bath which, as he knows very well, the majority of English, Irish, and Scotch people do not take, and which the majority of the inhabitants of the world do not even tell lies about.

Major Petkoff is quite right in his intuitive perception that soap, instead of being the radical remedy for dirt, is really one of its worst consequences. And his remark that the cultus of soap comes from the English because their climate makes them exceptionally dirty, is one of the most grimly and literally accurate passages in the play, as we who dwell in smoky towns know to our cost. However, I am sorry that my piece of realism should have been construed as an insult to the Bulgarian nation; and perhaps I should have hesitated to introduce it had I known that a passionate belief in the scrupulous cleanliness of the inhabitants of the Balkan peninsula is a vital part of Liberal views on foreign policy. But what is done is done. I close the incident by quoting from the daily papers of the 5th May last the following item of Parliamentary intelligence, which gives a basis for a rough calculation of the value of English cleanliness as measured by the pecuniary sacrifices we are willing to make for it: —

"ARMY BEDDING

"The SECRETARY for WAR, replying to Mr. Hanbury's question as to the provision made in the Army for the washing of soldiers' bedding, stated that soldiers are now allowed to have their sheets washed once a month, and their blankets once a year; and the right hon. gentleman stated that the cost of allowing clean sheets fortnightly instead of monthly would amount to something like £10,000 a year, money which might be spent more advantageously in other directions, he thought. (Hear, hear.)"

I am afraid most of my critics will receive the above explanations with an indignant sense of personal ingratitude on my part. The burden of their mostly very kind notices has been that I am a monstrously clever fellow, who has snatched a brilliant success by amusingly whimsical perversions of patent facts and piquantly cynical ridicule of human nature. I hardly have the heart to turn upon such friendly help with a cold-blooded confession that all my audacious originalities are simple liftings from stores of evidence which lie ready to everybody's hand. Even that triumph of eccentric invention which nightly brings down the house, Captain Bluntschli's proposal for the hand of Raïna, is a paraphrase of an actual proposal made by an Austrian hotel proprietor for the hand of a member of my own family. To that gentleman, and to him alone, is due the merit of the irresistible joke of the four thousand tablecloths and the seventy equipages of which twenty-four will hold twelve inside. I have plundered him as I have plundered Lord Wolseley and General Porter and everyone else who had anything that was good to steal. I created nothing; I invented nothing; I imagined nothing; I perverted nothing; I simply discovered drama in real life.

I now plead strongly for a theatre to supply the want of this sort of drama. I declare that I am tired to utter disgust of imaginary life, imaginary law, imaginary ethics, science, peace, war, love, virtue, villainy, and imaginary everything else, both on the stage and off it. I demand respect, interest, affection for human nature as it is, and life as we must still live it even when we have bettered it and ourselves to the utmost. If the critics really believe all their futile sermonising about "poor humanity" and the "seamy side of life" and meanness, cowardice, selfishness, and all the other names they give to qualities which are as much and as obviously a necessary part of themselves as their arms and legs, why do they not shoot themselves like men instead of coming whimpering to the dramatist to pretend that they are something else? I, being a man like to themselves, know what they are perfectly well; and as I do not find that I dislike them for what they persist in calling their vanity, and sensuality, and mendacity, and dishonesty, and hypocrisy, and venality, and so forth; as, furthermore, they would not interest me in the least if they were otherwise, I shall continue to put them on the stage as they are to the best of my ability, in the hope that some day it may strike them that if they were to try a little self-respect, and stop calling themselves offensive names, they would discover that the affection of their friends, wives, and sweethearts for them is not a reasoned tribute to their virtues, but a human impulse towards their very selves. When Raïna says in the play, "Now that you have found me out, I suppose you despise me," she discovers that that result does not follow in the least, Captain Bluntschli not being quite dramatic critic enough to feel bound to repudiate the woman who has saved his life as "a false and lying minx," because, at twenty-three, she has some generous illusions which lead her into a good deal of pretty nonsense.

I demand, moreover, that when I deal with facts into which the critic has never inquired, and of which he has had no personal experience, he shall not make his vain imaginings the criterion of my accuracy. I really cannot undertake, every time I write a play, to follow it up by a text-book on mortgages, or soldiering, or whatever else it may be about, for the instruction of gentlemen who will neither accept the result of my study of the subject (lest it should destroy their cherished ideals), nor undertake any study on their own account. When I have written a play the whole novelty of which lies in the fact that it is void of malice to my fellow creatures, and laboriously exact as to all essential facts, I object to be complimented on my "brilliancy" as a fabricator of cynical extravaganzas. Nor do I consider it decent for critics to call their own ignorance "the British public," as they almost invariably do.

It must not be supposed that the whole Press has gone wrong over "Arms and the Man" to the same extent and in the same direction. Several of the London correspondents of the provincial papers, accustomed to deal with the objective world outside the theatre, came off with greater credit than the hopelessly specialised critics. Some of the latter saved themselves by a strong liking for the play, highly agreeable to me; but most of them hopelessly misunderstood me. I should have lain open to the retort that I had failed to make myself comprehensible had it not been for the masterly critical exploit achieved by Mr. A. B. Walkley, whose article in the *Speaker* was a completely successful analysis of my position. Mr. Walkley here saved the critics from the reproach of having failed where the actors had succeeded. Nobody who has seen Mr. Yorke Stephens's impersonation of the Swiss captain will suspect him for a moment of mistaking his man, as most of the critics did, for "a poltroon who prefers chocolate to fighting." It was Mr. Walkley who recognised that Bluntschli, "dogged, hopelessly unromantic, incurably frank, always *terre à terre*, yet a man every inch of him, is one of the most artistic things Mr. Yorke Stephens has done."

Here we have the actor making Bluntschli appear to a fine critic, as he undoubtedly did to the gallery, a brave, sincere, unaffected soldier; and yet some of the other critics, unable to rise to the actor's level, moralised in a positively dastardly way about a "cowardly and cynical mercenary." Imagine English dramatic critics, who, like myself, criticise for the paper that pays them best, without regard to its politics, and whose country's regular army is exclusively a paid professional one, waxing virtuous over a "mercenary" soldier! After that, one hardly noticed their paying tribute to the ideal woman (a sort of female George Washington) by calling Raïna a minx, and feebly remonstrating with Miss Alma Murray for charming them in such a character; whilst as to the heroic Sergius, obsessed with their own ideals, and desperately resolved to live up to them in spite of his real nature, which he is foolish enough to despise, I half expected them to stone him; and I leave Mr. Bernard Gould and Mr. Walkley to divide the credit, as actor and critic, the one of having realised the man, and the other of having analysed him — the nicety of the second operation proving the success of the first.

Here I must break off, lest I should appear to talk too much about my own play. I should have broken off sooner but for the temptation of asserting the right of the authors to decide who is the best critic, since the critics take it upon themselves to decide who is the best author.

How to Become a Man of Genius

(*Town Topics,* New York, 6 December 1894)

The secret at the bottom of the whole business is simply this: there is no such thing as a man of genius. I am a man of genius myself, and ought to know. What there is, is a conspiracy to pretend that there are such persons, and a selection of certain suitable individuals to assume the imaginary character. The whole difficulty is to get selected.

On reflection I perceive that this explanation is too straightforward for anyone to understand. Let me try to come at it by another way. You will at least admit that Man, having, as he cynically believes, excellent private reasons for not thinking much of himself, has a praiseworthy desire to improve on himself — an aspiration after better things is what you probably call it. Now when a child wants something it has not got, what does it do? It pretends to have it. It gets astride of a walking stick and insists on a general conspiracy to pass that stick off as a horse. When it grows to manhood it gives up pretending that walking sticks are horses, not in the least because it has risen superior to the weakness of conspiring to cherish illusions, but because on leaving the nursery it has passed into a sphere in which real horses are attainable, at which point the pretence becomes unnecessary. The moment it becomes unnecessary, the pressure which kept all eyes closed to its absurdity ceases. Here you have the whole explanation of the fact that the grown man is more "sensible" than the child, or the civilized man than the savage. Because he is able to attain more, he pretends less. With regard to the things that are beyond his attainment, he pretends as arrantly as his five-year-old boy.

For example, he wants, as aforesaid, to improve on himself. But is such a want possible, seeing that Man, whatever he may suppose to the contrary, most certainly cannot conceive anything that is outside his own experience, and therefore in a sense cannot conceive anything higher than himself, nor desire a thing without conceiving it. But that difficulty is very easily got over. Pray, amiable sir or madam, what is the thing you call yourself? Is it yourself as you are with people you like or as you are with people who rub you the wrong way? Is it yourself before dinner or after it? Is it yourself saying your prayers or driving a bargain, listening to a Beethoven symphony or being hustled by a policeman to make way for a public procession, buying a present for your first love or paying your taxes, fascinating everyone in your best clothes or hiding your slippers and curl papers from the public eye? If your enemy might select some one moment of your life to judge you by, would you not come out mean, ugly, cowardly, vulgar, sensual, even though you be another Goethe; or if you might choose the moment yourself, would you not come out generous and handsome, though you may be, on an average of all your moments, a most miserly and repulsive person? At worst, you are brave when there is no danger, and openhanded when you are not asked for anything, as one may see by your sympathy with the heroes of your favorite novels and plays.

Our experience does, then, provide us with material for a concept of a superhuman person. You have only to imagine someone always as good as you were in the very loftiest ten seconds of your life, always as brave as you felt when you read The Three Musketeers, always as wise at a moment's notice as the books into which philosophers have garnered the corrected errors of their lifetime, always as selfless as you have felt in your hour of utmost satiety, always as beautiful and noble as your wife or husband appeared to you at the climax of the infatuation which led you to the matrimonial experiment which you may or may not have regretted ever since, and there you have your poet, your hero, your Cleopatra or whatever else you may require in the superhuman line, by a simple rearrangement of your own experience, much of which was itself arrived at by the same process.

Wise indeed and wisest among men would be he who could now say to me: Why should I deceive myself thus foolishly? Why not fix my affections, my hopes, my enthusiasms on men and women as they are, varying from day to day, and but rarely seeing the highest heaven through the clouds, instead of on these ideal monsters who never existed and never will exist, and for whose sake men and women now despise one another and make the earth ridiculous with Pessimism, which is the inevitable end of all Idealism? But the average man is not yet wise: he will have his ideals just as the child will have his walking stick horse. And the lower he is, the more extravagant are his demands. Everyone has noticed how severely fastidious a thorough-paced blackguard is about the character and conduct of the woman to whom he proposes to confide the honor of his name, whereas your great man scandalises his acquaintances by his tolerance of publicans and sinners. Again, if you are a dramatist writing plays for a theatre in a disreputable quarter, where every boy in the gallery is a pickpocket, your hero must be positively singing like a kettle with ebullient honesty, a thing which no law abiding audience could bear for half an hour.

Observe now that the actor who plays to the thieves' gallery is not really an outrageously honest man: he only lends himself to the desire of the audience to pretend that he is. But do not therefore conclude that he enjoys his position through no merit of his own. If that were so, why should he, and not the "extra gentleman" who silently carries a banner, and who vehemently covets his salary and his place in the cast, be the hero of the play? Clearly because of the superior art with which the hero is able to lend himself to the conspiracy. The audience craves intensely for every additional quarter inch of depth of belief in their illusion, and for every quarter inch they will pay solid money; whilst they will no less feelingly avoid the actor who fails to bear it out, or who, worse still, destroys it. Therefore the actor, though he may not have the merit they ascribe to him, has the merit of counterfeiting it well; and in this, as in all other things, it takes, as Dumas *fils* well said, "a great deal of merit to make even a small success." But that is only because the competition for leading parts is so tremendous in the modern world. The public is not exacting: it will choose the better of two actors for its hero when it has any choice; but it will have its hero anyhow, even when the best actor is a very bad one, as he often is.

Now let us go from the microcosm to the macrocosm — from the cheap theatre to Shakespeare's great stage of "all the world," which, also, be it observed, has its thieves' gallery. On that stage there are many parts to be cast, since the audience will have its ideal king, its President, its statesman, its saint, its hero, its poet, its Helen of Troy, and its man of genius. No one can *be* these figments; but somebody must act them or the gallery will pull the house down. Napoleon, called on, as a man who had won battles, to cast himself for Emperor, grasped the realities of the situation, and, instead of imitating the ideal Cæsar or Charlemagne, took lessons from Talma. Other king's parts are hereditary: your Romanoff, your Hohenzollern, your Guelph walks through his part at his ease, knowing that with a crown on his head his "How d'ye do?" will enchant everyone with its affability, his three platitudes and a peroration pass for royal eloquence, and his manners and his coat seem in the perfection of taste. The divinity that hedges a king wrecks itself as effectually on a born Republican as on an English court tailor. I have seen a book by an American lady in which the Princess of Wales is ecstatically compared to "a vestal kneeling at some shrine." In England a judge is as likely as not to be some vulgar promoted advocate who makes coarse jokes over breach-of-promise cases; passes vindictive sentences with sanctimonious unction; and amuses himself off the bench like an ostler. But he is always spoken and written of as a veritable Daniel come to judgment. Mr. Gladstone's opinions on most social subjects are too childish to be intelligible to the rising generation; and Lord Salisbury makes blunders about the functions of governing bodies which would disqualify him for employment as a vestry clerk: but both gentlemen are highly successful in the parts of eminent statesmen. The fool of the family scrapes through an examination in the Greek testament by the bishop's chaplain; buttons his collar behind instead of before; and is straightway revered as a holy man. And the policeman, with his club and buttons, represents unspeakable things to the child in the street. The public has invested them all with the attributes of its ideals; and thenceforth the man who betrays the truth about them profanes those ideals and is dealt with accordingly.

It is now plain how to proceed in order to become a man of genius. You must strike the public imagination in such a fashion that they will select you as the incarnation of their ideal of a man of genius. To do this no doubt demands some extraordinary qualities, and sufficient professional industry; but it is by no means necessary to be what the public will pretend that you are. On the contrary, if you believe in the possibility of the ideal yourself without being vain enough to fancy that you realize it — if you retire discouraged because you find that you are not a bit like it — if you do not know, as every conjuror knows, that the imagination of the public will make up for all your deficiencies and fight for your complete authenticity as a fanatic fights for his creed, then you will be a failure. "Act well your part: there all the honor lies."

It is possible, however, that circumstances may cast you for such a humble part that it may be difficult even by any extremity of good acting to raise it to any prominence. You must then either be content in obscurity or else do what Sothern did with the part of Lord Dundreary in "Our American Cousin" or what Frederic Lemaître did with the part of Robert Macaire in "L'Auberge des Adrets." You must throw over the author's intention and create for yourself a fantastic leading part out of the business designed for a mere walking gentleman or common melodramatic villain. This is the resource to which I myself have been driven. Very recently the production of a play of mine [*Arms and the Man*] in New York led to the appearance in the New York papers of a host of brilliant critical and biographical studies of a remarkable person called Bernard Shaw. I am supposed to be that person; but I am not. There is no such person; there never was any such person; there never will or can be any such person. You may take my word for this, because I invented him, floated him, advertised him, impersonated him, and am now sitting here in my dingy second floor lodging in a decaying London Square, breakfasting off twopenn'orth of porridge and giving this additional touch to his make-up with my typewriter. My exposure of him will not shake the faith of the public in the least: they will only say "What a cynic he is!", or perhaps the more sympathetic of them may say, "What a pity he is such a cynic!"

It is a mistake, however, to suppose that a man must be either a cynic or an idealist. Both of them have as a common basis of belief the conviction that mankind as it really is is hateful. From this dismal and disabling infidelity the idealist escapes by pretending that men can be trained and preached and cultivated and governed and educated and self-repressed into something quite different from what they really are. The cynic sees that this regeneration is an imposture, and that the selfish and sensual Yahoo remains a Yahoo underneath the scholar's gown, the priest's cassock, the judge's ermine, the soldier's uniform, the saint's halo, the royal diadem and the poet's wreath. But pray where do these idealists and cynics get their fundamental assumption that human nature needs any apology? What is the objection to man as he really is and can become any more than to the solar system as it really is? All that can be said is that men, even when they have done their best possible, cannot be ideally kind, ideally honest, ideally chaste, ideally brave and so on. Well, what does that matter, any more than the equally important fact that they have no eyes in the back of their heads (a most inconvenient arrangement), or that they live a few score years instead of a few thousand? Do fully occupied and healthy people ever cry for the moon, or pretend they have got it under a glass case, or believe that they would be any the better for having it, or sneer at themselves and other people for not having it? Well, the time is coming when grown up people will no more cry for their present ideals than they now do for the moon.

Even the idealist system itself is no proof of any want of veracity on the part of the human race. Moral subjects require some power of thinking: and the ordinary man very seldom thinks, and finds it so difficult when he tries that he cannot get on without apparatus. Just as he cannot calculate without symbols and measure without a foot rule, so, when he comes to reason deductively, he cannot get on without hypotheses, postulates, definitions and axioms that do not hold good of anything really existent. The actions of a capitalist as deduced by a political economist, the path of a bullet as deduced by a physicist, do not coincide with the reality, because the reality is the result of many more factors than the economist or physicist is able to take into account with his limited power of thinking. He must simplify the problem if he is to think it at all. And he does this by imagining an ideal capitalist, void of all but mercenary motives, an ideal gun, pointed in an ideal direction with ideal accuracy and charged with ideal gunpowder and an ideal bullet governed in its motion solely by the ideal explosion of the ideal powder and by gravitation. Allow him all these fictions and he can deduce an ideal result for you, which will be contradicted by the first bargain you drive or the first shot you fire, but which is nevertheless the only *thinkable* result so far. Bit by bit we shall get hold of the omitted factors in the calculation, replace the fictitious ones by real ones, and so bring our conclusions nearer to the facts. It is just the same in our attempts to think about morals. We are forced to simplify the problems by dividing men into heroes and villains, women into good women and bad women, conduct into virtue and vice, and character into courage and cowardice, truth and falsehood, purity and licentiousness, and so forth. All that is childish; and sometimes, when it comes into action in the form of one man, dressed up as Justice, ordering the slaughter of another man, caged up as Crime, it is sufficiently frightful. Under all circumstances, its pageant of kings, bishops, judges and the rest, is to the eye of the highest intellect about as valid in its pretension to reality as the Lord Mayor's Show in London is valid in its pretension to dignity. We shall get rid of it all some day. America has already got rid of two of its figures, the king and the subject, which were once esteemed vital parts of the order of nature, and defended with unmeasured devotion and bloodshed, as indeed they still are in many places. The America of to-day is built on the repudiation of royalty. The America of to-morrow will be built on the repudiation of virtue. That is the negative side of it. The positive side will be the assertion of real humanity, which is to morality as time and space are to clocks and diagrams.

A Degenerate's View of Nordau

(A critique on Max Nordau's *Degeneration* in an open letter to editor Benjamin R. Tucker, in *Liberty*, New York, 27 July 1895. Issued as a book, with a new preface and minor revision, under the title *The Sanity of Art*, 1908; reprinted with further minor revision in Shaw's *Major Critical Essays*, 1930)

My dear Tucker:

I have read Max Nordau's "Degeneration" at your request — two hundred and sixty thousand mortal words, saying the same thing over and over again. That, as you know, is the way to drive a thing into the mind of the world, though Nordau considers it a symptom of insane "obsession" on the part of writers who do not share his own opinions. His message to the world is that all our characteristically modern works of art are symptoms of disease in the artists, and that these diseased artists are themselves symptoms of the nervous exhaustion of the race by overwork.

To me, who am a professional critic of art, and have for many successive London seasons had to watch a grand march past of books, of pictures, of concerts and operas, and of stage plays, there is nothing new in Herr Nordau's outburst. I have heard it all before. At every new birth of energy in art the same alarm has been raised; and, as these alarms always had their public, like prophecies of the end of the world, there is nothing surprising in the fact that a book which might have been produced by playing the resurrection man in the old newspaper rooms of our public libraries, and collecting all the exploded bogey-criticisms of the last half century into a huge volume, should have a considerable success. To give you an idea of the heap of material ready to hand for such a compilation, let me lay before you a sketch of one or two of the Reformations in art which I have myself witnessed.

When I was engaged chiefly in the criticism of pictures, the Impressionist movement was struggling for life in London; and I supported it vigorously because, being the outcome of heightened attention and quickened consciousness on the part of its disciples, it was evidently destined to improve pictures greatly by substituting a natural, observant, real style for a conventional, taken-for-granted, ideal one. The result has entirely justified my choice of sides. I can remember

when Mr. Whistler, in order to force the public to observe the qualities he was introducing into pictorial work, had to exhibit a fine drawing of a girl with the head deliberately crossed out with a few rough
pencil strokes, knowing perfectly well that, if he left a woman's face
discernible, the British Philistine would simply look to see whether
she was a pretty girl or not, or whether she represented some of his
pet characters in fiction, and pass on without having seen any of the
qualities of artistic execution which made the drawing valuable. But
it was easier for the critics to resent the obliteration of the face as
an insolent eccentricity, and to show their own good manners by
writing of Mr. Whistler as "Jimmy," than to think out what he meant.
It took several years of "propaganda by deed" before the qualities which
the Impressionists insisted on came to be looked for as a matter of
course in pictures, so that even the ordinary picture-gallery frequenter,
when he came face to face with Bouguereau's "Girl in a Cornfield,"
instead of accepting it as a window-glimpse of nature, saw at a glance
that the girl is really standing in a studio with what the house agents
call "a good north light," and that the cornfield is a conventional
sham. This advance in public education was effected by persistently
exhibiting pictures which, like Mr. Whistler's girl with her head
scratched out, were propagandist samples of workmanship rather than
complete works of art. But the moment Mr. Whistler and other really
able artists forced the dealers and the societies of painters to exhibit
these studies, and, by doing so, to accustom the public to tolerate what
appeared to it at first to be absurdities, the door was necessarily opened
to real absurdities. It is exceedingly difficult to draw or paint well;
it is exceedingly easy to smudge paper or canvas so as to suggest a
picture just as the stains on an old ceiling or the dark spots in a glowing
coal-fire do. Plenty of rubbish of this kind was produced, exhibited,
and tolerated at the time when people could not see the difference
between any daub in which there were shadows painted in vivid ani-
line hues and a landscape by Monet. Not that they thought the daub
as good as the Monet: they thought the Monet as ridiculous as the
daub; but they were afraid to say so, because they had discovered that
people who were good judges did not think Monet ridiculous. Then,
besides the mere impostors, there were a certain number of highly
conscientious painters who produced abnormal pictures because they
saw abnormally. My own sight happens to be "normal" in the oculist's sense: that is, I see things with the naked eye as most people
can only be made to see them by the aid of spectacles. Once I had
a discussion with an artist who was shewing me a clever picture of
his in which the parted lips in a pretty woman's face revealed what
seemed to me like a mouthful of virgin snow. The painter lectured

me for not using my eyes, instead of my knowledge of facts. "You can't see the divisions in a set of teeth, when you look at a person's mouth," he said; "all you can see is a strip of white, or yellow, or pearl, as the case may be; but, because you know, as a matter of anatomic fact, that there are divisions there, you want to have them represented by strokes in a drawing. That is just like you art critics, &c., &c." I do not think he believed me when I told him that, when I looked at a row of teeth, I saw, not only the divisions between them, but their exact shape, both in contour and modelling, just as well as I saw their general color. Some of the most able of the Impressionists evidently did not see forms as definitely as they appreciated color relationship; and, since there is always a great deal of imitation in the arts, we soon had young painters with perfectly good sight looking at landscapes or at their models with their eyes half closed and a little asquint, until what they saw looked to them like one of their favorite master's pictures. Further, the Impressionist movement led to a busy study of the atmosphere, conventionally supposed to be invisible, but seldom really completely so, and of what were called "values": that is, the relation of light and dark between the various objects depicted, on the correctness of which relation truth of effect mainly depends. This proved very difficult in full outdoor light with the "local color" brilliantly visible, and comparatively easy in gloomy rooms where the absence of light reduced all objects to masses of brown or grey of varying depth with hardly any discernible local color. Whistler's portrait of Sarasate, a masterpiece in its way, looks like a study in monochrome beside a portrait by Holbein; and his cleverest followers could paint dark interiors, or figures placed apparently in coal cellars, with admirable truth and delicacy of "value" sense, whilst they were still helplessly unable to represent a green tree or a blue sky, much less paint an interior with the light and local color as clear as in the works of Peter de Hooghe. Naturally the public eye, with its utilitarian familiarity with local color, and its Philistine insensibility to values and atmosphere, did not at first see what the Impressionists were driving at, and dismissed them as mere perverse, notoriety-hunting cranks. Here, then, you had a movement in painting which was wholly beneficial and progressive; and in no sense insane or decadent. Nevertheless it led to the public exhibititon of daubs which even the authors themselves would never have presumed to offer for exhibition before; it betrayed aberrations of vision in painters who, on the old academic lines, would have hidden their defects by drawing objects (teeth, for instance) as they knew them to exist, and not as they saw them; it set hundreds of clear-sighted students practising optical distortion, so as to see things myopically; and it substituted canvases which looked like enlargements of obscure photographs for the familiar portraits of masters of the hounds in cheerfully unmistakable pink coats, mounted on bright chestnut horses. All of which, and much else, to man who looked on at it without any sense of the deficiencies in conventional painting, necessarily suggested that the Impressionists and their contemporaries were much less sane than their fathers.

Again, my duties as a musical critic compelled me to ascertain very carefully the exact bearings of the controversy which has raged round Wagner's music-dramas since the middle of the century. When you and I last met, we were basking in the sun between the acts of "Parsifal" at Bayreuth; but experience has taught me that an American may appear at Bayreuth without being necessarily fonder than most men of a technical discussion on music. Let me therefore put the case to you in a mercifully intelligible way. Music is like drawing in this respect — that it can be purely decorative, or purely dramatic, or anything between the two. A draughtsman may be a pattern-designer, like William Morris, or he may be a delineator of life and character, like Ford Madox Brown. Or he may come between these two extremes, and treat scenes of life and character in a decorative way, like Walter Crane or Burne Jones — both of them consummate pattern-designers, whose subject pictures and illustrations are also fundamentally figure-patterns, prettier, but much less convincingly human and real, than Madox Brown's. Now, in music we have these same alternative applications of the art to drama and decoration. You can compose a graceful, symmetrical sound-pattern that exists solely for the sake of its own grace and symmetry. Or you can compose music to heighten the expression of human emotion; and such music will be intensely affecting in the presence of that emotion, and utter nonsense apart from it. For examples of pure pattern-designing in music I should have to go back to the old music of the thirteenth, fourteenth, and fifteenth centuries, before the operatic movement gained the upper hand; but I am afraid my assertions that much of this music is very beautiful and hugely superior to the stuff our music publishers turn out today would not be believed in America; for, when I hinted at something of the kind lately in the American "Musical Courier,"* and pointed out also the beauty of the instruments for which this old music was written — viols, virginals, and so on — one of your leading musical critics [Henry T. Finck] rebuked me with an expatiation on the superiority (meaning apparently the greater loudness) of the modern concert grand pianoforte, and contemptuously ordered the middle ages out from the majestic presence of the nineteenth century. Perhaps, however, you will take my word for it that in England alone

* "The Musical Revolution," September 1894 — Ed.

a long line of composers, from Henry VIII to Henry Purcell, have left us quantities of instrumental music which was not dramatic music nor "programme music," but which was designed to affect the hearer solely by its beauty of sound and grace and ingenuity of pattern. This is the art which Wagner called "absolute music." It is represented today by the formal sonata and symphony; and we are coming back to it in something like its old integrity by a post-Wagnerian reaction led by that greatly gifted absolute musician and hopelessly commonplace and tedious dramatic composer, Johannes Brahms.

To understand the present muddle, you must know that modern dramatic music did not appear as an independent branch of musical art, but as an adulteration of absolute music. The first modern dramatic composers accepted as binding on them the rules of good pattern-designing in sound; and this absurdity was made to appear practicable by the fact that Mozart had such an extraordinary command of his art that his operas contain "numbers" which, though they seem to follow the dramatic play of emotion and character without reference to any other consideration whatever, are seen, on examining them from the point of view of the absolute musician, to be perfectly symmetrical sound-patterns. But these *tours de force* were no real justification for imposing the laws of pattern-designing on other dramatic musicians; and even Mozart himself broke away from them in all directions, and was violently attacked by his contemporaries for doing so, the accusations levelled at him — absence of melody, illegitimate and discordant harmonic progressions, and monstrous abuse of the orchestra — being exactly those with which the opponents of Wagner so often pester ourselves. Wagner, whose leading lay characteristic was his enormous common sense, completed the emancipation of the dramatic musician from these laws of pattern-designing, and we now have operas, and very good ones too, written by composers like Bruneau or Boito, who are not musicians in the old sense at all — that is, they do not compose music apart from drama, and, when they have to furnish their operas with instrumental preludes or intermezzos or the like, they either take themes from the dramatic part of their operas and rhapsodize on them, or else they turn out some perfectly simple song or dance tune, at the cheapness of which Haydn would have laughed heartily, in spite of its orchestral and harmonic fineries.

If I add now that music in the academic, professorial, Conservative, respectable sense always means absolute music, and that students are taught that the laws of pattern-designing are binding on all musicians, and that violations of them are absolutely "wrong"; and if I mention incidentally that these laws are themselves confused by the survivals from a still older tradition based on the church art, technically very

highly specialized, of writing perfectly smooth and beautiful vocal harmony, for unaccompanied voices, worthy to be sung by angelic doctors
round the throne of God (this was Palestrina's art) — you will understand why it was that all the professional musicians who could not
see beyond the routine which they were taught, and all the men and
women (and there are many of them) who have little or no sense
of drama, but a very keen sense of beauty of sound and prettiness of
pattern in music, regarded Wagner as a madman who was reducing
music to chaos, perversely introducing ugly and brutal sounds into a
region where beauty and grace had reigned alone, and substituting
an incoherent, aimless, endless meandering for the familiar symmetrical tunes in four-bar strains, like "Pop Goes the Weazel," in which
the second and third strains repeat, or nearly repeat, the first and
second, so that any one can remember them and treasure them like
nursery rhymes. It was the unprofessional, "unmusical" public which
caught the dramatic clue, and saw order and power, strength and
sanity in the supposed Wagner chaos; and now, his battle being won
and overwon, the professors, to avert the ridicule of their pupils, are
compelled to explain (quite truly) that Wagner's technical procedure
in music is almost pedantically logical and grammatical; that the "Lo-
hengrin" prelude is a masterpiece of the "form" proper to its aim; and
that his disregard of "false relations" and his free use of the most
extreme discords without "preparation," were straight and sensible instances of that natural development of harmony which has proceeded
continuously from the time when common six-four chords were considered "wrong," and such free use of unprepared dominant sevenths
and minor ninths as had become common in Mozart's time would have
seemed the maddest cacophony.

The dramatic development also touched purely instrumental music.
Liszt was no more an absolute musician than Wagner was. He
wanted a symphony to express an emotion and its development, not
to be a pretty sound-pattern. And he defined the emotion by con-
necting it with some known story, poem, or even picture — Mazeppa,
Victor Hugo's "Les Preludes," Kaulbach's "Die Hunnenschlacht," or
the like. But the moment you try to make an instrumental composition follow a story, you are forced to abandon the sound-pattern form,
since all patterns consist of some decorative form which is repeated
over and over again, and which generally consists in itself of a repetition of two similar halves; for example, if you take a playing card
— say the five of diamonds — as a simple example of a pattern, you
find not only that the diamond figure is repeated five times, but that
each side of each pip is a reversed duplicate of the other. Now, the
established form for a symphony is essentially a pattern form in-

volving just such symmetrical repetitions; and, since a story does not repeat itself, but pursues a continuous chain of fresh incident and correspondingly varied emotions, Liszt had either to find a new musical form for his musical poems, or else face the intolerable anomalies and absurdities which spoil the many attempts made by Mendelssohn, Raff, and others to handcuff the old form to the new matter. Consequently he invented the "symphonic poem," a perfectly simple and fitting common-sense form for his purpose, and one which makes "Les Preludes" much plainer sailing for the ordinary hearer than Mendelssohn's "Naiades" overture or Raff's "Lenore" or "Im Walde" symphonies, in both of which the formal repetitions would stamp Raff as a madman if we did not know that they were mere superstitions, which he had not the strength of mind to shake off as Liszt did. But still, to the people who would not read Liszt's explanations and cared nothing for his purpose, who had no taste for "tone poetry" and consequently insisted on judging the symphonic poems as sound-patterns, Liszt must needs appear, like Wagner, a perverse egotist with something fundamentally disordered in his intellect — in short, a lunatic.

The sequel was the same as in the Impressionist movement. Wagner, Berlioz, and Liszt, in securing tolerance for their own works, secured it for what sounded to many people absurd; and this tolerance necessarily extended to a great deal of stuff which was really absurd, but which the secretly-bewildered critics dared not denounce, lest it, too, should turn out to be great, like the music of Wagner, over which they had made the most ludicrous exhibition of their incompetence. Even at such stupidly conservative concerts as those of the London Philharmonic Society, I have seen ultra-modern composers, supposed to be representatives of the Wagnerian movement, conducting rubbish in no essential superior to Jullien's British army quadrilles. And then, of course, there are the young imitators, who are corrupted by the desire to make their harmonies sound like those of the masters whose purposes and principles of work they are too young to understand.

Here, again, you see, you have a progressive, intelligent, wholesome, and thoroughly sane movement in art, producing plenty of evidence to prove the case of any clever man who does not understand music, but who has a theory which involves the proposition that all the leaders of the art movements of our time are degenerate and, consequently, retrogressive lunatics.

There is no need for me to go at any great length into the grounds on which any development in our moral views must at first appear insane and blasphemous to people who are satisfied, or more than satisfied, with the current morality. Perhaps you remember the opening chapters of my "Quintessence of Ibsenism," in which I shewed why the

London press, now abjectly polite to Ibsen, received him four years ago with a shriek of horror.   Every step in morals is made by challenging the validity of the existing conception of perfect propriety of conduct; and, when a man does that, he must look out for a very different reception from the painter who has ventured to paint a shadow brilliant purple, or the composer who begins the prelude to his opera with an unprepared chord of the thirteenth. Heterodoxy in art is at worst rated as eccentricity or folly; heterodoxy in morals is at once rated as scoundrelism, and, what is worse, propagandist scoundrelism, which must, if successful, undermine society and bring us back to barbarism after a period of decadence like that which brought imperial Rome to its downfall. Your function as a philosophic Anarchist in American society is to combat the attempts that are constantly being made to arrest development by using the force of the State to suppress all departures from what the majority consider to be "right" in conduct or overt opinion. I dare say you will find the modern democratic voter a very troublesome person, chicken-heartedly diffident as to the value of his opinions on art or science, but cocksure about right and wrong in morals, politics, and religion — that is to say, in all the departments in which he can interfere effectively and mischievously. Happily, the individual is developing greatly in freedom and boldness nowadays.   Formerly our young people mostly waited in diffident silence until they were old enough to find their aspirations towards the fullest attainable activity and satisfaction working out in practice very much as they have worked out in the life of the race; so that the revolutionist of twenty-five, who saw nothing for it but a clean sweep of all our institutions, found himself, at forty, accepting and even clinging to them on condition of a few reforms to bring them up to date. But nowadays the young people do not wait so patiently for this reconciliation. They express their dissatisfaction with the wisdom of their elders loudly and irreverently, and formulate their heresy as a faith. They demand the abolition of marriage, of the State, of the Church; they preach the divinity of love and the heroism of the man who believes in himself and dares do the thing he wills; they contemn the slavery to duty and discipline which has left so many soured old people with nothing but envious regrets for a virtuous youth. They recognize their gospel in such utterances as that quoted by Nordau from Brandes: "To obey one's senses is to have character. He who allows himself to be guided by his passions has individuality." For my part, I think this excellent doctrine, both in Brandes's form and in the older form: "He that is unjust, let him be unjust still; and he which is filthy, let him be filthy still; and he that is righteous, let him be righteous still; and he that is holy, let him be holy still." This is not the opinion of

Nordau, who, with facile journalistic vulgarity, proceeds to express his horror of Brandes with all the usual epithets — "debauchery, dissoluteness, depravity disguised as modernity, bestial instincts, *maître de plaisir,* egomaniacal anarchist" — and such sentences as the following:

> It is comprehensible that an educator who turns the school-room into a tavern and a brothel should have success and a crowd of followers. He certainly runs the risk of being slain by the parents, if they come to know what he is teaching their children; but the pupils will hardly complain, and will be eager to attend the lessons of so agreeable a teacher. This is the explanation of the influence Brandes gained over the youth of his country, such as his writings, with their emptiness of thought and unending tattle, would certainly never have procured for him.

In order to thoroughly enjoy this spluttering, you must know that it is immediately followed by an attack on Ibsen for the weakness of "obsession by the doctrine of original sin." Yet what would the passage I have just quoted be without the doctrine of original sin as a postulate? If "the heart of man is deceitful above all things, and desperately wicked," then, truly, the man who allows himself to be guided by his passions must needs be a scoundrel, and his teacher might well be slain by his parents. But how if the youth thrown helpless on his passions found that honesty, that self-respect, that hatred of cruelty and injustice, that the desire for soundness and health and efficiency, were master passions — nay, that their excess is so dangerous to youth that it is part of the wisdom of age to say to the young: "Be not righteous overmuch: why shouldst thou destroy thyself?" I am sure, my dear Tucker, your friends have paraphrased that in vernacular American often enough in remonstrating with you for your Anarchism, which defies not only God, but even the wisdom of the United States congress. On the other hand, the people who profess to renounce and abjure their own passions, and ostentatiously regulate their conduct by the most convenient interpretation of what the Bible means, or, worse still, by their ability to find reasons for it (as if there were not excellent reasons to be found for every conceivable course of conduct, from dynamite and vivisection to martyrdom), seldom need a warning against being righteous overmuch, their attention, indeed, often needing a rather pressing jog in the opposite direction. The truth is that passion is the steam in the engine of all religions and moral systems. In so far as it is malevolent, the religions are malevolent too, and insist on human sacrifices, on hell, wrath, and vengeance. You cannot read Browning's "Caliban upon Setebos, or, Natural Theology on the Island" without admitting that all our religions have been made as Caliban made his, and that the difference between Caliban and Prospero is that Prospero is mastered by holier passions. And as Caliban imagined his theology, so did Mill reason out his essay on "Liberty" and Spencer his "Data of Ethics." In them we find the authors still trying to formulate abstract principles of conduct — still missing the fact that truth and justice are not abstract principles external to man, but human passions, which have, in their time, conflicted with higher passions as well as with lower ones. If a young woman, in a mood of strong reaction against the preaching of duty and self-sacrifice and the rest of it, were to tell Mr. Herbert Spencer that she was determined not to murder her own instincts and throw away her life in obedience to a mouthful of empty phrases, I suspect he would recommend the "Data of Ethics" to her as a trustworthy and conclusive guide to conduct. Under similar circumstances I should unhesitatingly say to the young woman: "By all means do as you propose. Try how wicked you can be; it is precisely the same experiment as trying how good you can be. At worst you will only find out the sort of person you really are. At best you will find that your passions, if you really and honestly let them all loose impartially, will discipline you with a severity which your conventional friends, abandoning themselves to the mechanical routine of fashion, could not stand for a day." As a matter of fact, I have seen over and over again this comedy of the "emancipated" young enthusiast flinging duty and religion, convention and parental authority, to the winds, only to find herself becoming, for the first time in her life, plunged into duties, responsibilities, and sacrifices from which she is often glad to retreat, after a few years' wearing down of her enthusiasm, into the comparatively loose life of an ordinary respectable woman of fashion. The truth is, laws, religions, creeds, and systems of ethics, instead of making society better than its best unit, make it worse than its average unit, because they are never up to date. You will ask me: "Why have them at all?" I will tell you. They are made necessary — though we all secretly detest them — by the fact that the number of people who can think out a line of conduct for themselves even on one point is very small, and the number who can afford the time for it still smaller. Nobody can afford the time to do it on all points. The professional thinker may on occasion make his own morality and philosophy as the cobbler may make his own boots; but the ordinary man of business must buy at the shop, so to speak, and put up with what he finds on sale there, whether it exactly suits him or not, because he can neither make a morality for himself nor do without one. This typewriter with which I am writing is the best I can get; but it is by no means a perfect instrument; and I have not the smallest doubt that in fifty years' time the authors of that day will wonder how men could have put up with so clumsy a contrivance. When a better one is invented, I shall buy it: until then, I must make the best of it, just as my Protestant and Roman Catholic and Agnostic friends make the best of their creeds and systems. This would be better recognized if people took consciously and deliberately to the use of creeds as they do to the use of typewriters. Just as the traffic of a great city would be impossible without a code of rules of the road which not one wagoner in a thousand could draw up for himself, much less promulgate, and without, in London at least, an unquestioning consent to treat the policeman's raised hand as if it were an impassable bar stretched half across the road, so the average man is still unable to get through the world without being told what to do at every turn, and basing such calculations as he is capable of on the assumption that every one else will calculate on the same assumptions. Even your man of genius accepts a thousand rules for every one he challenges; and you may lodge in the same house with an Anarchist for ten years without noticing anything exceptional about him. Martin Luther, the priest, horrified the greater half of Christendom by marrying a nun, yet was a submissive conformist in countless ways, living orderly as a husband and father, wearing what his bootmaker and tailor made for him, and dwelling in what the builder built for him, although he would have died rather than take his Church from the Pope. And when he got a Church made by himself to his liking, generations of men calling themselves Lutherans took that Church from him just as unquestioningly as he took the fashion of his clothes from his tailor. As the race evolves, many a convention which recommends itself by its obvious utility to every one passes into an automatic habit, like breathing; and meanwhile the improvement in our nerves and judgment enlarges the list of emergencies which individuals may be trusted to deal with on the spur of the moment without reference to regulations; but there will for many centuries to come be a huge demand for a ready-made code of conduct for general use, which will be used more or less as a matter of overwhelming convenience by all members of communities. Oh, Father Tucker, worshipper of Liberty! where shall I find a country where the thinking can be done without division of labor?

It follows that we can hardly fall into any error stupider than that of mistaking creeds and the laws founded on creeds for the applications to human conduct of eternal and immutable principles of good and evil. It sets people regarding laws as institutions too sacred to be tampered with, whereas in a progressive community nothing can make laws tolerable unless their changes and modifications are kept closely on the heels of the changes and modifications which are continuously proceeding in the minds and habits of the people; and it deadens the conscience of individuals by relieving them of the moral responsibility of their own actions. When this relief is made as complete as possible, it reduces a man to a condition in which his very virtues are contemptible. Military discipline, for example, aims at destroying the individuality and initiative of the soldier whilst increasing his mechanical efficiency, until he is simply a weapon with the power of hearing and obeying orders. In him you have duty, obedience, self-denial, submission to external authority, carried as far as it can be carried; and the result is that in England, where military service is voluntary, the common soldier is less respected than any other serviceable worker in the community. The police constable, who, though under discipline too, is a civilian and has to use his own judgment and act on his own responsibility in innumerable petty emergencies, is by comparison a popular and esteemed citizen. The Roman Catholic peasant who consults his parish priest instead of his conscience, and submits wholly to the authority of the Church, is mastered and governed either by statesmen or cardinals who despise his superstition, or by Protestants who are at least allowed to persuade themselves that they have arrived at their religious opinions through the exercise of their private judgment. The whole progress of the world is from submission and obedience as safeguards against panic and incontinence, to wilfulness and self-assertion made safe by reason and self-control, just as plainly as the physical growth of the individual leads from the perambulator and the nurse's apron-string to the power of walking alone, or his moral growth from the tutelage of the boy to the responsibility of the man. But it is useless for impatient spirits — you and I, for instance — to call on people to walk before they can stand. Without high gifts of reason and self-control — that is, without strong common sense — no man dare yet trust himself out of the school of authority. What he does is to claim gradual relaxations of the discipline, so as to have as much freedom as he thinks is good for him and as much government as he needs to keep him straight. We see this in the history of British-American Christianity. Man, as the hero of that history, starts by accepting as binding on him the revelation of God's will as interpreted by the Church. Then he claims a formal right to exercise his own judgment, which the Reformed Church, competing with the Unreformed for clients, grants him on condition that he arrive at the same conclusions as itself. Later on, he violates this condition in certain particulars, and "dissents," flying to America in the Mayflower from the prison of Conformity, but promptly building a new jail, suited to the needs of his sect, in his adopted country. For all these little mutinies he finds excellent arguments to prove that he is exchanging a false authority for *the* true one, never daring even to think of brazenly admitting that what he is really doing is substituting his own will, bit by bit, for what he calls the will of God or the laws of Nature. The arguments so accustom the world to submit authority to the test of discussion that he is at last emboldened to claim the right to do anything he can find good arguments for, even to the extent of questioning the scientific accuracy of the book of Genesis and the validity of the popular conception of God as an omniscient, omnipotent, and very serious old gentleman sitting on a throne above the clouds. This seems a giant stride towards emancipation; but it leaves our hero, as Rationalist and Materialist, regarding Reason as an eternal principle, independent of and superior to his erring passions, at which point it is easy to suggest that perhaps the experienced authority of a Roman Catholic Church might be better than the first crop of arguments raised by a handful of raw Rationalists in their sects of "Freethinkers" and "Secularists" for the working class, and "Positivists" or "Don't Knowists" (Agnostics) for the genteel votaries of the new fetich.

In the meantime came Schopenhauer to re-establish the old theological doctrine that reason is no motive power; that the true motive power in the world — otherwise life — is will; and that the setting up of reason above will is a damnable error. But the theologians could not open their arms to Schopenhauer, because he fell into the cardinal Rationalist error of making happiness instead of completeness of activity the test of the value of life, and of course came to the idiotic pessimist conclusion that life is not worth living, and that the will which urges us to live in spite of this is necessarily a malign torturer, the desirable end of all things being the Nirvana of the stilling of the will and the consequent setting of life's sun "into the blind cave of eternal night." Further, the will of the theologians was the will of God, standing outside man and in authority above him, whereas the Schopenhauerian will is a purely secular force of nature, attaining various degrees of organization, here as a jelly fish, there as a cabbage, more complexly as an ape or a tiger, and attaining its highest form so far in the human being. As to the Rationalists, they approved of Schopenhauer's secularism and pessimism, but of course could not stomach his metaphysical method or his dethronement of reason by will. Accordingly, his turn for popularity did not come until after Darwin's, and then mostly through the influence of two great artists, Richard Wagner and Ibsen, whose "Tristan" and "Emperor or Galilean" shew that Schopenhauer was a true pioneer in the forward march of the human spirit. We can now, as soon as we are strong-minded enough, drop the Nirvana nonsense, the pessimism, the rationalism, the theology, and all the other subterfuges to which we cling because we are afraid to look life straight in the face and see in it, not the fulfilment of a moral law or of the deductions of reason, but the satisfaction of a passion in us of which we can give no account whatever. It is natural for man to shrink from the terrible responsibility thrown on him by this inexorable fact. All his stock excuses vanish before it — "The woman tempted me," "The serpent tempted me," "I was not myself at the time," " I meant well," "My passion got the better of my reason," "It was my duty to do it," "The Bible says that we should do it," "Everybody does it," and so on. Nothing is left but the frank avowal: "I did it because I am built that way." Every man hates to say that. He wants to believe that his generous actions are characteristic of him, and that his meannesses are aberrations or concessions to the force of circumstances. Our murderers, with the assistance of the jail chaplain, square accounts with the devil and with God, never with themselves. The convict gives every reason for his having stolen something except the reason that he is a thief. Cruel people flog their children for their children's good, or offer the information that a guinea pig perspires under atrocious torture as an affectionate contribution to science. Lynched negroes are riddled by dozens of superfluous bullets, every one of which is offered as the expression of a sense of outraged justice and womanhood in the scamp and libertine who fires it. And such is the desire of men to keep one another in countenance that they positively demand such excuses from one another as a matter of public decency. An uncle of mine, who made it a rule to offer tramps a job when they begged from him, naturally very soon became familiar with every excuse that human ingenuity can invent for not working. But he lost his temper only once; and that was with a tramp who frankly replied that he was too lazy. This my uncle described with disgust as "cynicism." And yet our family arms bear the motto, in Latin, "Know thyself."

As you know, the true trend of this movement has been mistaken by many of its supporters as well as by its opponents. The ingrained habit of thinking of the propensities of which we are ashamed as "our passions," and our shame of them and our propensities to noble conduct as a negative and inhibitory department called generally our conscience, leads us to conclude that to accept the guidance of our passions is to plunge recklessly into the insupportable tedium of what is called a life of pleasure. Reactionists against the almost equally insupportable slavery of what is called a life of duty are nevertheless willing to venture on these terms. The "revolted daughter," exasperated at being systematically lied to by her parents on every subject of vital importance to an eager and intensely curious young student of life, allies herself with really vicious people and with humorists who like to shock the pious with gay paradoxes, in claiming an impossible license in personal conduct. No great harm is done beyond the inevitable and temporary excesses produced by all reactions; for, as I have said, the would-be wicked ones find, when they come to the point, that the indispensable qualification for a wicked life is not freedom, but wickedness. But the misunderstanding supports the clamor of the opponents of the newest opinions, who naturally shriek as Nordau shrieks in the passages about Brandes, quoted above. Thus you have here again a movement which is thoroughly beneficial and progressive presenting a hideous appearance of moral corruption and decay, not only to our old-fashioned religious folk, but to our comparatively modern scientific folk as well. And here again, because the press and the gossips have found out that this apparent corruption and decay is considered the right thing in some influential quarters, and must be spoken of with respect, and patronized and published and sold and read, we have a certain number of pitiful imitators taking advantage of their tolerance to bring out really silly and rotten stuff, which the reviewers are afraid to expose, lest it, too, should turn out to be the correct thing.

After this long preamble, you will have no difficulty in understanding the sort of book Nordau has written. Figure to yourself a huge volume, stuffed with the most slashing of the criticisms which were hurled at the Impressionists, the Tone Poets, and the philosophers and dramatists of the Schopenhauerian revival, before these movements had reached the point at which it began to require some real courage to attack them. Imagine a *rechauffée*, not only of the newspaper criticisms of this period, but actually of all its little parasitic paragraphs of small talk and scandal, from the long-forgotten jibes against Mr. Oscar Wilde's momentary attempt to bring knee-breeches into fashion years ago, to the latest scurrilities about "the New Woman." Imagine the general staleness and occasional putrescence of this mess disguised by a dressing of the terminology invented by Krafft-Ebing, Lombroso, and all the latest specialists in madness and crime, to describe the artistic faculties and propensities as they operate in the insane. Imagine all this done by a man who is a vigorous and capable journalist, shrewd enough to see that there is a good opening for a big reactionary book as a relief to the Wagner and Ibsen booms, bold enough to let himself go without respect to persons or reputations, lucky enough to be a stronger, clearer-headed man than ninety-nine out of a hundred of his critics, besides having a keener interest in science, a born theorist, reasoner, and busybody, and so able, without insight, originality, or even any very remarkable intensive industry (he is, like most Germans, *ex*tensively industrious to an appalling degree), to produce a book which has made a very considerable impression on the artistic ignorance of Europe and America. For he says a thing as if he meant it; he holds superficial ideas obstinately, and sees them clearly; and his mind works so impetuously that it is a pleasure to watch it — for a while. All the same, he is shallow and unfeeling enough to be the dupe of a theory which would hardly impose on one of those gamblers who have a system or martingale, founded on a solid rock of algebra, by which they can infallibly break the bank at Monte Carlo. "Psychiatry" takes the place of algebra in Nordau's martingale.

This theory of his is, at bottom, nothing but the familiar delusion of the used-up man that the world is going to the dogs. But Nordau is too clever to be driven back on ready-made mistakes; he makes them for himself in his own way. He appeals to the prodigious extension of the quantity of business that a single man can transact through the modern machinery of social intercourse — the railway, the telegraph and telephone, the post, and so forth. He gives appalling statistics of the increase of railway mileage and shipping, of the number of letters written per head of the population, of the newspapers which tell us things of which we used to know nothing.* "In the last fifty years," he says, "the population of Europe has not doubled, whereas the sum of its labors has increased tenfold — in part, even fiftyfold. Every civilized man furnishes, at the present time, from five to twenty-five times as much work as was demanded of him half a century ago."† Then follow more statistics of "the constant increase of crime, madness, and suicide," of increases in the mortality from diseases of the nerves and heart, of increased consumption of stimulants, of new nervous diseases like "railway spine and railway brain," with the general moral that we are all suffering from exhaustion, and that symptoms of degeneracy are visible in all directions, culminating at various points in such hysterical horrors as Wagner's music, Ibsen's dramas, Manet's pictures, Tolstoi's novels, Whitman's poetry, Dr. Jaeger's woollen clothing, vegetarianism, scep-

---

* Perhaps I had better remark in passing that, unless it were true — which it is not — that the length of the modern penny letter or halfpenny post-card is the same as that of the eighteenth-century letter, and that the number of persons who know how to read and write has not increased, there is no reason whatever to draw Nordau's conclusion from these statistics.

† Here again we have a statement which means nothing, unless it be compared with statistics as to the multiplication of the civilized man's power of production by machinery, which in some industries has multiplied a single man's power by hundreds and in others by thousands. As to crimes and disease, Nordau should state whether he counts convictions under modern laws — for offences against the Joint-Stock Company Acts, for instance — as proving that we have degenerated since those Acts were passed, and whether he regards the invention of new names for a dozen varieties of fever which were formerly counted as one single disease as an evidence of decaying health in the face of the increasing duration of life.

ticism as to the infallibility of vivisection and vaccination, Anarchism and humanitarianism, and, in short, everything that Herr Nordau does not happen to approve of.

You will at once see that such a case, if well got up and argued, is worth hearing, even though its advocate has no chance of a verdict, because it is sure to bring out a certain number of facts which are interesting and important. It is, I take it, quite true that, with our railways and our postal services, many of us are for the moment very like a pedestrian converted to bicycling, who, instead of using his machine to go forty miles with less labor than he used to walk twenty, proceeds to do a hundred miles instead, with the result that the "labor-saving" contrivance acts as a means of working its user to exhaustion. It is also, of course, true that under our existing industrial system machinery in industrial processes is regarded solely as a means of extracting a larger product from the unremitted toil of the actual wage-worker. And I do not think any person who is in touch with the artistic professions will deny that they are recruited largely by persons who become actors, or painters, or journalists and authors because they are incapable of steady work and regular habits, or that the attraction which the patrons of the stage, music, and literature find in their favorite arts has often little or nothing to do with the need which nerves great artists to the heavy travail of creation. The claim of art to our respect must stand or fall with the validity of its pretension to cultivate and refine our senses and faculties until seeing, hearing, feeling, smelling, and tasting become highly conscious and critical acts with us, protesting vehemently against ugliness, noise, discordant speech, frowsy clothing, and foul air, and taking keen interest and pleasure in beauty, in music, and in the open air, besides making us insist, as necessary for comfort and decency, on clean, wholesome, handsome fabrics to wear, and utensils of fine material and elegant workmanship to handle. Further, art should refine our sense of character and conduct, of justice and sympathy, greatly heightening our self-knowledge, self-control, precision of action, and considerateness, and making us intolerant of baseness, cruelty, injustice, and intellectual superficiality or vulgarity. The worthy artist or craftsman is he who responds to this cultivation of the physical and moral senses by feeding them with pictures, musical compositions, pleasant houses and gardens, good clothes and fine implements, poems, fictions, essays, and dramas which call the heightened senses and ennobled faculties into pleasurable activity. The great artist is he who goes a step beyond the demand, and, by supplying works of a higher beauty and a higher interest than have yet been perceived, succeeds, after a brief struggle with its strangeness, in adding this fresh extension of sense to the heritage of the race. This is why we value art; this is why we feel that the iconoclast and the Puritan are attacking something made holier, by solid usefulness, than their own theories of purity; this is why art has won the privileges of religion; so that London shopkeepers who would fiercely resent a compulsory church rate, who do not know "Yankee Doodle" from "God Save the Queen," and who are more interested in the photograph of the latest celebrity than in the Velasquez portrait in the National Gallery, tamely allow the London county council to spend their money on bands, on municipal art inspectors, and on plaster casts from the antique.

But the business of responding to the demand for the gratification of the senses has many grades. The confectioner who makes unwholesome sweets, the bull-fighter, the women whose advertisements in the Chicago papers are so astounding to English people, are examples ready to hand to shew what the art and trade of pleasing may be, not at its lowest, but at the lowest that we can speak of without intolerable shame. We have dramatists who write their lines in such a way as to enable low comedians of a certain class to give them an indecorous turn; we have painters who aim no higher than Giulio Romano did when he decorated the Palazzo Te in Mantua; we have poets who have nothing to versify but the commonplaces of amorous infatuation; and, worse than all the rest put together, we have journalists who openly profess that it is their duty to "reflect" what they believe to be the ignorance and prejudice of their readers, instead of leading and enlightening them to the best of their ability — an excuse for cowardice and time-serving which is also becoming well worn in political circles as "the duty of a democratic statesman." In short, the artist can be a prostitute, a pander, and a flatterer more easily, as far as external pressure goes, than a faithful servant of the community, much less the founder of a school or the father of a church. Even an artist who is doing the best he can may be doing a very low class of work: for instance, many performers at the rougher music halls, who get their living by singing coarse songs in the rowdiest possible way, do so to the utmost of their ability in that direction in the most conscientious spirit of earning their money honestly and being a credit to their profession. And the exaltation of the greatest artists is not continuous; you cannot defend every line of Shakspere or every stroke of Titian. Since the artist is a man and his patron a man, all human moods and grades of development are reflected in art; consequently the Puritan's or the Philistine's indictment of art has as many counts as the misanthrope's indictment of humanity. And this is the Achilles' heel of art at which Nordau has struck. He has piled the Puritan on the Philistine, the Philistine on the misanthrope, in order to make out his case. Let me describe to you one or two of his typical artifices as a special pleader making the most of the eddies at the sides of the stream of progress.

Chief among his tricks is the old and effective one of pointing out, as "stigmata of degeneration" in the person he is abusing, features which are common to the whole human race. The drawing-room palmist astonishes ladies by telling them "secrets" about themselves which are nothing but the inevitable experiences of ninety-nine people out of every hundred, though each individual is vain enough to suppose that they are peculiar to herself. Nordau turns the trick inside out by trusting to the fact that people are in the habit of assuming that uniformity and symmetry are laws of nature — for example, that every normal person's face is precisely symmetrical, that all persons have the same number of bones in their bodies, and so on. Nordau takes advantage of this popular error to claim asymmetry as a stigma of degeneration. As a matter of fact, perfect symmetry or uniformity is the rarest thing in nature. My two profiles, when photographed, are hardly recognizable as belonging to the same person by those who do not know me; so that the camera would prove me an utter degenerate if my case were exceptional. Probably, however, you would not object to testify that my face is as symmetrical as faces are ordinarily made. Another unfailing trick is the common one of having two names for the same thing — one of them abusive, the other complimentary — for use according to circumstances. You know how it is done: "We trust the government will be firm" in one paper, and "We hope ministers will not be obstinate" in another. The following is a typical specimen of Nordau's use of this device. When a man with a turn for rhyming goes mad, he repeats rhymes as if he were quoting a rhyming dictionary. You say "Come" to him, and he starts away with "Dumb, plum, sum, rum, numb, gum," and so on. This the doctors call "echolalia." Dickens gives a specimen of indulgence in it by sane people in "Great Expectations," where Mr. Jaggers's Jewish client expresses his rapture of admiration for the lawyer by exclaiming: "Oh, Jaggerth, Jaggerth, Jaggerth; all otherth ith Cag-Maggerth, give me Jaggerth!" There are some well-known verses by Swinburne, beginning, "If love were what the rose is," which, rhyming and tripping along very prettily, express a sentiment without making any intelligible statement whatsoever; and we have plenty of nonsensically inconsequent nursery rhymes, like "Ba, ba, black sheep," or "Old Daddy long legs," which please perfectly sane children just as Mr. Swinburne's verses please perfectly sane adults, simply as funny or pretty little word-patterns. People do not write such things for the sake of conveying information, but for the sake of amusing and pleasing, just as people do not eat strawberries and cream to nourish their bones and muscles, but to enjoy the taste of a toothsome dish. A lunatic may plead that he eats kitchen soap and tin tacks on exactly the same ground; and, as far as I can see, the lunatic would completely shut up Nordau by this argument: for Nordau is absurd enough, in the case of rhyming, to claim that every rhyme made for its own sake, as proved by the fact that it does not convey an intelligible statement of fact of any kind, convicts the rhymer of "echolalia," or the disease of the lunatic who, when you ask him to come in to dinner, begins to reel off "Sinner, skinner, thinner, winner," &c., instead of accepting the invitation or making a sensible answer. Nordau can thus convict any poet whom he dislikes of being a degenerate by simply picking out a rhyme which exists for its own sake, or a pun, or what is called a "burden" in a ballad, and claiming them as symptoms of "echolalia," supporting this diagnosis by carefully examining the poem for contradictions and inconsistencies as to time, place, description, or the like. It will occur to you probably that by this means he must bring out Shakspere as the champion instance of poetic degeneracy, since Shakspere was an incorrigible punster, delighted in "burdens" — for instance, "With hey, ho, the wind and the rain," which exactly fulfils all the conditions accepted by Nordau as symptomatic of insanity in Rossetti's case — and rhymed for the sake of rhyming in a quite childish fashion, whilst, as to contradictions and inconsistencies, "Midsummer Night's Dream," as to which Shakspere never seems to have made up his mind whether the action covered a week or a single night, is only one of a dozen instances of his slips. But no: Shakspere, not being a nineteenth-century poet, would have spoiled the case for modern degeneration by shewing that it could have been made out on the same grounds before the telegraph and the railway were dreamt of; and besides, Nordau likes Shakspere, just as he likes Goethe, and holds him up as a model of sanity against the nineteenth-century poets. Thus Wagner is a degenerate because he made puns; and Shakspere, who made worse ones, is a great poet. Swinburne, with his "unmeaning" refrains of "Small red leaves in the mill water," and "Apples of gold for the King's daughter," is a diseased madman; but Shakspere, with his "In spring time, the only merry ring time, when birds do sing hey ding a ding ding" (if this is not the worst case of "echolalia" in the world, what *is* echolalia?), is a sober master mind. Rossetti, with his Blessed Damozel leaning out from the gold bar of heaven, who weeps, although she is in paradise, which is a happy place, who describes the dead in one place as "dressed in white" and in another as "mounting like thin flames," and whose calculations of days and years do not resemble those in commercial diaries, is that dangerous and cranky thing, "a mystic"; whilst Goethe, the author of the second part of "Faust," if you please, is a hard-headed, accurate, sound scientific poet. As to the list of inconsistencies of which poor Ibsen is convicted, it is too long to be dealt with in detail. But I assure you I am not doing Nordau less than justice when I say that, if he had accused Shakspere of inconsistency on the ground that Othello is represented in the first act as loving his wife, and in the last as strangling her, the demonstration would have left you with more respect for his good sense than his pages on Ibsen, the folly of which goes beyond all patience.*

When Nordau deals with painting and music, he is less irritating, because he errs through ignorance, and ignorance, too, of a sort that is now perfectly well recognized and understood. We all know what the old-fashioned literary and scientific writer, who cultivated his intellect without ever dreaming of cultivating his eyes and ears, can be relied upon to say when painters and composers are under discussion. Nordau makes a fool of himself with laughable punctuality. He gives us "the most glorious period of the Renaissance" and "the rosy dawn of the new thought" with all the gravity of the older editions of Murray's guides to Italy. He tells us that "to copy Cimabue and Giotto is comparatively easy; to imitate Raphael it is necessary to be able to draw and paint to perfection." He lumps Fra Angelico with Giotto and Cimabue, as if they represented the same stage in the development of technical execution, and Pollajuolo with Ghirlandajo. "Here," he says, speaking of the great Florentine painters, from Giotto to Masaccio, "were paintings bad in drawing, faded or smoked, their coloring either originally feeble or impaired by the action of centuries, pictures *executed with the awkwardness of a learner . . .* easy of imitation, since, in painting pictures in the style of the early masters, faulty drawing, deficient sense of color, and *general artistic incapacity*, are

---

* Perhaps I had better give one example. Nordau first quotes a couple of speeches from "An Enemy of the People" and "The Wild Duck."

STOCKMANN: I love my native town so well that I had rather ruin it than see it flourishing on a lie. All men who live on lies must be exterminated like vermin. ("An Enemy of the People.")

RELLING: Yes, I said illusion [lie]. For illusion, you know, is the stimulating principle. Rob the average man of his life illusion, and you rob him of his happiness at the same time. ("The Wild Duck.")

Nordau proceeds to comment as follows:

Now, what is Ibsen's real opinion? Is a man to strive for truth or to swelter in deceit? Is Ibsen with Stockmann or with Relling? Ibsen owes us an answer to these questions, or, rather, he replies to them affirmatively and negatively with equal ardor and equal poetic power.

so many advantages." To make any comment on this would be to hit a man when he is down. Poor Nordau offers it as a demonstration that Ruskin, who gave this sort of ignorant nonsense its death-blow, was a delirious mystic. Also that Millais and Holman Hunt, in the days of the pre-Raphaelite brotherhood, strove to acquire the qualities of the early Florentine masters because the Florentine easel pictures were so much easier to imitate than those of the apprentices in Raphael's Roman fresco factory.

In music we find Nordau equally content with the theories as to how music is composed which were current among literary men fifty years ago. He tells us of "the severe discipline and fixed rules of the theory of composition, which gave a grammar to the musical babbling of primeval times, and made of it a worthy medium for the expression of the emotions of civilized men," and describes Wagner as breaking these "fixed rules" and rebelling against this "severe discipline" because he was "an inattentive mystic, abandoned to amorphous dreams." This notion that there are certain rules, derived from a science of counterpoint, by the application of which pieces of music can be constructed just as an equilateral triangle can be constructed on a given straight line by any one who has mastered Euclid's first proposition is highly characteristic of the generation of blind and deaf critics to which Nordau belongs. It is evident that, if there were "fixed rules" by which Wagner or any one else could have composed good music, there could have been no more "severe discipline" in the work of composition than in the work of arranging a list of names in alphabetical order. The severity of artistic discipline is produced by the fact that in creative art no ready-made rules can help you. There is nothing to guide you to the right expression for your thought except your own sense of beauty and fitness; and, as you advance upon those who went before you, that sense of beauty and fitness is necessarily often in conflict, not with fixed rules, because there are no rules, but with precedents, which are what Nordau means by "fixed rules," as far as he knows what he is talking about well enough to mean anything at all. If Wagner had composed the prelude to "Das Rheingold" with a half close at the end of the eighth bar and a full close at the end of the sixteenth, he would undoubtedly have followed the precedent of Mozart and other great composers, and complied with the requirements of Messrs. Hanslick, Nordau and Company. Only, as it happened, that was not what he wanted to do. His purpose was to produce a tone picture of the mighty flood in the depths of the Rhine; and, as the poetic imagination does not conceive the Rhine as stopping at every eight feet to take off its hat to Herren Hanslick and Nordau, the closes and half closes are omitted, and poor Herr Nordau, huffed at being passed by as if he were a person of no consequence, complains that the composer is "an inattentive mystic, abandoned to amorphous dreams." But, even if Wagner's descriptive purpose is left out of the question, Nordau's general criticism of him is an ignorant one; for the truth is that Wagner, like most artists who have great intellectual power, was dominated in the technical work of his gigantic scores by so strong a regard for system, order, logic, symmetry, and syntax that, when in the course of time his melody and harmony become perfectly familiar to us, he will be ranked with Händel as a composer whose extreme regularity of procedure must make his work appear drily mechanical to those who cannot catch its dramatic inspiration. If Nordau, having no sense of that inspiration, had said: "This fellow, whom you all imagine to be the creator of a new heaven and a new earth in music out of a chaos of poetic emotion, is really an arrant pedant and formalist," I should have pricked up my ears and listened to him with some curiosity, knowing how good a case a really keen technical critic could make out for that view. As it is, I have only to expose him as having picked up a vulgar error under the influence of a vulgar literary superstition. For the rest, you will hardly need any prompting of mine to appreciate the absurdity of dismissing as "inattentive" the Dresden conductor, the designer and founder of the Bayreuth enterprise, the humorous and practical author of "On Conducting," and the man who scored and stage-managed the four evenings of "The Niblung Ring." I purposely leave out the composer, the poet, the philosopher, the reformer, since Nordau cannot be compelled to admit that Wagner's eminence in these departments was real. Striking them all out accordingly, there remain the indisputable, objective facts of Wagner's practical professional ability and organizing power to put Nordau's diagnosis of Wagner as an "amorphous," inattentive person out of the question. If Nordau had one hundredth part of the truly terrific power of attention which Wagner must have maintained all his life almost as easily as a common man breathes, he would not now be so deplorable an example of the truth of his own contention that the power of attention may be taken as the measure of mental strength.

Nordau's trick of calling rhyme "echolalia" when he happens not to like the rhymer is reapplied in the case of authorship, which he calls "graphomania" when he happens not to like the author. He insists that Wagner, who was a voluminous author as well as a composer, was a graphomaniac; and his proof is that in his books we find "the restless repetition of one and the same strain of thought. . . . 'Opera and Drama,' 'Judaism in Music,' 'Religion and the State,' 'Art and Religion,' and 'The Vocation of Opera' are nothing more than the amplification of single passages in 'The Art-Work of the Future.' "

This is a capital example of Nordau's limited power of attention. The moment that limited power is concentrated on his theory of degeneration, he loses sight of everything else, and drives his one borrowed horse into every obstacle on the road. To those of us who can attend to more than one thing at a time, there is no observation more familiar, and more frequently confirmed, than that this growth of pregnant single sentences into whole books which Nordau discovers in Wagner, balanced as it always is by the contraction of whole boyish chapters into single epigrams, is the process by which all great writers, speakers, artists, and thinkers elaborate their life-work. Let me take a writer after Nordau's own heart — a specialist in lunacy, of course — one whom he quotes as a trustworthy example of what he calls "the clear, mentally sane author, who, feeling himself impelled to say something, once for all expresses himself as distinctly and impressively as it is possible for him to do, and has done with it": namely, Dr. Henry Maudsley. Dr. Maudsley is a clever and cultivated specialist in insanity, who has written several interesting books, consisting of repetitions, amplifications, and historical illustrations of the same idea, which is, if I may put it rather more bluntly than the urbane author, nothing less than the identification of religious with sexual ecstasy. And the upshot of it is the conventional scientific pessimism, from which Dr. Maudsley never gets away; so that his last book repeats his first book, instead of leaving it far behind, as Wagner's "State and Religion" leaves his "Art and Revolution" behind. But, now that I have prepared the way by quoting Dr. Maudsley, why should I not ask Herr Nordau himself to step before the looking-glass and tell us frankly whether, even in the ranks of his "psychiatrists" and lunacy doctors, he can pick out a crank more hopelessly obsessed with one idea than himself. If you want an example of "echolalia," can you find a more shocking one than this gentleman who, when you say "mania," immediately begins to gabble Egomania, Graphomania, Megalomania, Onomatomania, Pyromania, Kleptomania, Dipsomania, Erotomania, Arithmomania, Oniomania, and is started off by the termination "phobia" with a string of Agoraphobia, Claustrophobia, Rupophobia, Iophobia, Nosophobia, Aichmophobia, Belenophobia, Cremnophobia, and Trichophobia? After which he suddenly observes: "This is simply philologico-medical trifling" — a remark which looks like returning sanity until he follows it up by clasping his temples in the true bedlamite manner, and complaining that "psychiatry is being stuffed with useless and disturbing designations," whereas, if the psychiatrists would only listen to him, they would see that there is only one phobia and one mania — namely, degeneracy. That is, the philologico-medical triflers are not crazy enough for him. He is so utterly mad on the subject of degeneration that he finds the symptoms of it in the loftiest geniuses as plainly as is the lowest jail-birds, the only exceptions being himself, Lombroso, Krafft-Ebing, Dr. Maudsley, and — for the sake of appearances — Goethe, Shakspere, and Beethoven. Perhaps he would even except a case so convenient in many ways for his theory as Coleridge sooner than spoil the connection between degeneration and "railway spine." If a man's senses are acute, he is degenerate, hyperæsthesia having been observed in asylums. If he is particular as to what he wears, he is degenerate; silk dressing-gowns and knee-breeches are grave symptoms, and woollen shirts conclusive. If he is negligent in these matters, clearly he is inattentive, and therefore degenerate. If he drinks, he is neurotic; if he is a vegetarian and tee-totaller, let him be locked up at once. If he lives an evil life, that fact condemns him without further words; if, on the other hand, his conduct is irreproachable, he is a wretched "mattoid," incapable of the will and courage to realize his vicious propensities in action. If he writes verse, he is afflicted with echolalia; if he writes prose, he is a graphomaniac; if in his books he is tenacious of his ideas, he is obsessed; if not, he is "amorphous" and "inattentive." Wagner, as we have seen, contrived to be both obsessed and inattentive, as might be expected from one who was "himself alone charged with a greater abundance of degeneration than all the other degenerates put together." And so on and so forth.

There is, however, one sort of mental weakness, common among men who take to science, as so many people take to art, without the necessary brain power, which Nordau, with amusing unconsciousness of himself, has omitted. I mean the weakness of the man who, when his theory works out into a flagrant contradiction of the facts, concludes: "So much the worse for the facts; let them be altered," instead of: "So much the worse for my theory." What in the name of common sense is the value of a theory which identifies Ibsen, Wagner, Tolstoi, Ruskin, and Victor Hugo with the refuse of our prisons and lunatic asylums? What is to be said of the state of mind of an inveterate pamphleteer and journalist who, instead of accepting that identification as a *reductio-ad-absurdum* of the theory, desperately sets to work to prove it by pointing out that there are numerous resemblances — that they all have heads and bodies, appetites, aberrations, whims, weaknesses, asymmetrical features, erotic impulses, fallible judgments, and the like common properties, not merely of all human beings, but all vertebrate organisms. Take Nordau's own list — "vague and incoherent thought, the tyranny of the association of ideas, the presence of obsessions, erotic excitability, religious enthusiasm, feebleness of perception, will, memory, and judgment, as well as inattention and instability"; is there a single man capable of understanding these terms who will not plead guilty to some experience of all of them, especially when he is accused vaguely and unscientifically, without any statement of the subject, or the moment, or the circumstances to which the accusation refers, or any attempt to fix a standard of sanity? I could prove Nordau to be an elephant on more evidence than he has brought to prove that our greatest men are degenerate lunatics. The papers in which Swift, having predicted the death of the sham prophet Bickerstaff on a certain date, did, after that date, immediately prove that he was dead are much more closely and fairly reasoned than any of Nordau's chapters. And Swift, though he afterwards died in a madhouse, was too sane to be the dupe of his own logic. At that rate, where will Nordau die? Probably in a highly respectable suburban villa.

Nordau's most likeable point is the freedom and boldness with which he expresses himself. Speaking of Peladan (of whose works I know nothing), he says, whilst holding him up as a typical degenerate of the mystical variety: "His moral ideal is high and noble. He pursues with ardent hatred all that is base and vulgar, every form of egoism, falsehood, and thirst for pleasure; and his characters are thoroughly aristocratic souls, whose thoughts are concerned only with the worthiest, if somewhat exclusively artistic, interests of society." On the other hand, Maeterlinck is a "poor devil of an idiot"; Mr. W. D. O'Connor, for describing Whitman as "the good gray poet," is politely introduced as "an American driveller"; Nietzsche "belongs, body and soul, to the flock of the mangy sheep"; Ibsen is "a malignant, antisocial simpleton"; and so on. Only occasionally is he insincerely Pharisaical in his tone, as, for instance, when he pretends to become virtuously indignant over Wagner's dramas, and plays to Mrs. Grundy by exclaiming ironically: "How unperverted must wives and readers be, when they are in a state of mind to witness these pieces without blushing crimson and sinking into the earth for shame!" This, to do him justice, is only an exceptional lapse; a far more characteristic comment of his on Wagner's love-scenes is: "The lovers in his pieces behave like tom cats gone mad, rolling in contortions and convulsions over a root of valerian." And he is not always on the side of the police, so to speak; for he is as careless of the feelings of the "beer-drinking" German *bougeoisie* as of those of the æsthetes. Thus, though on one page he is pointing out that Socialism and all other forms of discontent with the existing social order are "stigmata of degeneration," on the next he is talking pure Karl Marx. For example, taking the two sides in their order:

Ibsen's egomania assumes the form of Anarchism. He is in a state of constant revolt against all that exists. . . . The psychological roots of his anti-social impulses are well known. They are the degenerate's incapacity for self-adaptation, and the resultant discomfort in the midst of circumstances to which, in consequence of his organic deficiencies, he cannot accommodate himself. "The criminal," says Lombroso, "through his neurotic and impulsive nature, and his hatred of the institutions which have punished or imprisoned him, is a perpetual latent political rebel, who finds in insurrection the means, not only of satisfying his passions, but of even having them countenanced for the first time by a numerous public.

Wagner is a declared Anarchist. . . . He betrays that mental condition which the degenerate share with enlightened reformers, born criminals with the martyrs of human progress — namely, deep, devouring discontent with existing facts. . . . He would like to crush "political and criminal civilization," as he calls it.

Now for Nordau speaking for himself.

Is it not the duty of intelligent philanthropy and justice, without destroying civilization, to adopt a better system of economy and transform the artisan from a factory convict, condemned to misery and ill health, into a free producer of wealth, who enjoys the fruits of his labor himself, and works no more than is compatible with his health and his claims on life?

Every gift that a man receives from some other man without work, without reciprocal service, is an alms, and as such is deeply immoral.

Not in the impossible "return to Nature" lies healing for human misery, but in the reasonable organization of our struggle with nature — I might say, in universal and obligatory service against it, from which only the crippled should be exempted.

In England it was Tolstoi's sexual morality that excited the greatest interest; for in that country economic reasons condemn a formidable number of girls, particularly of the educated classes, to forego marriage; and, from a theory which honored chastity as the highest dignity and noblest human destiny, and branded marriage with gloomy wrath as abominable depravity, these poor creatures would naturally derive rich consolation for their lonely, empty lives and their cruel exclusion from the possibility of fulfilling their natural calling.

So it appears that Nordau, too, shares "the degenerate's incapacity for self-adaptation, and the resultant discomfort in the midst of circumstances to which, in consequence of his organic deficiencies, he cannot accommodate himself." But he has his usual easy way out of the dilemma. If Ibsen and Wagner are dissatisfied with the world, that is because the world is too good for them; but, if Max Nordau is dissatisfied, it is because Max is too good for the world. His modesty does not permit him to draw the distinction in these exact terms. Here is his statement of it:

> Discontent shews itself otherwise in the degenerate than in reformers. The latter grow angry over real evils only, and make rational proposals for their remedy which are in advance of the time: these remedies may presuppose a better and wiser humanity than actually exists; but, at least, they are capable of being defended on reasonable grounds. The degenerate, on the other hand, selects among the arrangements of civilization such as are either immaterial or distinctly suitable, in order to rebel against them. His fury has either ridiculously insignificant aims, or simply beats the air. He either gives no earnest thought to improvement, or hatches astoundingly mad projects for making the world happy. His fundamental frame of mind is persistent rage against everything and every one, which he displays in venomous phrases, savage threats, and the destructive mania of wild beasts. *Wagner is a good specimen of this species.*

Wagner is only named here because the passage occurs in the almost incredibly foolish chapter which is headed with his name. In another chapter it might have been Ibsen, or Tolstoi, or Ruskin, or William Morris, or any other eminent artist who shares Nordau's objection, and yours and mine, to our existing social arrangements. In the face of this, it is really impossible to deny oneself the fun of asking Nordau, with all possible good humor, who he is and what he is, that he should rail in this fashion at great men. Wagner was discontented with the condition of musical art in Europe. In essay after essay he pointed out with the most laborious exactitude what it was he complained of, and how it might be remedied. He not only shewed, in the teeth of the most envenomed opposition from all the dunderheads, pedants, and vested interests in Europe, what the musical drama

ought to be as a work of art, but how theatres for its proper performance should be managed — nay, how they should be built, down to
the arrangement of the seats and the position of the instruments in
the orchestra. And he not only shewed this on paper, but he successfully composed the music dramas, built a model theatre, gave the
model performances, *did* the impossible; so that there is now nobody
left, not even [Edouard] Hanslick, who cares to stultify himself by
repeating the old anti-Wagner cry of craziness and Impossibilism —
nobody, save only Max Nordau, who, like a true journalist, is fact-
proof. William Morris objected to the abominable ugliness of early
Victorian decoration and furniture, to the rhymed rhetoric which
has done duty for poetry ever since the Renaissance, to kamptulicon
stained glass, and, later on, to the shiny commercial gentility of typography according to the American ideal, which was being spread
through England by "Harper's" and "The Century," and which had
not, like your abolition of "justifying" in Liberty, the advantage of
saving trouble. Well, did he sit down, as Nordau suggests, to rail
helplessly at the men who were at all events getting the work of the
world done, however inartistically? Not a bit of it; he designed and
manufactured the decorations he wanted, and furnished and decorated
houses with them; he put into public halls and churches tapestries and
picture-windows which cultivated people now travel to see as they
travel to see first-rate fifteenth-century work in that kind; the books
from his Kelmscott Press, printed with type designed by his own hand,
are pounced on by collectors like the treasures of our national museums, all this work, remember, involving the successful conducting
of a large business establishment and factory, and being relieved by
the incidental production of a series of poems and prose romances
which have placed their author in the position of the greatest living
English poet. Now let me repeat the terms in which Nordau describes
this kind of activity. "Ridiculously insignificant aims — beating the
air — no earnest thought to improvement — astoundingly mad projects for making the world happy — persistent rage against everything
and every one, displayed in venomous phrases, savage threats, and
destructive mania of wild beasts." Is there not something deliciously
ironical in the ease with which a splenetic pamphleteer, with nothing
to shew for himself except a bookful of blunders tacked on to a mock
scientific theory picked up at second hand from a few lunacy doctors
with a literary turn, should be able to create a European scandal by
declaring that the greatest creative artists of the century are barren
and hysterical madmen? I do not know what the American critics
have said about Nordau; but here the tone has been that there is much
in what he says, and that he is evidently an authority on the subjects

with which he deals. And yet I assure you, on my credit as a man who lives by art criticism, that from his preliminary description of a Morris design as one "on which strange birds flit among crazily ramping branches, and blowzy flowers coquet with vain butterflies" (which is about as sensible as a description of the Norman chapel in the Tower of London as a characteristic specimen of Baroque architecture would be) to his coupling of Cimabue and Fra Angelico as primitive Florentine masters; from his unashamed bounce about "the conscientious observance of the laws of counterpoint" by Beethoven and other masters celebrated for breaking them to his unlucky shot about "a pedal bass with correct harmonization" (a pedal bass happening to be the particular instance in which even the professor-made rules of "correct harmonization" are suspended), Nordau gives himself away time after time as an authority upon the fine arts. But his critics, being for the most part ignorant literary men like himself, with sharpened wits and neglected eyes and ears, have swallowed Cimabue and Ghirlandajo and the pedal bass like so many gulls. Here an Ibsen admirer may maintain that Ibsen is an exception to the degenerate theory and should be classed with Goethe; there a Wagnerite may plead that Wagner is entitled to the honors of Beethoven; elsewhere one may find a champion of Rossetti venturing cautiously to suggest a suspicion of the glaringly obvious fact that Nordau has read only the two or three popular ballads like "The Blessed Damozel," "Eden Bower," "Sister Helen," and so on, which every smatterer reads, and that his knowledge of the mass of pictorial, dramatic, and decorative work turned out by Rossetti, Burne Jones, Ford Madox Brown, William Morris, and Holman Hunt, without a large knowledge and careful study of which no man can possibly speak with any critical authority of the pre-Raphaelite movement, is apparently limited to a glance at Holman Hunt's "Shadow of the Cross," or possibly an engraving thereof. And, if Nordau were to convince me tomorrow that I am wrong, and that he knows all the works of the school thoroughly, I should only be forced to assure him regretfully that he was all the greater fool. As it is, I have nothing worse to say of his art criticism than that it is the work of a pretentious ignoramus, instantly recognizable as such by any expert. I copy his bluntness of speech as a matter of courtesy to him.

And now, my dear Tucker, I have told you as much about Nordau's book as it is worth. In a country where art was really known to the people, instead of being merely read about, it would not be necessary to spend three lines on such a work. But in England, where nothing but superstitious awe and self-mistrust prevents most men from thinking about art as Nordau boldly speaks about it; where to have a sense of art is to be one in a thousand, the other nine hundred and ninety-nine being Philistine voluptuaries or Puritan anti-voluptuaries — it is useless to pretend that Nordau's errors will be self-evident. Already we have native writers, without half his cleverness or energy of expression, clumsily imitating his sham scientific vivisection in their attacks on artists whose work they happen to dislike. Therefore, in riveting his book to the counter, I have used a nail long enough to go through a few pages by other people as well; and that must be my excuse for my disregard of the familiar editorial stigma of degeneracy which Nordau calls Agoraphobia, or Fear of Space.

G. Bernard Shaw.

On Going to Church

(*The Savoy*, London, January 1896. Reprinted, without authorization, in *The Roycroft Quarterly*, East Aurora, N.Y., August 1896, and as a book by the Roycroft Press, from the same plates, in September 1896, the text being slightly revised and abridged. A second unauthorized American edition by John W. Luce & Co., Boston, 1905, followed the text in *The Savoy*)

As a modern man, concerned with matters of fine art and living in London by the sweat of my brain, I dwell in a world which, unable to live by bread alone, lives spiritually on alcohol and morphia. Young and excessively sentimental people live on love, and delight in poetry or fine writing which declares that love is Alpha and Omega; but an attentive examination will generally establish the fact that this kind of love, ethereal as it seems, is merely a symptom of the drugs I have mentioned, and does not occur independently except in those persons whose normal state is similar to that induced in healthy persons by narcotic stimulants. If from the fine art of to-day we set aside feelingless or prosaic art, which is, properly, not fine art at all, we may safely refer most of the rest to feeling produced by the teapot, the bottle, or the hypodermic syringe. An exhibition of the cleverest men and women in London at five p.m., with their afternoon tea cut off, would shatter many illusions. Tea and coffee and cigarettes produce conversation; lager beer and pipes produce routine journalism; wine and gallantry produce brilliant journalism, essays and novels; brandy and cigars produce violently devotional or erotic poetry; morphia produces tragic exaltation (useful on the stage); and sobriety produces an average curate's sermon. Again, strychnine and arsenic may be taken as pick-me-ups; doctors quite understand that "tonics" mean drams of ether; chlorodyne is a universal medicine; chloral, sulphonal and the like call up Nature's great destroyer, artificial sleep; bromide of potassium will reduce the over-sensitive man of genius to a condition in which the alighting of a wasp on his naked eyeball will not make him wink; haschisch tempts the dreamer by the Oriental glamour of its reputation; and gin is a cheap substitute for all these anodynes. Most of the activity of the Press, the Pulpit, the Platform and the Theatre is only a symptom of the activity of the drug trade, the tea trade, the tobacco trade and the liquor trade. The world is not going from bad to worse, it is

378

true; but the increased facilities which constitute the advance of civilisation include facilities for drugging oneself. These facilities wipe whole races of black men off the face of the earth; and every extension and refinement of them picks a stratum out of white society and devotes it to destruction. Such traditions of the gross old habits as have reached me seem to be based on the idea of first doing your day's work and then enjoying yourself by getting drunk. Nowadays you get drunk to enable you to begin work. Shakespere's opportunities of meddling with his nerves were much more limited than Dante Rossetti's; but it is not clear that the advantage of the change lay with Rossetti. Besides, though Shakespere may, as tradition asserts, have died of drink in a ditch, he at all events conceived alcohol as an enemy put by a man into his own mouth to steal away his brains; whereas the modern man conceives it as an indispensable means of setting his brains going. We drink and drug, not for the pleasure of it, but for Dutch inspiration and by the advice of our doctors, as duellists drink for Dutch courage by the advice of their seconds. Obviously this systematic, utilitarian drugging and stimulating, though necessarily "moderate" (so as not to defeat its own object), is more dangerous than the old boozing if we are to regard the use of stimulants as an evil.

As for me, I do not clearly see where a scientific line can be drawn between food and stimulants. I cannot say, like Ninon de l'Enclos, that a bowl of soup intoxicates me; but it stimulates me as much as I want to be stimulated, which is, perhaps, all that Ninon meant. Still, I have not failed to observe that all the drugs, from tea to morphia, and all the drams, from lager beer to brandy, dull the edge of self-criticism and make a man content with something less than the best work of which he is soberly capable. He thinks his work better, when he is really only more easily satisfied with himself. Those whose daily task is only a routine, for the sufficient discharge of which a man need hardly be more than half alive, may seek this fool's paradise without detriment to their work; but to those professional men whose art affords practically boundless scope for skill of execution and elevation of thought, to take drug or dram is to sacrifice the keenest, most precious part of life to a dollop of lazy and vulgar comfort for which no true man of genius should have any greater stomach than the lady of the manor has for her ploughman's lump of fat bacon. To the creative artist stimulants are especially dangerous, since they produce that terrible dream-glamour in which the ugly, the grotesque, the wicked, the morbific begin to fascinate and obsess instead of disgusting. This effect, however faint it may be, is always produced in some degree by drugs. The mark left on a novel in the *Leisure Hour* by a cup of tea may be imperceptible to a bishop's wife who has just had two cups; but the effect is there as certainly as if De Quincey's eight thousand drops of laudanum had been substituted.

A very little experience of the world of art and letters will convince any open-minded person that abstinence, pure and simple, is not a practicable remedy for this state of things. There is a considerable commercial demand for maudlin or nightmarish art and literature which no sober person would produce, the manufacture of which must accordingly be frankly classed industrially with the unhealthy trades, and morally with the manufacture of unwholesome sweets for children or the distilling of gin. What the victims of this industry call imagination and artistic faculty is nothing but attenuated delirium tremens, like Pasteur's attenuated hydrophobia. It is useless to encumber an argument with these predestined children of perdition. The only profitable cases to consider are those of people engaged in the healthy pursuit of those arts which afford scope for the greatest mental and physical energy, the clearest and acutest reason and the most elevated perception. Work of this kind requires an intensity of energy of which no ordinary labourer or routine official can form any conception. If the dreams of Keeleyism could be so far realised as to transmute human brain energy into vulgar explosive force, the head of Shakespere, used as a bombshell, might conceivably blow England out of the sea. At all events, the succession of efforts by which a Shakesperean play, a Beethoven symphony, or a Wagner music-drama is produced, though it may not overtax Shakespere, Beethoven or Wagner, must certainly tax even them to the utmost, and would be as prodigiously impossible to the average professional man as the writing of an ordinary leading article to a ploughman. What is called professional work is, in point of severity, just what you choose to make it, either commonplace, easy and requiring only *ex*tensive industry to be lucrative, or else distinguished, difficult and exacting the fiercest *in*tensive industry in return, after a probation of twenty years or so, for authority, reputation and an income only sufficient for simple habits and plain living. The whole professional world lies between these two extremes. At the one, you have the man to whom his profession is only a means of making himself and his family comfortable and prosperous: at the other, you have the man who sacrifices everything and everybody, himself included, to the perfection of his work, to the passion for efficiency which is the true master-passion of the artist. At the one, work is a necessary evil and moneymaking a pleasure: at the other, work is the objective realisation of life and moneymaking a nuisance. At the one, men drink and drug to make themselves comfortable: at the other, to stimulate their working faculty. Preach mere abstinence at the one, and you are preaching nothing but diminution of happiness. Preach it at the other, and you are proposing a reduction of efficiency. If you are to prevail, you must propose a substitute. And the only one I have yet been able to hit on is — going to church.

It will not be disputed, I presume, that an unstimulated saint can work as hard, as long, as finely and, on occasion, as fiercely, as a stimulated sinner. Recuperation, recreation, inspiration seem to come to the saint far more surely than to the man who grows coarser and fatter with every additional hundred a year, and who calls the saint an ascetic. A comparison of the works of our carnivorous drunkard poets with those of Shelley, or of Dr. Johnson's dictionary with that of the vegetarian Littré, is sufficient to show that the secret of attaining the highest eminence either in poetry or in dictionary compiling (and all fine literature lies between the two), is to be found neither in alcohol nor in our monstrous habit of bringing millions of useless and disagreeable animals into existence for the express purpose of barbarously slaughtering them, roasting their corpses and eating them. I have myself tried the experiment of not eating meat or drinking tea, coffee or spirits for more than a dozen years past, without, as far as I can discover, placing myself at more than my natural disadvantages relatively to those colleagues of mine who patronise the slaughter-house and the distillery. But then I go to church. If you should chance to see, in a country churchyard, a bicycle leaning against a tombstone, you are not unlikely to find me inside the church if it is old enough or new enough to be fit for its purpose. There I find rest without languor and recreation without excitement, both of a quality unknown to the traveller who turns from the village church to the village inn and seeks to renew himself with shandygaff. Any place where men dwell, village or city, is a reflection of the consciousness of every single man. In my consciousness there is a market, a garden, a dwelling, a workshop, a lover's walk — above all, a cathedral. My appeal to the master-builder is: Mirror this cathedral for me in enduring stone; make it with hands; let it direct its sure and clear appeal to my senses, so that when my spirit is vaguely groping after an elusive mood my eye shall be caught by the skyward tower, showing me where, within the cathedral, I may find my way to the cathedral within me. With a right knowledge of this great function of the cathedral builder, and craft enough to set an arch on a couple of pillars, make doors and windows in a good wall and put a roof over them, any modern man might, it seems to me, build churches as they built them in the middle ages, if only the pious founders and the parson would let him. For want of that knowledge, gentlemen of Mr. Pecksniff's profession make fashionable pencil-drawings, presenting what Mr. Pecksniff's creator elsewhere calls an architectooralooral appearance, with which, having delighted the darkened eyes of the committee and the clerics, they have them translated into bricks and masonry and take a shilling in the pound on the bill, with the result that the bishop may consecrate the finished building until he is black in the face without making a real church of it. Can it be doubted by the pious that babies baptised in such places go to limbo if they die before qualifying themselves for other regions; that prayers said there do not count; nay, that such purposeless, respectable-looking interiors are irreconcilable with the doctrine of Omnipresence, since the bishop's blessing is no spell of black magic to imprison Omnipotence in a place that must needs be intolerable to Omniscience? At all events, the godhead in me, certified by the tenth chapter of St. John's Gospel to those who will admit no other authority, refuses to enter these barren places. This is perhaps fortunate, since they are generally kept locked; and even when they are open, they are jealously guarded in the spirit of that Westminster Abbey verger who, not long ago, had a stranger arrested for kneeling down, and explained, when remonstrated with, that if that sort of thing were tolerated, they would soon have people praying all over the place. Happily it is not so everywhere. You may now ride or tramp into a village with a fair chance of finding the church-door open and a manuscript placard in the porch, whereby the parson, speaking no less as a man and a brother than as the porter of the House Beautiful, gives you to understand that the church is open always for those who have any use for it. Inside such churches you will often find not only carefully-cherished work from the ages of faith, which you expect to find noble and lovely, but sometimes a quite modern furnishing of the interior and draping of the altar, evidently done, not by contract with a firm celebrated for its illustrated catalogues, but by someone who loved and understood the church, and who, when baffled in the search for beautiful things, had at least succeeded in avoiding indecently commercial and incongruous ones. And then the search for beauty is not always baffled. When the dean and chapter of a cathedral want not merely an ugly but a positively beastly pulpit to preach from — something like the Albert Memorial canopy, only much worse — they always get it, improbable and unnatural as the enterprise is. Similarly, when an enlightened country parson wants an unpretending tub to thump, with a few pretty panels in it and a pleasant shape generally, he will, with a little perseverance, soon enough find a craftsman who has picked up the thread of the tradition of his craft from the time when that craft was a fine art — as may be done nowadays more easily than was possible before we had cheap trips and cheap photographs*

---

* At the bookstall in the South Kensington Musêum, any young craftsman, or other person, can turn over hundreds of photographs taken by Alinari, of Florence, from the finest work in the churches and palaces of

— and who is only too glad to be allowed to try his hand at something in the line of that tradition. Some months ago, bicycling in the west country, I came upon a little church, built long before the sense of beauty and devotion had been supplanted by the sense of respectability and talent, in which some neat panels left by a modern carver had been painted with a few saints on gold backgrounds, evidently by some woman who had tried to learn what she could from the early Florentine masters and had done the work in the true votive spirit, without any taint of the amateur exhibiting his irritating and futile imitations of the celebrated-artist business. From such humble but quite acceptable efforts, up to the masterpiece in stained glass by William Morris and Burne-Jones which occasionally astonishes you in places far more remote and unlikely than Birmingham or Oxford, convincing evidence may be picked up here and there that the decay of religious art from the sixteenth century to the nineteenth was not caused by any atrophy of the artistic faculty, but was an eclipse of religion by science and commerce. It is an odd period to look back on from the churchgoer's point of view — those eclipsed centuries calling their predecessors "the dark ages," and trying to prove their own piety by raising, at huge expense, gigantic monuments in enduring stone (not very enduring, though, sometimes) of their infidelity. Go to Milan, and join the rush of tourists to its petrified christening-cake of a cathedral. The projectors of that costly ornament spared no expense to prove that their devotion was ten times greater than that of the builders of San Ambrogio. But every pound they spent only recorded in marble that their devotion was a hundred times less. Go on to Florence and try San Lorenzo, a really noble church (which the Milan Cathedral is not), Brunelleschi's masterpiece. You cannot but admire its intellectual command of form, its unaffected dignity, its power and accomplishment, its masterly combination of simplicity and homogeneity of plan with elegance and variety of detail: you are even touched by the retention of that part of the beauty of the older time which was perceptible to the Renascent intellect before its weaning from heavenly food had been followed by starvation. You understand the deep and serious respect which Michael Angelo had for Brunelleschi — why he said "I can do different work,

---

Italy. He will not be importuned to buy, or grudged access to the portfolios, which are, fortunately, in charge of a lady who is a first-rate public servant. He can, however, purchase as many of the photographs as he wants for sixpence each. This invaluable arrangement, having been made at the public expense, is carefully kept from the public knowledge, because, if it were properly advertised, complaints might be made by English shopkeepers who object to our buying Alinari's cheap photographs instead of their own dear photographs of the Great Wheel at Earl's Court.

but not better." But a few minutes' walk to Santa Maria Novella or Santa Croce, or a turn in the steam-tram to San Miniato, will bring you to churches built a century or two earlier; and you have only to cross their thresholds to feel, almost before you have smelt the incense, the difference between a church built to the pride and glory of God (not to mention the Medici) and one built as a sanctuary shielded by God's presence from pride and glory and all the other burdens of life. In San Lorenzo up goes your head — every isolating advantage you have of talent, power or rank asserts itself with thrilling poignancy. In the older churches you forget yourself, and are the equal of the beggar at the door, standing on ground made holy by that labour in which we have discovered the reality of prayer. You may also hit on a church like the Santissima Annunziata, carefully and expensively brought up to date, quite in our modern church-restoring manner, by generations of princes chewing the cud of the Renascence; and there you will see the worship of glory and the self-sufficiency of intellect giving way to the display of wealth and elegance as a guarantee of social importance — in another word, snobbery. In later edifices you see how intellect, finding its worshippers growing colder, had to abandon its dignity and cut capers to attract attention, giving the grotesque, the eccentric, the baroque, even the profane and blasphemous, until, finally, it is thoroughly snubbed out of its vulgar attempts at self-assertion, and mopes conventionally in our modern churches of St. Nicholas Without and St. Walker Within, locked up, except at service-time, from week's end to week's end without ever provoking the smallest protest from a public only too glad to have an excuse for not going into them. You may read the same history of the human soul in any art you like to select; but he who runs may read it in the streets by looking at the churches.

Now, consider for a moment the prodigious increase of the population of Christendom since the church of San Zeno Maggiore was built at Verona, in the twelfth and thirteenth centuries. Let a man go and renew himself for half an hour occasionally in San Zeno, and he need eat no corpses, nor drink any drugs or drams to sustain him. Yet not even all Verona, much less all Europe, could resort to San Zeno in the thirteenth century; whereas, in the nineteenth, a thousand perfect churches would be but as a thousand drops of rain on Sahara. Yet in London, with four millions and a quarter of people in it, how many perfect or usable churches are there? And of the few we have, how many are apparent to the wayfarer? Who, for instance, would guess from the repulsive exterior of Westminster Abbey that there are beautiful chapels and a noble nave within, or cloisters without, on the hidden side?

I remember, a dozen years ago, Parson Shuttleworth, of St. Nicholas

Cole Abbey in the city, tried to persuade the city man to spend his mid-day hour of rest in church; guaranteeing him immunity from sermons, prayers and collections, and even making the organ discourse Bach and Wagner, instead of Goss and Jackson. This singular appeal to a people walking in darkness was quite successful: the mid-day hour is kept to this day; but Parson Shuttleworth has to speak for five minutes — by general and insistent request — as Housekeeper, though he has placed a shelf of books in the church for those who would rather read than listen to him or the organ. This was a good thought; for all inspired books should be read either in church or on the eternal hills. St. Nicholas Cole Abbey makes you feel, the moment you enter it, that you are in a rather dingy rococo banqueting-room, built for a city company. Corpulence and comfort are written on every stone of it. Considering that money is dirt cheap now in the city, it is strange that Mr. Shuttleworth cannot get twenty thousand pounds to build a real church. He would, soon enough, if the city knew what a church was. The twenty thousand pounds need not be wasted, either, on an "architect." I was lately walking in a polite suburb of Newcastle, when I saw a church — a *new* church — with, of all things, a detached campanile; at sight of which I could not help exclaiming profanely: "How the deuce did *you* find your way to Newcastle?" So I went in and, after examining the place with much astonishment, addressed myself to the sexton, who happened to be about. I asked him who built the church, and he gave me the name of Mr. Mitchell, who turned out, however, to be the pious founder — a shipbuilder prince, with some just notion of his princely function. But this was not what I wanted to know; so I asked who was the — the word stuck in my throat a little — the architect. He, it appeared, was one Spence. "Was that marble carving in the altar and that mosaic decoration round the chancel part of his design?" said I. "Yes," said the sexton, with a certain surliness as if he suspected me of disapproving. "The ironwork is good," I remarked, to appease him; "who did that?" "Mr. Spence did." "Who carved that wooden figure of St. George?" (the patron saint of the edifice). "Mr. Spence did." "Who painted those four panels in the dado with figures in oil?" "Mr. Spence did: he meant them to be at intervals round the church, but we put them all together by mistake." "Then, perhaps, he designed the stained windows, too?" "Yes, most of 'em." I got so irritated at this — feeling that Spence was going too far — that I remarked sarcastically that no doubt Mr. Spence designed Mr. Mitchell's ships as well, which turned out to be the case as far as the cabins were concerned. Clearly, this Mr. Spence is an artist-craftsman with a vengeance. Many people, I learnt, came to see the church, especially in the first eighteen months; but some of the congregation thought it too ornamental. (At St. Nicholas Cole Abbey, by the way, some of the parishioners objected at first to Mr. Shuttleworth as being too religious). Now, as a matter of fact, this Newcastle church of St. George's is not ornamental enough. Under modern commercial conditions, it is impossible to get from the labour in the building-trade that artistic quality in the actual masonry which makes a good mediæval building independent of applied ornament. Wherever Mr. Spence's artist's hand has passed over the interior surface, the church is beautiful. Why should his hand not pass over every inch of it? It is true, the complete finishing of a large church of the right kind has hardly ever been carried through by one man. Sometimes the man has died: more often the money has failed. But in this instance the man is not dead; and surely money cannot fail in the most fashionable suburb of Newcastle. The chancel with its wonderful mosaics, the baptistry with its ornamented stones, the four painted panels of the dado, are only samples of what the whole interior should and might be. All that cold contract masonry must be redeemed, stone by stone, by the travail of the artist-churchmaker. Nobody, not even an average respectable Sabbath-keeper, will dare to say then that it is overdecorated, however out of place in it he may feel his ugly Sunday clothes and his wife's best bonnet. Howbeit, this church of St. George's in Newcastle proves my point, namely, that churches fit for their proper use can still be built by men who follow the craft of Orcagna instead of the profession of Mr. Pecksniff, and built cheaply, too; for I took the pains to ascertain what this large church cost, and found that £30,000 was well over the mark. For aught I know, there may be dozens of such churches rising in the country; for Mr. Spence's talent, though evidently a rare and delicate one, cannot be unique, and what he has done in his own style other men can do in theirs, if they want to, and are given the means by those who can make money, and are capable of the same want.

There is still one serious obstacle to the use of churches on the very day when most people are best able and most disposed to visit them. I mean, of course, the services. When I was a little boy, I was compelled to go to church on Sunday; and though I escaped from that intolerable bondage before I was ten, it prejudiced me so violently against churchgoing that twenty years elapsed before, in foreign lands and in pursuit of works of art, I became once more a churchgoer. To this day, my flesh creeps when I recall that genteel suburban Irish Protestant church, built by Roman Catholic workmen who would have considered themselves damned had they crossed its threshold afterwards. Every separate stone, every pane of glass, every fillet of ornamental ironwork — half-dog-collar, half-coronet — in that building must have sowed a separate evil passion in my young heart. Yes; all the vulgarity, savagery, and bad blood which has marred my literary work, was certainly laid upon me in that house of Satan! The mere nullity of the building could make no positive impression on me; but what could, and did, were the unnaturally motionless figures of the congregation in their Sunday clothes and bonnets, and their set faces, pale with the malignant rigidity produced by the suppression of all expression. And yet these people were always moving and watching one another by stealth, as convicts communicate with one another. So was I. I had been told to keep my restless little limbs still all through those interminable hours; not to talk; and, above all, to be happy and holy there and glad that I was not a wicked little boy playing in the fields instead of worshipping God. I hypocritically acquiesced; but the state of my conscience may be imagined, especially as I implicitly believed that all the rest of the congregation were perfectly sincere and good. I remember at that time dreaming one night that I was dead and had gone to heaven. The picture of heaven which the efforts of the then Established Church of Ireland had conveyed to my childish imagination was a waiting room with walls of pale sky-coloured tabbinet, and a pew-like bench running all round, except at one corner, where there was a door. I was, somehow, aware that God was in the next room, accessible through that door. I was seated on the bench with my ankles tightly interlaced to prevent my legs dangling, behaving myself with all my might before the grown-up people, who all belonged to the Sunday congregation, and were either sitting on the bench as if at church or else moving solemnly in and out as if there were a dead person in the house. A grimly-handsome lady who usually sat in a corner seat near me in church, and whom I believed to be thoroughly conversant with the arrangements of the Almighty, was to introduce me presently into the next room — a moment which I was supposed to await with joy and enthusiasm. Really, of course, my heart sank like lead within me at the thought; for I felt that my feeble affectation of piety could not impose on Omniscience, and that one glance of that all-searching eye would discover that I had been allowed to come to heaven by mistake. Unfortunately for the interest of this narrative, I awoke, or wandered off into another dream, before the critical moment arrived. But it goes far enough to show that I was by no means an insusceptible subject: indeed, I am sure, from other early experiences of mine, that if I had been turned loose in a real church, and allowed to wander and stare about, or hear noble music there instead of that most accursed Te Deum of Jackson's and a senseless droning of the Old Hundredth, I should never have seized the opportunity of a great evangelical revival, which occurred when I was still in my teens, to begin my literary career with a letter to the Press (which was duly printed), announcing with inflexible materialistic logic, and to the extreme horror of my respectable connections, that I was an atheist. When, later on, I was led to the study of the economic basis of the respectability of that and similar congregations, I was inexpressibly relieved to find that it represented a mere passing phase of industrial confusion, and could never have substantiated its claims to my respect if, as a child, I had been able to bring it to book. To this very day, whenever there is the slightest danger of my being mistaken for a votary of the blue tabbinet waiting-room or a supporter of that morality in which wrong and right, base and noble, evil and good, really mean nothing more than the kitchen and the drawing-room, I hasten to claim honourable exemption, as atheist and socialist, from any such complicity.

When I at last took to church-going again, a kindred difficulty beset me, especially in Roman Catholic countries. In Italy, for instance, churches are used in such a way that priceless pictures become smeared with filthy tallow-soot, and have sometimes to be rescued by the temporal power and placed in national galleries. But worse than this are the innumerable daily services which disturb the truly religious visitor. If these were decently and intelligently conducted by genuine mystics to whom the Mass was no mere rite or miracle, but a real communion, the celebrants might reasonably claim a place in the church as their share of the common human right to its use. But the average Italian priest, personally uncleanly, and with chronic catarrh of the nose and throat, produced and maintained by sleeping and living in frowsy, ill-ventilated rooms, punctuating his gabbled Latin only by expectorative hawking, and making the decent guest sicken and shiver every time the horrible splash of spitten mucus echoes along the vaulting from the marble steps of the altar: this unseemly wretch should be seized and put out, bell, book, candle and all, until he learns to behave himself. The English tourist is often lectured for his inconsiderate behaviour in Italian churches, for walking about during service, talking loudly, thrusting himself rudely between a worshipper and an altar to examine a painting, even for stealing chips of stone and scrawling his name on statues. But as far as the mere disturbance of the services is concerned, and the often very evident disposition of the tourist — especially the experienced tourist — to regard the priest and his congregation as troublesome intruders, a week spent in Italy will convince any unprejudiced person that this is a perfectly reasonable attitude. I have seen inconsiderate British behaviour often enough both in church and out of it. The slow-witted Englishman who refuses to get out of the way of the Host, and looks at the bellringer going before it with "Where the devil are you shoving to?" written in every pucker of his free-born British brow, is a familiar figure to me; but I have never seen any stranger behave so insufferably as the officials of the church habitually do. It is the sacristan who teaches you, when once you are committed to tipping him, not to waste your good manners on the kneeling worshippers who are snatching a moment from their daily round of drudgery and starvation to be comforted by the Blessed Virgin or one of the saints: it is the officiating priest who makes you understand that the congregation are past shocking by any indecency that you would dream of committing, and that the black looks of the congregation are directed at the foreigner and the heretic only, and imply a denial of your right as a human being to your share of the use of the church. That right should be unflinchingly asserted on all proper occasions. I know no contrary right by which the great Catholic churches made for the world by the great church-builders should be monopolised by any sect as against any man who desires to use them. My own faith is clear: I am a resolute Protestant; I believe in the Holy Catholic Church; in the Holy Trinity of Father, Son (or Mother, Daughter) and Spirit; in the Communion of Saints, the Life to Come, the Immaculate Conception, and the everyday reality of Godhead and the Kingdom of Heaven. Also, I believe that salvation depends on redemption from belief in miracles; and I regard St. Athanasius as an irreligious fool — that is, in the only serious sense of the word, a damned fool. I pity the poor neurotic who can say, "Man that is born of a woman hath but a short time to live, and is full of misery," as I pity a maudlin drunkard; and I know that the real religion of to-day was made possible only by the materialistic-physicists and atheist-critics who performed for us the indispensable preliminary operation of purging us thoroughly of the ignorant and vicious superstitions which were thrust down our throats as religion in our helpless childhood. How those who assume that our churches are the private property of their sect would think of this profession of faith of mine I need not describe. But am I, therefore, to be denied access to the place of spiritual recreation which is my inheritance as much as theirs? If, for example, I desire to follow a good old custom by pledging my love to my wife in the church of our parish, why should I be denied due record in the registers unless she submits to have a moment of deep feeling made ridiculous by the reading aloud of the *naïve* impertinences of St. Peter, who, on the subject of Woman, was neither Catholic nor Christian, but a boorish Syrian fisherman. If I want to name a child in the church, the prescribed service may be more touched with the religious spirit — once or twice beautifully touched — but, on the whole, it is time to dismiss our prayerbook as quite rotten with the pessimism of the age which produced it. In spite of the stolen jewels with which it is studded, an age of strength and faith and noble activity can have nothing to do with it: Caliban might have constructed such a ritual out of his own terror of the supernatural, and such fragments of the words of the saints as he could dimly feel some sort of glory in.

My demand will now be understood without any ceremonious formulation of it. No nation, working at the strain we face, can live cleanly without public-houses in which to seek refreshment and recreation. To supply that vital want we have the drinking-shop with its narcotic, stimulant poisons, the conventicle with its brimstone-flavoured hot gospel, and the church. In the church alone can our need be truly met, nor even there save when we leave outside the door the materialisations that help us to believe the incredible, and the intellectualisations that help us to think the unthinkable, completing the refuse-heap of "isms" and creeds with our vain lust for truth and happiness, and going in without thought or belief or prayer or any other vanity, so that the soul, freed from all that crushing lumber, may open all its avenues of life to the holy air of the true Catholic Church.

Socialism for Millionaires

(*Contemporary Review,* London, February 1896, and, unauthorized, in *Eclectic Magazine,* New York, March 1896. Extensively revised in 1901 as Fabian Tract No. 107, and reprinted in Shaw's *Essays in Fabian Socialism,* 1932)

The Sorrows of the Millionaire

The millionaire class, a small but growing one, into which any of us may be flung to-morrow by the accidents of commerce, is perhaps the most neglected in the community. As far as I know, this is the first Tract that has ever been written for millionaires. In the advertisements of the manufactures of the country I find that everything is produced for the million and nothing for the millionaire. Children, boys, youths, "gents," ladies, artizans, professional men, even peers and kings are catered for; but the millionaire's custom is evidently not worth having: there are too few of him. Whilst the poorest have their Rag Fair, a duly organized and busy market in Houndsditch, where you can buy a boot for a penny, you may search the world in vain for the market where the £50 boot, the special dear line of hats at forty guineas, the cloth of gold bicycling suit, and the Cleopatra claret, four pearls to the bottle, can be purchased wholesale. Thus the unfortunate millionaire has the responsibility of prodigious wealth without the possibility of enjoying himself more than any ordinary rich man. Indeed, in many things he cannot enjoy himself more than many poor men do, nor even so much; for a drum-major is better dressed; a trainer's stable-lad often rides a better horse; the first class carriage is shared by office-boys taking their young ladies out for the evening; everybody who goes down to Brighton for Sunday rides in the Pullman car; and of what use is it to be able to pay for a peacock's-brain sandwich when there is nothing to be had but ham or beef? The injustice of this state of things has not been sufficiently considered. A man with an income of £25 a year can multiply his comfort beyond all calculation by doubling his income. A man with £50 a year can at least quadruple his comfort by doubling his income. Probably up to even £250 a year doubled income means doubled comfort. After that the increment of comfort grows less in proportion to the increment of income until a point is reached at which the victim is satiated and even surfeited with everything that money can

391

procure. To expect him to enjoy another hundred thousand pounds because men like money, is exactly as if you were to expect a confectioner's shopboy to enjoy two hours more work a day because boys are fond of sweets. What can the wretched millionaire do that needs a million? Does he want a fleet of yachts, a Rotten Row full of carriages, an army of servants, a whole city of town houses, or a continent for a game preserve? Can he attend more than one theatre in one evening, or wear more than one suit at a time, or digest more meals than his butler? Is it a luxury to have more money to take care of, more begging-letters to read, and to be cut off from those delicious Alnaschar* dreams in which the poor man, sitting down to consider what he will do in the always possible event of some unknown relative leaving him a fortune, forgets his privation? And yet there is no sympathy for this hidden sorrow of plutocracy. The poor alone are pitied. Societies spring up in all directions to relieve all sorts of comparatively happy people, from discharged prisoners in the first rapture of their regained liberty to children revelling in the luxury of an unlimited appetite; but no hand is stretched out to the millionaire, except to beg. In all our dealings with him lies implicit the delusion that *he* has nothing to complain of, and that he ought to be ashamed of rolling in wealth whilst others are starving.

Millionaires Less Than Ever Able to Spend Their Money on Themselves

And please remember that his plight is getting worse and worse with the advance of civilization. The capital, the energy, the artistic genius that used to train themselves for the supply of beautiful things to rich men, now turn to supply the needs of the gigantic proletariats of modern times. It is more profitable to add an iron-mongery department to a Westbourne Grove emporium than it was to be a Florentine armorer in the fifteenth century. The very millionaire himself, when he becomes a railway director, is forced to turn his back on his own class, and admit that it is the third-class traffic that pays. If he takes shares in a hotel, he learns that it is safer, as a matter of commercial policy, to turn a lord and his retinue out of doors than to disoblige a commercial traveller or a bicyclist in the smallest reasonable particular. He cannot get his coat made to fit him without troublesome tryings-on and alterations unless he goes to the cheap ready-money tailors, who monopolize all the really expert cutters because their suits must fit infallibly at the first attempt if the low prices are to be made pay. The old-fashioned tradesman, servile to the great man and insolent to the earner of weekly

* A beggar in the *Arabian Nights,* who indulged in visions of riches and grandeur — Ed.

wages, is now beaten in the race by the universal provider, who attends more carefully to the fourpenny and tenpenny customers than to the mammoth shipbuilder's wife sailing in to order three grand pianos and four French governesses. ' In short, the shops where Dives is expected and counted on are only to be found now in a few special trades, which touch a man's life but seldom. For everyday purposes the customer who wants more than other people is as unwelcome and as little worth attending to as the customer who wants less than other people. The millionaire can have the best of everything in the market; but this leaves him no better off than the modest possessor of £5,000 a year. There is only one thing that he can still order on a scale of special and recklessly expensive pomp, and that is his funeral. Even this melancholy outlet will probably soon be closed. Huge joint-stock interment and cremation companies will refuse to depart to any great extent from their routine of Class I., Class II., and so on, just as a tramway company would refuse to undertake a Lord Mayor's Show. The custom of the great masses will rule the market so completely that the millionaire, already forced to live nine-tenths of his life as other men do, will be forced into line as to the other tenth also.

Why Millionaires Must Not Leave Too Much to Their Families

To be a millionaire, then, is to have more money than you can possibly spend on yourself, and to suffer daily from the inconsiderateness of those persons to whom such a condition appears one of utter content. What, then, is the millionaire to do with his surplus funds? The usual reply is, provide for his children and give alms. Now these two resources, as usually understood, are exactly the same thing, and a very mischievous thing too. From the point of view of society, it does not matter a straw whether the person relieved of the necessity of working for his living by a millionaire's bounty is his son, his daughter's husband, or merely a casual beggar. The millionaire's private feelings may be more highly gratified in the former cases; but the mischief to society and to the recipient is the same. If you want to spoil a young man's career, there is no method surer than that of presenting him with what is called "an independence," meaning an abject and total dependence on the labor of others. Anybody who has watched the world intelligently enough to compare the average man of independent means when he has just finished his work at the university, with the same man twenty years later, following a routine of fashion compared to which the round of a postman is a whirl of excitement, and the beat of a policeman a chapter of romance, must have sometimes said to himself that it would have been better for the man if his father had spent every penny of his money, or thrown it into the Thames.

Parasites on Property

In Ireland, the absentee landlord is bitterly reproached for not administering his estate in person. It is pointed out truly enough that the absentee is a pure parasite upon the industry of his country. The indispensable minimum of attention to his estate is paid by his agent or solicitor, whose resistance to his purely parasitic activity is fortified by the fact that the estate usually belongs mostly to the mortgagees, and that the nominal landlord is so ignorant of his own affairs that he can do nothing but send begging letters to the agent. On these estates generations of peasants (and agents) live hard but bearable lives; whilst off them generations of ladies and gentlemen of good breeding and natural capacity are corrupted in drifters, wasters, drinkers, waiters-for-dead-men's-shoes, poor relations, and social wreckage of all sorts, living aimless lives, and often dying squalid and tragic deaths. But is there any country in the world in which this same wreckage does not occur? The typical modern proprietor is not an Irish squire but a cosmopolitan shareholder; and the shareholder is an absentee as a matter of course. If his property is all the better managed for that, he himself is all the more completely reduced to the condition of a mere parasite upon it; and he is just as likely as the Irish absentee to become a centre of demoralization to his family connections. Every millionaire who leaves all his millions to his family in the ordinary course exposes his innocent descendants to this risk without securing them any advantage that they could not win more effectually and happily by their own activity, backed by a fair start in life. Formerly this consideration had no weight with parents, because working for money was considered disgraceful to a gentleman, as it is still, in our more belated circles, to a lady. In all the professions we have survivals of old pretences — the rudimentary pocket on the back of a barrister's gown is an example — by which the practitioner used to fob his fee without admitting that his services were for sale. Most people alive today, of middle age and upward, are more or less touched with superstitions that need no longer be reckoned with by or on behalf of young men. Such, for instance, as that the line which divides wholesale from retail trade is also a line marking a step in social position; or that there is something incongruous in a lord charging a shilling a head for admission to his castle and gardens, or opening a shop for milk, game, and farm produce; or that a merchant's son who obtains a commission in a smart regiment is guilty of an act of ridiculous presumption.

Dignity of Labor

Even the prejudice against manual labor is vanishing. In the artistic professions something like a worship of it was inaugurated when Ruskin took his Oxford class out of doors and set them to make roads. It is now a good many years since Dickens, when visiting a prison, encountered Wainewright the poisoner, and heard that gentleman vindicate his gentility by demanding of his fellow prisoner (a bricklayer, if I remember aright) whether he had ever condescended to clean out the cell, or handle the broom, or, in short, do any work whatever for himself that he could put on his companion. The bricklayer, proud of having so distinguished a cell mate, eagerly gave the required testimony. In the great Irish agitation against coercion in Ireland during Mr. Balfour's secretaryship, an attempt was made to add to the sensation by pointing to the spectacle of Irish political prisoners, presumably gentlemen, suffering the indignity of having to do housemaid's work in cleaning their cells. Who cared? It would be easy to multiply instances of the change of public opinion for the better in this direction. But there is no need to pile up evidence. It will be quite willingly admitted that the father who throws his son on his own exertions, after equipping him fully with education and a reasonable capital, no longer degrades him, spoils his chance of a well-bred wife, and forfeits the caste of the family, but, on the contrary, solidifies his character and widens his prospects, professional, mercantile, political, and matrimonial. Besides, public opinion, growing continually stronger against drones in the hive, begins to threaten, and even to execute, a differentiation of taxation against unearned incomes; so that the man who, in spite of the protests of parental wisdom and good citizenship, devotes great resources to the enrichment and probable demoralization of remote descendants for whose merit the community has no guarantee, does so at the risk of having his aim finally defeated by the income-tax collector. We, therefore, have the intelligent and public-spirited millionaire cut off from his old resource of "founding a family." All that his children can now require of him, all that society expects him to give them, all that is good for themselves, is a first-rate equipment, not an "independence."

And there are millionaires who have no children.

Why Almsgiving is a Waste of Money

The extremities to which the millionaire is reduced by this closing up of old channels of bequest are such that he sometimes leaves huge sums to bodies of trustees "to do good with," a plan as mischievous as it is resourceless; for what can the trustees do but timidly dribble the fund away on charities of one kind or another? Now I am loth to revive the harsh strains of the Gradgrind political economy: indeed, I would, if I could, place in every Board School a copy of Mr. [G. F.] Watts' picture of a sheet profiled by the outline of a man lying dead underneath it, with the inscription above, "What I saved, I lost: what I spent, I had: what I gave, I have." But woe to the man who takes from another what he can provide for himself; and woe also to the giver! There is no getting over the fact that the moment an attempt is made to organize almsgiving by entrusting the funds to a permanent body of experts, it is invariably discovered that beggars are perfectly genuine persons: that is to say, not "deserving poor," but people who have discovered that it is possible to live by simply impudently asking for what they want until they get it, which is the essence of beggary. The permanent body of experts, illogically instructed to apply their funds to the cases of the deserving poor only, soon become a mere police body for the frustration of true begging, and consequently of true almsgiving. Finally, their experience in a pursuit to which they were originally led by natural benevolence lands them in an almost maniacal individualism and an abhorrence of ordinary "charity" as one of the worst of social crimes. This may not be an amiable attitude; but no reasonable person can fail to be impressed by the certainty with which it seems to be produced by a practical acquaintance with the social reactions of mendicity and benevolence.

"The Deserving Poor"

Of course, this difficulty is partly created by the "deserving poor" theory. I remember once, at a time when I made daily use of the reading-room of the British Museum — a magnificent communistic institution — I gave a £2 copying job to a man whose respectable poverty would have moved a heart of stone: an ex-schoolmaster, whose qualifications were out of date, and who, through no particular fault of his own, had drifted at last into the reading-room as less literate men drifted into Salvation Army Shelters. He was a sober, well-spoken, well-conducted, altogether unobjectionable man, really fond of reading, and eminently eligible for a good turn of the kind I did him. His first step in the matter was to obtain from me an advance of five shillings; his next, to sublet the commission to another person in similar circumstances for one pound fifteen, and so get it entirely off his mind and return to his favorite books. This second, or rather, third party, however, required an advance from my acquaintance of one-and-sixpence to buy paper, having obtained which, he handed over the contract to a fourth party, who was willing to do it for one pound thirteen and sixpence. Speculation raged for a day or two as the job was passed on; and it reached bottom at last in the hands of the least competent and least sober copyist in the room, who actually did the work for five shillings, and borrowed endless sixpences from me from that time to the day of her death, which each sixpence probably accelerated to the extent of fourpence, and staved off to the extent of twopence. She was not a deserving person: if she had been she would have come to no such extremity. Her claims to compassion were that she could not be depended upon, could not resist the temptation to drink, could not bring herself to do her work carefully, and was therefore at a miserable disadvantage in the world: a disadvantage exactly similar to that suffered by the blind, the deaf, the maimed, the mad, or any other victims of imperfect or injured faculty. I learnt from her that she had once been recommended to the officials of the Charity Organization Society; but they, on inquiring into her case, had refused to help her because she was "undeserving," by which they meant that she was incapable of helping herself. Here was surely some confusion of ideas. She was very angry with the Society, and not unreasonably so; for she knew that their funds were largely subscribed by people who regarded them as ministers of pity to the poor and downcast. On the other hand, these people themselves had absurdly limited the application of their bounty to sober, honest, respectable persons: that is to say, to the persons least likely to want it, and alone able to be demoralized by it. An intelligent millionaire, if tempted to indulge himself by playing the almsgiving philanthropist (to the great danger of his own character) would earmark his gift for the use of the utterly worthless, the hopelessly, incorrigibly lazy, idle, easy-going, good-for-nothing. Only, such a policy would soon exhaust the resources of even a billionaire. It would convince the most sentimental of almsgivers that it is economically impossible to be kind to beggars. It is possible to treat them humanely, which means that they can be enslaved, brought under discipline, and forced to perform a minimum of work as gently as the nature of the process and their own intense objection to it permit; but there is no satisfaction for the compassionate instincts to be got out of that. It is a public duty, like the enforcement of sanitation, and should be undertaken by the public. Privately supported colonies of the unemployed, like that of the Salvation Army at Hadleigh, are only the experiments on which an inevitable extension of the Poor Law will have to be based. What is urgently needed at present by the poor is the humanization of the Poor Law, an end which is retarded by all attempts to supplant it by private benevolence. Take, for example, the hard case of the aged poor, who are not beggars at all, but veterans of industry who have in most cases earned an honorable pension (which we are dishonest enough to grudge them) by a lifetime of appalling drudgery. We have to deal with at least 350,000 of them every year. Very little can be done by private efforts to rescue these unfortunate people from the barbarity of the ratepayers by building a few almshouses here and there. But a great deal can be done by arousing the public conscience and voting for reasonably humane and enlightened persons at elections of guardians. The guardians of the West Derby (Liverpool) Union, instead of imprisoning aged couples separately and miserably in their workhouse, put them into furnished cottages, where, provided they keep them neat and clean, they are no more interfered with than if they were in a private almshouse. The difference in happiness, comfort, and self-respect, between the cottage and the workhouse, is enormous: the difference in cost is less than two shillings a week per pair. If a millionaire must build almshouses, he had better do it by offering to defray the cost of a set of cottages on condition that the guardians adopt the West Derby system. This, of course, is pauperizing the ratepayer; but the average ratepayer is a quite shameless creature, loud in his outcry against the immorality of pauperizing any one at his expense, but abject in his adulation of the rich man who will pauperize him by those subscriptions to necessary public institutions which act as subsidies in relief of the rates.

Never Endow Hospitals

Hospitals are the pet resource of the rich man whose money is burning a hole in his pockets. Here, however, the verdict of sound social economy is emphatic. Never give a farthing to an ordinary hospital. An experimental hospital is a different thing: a millionaire who is interested in proving that the use of drugs, of animal food, of alcohol, of the knife in cancer, or the like, can be and should be dispensed with, may endow a temporary hospital for that purpose; but in the charitable hospital, private endowment and private management mean not only the pauperization of the ratepayer, but irresponsibility, waste and extravagance checked by spasmodic stinginess, favoritism, almost unbridled licence for experiments on patients by scientifically enthusiastic doctors, and a system of begging for letters of admission which would be denounced as intolerable if it were part of the red tape of a public body. A safe rule for the millionaire is never to do anything for the public, any more than for an individual, that the public will do (because it must) for itself without his intervention. The provision of proper hospital accommodation is pre-eminently one of these things. Already more than a third of London's hospital accommodation is provided by the ratepayers. In Warrington the hospital rate, which was 2d. in the pound in 1887–8, rose in five years to 1s. 2d. If a billionaire had interposed to take this increase on his own shoulders, he would have been simply wasting money for which better uses were waiting, demoralizing his neighbors, and forestalling good hospitals by bad ones. Our present cadging hospital system will soon go the way of the old Poor Law; and no invalid will be a penny the worse.

Be Careful in Endowing Education

Education comes next to hospitals in the popular imagination as a thoroughly respectable mark for endowments. But it is open to the same objections. The privately endowed elementary school is inferior to the rate-supported one, and is consequently nothing but a catchpit in which children, on the way to their public school, are caught and condemned to an inferior education in inferior buildings under sectarian management. University education is another matter. But whilst it is easy to found colleges and scholarships, it is impossible to confine their benefits to those who are unable to pay for them. Besides, it is beginning to be remarked that university men, as a class, are specially ignorant and misinformed. The practical identity of the governing class with the university class in England has produced a quite peculiar sort of stupidity in English policy, the masterstrokes of which are so very frequently nothing but class solecisms that even the most crudely democratic legislatures of the Colonies and the most corrupt lobbies of the United States are superior to ours in directness and promptitude, sense of social proportion, and knowledge of contemporary realities. An intelligent millionaire, unless he is frankly an enemy of the human race, will do nothing to extend the method of caste initiation practised under the mask of education at Oxford and Cambridge. Experiments in educational method, and new subjects of technical education, such, for instance, as political science considered as part of the technical education of the citizen (who is now such a disastrously bungling amateur in his all-important political capacity as voter by grace of modern democracy); or economics, statistics, and industrial history, treated as part of the technical commercial education of the wielder of modern capitals and his officials: these, abhorrent to university dons and outside the scope of public elementary education, are the departments in which the millionaire interested in education can make his gold fruitful. Help nothing that is already on its legs is not a bad rule in this and other matters. It is the struggles of society to adapt itself to the new conditions which every decade of modern industrial development springs on us that need help. The old institutions, with their obsolete routine, and their lazy denials and obstructions in the interests of that routine, are but too well supported already.

Endowing Societies

The objection to supplanting public machinery by private does not apply to private action to set public machinery in motion. Take, for example, the National Society for the Prevention of Cruelty to Children. If that society were to undertake the punishment of cruel parents by building private prisons and establishing private tribunals, even the most thoughtless subscriber to private charities and hospitals would shake his head and button up his pocket, knowing that there are public laws and public prisons and tribunals to do the work, and that they alone should be trusted with such functions. But here the public machinery requires the initiative of an aggrieved person to set it in motion; and when the aggrieved person is a child, and its "next friend" the aggressor, the machinery does not get started. Under such circumstances, Mr. Waugh's society, by stepping in and taking the child's part, does a great deal of good; and this, observe, not by supplanting the State, or competing with it, but by co-operating with it and compelling it to do its duty. Generally speaking, all societies which are of the nature of Vigilance Committees are likely to be useful. The odium whch attaches to the name came from the old-fashioned American Vigilance Committee, which, in the true spirit of private enterprise, not only detected offenders, but lynched them on its own responsibility. We have certain State vigilance officers: sanitary inspectors, School Board visitors, a Public Prosecutor (of a sort), the Queen's Proctor, and others. The only one of these who is an unmitigated public nuisance is the censor of the theatre, who, instead of merely having power to hale the author of an obnoxious play before a public tribunal, has power to sentence him to suppression and execute him with his own hands and on his own responsibility, with the result that our drama is more corrupt, silly, and indecent than any other department of fine art, and our unfortunate censor more timid and helpless than any other official. His case shows the distinction which it is essential to observe in vigilance work. But though we have an official to prevent Tolstoy's plays from being performed, we have no official to prevent people from stealing public land and stopping up public footpaths. The millionaire who gives money to "Days in the Country" for city children, and will not help Commons Preservation Societies and the like to keep the country open for them, is unworthy of his millions.

All these considerations point in the same direction. The intelligent millionaire need not hesitate to subsidize any vigilance society or reform society that is ably conducted, and that recognizes the fact that it is not going to reform the world, but only, at best, to persuade the world to take its ideas into consideration in reforming itself. Subject to these conditions, it matters little whether the millionaire agrees with the society or not. No individual or society can possibly be absolutely and completely right; nor can any view or theory be so stated as to comprise the whole truth and nothing but the truth. A millionaire who will not subsidize forces that are capable of a mischievous application will subsidize nothing at all. Such justice as we attain in our criminal courts is the outcome of a vehemently partial prosecution and defence; and all parliamentary sanity is the outcome of a conflict of views. For instance, if we try to figure to ourselves a forcible reconstruction of society on lines rigidly deduced either from the Manchester School or from State Socialism we are at a loss to decide which of the two would be the more intolerable and disastrous. Yet who hesitates on that account, if such matters interest him, to back up the Fabian Society on the one hand, or the Personal Rights Association on the other, according to his bias? Our whole theory of freedom of speech and opinion for all citizens, rests, not on the assumption that everybody is right, but on the certainty that everybody is wrong on some point on which somebody else is right, so that there is a public danger in allowing anybody to go unheard. Therefore, any propagandist society which knows how to handle money intelligently and which is making a contribution to current thought, whether Christian or Pagan, Liberal or Conservative, Socialist or Individualist, scientific or humanitarian, physical or metaphysical, seems to me an excellent mark for a millionaire's spare money.

Yet after all, mere societies are good marks for anybody's spare money. Most of them may be left to the ordinary guinea subscriber; and though millionaires are such inveterate subscribers and donors that I dare not leave the societies out of account, I confess I despise a millionaire who dribbles his money away in fifties and hundreds, thereby reducing himself to the level of a mere crowd of ordinary men, instead of planking down sums that only a millionaire can. My idea of a millionaire is a man who never gives less than ten thousand pounds, ear-marked for the purchase of something of the best quality costing not a penny less than that amount. The millionaire should ask himself what is his favorite subject? Has it a school, with scholarships for the endowment of research and the attraction of rising talent? Has it a library, or a museum? If not, then he has an opening at once for his ten thousand or hundred thousand.

Starting Snowballs

There is always something fascinating to the imagination of a very poor man in the notion of leaving a million or so to accumulate at compound interest for a few centuries, and then descend in fabulous riches on some remote descendant and make a Monte Cristo of him. Now, even if there were likely to be any particular point in being Monte Cristo after a couple of hundred years further social and industrial development, a modern millionaire, for the reasons already stated, should be the last person in the world to be much impressed by it. Still, the underlying idea of keeping a great money force together, multiplying it, and finally working a miracle with it, is a tempting one. Here is a recent example, quoted from a local paper:

> "The gift of a farm to the Parish Council of St. Bees by the Rev. Mr. Pagan, of Shadforth, Durham, is accompanied by some peculiar conditions. The farm is 33a. 3r. 2p. in extent, and is valued at £1,098. The rent of the farm is to be allowed to accumulate, with two reservations. Should the grantor ever require it, the council may be called upon during his lifetime to pay him from time to time out of the accumulated investments any amounts not exceeding £1,098. Not more than £10 may be spent in charity, *but not in relief of the rates.* The balance is to be invested in land and houses until all the land and houses in the parish have been secured by the parish council. When that is accomplished, the sum of £1,098 may be handed over to some adjacent parish, which shall deal with the gift similarly to St. Bees."

Beware of the Ratepayer and the Landlord

In the above bequest, we have a remarkable combination of practical sagacity and colossal revolutionary visionariness. Mr. Pagan sets a thousand pound snowball rolling in such a way as to nationalize the land parish by parish until the revolution is complete. Observe — and copy — his clause, "not in relief of the rates." Let the millionaire never forget that the ratepayer is always lying in wait to malversate public money to the saving of his own pocket. Possibly the millionaire may sympathize with him, and say that he wishes to relieve him. But in the first place a millionaire should never sympathize with anybody: his destiny is too high for such petty self-indulgence; and in the second, you cannot relieve the ratepayer by reducing, or even abolishing, his rates, since freeing a house of rates simply raises the rent. The millionaire might as well leave his money direct to the landlords at once. In fact, the ratepayer is only a foolish catspaw for the landlord, who is the great eater-up of public bequests. At Tonbridge, Bedford, and certain other places, pious founders have endowed the schools so splendidly that education is nobly cheap there. But rents are equivalently high; so that the landlords reap the whole pecuniary value of the endowment. The remedy, however, is to follow the example of the Tonbridge and Bedford founders instead of avoiding it. If every centre of population were educationally endowed with equal liberality, the advantage of

Bedford would cease to be a *differential* one; *and it is only advantages which are both differential and pecuniarily realizable by the individual citizens that produce rent.* Meanwhile, the case points to another form of the general rule above deduced for the guidance of millionaires: namely, that bequests to the public should be for the provision of luxuries, never of necessaries. We must provide necessaries for ourselves; and their gratuitous provision in any town at present constitutes a pecuniarily realizable differential advantage in favor of living in that town. Now, a luxury is something that we not have, and consequently will not pay for except with spare or waste money. Properly speaking, therefore, it is something that we will not pay for at all. And yet nothing is more vitally right than the attitude of the French gentleman who said: "Give me the luxuries of life, and I will do without the necessaries."* For example, the British Library of Political Science is prodigiously more important to our well-being than a thousand new charitable soup-kitchens; but as ordinary people do not care a rap about it, it does not raise the rent of even students' lodgings in London by a farthing. But suppose a misguided billionaire, instead of founding an institution of this type, were to take on himself the cost of paving and lighting some London parish, and set on foot a free supply of bread and milk! All that would happen would be that the competition for houses and shops in that parish would rage until it had brought rents up to a point at which there would be no advantage in living in it more than in any other parish. Even parks and open spaces raise rents in London, though, strange to say, London statues do not diminish them. Here, then, is the simple formula for the public benefactor. Never give the people anything they want: give them something they ought to want and dont.

Create New Needs: the Old Ones Will Take Care of Themselves

Thus we find at the end of it all, appositely enough, that the great work of the millionaire, whose tragedy is that he has not needs enough for his means, is to create needs. The man who makes the luxury of yesterday the need of to-morrow is as great a benefactor as the man who makes two ears of wheat grow where one grew before. John Ruskin set a wise example in this respect to our rich men. He published his accounts with the public, and shewed that he had taken no more for himself than fair pay for his work of giving Sheffield a valuable museum, which it does not want and would cheerfully sell for a fortnight's

---

* Oliver Wendell Holmes, in *The Autocrat of the Breakfast-Table*, credits this aphorism to the American historian John Lothrop Motley — Ed.

holiday with free beer if it could. Was not that better than wasting it heartlessly and stupidly on beggars, on able-bodied relatives, on rate-payers, on landlords, and all the rest of our social absorbents? He has created energy instead of dissipating it, and created it in the only funda-mentally possible way, by creating fresh needs. His example shows what can be done by a rich expert in fine art; and if millions could bring such expertness to their possessor, I should have discoursed above of the beautification of cities, the endowment of a standard orchestra and theatre in every centre of our population, and the building of a wholesome, sincere, decent house for Parliament to meet in (noble legislation is impossible in the present monstrosity) as an example for parish halls and town halls all through the country, with many other things of the same order. But these matters appeal only to a religious and artistic faculty which cannot be depended on in millionaires — which, indeed, have a very distinct tendency to prevent their possessor from ever becoming even a thousandaire, if I may be permitted that equally justifiable word. The typical modern millionaire knows more about life than about art; and what he should know better than anyone else, if he has any reflective power, is that men do not succeed nowadays in industrial life by sticking to the methods and views of their grand-fathers. And yet not until a method or a view has attained a grand-fatherly age is it possible to get it officially recognized and taught in an old country like ours. In bringing industrial education up to date, the millionaire should be on his own ground. Experiment, propaganda, exploration, discovery, political and industrial information: take care of these, and the pictures and statues, the churches and hospitals, will take care of themselves.

Conscience Money and Ransom

I must not conclude without intimating my knowledge of the fact that most of the money given by rich people in "charity" is made up of conscience money, "ransom," political bribery, and bids for titles. The traffic in hospital subscriptions in the name of Royalty fulfils ex-actly the same function in modern society as Texel's traffic in indul-gences in the name of the Pope did before the Reformation. One buys moral credit by signing a cheque, which is easier than turning a prayer wheel. I am aware, further, that we often give to public objects money that we should devote to raising wages among our own employees or substituting three eight-hour shifts for two twelve-hour ones. But when a millionaire does not really care whether his money does good or not, provided he finds his conscience eased and his social status improved by giving it away, it is useless for me to argue with him. I mention him only as a warning to the better sort of donors that the mere disbursement of large sums of money must be counted as a distinctly suspicious circumstance in estimating personal character. Money is worth nothing to the man who has more than enough; and the wisdom with which it is spent is the sole social justification for leaving him in possession of it.

The Illusions of Socialism

(*The Home Journal,* New York, 21 and 28 October 1896. Reprinted in *Forecasts of the Coming Century,* ed. Edward Carpenter, London, 1897, and in an American limited edition of this work, under the title *Hand and Brain,* East Aurora, N.Y., 1898)

Do not suppose that I am going to write about the illusions of Socialism with the notion of saving anyone from them. Take from the activity of mankind that part of it which consists in the pursuit of illusions, and you take out the world's mainspring. Do not suppose, either, that the pursuit of illusions is the vain pursuit of nothing: on the contrary, there can no more be an illusion without a reality than a shadow without an object. Only, men are for the most part so constituted that realities repel, and illusions attract them. To take the simple instance much insisted on by Schopenhauer, young men and young women do not attract each other as they really are. The young man will not marry the young woman until he is persuaded that she is an angel, with whom life will be ecstasy; nor will she marry him until she believes him to be a hero. Under the spell of this illusion, they marry in haste; but it does not at all follow that they repent at leisure. If that were so, their married friends would warn them against marriage instead of encouraging them in it; and widows and widowers would not marry again, as they generally do when they can. The pair find one another out, it is true; but if the union is at all a fortunate one, the disillusion consists in the encouraging discovery that one real woman, faults and all, is worth a dozen angels, and, similarly, one real man, follies and all, worth all the heroes ever imagined. Consequently, these two dupes of a ridiculous illusion, instead of finding themselves cheated and disappointed, get more than they bargained for, and breed new generations for the world as well; and that is why they allow their own sons and daughters to pursue the same illusion when their turn comes.

Now, therefore, if I say flatly that Socialism as it appears to ninety-nine out of every hundred of the ardent young Socialists who will read this book, is an illusion, I do not say that there is no reality behind the illusion, nor that the reality will not be much better than the illusion. Only, I do say, very emphatically, that if the Socialist future were pre-

406

sented in its reality to those who are devoting all the energy they have to spare after their day's work, and all the enthusiasm of which they are capable, to "the Cause," many of them would not lift a finger for it, and would even disparage and loathe it as a miserably prosaic "bourgeois" development and extension of the middle class respectability of to-day. When any part of Socialism presents itself in the raw reality of a concrete proposal, capable of being adopted by a real Government, and carried out by a real Executive, the professed Socialists are the last people in the country who can be depended on to support it. At best, they will disparage it as "a palliative," and assure the public that it will do no good unless the capitalist system is entirely abolished as well. At worst, they will violently denounce it, and brand its advocates as frauds, traitors, and so on. This natural antagonism between the enthusiasts who conceive Socialism and the statesmen who have to reduce it to legislative and administrative measures, is inevitable, and must be put up with. But it need not be put up with silently. Every man, enthusiast or realist, has more or less power of self-criticism; and the more he is reasoned with, the more reasonable he is likely to be in his attitude.

And here the clever and attentive reader will say, "Aha! so you *are* going to try to reason away my illusions after all?" Well, no doubt I am; but there will be enough of them left when I am done to carry on propaganda with; so do not be alarmed.

First, let me carefully insist on the fact that the cheerful view I have put forward of illusions as useful incentives to men to strive after still better realities, is not true of all illusions. If a man sets his heart on being a millionaire, or a woman on becoming the spouse of Christ, and attaining to eternal beatitude by living a nun and dying a saint, there is not the smallest likelihood that the results will be worth exchanging for the lot of a decent railway porter or factory girl. Similarly, if a Socialist is merely a man crying out for the millennium because he wants unearned happiness for himself and the world, not only will he not get it, but he will be just as dissatisfied with what he will get as with his present condition. There are foolish illusions as well as wise ones; and a man may be opposed to our existing social system because he is not good enough for it just as easily as because it is not good enough for him.

Illusions are of two kinds, flattering ones and necessary ones. (For that matter, they are of two million kinds; but I am only concerned here with these two.) Flattering illusions nerve us to strive for things we do not know how to value in their naked reality, and reconcile us to the discomfort of our lot or to inevitable actions which are against our consciences. The enthusiasm of the average Conservative or Liberal for his party and its leader is excited, not by facts, but by the illusion that his leader is a transcendently great statesman, and his party the champion of all the great reforms, and the opponent of all the mischievous innovations and reactions, which have occurred in the political history of the century. When, as a civilized nation, we dispossess and destroy an uncivilized one, a proceeding which, though often quite proper and unavoidable, would be plain robbery and murder between one civilized citizen and another, we invest it with the illusion of military glory, empire, patriotism, the spread of enlightenment, and so on. When a laborer boasts of being a free Englishman, and declares that he will not stand any nonsense from the German Emperor, or that he would like to see anyone lay a finger on the English Throne or the English Church, he is reconciling himself to his real slavery by the illusion of "Rule Britannia."

The foolishest of the flattering illusions is the common one by which men conceive themselves as morally superior to those with whom they differ in opinion. A Socialist who thinks that the opinions of Mr. Gladstone on Socialism are unsound and his own sound, is within his rights; but a Socialist who thinks that his opinions are virtuous and Mr. Gladstone's vicious, violates the first rule of morals and manners in a Democratic country: namely, that you must not treat your political opponent as a moral delinquent. Yet this conceited illusion, it appears, is indispensable in political organization at present. A speech by one of our eminent party leaders usually takes the form of an explosion of virtuous indignation at the proceedings of his opponent. Mr. Chamberlain lectures Sir William Harcourt; Sir William Harcourt lectures Mr. Balfour; Mr. Balfour lectures Mr. Morley; Mr. Morley lectures Lord Salisbury, and so on. The same thing occurs, only more narrowly and virulently, between the Church party and the Non-conformists, and the Protestants and Roman Catholics in Ireland; whilst the Socialists, I regret to say, usually outdo all the other factions in their habitual assumption that their opponents — typified as "the capitalist" — are robbers, rogues, liars, and hypocrites, without a redeeming trait in their characters. Labour is commonly described by them as crucified between two thieves, a fancy picture which implies, not only the villainy of the landlord and capitalist, but the martyred sinlessness of the Socialist, who is represented (by himself) as standing to his opponents in the relation of good to evil. Now, this is an exceedingly flattering illusion. Unfortunately, it is a necessary illusion too, and therefore cannot be exorcised by a mere genteel deprecation of its uncharitableness, folly, and bad manners.

What, then, is a necessary illusion? It is the guise in which reality must be presented before it can rouse a man's interest, or hold his attention, or even be consciously apprehended by him at all. The ordinary man can be depended on to like and dislike, to admire and despise, to court life and shun death; and these impulses of his will set him thinking and working to benefit and to injure, to give and to grab, to create and destroy, to produce and consume, to maintain and demolish, with sufficient energy and interest to produce civilization as we now have it. But if you present some problem to him which appeals to none of his passions — say a purely mathematical one — you will find great difficulty in making him understand it. He is not sufficiently interested in it to make the effort, even when he has been forced for years to acquire some practice and skill in such efforts as a schoolboy and university graduate. He only devotes himself to dispassionate thought under the compulsion of having to earn his livelihood, and then only when his training, his circumstances, and his capacity make daily work at science or philosophy less irksome to him, on the whole, than business or manual labour. Take an average skipper for example. He will master just as much science as is necessary to qualify him to obtain the indispensable Board of Trade certificates in scientific navigation. But ask him to take a gratuitous interest in science, like that of Galileo or Newton, and you will ask in vain. Mathematics, economics, physics, metaphysics, and so forth, are to him what he calls "dry subjects," which means, practically, that he will not study them unless he is paid, and not then, even, if he can get his living in any more congenial way. But he will, without any payment or external compulsion, buy and read story books or sermons, and go to the theatre or to religious services at his own expense. He is easily, willingly, pleasurably susceptible to art and religion, which appeal either to his passions and emotions, or to his direct physical sense of beauty of form, sound or color; but to science he is refractory and reluctant.

Science, accordingly, never appeals successfully to the people without disguising itself. It must either bribe them by promising to increase their wealth, prolong their lives, and cure their diseases without interfering with their unhealthy habits; or else it must excite their romantic love of adventures and marvels by voyages in search of the pole, explorations of hidden continents, or a parade of billions and trillions of miles of interstellar space. Such devices for interesting the public are called "the popularization of science," and are privately ridiculed by scientific men (exactly as statesmen privately ridicule their own electioneering speeches), who only tolerate them to obtain the recognition and endowments necessary for their work. If Newton were alive now, he would be much less popular as "a man of science" than Mr. Edison, the American inventor; and even Mr. Edison is not popular as an inventor, but as a magician.

But do not, merely for the sake of argument, run away with the idea that the human race is divided into a few scientific Newtons, and Keplers, and Darwins, and a great many wholly unscientific Smiths and Robinsons. Newton's intellect was so powerful that he worked gratuitously at the mathematical theory of fluxions to exercise it, much as a man of great muscular power will work gratuitously at gymnastics and record breaking. But though every man is not a Newton any more than an athletic champion, every man has a certain degree of intellectual power, just as he has a certain degree of muscular power. If his daily work does not use up all his muscular power, he describes his occupation as "sedentary," and works off the surplus by "taking exercise" in the evening. If it does not use up all his mental power, he amuses himself with puzzles, or plays games of skill, or reads treatises.

Now please consider very attentively the fact that the intellect cannot prompt its own actions, any more than the muscles can. When a man kisses a woman, the action is a purely muscular one; yet everyone knows that it never takes place until the man's purpose is formed by his feelings and his imagination. The athlete is not an automatic muscular machine: he is prompted by vanity, pugnacity, emulation, and all sorts of instincts. The same thing is true of the intellect. It does not work out fluxions or play chess of its own accord: it must be directed to that particular form of activity by some purpose or fancy in its possessor; and that purpose can only be roused by an appeal to his feelings and imagination. The only initiative power enjoyed by the intellect or the muscles is that of making a man feel restless in mind or body until he has exercised them sufficiently in some way. Hence it used to be said, in the words of a once popular corrupter [Isaac Watts] of children's minds, that

> Satan will find mischief still
> For idle hands to do.

If this gentleman had believed in his god as devoutly as he believed in his devil, he would not have taught, in the face of the infinite benefits conferred on him in common with the rest of the world by voluntary work, that mischief comes any more or less naturally to men than suicide does.

Thus we see that though the popularization of science must be effected by presenting it as a story or drama to the feelings and the imagination, the result of the interest thus aroused will be a certain degree of scientific curiosity about it, especially among people whose daily work consists of some sedentary routine which leaves their minds only half exercised, and does not, like the heavier forms of manual labor, so exhaust the energies of the worker that the least effort to think sends him to sleep at once. Hence we have a popular demand for "scientific explanations."

And here a subtler difficulty, only to be overcome by a fresh illusion, arises. "Explaining a science" means making it intelligible as a subject of thought. Just as the science had to be arranged as a story or drama before the public could be sufficiently interested to think about it, so it now has to be arranged as a logical theory before the human mind, however willing, can grasp it or apprehend it. The human mind is like the human hand in being able to grasp things only when they are shaped in a certain way. Take a plain wooden chair, and ask a man to lift it. He takes it by the back, or by one of the rails or legs, or by the edge of the seat, and lifts it with more or less ease. But ask him to lift it by the centre of the seat, and he cannot do it even if he were as strong as Sandow, because he cannot grasp a flat surface. He can only leave it as he finds it, and put it to its proper use by sitting down on it. Now, if instead of asking him to exercise his hands on chairs, you ask him to exercise his brain on subjects of thought, you will find him under just the same necessity to have a handle to his subject, so to speak, before he can apprehend it. And a logical theory, with its assumptions of cause and effect, time and space, and so on, is just such a mental handle and nothing else. Without a theory, natural occurrences may be put to use; but they cannot be thought out. Men construct windmills and watermills, and grind wheat in them, long before they trouble themselves about the science of winds and currents. When they do, they have to wait until a professional thought-carpenter fits a theory to them. Then everyone can "understand the subject," provided the theory is simple enough. When I was a child I was given this handle to lay hold of the universe by:

God made Man; and Man made Money.
God made Bees; and Bees made Honey.
God made Satan; and Satan made Sin;
And God made a hole to put Satan in.

That was a somewhat rough handle; but for many ages it served, as it still serves, great masses of men to arrange the facts of the world in their own heads so that they can think coherently about them. Its absolute, self-evident validity and sufficiency once seemed as plain and certain to very able men as the validity of gravitation or evolution is to very able men at present; and there is not the smallest reasonable doubt that gravitation and evolution will some day appear quite as crude and childish as the above quatrain appeared to Darwin.

We have now before us the conditions upon which science can be received by the mass of the people at the present stage of human development. If it cannot be forced upon them as the multiplication table is forced on children, or paid for as the ship captain's study of mathematical geography is paid for, it must be dramatized, either in an artistic or a religious form, to rouse popular sympathy and enchain popular attention. And, when intellectual curiosity follows sympathy and interest, drama must be followed by theory in order that people may think it as well as feel and imagine it.

Now it will not be questioned that Socialism, if it is to gain serious attention nowadays, must come into the field as political science and not as sentimental dogma. It is true that it is founded on sentimental dogma, and is quite unmeaning and purposeless apart from it. But so are all modern democratic political systems. The American constitution affirms, quite accurately and inevitably, that every man has a natural right to life, liberty, and the pursuit of happiness. This is the formal expression of the fact that a democratic political system must start from the assumption of an absolutely dogmatic, unreasonable, unjustifiable, unaccountable, in short, "natural" determination on the part of every citizen to live, do, and say as he pleases, and to use his powers to make himself happy in his own way. Moralizers have proved again and again that life, estimated on the rational basis of a comparison of its pleasures with its pains, anxieties, and labours, is not worth living. High Tories have proved, and can still prove, that slaves purchase freedom at the exorbitant cost of guaranteed subsistence, good government, peace, order, and security. Philosophers have warned us that the pursuit of happiness is of all pursuits the most wretched, and that happiness has never yet been found except on the way to some other goal. Every man's reason assents to these propositions; and every man's will utterly ignores them. Mankind is, by definition, unreasonable on these subjects; and we affirm our unreason by claiming what we call natural rights, and agitating for political recognition of these rights as postulates from which all legislation must start, and to the practical satisfaction and enlargement of which it must all be directed. Every political document in which these rights find a fuller and more conscious expression, however ineffectual it may be practically, becomes a historic landmark, as, for example, Magna Charta, the Petition of Rights, the Habeas Corpus Act, and the American Constitution. The final recognition of "natural rights" for every man in the Declaration of Independence, in spite of the practical exclusion of women and blacks from the definition, was the formal inauguration of modern Democracy on its firm dogmatic basis.

But it is one thing to ascertain what you want to secure, and quite another to ascertain the right method of securing it. The American Constitution is often such an exasperating obstruction to the life, liberty, and pursuit of happiness of the American nation, that American reformers long to tear it up; and every gentleman who has been mentally disabled at a University explains that natural rights cannot exist because they are illogical — as if that were not the whole point of them. A nation making its first attempts to secure its natural rights is like a lady trying to relieve the thirsty discomfort of a very hot day by eating ices. The most obvious steps are not merely ineffectual: they defeat their own object. The early democrats, having become accustomed, under oligarchical or autocratic systems, to associate the denial of their natural rights with governmental action, began by systematically attempting to extend the power of the individual and to curtail that of the State. Hence we get, as the first fruits of Democracy, the triumph of the Whig and his principles of Freedom of Contract, Laissez-faire, and so on, with the Manchester School in his van, and the Anarchists* as his extreme left wing, just as Cromwell had his left wing of Levellers. But a brief experience of Whig Anarchism, as a safeguard for natural rights, shows that the problem of securing their fullest practicable exercise is much more complicated than it once seemed. It is perceived that just as science throws no light on the dogmatic foundation of Democracy, so the natural right dogmas throw no light on the science of politics. The most immediate and obvious inferences from these dogmas have produced a state of things which, at its worst, is a perfect hell of slavery, misery, and destruction of life in the factory and mine, and at its best, though better, on the whole, than anything that has gone before, is out of the question as a permanently satisfactory social adjustment. It has been discovered that the dominant factor in human society is not political organization, but industrial organization; and that to secure to the people control of the political organization, whilst letting the industrial organization slip

---

* Perhaps I had better explain that by Anarchists I do not mean the unfortunate criminals who, having read in the newspapers that Anarchists are incendiaries, thieves and murderers, try to dignify their outbreaks by announcing themselves as Anarchists. Nor do I mean those materialist-rationalists who believe that because dynamite is logical its use is humanly valid. I mean those theorists who, like Mr. Herbert Spencer or Kropotkin, would solve the social problem by abolishing State compulsion and State enterprise, and substituting the power and action of the free individual.

through their fingers, is to intensify slavery under the political forms and pretensions of freedom and equality. In short, unless the Government controls industry, it is useless for the people to control the Government.

When this became plain, the Manchester School was superseded by the Collectivist or Socialist School;* and Democracy became Social-Democracy, their objects being the regulation, and finally the proprietorship, organization, and control of industry by the State. Now it is to be observed that we have here no recantation or revision of the dogmas of the American constitution. Democracy still pursues happiness, and strains after wider life and liberty; and it still disregards the teachings of Asceticism and Pessimism. And Socialism is quite on the side of Democracy — quite agrees that the system it proposes must stand or fall by its success in making the people livelier, freer, and happier than they can be without it. Consequently Socialism is not distinguishable on its dogmatic side from the older-fashioned Democracy, Republicanism, Radicalism or Liberalism, or even from English Conservatism, which no longer pretends to be the organ of a class as against the people, and which is, in fact, more advanced practically than German Social-Democracy. The sole distinction lies in its contention that industrial Collectivism is the true political science of Democracy. The Socialists do not say to the Manchesterists, "Your humanitarian objects are misinterpretations of Man's will," but "Your methods of fulfilling our common object are mistaken, because your social science is erroneous. In your induction you have missed the greater part of the facts, because your interest and class prejudices have turned your attention exclusively towards the lesser part. You have relied too much on deduction and too little on historical research and contemporary investigation. You have ludicrously underrated the complexity of the problem to be solved, and have allowed yourselves to be hampered and stopped in your reasoning by old associations of ideas which you have mistaken for principles. To the politicians, as the engineers who must work the political machine, and the artificers who must repair and enlarge it, you have given and are giving bad advice and impracticable directions. We therefore propose to persuade the people to dismiss you and elect us in your place."

The whole question at issue, then, is one of political science and practice, and of them alone. Just as the introduction of the screw-

---

* The Socialists, by the way, should not forget their obligations to the Positivists — obligations so great that Mr. Sidney Webb has declared that the most obvious modern application of Comte's "law of the three stages" is that Comtism is the metaphysical stage of Collectivism, and Collectivism the positive stage of Comtism.

steamer, or the cutting of the Suez Canal, did not affect the emigrant's desire to go to America or Ceylon, but simply provided him with a better method of getting there, so Socialism does not affect the goal of Democracy, but simply offers a better means of reaching it. There is no disposition to question this — at least verbally — on the Socialist side. Ever since Marx and Engels, in the Communist Manifesto, declared that all other human institutions have been and still are and ever must be only the reflection, in politics, art, religion, and what not, of industrial institutions, we have had the utmost ostentation of the scientific character of Socialism, first as against the Utopian Socialism of Fourier, and more recently as against the pure Opportunism of the established political parties. Manchesterism was the first modern political system that came into the field with absolute integrity as an application of pure political and industrial science, and not of supernatural religion or duty. Socialism is equally secular, and more materialistic and fatalistic, because it attributes more importance to circumstances as a factor in personal character and to industrial organization as a factor in society. The data of Collectivism are to be found in Blue Books, statistical abstracts, reports, records and observations of the actual facts and conditions of industrial life, not in dreams, ideals, prophecies and revelations. In theorizing from these data, Socialists have blundered often enough — Marx, for instance, was as faulty in his abstract economics as Adam Smith — but the blunder has never been due to any intentional vitiation of the secularity of the argument by unscientific considerations.

And now, what faces us as to the consequence of this scientific character of Socialism? Clearly, it must obey the law to which all science bows when it requires the support of the people. It must be popularized by being first dramatized and then theorized. It must be hidden under a veil of illusions embroidered with promises, and provided with a simple mental handle for the grasp of the common mind. I do not propose to attempt an account of all these illusions and carpenterings: in demonstrating their necessity I have done as much as I can do with profit. What follows is by way of illustration merely.

The dramatic illusion of Socialism is that which presents the working-class as a virtuous hero and heroine in the toils of a villain called "the capitalist," suffering terribly and struggling nobly, but with a happy ending for them, and a fearful retribution for the villain, in full view before the fall of the curtain on a future of undisturbed bliss. In this drama, the proletarian finds somebody to love, to sympathize with, and to champion, whom he identifies with himself; and somebody to execrate and feel indignantly superior to, whom he can identify with the social tyranny from which he suffers. Socialism is thus presented on the platform exactly as life is presented on the stage of the Adelphi Theatre, quite falsely and conventionally, but in the only way in which the audience can be induced to take an interest in it.

Closely allied to the dramatic illusion, and indeed at bottom the same thing, is the religious illusion. This illusion presents Socialism as consummating itself by a great day of wrath, called "The Revolution," in which capitalism, commercialism, competition, and all the lusts of the Exchange, shall be brought to judgment and cast out, leaving the earth free for the kingdom of heaven on earth, all of which is revealed in an infallible book by a great prophet and leader. In this illusion the capitalist is not a stage villain, but the devil; Socialism is not the happy ending of a drama, but heaven; and Karl Marx's "Das Kapital" is "the Bible of the working-classes." The working-man who has been detached from the Established Church or the sects by the Secularist propaganda, and who, as an avowed Agnostic or Atheist, strenuously denies or contemptuously ridicules the current beliefs in heavens and devils and bibles, will, with the greatest relief and avidity, go back to his old habits of thought and imagination when they reappear in this secular form. The Christian who finds the supernatural aspect of his faith slipping away from him, recaptures it in what seems to him a perfectly natural aspect as Christian Socialism.

A popular drama must have plenty of sensational incidents — combats, trials, plots, hair-breadth escapes, and so forth. They are copiously supplied by the history of revolutionary Socialism, which has been as romantically told as any history in the world. What incidents are to a drama, persecutions and salvational regenerations are to a religion. Accordingly we have, in the religious illusion of Socialism, a profuse exploitation of the calamities of martyrs exiled, imprisoned, and brought to the scaffold for "The Cause"; and we are told of the personal change, the transfigured, lighted-up face, the sudden accession of self-respect, the joyful self-sacrifice, the new eloquence and earnestness of the young working man who has been rescued from a purposeless, automatic loafing through life, by the call of the gospel of Socialism.*

* These transfigurations are very remarkable and touching to the observer who has not had any opportunities of following them up. They are as common in Socialist propaganda campaigns as in the Salvation Army. But to the old hand, they are dangerous symptoms of a too rapid and facile exaltation. If they are followed by a long campaign of insatiable and urgent public speaking, indoors and out, several times a week, they end in a peculiar exhaustion and emptiness of mind and character, leaving their victim a dull, hopeless windbag, opinionated without opinions, and conceited without qualities. I remember once, when lecturing, being opposed by an ex-apostle of Robert Owen, on the ground that he had observed, in the eighteen-thirties, that the propaganda had an unfavourable effect on the character of the propagandists. I quite believed him. The same qualities —

In describing the dramatic and the religious illusions separately, I do not lose sight of the fact that most men are subject to both, just as most civilized men go both to the theatre and the church, though some go to one and not to the other. But, mixed or apart, they are the chief means by which Socialism has laid hold of its disciples. Cruder and narrower dramatic and religious versions of the social problem still hold the field against them; but the wider, humaner, more varied and interesting character of the Socialist version, its optimism, its power of bringing happiness and heaven from dreamland and from beyond the clouds down into living, breathing reach, and the power it gains from its contact with and constant reference to contemporary fact and experience, give it an appearance of immense modernity and practicability as compared to the more barbarous and imaginary conceptions which it is superseding. But it is none the less illusory; and the more the Socialist leaders yield to the temptation to wallow recklessly in the enthusiasm and applause it creates, the more certain they are, when the moment for action arrives, to find themselves thwarted by its wrongheadedness. For when the reality at last comes to the men who have been nursed on dramatizations of it, they do not recognize it. Its prosaic aspect revolts them; and since it must necessarily come by penurious instalments, each maimed in the inevitable compromise with powerful hostile interests, its advent has neither the splendid magnitude nor the absolute integrity of principle dramatically and religiously necessary to impress them. Hence they either pass it by contemptuously or join the forces of reaction by opposing it vehemently. Worse still, to prevent the recurrence of such scandals, and maintain the purity of their faith, they begin to set up rigid tests of orthodoxy; to excommunicate the genuinely scientific Socialists; to entrust the leadership of their organizations to orators and preachers: in short, to develop all the symptoms of what the French call Impossibilism.

The first condition of an illusion is, of course, that its victim should mistake it for a reality. The dramatic and religious illusions of Socialism, in their extreme forms, are too gross, too mercilessly and insistently contradicted by experience to impose on a capable man when once he is confronted with practical political work and responsibility. Though very few Socialists gain sufficient practical experi-

---

or lack of qualities — that make a man suddenly and fervently impressionable, and incontinently rhapsodic and vehement in oratory, may, and sometimes do, land him in prison later on as a common, non-political offender. But in the meantime the apparent miracle of his conversion will have made a strong impression on those religiously susceptible persons who have witnessed it.

ence nowadays to be completely cured of Impossibilism, partial cures occur every day. The invaluable habit of mind which we modern Socialists have learnt from our Jevonian economics should therefore save us from the error of regarding Socialists as either out-and-out Possibilists or out-and-out Impossibilists. Neither in Socialism or anything else is it true that whatever is not white is black. Every gradation of credulity, from the crudest dreaming to the most sceptical practicality, is represented in the Socialist movement. In the extreme sections of the Social-Democratic Federation, in the Communist-Anarchist side of the Independent Labour Party, and in the Anarchist groups, the dramatic and religious illusions will be found just as I have described them. At the other extremity you have the typical Fabian, who flatly declares that there will be no revolution; that there is no class war; that the wage earners are far more conventional, prejudiced, and "bourgeois," than the middle class; that there is not a single democratically constituted authority in England, including the House of Commons, that would not be much more progressive if it were not restrained by fear of the popular vote; that Karl Marx is no more infallible than Aristotle or Bacon, Ricardo or Buckle, and, like them, made mistakes which are now plain to any undergraduate; that a professed Socialist is neither better nor worse morally than a Liberal or Conservative, nor a working-man than a capitalist; that the working-man can alter the present system if he chooses, whereas the capitalist cannot because the working-man will not let him; that it is perverse stupidity to declare in one breath that the working-classes are starved, degraded, and left in ignorance by a system which heaps victuals, education and refinement on the capitalist, and to assume in the next that the capitalist is a narrow, sordid scoundrel, and the working-man a high-minded, enlightened, magnanimous philanthropist; that Socialism will come by prosaic instalments of public regulation and public administration enacted by ordinary parliaments, vestries, municipalities, parish councils, school boards, and the like; and that not one of these instalments will amount to a revolution, or will occupy a larger place in the political program of its day than a Factory Bill or a County Government Bill now does: all this meaning that the lot of the Socialist is to be one of dogged political drudgery, in conflict, not with the wicked machinations of the capitalist, but with the stupidity, the narrowness, in a word the idiocy (using the word in its precise and original meaning) of all classes, and especially of the class which suffers most by the existing system.

Taking these as the two extremes between which all avowed and conscious Socialists, and a good many unavowed and unconscious ones, are to be found, we see that the scale is apparently one of diminishing illusion. But the real scale is one of acuteness of intellect, political experience, practical capacity, the strength of character which gives a man power to look unpleasant facts in the face, and doubtless also the comfortable circumstances which enable clever professional men, with fair incomes, to be more philosophical than poor and worried ones. That is why a very crude illusion will impose on the men at one end of the scale, whilst it requires a comparatively very subtle one to impose on the men at the other. I remember once, shortly after the great London Dock Strike of 1889, addressing a rather bigoted Socialist audience from the Fabian point of view. One speaker was so strongly possessed by the dramatic illusion, that in criticising the parts played by Mr. John Burns and the late Cardinal Manning in that struggle, he vehemently denounced Mr. Burns, with many sanguinary expletives, as a cowardly trimmer and apostate, because he had not taken the cardinal by the neck and pitched him into the river. Another speaker, of acuter mind, illustrated the danger of having any dealings with Radicals who were coming round to our opinions, by the analogy of his own experience as a sprint runner, in which he had found, he said, that the man to be feared in the race was not the man farthest behind him, but the one close on his heels. Therefore, he argued, the bigoted Tory was less dangerous to us than the Radical Land Nationalizer. Now if these two Socialists be compared with, say, Shelley and Lassalle, it will not be disputed that they were enormously less capable men. But to say that the ideals of Shelley and Lassalle, however immeasurably they may have transcended those of the fraternal gentleman who wanted to have the Cardinal pitched into the river, were any less illusory in the forms in which they presented themselves to their consciousness, is more than any wise man will venture to affirm.

My reader must now beware of the illusion that other Socialists do not recognize this scale. On the contrary, all Socialists do; but each considers himself as being at the sensible, hard-headed end of it. And the more completely a Socialist is the dupe of the dramatic and religious illusions in their crudest form, the more positively is he convinced that he is founded on a triple rock of "scientific political economy," history, and social evolution. The way in which a man, out of the abysses of an ignorance of the subject ten times deeper than any ordinary honest unconsciousness of it, will expound to you such blurred notions as he has been able to pick up of "surplus value," over-production, commercial crises, the imminent breakdown of the capitalist system by the laws of its own development, and so on, is quite as funny as the way in which the man who opposes him will retort with scraps from the economic prophets of the Manchester school — supply and demand, the population question, the law of diminishing return, and what not?

And here we come to the second line of illusion — that which supplies the demand for a theory, not only as a sort of trapeze for the intellect, but as a scientific basis for faith. This demand is now a thoroughly popular one: even the narrowest chapel-goer likes to hear that fossils have been discovered on the tops of mountains (showing that the Deluge is scientifically proved), and that the name of Nebuchadnezzar has been deciphered on Babylonian bricks. But the popularization of genuine scientific theories is becoming daily more impossible among people who have not had an elaborate secondary education — that is, the vast majority of citizens — because the theories, as they are followed up, lose their original crude and simple forms, and become not only complex in themselves, but unintelligible without reference to other theories. For example, the old theory of light, which had the great authority of Newton to recommend it, presented the solar spectrum (popularly, the rainbow) as consisting of three primary colours, with three secondary ones produced by the overlapping and mixing of the primaries. This was a very easy explanation: every child could take his penny paints, red, blue and yellow, and mix them into purple, green, and orange. But the modern theory of the spectrum which has prevailed since Young's time, is no such simple matter: it cannot be made intelligible to anyone who does not know something of the whole theory of light. The result is that to this day the notion of primary and secondary colours remains the popular theory.

Now Socialism, as it happens, has for its economic basis two theories, the theory of Rent and the theory of Value. The first of these seems simple to those who have mastered it; but it is neither obvious nor easy to the average sympathetic man: indeed, men of first-rate ability, among them Adam Smith, Marx, and Ruskin, have blundered over it, although writers of much less imposing eminence mastered it and formulated it for the instruction of later generations. Nobody, not even Mr. Henry George, has succeeded in popularizing it. The theory of value has a different history. Like the rainbow theory, it began by being simple enough for the most unsophisticated audience, and ended by becoming so subtle that its popularization is out of the question, especially as the old theory is helped by the sentiments of approbation it excites; whereas the scientific theory is ruthlessly indifferent to the moral sense. The result is that the old theory is the only one available for general use among Socialists. It has accordingly been adopted by them in the form (as far as that form is popularly intelligible) laid down in the first volume of Karl Marx's "Capital."

It is erroneous and obsolete; it has been modified out of existence by Marx himself in his third volume;* it would, if it were valid, disprove the existence of "surplus value" instead of proving it; it has been used again and again to discredit the economic soundness of Socialism; but any child can understand its elementary proposition that the value of a commodity is created by the labour put into it, and can be measured, as labour customarily is in the market, by hours and days; whereas the scientific theory, though based on the sufficiently plain, acceptable fact that things have value because people want them, labour being thus the consequence and not the cause of value, proved so baffling and elusive when the first attempts were made to reduce it to a rule, that until Jevons conquered it the economists gave it up as unworkable, and boldly treated commodities as possessing two distinct sorts of value — use value and exchange value — which was, of course, absurd. But, absurd as it was, it was the only handle by which men so clever as Adam Smith, Ricardo, De Quincey, John Stuart Mill, and Karl Marx† could lay hold of the problem; and what

* Exact references on this point will be found in "German Social Democracy," by Bertrand Russell. (Longmans, 1896.)

† It must not be inferred, however, that De Quincey and Karl Marx were inferior to Jevons in intellectual subtlety. If either of them had been economists pure and simple, like Jevons, they would probably have anticipated him. But De Quincey's profession was literature, not economics; and all he aimed at was a perfectly lucid and artistic statement of the theories of Ricardo, who, not being an artist in literature, was apt to convey his meaning by saying exactly the opposite of what he meant. As it was, De Quincey stated the labour value theory and its more obvious modifications by supply and demand so artistically that Mill declared that the theory was complete, and that there was nothing left to be said on the subject.

Karl Marx failed because he was not an economist, but a revolutionary Socialist using political economy as a weapon against his opponents. The conclusion that labour is the source of value was foregone with him: he only attempted to do for a long line of theorizers, from Petty in the seventeenth century up to Hodgskin and Thompson in the nineteenth, what De Quincey had done for Ricardo: that is, supply them with a new and more closely reasoned logical process of demonstration. This he did in his analysis of a commodity, which brings him within one step of Jevons. Had he been a scientific economist seeking a theory of value with the most complete indifference to the political inferences that might be drawn from it, he would never have stopped at his consideration of a commodity as an embodiment of "abstract labor," with its aspect as an embodiment of "abstract desirability" staring him in the face as an equally obvious result of his method. But he stopped when he had, as he thought, carried his political point; and Socialism has suffered for it ever since. Possibly if Jevons had foreseen that his theory would make Socialism economically irrefutable, and extinguish the last ray of the optimistic illusion that labour power, being the product of the labour of those who produce its subsistence, must always have the baffled brains as able and specially trained as theirs, is hardly likely to come easily to amateur Socialist lecturers, much less to their audiences, who generally regard the intelligible theory as favourable to Labor, and the unintelligible one as hostile to it — a mistake, but a very convenient one for the lecturers, since it saves them the necessity of explaining the theory they do not understand, and enables them to ask whether it is likely that Jevons (whose renown is purely academic) was a greater man than the world-renowned Marx, forgetting that a very ordinary person may now be of opinion that the earth is round without necessarily being a greater man than Saint Augustine, who believed it to be flat.

However, a Socialist is a Socialist; and whichever theory he adopts, he arrives at the same conclusion: the advocacy of a transfer of "the means of production, distribution, and exchange" from private to collective ownership. If he could be persuaded that the old theory did not support this "principle," as he calls it, he would give up the old theory, even if Jevons were still too hard for him. And thereby comes the cherished illusion that all Socialists are agreed in principle though they may differ as to tactics. This is perhaps the most laughable of all the illusions of Socialism, so outrageously is it contradicted by the facts. It is quite true that the Socialists are in perfect agreement with one another except on those points on which they happen to differ. They can claim that happy understanding not only among themselves, but with the Liberals and Conservatives as well. But the notion that their differences are at present any less fundamental than their agreements is an illusion, as the following examination will show.

With the Socialists who are under the religious illusion in its most Calvinistic mode, the formula about the means of production represents a principle to be carried out to its logical extreme in unbroken integrity — Man, from their point of view, being made for Socialism and not Socialism for Man. The toleration of even such a convenient infraction of the principle as allowing an individual to keep a typewriter or a bicycle for his own exclusive use without some very explicit and constant affirmation of the fact that it was common property, would be resisted by them as determinedly as an old-fashioned New

---

value of that subsistence; so that men can never starve as long as "freedom of contract" is maintained (an exquisite consolation to the unemployed), his scientific integrity also might have gone by the board. A comparison of his shilling primer of Economics, for the use of working men, with the expensive and cryptic treatise in which his scientific theory is circulated, shows that the moment he began to write with the social and political consequences of his works in his mind, he instinctively became as much a special pleader as Marx or Adam Smith.

England Methodist resists the introduction of an organ into his meeting house. Other Socialists — the Fabians, for instance — openly and expressly treat the question of private property as one of pure convenience, and declare that as long as the livelihood of the people is made independent of private capital and enterprise, the more private property and individual activity we have the better. Here, clearly, far from the Calvinistic Socialist being agreed with the Fabian Socialist in principle, it is just on the question of principle that they are irreconcileable, though circumstances may at any moment bring them to an agreement as to tactics. I myself am firmly persuaded that Socialism will not prove worth carrying out in its integrity — that long before it has reached every corner of the political and industrial organization, it will have so completely relieved the pressure to which it owes its force that it will recede before the next great movement in social development, leaving relics of untouched Individualist Liberalism in all directions among the relics of feudalism which Liberalism itself has left. I believe that its dissolution of the petty autocracies and oligarchies of private landlordism and capitalism will enormously stimulate genuine individual enterprise instead of suppressing it; and I strongly suspect that Socialist States will connive at highly undemocratic ways of leaving comparatively large resources in the hands of certain persons, who will thereby become obnoxious as a privileged class to the consistent levellers. If I am right, Socialism at its height will be as different from the ideal of the "Anti-State Communists" of the Socialist League in 1885, and of Domela Nieuwenhuis and his Dutch Communist Anarchist comrades to-day, as current Christianity is from the ideal of the apostles and of Tolstoi. This, of course, is not my "principle": it is my practical view of the situation; but the fact that I do not think it wrong to take that view, and should unhesitatingly vote for a man who took it as against a man who took what I have called the Calvinist view, appears to the Calvinist mind to be conclusive evidence either that I am no Socialist, or else that I am so cynically indifferent to "principle" in the abstract that I cannot properly be said to be anything at all. To settle the matter, let us again apply the Jevonian method. Instead of asking "Are you a Socialist or not?" let us say, "How much are you a Socialist?" or, more practically still, "What do you want to Socialize; and how much and when do you propose to Socialize it?" The moment the case is put in this way, all pretence of agreement vanishes. Let me suggest a few detailed questions. Do you advocate the socialization of the cotton industry, of shipbuilding, of railways, of coal mines, of building, of food supply, and of the clothing trades? If so, do you contemplate the socialization of the book industry? and do you, in that case, conceive that the

Kelmscott Press and the Doves Bindery would be incorporated with the Stationery Office, with Mr. William Morris and Mr. Cobden Sanderson as salaried officials, under the orders of an Under Secretary and a Cabinet Minister?* Do you advocate the socialization of the church, the chapel, the "hall of science," the services of the Ethical Society, and of the Salvation Army? If so, do you advocate the socialization of the theatre and concert room? Do you propose merely to extend State enterprise to industry, or to enforce State monopoly by suppressing all private enterprise in industry? Or would you monopolize in some cases and not in others, according to circumstances? For instance, if you socialized surgery and painting, would you punish a dentist for making a private contract with a citizen to extract his tooth for a guinea, or fine Sir Edward Burne Jones for painting his daughter's portrait out of office hours for nothing?

I might devise pages of such questions; but the above are quite sufficient to divide Socialists into two sections: first, the fanatics who are prepared to sacrifice all considerations of human welfare and convenience sooner than flinch from the rigorous application of "their principles,"† even to the point of burlesquing their own creed; and, second, the more or less practical men, among whom there would be as much diversity of opinion on each particular point as there is on any ordinary question in the House of Commons. Thus the unity of Socialism, and the existence of definite boundary lines between it and Progressivism, prove to be mere illusions. Notwithstanding which, the battle cry of the Communist Manifesto, "Proletarians from every land, unite!" still inspires us; and we gain a foolish but effective courage from the imaginary tread of millions of workers joining the mighty columns of the Revolution.

The double rampart of illusion is now complete. Socialism wins its disciples by presenting civilization to them as a popular melodrama, or as a Pilgrim's Progress through suffering, trial, and combat against the powers of evil to the bar of poetic justice with paradise beyond; by holding up its leaders as heroes, prophets, and seers; and by satisfying the intellectual curiosity and criticism which the picture arouses

---

* The death [on 3 October 1896] of William Morris since the above sentence was written only adds force to the question, since it has brought home to us our complete dependence for eminent work on the free initiative of eminent men.

† I put it in this flattering way so as not to hurt anyone's feelings. But I am bound to say that I am extremely sceptical about the fanaticism of our friends who are so determined not to "compromise their principles." I suspect some of them of using a formula to save themselves the trouble of finding sensible answers for practical questions, and the humiliation of confessing that their panacea will not cure all ailments.

with a few links of logic held up and jingled as scientific formulæ. It is in such ways that the will of the world accomplishes itself. Out of the illusion of "the abolition of the wage system" we shall get steady wages for everybody, and finally discredit all other sources of income as disreputable. By the illusion of the downfall of Capitalism we shall turn whole nations into Joint Stock Companies; and our determination to annihilate the *bourgeoisie* will end in making every workman a *bourgeois gentilhomme*. By the illusion of Democracy, or government by everybody, we shall establish the most powerful bureaucracy ever known on the face of the earth, and finally get rid of popular election, trial by jury, and all the other makeshifts of a system in which no man can be trusted with power. By the illusion of scientific materialism we shall make life more and more the expression of our thought and feeling, and less and less of our craving for more butter on our bread. But in the meantime we shall continue to make fools of ourselves; to make our journals bywords for slander and vituperation in the name of fraternity; to celebrate the advent of universal peace by the most intemperate quarrelling; to pose as uneducated men of the people whilst advancing claims to scientific infallibility which would make Lord Kelvin ridiculous; to denounce the middle class, to which we ourselves mostly belong: in short, to wallow in all the follies and absurdities of public life with the fullest conviction that we have attained a Pisgah region far above such Amalekitish superstitions. No matter: it has to be done in that way, or not at all. Only, please remember, still in the true Jevonian spirit, that the question is not whether illusions are useful or not, but exactly how useful they are.

Up to a certain point, illusion — or, as it is commonly called by Socialists, "enthusiasm" — is, more or less, precious and indispensable; but beyond that point it gives more trouble than it is worth: in Jevonese language, its utility becomes disutility. There are some Socialists who, to put it plainly, are such fools that they do more harm than good, even in the roughest sort of preliminary propaganda. Others, more sensible, do excellent work as preachers and revivalists, but are nuisances when the work of formal political organization begins. Others, who can get as far as organizing an election without being disqualified by the vehemence of their partisanship, would, if elected themselves, be worse than useless as legislators and administrators. Others are good parliamentary orators and debaters, but bad committee men. As the work requires more and more ability and temper, it requires more and more freedom from the cruder illusions, especially those which dramatize one's opponents as villains and fiends, and more and more of that quality which is the primal republican material —

that sense of the sacredness of life which makes a man respect his fellow without regard to his social rank or intellectual class, and recognizes the fool of Scripture only in those persons who refuse to be bound by any relations except the personally luxurious ones of love, admiration, and identity of political opinion and religious creed. Happily none of us is quite without this republican quality; for it is not a question of having it or not, but of having it more or less (the inevitable Jevons again, you see); and it is certain that unless it is so strong in a man that he is habitually at least a little conscious of it, he is hardly good enough for the world as it is, much less for the Socialist world to come. To such a man alone can Equality have any sense or validity in a society where men differ from one another through an enormous compass of personal ability, from the peasant to the poet and philosopher. Perhaps to such a one alone will it be plain that a Socialist may, without offence or arrogance, or the least taint of intentional cynicism, discourse as freely as I have done on the illusions of his own creed.

Tolstoy on Art

(A review of Aylmer Maude's translation of Leo Tolstoy's
What is Art? Daily Chronicle, London, 10 September 1898.
Reprinted in Maude's *Tolstoy on Art and Its Critics*, 1925, and,
with minor revisions, in Shaw's *Pen Portraits and Reviews*,
1931)

Like all Tolstoy's didactic writings, this book is a most effective
booby-trap. It is written with so utter a contempt for the objections
which the routine critic is sure to allege against it, that many a dilet-
tantist reviewer has already accepted it as a butt set up by Providence
to show off his own brilliant marksmanship. It seems so easy to dis-
pose of a simpleton who moralizes on the Trojan war as if it were an
historical event!

Yet Tolstoy will be better understood in this volume than in his
Christian epistles because art is at present a more fashionable subject
than Christianity. Most people have a loose impression that Tolstoy
as a Christian represents Evangelicalism gone mad. As a matter of
fact, Tolstoy's position, as explained by himself, is, from the Evangelical point of view, as novel as it is blasphemous. What Evangelicalism calls revelation, vouchsafed to man's incapacity by Divine wisdom, Tolstoy declares to be a piece of common sense so obvious as to
make its statement in the Gospels superfluous. "I will go further,"
he says. "This truth [Resist not evil] appears to me so simple and
so clear that I am persuaded I should have found it out by myself,
even if Christ and his doctrine had never existed." Blasphemy can
go no further than this from the point of view of the Bible-worship-
per. Again he says, "I beg you, in the name of the God of truth whom
you adore, not to fly out at me, nor to begin looking for arguments
to oppose me with, before you have meditated, not on what I am going
to write to you, but on the Gospel; and not on the Gospel as the
word of God or of Christ, but on the Gospel considered as the neatest,
simplest, most comprehensible and most practical doctrine on the
way in which men ought to live."

What makes this attitude of Tolstoy's so formidable to Christians
who feel that it condemns their own systematic resistance to evil, is the
fact that he is a man with a long, varied, and by no means exclusively

427

pious experience of worldly life. In vain do we spend hours in a highly superior manner in proving that Tolstoy's notions are unpractical, visionary: in short, cranky. We cannot get the sting and the startle out of his flat challenge as to how much we have done and where we have landed ourselves by the opposite policy. No doubt the challenge does not make all of us uneasy. But may not that be because he sees the world from behind the scenes of politics and society, whilst most of us are sitting to be gulled in the pit? For, alas! nothing seems plainer to the dupe of all the illusions of civilization than the folly of the seer who penetrates them.

If Tolstoy has made himself so very disquieting by criticizing the world as a man of the world, he has hardly made himself more agreeable by criticizing art as an artist of the first rank. Among the minor gods of the amateur he kindles a devastating fire. Naturally, the very extensive literary output of delirium tremens in our century receives no quarter from him: he has no patience with nonsense, especially drunken nonsense, however laboriously or lusciously it may be rhymed or alliterated. But he spares nobody wholly, dealing unmercifully with himself, sweeping away Mr. Rudyard Kipling with the French decadents, and heaping derision on Wagner. Clearly, this book of his will not be valued for its specific criticisms, some of which, if the truth must be told, represent nothing but the inevitable obsolescence of an old man's taste in art. To justify them, Tolstoy applies a test highly characteristic of the Russian aristocrat. A true work of art, he maintains, will always be recognized by the unsophisticated perception of the peasant folk. Hence Beethoven's Ninth Symphony, not being popular among the Russian peasantry, is not a true work of art!

Leaving the Ninth Symphony to take care of itself, one cannot help being struck by the fact that Russian revolutionists of noble birth invariably display what appears to us a boundless credulity concerning the virtues of the poor. No English county magnate has any doubt as to which way an English agricultural laborer would choose between Tolstoy's favorite Chopin nocturne (admitted by him to be true art) and the latest music-hall tune: we know perfectly well that the simplicity of our peasants' lives is forced on them by their poverty, and could be dispelled at any moment by a sufficient legacy. We know that the equality which seems to the rich man to be accepted among laborers (because he himself makes no distinction among them) is an illusion, and that social distinctions are more pitifully cherished by our poor than by any other class until we get down to the residuum which has not self-respect enough even for snobbery. Now, whether it is that the Russian peasantry, being illiterate and outlandish, has never been absorbed by European civilization as ours has been, or else that the distance between peasant and noble in Russia is so great that the two classes do not know one another, and fill up the void in their knowledge by millennial romancing, certain it is that the Russian nobles Kropotkin and Tolstoy, who have come into our counsels on the side of the people, seem to assume that the laboring classes have entirely escaped the class vices, follies, and prejudices of the bourgeoisie.

If it were not for this very questionable premiss, it would be very difficult to dissent from any of Tolstoy's judgments on works of art without feeling any danger of merely providing him with an additional example of the corruption of taste which he deplores. But when his objection to a masterpiece is based solely on the incapacity of a peasant to enjoy it or understand it, the misgiving vanishes. Everything that he says in condemnation of modern society is richly deserved by it; but if it were true that the working classes, numbering, say, four-fifths of the population, had entirely escaped the penalties of civilization, and were in a state so wholesomely natural and benevolent that Beethoven must stand condemned by their coldness towards his symphonies, then his whole case against civilization must fall to the ground, since such a majority for good would justify any social system. In England, at least, one cannot help believing that if Tolstoy were reincarnated as a peasant he would find that the proletarian simplicity in which he has so much faith is nothing but the morality of his own class, modified, mostly for the worse, by ignorance, drudgery, insufficient food, and bad sanitary conditions of all kinds. It is true that the absolutely idle class has a peculiar and exasperating nonentity and futility, and that this class wastes a great deal of money in false art; but it is not numerically a very large class. The demand of the professional and mercantile classes is quite sufficient to maintain a considerable body of art, the defects of which cannot be ascribed to the idleness of its patrons.

If due allowance be made for these considerations, which, be it remembered, weaken Society's defence and not Tolstoy's attack, this book will be found extraordinarily interesting and enlightening. We must agree with him when he says, "To thoughtful and sincere people there can be no doubt that the art of the upper classes can never be the art of the whole people." Only, we must make the same reservation with regard to the art of the lower classes. And we must not forget that there is nothing whatever to choose between the average country gentleman and his gamekeeper in respect of distaste for the Ninth Symphony.

Tolstoy's main point, however, is the establishment of his definition of art. It is, he says, "an activity by means of which one man, having experienced a feeling, intentionally transmits it to others." This is the simple truth: the moment it is uttered, whoever is really conversant with art recognizes in it the voice of the master. None the less is Tolstoy perfectly aware that this is not the usual definition of art, which amateurs delight to hear described as that which produces beauty. Tolstoy's own Christian view of how he should treat the professors of this or any other heresy is clearly laid down in these articles of faith, already quoted above, which conclude his *Plaisirs Cruels*. "To dispute with those who are in error is to waste labor and spoil our exposition of truth. It provokes us to say things that we do not mean, to formulate paradoxes, to exaggerate our thought, and, leaving on one side the essential part of our doctrine, play off tricks of logic on the slips which have provoked us." Fortunately for the entertainment of the readers of *What is Art?* Tolstoy does not carry out his own precepts in it. Backsliding without the slightest compunction into the character of a first-rate fighting man, he challenges all the authorities, great and small, who have committed themselves to the beauty theory, and never quits them till he has left them for dead. There is always something specially exhilarating in the spectacle of a Quaker fighting; and Tolstoy's performance in this kind will not be soon forgotten. Our generation has not seen a heartier bout of literary fisticuffs, nor one in which the challenger has been more brilliantly victorious.

Since no man, however indefatigable a reader he may be, can make himself acquainted with all that Europe has to say on any subject of general interest, it seldom happens that any great champion meets the opponent we would most like him to join issue with. For this reason we hear nothing from Tolstoy of William Morris's definition of art as the expression of pleasure in work. This is not exactly the beauty doctrine: it recognizes, as Tolstoy's definition does, that art is the expression of feeling; but it covers a good deal of art work which, whilst proving the artist's need for expression, does not convince us that the artist wanted to convey his feeling to others. There have been many artists who have taken great pains to express themselves to themselves in works of art, but whose action, as regards the circulation of those arts, has very evidently been dictated by love of fame or money rather than by any yearning for emotional intercourse with their fellow-creatures. It is, of course, easy to say that the works of such men are not true art; but if they convey feeling to others, sometimes more successfully and keenly than some of the works which fall within Tolstoy's definition, the distinction is clearly not a practical one. The truth is that definitions which are applied on the principle that whatever is not white is black never are quite practical. The only safe plan is to ascertain the opposite extremes of artistic motive; determine which end of the scale between them is the higher and which the lower; and place each work in question in its right position on the scale. There are plenty of passages in this very book of Tolstoy's — itself a work of art according to his own definition — which have quite clearly been written to relieve the craving for expression of the author's own combativeness, or fun, or devotion, or even cleverness, and would probably have been written equally had he been the most sardonic pessimist that ever regarded his fellow-creatures as beyond redemption.

Tolstoy's justification in ignoring these obvious objections to the accuracy and universality of his treatise is plain enough. Art is socially important — that is, worth writing a book about — only in so far as it wields that power of propagating feeling which he adopts as his criterion of true art. It is hard to knock this truth into the heads of the English nation. We admit the importance of public opinion, which, in a country without intellectual habits (our own, for example), depends altogether on public feeling. Yet, instead of perceiving the gigantic importance which this gives to the theatre, the concert-room, and the bookshop as forcing-houses of feeling, we slight them as mere places of amusement, and blunder along upon the assumption that the House of Commons, and the platitudes of a few old-fashioned leader-writers, are the chief fountains of English sentiment. Tolstoy knows better than that.

"Look carefully," he says, "into the causes of the ignorance of the masses, and you may see that the chief cause does not at all lie in the lack of schools and libraries, as we are accustomed to suppose, but in those superstitions, both ecclesiastical and patriotic, with which the people are saturated, and which are unceasingly generated by all the methods of art. Church superstitions are supported and produced by the poetry of prayers, hymns, painting; by the sculpture of images and of statues; by singing, by organs, by music, by architecture, and even by dramatic art in religious ceremonies. Patriotic superstitions are supported and produced by verses and stories, which are supplied even in schools; by music, by songs, by triumphal processions, by royal meetings, by martial pictures, and by monuments. Were it not for this continual activity in all departments of art, perpetuating the ecclesiastical and patriotic intoxication and embitterment of the people, the masses would long ere this have attained to true enlightenment."

It does not at all detract from the value of Tolstoy's thesis that what he denounces as superstitions may appear to many to be wholesome enthusiasms and fruitful convictions. Still less does it matter that his opinions of individual artists are often those of a rather petulant veteran who neither knows nor wants to know much of works that are too new to please him. The valid point is that our artistic institutions are vital social organs, and that the advance of civilization tends constantly to make them, especially in the presence of democratic institutions and compulsory schooling, more important than the political and ecclesiastical institutions whose traditional prestige is so much greater. We are too stupid to learn from epigrams; otherwise Fletcher of Saltoun's offer to let whoever wished make the laws of the nation provided he made its songs, would have saved Tolstoy the trouble of telling us the same thing in twenty chapters. At all events, we cannot now complain of want of instruction. With Mr. Ashton Ellis's translation of Wagner's prose works to put on the shelves of our libraries beside the works of Ruskin, and this pregnant and trenchant volume of Tolstoy's to drive the moral home, we shall have ourselves to thank if we do not take greater care of our art in the future than of any other psychological factor in the destiny of the nation.

In the Days of My Youth

(An open letter to editor T. P. O'Connor, in *M.A.P.* [*Mainly About People*], London, 17 September 1898. Revised versions in *Shaw Gives Himself Away,* 1939, and *Sixteen Self Sketches,* 1949)

My dear T. P., —

All autobiographies are lies. I do not mean unconscious, unintentional lies: I mean deliberate lies. No man is bad enough to tell the truth about himself during his lifetime, involving, as it must, the truth about his family and friends and colleagues. And no man is good enough to tell the truth to posterity in a document which he suppresses until there is nobody left alive to contradict him.

I speak with the more confidence on the subject because I have myself tried the experiment, within certain timid limits, of being candidly autobiographical. But I have produced no permanent impression, because nobody has ever believed me. I once told a brilliant London journalist [A. B. Walkley] some facts about my family. It is a very large family, running to about forty first cousins and to innumerable second and thirds. Like most large families, it did not consist exclusively of teetotalers; nor did all its members remain until death up to the very moderate legal standard of sanity. One of them discovered an absolutely original method of committing suicide. It was simple to the verge of triteness; yet no human being had ever thought of it before. It was also amusing. But in the act of carrying it out, my relative jammed the mechanism of his heart — possibly in the paroxysm of laughter which the mere narration of his suicidal method has never since failed to provoke — and, if I may be allowed to state the result in my Irish way, he died about a second before he succeeded in killing himself. The coroner's jury found that he died "from natural causes"; and the secret of the suicide was kept, not only from the public, but from most of the family.

I revealed that secret in private conversation to the brilliant journalist aforesaid. He shrieked with laughter, and printed the whole story in his next *causerie.* It never for a moment occurred to him that it was true. To this day he regards me as the most reckless liar in London. Meanwhile, the extent to which I stood compromised with my relative's widow and brothers and sisters may be imagined.

433

If I were to attempt to write genuine autobiography here the same difficulty would arise. I should give mortal offence to the few relatives who would know that I was writing the truth; and not one of the thousands of readers of M.A.P. would believe me.

I am in the further difficulty that I have not yet ascertained the truth about myself. For instance, am I mad or sane? I really do not know. Doubtless I am clever in certain directions: my talent has enabled me to cut a figure in my profession in London. But a man may, like Don Quixote, be clever enough to cut a figure and yet be stark mad. A critic has described me, with deadly acuteness, as having "a kindly dislike of my fellow creatures." Perhaps dread would have been nearer the mark than dislike; for man is the only animal of which I am thoroughly and cravenly afraid. I have never thought much of the courage of a lion tamer.

Inside the cage he is at least safe from other men. There is not much harm in a lion. He has no ideals, no religion, no politics, no chivalry, no gentility; in short, no reason for destroying anything that he does not want to eat. In the Spanish-American War the Americans burnt the Spanish fleet, and finally had to drag the wounded men out of the hulls which had become furnaces. The effect of this on one of the American commanders was to make him assemble his men and tell them that he wished to declare before them that he believed in God Almighty. No lion would have done that. On reading it, and observing that the newspapers, representing normal public opinion, seemed to consider it a very creditable, natural and impressively pious incident, I came to the conclusion that I must be mad. At all events, if I am sane, the rest of the world ought not to be at large. We cannot both see things as they really are.

My father was an Irish Protestant gentleman. He had no money, no education, no profession, no manual skill, no qualification of any sort for any definite social function. But he had been brought up to believe that there was an inborn virtue of gentility in all Shaws, since they revolved impecuniously in a sort of vague second cousinship round a baronetcy. He had by some means asserted his family claim on the State with sufficient success to attain a post in the Four Courts (the Irish Palais de Justice).

The post was abolished, and he was pensioned off. He sold the pension, and embarked with the proceeds in the corn trade, of which he had not the slightest knowledge; nor did he acquire much, as far as I can judge, to the day of his death. There was a mill a little way out in the country, which was attached to the business as a matter of ceremony, and which perhaps paid its own rent, since the machinery was generally in motion. But its chief use, I believe, was to amuse me and my boon companions, the sons of my father's partner.

I believe Ireland, as far as the Protestant gentry are concerned, to be the most irreligious country in the world. I was christened by a clerical uncle; and as my godfather was intoxicated and did not turn up, the sexton was ordered to promise and vow in his place, precisely as my uncle might have ordered him to put more coals on the vestry fire. I was never confirmed, and I believe my parents never were, either. The seriousness with which English families take this rite, and the deep impression it makes on many children, was a thing of which I had no conception. Protestantism in Ireland is not a religion: it is a side in political faction, a class prejudice, a conviction that Roman Catholics are socially inferior persons, who will go to hell when they die, and leave Heaven in the exclusive possession of ladies and gentlemen.

In my childhood I was sent on Sundays to a Sunday-school, where genteel little children repeated texts, and were rewarded with little cards inscribed with other texts. After an hour of this we were marched into the adjoining church, to fidget there until our neighbours must have wished the service over as heartily as we did. I suffered this, not for my salvation, but because my father's respectability demanded it. When we went to live in the country, remote from social criticism, I broke with the observance and never resumed it.

What helped to make this church a hotbed of all the social vices was that no working folk ever came to it. In England the clergy go among the poor, and sometimes do try desperately to get them to come to church. In Ireland the poor are Catholics — "Papists," as my Orange grandfather called them. The Protestant Church has nothing to do with them. I cannot say that in Ireland every man is the worse for what he calls his religion. I can only say that all the people I knew were.

One evening I was playing in the street with a schoolfellow of mine when my father came home. He questioned me about this boy, who was the son of a prosperous ironmonger. The feelings of my father, who was not prosperous, and who sold flour by the sack, when he learnt that his son had played in the public street with the son of a man who sold nails by the pennyworth in a shop, are not to be described. He impressed on me that my honour, my self-respect, my human dignity all stood upon my determination not to associate with persons engaged in retail trade. Probably this was the worst crime my father ever committed. And yet I do not see what else he could have taught me, short of genuine republicanism, which is the only possible school of good manners.

I remember Stopford Brooke one day telling me that he discerned in my books an intense and contemptuous hatred for society. No wonder! — though, like him, I strongly demur at the usurpation of the word "Society" by an unsocial system of setting class against class and creed against creed.

If I had not suffered from these things in my childhood perhaps I could keep my temper about them. To an outsider there was nothing but comedy in the spectacle of a forlorn set of Protestant merchants in a Catholic country, led by a miniature plutocracy of stockbrokers, doctors and land agents, and flavoured by that section of the landed gentry who were too heavily mortgaged to escape to London, playing at being a Court and an aristocracy with the assistance of the unfortunate exile who had been persuaded to accept the post of Lord-Lieutenant. To this pretence, involving a prodigious and continual lying as to incomes and the social standing of relatives, were sacrificed citizenship, self-respect, freedom of thought, sincerity of character, and all the realities of life, its votaries gaining in return the hostile estrangement of the great mass of their fellow-countrymen, and in their own class the supercilious snubs of those who had outdone them in pretension and the jealous envy of those whom they had outdone.

And now, what power did I find in Ireland religious enough to redeem me from this abomination of desolation? Quite simply, the power of Art.

My mother, as it happened, had a considerable musical talent. In order to exercise it seriously she had to associate with other people who had musical talent. My first childish doubt as to whether God could really be a good Protestant was suggested by my observation of the deplorable fact that the best voices available for combination with my mother's in the works of the great composers had been unaccountably vouchsafed to Roman Catholics. Even the Divine gentility was presently called in question; for some of these vocalists were undeniably connected with retail trade.

There was no help for it: if my mother was to do anything but sing silly ballads in drawing-rooms, she had to associate herself on an entirely republican footing with people of like artistic gifts, without the smallest reference to creed or class.

Nay, if she wished to take part in the Masses of Haydn and Mozart, which had not then been forgotten, she must actually permit herself to be approached by Roman Catholic priests, and even, at their invitation, to enter that house of Belial the Roman Catholic Chapel (in Ireland the word church, as applied to a place of worship, denoted the Protestant denomination), and take part in their services. All of which led directly to the discovery, hard to credit at first, that a Roman Catholic priest could be as agreeable and cultivated a person as a Protestant clergyman was supposed, in defiance of bitter experience, always to be; and, in short, that the notion that the courtly distinctions of Dublin society corresponded to any real human distinctions was as ignorant as it was pernicious. If religion is that which binds men to one another, and irreligion that which sunders, then must I testify that I found the religion of my country in its musical genius, and its irreligion in its churches and drawing-rooms.

GEORGE BERNARD SHAW.

Mr. Shaw's Method and Secret

(A letter to the Editor of *The Daily Chronicle*, London, 30
April 1898)

28th April 1898.

Sir, —

I notice that your columns are agitated at present by the question
whether my dramatic works are due to the influence of Ibsen or De
Maupassant.

Allow me to give you a few instances of the real living influences
under which I work. I live in the parish of St. Pancras, and am a
vestryman thereof. St. Pancras contains quarter of a million inhabitants. An appalling number of them live in single-room tenements.
The districts in which these tenements are most plentiful have been
frankly given up by our most energetic sanitary inspectors, who
have no time to do anything more than attend to complaints which,
I need hardly say, are only made by the people who are enlightened
enough to be least in need of attention. A recent very careful inquiry
by a sub-committee in the Health Department pointed out the means
of dealing with this evil. The vestry positively declined to take them.
It gave no reasons. It freely accused its Health Committee of incompetence and its Sanitary Staff of negligence; but it took no steps to
reconstitute the committee, nor to set on foot an inquiry into the alleged negligence. It knew perfectly well that more sanitary inspectors
were required; and it was resolved not to pay for them even at the
risk of being ignominiously compelled by the County Council to do
its duty.

There is in St. Pancras the usual public sanitary accommodation, including a single underground convenience for women. The accommodation is perfectly free to men, and is used by thousands daily without
payment. It is only when the lavatory or a closet is used that a charge
is made. Free accommodation is refused altogether to women. Six
months ago the one woman on the vestry, supported by a few humane
and decent men, succeeded in shaming the vestry into making the
accommodation in the women's convenience partly free. Since then,
1,725 women, or thirteen per cent., of the total number using the

convenience, have availed themselves of the free accommodation. Yesterday the vestry deliberately abolished it. I remonstrated, and was seconded by our lady member. An eminent member of the vestry immediately rose and expressed his horror at my venturing to speak in public on so disgusting a subject. He then accused my seconder of indecency. At this point the vestrymen, to their credit, revolted, and squashed the unhappy apostle of gentlemanly delicacy; but they voted on his side in a majority of about seven to one, and the poor women of St. Pancras will in future have to pay a penny for the privilege, enjoyed for nothing by the men, of observing the common decencies of traffic in a city.

Later on we came to a subject which has lately been well in evidence in the "Chronicle" — I mean the Bill now before Parliament for interfering very mildly with shop slavery. The vestry was warned by its Parliamentary Committee that this Bill would compel the provision of sitting accommodation for women employed in shops; would save them from being kept more than a certain number of hours without rest or refreshment; and would secure proper sanitary accommodation and ventilation for them. We were told that the vestry of St. Anne, Limehouse, has resolved to oppose the Bill, "for the reason that it would injuriously affect the interests of retail traders." The vestry of St. Pancras, a ghastly centre of shop slavery, promptly assured St. Anne of its approval and cordial agreement.

It must not be inferred that vestrymen are an inhuman and merciless class. On the contrary, they are stuffed, every man of them, with good intentions, intense respectability, piety, theoretical humanity and the most exalted ideas of womanly purity. All their finest instincts are jarred unendurably when their minds are dragged down from the contemplation of photographs of princesses to sanitary conveniences for charwomen. Every drop of their blood is so sweetened by charity that they pay starvation wages to their scavengers lest they should be compelled to discharge the worn-out men whom they have employed out of benevolence. At most of their meetings they commit crimes against society for which they would get twenty years' penal servitude if they committed them as individuals against private property instead of as public representatives against the common weal. But they do it from the loftiest, kindliest, most self-sacrificing reasons; and all remonstrance strikes them as being half ludicrous, half cynical, and altogether a breach of good sense and good manners — much as "The Philanderer" strikes my friend Mr. Archer, in fact.

Looking away from local politics to the broader world-horizon, I see two nations busily engaged in shiplifting, arson and murder, and all the newspapers gravely calling it war, patriotism, "Feeling in America," "Feeling in Spain," and so forth. And if I were to propose that the European Concert should promptly take steps to capture the shiplifters and restrain them by force, I daresay I should discover that the European Press is precisely like the St. Pancras Vestry; and your literary columns would proceed to discuss whether my proposals were borrowed from Ibsen or Maupassant.

If a dramatist living in a world like this has to go to books for his ideas and his inspiration, he must be both blind and deaf. Most dramatists are.

For the satisfaction of my friend Cunninghame Graham, I may say that if I have fallen into the ways of De Maupassant, the fault is Mr. Archer's. He once lent me, and insisted on my reading, a book by that author entitled "Une Vie." It took me two years to get through it; but it was a very honest and able bit of photography. I believe I also once read a short Maupassant story about a man who shot himself because he was afraid to fight a duel. As to "Mrs. Warren's Profession," it came about in this way. Miss Janet Achurch mentioned to me a novel by some French writer [De Maupassant's *Yvette*] as having a dramatisable story in it. It being hopeless to get me to read anything, she told me the story, which was ultra-romantic. I said, "Oh, I will work out the real truth about that mother some day." In the following autumn I was the guest of a lady [Beatrice Webb] of very distinguished ability — one whose knowledge of English social types is as remarkable as her command of industrial and political questions. She suggested that I should put on the stage a real modern lady of the governing class — not the sort of thing that theatrical and critical authorities imagine such a lady to be. I did so; and the result was Miss Vivie Warren, who has laid the intellect of Mr. William Archer in ruins. The fact is the modern lady expresses so freely the ideas that were first introduced to Mr. Archer by me in the course of the fruitless pains I have bestowed for years on his neglected sociological education, that he sees nothing in her but a Shaw in petticoats — a dreadful phenomenon. Mrs. Warren herself was my version of the heroine of the romance narrated by Miss Achurch. The tremendously effective scene — which a baby could write if its sight were normal — in which she justifies herself, is only a paraphrase of a scene in a novel of my own, "Cashel Byron's Profession" (hence the title, "Mrs. Warren's Profession"), in which a prize-fighter shows how he was driven into the ring exactly as Mrs. Warren was driven on the streets. Never was there a more grossly obvious derivation. I finally persuaded Miss Achurch, who is clever with her pen, to dramatise her story herself on its original romantic lines. Her version is called "Mrs. Daintry's Daughter." That is the history of "Mrs. Warren's Profession." I never dreamt of Ibsen or De Maupassant, any more than a blacksmith shoeing a horse thinks of the blacksmith in the next county.

Yours truly,
G. Bernard Shaw.

Trials of a Military Dramatist

(*Review of the Week*, London, 4 November 1899)

On returning from a trip to the South of Europe, where I have found the two soundly-beaten nations, Spain and Greece, so effectually brought back to the sober realities of national character and industry that I am almost in love with defeat, I find myself for the second time in my life enjoying a nine days' infamy as a malignant scoffer at everything that is noblest in war: in other words, at the British Army. This situation, however flattering to my private sense of my own importance, would not in time of peace have any interest for the public at large. As it is, with every newspaper full of cannon and trumpet, drum and death-roll, the most trivial instance of the cloud of melodramatic illusions which constitutes the military consciousness of the country, has its significance.

As I write, news comes in that a couple of British battalions concerning whom our general naïvely telegraphed yesterday that they were "expected that evening, but had not yet returned," have surrendered, and are prisoners. And our editors, appalled into seriousness, observe that nothing of the kind has happened since Burgoyne surrendered to the Americans at Saratoga 122 years ago. Now, it is but the other day that I called up on the stage the ghost of this very Burgoyne, and was told that he was nothing but my own sardonic self in an eighteenth century uniform. This was natural enough; for instead of simply putting on the stage the modern conception of a British general, half idealised prize-fighter, half idealised music-hall chairman, I had taken some pains to ascertain what manner of person the real Burgoyne was, and had found him a wit, a rhetorician, and a successful dramatic author. Also, of course, an eighteenth century gentleman, independent of a public of grown-up schoolboys. He was sent out to quell the American rebellion with a force of Hessians, English, and Indians. It was arranged that he should march from Boston to Albany, and there join a force marching thither simultaneously from New York. Unfortunately the civil servant in London, whose duty it was to send the necessary orders to the New York force, went down to Brighton and forgot all about it (observe how farcical history can be), much as somebody appears to have forgotten to send troops to South Africa in time for war the other day, or stores to the Crimea forty-five years ago. Burgoyne marched into the wilderness, where, instead of meeting his colleague's battalions, he met the Americans in overwhelming numbers, and in an impregnable position. He fought until his sense of dramatic effect was satisfied, and then capitulated. The Americans thereupon propounded articles of surrender to him; and the dramatic style and character of the man are in his answers. For example, it was set forth by way of preamble that he was completely beaten. His written comment was: — "Lieut.-General Burgoyne's army, however reduced, will never admit that their retreat is cut off while they have arms in their hands." The Americans further said that they would imprison British officers who broke their parole. Burgoyne replied, "There being no officer in this army under, or capable of being under, the description of breaking parole, this article needs no answer." And finally, in reply to Article VI., "This article is inadmissible in any extremity. Sooner than this army will consent to ground their arms in their encampments, they will rush on the enemy determined to take no quarter." In the final scene, when he handed his sword to the "rebel" commander, he played that worthy man, who was awkward and nervous, clean off the stage, although, as the defeated general, his part was painfully secondary. Finding himself, on his return to England, made a scapegoat, in the matter of the loss of America for the king and the gentleman [Lord George Germain] who went to Brighton, he took refuge in the House of Commons and there exercised his rhetorical talents to his heart's content.

This is authentic history; but like all authentic histories of great events enacted by men not great, its details produce an effect of comic opera on the multitude, who can recognise tragedy only when she brandishes her bowl and dagger. Its central event, the surrender at Saratoga, was just such an event as the surrender of last Monday. The Americans, like the Boers, were farmers who could shoot. They systematically picked off the English officers, Burgoyne himself narrowly escaping with bullet holes in his hat and waistcoat. My stage Burgoyne convulsed the playgoers of Kennington by asking a rebel who demanded to be "shot like a man instead of hanged like a dog," whether he had any idea of the average marksmanship of the British Army, and earnestly recommending him to be hanged. Everybody shrieked with laughter, and exclaimed that this was not General Burgoyne, but myself disguised as General Boum.* And yet, like all my wildest extravagances, it was an uncooked "slice of life." In my youth I was conversing one day, I and others, with a British general, who prophesied rain on the authority of a bullet in his shoulder which

* A character in Offenbach's *La Grande Duchesse de Gérolstein* — Ed.

had served him faithfully for many years as a barometer. We set him talking about the campaign in which he acquired this instrument, and found, among other things, that he had conducted many military executions. On our assuming that these were carried out by shooting parties, he told us, with great earnestness, what indeed the famous case of the Mexican Maximilian should have suggested to us already, that no humane person who had ever seen an execution by shooting — horrible, sanguinary, and demoralising even when it was successful (which seldom happened) — would ever adopt it if a rope, a tree, and camp table were equally available for the swift and certain death, and comparatively bearable spectacle, of an execution by hanging. He declared that he would infinitely prefer hanging himself, and recommended us, as an elderly man speaking to his juniors, to choose it without hesitation should the alternative be presented to us.

A moment's reflection will convince anybody that this is not comic opera, but common-sense. Unhappily, in this country the people who reflect do not go to the theatre.

In transferring the counsels of my military acquaintance to Burgoyne, I incurred reprobation, not only for wilful farce, but for insulting the British Army by disparaging its marksmanship. From the many generous excuses made for me by my fellow critics, I select the following as typical: — "Of Mr. Shaw's remarks, put into the mouth of General Burgoyne, as to the marksmanship of the army, I think nothing as a matter of patriotism. To begin with, the army can scarcely be called a British Army at all; and, in addition, it was and is notorious that up to the time of the Crimea it took a ton of lead to kill a man." Up to the time of the Crimea! *Sancta simplicitas!* is any man so ignorant as to suppose that now, or at any other period, it has been possible to make the British taxpayer pay for cartridges enough to make the British soldier an efficient shooter? Why, only the other day, at Omdurman, the whole British and Egyptian forces of the Sirdar, blazing away for twenty minutes with modern magazine rifles, machine guns and field artillery, and using bullets each capable of penetrating several men, did not score more hits than a single machine gun might have done in skilful hands in half the time. The Crimean ton of lead is now a mountain. During the Dreyfus case, we had some grotesque instances of the French deference to "the honour of the army"; but the silliest of them must yield the palm to the assumption that Tommy Atkins is a marksman. It is just about as possible for him to be a marksman as it is for him to play the fiddle like Sarasate. How exquisitely English it is to refuse him the money for practice cartridges, and then pretend that he is a dead shot; to enlist him at twenty-five years of age with a 31 inch chest, and pretend that he is a youth of eighteen who will grow up to the standard; to tell him that flogg. abolished in the Army, and then flog him soundly the moment he ge. into a military prison; to deprive him of our common political rights, and leave him to the mercy of the worst form of lynch law in the world (recognised as such lately at Rennes); to promise him a shilling a day, and filch pennies back from him under mean pretexts: in short, to take every conceivable shabby advantage of him until we are at last actually face to face with conscription — flat slavery — because we will not pay another sixpence a day and get an invincible army for it as Cromwell did. And, if you please, I, the dramatist, knowing all this, am to join the War Office in persuading the foolish man in the street that the British Army is perfect. Pray, why should I? The War Office may reply, Because it pays. But suppose I am of a perverse disposition, and get as much satisfaction out of exposing perilous humbug and befriending the unfortunate soldier, as a War Office apologist gets out of a large official salary, or a popular melodramatist out of the royalties on "One of the Best" or "In the Ranks"! Suppose, even, I were a military enthusiast and British patriot! Nobody will question the sincerity of Mr. Arnold Foster in both capacities. I wonder what would be said if I dramatised everything in Mr. Arnold Foster's Army letters to the *Times,* representing "the views of at least nine-tenths of the officers and men actually serving or on the retired list." Dreyfus's fate would be considered too merciful for me.

I remain astonished at my moderation.

Who I Am, and What I Think

(Replies to a questionnaire by editor Frank Harris, in *The Candid Friend*, London, 11 and 18 May 1901. Revised versions in *Shaw Gives Himself Away*, 1939, and *Sixteen Self Sketches*, 1949)

Won't you begin by telling me something of your parents and their influence on your life?

It is impossible to give you the Rougon-Macquart view of myself in less than twenty volumes. Let me tell you a story of my father. When I was a child, he gave me my first dip in the sea in Killiney Bay. He prefaced it by a very serious exhortation on the importance of learning to swim, culminating in these words: "When I was a boy of only fourteen, my knowledge of swimming enabled me to save your Uncle Algernon's life." Then, seeing that I was deeply impressed, he stooped, and added confidentially in my ear — "and, to tell you the truth, I never was so sorry for anything in my life afterwards." He then plunged into the ocean, enjoyed a thoroughly refreshing swim, and chuckled all the way home. Now, only the other day, Mr. Granville Barker, in rehearsing the part of Napoleon in my play, "The Man of Destiny," said to me that the principle of the whole play was anti-climax. Mr. Henry Norman once said of me that no man could butter a moral slide better than Shaw. That was before he became serious and went into Parliament. Now I protest that I do not aim at anti-climax; it occurs as naturally in my work as night follows day. But there is no doubt some connection between my father's chuckling and the observations of Granville Barker and Norman. My father was an ineffective, unsuccessful man, in theory a vehement teetotaller, but in practice often a furtive drinker. He might have been a weaker brother of Charles Lamb. My mother you can interview for yourself if you want to know about her. But her musical activity was of the greatest importance in my education. I never learnt anything at school, a place where they put "Cæsar" and "Horace" into the hands of small boys and expected the result to be an elegant taste and knowledge of the world. I took refuge in total idleness at school, and picked up at home, quite unconsciously, a knowledge of that extraordinary literature of modern music, from Bach to Wagner, which has saved me from being at the smallest disadvantage in competition with men who only

446

know the grammar and mispronunciation of the Greek and Latin poets and philosophers. For the rest, my parents went their own way and let me go mine. Thus the habit of freedom, which most Englishmen and Englishwomen of my class never acquire and never let their children acquire, came to me naturally.

When did you first feel inclined to write?

I never felt inclined to write, any more than I ever felt inclined to breathe. I felt inclined to draw: Michael Angelo was my boyish ideal. I felt inclined to be a wicked baritone in an opera when I grew out of my earlier impulse towards piracy and highway robbery. You see, as I couldn't draw, I was perfectly well aware that drawing was an exceptional gift. But it never occurred to me that my literary sense was exceptional. I gave the whole world credit for it. The fact is, there is nothing miraculous, nothing particularly interesting even, in a natural faculty to the man who has it. The amateur, the collector, the enthusiast in an art, is the man who lacks the faculty for producing it. The Venetian wants to be a soldier; the Gaucho wants to be a sailor; the fish wants to fly, and the bird to swim. No, I never wanted to write. I know now, of course, the value and the scarcity of the literary faculty (though I think it over-rated); but I still don't want it. You cannot want a thing and have it too.

What form did your literary work first take?

I vaguely remember that when I was a small boy I concocted a short story and sent it to some boys' journal — something about a man with a gun attacking another man in the Glen of the Douns. The gun was the centre of interest to me. Some years ago, Arnold's, of Covent Garden, published a couple of really original Irish novels called "Misther O'Ryan" and "The Son of a Peasant," by Edward McNulty. McNulty was a schoolfellow of mine for a short time. Then I drifted into an office in Dublin, and he drifted into the Newry branch of the Bank of Ireland. We had struck up one of those romantic friendships that occur between imaginative boys; and from the ages of fifteen to twenty we kept up a voluminous correspondence between Dublin and Newry, exchanging long letters by return of post. That correspondence worked off the literary energy which usually produces early works. I believe my first appearance in print was on the occasion of the visit of the American evangelists, Moody and Sankey, to Dublin. Their arrival created a great sensation on this side of the Atlantic; and I went to hear them. I was wholly unmoved by their eloquence, and felt bound to inform the public that I was, on the whole, an Atheist. My letter was solemnly printed in *Public*

Opinion, to the extreme horror of my numerous uncles. I perpetrated one more long correspondence, this time with an English lady [Elinor Huddart] whose fervidly imaginative novels would have made her known if I could have persuaded her to make her own name public, or at least to stick to the same pen name, instead of changing it for every book. Virtually, my first works were the five novels I wrote from 1879 to 1883, which nobody would publish. They got into print later on as pure padding for Socialist magazines, and are now raging in America, in unauthorised editions, as the latest fruits of my genius. I came to London in 1876; and between 1876 and 1879 I did a little devilling at musical criticism, and began a Passion Play in blank verse, with the mother of the hero represented as a termagant; but I never carried these customary follies of young authors through: I was always, fortunately for me, a failure as a trifler. All my attempts at Art for Art's sake broke down; it was like hammering tenpenny nails into sheets of notepaper.

When did you begin to be interested in political questions? In what way did these affect your work?

Well, at the beginning of the eighties I happened to hear an address by Henry George at the Memorial Hall in Farringdon Street. It flashed on me then for the first time that the "conflict between Religion and Science" — you remember [John William] Draper's book? — the overthrow of the Bible, the higher education of women, Mill on liberty, and all the rest of the storm that raged round Darwin, Tyndall, Huxley, Spencer, and the rest, on which I had brought myself up intellectually, was a mere middle-class business. Suppose it could have produced a nation of Matthew Arnolds and George Eliots! — you may well shudder. The importance of the economic basis dawned on me: I read Marx, and was exactly in the mood for his reduction of all the conflicts to the conflict of classes for economic mastery, of all social forms to the economic forms of production and exchange. But the real secret of Marx's fascination was his appeal to an unnamed, unrecognised passion — a new passion — the passion of hatred in the more generous souls among the respectable and educated sections for the accursed middle-class institutions that had starved, thwarted, misled, and corrupted them from their cradles. Marx's "Capital" is not a treatise on Socialism; it is a jeremiad against the bourgeoisie, supported by such a mass of evidence and such a relentless Jewish genius for denunciation as had never been brought to bear before. It was supposed to be written for the working classes; but the working man respects the bourgeoisie, and wants to be a bourgeois; Marx never got hold of him for a moment. It was the revolting sons of the bourgeoisie itself — Lassalle, Marx, Liebknecht, Morris, Hyndman, Bax, all, like myself, bourgeois crossed with squirearchy — that painted the flag red. Bakunin and Kropotkin, of the military and noble caste (like Napoleon), were our extreme left. The middle and upper classes are the revolutionary element in society; the proletariat is the Conservative element, as Disraeli well knew. Hyndman and his Marxists, Bakunin and his Anarchists, would not accept this situation; they persisted in believing that the proletariat was an irresistible mass of unawakened Felix Pyats and Ouidas. I did accept the situation, helped, perhaps, by my inherited instinct for anti-climax. I threw Hyndman over, and got to work with Sidney Webb and the rest to place Socialism on a respectable bourgeois footing; hence Fabianism. [John] Burns did the same thing in Battersea by organising the working classes there on a genuine self-respecting working-class basis, instead of on the old romantic middle-class assumptions. Hyndman wasted years in vain denunciations of the Fabian Society and of Burns; and though facts became too strong for him at last, he is still at heart the revolted bourgeois. So am I, for the matter of that; you can see it in every line of my plays. So is Ibsen; so is Tolstoy; so is Sudermann; so is Hauptmann; so are you, my CANDID FRIEND (else you would be "The Hypocrite"); so are all the writers of the day whose passion is political and sociological. And that is the answer to your question as to how my politics and economics affect my work. What is a modern problem play but a clinical lecture on society; and how can one lecture like a master unless one knows the economic anatomy of society? Besides, at their simplest, politics save you from becoming a literary man. Feeding a man on books exclusively is like feeding a lap-dog on gin; both books and gin are products of distillation, and their effect on the organism is much the same.

To what do you owe your marvellous gift for public speaking?

My marvellous gift for public speaking is only part of the G.B.S legend. I am no orator, and I have neither memory enough nor presence of mind enough to be a really good debater, though I often seem to be one when I am on ground that is familiar to me and new to my opponents. I learnt to speak as men learn to skate or to cycle — by doggedly making a fool of myself until I got used to it. Then I practised it in the open air — at the street corner, in the market square, in the park — the best school. I am comparatively out of practice now, but I talked a good deal to audiences all through the eighties, and for some years afterwards. I should be a really remarkable orator after all that practice if I had the genius of the born orator. As it is, I am simply the sort of public speaker anybody can become by going through the same mill. I don't mean that he will have the same things to say, or that he will put them in the same words, for naturally I don't leave my ideas or my vocabulary behind when I mount the tub; but I *do* mean that he will say what he has to say as movingly as I say what I have to say — and more, if he is anything of a real orator. Of course, as an Irishman, I have some fluency, and can manage a bit of rhetoric and a bit of humour on occasion; and that goes a long way in England. But "marvellous gift" is all my eye.

What was your first real success? Tell me how you felt about it? Did you ever despair of succeeding?

Never had any. Success, in that sense, is a thing that comes to you, and takes your breath away. What came to me was invariably failure. By the time I wore it down I knew too much to care about either failure or success. Life is like a battle; you have to fire a thousand bullets to hit one man. I was too busy firing to bother about the scoring. As to whether I ever despaired, you will find somewhere in my works this line: "He who has never hoped can never despair." I am not a fluctuator.

Do you think that poverty stands in the way of success, or that it acts rather as an incentive to it?

If by poverty you mean shortness of cash, then all I can say is that our social system is so ingeniously arranged that it is impossible to say which is the greater obstruction to the development of a writer — money or the want of it. I could not undertake to rewrite "The Pilgrim's Progress" and "Fors Clavigera" as they would have been if Ruskin had been a tinsmith and Bunyan a gentleman of independent means. But whilst I am not sure that the want of money lames a poor man more than the possession of it lames a rich one, I am quite sure that the class which has the pretensions and prejudices and habits of the rich without its money, and the poverty of the poor without the freedom to avow poverty — in short, the people who don't go to the theatre because they cannot afford the stalls, and are ashamed to be seen in the gallery — are the worst-off of all. To be on the down grade from the *haute bourgeoisie* and the landed gentry to the nadir at which the younger son's younger great-grandson gives up the struggle to keep up appearances; to have the pretence of culture without the reality of it; to make £300 a year look like £800 in Ireland or Scotland; or £500 look like £1,000 in London; to be educated neither at the Board school and the Birkbeck, nor at the University, but at some rotten private adventure academy for the sons of gentlemen; to try to maintain a select circle by excluding all the frankly poor people from it, and then find that all the rest of the world excludes you — that is poverty at its most damnable; and yet from that poverty a great deal of our literature and journalism has sprung. Think of the frightful humiliation of the boy Dickens in the blacking warehouse, and his undying resentment of his mother's wanting him to stay there — all on a false point of genteel honour. Think of Trollope, at an upper-class school with holes in his trousers, because his father could not bring himself to dispense with a manservant. Ugh! Be a tramp or be a millionaire — it matters little which — what *does* matter is being a poor relation of the rich; and that is the very devil. Fortunately, that sort of poverty can be cured by simply shaking off its ideas — cutting your coat according to your cloth, and not according to the cloth of your father's second cousin, the baronet. As I was always more or less in rebellion against those ideas, and finally shook them off pretty completely, I cannot say that I have much experience of real poverty — quite the contrary. Before I could earn anything with my pen, I had a magnificent library in Bloomsbury, a priceless picture-gallery in Trafalgar Square, and another at Hampton Court, without any servants to look after or rent to pay. As to music, I actually got paid later on for saturating myself with the best of it from London to Bayreuth. Nature and mankind are common property. Friends! Lord bless me, my visiting list has always been of an unpurchasable value and exclusiveness. What could I have bought with more than enough money to feed and clothe me? Cigars? I don't smoke. Champagne? I don't drink. Thirty suits of fashionable clothes? The people I most avoid would ask me to dinner if I could be persuaded to wear such things. Horses? They're dangerous. Carriages? They're sedentary and tiresome. By this time I can afford to sample them; but I buy nothing that I didn't buy before. Besides, I have an imagination. Ever since I can remember, I have only had to go to bed and shut my eyes to be and do whatever I pleased. What are your trumpery Bond Street luxuries to me, George Bernard Sardanapalus? Why, such insight as I have in criticism is due to the fact that I exhausted romanticism before I was ten years old. Your popular novelists are now gravely writing the stories I told to myself before I replaced my first set of teeth. Some day I will try to found a genuine psychology of fiction by writing down the history of my imagined life, duels, battles, love affairs with queens and all. They say that man in embryo is successively a fish, a bird, a mammal, and so on, before he develops into a man. Well, popular novel writing is the fish stage of your Jonathan Swift. I have never been so dishonest as to sneer at our popular novelists. I once went on like that myself. Why does the imaginative man always end by writing comedy if only he has also a sense of reality? Clearly because of the stupendous irony of the contrast between his imaginary adventures and his real circumstances and powers. At night, a conquering hero, an Admirable Crichton, a Don Juan; by day, a cowardly little brat cuffed by his nurse for stealing lumps of sugar. Poverty! Nonsense: my real name is Alnaschar. For Heaven's sake change the ridiculous subject.

Where did you live in your developing period, and how? By journalism?

My parents pulled me through the years in which I earned nothing. My mother came to London, and became a professional musician late in life to keep things together. It was a frightful squeeze at times; but I never went back to the office work I did from fifteen to twenty, and finally I got journalistic work enough to fill the larder. As to my developing period, I hope it's not over. At all events leave me the illusion that it isn't.

What do you think of journalism as a profession?

Daily journalism is a superhuman profession; excellence in it is quite beyond mortal strength and endurance. Consequently, it trains literary men to scamp their work. A weekly *feuilleton* is at least possible: I did one for ten years. I took extraordinary pains — all the pains I was capable of — to get to the bottom of everything I wrote about. There is an indescribable levity — not triviality, mind, but levity — something spritelike about the final truth of a matter; and this exquisite levity communicates itself to the style of the writer who will face the labour of digging down to it. It is the half truth which is congruous, heavy, serious, and suggestive of a middle-aged or elderly philosopher. The whole truth is often the first thing that comes into the head of a fool or a child; and when a wise man forces his way to it through the many strata of his sophistications, its wanton, perverse air reassures him instead of frightening him. Ten years of such work, at the rate of two thousand words a week or thereabouts — say, roughly, a million words — all genuine journalism, dependent on the context of the week's history for its effect, was an apprenticeship which made me master of my own style. But I don't think it was practicable journalism. I could not have kept up the quality of my work if I had undertaken more than one *feuilleton;* and even that I could not have done without keeping myself up to the neck all the rest of the week in other activities — gaining other efficiencies and gorging myself with life and experience as well. My income as a journalist began in 1885 at £117 0s. 3d.; and it ended at about £500, by which time I had reached the age at which we discover that journalism is a young man's stand-by, not an old man's livelihood. So I am afraid that even weekly journalism is superhuman except for young men. The older ones *must* scamp it; and the younger ones must live plainly and cheaply, if they are to get their work up to the pitch at which they can command real freedom to say what they think. Of course, they do nothing of the sort. If they did, journalism would train them in literature as nothing else could. Would, but doesn't. It spoils them instead. If you want a problem stated, a practised journalist will do it with an air that is the next best thing to solving it. But he never solves it: he hasn't time, and wouldn't get paid any more for the solution if he *had* time. So he chalks up the statement, and runs away from the solution.

Were you always a vegetarian? How did you first become one?

No: I was a cannibal for twenty-five years; for the other twenty I have been a vegetarian. Shelley first opened my eyes to the infamy of my habits; but it was not until 1880 or thereabouts that the establishment of vegetarian restaurants made reform practicable without disastrous private experiments. The great secret of vegetarianism is never to eat vegetables. There is no doubt that my vegetarianism has produced an extraordinary effect on the conscience of my critics. You have noticed, no doubt, that no other author is written about quite as I am. You see a long article, purporting to be a notice of my latest book. You take it up, and presently discover that what the critic is really doing is defending his private life against mine — that it is all the *apologia pro sua vita* of a deeply-wounded man. The critic tries to go through his usual brilliant pen performance; but the blood of the Deptford Victualling Yard chokes him, and the horrible carcass groves of Farringdon Market rise up and appall him. This is a most curious phenomenon: you cannot have failed to notice it. The theatre critics are at their ease with Jones, Pinero, Grundy, Chambers, Carton, Esmond, even with THE CANDID FRIEND: but when I am their theme, Archer becomes Macbeth thinking of Duncan; Walkley's airiness is the attempt of the West-End clubman to outface the Hallelujah lass who has asked him where he will spend eternity; Max [Beerbohm]'s flatteries are thinly-veiled exorcisms. All that *mauvaise honte* is the remorse of the meat-eater in the presence of the man who is a living proof that meat is not indispensable to success in literature. All my other peculiarities are familiar to them, and even shared by them in one point or another. But this is a matter of bloodguilt; and *Blut ist ein ganz besondrer Saft.*

Does married life make a difference in your views?

What do you call married life? Real married life is the life of the youth and maiden who pluck a flower and bring down an avalanche on their shoulders — thirty years of the work of Atlas, and then rest as pater and materfamilias. What can people with independent incomes, marrying at forty, tell you about marriage? A comfortable marriage exacerbates a man's views; a wretched one softens them. My views, as far as they are modified at all, are exacerbated.

What is your honest opinion of G.B.S?

Oh, one of the most successful of my fictions, but getting a bit tiresome, I should think. G.B.S. gets on my nerves and bores me, except when he is working out something solid for me, or saying what I want said. G.B.S. be blowed!

What is your definition of humour?

Anything that makes you laugh. But the finest sort draws a tear along with the laugh.

I want one word as to the meaning of the world-comedy from your point of view.

It is this premature search for a meaning that produces the comedy. We are not within a million years, as yet, of being concerned with the meaning of the world. Why do we recognise that philosophy is not a baby's business, although its facial expression so strongly suggests the professional philosopher? Because we know that all its mental energy is absorbed by the struggle to attain ordinary physical consciousness. It is learning to interpret the sensations of its eyes and ears and nose and tongue and finger-tips. It is ridiculously delighted by a silly toy, absurdly terrified by a harmless bogey, because it cannot as yet see these things as they really are. Well, we are all still as much babies in the world of thought as we were in our second year in the world of sense. Men are not real men to us; they are heroes and villains, respectable persons and criminals. Their qualities are virtues and vices; the natural laws that govern them are gods and devils; their destinies are rewards and expiations; their conditions are innocence and guilt — there is no end to the amazing transubstantiations and childish imaginings which delight and terrify us because we have not yet grown up enough to be capable of genuine natural history. And then people come to you with their heads full of these figments, which they call, if you please, "the world," and ask you what is the meaning of them. The answer is, that they have not even an existence, much less a meaning. The blank incredulity of men to that reply, and their absurd attempts to act on their illusions, are as funny as the antics of a baby: that is what you call the world-comedy. But when they try to force others to act on them, when they ostracise, punish, murder, make war, impose by force their grotesque religions and hideous criminal codes, then the comedy becomes a tragedy. And only the dramatist sees through it; all the rest, the Army, the Navy, the Church, and the Bar are busy bolstering up the imposture. The dramatic faculty is nothing more nor less than a little more than common forwardness in natural history, a little more than common freedom from illusion, or, to put it as the average dupe sees it, and as Ruskin flatly expressed it concerning Shakespeare, a little less than common conscience. What is your own speciality, my CANDID FRIEND? Not conscience, but a more penetrating consciousness. What is your motto? "To comprehend everything is to pardon everybody" — Heaven and hell, the gallows and the Garter, abolished in a single phrase. And you, too, are a dramatist. Only a dramatist could play this new part of yours. But let us break off the conversation lest a worst thing befall; for, look you, if the playgoer could see the dramatist's mind, all the dramatists would be hanged, just as all the men and women of forty would be massacred by all the youths and maidens of twenty, if these young ones only knew. So mum! and good morning.

A B C D E F G H I J — R — 7 3 2 1 0 / 6 9 8 7 6 5